TONY HILLERMAN

The Leaphorn and Chee Novels

Skinwalkers

A Thief of Time

Coyote Waits

Also by Tony Hillerman

Fiction

Skeleton Man
The Sinister Pig
The Wailing Wind
Hunting Badger
The First Eagle
The Fallen Man
Finding Moon
Sacred Clowns
Coyote Waits
Talking God
A Thief of Time
Skinwalkers
The Ghostway
The Dark Wind
People of Darkness
Listening Woman
Dance Hall of the Dead
The Fly on the Wall
The Blessing Way
The Boy Who Made Dragonfly (for children)
Buster Misquite's Cowboy Bond (for children)

Nonfiction

Seldom Disappointed
Hillerman Country
The Great Taos Bank Robbery
Rio Grande
New Mexico
The Spell of New Mexico
Indian Country
Talking Mysteries (with Ernie Bulow)
Kilroy Was There
The American Detective
The Best American Detective Stories of the Century

TONY HILLERMAN

The Leaphorn and Chee Novels

Skinwalkers
A Thief of Time
Coyote Waits

HarperCollins*Publishers*

Skinwalker, *A Thief of Time*, and *Coyote Waits* were originally published in 1986, 1988, and 1990 respectively by HarperCollins Publishers Inc.

Map in *A Thief of Time* by Mario Ferro, based on a design by David Lindroth

Designed by Elliott Beard

ISBN 0-06-075338-2

Contents

Skinwalkers

This book is dedicated to Katy Goodwin, Ursula Wilson, Faye Bia Knoki, Bill Gloyd, Annie Kahn, Robert Bergman, and George Bock, and all the Medicine People, Navajo and *belagana*, who care for The People—and about them. My thanks to Dr. Albert Rizzoli for his kindness and his help, and a tip of my hat to the good work of the too often unappreciated Indian Health Service.

Author's Note

THOSE WHO READ these Navajo mysteries with a map of the Big Reservation beside them should be warned that Badwater Wash, its clinic, and its trading post are as fictional as the people who inhabit them. The same is true of Short Mountain. I also use an unorthodox form of the Navajo noun for shaman/medicine man/singer, which is commonly spelled "hataalii." Finally my good friend Ernie Bulow correctly reminds me that more traditional shamans would disapprove of both the way Jim Chee was invited to do the Blessing Way mentioned in this book (such arrangements should be made face-to-face and not by letter) and of Chee practicing a sandpainting on the ground under the sky. Such sacred and powerful ritual should be done only in the hogan.

We Navajo understand Coyote is always waiting out there, just out of sight. And Coyote is always hungry.

—ALEX ETCITTY, born to the *Water Is Close* People

1

WHEN THE CAT came through the little trapdoor at the bottom of the screen it made a *clack-clack* sound. Slight, but enough to awaken Jim Chee. Chee had been moving in and out of the very edge of sleep, turning uneasily on the narrow bed, pressing himself uncomfortably against the metal tubes that braced the aluminum skin of his trailer. The sound brought him enough awake to be aware that his sheet was tangled uncomfortably around his chest.

He sorted out the bedclothing, still half immersed in an uneasy dream of being tangled in a rope that he needed to keep his mother's sheep from running over the edge of something vague and dangerous. Perhaps the uneasy dream provoked an uneasiness about the cat. What had chased it in? Something scary to a cat—or to this particular cat. Was it something threatening to Chee? But in a moment he was fully awake, and the uneasiness was replaced by happiness. Mary Landon would be coming. Blue-eyed, slender, fascinating Mary Landon would be coming back from Wisconsin. Just a couple of weeks more to wait.

Jim Chee's conditioning—traditional Navajo—caused him to put that thought aside. All things in moderation. He would think more about that later. Now he thought about tomorrow. Today, actually, since it must be well after midnight. Today he and Jay Kennedy would go out and arrest Roosevelt Bistie so that Bistie could be charged with some degree of homicide—probably with murder. Not a complicated job, but unpleasant enough to cause Chee to change the subject of his thinking again. He thought about the cat. What had driven it in? The coyote, maybe. Or what? Obviously something the cat considered a threat.

The cat had appeared last winter, finding itself a sort of den under a juniper east of Chee's trailer—a place where a lower limb, a boulder, and a rusted barrel formed a closed cul-de-sac. It had become a familiar, if suspicious, neighbor. During the spring, Chee had formed a habit of leaving out table scraps to feed it after heavy snows. Then when the snow melt ended and the spring drought arrived, he began leaving out water in a coffee can. But easy water attracted other animals, and birds, and sometimes they turned it over. And so, one afternoon when there was absolutely nothing else to do, Chee had removed the door, hacksawed out a cat-sized rectangle through its bottom frame, and then attached a plywood flap, using leather hinges and Miracle Glue. He had done it on a whim, partly to see if the ultracautious cat could be taught to use it. If the cat did, it would gain access to a colony of field mice that seemed to have moved into Chee's trailer. And the watering problem would be solved. Chee felt slightly uneasy about the water. If he hadn't started this meddling, nature would have taken its normal course. The cat would have moved down the slope and found itself a den closer to the San Juan—which was never dry. But Chee had interfered. And now Chee was stuck with a dependent.

Chee's interest, originally, had been simple curiosity. Once, obviously, the cat had been owned by someone. It was skinny now, with a long scar over its ribs and a patch of fur missing from its right leg, but it still wore a collar, and, despite its condition, it had a purebred look. He'd described it to the woman in the pet store at Farmington—tan fur, heavy hind legs, round head, pointed ears; reminded you of a bobcat, and like a bobcat it had a mere stub of a tail. The woman had said it must be a Manx.

"Somebody's pet. People are always bringing their pets along on vacations," she'd said, disapproving, "and then they don't take care of them and they get out of the car and that's the end of them." She'd asked Chee if he could catch it and bring it in, "so somebody can take care of it."

Chee doubted if he could get his hands on the cat, and hadn't tried. He was too much the traditional Navajo to interfere with an animal without a reason. But he was curious. Could such an animal, an animal bred and raised by the white man, call up enough of its hunting instincts to survive in the Navajo world? The curiosity gradually turned to a casual admiration. By early summer, the animal had accumulated wisdom with its scar tissue. It stopped trying to hunt prairie dogs and concentrated on small rodents and birds. It learned how to hide, how to escape. It learned how to endure.

It also learned to follow the water can into Chee's trailer rather than make the long climb down to the river. Within a week the cat was using the flap when Chee was away. By midsummer it began coming in when he was at home. At first it had waited tensely at the step until he was away from the door, kept a nervous eye on him while it drank, and bolted through the flap at his first motion. But now, in August, the cat virtually ignored him. It had come inside at night only once before—driven in by a pack of dogs that had flushed it out of its den under the juniper.

Chee looked around the trailer. Far too dark to see where the cat had gone. He pushed the sheet aside, swung his feet to the floor. Through the screened window beside his bed he noticed the moon was down. Except far to the northwest, where the remains of a thunderhead lingered, the sky was bright with stars. Chee yawned, stretched, went to the sink, and drank a palmful of water warm from the tap. The air smelled of dust, as it had for weeks. The thunderstorm had risen over the Chuskas in the late afternoon, but it had drifted northward over the Utah border and into Colorado and nothing around Shiprock had gotten any help. Chee ran a little more water, splashed it on his face. The cat, he guessed, would be standing behind the trash canister right beside his feet. He yawned again. What had driven it in? He'd seen the coyote's tracks along the river a few days ago, but it would have to be terribly hungry to hunt this close to his trailer. No dogs tonight, at least he hadn't heard any. And dogs, unlike coyotes, were easy enough to hear. But probably it was dogs, or the coyote. Probably a coyote. What else?

Chee stood beside the sink, leaning on it, yawning again. Back to bed. Tomorrow would be unpleasant. Kennedy said he would be at Chee's trailer at 8 A.M. and the FBI agent was never late. Then the long drive into the Lukachukais to find the man named Roosevelt Bistie and ask him why he had killed an old man named Dugai Endocheeney with a butcher knife. Chee had been a Navajo Tribal Policeman for seven years now—ever since he'd graduated from the University of New Mexico—and he knew now he'd never learn to like this part of the job, this dealing with sick minds in a way that would never bring them back to harmony. The federal way of curing Bistie would be to haul him before a federal magistrate, charge him with homicide on a federal reservation, and lock him away.

Ah, well, Chee thought, most of the job he liked. Tomorrow he would endure. He thought of the happy times stationed at Crownpoint. Mary Landon teaching in the elementary school. Mary Landon always there. Mary Landon always willing to listen. Chee felt relaxed. In a moment he would go back to bed. Through the screen he could see only a dazzle of stars above a black landscape. What was out there? A coyote? Shy Girl Beno? That turned his thoughts to Shy Girl's opposite. Welfare Woman. Welfare Woman and the Wrong Begay Incident. That memory produced a delighted, reminiscent grin. Irma Onesalt was Welfare Woman's name, a worker in the tribal Social Services office, tough as saddle leather, mean as a snake. The look on her face when they learned they had hauled the wrong Begay out of the Badwater Clinic and delivered him halfway across the reservation was an image he would treasure. She was dead now, but that had happened far south of the Shiprock district, out of Chee's jurisdiction. And for Chee, the shooting of Irma Onesalt didn't do as much as it might have to diminish the delight of the Wrong Begay Incident. It was said they'd never figure out who shot Welfare Woman because everybody who ever had to work with her would be a logical suspect with a sound motive. Chee couldn't remember meeting a more obnoxious woman.

He stretched. Back to bed. Abruptly he thought of an alternative to the coyote-scared-the-cat theory. The Shy Girl at Theresa Beno's camp. She had wanted to talk to him, had hung on the fringes while he talked to Beno, and Beno's husband, and Beno's elder daughter. The shy one had the long-faced, small-boned beauty that seemed to go with Beno women. He had noticed her getting into a gray Chevy pickup when he was leaving the Beno camp, and when he had stopped for a Pepsi at the Roundtop Trading Post, the Chevy had driven up. Shy Girl had parked well away from the gasoline pumps. He'd noticed her watching him, and waited. But she had driven away.

Chee moved from the sink and stood by the screen door, looking out into the darkness, smelling the August drought. She knew something about the sheep, he thought, and she wanted to tell me. But she wanted to tell me where no one could see her talking to me. Her sister's husband is stealing the sheep. She knows it. She wants him caught. She followed me. She waited. Now she will come up to the door and tell me as soon as she overcomes her shyness. She is out there, and she frightened the cat.

It was all, of course, a silly idea, product of being half asleep. Chee could see nothing through the screen. Only the dark shape of the junipers, and a mile up the river the lights that someone had left on at the Navajo Nation Shiprock Agency highway maintenance yards, and beyond that the faint glow that attempted to civilize the night at the town of Shiprock. He could smell dust and the peculiar aroma of wilted, dying leaves—an odor familiar to Chee and to all Navajos, and one that evoked unpleasant boyhood memories. Of thin horses, dying sheep, worried adults. Of not quite enough to eat. Of being very careful to take into the gourd dipper no more of the tepid water than you would drink. How long had it been since it had rained? A shower at Shiprock at the end of April. Nothing since then. Theresa Beno's shy daughter wouldn't be out there. Maybe a coyote. Whatever it was, he was going back to bed. He ran a little more water into his palm, sipped it, noticing the taste. The reservoir on his trailer would be low. He should flush it out and refill it. He thought of Kennedy again. Chee shared the prejudices of most working policemen against the FBI, but Kennedy seemed a better sort than most. And smarter. Which was good, because he would probably be stationed at Farmington a long time and Chee would be working . . .

Just then he became aware of the form in the darkness. Some slight motion, perhaps, had given it away. Or perhaps Chee's eyes had finally made the total adjustment to night vision. It was not ten feet from the window under which Chee slept, an indistinct black-against-black. But the shape was upright. Human. Small? Probably the woman at Theresa Beno's sheep camp. Why did she stand there so silently if she had come all this way to talk to him?

Light and sound struck simultaneously—a white-yellow flash which burned itself onto the retina behind the lens of Chee's eyes and a boom which slammed into his eardrums and repeated itself. Again. And again. Without thought, Chee had dropped to the floor, aware of the cat clawing its way frantically over his back toward the door flap.

Then it was silent. Chee scrambled to a sitting position. Where was his pistol? Hanging on his belt in the trailer closet. He scrambled for it on hands and knees, still seeing only the white-yellow flash, hearing only the ringing in his ears. He pulled open the closet door, reached up blindly and fumbled until his fingers found the holster, extracted the pistol, cocked it. He sat with his back pressed against the closet wall, not daring to breathe, trying to make his eyes work again. They did, gradually. The shape of the open door became a rectangle of black-gray in a black-black field. The light of the dark night came through the window above his bed. And below that small square, he seemed to be seeing an irregular row of roundish places—places a little lighter than the blackness.

Chee became aware of his sheet on the floor around him, of his foam-rubber mattress against his knee. He hadn't knocked it off the bunk. The cat? It couldn't. Through the diminishing ringing in his ears he could hear a dog barking somewhere in the distance toward Shiprock. Awakened by the gunshots, Chee guessed. And they must have been gunshots. A cannon. Three of them. Or was it four?

Whoever had fired them would be waiting out there. Waiting for Chee to come out. Or trying to decide whether four shots through the aluminum skin of the trailer into Chee's bed had been enough. Chee looked at the row of holes again, with his vision now clearing. They looked huge—big enough to stick your foot through. A shotgun. That would explain the blast of light and sound. Chee decided going through the door would be a mistake. He sat, back to the closet wall, gripping the pistol, waiting. A second distant dog joined the barking. Finally, the barking stopped. Air moved through the trailer, bringing in the smells of burned gunpowder, wilted leaves, and the exposed mud flats along the river. The white-yellow blot on Chee's retina faded away. Night vision returned. He could make out the shape of his mattress now, knocked off the bed by the shotgun blasts. And through the holes punched in the paper-thin aluminum walls, he could see lightning briefly illuminate the dying thunderhead on the northwest horizon. In Navajo mythology, lightning symbolized the wrath of the *yei*, the Holy People venting their malice against the earth.

2

LIEUTENANT JOE LEAPHORN had gone to his office early. He'd awakened a little before dawn and lay motionless, feeling Emma's hip warm against his own, listening to the sound of her breathing, feeling a numbing sense of loss. He had decided, finally, that he would force her to see a doctor. He would take her. He would tolerate no more of her excuses and delays. He had faced the fact that he had humored Emma's reluctance to see a *belagana* doctor because of his own fear. He knew what the doctor would say. Hearing it said would end his last shred of hope. "Your wife has Alzheimer's disease," the doctor would say, and his face would be sympathetic, and he would explain to Leaphorn what Leaphorn already knew too well. It was incurable. It would be marked by an episodic loss of function of that territory of the brain which stored the human memory and which controlled other behavior. Finally, this loss would be so severe that the victim would simply forget, as it seemed to Leaphorn, to remain alive. It also seemed to Leaphorn that this disease killed its victim by degrees—that Emma was already partly dead. He had lain there, listening to her breathing beside him, and mourned for her. And then he had gotten up, and put on the coffeepot, and dressed, and sat at the kitchen table and watched the sky begin to brighten behind the upthrust wall of stone that gave the little town of Window Rock its name. Agnes had heard him, or smelled the coffee. He had heard water running in the bathroom, and Agnes joined him, face washed, hair combed, wearing a dressing gown covered with red roses.

Leaphorn liked Agnes, and had been happy and relieved when Emma had told him—as her headaches and her forgetfulness worsened—that Agnes would come and stay until health returned. But Agnes was Emma's sister, and Agnes, like Emma, like everyone Leaphorn knew in their branch of the Yazzie family, was deeply traditional. Leaphorn knew they were modern enough not to expect him to follow the old way and take another wife in the family when Emma died. But the thought would be there. And thus Leaphorn found himself uneasy when he was alone with Agnes.

And so he'd finished his coffee and walked through the dawn to the tribal police building, moving away from fruitless worry about his wife to a problem he thought he could solve. He would spend some quiet time before the phone began to ring, deciding, once and for all, whether he was dealing with a coincidence in homicides. He had three of them. Seemingly, absolutely nothing connected them except the exquisite level of frustration with which they confronted Joe Leaphorn. Everything in Leaphorn's Navajo blood, bones, brains, and conditioning taught him to be skeptical of coincidences. Yet for days he had seemed stuck with one—a problem so intractable and baffling that in it he was able to find shelter from the thought of Emma. This morning he intended to take a preliminary step toward solving this puzzle. He would leave the phone off the hook, stare at the array of pins on his map of the Navajo Reservation, and force his thinking into some sort of equal order. Given quiet, and a little time, Leaphorn's mind was very, very good at this process of finding logical causes behind apparently illogical effects.

A memo lay in his in-basket.

> FROM: *Captain Largo, Shiprock.*
> TO: *Lieutenant Leaphorn, Window Rock.*

"*Three shots fired into trailer of Officer Jim Chee about 2:15* A.M. this date," the memo began. Leaphorn read it quickly. No description of either the suspect or the escape vehicle. Chee unharmed. "*Chee states he had no idea of the motive,*" the memo concluded.

Leaphorn reread the final sentence. Like hell, he thought. Like hell he doesn't. Logically, no one shoots at a cop without a motive. And logically, the cop shot at knows that motive very well indeed. Logically, too, that motive reflects so poorly upon the conduct of the policeman that he's happy not to remember it. Leaphorn put the memo aside. When the more normal working day began, he'd call Largo and see if he had anything to add. But now he wanted to think about his three homicides.

He swiveled his chair and looked at the reservation map that dominated the wall behind him. Three pins marked the unsolved homicides: one near Window Rock, one up on the Arizona-Utah border, one north and west in the empty country not far from Big Mountain. They formed a triangle of roughly equal sides—some 120 miles apart. It occurred to Leaphorn that if the man with the shotgun had killed Chee, the triangle on his map would become an oddly shaped rectangle. He would have four unsolved homicides. He rejected the thought. The Chee business wouldn't be unsolved. It would be simple. A matter of identifying the malice, uncovering the officer's malfeasance, finding the prisoner he had abused. It would not, like the three pins, represent crime without motive.

The telephone rang. It was the desk clerk downstairs. "Sorry, sir. But it's the council-woman from Cañoncito."

"Didn't you tell her I won't get in until eight?"

"She saw you come in," the clerk said. "She's on her way up."

She was, in fact, opening Leaphorn's door.

And now the councilwoman was sitting in the heavy wooden armchair across from Leaphorn's desk. She was a burly, big-bosomed woman about Leaphorn's middle age and middle size, dressed in an old-fashioned purple reservation blouse and wearing a heavy-silver squash blossom necklace. She was, she informed Leaphorn, staying at the Window Rock Motel, down by the highway. She had driven in all the way from Cañoncito yesterday afternoon following a meeting with her people at the Cañoncito Chapter House. The people of the Cañoncito Band were not happy with Navajo Tribal Police. They didn't like the police protection they were getting, which was no protection at all. And so she had come by the Law and Order Building this morning to talk to Lieutenant Leaphorn about this, only to find the building locked and only about two people at work. She had waited in her car for almost half an hour before the front door had been unlocked.

This discourse required approximately five minutes, giving Leaphorn time to think that the councilwoman had actually driven in to attend the Tribal Council meeting, which began today, that the Cañoncito Band had not been happy with the tribal government since 1868, when the tribe returned from its years of captivity at Fort Stanton, that the councilwoman unquestionably knew it wasn't fair to expect more than a radio dispatcher and a night staffer to be on duty at dawn, that the councilwoman had gone over this complaint with him at least twice before, and that the councilwoman was making a lot of her early rising to remind Leaphorn that Navajo bureaucrats, like all good Navajos, should be up at dawn to bless the rising sun with prayer and a pinch of pollen.

Now the councilwoman was silent. Leaphorn, Navajo fashion, waited for the signal that would tell him whether she had finished with what she had to say or was merely pausing to collect her thoughts. The councilwoman sighed, and shook her head.

"Not no Navajo police at all," she summarized. "Not one on the whole Cañoncito Reservation. All we got is a Laguna policeman, now and then, part of the time." She paused again. Leaphorn waited.

"He just sits there in that little building by the road and he doesn't do nothing. Most of the time he's not even there." The councilwoman, aware that Leaphorn had heard all this before, wasn't bothering to look at him while she recited it. She was studying his map.

"You call on the telephone and nobody answers. You go by there and knock, nobody home." Her eyes drifted from map to Leaphorn. She was finished.

"Your Cañoncito policeman is an officer of the Bureau of Indian Affairs," Leaphorn said. "He's a Laguna Indian, but he's actually a BIA policeman. He doesn't work for the Lagunas. He works for you." Leaphorn explained, as he had twice before, that since the Cañoncito Band lived on a reservation way over by Albuquerque, so far from the Big Reservation, and since only twelve hundred Navajos lived there, the Judicial Committee of the Tribal Council had voted to work out a deal with the BIA instead of keeping a full shift of the NTP stationed there. Leaphorn did not mention that the councilwoman was a member of that committee, and neither did the councilwoman. She listened with patient Navajo courtesy, her eyes wandering across Leaphorn's map.

"Just two kinds of pins on the Cañoncito," she said when Leaphorn had finished.

"Those are left over from before the Tribal Council voted to give jurisdiction to the Bureau of Indian Affairs," Leaphorn said, trying to avoid the next question, which would be What do the pins mean? The pins were all in shades of red or were black, Leaphorn's way of marking alcohol-related arrests and witchcraft complaints. The two were really Cañoncito's only disruptions of the peace. Leaphorn did not believe in witches, but there were those on the Big Reservation who claimed everybody at Cañoncito must be a skinwalker.

"Because of that decision by the Tribal Council, the BIA takes care of Cañoncito," Leaphorn concluded.

"No," the councilwoman said. "The BIA don't."

The morning had gone like that. The councilwoman finally left, replaced by a small freckled white man who declared himself owner of the company that provided stock for the Navajo rodeo. He wanted assurance that his broncos, riding bulls, and roping calves would be adequately guarded at night. That pulled Leaphorn into the maze of administrative decisions, memos, and paperwork required by the rodeo—an event dreaded by all hands in the Window Rock contingent of the tribal police. Before he could finish the adjustments required to police this three-day flood of macho white cowboys, macho Indian cowboys, cowboy groupies, drunks, thieves, con men, Texans, swindlers, photographers, and just plain tourists, the telephone rang again.

It was the principal of Kinlichee Boarding School, reporting that Emerson Tso had reopened his bootlegging operation. Not only was Tso selling to any Kinlichee student willing to make the short walk over to his place; he was bringing bottles to the dorm at night. The principal wanted Tso locked up forever. Leaphorn, who detested whiskey as ardently as he hated witchcraft, promised to have Tso brought in that day. His voice was so grim when he said it that the principal simply said thank you and hung up.

And so finally, just before lunch, there was time for thinking about three unsolved homicides and the question of coincidence. But first Leaphorn took the telephone off the hook. He walked to the window and looked out across the narrow asphalt of Navajo Route 27 at the scattered red-stone buildings that housed the government bureaucracy of his tribe, at the sandstone cliffs behind the village, and at the thunderclouds beginning to form in the August sky, clouds that in this summer of drought would probably not climb quite high enough up the sky to release any moisture. He cleared his mind of Tribal Council members, rodeos, and bootleggers. Sitting again, he swiveled his chair to face the map.

Leaphorn's map was known throughout the tribal police—a symbol of his eccentricity. It was mounted on corkboard on the wall behind his desk—a common "Indian Country" map published by the Auto Club of Southern California and popular for its large scale and its accurate details. What drew attention to Leaphorn's map was the way he used it.

It was decorated in a hundred places with colored pins, each color representing its own sort of crime. It was inscribed in a hundred places with notes written in Leaphorn's cryptic shorthand. The notes reminded Leaphorn of information he'd accumulated in a lifetime of living on the reservation and half a lifetime of working it as a cop. The tiny *q* west of Three Turkey Ruins meant quicksand in Tse Des Zygee Wash. The *r* beside the road to Ojleto on the Utah border (and beside dozens of other such roads) recalled spots where rainstorms made passage doubtful. The *c*'s linked with family initials marked the sites of summer sheep camps along the mountain slopes. Myriad such reminders freckled the map. *W*'s marked places where witchcraft incidents had been reported. *B*'s marked the homes of bootleggers.

The notes were permanent, but the pins came and went with the ebb and flow of misbehavior. Blue ones marked places where cattle had been stolen. They disappeared when the cattle thief was caught driving a truckload of heifers down a back road. Gaudy rashes of scarlet, red, and pink ones (the colors Leaphorn attached to alcohol-related crimes) spread and subsided inside the reservation with the fate of bootleggers. They made a permanent rosy blotch around reservation border towns and lined the entrance highways. Markers for rapes, violent assaults, family mayhem, and other, less damaging, violent losses of control tended to follow and mingle with the red. A few pins, mostly on the reservation's margins, marked such white-man crimes as burglary, vandalism, and robbery. At the moment, Leaphorn was interested only in three brown pins with white centers. They marked his homicides.

Homicides were unusual on the reservation. Violent death was usually accidental: a drunk stumbling in front of a passing car, drunken fights outside a bar, an alcohol-primed explosion of family tensions—the sort of unpremeditated violence that lends itself to instant solutions. When brown-and-white pins appeared, they rarely remained more than a day or two.

Now there were three. And they'd been stuck in Leaphorn's corkboard, and in his consciousness, for weeks. In fact, the oldest had been there almost two months.

Irma Onesalt was her name—pin number one. Leaphorn had stuck it beside the road between Upper Greasewood and Lukachukai fifty-four days ago. The bullet that killed her was a 30-06, the second most popular caliber in the world and the one that hung on the rifle rack across the rear window of every third pickup truck on the reservation, and around it. Everybody seemed to own one, if they didn't own a 30-30. And sometimes even if they did. Irma Onesalt, born to the Bitter Water Clan, born for the Towering House People, daughter of Alice and Homer Onesalt, thirty-one years old, unmarried, agent of the Navajo Office of Social Services, found in the front seat of her overturned Datsun two-door, hit in the jaw and throat by a bullet that smashed through the driver's-side window and, after destroying her, lodged in the opposite door. They had found a witness, more or less and maybe. A student from the Toadlena Boarding School had been en route home to visit her parents. She had noticed a man—an old man, she'd said—sitting in a pickup truck parked about where the shot would have been fired from. That theory presumed that Irma Onesalt had lost control of the Datsun the moment she'd been hit. Leaphorn had seen the body. It seemed a safe presumption.

Pin two, two weeks later, represented Dugai Endocheeney, born to the Mud People, born for the Streams Come Together Clan. Maybe seventy-five, maybe seventy-seven, depending on whom you believed. Stabbed (the butcher knife left in his body) at the sheep pen behind his hogan on the Nokaito Bench, not far from where Chinle Creek runs into the San Juan River. Dilly Streib, the agent in charge, had said there was an obvious connection between pin one and pin two. "Onesalt didn't have any friends, and Endocheeney didn't have any enemies," Dilly had said. "Somebody is working from both ends. Going to keep knocking off good ones and bad ones until there's nothing left but the middle."

"Just us average ones," Leaphorn said.

Streib had laughed. "I think he'll get to you pretty quick, on the obnoxious end."

Delbert L. Streib wasn't your usual FBI agent. It had always seemed to Leaphorn, who had spent a tour at the FBI Academy and half his life running errands for the Agency, that Streib was smarter than most. He had a quick, innovative intelligence, which had made him a terrible misfit in the J. Edgar Hoover years and got him exiled to Indian country. But Streib, whose case it was since it was a homicide committed on a federal reservation, had drawn a blank on Onesalt. And on Endocheeney. And so had Leaphorn.

When he had seen Leaphorn's map, Streib had argued that pin two should be pin three. And maybe he was right. Leaphorn had assigned the third pin to Wilson Sam, born to the One Walks Around Clan, and born for the Turning Mountain People. The late Mr. Sam was fifty-seven, a herder of sheep who sometimes worked on Arizona Highway Department grader crews. He had been hit on the back of the neck with the blade of a shovel, so very, very hard that there was no question he had died instantly. But there was a question of when he had been hit. Sam's nephew had found the victim's sheepdog, voiceless from howling and half dead from thirst, sitting on the rim of Chilchinbito Canyon. Wilson Sam's body was on the canyon floor below—apparently dragged to the edge and tumbled over. The autopsy suggested a time of death about the same as Endocheeney's. So who died first? Anyone's guess. Again, no witnesses, no clues, no apparent motive, not much of anything except the negative fact that if the coroner was right, it would have been very difficult for the same man to have killed them both.

"Unless he was a skinwalker," Dilly Streib had said, looking somber, "and you guys are right about skinwalkers being able to fly, and outrun turbocharged pickup trucks, and so forth."

Leaphorn didn't mind Streib kidding him, but he didn't like anyone kidding him about witches. He hadn't laughed.

Remembering it now, he still didn't laugh. He sighed, scratched his ear, shifted in the chair. Staring at the map today took him exactly where it had taken him the last time he tried it. One pin was a Window Rock pin, relatively speaking. The first one. The next two were out-in-the-boondocks pins.

The first victim was a bureaucrat, younger, female, more sophisticated. Shot. The last two were men who had followed their flocks, traditional people, probably spoke little English, killed at close quarters. Did he have two separate cases? So it would seem. In the Window Rock case, premeditation—rarity of rarities on the reservation—was obvious. In the boondocks cases, it was possible but didn't look probable. A shovel hardly seemed a likely weapon of choice. And if you were determined to kill someone, most Navajos Leaphorn knew could take along an easier weapon than a butcher knife.

Leaphorn thought about his cases separately. He got nowhere. He thought about them as a trio. Same results. He isolated the Onesalt killing, considered everything they had learned about the woman. Mean as a snake, it seemed. People hesitated to badmouth the dead, but they had trouble finding anything good to say about Irma. No, Irma was a busybody. Irma was a militant. Irma was an angry young woman. Irma made trouble. As far as he could learn, she had no jilted lovers. In fact, the only one who seemed to mourn her aside from her immediate family was a longtime and apparently devoted live-in boyfriend—a schoolteacher at Lukachukai. Leaphorn always suspected devoted boyfriends in homicide cases. But this one had been standing in front of twenty-eight students talking about math when Onesalt was killed.

The mail arrived. Without breaking his concentration on the problem, idly, he sorted through it, mind still on Onesalt. Two telexes from the FBI were on top of the stack. The first one contained the details of the Jim Chee affair. He read the telex quickly. Nothing much new. Chee had not given chase. Chee said he had no idea who might have fired the shots. Tracks left by size seven rubber-soled running shoes had been found adjoining the trailer. They led about four hundred yards to a point where a vehicle had been parked. Tracks indicated worn tires. Drippage where vehicle had parked indicated either a lengthy stay or a serious oil leak.

Leaphorn set the message aside, expression glum. Again, no motive. But there was a motive, of course. When someone tries to ambush a cop there is a strong motive, and the motive tends to be unpleasant. Well, Chee was Captain Largo's boy, and finding out what Officer Chee was doing to provoke such a reaction would be Largo's problem.

The second telex reported that Agent Jay Kennedy of the Farmington office would this date locate and interrogate subject Roosevelt Bistie in connection with the Dugai Endocheeney homicide. Two witnesses had been located who placed a vehicle owned by Bistie at the Endocheeney hogan at the time of the killing. Another witness indicated that the driver of the vehicle had said he intended to kill Endocheeney. Any officer with any information about subject Roosevelt Bistie was asked to contact Agent Kennedy.

Leaphorn turned the paper over and looked at the back. Blank, of course. He glanced at the map, mentally removing the Endocheeney pin. The triangle of unsolved crimes became a line—two dots and no real reason to link them. It looked suddenly as if his rash of homicides were, in fact, coincidences. Two unsolved was a hell of a lot better than three. And perhaps Bistie would also prove to be the Wilson Sam killer. That seemed logical. The lives of the two men might be linked in many ways. Leaphorn felt much better. Order was returning to his world.

The telephone buzzed.

"This is your day for politicians, Lieutenant," the desk clerk said. "Dr. Yellowhorse wants to talk to you."

Leaphorn tried to think of some workable reason to justify not seeing Dr. Yellowhorse, who was a tribal councilman representing the Badwater Chapter and a member of the Tribal Council Judiciary Committee, as well as a doctor. And who, as a doctor, was founder and chief of medical staff of the Badwater Clinic.

No reason occurred to Leaphorn. "Tell him to come up," he said.

"I think he's already up," the clerk said.

Leaphorn's office door opened.

Dr. Bahe Yellowhorse was a barrel of a man. He wore a black felt reservation hat with a silver-and-turquoise band and a turkey feather. A closely braided rope of hair hung, Sioux fashion, behind each ear, the end of each tied with a red string. The belt that held his jeans over his broad, flat belly was two inches wide, studded with turquoise and buckled with a sand-cast silver replica of Rainbow Man curved around the symbol of Father Sun.

"*Ya-tah*," said Yellowhorse, grinning. But the grin looked mechanical.

"*Ya-tah-hey*," Leaphorn said. "Have a ch—"

"Going to have a meeting of Judicial Committee this afternoon," Yellowhorse said, easing himself into the chair across from Leaphorn's desk. "My people want me to talk to the committee about doing something to catch that fellow that killed Hosteen Endocheeney."

Yellowhorse dug in the pocket of his denim shirt and dug out a package of cigarets, giving Leaphorn an opportunity to comment. Leaphorn didn't. Old Man Endocheeney had been a resident of that great sprawl of Utah-Arizona borderlands included in the Badwater Chapter. Leaphorn didn't want to discuss the case with Tribal Councilman Bahe Yellowhorse.

"We're working on it," he said.

"That means you're not getting nowhere," said Yellowhorse. "You having any luck at all?"

"The FBI has jurisdiction," Leaphorn said, thinking that this was his day for telling people what they already knew. "Felony committed on federal trust land comes under—"

Yellowhorse held up a huge brown hand. "Save it," he said. "I know how it works. The feds don't know anything unless you guys tell 'em. You finding out who killed Endocheeney? I need to know something to tell my people back at the chapter house."

He leaned back in the wooden chair, extracted a cigaret from the package, and tapped its filtered end uselessly against his thumbnail, eyes on Leaphorn.

Leaphorn considered his police academy conditioning against ever telling anybody anything about anything, weighed it against common sense. Yellowhorse was sometimes an unusually severe pain in the ass, but he did have a legitimate interest. Beyond that, Leaphorn admired the man and respected what he was trying to do. Bahe Yellowhorse, born to the Dolii Dinee, the Blue Bird People of his mother. But he had no paternal clan. His father was an Oglala Sioux. Yellowhorse had founded the Bad Water Clinic mostly with his own money. True, there was a big Kellogg Foundation grant in it, and some other foundation money, and some federal funds. But from what Leaphorn knew, most of the money, and all of the energy, had come from Yellowhorse himself.

"You can tell them we have a suspect in the Endocheeney homicide," Leaphorn said. "Witnesses put him at the hogan at the right time. Expect to pick him up today and talk to him."

"You got the right fellow?" Yellowhorse asked. "He have a motive?"

"We haven't talked to him," Leaphorn said. "We're told he said he wanted to kill Endocheeney, so you can presume a motive."

Yellowhorse shrugged. "How about the other killing? Whatever his name was?"

"We don't know," Leaphorn said. "Maybe they're connected."

"Your suspect," Yellowhorse said. He paused, put the cigaret between his lips, lit it with a silver lighter, and exhaled smoke. "He another one of my constituents?"

"Seems to live up in the Lukachukais. Long way from your country."

Yellowhorse stared at Leaphorn, waiting for further explanation. None came. He inhaled smoke again, held it in his lungs, let it trickle from his nostrils. He extracted the cigaret and came just close enough to pointing it at Leaphorn to imply the insult without delivering it. Navajos do not point at one another.

"You guys s'posed to be out of the religion business, aren't you? Since the court cracked down on you for hassling the peyote people?"

Leaphorn's dark face turned a shade darker. "We haven't been arresting anyone for possession of peyote for years," Leaphorn said. He had been very young when the Tribal Council had passed its ill-fated law banning the use of hallucinogens, a law openly aimed at suppressing the Native American Church, which used peyote as a sacrament. He hadn't liked the law, had been glad when the federal court ruled it violated the First Amendment, and he didn't like to be reminded of it. He especially didn't like to be reminded of it in this insulting way by Yellowhorse.

"How about the Navajo religion?" Yellowhorse asked. "The tribal police got any policies against that these days?"

"No," Leaphorn said.

"I didn't think you did," Yellowhorse said. "But you got a cop working out of Shiprock who seems to think you have."

Yellowhorse inhaled tobacco smoke. Leaphorn waited. Yellowhorse waited. Leaphorn waited longer.

"I'm a crystal gazer," Yellowhorse said. "Always had a gift for it, since I was a boy. But only been practicing for the last few years. People come to me at the clinic. I tell 'em what's wrong with 'em. What kind of cure they need."

Leaphorn said nothing. Yellowhorse smoked, exhaled. Smoked again.

"If they have been fooling with wood that's been struck by lightning, or been around a grave too much, or have ghost sickness, then I tell them whether they need a Mountaintop sign, or an Enemy Way, or whatever cure they need. If they need a gallstone removed, or their tonsils out, or a course of antibiotics to knock a strep infection, then I check them into the clinic for that. Now, the American Medical Association hasn't approved it, but it's free. No charge. And a lot of the people out there are getting to know about me doing it, and it brings 'em in where we can get a look at 'em. The sick ones come in. Wouldn't have come in otherwise. They'd have gone to some other medicine man instead of me. And that way we catch a lot of early diabetic cases, and glaucoma, and skin cancer, blood poisoning, and God knows what."

"I've heard about it," Leaphorn said. He was remembering what else he'd heard. He'd heard that Yellowhorse liked to tell how his mother had died out there in that empty country of a little cut on her foot. It had led to an infection, and gangrene, because she never got any medical help. That, so the story went, was how Yellowhorse was orphaned, and got stuck in a Mormon orphanage, and got adopted into a large amount of Midwestern farm machinery money, and inherited a way to build himself a clinic—sort of a perfect circle.

"Sounds like a good idea to me," Leaphorn said. "We damn sure wouldn't have any policy against it."

"One of your cops does," Yellowhorse said. "He's telling people I'm a fake and to stay away from me. I hear the little bastard is trying to be a *yataalii* himself. Maybe he thinks I'm unfair competition. Anyway, I want you to tell me how what he's doing squares with the law. If it doesn't square, I want it stopped."

"I'll check into it," Leaphorn said. He reached for his notepad. "What's his name?"

"His name's Jim Chee," Yellowhorse said.

3

ROOSEVELT BISTIE WASN'T at home, his daughter informed them. He had gone into Farmington to get some medicine yesterday, and was going to spend the night with his other daughter, at Shiprock, and then drive back this morning.

"When do you expect him?" Jay Kennedy asked. The relentless high desert sun of the reservation had burned the yellow out of Kennedy's short blond hair and left it almost white, and his skin was peeling. He looked at Chee, waiting for the translation. Bistie's Daughter probably understood English as well as Kennedy, and spoke it as well as Chee, but the way she had chosen to play the game today, she knew only Navajo. Chee guessed she was a little uneasy—that she hadn't seen many sunburned blond white men up close before.

"That's the kind of questions *belagana* ask," Chee told her in Navajo. "I'm going to tell him you expect your father when you see him. How sick is he?"

"Bad, I think," Bistie's Daughter said. "He went to a crystal gazer down there at Two Story and the crystal gazer told him he needed a Mountaintop sing. I think he's got something wrong with his liver." She paused. "What do you policemen want him for?"

"She says she expects him when he gets here," Chee told Kennedy. "We could start back and maybe meet him on the road. Or we could just wait here. I'll ask her if she knows where the old man went—what was it—two weeks ago?"

"Just a minute." Kennedy motioned Chee over toward the Agency's carryall. "I think she can understand some English," he said in just above a whisper. "We have to be careful of what we say."

"I wouldn't be surprised," Chee said. He turned back to Bistie's Daughter.

"Two weeks ago?" she asked. "Let's see. He went to see the crystal gazer the second Monday in July. That's when I go in and get all my laundry done down at Red Rock Trading Post. He took me down there. And then it was . . ." She thought, a sturdy young woman in an "I Love Hawaii" T-shirt, jeans, and squaw boots. Pigeon-toed, Chee noticed. He remembered his sociology professor at the University of New Mexico saying that modern dentistry had made crooked teeth an identifying mark of those who were born into the bottommost fringe of the American socioeconomic classes. Unstraightened teeth for the white trash, uncorrected birth defects for the Navajo. Or, to be fair, for those Navajos who lived out of reach of the Indian Health Service. Bistie's Daughter shifted her weight on those bent ankles. "Well," she said, "it would have been about a week later. About two weeks ago. He took the truck. I didn't want him to go because he had been feeling worse. Throwing up his food. But he said he had to go find a man somewhere way over there around Mexican Hat or Montezuma Creek." She jerked her chin in the general direction of north. "Over by Utah."

"Did he say why?"

"What you want to see him about?" Bistie's Daughter asked.

"She says Bistie went to see a man over by the Utah border two weeks ago," Chee told Kennedy.

"Ah," Kennedy said. "Right time. Right place."

"I don't think I will talk to you anymore," Bistie's Daughter said. "Not unless you tell me what you want to talk to my father. What's wrong with that *belagana*'s face?"

"That's what sunshine does to white people's skin," Chee said. "Somebody got killed over there around Mexican Hat two weeks ago. Maybe your father saw something. Maybe he could tell us something."

Bistie's Daughter looked shocked. "Killed?"

"Yes," Chee said.

"I'm not going to talk to you anymore," Bistie's Daughter said. "I'm going into the house now." And she did.

Chee and Kennedy talked it over. Chee recommended waiting awhile. Kennedy decided they would wait one hour. They sat in the carryall, feet hanging out opposite doors, and sipped the cans of Pepsi-Cola that Bistie's Daughter had given them when they arrived. "Warm Pepsi-Cola," Kennedy said, his voice full of wonder. This remark caught Chee thinking of the way the buckshot had torn through the foam rubber of his mattress, fraying it, ripping away chunks just about over the place where his kidneys would have been. Thinking of who wanted to kill him. Of why. He had thought about the same subjects all day, interrupting his gloomy ruminations only with an occasional yearning thought of Mary Landon's impending return to Crownpoint. Neither produced any positive results. Better to think of warm Pepsi-Cola. For him, it was a familiar taste, full of nostalgia. Why did the white culture either cool things or heat them before consumption? The first time he had experienced a cold bottle of pop had been at the Teec Nos Pos Trading Post. He'd been about twelve. The school bus driver had bought a bottle for everyone on the baseball team. Chee remembered drinking it, standing in the shade of the porch. The remembered pleasure faded into the thought that anyone with a shotgun in any passing car could have mowed him down. Someone now, on the ridgeline behind Bistie's hogan, could be looking over a rifle sight at the center of his back.

Chee moved his shoulders uneasily. Took a sip of the Pepsi. Turned his thoughts back to why whites always iced it. Less heat. Less energy. Less motion in the molecules. He poked at that for a cultural conclusion, found himself drawn back to the sound of the shotgun, the flash of light. What had he, Jim Chee, done to warrant that violent reaction?

Suddenly, he badly wanted to talk to someone about it. "Kennedy," he said. "What do you think about last night? About . . ."

"You getting shot at?" Kennedy said. They had covered that question two or three times while driving out from Shiprock, and Kennedy had already said what he thought. Now he said it again, in slightly different words. "Hell, I don't know. Was me, I'd been examining my conscience. Whose lady I'd been chasing. Anybody's feelings I'd hurt. Any enemies I'd made. Anybody I'd arrested who just recently got out of jail. That sort of thing."

"The kind of people I arrest are mostly too drunk to remember who arrested 'em. Or care," Chee said. "If they have enough money to buy shotgun shells they buy a bottle instead. They're the kind of people who have eaten a lot of shaky soup." As for whose lady he had been chasing, there hadn't been any lady lately.

"Shaky soup?" Kennedy asked.

"Local joke," Chee said. "Lady down at Gallup runs her own soup line for drunks when the cops let 'em out of the tank. They're shaking, so everybody calls it shaky soup." He decided not to try to explain another reason it was called shaky soup: the combination of Navajo gutturals used to express it was almost identical to the sounds that said penis—thereby producing the material for one of those earthy puns Navajos treasure. He had tried once to explain to Kennedy how the similarity of Navajo words for rodeo and chicken could be used to produce jokes. Kennedy hadn't seen the humor.

"Well," Kennedy said. "I'd examine my conscience, then. Somebody shoots at a cop . . ." Kennedy shrugged, let the sentence trail off without finishing the implication.

Captain Largo had not bothered to be so polite this morning in Largo's office. "It's been my experience," the captain had rumbled, "that when a policeman has got himself in a situation where somebody is coming after him to kill him, then that policeman has been up to something." Captain Largo had been sitting behind his desk, examining Chee pensively over his tented fingers, when he said it, and it hadn't angered Chee until later, when he was back in his patrol car remembering the interview. Now the reaction was quicker. He felt a flush of hot blood in his face.

"Look," Chee said. "I don't like—"

Just then they heard a vehicle clanking and groaning up the track.

Kennedy removed the pistol from the holster under his jacket on the seat, put on the jacket, dropped the pistol into the jacket pocket. Chee watched the track. An elderly GMC pickup, rusty green, emerged from the junipers. A 30-30 lever-action carbine was in the rack across the back window. The pickup eased to a slow, almost dustless stop. The man driving it was old and thin, with a black felt reservation hat pushed back on his head. He looked at them curiously while the engine wheezed to a stop, sat for a moment considering them, and then climbed out.

"*Ya-tah-hey,*" Chee said, still standing beside the carryall.

Bistie responded gravely with the Navajo greeting, looking at Chee and then at Kennedy.

"I am born for Red Forehead People, the son of Tessie Chee, but now I work for all of the Dinee. For the Navajo Tribal Police. This man"—Chee indicated Kennedy Navajo fashion, by shifting his lips in Kennedy's direction—"is an FBI officer. We have come here to talk to you."

Roosevelt Bistie continued his inspection. He dropped his ignition key in his jeans pocket. He was a tall man, stooped a little now by age and illness, his face the odd copper color peculiar to advanced jaundice. But he smiled slightly. "Police?" he said. "Then I guess I hit the son-of-a-bitch."

It took Chee a moment to digest this—the admission, then the nature of the admission.

"What did he—" Kennedy began. Chee held up his hand.

"Hit him?" Chee asked. "How?"

Bistie looked surprised. "Shot the son-of-a-bitch," he said. "With that rifle there in the truck. Is he dead?"

Kennedy was frowning. "What's he saying?"

"Shot who?" Chee asked. "Where?"

"Over there past Mexican Hat," Bistie said. "Over there almost to the San Juan River. He was a Mud Clan man. I forget what they call him." Bistie grinned at Chee. "Is he dead? I thought maybe I missed him."

"Oh, he's dead," Chee said. He turned to Kennedy. "We have a funny one here. He says he shot Old Man Endocheeney. With his rifle."

"Shot?" Kennedy said. "What about the butcher knife? He wasn't—"

Chee stopped him. "He probably speaks some English. Let's talk. I think we should take him back over there. Have him show us what happened."

Kennedy's face flushed under the peeling epidermis. "We haven't read him his rights," he said. "He's not supposed—"

"He hasn't told us anything in English yet," Chee said. "Just in Navajo. He's still got a right to remain silent in English until he talks to a lawyer."

Bistie told them just about everything on the long, dusty drive that took them out of the Lukachukais, and back through Shiprock, and westward into Arizona, and northward into Utah.

"Navajo or not," Kennedy had said, "we better read him his rights." And he did, with Chee translating it into Navajo.

"Better late than never, I guess," Kennedy said. "But who would guess a suspect would walk right up and tell you he shot the guy?"

"When he didn't," Chee said.

"When he stuck him with a butcher knife," Kennedy said.

"Why is the white man talking all this bullshit about a knife?" Bistie asked.

"I'll explain that," Chee said. "You haven't told us why you shot him."

And he didn't. Bistie continued his account. Of making sure the 30–30 was loaded. Of making sure the sights were right, because he hadn't fired it since shooting a deer last winter. Of the long drive to Mexican Hat. Of asking people there how to find the Mud Clan man. Of driving up to the hogan of the Mud Clan man, just about this time of day, with a thunderstorm building up, and taking the rifle down off the rack, and cocking it, and finding nobody at the hogan, but a pickup truck parked there, and guessing that the Mud Clan man would be around somewhere. And hearing the sound of someone hammering, and seeing the Mud Clan man working on a shed back in an arroyo behind the hogan—nailing on loose boards. And then Bistie described standing there looking over the sights at the Mud Clan man, and seeing the man looking back at him just as he pulled the trigger. And he told them how, when the smoke had cleared, the man was no longer on the roof. He told them absolutely everything about the chronology and the mechanics of it all. But he told them absolutely nothing about why he had done it. When Chee asked again, Bistie simply sat, grimly silent. And Chee didn't ask why he was claiming to have shot a man who had been knifed to death.

While Roosevelt Bistie talked, describing this insanity in a calm, matter-of-fact, old man's voice, Chee found other questions forming in his mind.

"You were in Shiprock last night? At your daughter's house? Tell me her name. Where she lives."

Chee wrote the name and place in his notebook. It would have taken Old Man Bistie ten minutes to drive from that Shiprock address to Chee's trailer.

"What are you writing?" Kennedy asked.

Chee grunted.

"Do you have a shotgun?" he asked Bistie.

There is no Navajo word for shotgun and Kennedy caught the noun.

"Hey," he said. "What are you getting into?"

"Just the rifle," Bistie said.

"I'm getting into who tried to shoot Jim Chee," Jim Chee said.

4

AWAKENING WAS ABRUPT. An oblong of semi-blackness against the total darkness. The door of the summer hogan left open. Through it, against the eastern horizon, the faint glow of false dawn. Had the boy cried out? There was nothing but silence now. No air moved. No night insect stirred. Anxiety alone seemed to have overcome sleep. There was the smell of dust, of the endless, sheep-killing drought. And the smell, very faint, of something chemical. Oil, maybe. More and more, the truck engine leaked oil. Where it stood in the yard beside the brush arbor, the earth was hard and black with the drippings. A quart, at least, every time they drove it. More than a dollar a quart. And not enough money, not now, to get it fixed. All the money had gone with the birth of the boy, with the time they had had to spend at the hospital while the doctors looked at him. Anencephaly, the doctor had called it. The woman had written the word on a piece of paper for them, standing beside the bed in a room that seemed too cold, too full of the smell of white-man medicines. "Unusual," the woman had said. "But I know of two other cases on the reservation in the past twenty years. It happens to everybody. So it happens to Navajos too."

What did anencephaly mean? It meant Boy Child, the son, would live only a little while. "See," the woman had said, and she had brushed back the thin hair on the top of Boy Child's head. But it had already been apparent. The top of the head was almost flat. "The brain has not formed," the woman had said, "and the child cannot live long without that. Just a few weeks. We don't know what causes it. And we don't know anything to do about it."

Well, there were things that the *belagana* doctors didn't know. There was a cause, for this and for everything. And because there was a cause, something could be done about it. The cure lay in undoing that cause, restoring the harmony inside the small, fragile skull of Boy Child. The skinwalker had caused it, for some reason lost in the dark heart of malicious evil. Thus the skinwalker must die. His brain must shrivel so the brain of Boy Child could grow. And quickly. Quickly. Quickly. Kill the witch. The anxiety rose into something close to panic. Stomach knotted. Despite the predawn chill, the blanket roll against the cheek was damp with sweat.

The shotgun had seemed a good idea—fired through the thin skin of the trailer into the bed where the witch was sleeping. But skinwalkers were hard to kill. Somehow the skinwalker had known. It had flown from the bed and the bone had missed.

Boy Child stirred now. Sleep for him was always momentary, a fading out of consciousness that rarely lasted an hour. And then the whimpering would start again. A calling out to those who loved him, were bone of his bone and flesh of his flesh. The whimpering began, the only sound in the darkness. Just a sound, like that the newborn young of animals make. It seemed to say: Help me. Help me. Help me.

There would be no more sleep now. Not for a while. No time to sleep. Boy Child seemed weaker every day. He had already lived longer than the *belagana* woman at the hospital had said he would. No time for anything except finding the way to kill the witch. There had to be a way. The witch was a policeman, and hard to kill, and being a skinwalker, he had the powers skinwalkers gain—to fly through the air, to run as fast as the wind can blow, to change themselves into dogs and wolves and maybe other animals. But there must be a way to kill him.

The rectangle of the door frame grew lighter. Possibilities appeared and were considered, and modified, and rejected. Some were rejected because they might not work. Most were rejected because they were suicidal: The witch would die, but there would be no one left to keep Boy Child from starving. There must be a way to escape undetected. Nothing else was a useful solution.

In the cardboard box where he was kept, Boy Child whimpered endlessly—a pattern of sound as regular and mindless as an insect might make. A faint breeze moved the air, stirring the cloth that hung beside the hogan doorway—Dawn Girl awakening to prepare the day. About then the thought came: how it could be done. It was simple. It would work. And the witch they called Jim Chee would surely die.

5

LIEUTENANT JOE LEAPHORN nosed his patrol car into the shade of the Russian olive tree at the edge of the parking lot. He turned off the ignition. He eased himself into a more comfortable position and considered again how he would deal with Officer Chee. Chee's vehicle was parked in a row of five patrol cars lined along the sidewalk outside the entrance of the Navajo Tribal Police Station, Shiprock subagency. Unit 4. Leaphorn knew Chee was driving Unit 4 because he knew everything officially knowable about Chee. He had called the records clerk at 9:10 this morning and had Chee's personnel file sent upstairs. He'd read every word in it. Just a short time earlier, he had received a call from Dilly Streib. Streib had bad news.

"Weird one," Streib had said. "Kennedy picked up Roosevelt Bistie, and Roosevelt Bistie said he shot Endocheeney."

It took only a millisecond for the incongruity to register. "Shot," Leaphorn said. "Not stabbed?"

"Shot," Streib said. "Said he'd gone over to Endocheeney's hogan, and Endocheeney was fixing the roof of a shed, and Bistie shot him, and Endocheeney disappeared—fell off, I guess—and Bistie drove on home."

"What do you think?" Leaphorn asked.

"Kennedy didn't seem to have any doubt Bistie was telling the truth. Said they were waiting at Bistie's house, and he drove up and saw they were cops, and right away said something about shooting Endocheeney."

"Bistie speak English?"

"Navajo," Streib said.

"Who'd we have along? Who interpreted?" What Streib was telling him seemed crazy. Maybe there had been some sort of misunderstanding.

"Just a second." Leaphorn heard papers rustling. "Officer Jim Chee," Streib said. "Know him?"

"I know him," said Leaphorn, wishing he knew him better.

"Anyhow, I'll send you the paperwork on it. Thought you'd want to know it turned funny."

"Yeah. Thanks," Leaphorn said. "Why did Bistie want to kill Endocheeney?"

"Wouldn't say. Flatass refused to talk about it at all. Kennedy said he seemed to think he might have missed the man, and then he was glad when he found out the guy was dead. Wouldn't say a word about what he had against him."

"Chee did the questioning?"

"Sure. I guess so. Kennedy doesn't speak Navajo."

"One more thing. Was it Chee on this from the beginning? Working with Kennedy, I mean, back when the investigation opened?"

"Just a sec," Streib said. Papers rustled. "Here it is. Yeah. Chee."

"Well, thanks," Leaphorn said. "I'll look for the report."

He clicked the receiver cradle down with a finger, got the file room, and ordered Chee's folder.

While he waited for it, he pulled open the desk drawer, extracted a brown pin with a white center, and carefully stuck it back in the hole where the Endocheeney pin had been. He looked at the map a minute. Then he reached into the drawer again, took out another brown-and-white pin, and stuck it at the *p* in "Shiprock." Four pins now. One north of Window Rock, one on the Utah borderlands, one on Chilchinbito Canyon, one over in New Mexico. And now there was a connection. Faint, problematical, but something. Jim Chee had investigated the Endocheeney killing before someone had tried to kill Chee. Had Chee learned something that made him a threat to Endocheeney's killer?

Leaphorn had been smiling, but as he thought, the smile thinned and disappeared. He could see no possible way this helped. Getting old, Leaphorn thought. He had reached the ridge and now the slope was downward. The thought didn't depress him, but it gave him an odd sense of pressure, of time moving past him, of things that needed to be done before time ran out. Leaphorn considered this, and laughed. Most un-Navajo thinking. He had been around white men far too long.

He picked up the phone and called Captain Largo at Shiprock. He told Largo he wanted to talk to Jim Chee.

"What's he done now?" Largo said. And he sounded relieved, Leaphorn thought, when Leaphorn explained.

The short route from Window Rock to Shiprock, through Crystal and Sheep Springs, is a 120-mile drive over the hump of the Chuska Mountains. Leaphorn, who rarely broke the speed limit, drove it far too fast. It was mostly a matter of nerves.

And sitting here in the parking lot at Shiprock, he was still tense. Cumulus clouds climbing the sky over the Chuskas were tall enough to form the anvil tops that promised rain. But here the August sun glared off the asphalt beyond the small shade of Leaphorn's olive. He'd told Largo he'd be here by one, almost forty-five minutes away. Largo had said he'd have Chee on hand at one. Now Largo would be out to lunch. Leaphorn considered lunch for himself. A quick hamburger at the Burgerchef out on the highway. But he wasn't hungry. He found himself thinking of Emma, of the appointment he'd made with the neurologist at the Indian Health Service hospital in Gallup.

("Joe," Emma had said. "Please. You know how I feel about it. What can they do? It's headaches. I am out of *hozro*. I will have a sing and be well again. What can the *belagana* do? Saw open my head?" She'd laughed then, as she always laughed when he wanted to talk about her health. "They would cut open my head and let all the wind out," she'd said, smiling at him. He had insisted, and she had refused. "What do you think is wrong with me?" she asked, and he could see that she was, for once, half serious. He had tried to say "Alzheimer's disease," but the words wouldn't form, and he had simply said, "I don't know, but I worry," and she had said, "Well, I'm not going to have any doctor poking around in my head." But he had made the appointment anyway. He inhaled, exhaled. Maybe Emma was right. She could go to a listener, or a hand trembler, or a crystal gazer like Yellowhorse pretended to be, and have a curing ceremonial prescribed.

Then call in the singer to perform the cure, and all the kinfolks to join in the blessing. Would that make her any worse than she'd be when the doctors at Gallup told her that something they didn't understand was killing her and there was nothing they could do about it? What would Yellowhorse tell her if she went to him? Did he know the man well enough to guess? What did he know about him? He knew Yellowhorse was pouring his inherited money and his life into Badwater Clinic, feeding an obsession. He knew he was hiring foreign-trained refugee doctors and nurses—a Vietnamese, a Cambodian, a Salvadoran, a Pakistani—because he could no longer afford the domestic brand. So maybe the money was smaller than the obsession. He knew Yellowhorse was an adept politician. But he didn't know him well enough to guess what his prescription would be for Emma. Would he leave her to the singers or to the neurologists?)

The door of the station opened and three men in the khaki summer uniforms of Navajo Policemen emerged. One was George Benaly, who long ago had worked with Leaphorn out of Many Farms. One was a jolly-looking, plump young man with a thin mustache whom Leaphorn didn't recognize. The other was Jim Chee. The round brim of Chee's hat was tilted, shading his face, but Leaphorn could see enough of it to match the photo in Chee's personnel file. A longish, narrow face fitting a longish, narrow body—all shoulders and no hips. The "Tuba City Navajo," as some anthropologist had labeled the type. Pure Athapaskan genetics. Tall, long torso, narrow pelvis, destined to be a skinny old man. Leaphorn himself fell into the "Checkerboard type." He represented—according to this authority—a blood/gene mix with the Pueblo peoples. Leaphorn didn't particularly like the theory, but it was useful ammunition when Emma pressed him to get his weight and belt size down a bit.

The three officers, still talking, strolled toward their patrol cars. Leaphorn watched. The plump officer had not noticed Leaphorn's car parked under the olive tree. Benaly had seen it without registering any interest. Only Chee was conscious of it, instantly, aware that it was occupied, that the occupant was watching. Perhaps that alertness was the product of being shot at two nights earlier. Leaphorn suspected it was permanent—a natural part of the man's character.

Benaly and Plump Cop climbed into their cars and drove out of the lot.

Chee extracted something from the back seat of his vehicle and strolled back toward the station, conscious of Leaphorn's watching presence. Why wait? Leaphorn thought. He would check in with Largo later.

At Leaphorn's suggestion, they took Chee's police car to Chee's trailer. Chee drove, erect and nervous. The trailer, battered, dented, and looking old and tired, sat under a cluster of cottonwoods not a dozen yards from the crumbling north bank of the San Juan River. Cool, Leaphorn thought. Great spot for someone who wasn't bothered, as Leaphorn was, by mosquitoes. He inspected the three patches of duct tape Chee had used to heal the shotgun wounds in the aluminum skin of his home. About evenly spaced, he noticed. About two feet apart. Each a little more than hip high. Nicely placed to kill somebody in bed if you knew exactly where the bed was located in such a trailer.

"Doesn't look random," Leaphorn said, half to himself.

"No," Chee said. "I think some thought went into it."

"Trailer like this . . . Any trouble for anyone to find out where the bed would be located? How far off the floor?"

"How high to shoot?" Chee said. "No. It's a common kind. When I bought it in Flagstaff there were three just about like it on the used lot. See 'em all the time. Anyway, I think they're all pretty much alike. Where they put the beds."

"I think we'll ask around, anyway. See if somebody who sells them at Farmington, or Gallup, or Flag, can remember anything." He glanced at Chee. "Maybe a customer came in and asked to see this particular model, and pulled out a tape measure and said he had to measure the bed off to see where to hold the shotgun to get himself a Navajo Policeman."

Chee's expressionless face eased into what might have been a smile. "I'm not usually that lucky."

Leaphorn's fingers were on the tape that covered the hole nearest the front of the trailer. He glanced at Chee again.

"Pull it off," Chee said. "I've got more tape."

Leaphorn peeled off the patch, inspected the ragged hole punched through the aluminum, then stooped to peer inside. He could see only blue-and-white cloth. Flowers. Chee's pillow slip. It looked new. Hole torn in the old one, Leaphorn guessed. He was impressed that a bachelor would put a pillowcase on his pillow. Pretty tidy.

"You were lucky when this happened," said Leaphorn, who was always skeptical about luck, who was always skeptical about anything that violated the orderly rules of probability. "The report said your cat woke you up. You keep a cat?"

"Not exactly," Chee said. "It's a neighbor. Lives out there." Chee pointed upstream to a sun-baked slope of junipers. But Leaphorn was still looking thoughtfully at the shotgun hole—measuring its width with his fingers. "Lives out there under that juniper," Chee added. "Sometimes when something scares it, it comes in."

"How?"

Chee showed him the flap he'd cut in the trailer door. Leaphorn examined it. It didn't look new enough to have been put there after the shooting. He noticed that Chee was aware of his examination, and of the suspicion it suggested.

"Who tried to kill you?" Leaphorn asked.

"I don't know," Chee said.

"A new woman?" Leaphorn suggested. "That can cause trouble." Chee's expression became totally blank.

"No," Chee said. "Nothing like that."

"It could be something mild. Maybe just talking too often to a woman with a boyfriend who's paranoid."

"I've got a woman," Chee said slowly.

"You've thought all this out?" Leaphorn asked. He motioned toward the holes in the side of the trailer. "It's your ass somebody's after."

"I've thought about it," Chee said. He threw his hands apart, an angry gesture aimed at himself. "Absolutely damned nothing."

Leaphorn studied him, and found himself half persuaded. It was the gesture as much as the words. "Where did you sleep last night?"

"Out there," Chee said, gesturing toward the hillside. "I have a sleeping bag."

"You and the cat," Leaphorn said. He paused, dug out his pack of cigarets, offered one to Chee, took one himself. "What do you think about Roosevelt Bistie? And Endocheeney?"

"Funny," Chee said. "That whole thing's odd. Bistie's . . ." He paused, hesitated. "Why not come on in," Chee said. "Have a cup of coffee."

"Why not," Leaphorn said.

It was left-over-from-breakfast coffee. Leaphorn, made an authority on bad coffee by more than two decades of police work, rated it slightly worse than most. But it was warm, and it was coffee, and he sipped it appreciatively while Chee, sitting on the bunk where he had so nearly died, told him about meeting Roosevelt Bistie.

"I don't believe he was faking anything," Chee concluded. "He didn't act surprised to see us. Seemed pleased when he heard Endocheeney was dead, and then the whole business about shooting at Endocheeney on the roof, thinking he'd killed him, not really wondering about it until he got home, not going back to make sure because he figured if he hadn't killed him, Endocheeney wouldn't have stuck around to give him a second chance at it." Chee shrugged, shook his head. "Genuine satisfaction when he heard Endocheeney was dead. I just don't think he could have been faking any of that. No reason to. Why not just deny everything?"

"All right," Leaphorn said. "Now, tell me again exactly what he said when you asked him why he wanted to kill Endocheeney."

"Just like I said," Chee said.

"Tell me again."

"He wouldn't say anything. Just shut his mouth and looked grim and wouldn't say a word."

"What do you think?"

Chee shrugged. The light through the window over the trailer sink dimmed slightly. The shadow of the thunderhead over the Chuskas had moved across the Shiprock landscape. With the shadow, the cloud's advance guard of breeze sighed through the window screen. But it wouldn't rain. Leaphorn had studied the cloud. Now he was considering Chee's face, which wore a look of uneasy distaste. Leaphorn felt his own face beginning a smile, a wry one. Here we go again, he thought.

"Witchcraft?" Leaphorn asked. "A skinwalker?"

Chee said nothing. Leaphorn sipped the stale coffee. Chee shrugged. "Well," he said. "That could explain why Bistie wouldn't talk about it."

"That's right," Leaphorn said. He waited.

"Of course," Chee added, "so could other things. Protecting somebody in the family."

"Right," Leaphorn said. "If he tells us his motive, it's also the motive for the guy with the butcher knife. Brother. Cousin. Son. Uncle. What relatives does he have?"

"He's born to the Streams Come Together Dinee," Chee said, "and born for the Standing Rock People. Three maternal aunts, four uncles. Two paternal aunts, five uncles. Then he's got three sisters and a brother, wife's dead, and two daughters and a son. So not even counting his clan brothers and sisters, he's related to just about everybody north of Kayenta."

"Anything else you can think of? For why he won't talk?"

"Something he's ashamed of," Chee said. "Incest. Doing something wrong to some relative. Witchery."

Leaphorn could tell Chee didn't like the third alternative any better than he did.

"If it's witchcraft, which one is the skinwalker?"

"Endocheeney," Chee said.

"Not Bistie," Leaphorn said, thoughtfully. "So if you're right, Bistie killed himself a witch, or intended to." Leaphorn had considered this witch theory before. Nothing much wrong with the idea, except proving it. "You pick up anything about Endocheeney to support it? Or try it on Bistie?"

"Tried it on Bistie. He just looked stubborn. Talked to people up there on the Utah border who knew Endocheeney. Got nothing." Chee was looking at Leaphorn, judging the response.

He's heard about me and witches, Leaphorn thought. "In other words, everybody just shut up," he said. "How about Wilson Sam. Anything there?"

Chee hesitated. "You mean any connection?"

Leaphorn nodded. It was exactly what he was driving at. They were right. Chee was smart.

"That's out of our jurisdiction here," Chee said. "Where he was killed, that's in Chinle's territory. The subagency at Chinle has that case."

"I know that," Leaphorn said. "Did you go out there and look around? Ask around?" It was exactly what Leaphorn would have done under the circumstances—with two killings almost the same hour.

Chee looked surprised, and a little abashed. "On my day off," he said. "Kennedy and I hadn't gotten anything helpful on the Endocheeney thing yet, and I thought—"

Leaphorn held up his palm. "Why not?" he said. "You seeing anything that links them?"

Chee shook his head. "No family connections. Or clan connections. Endocheeney ran sheep, used to work when he was younger with that outfit that lays rails for the Santa Fe railroad. He got food stamps, and now and then sold firewood. Wilson Sam was also a sheepherder, had a job as a flagman on a highway construction job down near Winslow. He was fifty-something years old. Endocheeney was in his middle seventies."

"Did you try Sam's name on people who knew Endocheeney? To see if . . ." Leaphorn made a sort of inclusive gesture.

"No luck," Chee said. "Didn't seem to know the same people. Endocheeney's people didn't know Sam. Sam's people never heard of Endocheeney."

"Did you know either one of them? Ever? In any way? Even something casual?"

"No connection with me, either," Chee said. "They're not the kind of people policemen deal with. Not drunks. Not thieves. Nothing like that."

"No mutual friends?"

Chee laughed. "And no mutual enemies, as far as I can learn."

The laugh, Leaphorn thought, seemed genuine.

"Okay," he said. "How about the shooting-at-you business."

Chee described it again. While he talked, the cat came through the flap in the screen.

It was a large cat, with short tan hair, a stub of a tail, and pointed ears. It stopped just inside the screen, frozen in the crouch, staring at Leaphorn with intense blue eyes. Quite a cat, Leaphorn thought. Heavy haunches like a bobcat. The hair was matted on the left side of its head, and what looked like a scar distorted the smoothness of its flank. Some *belagana* tourist's pet, he guessed. Probably taken along on a vacation and lost. Leaphorn listened to Chee with half of his mind, alert only for some variation in an account he had already read twice in the official report, and heard from Largo over the phone. The other half of his consciousness focused on the cat. It still crouched by the door—judging whether this strange human was a threat. The flap probably had made enough noise when the cat came in to waken a man sleeping lightly, Leaphorn decided. The cat was thin, bony; its muscles had the ropy look of wild predators. If it had, in fact, been a pampered pet, it had adapted well. It had got itself in harmony with its new life. Like a Navajo, it had survived.

Chee had finished his account, without saying anything new. Or anything different. The metal seat of the folding chair was hard against Leaphorn's tailbone. He felt more tired than he should have felt after nothing much more than the drive from Window Rock. Chee was said to be smart. He seemed smart. Largo insisted he was. A smart man should have some idea who was trying to kill him. And why. If he wasn't a fool, was he a liar?

"When it got light, you looked outside," Leaphorn prompted. "What did you find?"

"Three empty shotgun shells," Chee said. His eyes said he knew Leaphorn already knew all this. "Twelve gauge. Center fire. Rubber sole tracks of a small shoe. Size seven. Fairly new. Led off up the slope to the road up there. Top of the slope, a vehicle had been parked. Tires were worn and it leaked a lot of oil."

"Did he come in the same way?"

"No," Chee said. The question had interested him. "Tracks down along the bank of the river."

"Past where this cat has its den."

"Right," Chee said.

Leaphorn waited. After a long silence, Chee said, "It seemed to me that something might have happened there. To spook the cat out of his hiding place. So I looked around." He made a deprecatory gesture. "Ground was scuffed. I think somebody had knelt there behind the juniper. It's not far from where people dump their trash and there's always a lot of stuff blowing around. But I found this." He got out his billfold, extracted a bit of yellow paper, and handed it to Leaphorn. "It's new," he said. "It hadn't been out there in the dirt very long."

It was the wrapper off a stick of Juicy Fruit gum. "Not much," Chee said, looking embarrassed.

It *wasn't* much. Leaphorn couldn't imagine how it would be useful. In fact, it seemed to symbolize just how little they had to work on in any of these cases. "But it's something," he said. His imagination made the figure squatting behind the juniper, watching the Chee trailer, a small figure holding a pump shotgun in his right hand, reaching into his shirt pocket with his left hand, fishing out a package of gum. No furious emotion here. Calm. A man doing a job, being careful, taking his time. And, as an accidental byproduct, giving the cat crouched under the juniper a case of nerves, eroding its instinct to stay hidden until this human left, sending it into a panicky dash for a safer place. Leaphorn smiled slightly, enjoying the irony.

"We know he chews gum. Or she does," Chee said. "And what kind he sometimes chews. And that he's . . ." Chee searched for the right word. "Cool."

And I know, Leaphorn thought, that Jim Chee is smart enough to think about what might have spooked the cat. He glanced at the animal, which was still crouched by the flap, its blue eyes fixed on him. The glance was enough to tilt the decision. Two humans in a closed place were too many. The cat flicked through the flap, *clack-clack*, and was gone. Loud enough to wake a light sleeper, especially if he was nervous. Did Chee have something to be nervous about? Leaphorn shifted in the chair, trying for a more comfortable position. "You read the report on Wilson Sam," Leaphorn said. "And you went out there. When? Let's go over that again."

They went over it. Chee had visited the site four days after the killing and he'd found nothing to add significant data to the original report. And that told little enough. A ground-water pond where Wilson Sam's sheep drank was going dry. Sam had been out looking for a way to solve that problem—checking on his flock. He hadn't returned with nightfall. The next morning some of the Yazzie outfit into which Sam was married had gone out to look for him. A son of his sister-in-law had remembered hearing a dog howling. They found the dog watching the body in an arroyo that runs into Tyende Creek south of the Greasewood Flats. The investigating officers from Chinle had arrived a little before noon. The back of Sam's head had been crushed, just above where head and neck join. The subsequent autopsy confirmed that he'd been struck with a shovel that was found at the scene. Relatives agreed that it wasn't Sam's shovel. The body apparently had fallen, or had rolled, down the bank and the assailant had climbed down after it. The nephew had driven directly out to the Dennehotso Trading Post, called the police, and then followed instructions to keep everybody away from the body until they arrived.

"There were still some pretty good tracks when I got there," Chee said. "Been a little shower there the day before the killing and a little runoff down the arroyo bottom. Cowboy boots, both heels worn, size ten, pointed toes. Heavy man, probably two hundred pounds or over, or he was carrying something heavy. He walked around the body, squatted beside it." Chee paused, face thoughtful. "He got down on both knees beside the body. Spent a little time, judging from the scuff marks and so forth. I thought maybe they were made by our people when they picked up the body. But I asked Gorman, and he said no. They were there when he'd checked originally."

"Gorman?"

"He's back with us now," Chee said. "But he was loaned out to Chinle back in June. Vacation relief. He was that guy who was walking out in the parking lot with me at noon. Gorman and Benaly. Gorman is the sort of fat one."

"Was the killer a Navajo?" Leaphorn asked.

Chee hesitated, surprised. "Yes," he said. "Navajo."

"You sound sure," Leaphorn said. "Why Navajo?"

"Funny. I knew he was Navajo. But I didn't think about why," Chee said. He counted it off on his fingers. "He didn't step over the body, which could have just happened that way. But when he walked down the arroyo, he took care not to walk where the water had run. And on the way back to the road, a snake had been across there, and when he crossed its path he shuffled his feet." Chee paused. "Or do white men do that too?"

"I doubt it," Leaphorn said. The don't-step-over-people business grew out of families living in one-room hogans, sleeping on the floor. A matter of respect. And the desert herders' respect for rain must have produced the taboo against stepping in water's footprints. Snakes? Leaphorn tried to remember. His grandmother had told him that if you walk across a snake's trail without erasing it by shuffling your feet, the snake would follow you home. But then his grandmother had also told him it was taboo for a child to keep secrets from grandmothers, and that watching a dog urinate would cause insanity. "How about the killer at Endocheeney's place? Another Navajo? Could it have been the same person?"

"Not many tracks there," Chee said. "Body was about a hundred yards from the hogan, with the whole family milling around after he was found. And we hadn't had the rain there. Everything dry."

"But what do you think? Another Navajo?"

Chee thought. "I don't know," he said. "Couldn't be absolutely sure. But when we eliminated what everybody who lived there was wearing, I think it was a boot with a flat rubber heel. And probably a smallish hole worn in the right sole."

"Different suspect, then," Leaphorn said. "Or different shoes." In fact, three different suspects. In fact, maybe four different suspects, counting Onesalt. He shook his head, thinking of the implausible, irrational insanity of it. Then he thought of Chee. An impressive young man. But why didn't he have at least an inkling of who had tried to kill him? Or why? Could he possibly not know? Leaphorn's back hurt. Sitting too long always did it these days. Easing himself out of the chair, he walked to the window over the sink and looked out. He felt something gritty under his boot sole, leaned down, and found it. The round lead pellet from a shotgun shell.

He showed it to Chee. "This one of them?"

"I guess so," Chee said. "I swept up, but when they went through the bedclothes, they bounced around. Got into everything."

Into everything except Jim Chee, Leaphorn thought. Too bad he had so much trouble learning to believe in luck. "Did you see anything at all that would connect the Endocheeney and Sam things? Anything at all? Anything to connect either one of them to this?" Leaphorn gestured at the three patched shotgun holes.

"I've thought about that," Chee said. "Nothing."

"Did the name Irma Onesalt turn up either place?"

"Onesalt? The woman somebody shot down near Window Rock? No."

"I'm going to ask Largo to take you off of everything else and have you rework everything about Endocheeney and Sam," Leaphorn said. "You willing? I mean talk to everybody about everything. Who people talked to. Who people saw. Try to get a fix on whatever the killers were driving. Just try to find out every damn thing. Work on it day after day after day until we get some feeling for what the hell went on. All right?"

"Sure," Chee said. "Fine."

"Anything else about this shooting of your own here that didn't seem to fit on the FBI report?"

Chee thought about it. His lips twitched in a gesture of doubt or deprecation.

"I don't know," he said. "Just this morning, I found this. Might not have anything to do with anything. Probably doesn't." He pulled out his wallet again and extracted from it something small and roundish and ivory-colored. He handed it to Leaphorn. It was a bead formed, apparently, from bone.

"Where was it?"

"On the floor under the bunk. Maybe it fell out when I changed the bedding."

"What do you think?" Leaphorn asked.

"I think I never had anything that had beads like that on it, or knew anybody who did. And I wonder how it got here."

"Or why?" Leaphorn asked.

"Yes. Or why."

If you believed in witches, Leaphorn thought, as Chee probably did, you would have to think of a bone bead as a way witches killed—the bone being human, and the fatal illness being "corpse sickness." And if you loaded your own shotgun shells, or even if you didn't, you would know how simple it would be to remove the little plug from the end, and the wadding, and add a bone bead to the lead pellets.

6

THE WIND BLEW out of the southwest, hot and dry, whipping sand across the rutted track in front of Jim Chee's patrol car. Chee had backed the car a hundred yards up the gravel road that led to Badwater Wash Trading Post. He'd parked it under the gnarled limbs of a one-seed juniper—a place that gave him a little shade and a long view back down the road he had traveled. Now he simply sat, waiting and watching. If anyone was following, Chee intended to know it.

"I'm going to go along with the lieutenant," Captain Largo had told him. "Leaphorn wants me to rearrange things and let you work on our killings." As usual when he talked, Captain Largo's hands were living their separate life, sorting through papers on the captain's desk, rearranging whatever the captain kept in the top drawer, trying to reshape a crease in the captain's hat. "I think he's wrong," Largo said. "I think we ought to leave those cases to the FBI. The FBI's not going to break them, and neither are we, but the FBI's getting paid for it, and nobody's going to do any good on them until we have some luck—and taking you off your regular work isn't going to make us lucky. Is it?"

"No, sir," Chee had said. He wasn't sure Largo expected an answer, or wanted one, but being agreeable seemed a good policy. He didn't want the captain to change his mind.

"I think that Leaphorn thinks you getting shot is connected with one or the other of those killings, or maybe both of them. He didn't say so, but that's what I think he thinks. I can't see any connection. How about it?"

Chee shrugged. "I don't see how there could be."

"No," Largo agreed. His expression, as he looked at Chee, was skeptical. "Unless you're not telling me something." The tone of the statement included a question mark.

"I'm not not telling you anything," Chee said.

"Sometimes you haven't," Largo said. But he didn't pursue it. "Real reason I'm going along with this is I want you to stay alive. Just getting shot at is bad enough." Largo pointed to the folder on his desk. "Look at that, and it's not finished yet. If somebody kills you, think how it would be." Largo threw out his arms in a gesture encompassing mountains of forms. "When we had that man killed over in the Crownpoint subagency back in the sixties, they were doing reports on that for two years."

"Okay," Chee said. "That's okay with me."

"What I mean is, poke around on Endocheeney and Wilson Sam and see what you can hear, but mostly I want you out where it would be hard for anybody to get a shot at you. In case they're still trying. Let 'em cool off. Be careful."

"Good," Chee had said, meaning it.

And while he was out there, Largo had added, he might as well get some useful work done. For instance, the people at the refinery over at Montezuma Creek were sore because somebody was stealing drip gasoline out of the collector pipeline. And somebody seemed to be hanging out around the tourist parking places at the Goosenecks, and other such places, and stealing stuff out of the cars. And so forth. The litany had been fairly long, indicating that the decline of human nature on the Utah part of the reservation was about the same as it was in Chee's usual New Mexico jurisdiction. "I'll get you the paperwork," Largo said, shuffling papers out of various files into a single folder. "Xerox copies. I wish we could put a stop to this getting into people's cars," he added. "People raise hell about it, and it gets to the chairman's office and then he raises hell. Be careful. And get some work done."

And now, parked here out of sight watching his back trail, Chee was being careful, exactly as instructed. If the man (or the woman) with the shotgun was following, it would have to be down this road. The only other way to get to the trading post at Badwater Wash was to float down the San Juan River, and then take one of the tracks that connected it to the hogans scattered where terrain allowed along the river. Badwater wasn't a place one passed through by accident en route to anywhere else.

And now the only dust on the Badwater road was wind dust. The afternoon clouds had formed over Black Mesa, far to the south, producing lightning and air turbulence. As far as Chee could estimate from thirty miles away, no rain was falling. He studied the cloud, enjoying the range of blues and grays, its shapes and its movement. But he was thinking of more somber things. The hours of thinking he had done about who would want to kill him had depressing effects. His imagination had produced an image in his mind—himself standing at the face of a great cliff of smooth stone, as blank as a mirror, feeling hopelessly for fingerholds that didn't exist. There was a second unpleasant effect. This persistent hunt for malice, for ill will, for hatred—examining relationships with friends and associates with cynical skepticism—had left him gloomy. And then there was Lieutenant Leaphorn. He'd gotten what he wanted from the man—more than he'd expected. But the lieutenant hadn't trusted him when they'd met, and he hadn't trusted him when they'd parted. Leaphorn hadn't liked the bone bead. When Chee had handed it to him, the lieutenant's face had changed, expressing distaste and what might have been contempt. In the small universe of the Navajo Police, total membership perhaps less than 120 sworn officers, Lieutenant Leaphorn was a Fairly Important Person, and somewhat of a legend. Everybody knew he hated bootleggers. Chee shared that sentiment. Everybody also knew Leaphorn had no tolerance for witchcraft or anything about it—for those who believed in witches, or for stories about skinwalkers, corpse sickness, the cures for same, and everything connected with the Navajo Wolves. There were two stories about how Leaphorn had acquired this obsession. It was said that when he was new on the force in the older days he had guessed wrong about some skinwalker rumors on the Checkerboard. He hadn't acted on what he'd heard, and a fellow had killed three witches and got a life term for murder and then committed suicide. That was supposed to be why the lieutenant didn't like witchcraft, which was a good enough reason. The other story was that he was a descendant of the great Chee Dodge and had inherited Dodge's determination that belief in skinwalkers had no part in the Navajo culture, that the tribe had been infected with the notion while it was held captive down at Fort Sumner. Chee suspected both stories were true.

Still, Leaphorn had kept the bone bead.

"I'll see about it," he'd said. "Send it to the lab. Find out if it is bone, and what kind of bone." He'd torn a page from his notebook, wrapped the bead in it, and placed it in the coin compartment of his billfold. Then he'd looked at Chee for a moment in silence. "Any idea how it got in here?"

"Sounds strange," Chee had said. "But you know you could pry out the end of a shotgun shell and pull out the wadding and stick a bead like this in with the pellets."

Leaphorn's expression became almost a smile. Was it contempt? "Like a witch shooting in the bone?" he asked. "They're supposed to do that through a little tube." He made a puffing shape with his lips.

Chee had nodded, flushing just a little.

Now, remembering it, he was angry again. Well, to hell with Leaphorn. Let him believe whatever he wanted to believe. The origin story of the Navajos explained witchcraft clearly enough, and it was a logical part of the philosophy on which the Dinee had founded their culture. If there was good, and harmony, and beauty on the east side of reality, then there must be evil, chaos, and ugliness to the west. Like a nonfundamentalist Christian, Chee believed in the poetic metaphor of the Navajo story of human genesis. Without believing in the specific Adam's rib, or the size of the reed through which the Holy People emerged to the Earth Surface World, he believed in the lessons such imagery was intended to teach. To hell with Leaphorn and what he didn't believe. Chee started the engine and jolted back down the slope to the road. He wanted to get to Badwater Wash before noon.

But he couldn't quite get Leaphorn out of his mind. Leaphorn posed a problem. "One more thing," the lieutenant had said. "We've got a complaint about you." And he'd told Chee what the doctor at the Badwater Clinic had said about him. "Yellowhorse claims you've been interfering with his practice of his religion," Leaphorn said. And while the lieutenant's expression said he didn't take the complaint as anything critically important, the very fact that he'd mentioned it implied that Chee should desist.

"I have been telling people that Yellowhorse is a fake," Chee said stiffly. "I have told people every chance I get that the doctor pretends to be a crystal gazer just to get them into his clinic."

"I hope you're not doing that on company time," Leaphorn said. "Not while you're on duty."

"I probably have," Chee said. "Why not?"

"Because it violates regulations," Leaphorn said, his expression no longer even mildly amused.

"How?"

"I think you can see how," Leaphorn had said. "We don't have any way to license our shamans, no more than the federal government can license preachers. If Yellowhorse says he's a medicine man, or a hand trembler, or a road chief of the Native American Church, or the Pope, it is no business of the Navajo Tribal Police. No rule against it. No law."

"I'm a Navajo," Chee said. "I see somebody cynically using our religion . . . somebody who doesn't believe in our religion using it in that cynical way . . ."

"What harm is he doing?" Leaphorn asked. "The way I understand it, he recommends they go to a *yataalii* if they need a ceremonial sing. And he points them at the white man's hospital only if they have a white man's problem. Diabetes, for example."

Chee had made no response to that. If Leaphorn couldn't see the problem, the sacrilege involved, then Leaphorn was blind. But that wasn't the trouble. Leaphorn was as cynical as Yellowhorse.

"You, yourself, have declared yourself to be a *yataalii*, I hear," Leaphorn said. "I heard you performed a Blessing Way."

Chee had nodded. He said nothing.

Leaphorn had looked at him a moment, and sighed. "I'll talk to Largo about it," he said.

And that meant that one of these days Chee would have an argument with the captain about it and if he wasn't lucky, Largo would give him a flat, unequivocal order to say nothing more about Yellowhorse as shaman. When that happened, he would cope as best he could. Now the road to Badwater had changed from bad to worse. Chee concentrated on driving.

It was the policy of the Navajo Tribal Police, as a matter of convenience, to consider Badwater to be in the Arizona portion of the Big Reservation. Local wisdom held that the store itself was actually in Utah, about thirty feet north of the imaginary line that marked the boundary. One of the local jokes was that Old Man Isaac Ginsberg, who built the place, used to move out of his room behind the trading post and into a stone hogan across the road one hundred yards to the south because he couldn't stand the cold Utah winters. Nobody seemed to know exactly where the place was, map-wise. Its location, in a narrow slot surrounded by the fantastic, thousand-foot, red-black-blue-tan cliffs, made pinpointing it on surveys mostly guesswork. And nobody cared enough to do more than guess.

Historically, it had been a watering place for herdsmen. In the immense dry badlands of Casa del Eco Mesa, it was a rare place where a reliable spring produced pools of drinkable water. Good water is a magnet anywhere in desert country. In a landscape like Caso del Eco, where gypsum and an arsenal of other soluble minerals tainted rainwater almost as fast as it fell, the stuff that seeped under the sandy arroyo bottoms was such a compound of chemicals that it would kill even tumbleweeds and salt cedar. Thus, the springs in Badwater Wash were a magnet for all living things. They attracted those tough little mammals and reptiles which endure in such hostile places. Eventually it attracted goats that strayed from the herds the Navajos had stolen from the Pueblo Indians. Then came the goatherders. Next came sheepherders. Finally, geologists discovered the shallow but persistent Aneth oil deposit, which brought a brief, dusty boom to the plateau. The drilling boom left behind a little refinery at Montezuma Creek, a scattering of robot pumps, and a worn-out spiderweb of truck trails connecting them with the world. Sometime in this period between boom and dust, it had attracted Isaac Ginsberg, who built the trading post of slabs of red sandstone, earned the Navajo name Afraid of His Wife, and died. The wife to whom Ginsberg owed his title was a Mud Clan Navajo called Lizzie Tonale, who had married Ginsberg in Flagstaff, had converted to Judaism, and, it was locally believed, had persuaded Ginsberg to establish his business in such an incredibly isolated locale because it was the hardest possible place for her relatives to reach. It would have been a sensible motive. Otherwise, the trading post would have been bankrupt in a month, since Lizzie Tonale could refuse no kin who needed canned goods, gasoline, or a loan, and maintain her status as a respectable woman. Whatever her motives, the widow Tonale-Ginsberg had run the post for twenty years before her own death, steadfastly closing on the Sabbath. She had left it to their daughter, the only product of their union. Chee had met this daughter only twice. That was enough to understand how she had earned her local name, which was Iron Woman.

Now, as he rolled his patrol car down the final slope and into the rutted yard of Badwater Wash Trading Post, he saw the bulky form of Iron Woman standing on the porch. Chee parked as much of the car as he could in the scanty shade of a tamarisk and waited. It was a courtesy learned from boyhood in a society where modesty is prized, privacy is treasured, and visitors, even at a trading post, are all too rare. "You don't just go run up to somebody's hogan," his mother had taught him. "You might see something you don't want to see."

So Chee sat, without giving it a thought, to allow the residents of Badwater Wash to get in harmony with the idea of a visit from a tribal policeman, to button up and tidy up, or to do whatever was required by Navajo good manners. While he sat, perspiring freely, he looked in his rearview mirror at the people on the porch. Iron Woman had been joined by another woman, as thin and bent as Iron Woman was stout and ramrod rigid. Then two young men appeared in the front door, seeming, in the dusty rearview glass, to be dressed exactly alike. Each wore a red sweatband around the forehead, a faded red plaid shirt, jeans, and cowboy boots. Iron Woman was saying something to the bent woman, who nodded and looked amused. The two young men, standing side by side, stared with implacable rudeness at Chee's car. An old Ford sedan was parked at the corner of the building, a cinder block supporting the right rear axle. Beside it, perched high on its backcountry suspension, was a new GMC four-by-four. It was black with yellow pinstripes. Chee had priced a similar model in Farmington and couldn't come close to affording it. He admired it now. A vehicle that would go anywhere. But richer than anything you expected to see parked at Badwater Wash.

Through his windshield, beyond the thin screen of Russian olive leaves, the red mass of the cliff rose to the sky, reflecting the sun. The patrol car was filled with dry heat. Chee felt uneasiness stirring. He was getting used to it, finding the anxiety familiar but not learning to like it. He got out of the car and walked toward the porch, keeping his eyes on the men, who kept their eyes on him.

"*Ya-tah-hey*," he said to Iron Woman.

"*Ya-tah*," she said. "I remember you. You're the new policeman from Shiprock."

Chee nodded.

"Out here the other day with the government officer seeing about the Endocheeney business."

"Right," Chee said.

"This man is born to the Slow Talking People and born for the Salts," Iron Woman told the bent woman. She named Chee's mother, and his maternal aunt, and his maternal grandmother, and then recited his father's side of the family.

Bent Woman looked pleased. She faced Chee with her head back and her eyes almost closed, looking at him under her lids, a technique the descending blindness of glaucoma and cataracts taught its victims. "He is my nephew," Bent Woman said. "I am born to the Bitter Water People, born for the Deer Spring Clan. My mother was Gray Woman Nez."

Chee smiled, acknowledging the relationship. It was vague—the Bitter Waters being linked to the Salt Clan and thereby to his father's family. The system meant that Chee, and all other Navajos, had wholesale numbers of relatives.

"On business?" Iron Woman asked.

"Just out poking around," Chee said. "Seeing what I can see."

Iron Woman looked skeptical. "You don't get out here much," she said. "Nobody gets out here except on purpose."

Chee was aware of the two men watching him. Barely men. Late teens, he guessed. Obviously brothers, but not twins. The one nearest him had a thinner face, and a half-moon of white scar tissue beside his left eye socket. Under the old rules of Navajo courtesy, they would have identified themselves first, since he was the stranger in their territory. They didn't seem to care about the old rules.

"My clan is Slow Talking People," Chee said to them. "Born for the Salt Dinee."

"Leaf People," the thinner one said. "Born for Mud." His face was sullen.

Chee's efficient nose picked up a whiff of alcohol. Beer. The Leaf Clan man let his eyes drift from Chee to study the police car. He gestured vaguely toward the other man. "My brother," he said.

"What's happening over your way?" Iron Woman asked. "I heard on the radio they had a knifing at a wedding over at Teec Nos Pos. One of the Gorman outfit got cut. Anything to that?"

Chee knew very little about that one—just what he'd overheard before the morning patrol meeting. Normally he worked east and south out of Shiprock—not this mostly empty northwestern area. He put the beer (possession illegal on the reservation) out of his mind and tried to remember what he had heard.

"Didn't amount to much," Chee said. "Fella was fooling with a girl and she had a knife. Stuck him in the arm. I think she was a Standing Rock girl. Not much to it."

Iron Woman looked disappointed. "It got on the radio, though," she said. "Lot of people around here related to the Gorman outfit."

Chee had gone to the battered red pop cooler just inside the front door, inserted two quarters, and tried to open the lid.

"Takes three," Iron Woman said. "Costs too much to get that stuff hauled way out here. And icing it down. Now everybody wants it cold."

"No more change," Chee said. He fished out a dollar and handed it to Iron Woman. It was dark inside the store and much cooler. At the cash register, Iron Woman handed him four quarters.

"Last time you were with that FBI man—asking about the one that got killed," she said, respecting the Navajo taboo of not speaking the name of the dead. "You find out who killed that man?"

Chee shook his head.

"That fellow that came through here looking for him the day he was killed. Sounded to me like he did it."

"That's a crazy thing," Chee said. "We found that man at his hogan over in the Chuskas. A man they call Roosevelt Bistie. Bistie told us he came over here to kill that man who got killed. And the man Bistie was after was up on his roof fixing something, and Bistie shot at him and he fell off. But whoever killed the man did it with a butcher knife."

"That's right," Iron Woman said. "Sure as hell, it was a knife. I remember his daughter telling me that." She shook her head, peered at Chee again. "Why would that fellow tell you he shot him?"

"We can't figure that out, either," Chee said. "Bistie said he wanted to kill the man, but he won't say why."

Iron Woman frowned. "Roosevelt Bistie," she said. "Never heard of him. I remember when he stopped in here asking directions, I never had seen him before. The man's kinfolks, do they know this Bistie?"

"None of them we've talked to," Chee said. He was thinking of how disapproving Kennedy would be if he could hear Chee discussing this case with a layman. Captain Largo too, for that matter, Largo having been a cop long enough to start acting secretive. But Kennedy was FBI to the bone, and the first law of the Agency was, Say nothing to nobody. If Kennedy were here, listening to this Navajo talk, he'd be waiting impatiently for a translation—knowing that Chee must be telling this woman more than she needed to know. However, Kennedy wasn't here, and Chee had his own operating theory. The more you tell people, the more people tell you. Nobody, certainly no Navajo, wants to be second in the business of telling things.

Chee dropped in quarters and selected a Nehi Orange. Cold and wonderful. Iron Woman talked. Chee sipped. Outside, noonday heat radiated from the packed earth of the yard, causing the light to shimmer. Chee finished his soda pop. The four-by-four drove away with a roar, dust spurting from its wheels. Beer in the four-by-four, Chee guessed. Unless the boys had bought it here. But if Iron Woman was a bootlegger, he hadn't heard it, and he hadn't remembered seeing this place on the map Largo kept of liquor sources in his subagency territory. Beer in the morning, and an expensive rig to drive. Iron Woman had said the two were part of the Kayonnie outfit, which ran goats down along the San Juan to the north and sometimes worked in the oil fields. But Iron Woman obviously did not want to discuss the Kayonnie boys, her neighbors, with a stranger. The local murder victim was another matter. She couldn't understand who would do it. He was a harmless old man. He stayed at home. Since his wife had died, he rarely came even as far as the trading post. Maybe two or three times a year, sometimes riding in on a horse, sometimes coming with a relative when a relative came to see him. No Endocheeney daughters to bring home their husbands, so the old man had lived alone. Only thing important she could remember happening involving him was a Red Ant Way sing done for him six or seven years ago to cure him of something or other after his woman died. In all the years she'd been at Badwater, which was all her life, she couldn't remember him getting into any kind of trouble, or being involved in bad problems. "Like getting your wood on somebody else's wood-gathering place, or getting into some other family's water, or running his sheep where they shouldn't be, or not helping out somebody that needed it. Never heard anything bad about him. Never been in any trouble. Always helping out at sheep dippings, always tried to take care of his kinfolks, always there when somebody was having a sing."

"I don't know if I ever told you that I have studied to be a *yataalii* myself," Chee said. "I do the Blessing Way and some others." He got out his billfold, extracted a card, and handed it to Iron Woman. The card said:

THE BLESSING WAY
and other ceremonials sung
by a singer who studied with
Frank Sam Nakai
Contact Jim Chee

The next lines provided his address and telephone number at the Shiprock Police Station. He had mentioned this to the dispatcher, thinking he would square it with Captain Largo if the captain ever learned about it. So far, the risk seemed small. There had been no calls, and no letters.

Iron Woman seemed to share the general lack of enthusiasm. She glanced at the card and laid it on the counter.

"Everybody liked him," Iron Woman said, getting back on the subject. "But now he's dead, some people are saying he was a skinwalker." Her face reflected distaste. "Sons-a-bitches," she added, clarifying that the distaste was not for skinwalkers but for the gossips. "When you live by yourself, people say things like that."

Or when you get stabbed to death, Chee thought. Violent death always seemed to provoke witch talk.

"If everybody around here liked him," Chee said, "then whoever killed him must have come from someplace else. Like Bistie. Did he know anybody anywhere else?"

"I don't think so," Iron Woman said. "Long as I been here, he only got one letter."

Chee felt a stir of excitement. Something at last. "You remember anything about it? Who it was from?" Of course she would remember. The arrival of any mail on this isolated outpost would be something to talk about, especially a letter to a man who never received letters and who couldn't read them if he did. It would lie in the little shoebox marked MAIL on the shelf above Iron Woman's cash register, the subject of conjecture and speculation until Endocheeney came in, or a relative showed up who might be trusted to deliver it to him.

"Wasn't from anybody," Iron Woman said. "It was from the tribe. There in Window Rock."

The excitement evaporated. "One of the tribal offices?"

"Social Services, I think it was. One of those that are always messing around with people."

"How about his pawn?" Chee asked. "Anything unusual in that?"

Iron Woman led him behind the counter, fished a key out of the folds of her voluminous reservation skirt, and unlocked the glass-topped cabinet where she kept the pawn.

The Endocheeney possessions held hostage for credit included one belt of heavy, crudely hammered conchas, old-fashioned and heavily tarnished; a small sack containing nine old Mexican twenty-peso coins, their silver as tarnished as the belt; two sand-cast rings; and a belt buckle of sand-cast silver. The buckle was beautiful, a simple geometric pattern that Chee favored, with a single perfect turquoise gem set in its center. He turned it in his hand, admiring it.

"And this," Iron Woman said. She thumped a small deerskin pouch on the countertop and poured out a cluster of unset turquoise nuggets and fragments. "The old man made some jewelry now and then. Or he used to. Guess he got too old for it after the old woman died."

There was nothing remarkable about the turquoise. It was worth maybe two hundred dollars. Add another two hundred for the belt and maybe one hundred for the buckle and probably fifteen or twenty dollars each for the old pesos. They were once standard raw material for belt conchas on the reservation, and cheap enough, but Mexico had long since stopped making them, and the price of silver had soared. Nothing remarkable about any of this, except the beauty of the buckle. He wondered if Endocheeney had cast it himself. And he wondered why some of his kin had not claimed these belongings. Once, tradition would have demanded that such personal stuff be disposed of with the body. But that tradition was now often ignored. Or perhaps Endocheeney's relatives didn't know about this pawn. Or perhaps they didn't have the cash to redeem it.

"How much do you have on the old man's bill?" Chee asked.

Iron Woman didn't have to look it up. "One hundred eighteen dollars," she said. "And some cents."

Not much, Chee thought. Far less than the stuff was worth. Someone without any cash could raise that much by selling a few goats.

"And then there's them," Iron Woman said. She tilted her head toward a corner behind the counter. There stood a posthole digger, two axes, a pair of crutches, a hand-turned ice cream freezer, and what seemed to be an old car axle converted into a wrecking bar.

Chee looked puzzled.

"The crutches," Iron Woman said impatiently. "He wanted to pawn them too, but hell, who wants crutches? They loan 'em to you free, up there at the Badwater Clinic, so I didn't want to get stuck with 'em as pawn. Anyway, he just left 'em there. Said give him half if I could sell 'em."

"Was he hurt?" Chee asked, thinking as he did that he could have found a smarter way to ask the question.

Iron Woman seemed to think so too. "Broke his leg. Fell off of something and they had to put a cast on it over at the clinic and he came back with the crutches."

"And then he climbed right back on the roof," Chee said. "Sounds like he was a slow learner."

"No, no," Iron Woman said. "Broke his leg way last autumn doing something else. Think he fell off of a rail fence. Leg caught." Iron Woman broke an imaginary stick with her fingers. "Snap," she said.

Chee was thinking of relatives who didn't come in and collect pawn. "Who buried the old man?" he asked.

"They got a man that works on those old well pumps out there." Iron Woman made a sweeping gesture with both hands to take in the entire plateau. "White man. He does that sometimes for people. Doesn't mind about corpses."

"This witch talk. You hear that a long time or just now?"

Iron Woman looked uneasy. From what Chee had heard about her, she had gone to school over at Ganado, at the College of Ganado, a good school. And she was a Jew, more or less, raised in that religion. But she was also a Navajo, a member of the Halgai Dinee, the People of the Valley Clan. She didn't like talking about witches in any specific way with a stranger.

"I heard about it just now," she said. "Since the killing."

"Was it just the usual stuff? What you'd expect when somebody gets killed?"

Iron Woman licked her lips, caught the lower lip between her teeth, looked at Chee carefully. She shifted her weight and in the silence the creak of the floorboard plank under her shoe was a loud groaning sound. But her voice was so faint when she finally spoke that, even in the silence, he had to strain to hear.

"They say that when they found him, they found a bone in the wound—where the knife had gone in."

"A bone?" Chee asked, not sure that he'd heard it.

Iron Woman held her thumb and forefinger up—an eighth of an inch apart. "Little corpse bone," she said.

She didn't need to explain it more than that. Chee was remembering the bone bead he'd found in his trailer.

7

DR. RANDALL JENKS held a sheet of paper in his fist. Presumably it was the laboratory report on the bead, since Jenks's office had called Leaphorn to tell him the report was ready. But Jenks gave no sign he was ready to hand it over.

"Have a seat," Dr. Jenks said, and sat down himself beside the long table in the meeting room. He wore a headband of red fabric into which the Navajo symbol of Corn Beetle had been woven. His blond hair was shoulder length and under his blue laboratory jacket Leaphorn could see the uniform—a frayed denim jacket. Leaphorn, who resented those who stereotyped Navajos, struggled not to stereotype others. But Dr. Jenks fell into Leaphorn's category of Indian Lover. That meant he irritated Leaphorn even when he was doing him favors. Now Leaphorn was in a hurry. But he sat down.

Jenks looked at him over his glasses. "The bead is made out of bone," he said, checking for reaction.

Leaphorn was not in the mood to pretend surprise. "I thought it might be," he said.

"Bovine," Jenks said. "Modern but not new, if you know what I mean. Dead long enough to be totally dehydrated. Maybe twenty years, maybe a hundred—more or less."

"Thanks for the trouble. Appreciate it," Leaphorn said. He got up, put on his hat.

"Did you expect it to be human?" Jenks asked. "Human bone?"

Leaphorn hesitated. He had work to do back at Window Rock—a rodeo that would probably be causing problems by now and a meeting of the Tribal Council that certainly would. Getting that many politicians together always caused some sort of problem. He wanted to confirm Emma's appointment before he left the hospital, and talk to the neurologist about her if he could. And then there were his three homicides. Three and a half if you counted Officer Chee. Besides, he wanted to think about what he had just learned—that the bone wasn't human. And what he had expected was none of Jenks's business. Jenks's business was public health, more specifically public health of the Navajos, Zunis, Acomas, Lagunas, and Hopis served by the U.S. Indian Service hospital at Gallup. Jenks's business, specifically, was pathology—a science that Lieutenant Leaphorn often wished he knew more about so he wouldn't be asking favors of Jenks.

"I thought it might be human," Leaphorn said.

"Any connection with Irma Onesalt?"

The question startled Leaphorn. "No," he said. "Did you know her?"

Jenks laughed. "Not exactly. Not socially. She was in here a time or two. Wanting information."

"About pathology?" Why would the Onesalt woman want information from a pathologist?

"About when a bunch of people died," Jenks said. "She had a list of names."

"Who?"

"I just glanced at it," Jenks said. "Looked like Navajo names, but I didn't really study it."

Leaphorn took off his hat and sat down.

"Tell me about it," he said. "When she came in, everything you can remember. And tell me why this bone bead business made you think of Onesalt."

Dr. Jenks told him, looking pleased.

Irma Onesalt had come in one morning about two months earlier.

Maybe a little longer. If it was important, maybe he could pin down the date. He had known her a little bit before. She had come to see him way back when the semiconductor plant was still operating at Shiprock—wanting to know if that kind of work was bad for the health. And he had looked stuff up for her a couple of times since.

Jenks paused, getting his thoughts in order.

"What kind of stuff?" Leaphorn asked.

Jenks's long, pale face looked slightly embarrassed. "Well, one time she wanted some details about a couple of diseases, how they are treated, if hospitalization is needed, how long, so forth. And one time she wanted to know if an alcohol death we had in here might have been beaten."

Jenks didn't say beaten by whom. He didn't need to say. Irma Onesalt would have been interested, Leaphorn suspected, only if police, and preferably Navajo Tribal Police, had been the guilty party. Irma Onesalt did not like police, particularly Navajo Police. She called them Cossacks. She called them oppressors of The People.

"This time she had a sheet of paper with her—just names typed on it. She wanted to know if I could go back through my records and come up with the date each one had died."

"Could you?" Leaphorn asked.

"A few of them, maybe. Only if they had died in this hospital, or if we did the postmortem workup for some reason. But you know how that works. Most Navajo families won't allow an autopsy and usually they can stop it on religious grounds. I'd have a record of it only if they died here, and then only if there was some good reason—like suspicious causes, or the FBI was interested, or something like that."

"She wanted to know cause of death?"

"I don't think so. All she seemed to want was dates. I told her the only place I could think of she could get them all was the vital statistics offices in the state health departments. In Santa Fe and Phoenix and Salt Lake City."

"Dates," Leaphorn said. "Dates of their death." He frowned. That seemed odd. "She say why?"

Jenks shook his head, causing the long blond hair to sway. "I asked her. She said she was just curious about something." Jenks laughed. "She didn't say what, but that little bone bead of yours made me think of her because she was talking about witchcraft. She said something about the problem with singers and the health situation. People getting scared by the singers into thinking a skinwalker has witched them, and then getting the wrong medical treatment, or treatment they don't need because they're not really sick. So when I saw your little bead I made the connection." He studied Leaphorn to see if Leaphorn understood. "You know. Witches blowing a little piece of bone into somebody to give 'em the corpse sickness. But she never said that had anything to do with her list of names and what she was curious about. She said it was too early. She shouldn't talk about it yet—not then, she meant—and she said if anything came of it she would let me know."

"But she didn't come back?"

"She came back," Jenks said. He looked thoughtful, running the tip of his thumb under the headband, adjusting it. "Must have been a couple of weeks before she got killed. This time she wanted to know what sort of treatment would be indicated for two or three diseases, and how long you'd be hospitalized. Things like that."

"What diseases?" Leaphorn asked, although when he asked it he couldn't imagine what the answer would mean to him.

"One was TB," Jenks said. "I remember that. And I think one was some sort of liver pathology." He shrugged. "Nothing unusual. Sort of routine ailments we deal with around here, I remember that."

"And did she tell you then? I mean tell you why she wanted the dates those people died?" He was thinking of Roosevelt Bistie—the man who tried to kill Endocheeney—the man they had locked up at Shiprock, with not much reason to keep him, according to Kennedy's report. Roosevelt Bistie had something wrong with his liver. But so did a lot of people. And what the hell could that mean, anyway?

"I was in a hurry," Jenks said. "Two of our staff were on vacation and I was covering for one of them and I was trying to get my own operation caught up so I could go on vacation myself. So I didn't ask any questions. Just told her what she wanted to know and got rid of her."

"Did she ever explain it to you? In any way at all?"

"When I got back from vacation—couple of weeks after that—somebody told me somebody had shot her."

"Yeah," Leaphorn said. Shot her and left Leaphorn to guess why, since nobody else seemed to care a lot. And here might be the motive—this further example of Irma Onesalt in the role of busybody, to use the *belagana* term for it. His mother would have called her, in Navajo, a "one who tells sheep which weed to eat." Onesalt's job in the Navajo Office of Social Services, obviously, had no more to do with death statistics than it did with the occupational hazards of the semiconductor plant or, to get closer to Leaphorn's own emotional scar tissue, with punishing bad judgment in the Navajo Tribal Police.

"Do you think what she was working on had anything to do with why . . ." Jenks didn't complete the sentence.

"Who knows," Leaphorn said. "FBI handles homicides on Indian reservations." He heard himself saying it, his voice curt and unfriendly, and felt a twinge of self-disgust. Why this animus against Jenks? It wasn't just that he felt Jenks's attitude was patronizing. It was part of a resentment against all doctors. They seemed to know so much, but when he gave them Emma, the only thing that mattered, they would know absolutely nothing. That was the principal source of this resentment. And it wasn't fair to Jenks, or to any of them. Jenks had come to the Big Reservation, as many of the Indian Health Service doctors did, because the federal loans that had financed his education required two years in the military or the Indian Health Service. But Jenks had stayed beyond the two-year obligation, as some other IHS doctors did—delaying the Mercedes, the country club membership, the three-day work week, and the winters in the Bahamas—to help Navajos fight the battle of diabetes, dysentery, bubonic plague, and all those ailments that follow poor diets, bad water, and isolation. He shouldn't resent Jenks. Not only wasn't it fair; showing it would hurt his chances of learning everything Jenks could tell him.

"However," Leaphorn added, "we know something about it. And from what we know, the FBI hasn't a clue about motive." Nor do I, Leaphorn thought. Not about motive. Not about anything else. Certainly not about how to connect three and a half murders whose only connection seems to be an aimless lack of motive. "Maybe this list Irma had would help. All Navajo names, you said. Right? Could you think of any of them?"

Jenks's expression suggested he was probing his brain for names. All the homicide victims were still alive when Jenks had seen the list, Leaphorn thought, but wouldn't it be wonderful and remarkable if . . .

"One was Ethelmary Largewhiskers," Jenks said, faintly amused. "One was Woody's Mother."

Leaphorn rarely allowed his face to show irritation, and he didn't now. These were exactly the sort of names he'd expect Jenks to remember: names that were quaint, or cute, that would provoke a smile at a cocktail party somewhere when Dr. Jenks had become bored with Navajos—when too few of them drove wagons, and hauled drinking water forty miles, and slept in the desert with their sheep, and too many drove station wagons and got their teeth straightened by the orthodontist.

"Any others?" Leaphorn asked. "It might be important."

Jenks put on the expression of a man trying hard for a recall. And failing. He shook his head.

"Would you remember any, if you heard?"

Jenks shrugged. "Maybe."

"How about Wilson Sam?"

Jenks wrinkled his face. Shook his head. "Isn't he that guy who got killed early this summer?"

"Right," Leaphorn said. "Was his name on the list?"

"I don't remember," Jenks said. "But he was still alive then. He didn't get killed until after Onesalt. If I remember it right, and I think I do because they did the autopsy at Farmington and the pathologist there called me about it."

"You're right. I'm just fishing around. How about Dugai Endocheeney?"

Jenks produced the expression that signifies deep thought. "No," he said. "I mean no, I can't remember. Been a long time." He shook his head. Stopped the gesture. Frowned. "I've heard the name," he said. "Not on the list, I think, but . . ." He paused, adjusted the headband. "Wasn't he a homicide victim too? The other one that was killed about then?"

"Yes," Leaphorn said.

"Joe Harris did the autopsy too, at Farmington," Jenks said. "He told me he got a dime out of one of the wounds. That's why I remembered it, I guess."

"Harris found a dime in the wound?" Harris was the San Juan County coroner working out of the Farmington hospital. Pathologists, like police, seemed to know one another and swap yarns.

"He said Endocheeney got stabbed a bunch of times through the pocket of his jacket. In knifings we're always finding threads and stuff like that in the wound. Whatever the knife happens to hit on the way in through the clothing. Buttons. Paper. Whatever. This time it hit a dime."

Leaphorn, whose memory was excellent, recalled reading the autopsy report in the FBI file. No mention of a dime. But there had been mention of "foreign objects," which would cover a dime as well as the more usual buttons, thread, gravel, and broken glass. Could a knife punch a dime into a wound? Easily enough. It seemed odd, but not unreasonable.

"But Endocheeney wasn't on the list."

"I don't think so," Jenks said.

Leaphorn hesitated. "How about Jim Chee?" he asked.

Dr. Jenks thought hard again. But he couldn't remember whether or not Jim Chee's name was on the death date list.

8

IT WAS ALMOST dark when Chee pulled into the police parking lot in Shiprock. He parked where a globe willow would shade the car from the early sun the next morning and walked, stiff and weary, toward his pickup truck. He had left it that morning where another of the police department willows would shade it from the afternoon sun. Now the same tree hid it from the dim red twilight in a pool of blackness. The uneasiness Chee had shaken off at Badwater Wash and on the long drive home was suddenly back in possession. He stopped, stared at the truck. He could see only its shape in the shadows. He turned abruptly and hurried into the Police Building.

Nelson McDonald was working the night shift, lounging behind the switchboard with the two top buttons of his uniform shirt open, reading the sports section of the Farmington *Times*. Officer McDonald glanced up at Chee, nodded.

"You still alive?" he asked, with no hint of a smile.

"So far," Chee said. But he didn't think it was funny. He would later, perhaps. Ten years later. Crises past, in police work, tended to transmute themselves from fear into the stuff of jokes. But now there was still the fear, a palpable something affecting the way Chee's stomach felt. "I guess nobody noticed anyone tinkering around with my truck?"

Officer McDonald sat up a little straighter, noticing Chee's face and re-getting the joke. "Nobody mentioned it," he said. "And it's parked right out there where everybody could see it. I don't think . . ." He decided not to finish the sentence.

"No messages?" Chee asked.

McDonald sorted through the notes impaled on a spindle on the clerk's desk. "One," he said, and handed it to Chee.

"Call Lt. Leaphorn as soon as you get in," it said, and listed two telephone numbers.

Leaphorn answered at the second one, his home.

"I want to ask you if you learned anything new about Endocheeney," Leaphorn said. "But there's a couple of other loose ends. Didn't you say you met Irma Onesalt just recently? Can you tell me exactly when?"

"I could check my logs," Chee said. "Probably in April. Late April."

"Did she say anything to you about a list of names she had? About trying to find out what date the people on that list died?"

"No, sir," Chee said. "I'm sure I'd remember something like that."

"You said you went to the Badwater Clinic and picked up a patient there and took him to a chapter meeting for her and they gave you the wrong man. And she was sore about it. That right?"

"Right. Old man named Begay. You know how it is with Begays." How it was with Begays on the reservation is how it is with Smiths and Joneses in Kansas City or Chavezes in Santa Fe. It was the most common name on the reservation.

"She said nothing about names? Nothing about a list of names? Nothing about how to go about finding out dates of deaths? Nothing that might lead into that?"

"No, sir," Chee said. "She just said a word or two when I got to the chapter house. She was waiting. Wanted to know why I was late. Then she took the old man in to the meeting. I waited because I was supposed to take him back after he had his say. After a while, she came out and raised hell with me for bringing her the wrong Begay, and then he came out and got in and I took him back to the clinic. Not much of a chance for chatting."

"No," Leaphorn said. "I had some dealing with the woman myself." Chee heard the sound of a chuckle. "I imagine you learned a few new dirty words?"

"Yes, sir," Chee said. "I did."

A long silence. "Well," Leaphorn said. "Just remember that a little while before she was shot she showed up at the pathologist's office at the Gallup hospital with a list of names. She wanted to know how to find out when each of them died. If you hear anything that helps explain that, I want to know about it right away."

"Right," Chee said.

"Now. What did you learn out around Badwater?"

"Not much," Chee said. "He had several hundred dollars' worth of pawn left at the post there—a lot more than he owed for—and his kinfolks haven't picked it up. And he broke a leg last summer falling off a fence. Nothing much."

Silence again. Then Leaphorn said, in a very mild voice: "I've got a funny way of working. Instead of telling me 'Not much,' I like people to tell me all the details and then I'll say, 'Well, that's not much,' or maybe I'll say, 'Hey, that part about the pawn explains something else I heard.' Or so forth. What I'm saying is, give me all the details and let me sort it out."

And so Chee, feeling slightly resentful, told Leaphorn of the bent woman, and the Kayonnie brothers with morning beer on their breath, and the letter from Window Rock, and the crutches which Iron Woman wouldn't accept as pawn and couldn't sell, and all the other details. He finished, and listened to a silence so long that he wondered if Leaphorn had put down the telephone. He cleared his throat.

"That letter," Leaphorn said. "From Window Rock. But what agency? And when?"

"Navajo Social Services," Chee said. "That's what Iron Woman remembered. It came back in June."

"That's who Irma Onesalt worked for," Leaphorn said.

"Oh," Chee said.

"Where'd he get the crutches?"

"Badwater Clinic," Chee said. "They set his leg. Guess they loan out their crutches."

"And don't get them back," Leaphorn said. "You learn anything else you're not telling me?"

"No, sir," Chee said.

Leaphorn noticed the tone. "You can see why I need the details. You haven't been working on the Onesalt case, so you had no way of knowing—or giving a damn—who she worked for. Now we have a link. Victim Onesalt wrote a letter to victim Endocheeney. Or somebody in her office did."

"That help?"

Leaphorn laughed. "I don't see how. But nothing else helps, either. You figured out yet why you got shot at?"

"No, sir."

Another pause. "Something I want you to think about." Silence. "I'm going to bet you that when we find out who did it and why, it's going to be based on something you know. You're going to say, 'Hell, I should have thought of that.' "

"Maybe," Chee said. But he thought about it as he put down the telephone. And he doubted it. Leaphorn was a hotshot. But Leaphorn was wrong about this.

He glanced at McDonald, immersed again in the *Times*. Chee had come in mostly to get the station's portable spotlight out of the storeroom and shine it on his truck. But now, in this well-lit room with his friend waiting behind the newspaper, curious and embarrassed, doing that seemed ridiculous. Instead he went to his typewriter and pounded out a note to Largo.

TO: *Commanding Officer*
FROM: *Chee*
SUBJECT: *Investigation thefts from vehicles at tourist parking sites and theft of drip gasoline in Aneth field.*

At Badwater Wash Trading Post ran into two young men, Kayonnie family, driving a new GMC 4 × 4 and drinking in the morning. Am told they are unemployed. Will check more out there again.

He initialed the memo and handed it to Officer McDonald.

"Going home," he said, and left.

He stood a moment in the darkness beyond the entrance until his eyes adjusted enough to make his pickup visible. By then the fear had reestablished itself, and the thought of walking up to that truck in the darkness, and then of driving into the darkness surrounding his trailer, was more than he wanted to handle. He'd walk. It was less than two miles from the station down along the river to his homesite under the cottonwoods. An easy walk, even at night. It would work out the stiffness of a day spent mostly in his patrol car. He trotted across the asphalt of U.S. 666 and found the path that led toward the river.

Chee was a fast walker and normally this trip took less than thirty minutes. Tonight, moving soundlessly, he took almost forty and used another ten carefully scouting, pistol in hand, the places around his trailer where someone with a shotgun might wait. He found nothing. That left the trailer itself.

He paused behind a juniper and studied it. Light from a half-moon made the setting a pattern of cottonwood shadows. The only sound on the breezeless air was a truck changing gears on the highway far behind him, growling up the long slope out of the valley en route to Colorado. As to whether someone with a shotgun was waiting in the trailer, Chee could think of no safe way to answer that question. He'd left the door locked, but the lock would be easy to pick. He slipped the pistol out of its holster again, thinking that this was a hell of a way to live, thinking that he might give up on the trailer, walk back to the station, get his patrol car, and spend the night in a motel, thinking that he might just say to hell with it and walk up to the door, pistol cocked, and unlock it, and go in. Then he remembered the cat.

The cat was probably out hunting the nocturnal rodents it had lived on until Chee began supplementing its diet with his table scraps. But maybe not. Maybe it was still a little early for rodents and the predators that hunt them. More than once when he had risen early he'd seen Cat returning to its den about dawn. So perhaps it slept early and hunted late. The juniper under which Cat made its home was along the slope to Chee's left. He picked up a handful of dirt and gravel and threw it into the bush.

Later, he thought that the cat must have been crouched, alert, under the juniper listening to his prowling. It shot from the bush, moving almost too fast to be seen in the poor light for its refuge in the trailer. He heard the *clack-clack* of the cat door. He relaxed. No one would be waiting for him inside.

But now he knew he couldn't sleep in the trailer. He got out his sleeping bag, packed his toothbrush and a change of clothing, and walked back to the police station. He was tired now, and the incident of the cat had broken the tension. The fear that had lived in his truck was gone now. It was simply a friendly, familiar vehicle. He unlocked the door, climbed in, and started the engine. He drove across the San Juan and then west on 504, with the dark shape of the Chuskas looming in the moonlight to the south. Just past Behclahbeto, he pulled onto the shoulder, turned off his lights, and waited. The car lights he'd noticed miles behind him turned out to belong to a U-Haul truck, which roared past him and disappeared over the hill. He restarted his engine and turned onto a dirt road that jolted through the dusty sagebrush and dipped into an arroyo. Up the arroyo, he parked and rolled out his sleeping bag. He lay on his back, looking up at the stars, thinking about the nature of fear and how it affected him, and about what Iron Woman had told him of the bone being found in Dugai Endocheeney. It could be false, one of those witch rumors that spring up like tumbleweeds after rain when bad things happen. Or it could be true. Perhaps someone thought he had been witched by Endocheeney, and had killed him and returned the bone of corpse poison to reverse the witching. Or it could be that a witch had killed Dugai Endocheeney and left the bone as its marker. In either case, how would the people at Badwater Wash have learned of it? Chee considered that and found an answer. The bone would have shown up in the autopsy. The surgeon would have seen it only as a piece of foreign matter lodged in the wound. But it was odd, and he would have mentioned it. The word would have spread. A Navajo would have heard it—a nurse, an orderly. To a Navajo, any Navajo, the significance would have been apparent. The word of the bone would have reached Badwater Wash with the speed of light.

So why hadn't he mentioned the bone gossip to the lieutenant who insisted on knowing every detail? Chee examined his motives. It was too vague to mention, he thought, but the real reason was his expectation of Leaphorn's reaction to anything associated with witchery. Ah, well, perhaps he would mention it to Leaphorn the next time he saw him.

Chee rolled onto his side, seeking comfort and sleep. Tomorrow he would go to the Farmington jail, where Roosevelt Bistie was being held until the federals could decide what to do with him. He would try to get Bistie to talk about witchcraft.

9

I THINK YOU'RE too late," the officer on the jail information desk telephone said. "I think his lawyer's coming to get him."

"Lawyer?" Chee asked. "Who?"

"Somebody from DNA," the deputy said. "Some woman. She's driving over from Shiprock."

"So am I," Chee said, checking his memory for the name to go with the deputy's voice, and finding it. "Listen, Fritz, if she gets there first, maybe you could stall around a little. Take some time getting him checked out."

"Maybe so, Jim," Fritz said. "Sometimes people say we're slow. Can you be here by nine?"

Chee glanced at his watch. "Sure," he said.

From the police station in Shiprock to the jail in Farmington is about thirty miles. While he drove it, Chee considered how he would deal with the lawyer, or try to deal with her. DNA was the popular acronym for Dinebeiina Nahiilna be Agaditahe, which translates roughly into "People Who Talk Fast and Help the People Out," and which was the Navajo Nation's version of Legal Aid Society/public defender organization. Earlier in its career it had attracted mostly young militant social activists whose relationship with the Navajo Tribal Police had ranged from icy to hostile. Things had improved gradually. Now, generally, the iciness had modified to coolness, and the hostility to suspicion. Chee expected no trouble.

However . . .

The young woman in the white silk shirt sitting against the wall in the D Center reception room was looking at him with something stronger than suspicion. She was small, skinny, a Navajo, with short black hair and large angry black eyes. Her expression, if not hostile, showed active distaste.

"You're Chee," she said, "the arresting officer?"

"Jim Chee," Chee said, checking his reflex offer of a handshake in midmotion. "Not the arresting officer, technically. The federal—"

"I know that," said Silk Shirt, getting to her feet with a graceful motion. "Did Agent Kennedy explain to you . . . did Agent Kennedy explain to Mr. Bistie . . . that a citizen, even a Navajo citizen, has a right to consult with an attorney before he undergoes a cross-examination?"

"We read him—"

"And do you know," Silk Shirt asked, forming each word with icy precision, "that you have absolutely no legal right to hold Mr. Bistie here in this jail with no charge against him whatsoever, and knowing that he didn't commit the homicide you arrested him for, just because you 'want to talk to him'?"

"He's being held for investigation," Chee said, aware that his face was flushed, aware that Officer Fritz Langer of the Farmington Police Department was standing there behind the reception desk, watching all this. Chee shifted his position. From the corner of his eye he could see Langer was not only listening, he was grinning. "He admitted taking a shot—"

"Without advice of counsel," Silk Shirt said. "And now, just at your request and without any legal grounds at all, Mr. Bistie is being held here by the police while you take your time driving over from Shiprock so you can talk to him. Just a favor from one good old boy to another."

The grin disappeared from Langer's face. "The paperwork," he said. "It takes time when the federals are involved."

"Paperwork, my butt," Silk Shirt snapped. "It's the good old boy network at work." She pointed a thumb in Chee's direction, something one polite Navajo did not do to another. "Your buddy here calls you and says keep him locked up until I can get around to talking to him. Stall around all day if you have to."

"Naw," Langer said. "Nothing like that. You know how the Federal Bureau of Investigation is about crossing all the *t*'s and dotting the *i*'s."

"Well, Mr. Chee is here now. Can you get the *i* dotted and release Mr. Bistie?"

Langer made a wry face at Chee, lifted the telephone, and talked to someone. "He'll be out in a minute," he said. He reached under the counter, extracted a brown paper grocery bag, and put it on the countertop. It bore the legend R. BISTIE, WEST WING in red Magic Marker. Chee felt a yearning to explore that paper sack. He should have thought of it earlier. Much earlier. Before Silk Shirt arrived. He smiled at Silk Shirt.

"All I need is just a few minutes. Just some information."

"About what?"

"Well," Chee said, "if we knew why Bistie wanted to kill Endocheeney—and he says he wanted to kill him," he inserted hastily, "then maybe we'd know more about why someone else did kill Endocheeney. Stabbed Endocheeney. Later."

"Make an appointment," Silk Shirt said. "Maybe he'll want to talk to you." She paused, looking at Chee. "And maybe he won't."

"I guess we could pick him up again," Chee said. "As a material witness. Something like that."

"I guess you could," she said. "But it better be legal this time. Now he'll be represented by someone who understands that even a Navajo has some constitutional rights."

Roosevelt Bistie came through the door, trailed by an elderly jailer. The jailer patted him on the shoulder. "Come see us," he said, and disappeared back through the doorway.

"Mr. Bistie," Silk Shirt said. "I am Janet Pete. We were told you needed legal counsel and the DNA sent me over to represent you. To be your lawyer."

Bistie nodded to her. "*Ya-tah-hey*," he said. He looked at Chee. Nodded. Smiled. "I don't need no lawyer," he said. "They told me somebody else killed the son-of-a-bitch. I missed him." Bistie chuckled when he said it, but to Chee he still looked sick.

"You need a lawyer to tell you to be careful what you say," Janet Pete said, glancing at Chee. And then, to Langer: "And we need a place where my client and I can talk. In private."

"Sure," Langer said. He handed Bistie the sack and pointed. "Down the hall. First door to the left."

"Miss Pete," Chee said. "When you're talking to your client, would you ask him if I can talk to him for a minute or two? Otherwise . . ."

"Otherwise what?"

"Otherwise I'll have to drive all the way up into the Lukachukais to his place and talk to him there," Chee said meekly. "And just to ask three or four questions I forgot to ask him earlier."

"I'll see," Janet Pete said, and disappeared down the hall after Bistie.

Chee looked out the window. The lawn needed water. What was it about white men that caused them to plant grass in places where grass couldn't possibly grow without them fiddling with it all the time? Chee had thought about that a lot, and talked to Mary Landon about it. He'd told Mary he thought it represented a subconscious need to remind themselves that they could defy nature. Mary said no, it was a need for remembered beauty. Chee looked at the lawn, and at the desert country visible across the San Juan beyond it. He preferred the desert. Today even the fringe of tumbleweeds along the sidewalk looked wilted. Dry heat everywhere and the sky almost cloudless.

"I didn't tell her you'd asked me to stall," Langer said, apologetically. "She figured that out for herself."

"Oh, well," Chee said. "I don't think she likes cops, anyway." A thought materialized abruptly. "You remember what was in Bistie's sack?"

Langer looked surprised at the question. He shrugged. "Usual stuff. Billfold. Keys to his truck. Pocket knife. One of those little deerskin sacks some of you guys carry. Handkerchief. Nothing unusual."

"Did you look in the billfold?"

"We have to inventory the money," Langer said. He sorted through papers on a clipboard. "Had a ten and three ones and seventy-three cents in change. Driver's license. So forth."

"Anything else you remember?"

"I didn't check him in," Langer said. "Al did. On the evening shift. Says here: 'Nothing else of value.' "

Chee nodded.

"What you looking for?"

"Just fishing," Chee said.

"Speaking of which," Langer said, "can you get a permit for fishing up there at Wheatfields Lake? Free, I mean."

"Well," Chee said. "I guess you know—"

Janet Pete appeared at the hall door. "He says he'll talk to you."

"I thank you," Chee said.

The room held a bare wooden table and two chairs. Roosevelt Bistie sat in one of them, eyes half closed, face sagging. But he returned Chee's salutation. Chee put his hand on the back of the other chair, glanced at Janet Pete. She was leaning against the wall behind Bistie, watching Chee. The paper sack was under Bistie's chair.

"Could we talk in private?" Chee asked her.

"I'm Mr. Bistie's legal counsel," she said. "I'll stay."

Chee sat down, feeling defeated. It had never been likely that Bistie would talk. He hadn't, after all, in the past. It was even less likely that he would talk about the subject Chee intended to raise, which was witchcraft. There was a simple enough reason for that. Witches hated to be talked about—to even have their evil business discussed. Therefore the prudent Navajo discussed witchcraft, if at all, only with those known and trusted. Not with a stranger. Certainly not with two strangers. However, there was no harm in trying.

"I have heard something which I think you would like to know," Chee said. "I will tell you what I heard. And then I will ask you a question. I hope you will give me an answer. But if you won't, you won't."

Bistie looked interested. So did Janet Pete.

"First," Chee said, speaking slowly, intent on Bistie's expression, "I will tell you what the people over at the Badwater Wash Trading Post hear. They hear that a little piece of bone was found in the body of that man you took a shot at."

There was a lag of a second or two. Then Bistie smiled a very slight smile. He nodded at Chee.

Chee glanced at Janet Pete. She looked puzzled. "Understand that I do not know if this is true," Chee said. "I will go to the hospital where the body of that man was taken and I will try to find out if it was true. Should I tell you what I find out?"

No smile now. Bistie was studying Chee's face. But he nodded.

"Now I have a question for you to answer. Do you have a little piece of bone?"

Bistie stared at Chee, face blank.

"Don't answer that," Janet Pete said. "Not until I find out what's going on here." She frowned at Chee. "What's this all about? It sounds like an attempt to get Mr. Bistie to incriminate himself. What are you driving at?"

"We know Mr. Bistie didn't kill Endocheeney," Chee said. "Somebody else killed him. We don't know who. We aren't likely to find out who until we know why. Mr. Bistie here seems to have had a good reason to kill Endocheeney, because he tried to do it. Maybe it was the same reason. Maybe it was because Endocheeney was a skinwalker. Maybe he witched Mr. Bistie. Put the witch bone into him. Maybe Endocheeney witched somebody else. If what I heard at Badwater Wash isn't just gossip, maybe Mr. Endocheeney had a bone put in him because that other person, the one who knifed Endocheeney, put it in him when he stabbed Endocheeney to turn the witching around." Chee was talking directly to Janet Pete, but he was watching Bistie from the corner of his eye. If Bistie's face revealed any emotion, it was satisfaction.

"It sounds like nonsense to me," Janet Pete said.

"Would you recommend to your client that he answer my question, then?" Chee asked. "Did he believe Mr. Endocheeney was a witch?"

"I'll talk to him about this," she said. "There are no charges against him. None. He's not accused of anything. You're just holding him to satisfy your curiosity."

"About a murder," Chee said. "And there may be a charge filed by now. Attempted homicide."

"Based on what?" Janet Pete asked. "On what he told you and Kennedy before consulting with his attorney? That's absolutely all you have."

"That, and some other stuff," Chee said. "Witnesses who put him where it happened. His license number. The ejected shell from his rifle." Which, as far as Chee knew, hadn't been found and wasn't being looked for. Why look for a shell casing from a shot that missed when they had a butcher knife, which didn't miss? But Janet Pete wouldn't know they hadn't found it.

"I don't think there's any basis for charges," Janet Pete said.

Chee shrugged. "It's not up to me. I think Kennedy—"

"I think I will call Kennedy," Janet Pete said. "Because I don't believe you." She walked to the door, stopped with her hand on the knob, smiled at Chee. "Are you coming?"

"I'll just wait," Chee said.

"Then my client is coming," she said. She motioned to Bistie. He got up, steadied himself with a hand on the tabletop.

"This interview is over," Janet Pete said, and she closed the door behind them.

Chee waited. Then he went to the door and glanced down the hall. Janet Pete was using the telephone in the pay booth. Chee closed the door again, picked up Bistie's sack, sorted quickly through it. Nothing interesting. He extracted Bistie's billfold.

In it, in the corner of the currency pocket that held a ten and three ones, Chee found a bead. He turned it over between thumb and first finger, examining it. Then he put it back where he had found it, put the wallet back in the sack, and the sack back on the floor under Bistie's chair. The bead seemed to be made of bone. In fact, it looked exactly like the one he'd found on the floor of his trailer.

10

THE TURBULENCE CAUSED by the thunderhead was sweeping across the valley floor toward them. It kicked up an opaque gray-white wall of dust which obscured the distant shape of Black Mesa and spawned dust devils in the caliche flats south of them. They were standing, Officer Al Gorman and Joe Leaphorn, beside Gorman's patrol car on the track that led across the sagebrush flats below Sege Butte toward Chilchinbito Canyon.

"Right here," Gorman said. "Here's where he parked his car, or pickup, or whatever."

Leaphorn nodded. Gorman was sweating. A trickle of it ran down his neck and under his shirt collar. It was partly the heat, and partly that Gorman should lose a few pounds, and partly, Leaphorn knew, because he made Gorman nervous.

"Tracks lead right back here." Gorman pointed. "From over there near the rim of Chilchinbito Canyon, where he killed Sam, and down that slope there, where the shale outcrops are, and then across the sagebrush right up to here."

Leaphorn grunted. He was watching the dust storm moving down the valley with its outrider of whirlwinds. One of them had crossed a gypsum sink, and its winds had sucked up that heavier mineral. The cone changed from the yellow-gray of the dusty earth to almost pure white. It was the sort of thing Emma would have noticed, and found beauty in, and related in some way or other to the mythology of The People. Emma would have said something about the Blue Flint Boys playing their games. They were the *yei* personalities credited with stirring up whirlwinds. He would describe it to her tonight. He would if she was awake and aware—and not in that vague world she now so often retreated into.

Beside him, Gorman was describing the sign he had followed from killing scene to car, and the sign the car had left, and his conclusion that the killer had raced away. "Spun his wheels in the grass," Gorman was saying. "Tore it up. Threw dirt. And then, right down there, he backed around and drove on back toward the road."

"Where was the killing?"

"See that little bunch of juniper? Look across the shale slope, and then to the right. That man . . ." Gorman stopped, glanced at Leaphorn for a reading of whether the lieutenant would allow him to avoid "wearing out the name" of a dead man. He made his decision and restated the sentence. "That's where Wilson Sam was, by the juniper. Looked like it was a regular stopping place for him when he was out with the sheep. And the killer got him about twenty-five, thirty yards to the right of those junipers."

"Looks like he took sort of a roundabout way to get back here, then," Leaphorn said. "If he circled all the way around and came down that shale."

"Looks that way," Gorman said. "But it's not. It fools you. You can't see it from here because of the way the land folds, but if you try to go straight across, then over that ridge there—the ridge that shale is in—over that there's an arroyo. Cut deep. To get across it you got to skirt way up, or way down, where there's sheep crossing. So the short way—"

Leaphorn interrupted him. "Did he go the same way he came back?"

Gorman looked puzzled.

Leaphorn rephrased the question, partly to clarify his own thinking. "When he drove along here, we'll say he was looking for Sam. Hunting him. He sees Sam, or maybe just the flock of sheep Sam was watching, over there across the flats by the junipers. This is as close as he can get the vehicle. So he parks here. Gets out. Heads for Sam. You say the fastest way to get there is angling way to the right, and then up that shale slope over there, and across the ridge, and then across an arroyo at a sheep crossing, and then swing left again. Long way around, but quickest. And that's the way he came back. But is that the way he went?"

"Sure," Gorman said. "I guess so. I didn't notice. I wasn't looking for that. Just tracking him to see where he went."

"Let's see if we can find out," Leaphorn said. It wouldn't be easy, but for the first time since he'd awakened that morning, with the homicides instantly on his mind, he felt a stirring of hope. This might be a way to learn whether or not the person who'd killed Wilson Sam was a stranger to Sam's territory. Small though that would be, it would satisfy Leaphorn's quota for this unpromising day.

Leaphorn had given himself the quota as he'd eaten his breakfast: Before the day was done, he would add one single hard fact to what he knew about his unsolved homicides. He'd eaten a bowl of cornmeal mush, a piece of Emma's fried bread, and some salami from the refrigerator. Emma, who for all the almost thirty years of their marriage had risen with the dawn, was still asleep. He'd dressed quietly, careful not to disturb her.

She'd lost weight, he thought. Not eating. Before Agnes had come to help, she would simply forget to eat when he wasn't home. He would make her a lunch before he left for the office and find it untouched when he came home at the end of the day. Now she would sometimes forget to eat even when the food was on her plate in front of her. "Emma," he would say. "Eat." And she would look at him with that embarrassed, confused, disoriented smile and say, "It's good, but I forget." He had looked down at her as he buttoned his shirt, seeing an unaccustomed hollowness below the cheekbones, under the eyes. When he was away from her, her face would always have the same smooth roundness he'd noticed that day he first saw her—walking with two other Navajo girls across the campus at Arizona State.

Arizona State. His mother had buried his umbilical cord at the roots of a piñon beside their hogan—the traditional Navajo ritual for binding a child to his family and his people. But for Leaphorn, Emma was the tie. A simple physical law. Emma could not be happy away from the Sacred Mountains. He could not be happy away from Emma. He had frowned down at her, studying her, seeing the flatness of her cheek, the lines under her eyes and at the corners of her mouth. ("I'm feeling fine," she would say. "I never felt better. You must not have any work to do down at the police to be worrying about me all the time.") But now she would admit the headaches. And there was no way she could hide the forgetfulness, nor those odd blank moments when she seemed to be awakening, confused, from some bad dream. Day after tomorrow was the appointment. At 2 P.M. They would leave early, and drive to Gallup, and check her in at the Indian Health Service hospital. And then they would find out. Now there was no reason to think about it, about what it might be. No reason to let his mind reexamine again and again and again all he had heard and read of the horrors of Alzheimer's disease. Maybe it wasn't that. But he knew it was. He'd called the toll-free number of the Alzheimer's Disease and Related Disorders Association, and they had sent him a package of information.

. . . initially a patient with AD exhibits the following symptoms:

1. *Forgetfulness.*
2. *Impairment of judgment.*
3. *Inability to handle routine tasks.*
4. *Lack of spontaneity.*
5. *Lessening of initiative.*
6. *Disorientation of time and place.*
7. *Depression and terror.*
8. *Disturbance of language.*
9. *Episodic confusional states.*

He had read it in the office, checking them off. The suddenly faltering unfinished sentences, the business of always thinking today was his day off, the lethargy, the trouble with getting the garbage bag installed in the garbage can, the preparation for Agnes's arrival two days after Agnes had arrived. Worst of all, his awakening in the night to find Emma clutching at him, frantic with some nightmare fear. He had, as was his fashion, made notes in the margin. Emma had scored nine for nine.

Leaphorn had every reason to think of something else.

And so that morning he had thought, first, of Irma Onesalt's list of the dead, and why death dates would be important to her. As he left Emma still sleeping he heard Agnes stirring in her room. He drove to his office in the clear, sunrise light of another day of heat and drought. Dust was already rising from the rodeo grounds down at the highway intersection—

the dust of stock feeding. Sometime today he would think of the rodeo and the myriad of problems it always brought. Now he wanted to think of his homicides.

At the office, he composed a letter to go to the various county health departments in Arizona, New Mexico, and Utah that would have been contacted by Onesalt if she followed the advice of Dr. Randall Jenks. It was too complicated, and too sensitive, to be handled by the half-dozen telephone calls it would require. And there was no real urgency. So he put the letter together—very carefully. He explained who he was, explained that the investigation of the murder of Irma Onesalt was involved, described the list as best he could, trying to recall for them the question she might have asked. Finally, with these needed preliminaries out of the way, he inquired if anyone in the department had received a letter or a telephone call from Ms. Onesalt concerning these names, asking death dates. If so, could he have a copy of the letter, or the name of the person who had handled the telephone call, so he could question that person more closely.

He wrote a clean copy of the final draft and a cover memo for the clerk, listing to whom copies should be sent. That done, he considered what Jenks had told him about Chee's bone bead. It was made of cow bone. A witch, if one believed bona fide witches existed, would have used human bone, presuming the bona fide witch believed Navajo witchcraft mythology in a literal meaning. So if a real witch was involved, presuming such existed, said witch had been swindled by his bone supplier. On the other hand, if someone was merely pretending to be a witch, such things didn't matter. Those who believed witches magically blew bone particles into their victims would hardly subject said bone to the microscope. And of course, cow-bone beads would be easy to get. Or would they? It seemed likely. Every slaughterhouse would produce mountains of cattle bones. Raw material for mass producing beads for the costume jewelry market. Leaphorn found his thought process leading him into the economics of producing bone beads as opposed to molding plastic beads. Chee's bone beads would certainly be old, something from old jewelry, or perhaps clothing. Jenks had said the bead was fairly old. Perhaps the FBI, with its infinite resources, could track down the source. But he couldn't imagine how. He tried to imagine Delbert Streib phrasing the memo about corpse poison and witches to touch off such an effort. Streib would simply laugh at the idea.

Leaphorn wrote another memo, instructing Officer Jimmy Tso, who handled liaison with the Gallup police department, to check suppliers for jewelry makers, pawnshops, and wherever else he could think of, to learn how a Navajo/Zuni/Hopi jewelry maker might obtain beads, and particularly bone beads. He dropped that memo in his out-basket atop the drafted letter. Then he extracted his homicide folders from the cabinet, put them on his desk, and looked at them.

He pushed the Onesalt file aside. Onesalt had been the first to die. Something in his instinct told him she was the key, and he knew her file by heart. It baffled him. It seemed as lacking in purpose as death by lightning—as cruel and casual as the malicious mischief of the Holy People. He picked up the file labeled WILSON SAM, opened it, and read. He saw nothing that he hadn't remembered. But when he'd first read it, he hadn't noticed that the tribal policeman working with Jay Kennedy on this investigation was Officer Al Gorman. The name then had meant nothing to him. It had simply identified a new, probably young, officer whom Leaphorn did not know. Now the name carried with it a visual image.

Leaphorn put the file on the desk and looked out his window at the early morning sunlight on the scattered roofs of Window Rock village. Gorman. The plump cop walking across the Shiprock parking lot with Chee and Benaly. Chee instantly conscious of the parked car, of what car it was, of its occupant, all with hardly a glance. But the walk became a little stiffer, the shoulders a little straighter, knowing he was watched. Benaly becoming aware of Chee's awareness, noticing the car, not being interested. And Gorman, talking, noticing nothing. Oblivious. Blind to everything except the single thought that occupied him. Officer Gorman had never noticed Leaphorn sitting in the shade in his car. If he missed that, what had he missed at the scene of Wilson Sam's death? Maybe nothing, but it was worth checking. To be honest, perhaps he should say it gave him an excuse.

It was nine minutes until eight. In nine minutes his telephone would start ringing. The world of the troublesome rodeo, the Tribal Council meeting, indignant school principals, bootleggers, too few men and too many assignments, would capture him for another day. He looked past the clock at the world outside the window, the highway leading away over the ridge toward everywhere but Window Rock, the world in which his job had once allowed him to pursue his own curiosity and to hell with the paperwork. He picked up the telephone and called the Shiprock station. He asked for Officer Al Gorman.

Now it was early afternoon. Gorman had met him, as requested, at the Mexican Water Trading Post. They'd made the bone-jarring drive back into the Chilchinbito Canyon country. Rather quickly, Officer Gorman had proved he was the sort of man who—as Leaphorn's grandmother would have said—counted the grass and didn't see the grazing.

Gorman was sitting now in Leaphorn's car, waiting (uneasily, Leaphorn hoped) for Leaphorn to finish whatever the hell Leaphorn was doing. What Leaphorn was doing was looking past the grass at the grazing. They had established by two hours of dusty work that the route the killer had taken to reach the growth of junipers where Wilson Sam was waiting was very different from his return route. Broken twigs here, dislodged rocks there, a footprint sheltered enough to survive two months of rainless days, showed them that he had headed in an almost straight line through the sagebrush toward the junipers. He had crossed the ridge, maintaining that direction except when heavy brush forced a detour, until he reached the arroyo. He had walked down its bank perhaps a hundred yards, presumably looking for a crossing point. Then he had reversed direction almost a quarter mile, to cross at a sheep trail—the same trail he'd used on his return trip.

Leaphorn spent the remainder of the morning having Gorman shown him just what he had found, and where he had found it, when Gorman had worked this scene for Kennedy early in the summer. Gorman had shown him where Wilson Sam's body had been found on the bottom of the narrow wash draining into Chilchinbito. He had pointed out the remains of the little rock slides that showed Sam had been tumbled down from above. The rainless summer had left the sign pretty much undisturbed. Ants had carried away most of the congealed blood from the sand where the body had lain, but you could still find traces. In this protected bottom, the winds had only smoothed the tracks of those who had come to carry Sam away.

Above, the scouring had been more complete. Gorman had shown Leaphorn where Sam had been and where the killer had come from. "Easy enough to tell 'em apart," Gorman said. "The ground was softer then. Sam had boots on. Flat heels. Easy to match them with his tracks. And the other fellow had on cowboy boots." He glanced at Leaphorn. "Bigger. Maybe size eleven."

All that had been in Kennedy's report. So had the answer to the question Leaphorn had decided to ask. But he wanted to hear it for himself.

"And they didn't stand and talk at all? No sign of that?"

"No, sir," Gorman said. "No sign of that. When I tracked the suspect back, it showed he started running about forty yards out there." Gorman had pointed into the sparse sagebrush to the south. "No more heel prints. He was running."

"And Sam? Where did he start running away?"

Gorman showed him. Sam had not run far. Perhaps twenty-five yards. Old men are poor runners, even when they are running for their life.

Back at the car, Leaphorn stood where the killer had parked and stared across the broken landscape toward the junipers where this person must have seen Sam, or Sam's sheep. He stood with his lower lip held between his teeth, nibbling thoughtfully, trying to recreate what the killer must have been thinking, retracing with his eyes the route the man had taken.

"Let's make sure we agree—that I'm not overlooking anything," Leaphorn said. "He's driving along here. He sees Sam, or maybe Sam's flock, over there by the junipers. He parks. He heads directly toward Sam." Leaphorn glanced at Gorman, saw no sign of disagreement. "In a hurry, I'd say, because of the way he crashed through the sagebrush. He didn't know the arroyo was there behind the ridge, and couldn't get across it there, so he had to skirt upstream to where the banks get lower."

"Not too smart," Gorman said.

"Could be that," Leaphorn said, although being smart had nothing to do with it. "And when he got close to Sam he was in such a hurry to kill him that he started running. Right?"

"I'd say so," Gorman said.

"Why did Sam start running?"

"Scared," Gorman said. "Maybe the guy was yelling at him. Or waving that shovel he killed him with."

"Yeah," Leaphorn said. "That's what I'd guess. When we catch him, who do you think it will turn out to be?"

Gorman shrugged. "No way of telling," he said. "It'd be a man. Big, man-sized feet. Probably some kinfolks or other." He looked at Leaphorn, smiling slightly. "You know how it is. It's always some sort of fight with some of his wife's folks, or some fight with some neighbor over where he's grazing his sheep. That's the way it always is."

It was, in fact, the way it always was. But this time it wasn't. "Think about him not knowing the arroyo was there. Not knowing where to find the sheep crossing," Leaphorn said. "That tell you anything?"

Gorman's pleasant round face looked puzzled. He thought. "I didn't think about that," he said. "I guess it wasn't a neighbor. Anybody lives around here, they'd know how the land lays. How it drains."

"So our man was a stranger."

"Yeah," Gorman said. "That's funny. Think it will help any?"

Leaphorn shrugged. He couldn't see how. It did form a sort of crazy harmony with the Endocheeney affair. Bistie and Endocheeney seemed to have been strangers. What did that mean? But he'd met his quota. He'd added one fact to his homicide data. Wilson Sam had been killed by a stranger.

11

AFTER MANY PAINSTAKING reconsiderations, Jim Chee finally decided he didn't know what the hell to do about the bone bead in Roosevelt Bistie's billfold. He had walked out of the visiting room and closed the door behind him, leaving Bistie's paper sack of belongings on the floor beside the chair, exactly where Bistie had put it. Then he stood by the door, looking at Bistie with a curiosity intensified by the thought that Bistie had tried to blast him out of bed with a shotgun. Bistie was sitting on the hard bench against the wall looking out of the window at something, his face in profile to Chee. Chee memorized him. A witch? Why had this man fired the shotgun through the skin of his trailer? He looked no different from any other human, of course. None of those special characteristics that the white culture sometimes gives its witches. No pointy nose, sharp features, broomstick. Just another man whose malice had led him to try to kill. To shoot Dugai Endocheeney, a stranger, on the roof of his hogan. To shoot Jim Chee, another stranger, asleep in his bed. To butcher Wilson Sam amid his sheep. As Bistie sat now, slumped on the bench, Chee had no luck relating his shape to the shape he had seen, or dreamed he had seen, in the darkness outside his trailer. His only impression had been that the shape had been small. Bistie seemed a little larger than the remembered shape. Could Bistie actually be the man?

Bistie lost interest in whatever he'd been watching through the window and glanced down the hall toward Chee. Their eyes met. Chee read nothing in Bistie's expression except a mild and guarded interest. Then the door of the phone booth pushed open and Janet Pete emerged. Chee walked down the hall, away from her, and out the exit into the parking lot and to his car, away from all the impulsive actions his instinct urged. He wanted to rearrest Bistie. He wanted to take the wallet and confront Bistie—in front of witnesses—with the bone bead. He wanted to make Bistie's possession of the bone a matter of record. But keeping a bone bead in one's billfold was legal enough. And Chee had absolutely no right to know it was there. He'd found it in an illegal search. There was a law against that. But not against bone possession or—for that matter—against being a skinwalker.

Having thought of nothing he could do, he sat in his car waiting for Pete and Bistie to emerge. Maybe they would leave without Bistie's sack. Simply forget it. If that happened, he would go to the jail, tell Langer that Bistie had left his belongings behind, get Langer to make another, more complete inventory, which would include all the billfold's contents. But when Pete and Bistie emerged, Bistie had the sack clutched in his hand. They drove out of the jail lot, turning toward Farmington. Chee turned west, toward Shiprock.

His mind worked on it as he drove. Reason told him that Bistie might not have been the shape in the darkness that had fired the shotgun into his trailer. Bistie had used the 30-30 on the rack across the back window of his pickup to shoot at Endocheeney. Or said he did. Not a shotgun. There had been no reason to search Bistie's place for a shotgun. Maybe he didn't have one. And the complex mythology of Navajo witchcraft, which Chee knew as well as any man, usually attached a motive to the malice of the skinwalkers. Bistie had no conceivable motive for wanting to kill Chee. Perhaps Bistie was not the one who had tried to kill him.

But even as he thought this, he was aware that his spirit was light again. The dread had lifted. He was not afraid of Bistie, as he had been afraid of the unknown. He felt an urge to sing.

The in-basket on his desk held two envelopes and one of the While You Were Out memos the tribal police used to record notes and telephone calls. One envelope, Chee noticed with instant delight, was the pale blue of Mary Landon's stationery. He put it in his shirt pocket and looked at the other one. It was addressed to Officer Chee, Police Station, Shiprock, in clumsy letters formed with a pencil. Chee glanced at the telephone memo, which said merely: "Call Lt. Leaphorn immediately," and tore open the envelope.

The folded letter inside had been written on the pulpy lined tablet paper schoolchildren use, in the format students are taught in grade school.

In the block where one is taught to put one's return address, the writer had printed:

Alice Yazzie
Sheep Springs Trading Post
Navajo Nation 92927

Dear Nephew Jim Chee:

I hope you are well. I am well. I write you this letter because your Uncle Frazier Denetsone is sick all this summer and worst sick about this month. We took him to the Crystal Gazer over at the Badwater Clinic and the Crystal Gazer said he should let the belagana doctor there give him some medicine. He is taking that green medicine now but he is still sick. The Crystal Gazer said he should take that medicine but that he needs a sing too. That will get him better faster, having the sing. And the sing should be a Blessing Way. I heard that you did the Blessing Way sing for the Niece of Old Grandmother Nez and everybody said it was good. Everybody said you got it all right and the dry paintings were right. They said the Niece of Old Grandmother Nez got better after that.

We want you to talk about it. We want you to come to the place of Hildegarde Goldtooth and we will talk to you about having the sing. We have about $400 but maybe there could be more.

Chee read with intense satisfaction. The Blessing Way he had conducted last spring had been his first job as a *yataalii*. And his last. The niece of Old Grandmother Nez was a niece by the broad Navajo definition—the daughter of a first cousin on the maternal side of Chee's family—and hiring him as singer had been family courtesy. In fact, the event had been a trial balloon—as much to inform the north central slice of the Big Reservation that Chee had begun his practice as to cure the girl of nothing more serious than the malaise of being sixteen.

Now, finally, a summons had come. Alice Yazzie called him nephew, but the title here reflected good manners and not ties of either clan or family. Frazier Denetsone was probably some sort of uncle, as Navajos defined such things, through linkage with his father's paternal clan. But a call for a *yataalii* didn't come from the patient. It came from whoever in the patient's circle of family took responsibility for such things. Chee glanced at Alice Yazzie's signature, which included, in the custom of old-fashioned Navajos, her clan. Streams Come Together Dinee. Chee was born to the Slow Talking People, and for the Salt Clan. No connections with the Streams Clan. Thus her invitation was the first clue that Jim Chee was becoming accepted as a singer outside his own kinfolk.

He finished the letter. Alice Yazzie wanted him to come to Hildegarde Goldtooth's place the next Sunday evening, when she and the patient's wife and mother could be there to work out a time for the ceremony. "We want to hold it as soon as we can because he is not good. He is not going to last long, I think."

That pessimistic note diminished Chee's jubilation. It was much better for a *yataalii* to begin his career with a visible cure—with a ceremony that not only restored the patient to harmony with his universe but also returned him to health. But Chee would tolerate nothing negative today. It would be better still to effect a cure on a hopeless case. If Frazier Denetsone's illness was indeed subject to correction by the powers evoked by the Blessing Way ritual, if Jim Chee was good enough to perform it precisely right, then all things were possible. Chee believed in penicillin and insulin and heart bypass surgery. But he also believed that something far beyond the understanding of modern medicine controlled life and death. He folded Alice Yazzie's letter into his shirt pocket. With his thumbnail he opened the letter from Mary Landon.

Dearest Jim:

I think of you every day (and even more every night). Miss you terribly. Can't you get some more leave and come back here for a while? I could tell you didn't enjoy yourself on your visit in May, but now we are having our annual two weeks of what passes for summer in Wisconsin. Everything is beautiful. It hasn't rained for two or three hours. You would like it now. In fact, I think you could learn to love it—to live somewhere away from the desert—if you would give it a chance.

Dad and I drove down to Madison last week and talked to an adviser in the College of Arts and Sciences. I will be able to get my master's degree—with a little luck—in just two more semesters because of those two graduate courses I took when I was an undergraduate. Also found a cute efficiency apartment within walking distance of the university and picked up the application papers for graduate admission. I can start taking classes on nondegree status while they process the grad school admission. The adviser said there shouldn't be any problem.

Classes will start the first week of September, which means that, if I enroll, I won't have time to come back out to see you until semester break, which I think is about Thanksgiving. I'm going to hate not seeing you until then, so try to find a way to come. . . .

Chee read the rest of it without much sense of what the words meant. Some chat about something that had happened when he'd visited her in Stevens Point, a couple of sentences about her mother. Her father (who had been painfully polite and had asked Chee endless questions about the Navajo religion and had looked at him as Chee thought Chee might look at a man from another planet) was well and thinking about retirement. She was excited about the thought of returning to school. Probably she would do it. There were more personal notes too, tender and nostalgic.

He read the letter again, slowly this time. But that changed nothing. He felt a numbness—a lack of emotion that surprised him. What did surprise him, oddly, he thought, was that he wasn't surprised. At some subconscious level he seemed to have been expecting this. It had been inevitable since Mary had arranged the leave from the teaching job at Crownpoint. If he hadn't known it then, he must have learned it during that visit to her home—which had left him on the flight back to Albuquerque trying to analyze feelings that were a mixture of happiness and sorrow. He glanced at the opening salutation again. "Dearest Jim . . ." The notes she'd sent him from Crownpoint had opened with "Darling . . ."

He stuffed the letter into his pocket with the Yazzie letter and picked up the memo.

It still said: "Call Lt. Leaphorn immediately."

He called Lieutenant Leaphorn.

12

THE TELEPHONE ON Joe Leaphorn's desk buzzed.

"Who is it?"

"Jim Chee from Shiprock," the switchboard said.

"Tell him to hold it a minute," Leaphorn said. He knew what to learn from Chee, but he took a moment to reconsider exactly how he'd go about asking the questions. He held the receiver lightly in his palm, going over it.

"Okay," he said. "Put him on."

Something clicked.

"This is Leaphorn," Leaphorn said.

"Jim Chee. Returning your call."

"Do you know any of the people who live out there around Chilchinbito Canyon. Out there where Wilson Sam lived?"

"Let me think," Chee said. Silence. "No. I don't think so."

"You ever worked anything out there? Enough to be familiar with the territory?"

"Not really," Chee said. "Not my part of the reservation."

"How about the country around Badwater Wash? Around where Endocheeney lived?"

"A lot better," Chee said. "It's not what Captain Largo has me patrolling, but I spent some time out there trying to find a kid who got washed down the San Juan last year. Several days. And then I handled the Endocheeney business. Went out there twice on that."

"I'm right that Bistie wouldn't say anything about whether he knew Endocheeney?"

"Right. He wouldn't say anything. Except he was glad Endocheeney was dead. He made that plain. So you guess he knew the man."

You do, Leaphorn thought. But maybe you guess wrong.

"Did he say anything that would give you an idea whether he knew that Badwater country? Like about having trouble finding Endocheeney's place? Anything like that?"

"You mean beyond stopping at the trading post to ask directions? He did that."

"That was in Kennedy's report," Leaphorn said. "What I meant was did you hear anything from him, or from the people you talked to at Badwater, that would tell you he was totally strange to that country? Afraid of not finding the road? Getting lost? Anything like that?"

"No." The word was said slowly, indicating the thought wasn't finished. Leaphorn waited. "But I didn't press it. We just got his description, and a make on his truck. Didn't look for that sort of information."

Obviously it wouldn't have seemed to have any meaning at that stage of the game. Perhaps it didn't now. He waited for Chee to make unnecessary excuses. None materialized. Leaphorn began phrasing his next question, but Chee interrupted the thought.

"You know," he said slowly, "I think the fellow who knifed Endocheeney was a stranger too. Didn't know the country."

"Oh?" Leaphorn said. He'd heard Chee was smart. He'd heard right. Chee was saving him his question.

"He came down out of the rocks," Chee said. "Have you seen that Endocheeney place? It's set back from the San Juan maybe a hundred yards. Cliffs to the south of it. The killer came down off of those. And went back the same way to get to where he'd left his car. I spent some time looking around. There were two or three easier ways to get down to Endocheeney. Easier than the way he took."

"So," Leaphorn said, half to himself. "Two strangers show up the same day to kill the same man. What do you think of that?"

There was silence. Through his window Leaphorn watched an unruly squadron of crows flying in from the cottonwoods along Window Rock Ridge toward the village. Lunchtime for crows in the garbage cans. But he wasn't thinking of crows. He was thinking of Chee's intelligence. If he told Chee now that the man who killed Wilson Sam was also a stranger, and how he knew it, Chee would quickly detect the reason for his first question. They had established that Chee, too, was a stranger to Wilson Sam's landscape. They established Leaphorn's suspicions. But to hell with that. A cop who got himself shot at from ambush should expect to be under close scrutiny. Chee might as well. He would tell Chee what he'd learned.

"It's possible," Chee was saying, slowly, "that there weren't two strangers coming to find Endocheeney. Maybe there was just one."

"Ah," said Leaphorn, who had the very same thought.

"It could be," Chee went on, "that Bistie knew he missed Endocheeney when he shot at him on the roof. So he drove away, parked up on the mesa, climbed down, and killed Endocheeney with the knife. And then—"

"He confesses to shooting Endocheeney," Leaphorn concluded. "Pretty smart. Is that what happened?"

Chee sighed. "I don't think so," he said.

Neither did Leaphorn. It violated what he'd learned of people down the years. People who prefer guns don't use knives, and vice versa. Bistie had preferred a rifle. He still had the rifle. Why not use it on the second attempt?

"Why not?" Leaphorn asked.

"Different tracks. I don't think Bistie would have brought along a change of footwear, and what few tracks I found at Endocheeney's didn't match Bistie's boots. Anyway, why would he do that? And why not shoot him on the second attempt? Why use a knife? It gave him an alibi, sure. And fooled us. But think of the advance planning it would take to make it all work out like that. And the things that could go wrong. It doesn't match my impression of Bistie."

"Okay," Leaphorn said. "Do you know anything from talking to Bistie, or from anything, that would suggest that Bistie might have known Wilson Sam?"

"No, sir. Nothing."

"Well, we seem to have another strange situation, then." He told Chee what he'd learned at Chilchinbito Canyon.

"Doesn't make much sense," Chee said. "Does it?"

"That bone bead in your trailer," Leaphorn said. "It turned out to be bovine. Made out of old cow bone."

Chee made a noncommittal sound.

"Anything else happened with you? Anything suspicious?"

"No, sir."

"You learning anything?"

"Well . . ." Chee hesitated. "Nothing much. I heard gossip at Badwater Trading Post. They say a bone was found in Endocheeney's corpse."

Leaphorn exhaled, surprised. "Like he had been witched?"

"Yeah," Chee said. "Or like he'd witched somebody else and they put it back into him."

And this was, in Leaphorn's thinking, the very worst part of a sick tradition—this cruel business of killing a scapegoat when things went wrong. It was what Chee Dodge had railed against when he tried to stamp it out. It was what had made Joe Leaphorn, young then and new to the Navajo Tribal Police, responsible for the deaths of four people. Two men. Two women. Three witches and the man who killed them. He had heard the gossip. He had laughed at it. He had collected the bodies—three murders and a suicide. That was twenty years ago. It had converted Leaphorn's contempt for witchcraft into hatred.

"Nothing about any foreign bone fragment showed up in the autopsy," Leaphorn said. But even as he said it, he knew it wasn't necessarily true. The pathologist might not list—probably wouldn't list—such odds and ends. When the cause of death was so obvious—a butcher knife blade driven repeatedly through clothing into the victim's abdomen and side—why list the threads and buttons, lint and gum wrappers, the blade might drive through the skin?

"I thought it might be worth asking about," Chee said.

"It is," Leaphorn said. "I will."

"Also," Chee said. And then paused.

Leaphorn waited.

"Also, Bistie had a bone bead in his wallet. Just like the one I found in my trailer. Looked like it, anyway."

Leaphorn exhaled again. "He did? What did he say about it?"

"Well, nothing," Chee said. He explained what had happened at the jail. "So I just put it back where I found it."

"I think we better go talk to Bistie again," Leaphorn said. "In fact, I think we better pick him up, and lock him up until we get this sorted out a little better." Leaphorn imagined trying to persuade Dilly to file the complaint. Dilly Streib would be hard to persuade. Dilly had been FBI too long not to care about his batting average. The Agency didn't like cases it didn't win. Still . . .

Leaphorn swiveled in his chair and looked at his map. A line of bone beads now connected two of his dots. And Roosevelt Bistie must know how they connected. And why.

"We can charge him with attempted murder, or attempted assault, or hold him as a material witness."

"Umm," Chee said. A sound full of doubt.

"I'll call the feds," Leaphorn said. He glanced at his watch. "Can you meet me in an hour at . . ." He looked at the map again, picking the most practical halfway point between Window Rock and Shiprock for their drive into the Chuskas. "At Sanostee," he concluded. "Sanostee in an hour?"

"Yes, sir," Chee said. "Sanostee in an hour."

13

SANOSTEE WAS HARDLY a halfway point, but it was convenient for where they were going. For Chee it was fast—twenty miles south on the worn pavement of U.S. 666 to Littlewater, and then nine miles westward, into the teeth of the gusting, dusty wind, up the long slope of the Chuska range to the trading post. For Leaphorn it was triple that distance—from Window Rock to Crystal and over Washington Pass to Sheep Springs, then north to the Littlewater intersection. When Leaphorn reached Sanostee it was sundown, the copper-colored twilight of one of those days when the desert sky is translucent with hanging dust.

Chee was sitting under his steering wheel, feet out the door, drinking an orange crush. They left Leaphorn's car and took Chee's. Leaphorn asked questions. Chee drove. They were astute questions, intended to duplicate as much of Chee's memory in Leaphorn's as was possible. At first the focus was on Bistie, on everything he'd said and how he'd said it, and then on Endocheeney, and finally on Janet Pete.

"I had a little mixup with her last year," Leaphorn said. "She thought we'd roughed up a drunk—or said she did."

"Had we?"

Leaphorn glanced at him. "Somebody had. Unless the officer was lying about it, it was somebody else."

The road that wandered northward from Sanostee had been graded once, and graveled at some time in the dim past when this part of the Chuskas had elected an unusually fierce advocate to the Tribal Council. The perpetual cycle of January snows and April thaws had swallowed the gravel long ago, and the highway superintendent for that district had solved the problem by erasing the road from his map. But it was still passable in dry weather and still used by the few families who grazed their sheep in this part of the highlands. Chee drove it carefully, skirting washouts and avoiding its washboard pattern of surface erosion when he could. Sunrays from below the curve of the planet lit cloud banks on the western horizon and reflected red now, converting the yellow hue of the universe into a vague pink tint.

"I've been wondering who called her in on this," Chee said. "When we told Bistie he could call a lawyer, he wasn't interested."

"Probably his daughter," Leaphorn said.

"Probably," Chee agreed. He remembered the daughter standing in the yard of Bistie's house. Would she have thought of calling a lawyer? Driven back to Sanostee to make the call? Known whom to call? He amended the "probably." "Maybe so," he said.

That concluded the conversation. They rode in silence. Leaphorn sat back straight against the seat, his eyes memorizing what he could see of the landscape in fading yellow light, his mind drawn to the intolerable problem of Emma's illness and then flinching away from that to escape into the merely frustrating puzzle of the four pins on his map. Chee rode slumped against the door, right hand on the wheel, a taller man and slender, thinking of the bone bead in Bistie's wallet, of what questions he might ask to cause the stubborn Bistie to talk about witchcraft to hostile strangers, of whether Leaphorn would allow him any questions, of how Leaphorn, the famous Leaphorn, the Leaphorn of tribal police legends, would handle this. And thinking of Mary Landon's letter. He found he could see the words, dark blue ink against the pale blue of the paper.

"Dad and I drove down to Madison last week and talked to an adviser in the College of Arts and Sciences. I will be able to get my master's degree—with a little luck—in just two more semesters . . ."

Just two semesters. Only two semesters. Only two. Or, put another way, I will only take two long steps away from you. Or, I promised I would come back to you at the end of summer, but now I am going away. Or, rephrased again, former lover, you are now a friend. Or . . .

The patrol car slanted up into the thicket of piñon and stunted ponderosa. Chee shifted into second gear.

"Just over this ridge," he said.

Just over the ridge, the light became visible. It was below them, still at least half a mile away, a bright point in the darkening twilight. Chee remembered it from the afternoon they had arrested Bistie. A single bare bulb protected by a metal reflector atop a forty-foot ponderosa pine stem. Bistie's ghost light. Would a witch be worried about ghosts? Would a witch keep a light burning to fend off the *chindi* which wandered in the darkness?

"His place?" Leaphorn asked.

Chee nodded.

"He's got electricity out here?" Leaphorn sounded surprised.

"There's a windmill generator behind the house," Chee said. "I guess he runs that light off batteries."

Bistie's access route required a right turn off the road, bumped over a rocky hummock and past a scattering of piñons, to drop again down to his place. In the harsh yellow light it looked worse than Chee had remembered it—a rectangular plank shack, probably with two rooms, roofed with blue asphalt shingles. Behind it stood a dented metal storage shack, a brush arbor, a pole horse corral, and, up the slope by the low cliff of the mesa, a lean-to for hay storage. Beyond that, against the cliff, the yellow light reflected from a hogan made of stacked stone slabs. Beside the shack, side by side and with their vanes turned away from the gusting west wind, were Bistie's windmill and his wind generator.

Chee parked his patrol car under Bistie's yard light.

There was no sign of the truck and no light on in the house.

Leaphorn sighed. "You know enough about him to do any guessing about where he might be?" he said. "Visiting kinfolks or anything?"

"No," Chee said. "We didn't get into that."

"Lives here with his daughter. Right?" Leaphorn said.

"Right."

They waited for someone to appear at the door and acknowledge the presence of visitors, delaying the moment when they'd admit the long drive had been for nothing. Delaying what would be either a return trip to Sanostee or a fruitless hunt for neighbors who might know where Roosevelt Bistie had gone.

"Maybe he didn't come back here when the lawyer got him out," Chee said.

Leaphorn grunted. The yellow light from the bare bulb above them lit the right side of his face, giving it a waxy look.

No one appeared at the door.

Leaphorn got out of the car, slammed the door noisily behind him, and leaned against the roof, eyes on the house. The door wouldn't be locked. Should he go in, and look around for some hint of where Bistie might be?

The wind gusted against him, blowing sand against his ankles above his socks and pushing at his uniform hat. Then it died. He heard Chee's door opening. He smelled something burning—a strong, acrid odor.

"Fire," Chee said. "Somewhere."

Leaphorn trotted toward the house, rapped on the door. The smell was stronger here, seeping between door and frame. He turned the knob, pushed the door open. Smoke puffed out, and was whipped away by another gust of the dry wind. Behind him, Chee yelled: "Bistie. You in there?"

Leaphorn stepped into the smoke, fanning with his hat. Chee was just behind him. The smoke was coming from an aluminum pot on top of a butane stove against the back wall of the room. Leaphorn held his breath, turned off the burner under the pan and under a blue enamel coffeepot boiling furiously beside it. He used his hat as a potholder, grabbed the handle, carried it outside, and dropped it on the packed earth. It contained what seemed to have been some sort of stew, now badly charred. Leaphorn went back inside.

"No one's here," Chee said. He was fanning the residual smoke with his hat. A chair lay on its side on the floor.

"You checked the back room?"

Chee nodded. "Nobody home."

"Left in a hurry," Leaphorn said. He wrinkled his nose against the acrid smell of burned meat and walked back into the front yard. With the butt of his flashlight, he poked into the still-smoking pan, inspected the residue it collected.

"Take a look at this," he said to Chee. "You're a bachelor, aren't you? How long does it take you to burn stew like this?"

Chee inspected the pot. "The way he had the fire turned up, maybe five, ten minutes. Depends on how much water he put in it."

"Or she," Leaphorn said. "His daughter. When you were here with Kennedy, they just have one truck?"

"That's all," Chee said.

"So they must be off somewhere in it," Leaphorn said. "One or both. And they drove off the other way from the way we were coming. But if it was that way, why didn't we see their headlights? They would have just left." Leaphorn straightened, put his hands on his hips, stretched his back. He stared into the deepening twilight, frowning. "Just one plate on the table. You notice that?"

"Yeah," Chee said. "And the chair turned over."

"Five or ten minutes," Leaphorn said. "If you know how long it takes to incinerate stew, then we didn't scare him off. The truck was already gone. And the stew was already burning before we got here."

"I'll go in and look around again," Chee said. "A little closer."

"Let me do it," Leaphorn said. "See if you can find anything out here."

Leaphorn stood at the doorway first, not wishing to further disturb any signs that might have been left. He suspected Chee might be good at this, but he knew he was good. The floor was covered with dark red linoleum, seamed near the middle of the room. It was fairly new, which was good, and dusty, which was almost inevitable considering the weather, and absolutely essential considering what Leaphorn hoped to do. But before he did anything, he looked. This front room was used for cooking, eating, general living, and the woman's bedroom. One corner of the bed, a single wooden frame neatly made up, was visible behind a curtain of blankets which walled off a corner. Shelves loaded with canned goods, cooking utensils, and an assortment of boxes lined the partition wall. Except for the overturned chair, nothing seemed odd or out of place. The room showed the habitual neatness imposed by limited living space.

But the floor was dusty.

Leaphorn squatted on the step and inspected the linoleum with his eyes just an inch or so above its surface. The pattern of dust newly disturbed by his footsteps, and Chee's, was easy enough to make out. He could easily separate the treads of Chee's bigger feet from his own. But the angle of light was wrong. Walking carefully, he went in and pulled the chain to turn off the light bulb. He clicked on his flashlight. Working the light carefully, squatting at first and then on his stomach with his cheek against the floor, he studied the marks left in the dust.

He ignored the fresh scuffs he and Chee had made—looking for other marks. He found them. Dimmer but fairly fresh and plain enough to an eye as experienced at this as Leaphorn's. Waffle marks left by the soles of someone who had apparently sat beside the table, someone who had pulled his feet back under the chair, leaving the drag marks of the toes. Also under the table, and near the fallen chair, another pattern, left by a rubber sole. Some sort of jogging or tennis shoes, perhaps. Smaller than the big-footed person who wore the waffle soles. Bistie and daughter? If so, Bistie's Daughter had large feet.

Leaphorn emerged from under the table, whacking his ear in the process. Behind the curtain of blankets, on a chest beside the bed, stood two pair of shoes. Worn tan squaw boots and low-heeled black slippers. They were narrow and about size six. He took a left slipper back to the table, relocated the track, and made the comparison. The slipper was far too small. Bistie had been entertaining a visitor not long before Leaphorn and Chee arrived.

But where the devil had they gone? And why had they left the stew to burn and the coffee to boil away?

He found nothing interesting in the back room. Against the wall, a bedroll on which Bistie apparently slept was folded neatly. Bistie's clothing hung with equal neatness from a wire strung taut along the wall—two pairs of well-worn jeans, a pair of khaki trousers with frayed cuffs. A plaid wool jacket, four shirts, all with long sleeves and one with a hole in the elbow. Leaphorn clicked his tongue against his teeth, thinking, studying the room. He pushed his forefinger into the enamel washbasin on the table beside Bistie's bedroom, testing water temperature without thinking why. It was tepid. Exactly what one would expect. He picked up the crumpled washcloth beside the basin. It was wet. Leaphorn looked at it, frowning. Not what one would expect.

The cloth had been used to clean something. Leaphorn studied it in the flashlight beam. In three places the cloth was heavily smudged with dirt—

as if to clean spots from the dusty floor. He held one of the spots to his nose and smelled it.

"Chee!" he shouted. "Chee!"

He examined the floor, moving the flash beam methodically back and forth, looking for a wiped place and seeing none. Perhaps it had been done in the front room. He squatted, holding the flash close to the linoleum, looking for tracks. He saw, instead, a path. It was fairly regular, possibly eighteen inches wide—a strip of the plastic surface wiped clean of dust. A pathway leading from the doorway into the front room, down the center of this back room, to the back door.

The back door opened and Chee looked in. "I think somebody, or maybe something, got dragged out of here," Chee said. "Drag marks leading up toward the rocks."

"Through here too," Leaphorn said. He drew the flashlight beam along the polished, dust-free path. "To the back door. But look at this." He handed Chee the damp cloth. "Smell it," he said.

Chee smelled.

"Blood," Chee said. "Smells like it." He glanced at Leaphorn. "Wonder what was in that stew. Fresh mutton, you think?"

"I doubt it," Leaphorn said. "I think we ought to find where those drag marks take us. I want to know what's being dragged."

"Or who's being dragged," Chee said.

Bare earth that has been lived on for years and as dry as drought can make it becomes almost as hard as concrete. From the back door, Leaphorn saw nothing until Chee's flashlight beam, held close to the earth, created shadows where something even harder had been pulled across its surface. Scratches. The scratches led past the windmill tower, past the metal storage building, and beyond. On the slope, where the earth was less pounded, the scratches became scuff marks between the scattering of wilted weeds and clumps of grass.

"Up toward the hogan," Leaphorn said. "It leads that way."

Even in the less compacted earth the drag marks were hard to follow. The twilight had faded into almost full dark now, with only a flush of dark red in the west. The wind had risen again, kicking up dust in front of Leaphorn. He walked with his flashlight focused on the ground, picking up the sign of dislodged earth and crushed weeds.

Even in retrospect, Leaphorn didn't remember hearing the shot—being aware first of pain. Something that felt like a hammer struck his right forearm and the flashlight was suddenly gone. Leaphorn was sitting on the ground, aware of Chee's voice yelling something, aware that his forearm hurt so badly that something must have broken it. The sound of Chee's pistol firing, the muzzle flash, brought him out of the shock and made him aware of what had happened. Roosevelt Bistie, that son-of-a-bitch, had shot him.

14

THE "OFFICER DOWN" call provokes a special reaction in each police jurisdiction. In the Shiprock subagency of the Navajo Tribal Police, Captain A. D. Largo commanding, it produced an immediate call to Largo himself, who was home watching television, and almost simultaneous radio calls to all Navajo Police units on duty in the district, to the New Mexico State Police, and the San Juan County Sheriff's Office. Then, since the Chuska Mountains sprawl across the New Mexico border into Arizona, and Sanostee is only a dozen or so miles from the state boundary, and neither the dispatcher at Shiprock nor anyone else was quite sure in which state all this was happening, the call also went out to the Arizona Highway Patrol and, more or less out of courtesy, to the Apache County Sheriff's Office, which might have some legitimate jurisdiction even though it was a hundred miles south, down at St. Johns.

The Farmington office of the Federal Bureau of Investigation, which had ultimate jurisdiction when such a lofty crime is committed on an Indian reservation, got the word a little later via telephone. The message was relayed to Jay Kennedy at the home of a lawyer, where he was engaged in a penny-a-point rotating-partner bridge game. Kennedy had just won two consecutive rubbers and was about to make a small slam, properly bid, when the telephone rang. He took the call, finished the slam, added up the score, which showed him to be ahead 2,350 points, collected his $23.50, and left. It was a few minutes after 10 P.M.

A few minutes after 10:30, Jim Chee got back to the Bistie place. He had met the ambulance from Farmington at Littlewater on U.S. 666. While Leaphorn was being tucked away in the back, Captain Largo had arrived—Gorman riding with him—and had taken charge. Largo asked a flurry of questions, sent the ambulance on its way, and made a series of quick radio checks to ensure roadblocks were in place. He'd hung up the microphone and sat, arms folded, looking at Chee.

"Too late for roadblocks, probably," he said.

It had been a long day for Chee. He was tired. All the adrenaline had drained away. "Who knows," he said. "Maybe he stopped to fix a flat. Maybe he didn't even have a car. If it was Bistie himself, maybe he just went back to his house. If—"

"You think it might be somebody besides Bistie?"

"I don't know," Chee said. "It's his place. He shoots at people. But then maybe somebody doesn't like him any better than he likes other people, and they came and shot him and dragged him off into the rocks."

Largo's expression, which had already been sour, suggested he didn't like Chee's tone. He stared at Chee.

"How did it happen?" he asked. "One old man, sick, and two cops with guns?"

Largo obviously didn't expect an answer and Chee didn't attempt one.

"You and Gorman go back up there and see if you can find him," Largo said. "I'll have the state police and the sheriff's people follow you. Don't let 'em get lost."

Chee nodded.

"I'm meeting Kennedy here," Largo said. "Then we'll come along and join you."

Chee headed for his car.

"One more thing," Largo shouted. "Don't let Bistie shoot you."

And now, at 10:55, Chee parked beside Bistie's now-dark light pole, got out, and waited for the entourage to finish its arrival. He felt foolish. Bistie's truck was still absent. Bistie's shack was dark. Everything seemed to be exactly as they had left it. The chance of Bistie's hanging around to await this posse simply didn't exist.

There was a general slamming of doors.

Chee explained the layout, pointed up into the darkness to the hogan from which the shots had come. They moved up the slope, weapons drawn, the state policeman carrying a riot gun, the deputy carrying a rifle. What had happened here two hours before already seemed unreal to Chee, something he had imagined.

No one was at the hogan, or in it.

"Here's some brass," the state policeman said. He was an old-timer, with red hair and a freckled, perpetually sunburned face. He stood frowning down at a copper-colored metal cylinder which reflected the beam of his flashlight. "Looks like thirty-eight caliber," he said. "Who'll be handling the evidence?"

"Just leave it there for Kennedy," Chee said. "There should be another one." He was thinking that the empty cartridge certainly wasn't from a 30-30. It was shorter. Pistol ammunition. And, since it had been ejected, probably from an automatic—not a revolver. If Bistie had fired it, he seemed to have quite an arsenal.

"Here it is," the state policeman said. His flashlight was focused on the ground about a long step from where the first cartridge lay. "Same caliber."

Chee didn't bother to look at it. He considered asking everyone to be careful of where they walked, to avoid erasing any useful tracks. But as dry and windy as it was, he couldn't imagine tracking as anything but a waste of time. Except for the drag marks. Whatever had been dragged up here should be easy to find.

It was.

"Hey," Gorman shouted. "Here's a body."

It was half hidden in a clump of chamiso, head downhill, feet uphill, legs still spraddled apart as if whoever had dragged it there had been using them to pull the body along and had simply dropped them.

The body had been Roosevelt Bistie. In the combined lights of Chee's and Gorman's flashlights, the yellow look of his face was intensified—but death had done little to change his expression. Bistie still looked grim and bitter, as if being shot was only what he'd expected—a fitting ending for a disappointing life. The dragging had pulled his shirt up over his shoulders, leaving chest and stomach bare. The waxy skin where the rib cage joined at the sternum showed two small holes, one just below the other. The lower one had bled a little. Very small holes, Chee thought. It seemed odd that such trivial holes would let out the wind of life.

Gorman was looking at him, a question in his face.

"This is Bistie," Chee said. "Looks like the guy who shot Lieutenant Leaphorn had shot this guy. I guess he was dragging him up here when we drove up, the lieutenant and me."

"And after he shot the lieutenant he just took off," Gorman said.

"And got clean away," Chee added.

Four flashlights now were illuminating the body. Only the San Juan County deputy was still out in the darkness, doing his fruitless job.

Down in Roosevelt Bistie's yard below, two more vehicles parked. Chee heard doors slam, the voice of Kennedy, the sound of Kennedy and Captain Largo coming up the slope. Chee's flashlight now was focused above the bullet wounds at a place on Bistie's left breast—a reddish mark, narrow, perhaps a half-inch long, where a cut was healing. It would seem, normally, an odd place for such a cut. It made Jim Chee think of Bistie's wallet, and the bone bead he had seen in it, and whether the wallet would have been dragged out of Bistie's hip pocket on his heels-first trip up this rocky slope, and whether the bone bead would still be in it when it was found.

He squatted beside Bistie, taking a closer look, imagining the scene at which this little healing scar had been produced. The hand trembler (or stargazer, or listener, or crystal gazer, or whatever sort of shaman Bistie had chosen to diagnose his sickness) explaining to Bistie that someone had witched him, telling Bistie that a skinwalker had blown the fatal bone fragment into him. And then the ritual cut of the skin, the sucking at the breast, the bone coming out of Bistie, appearing on the shaman's tongue. And Bistie putting the bone in his billfold, and paying his fee, and setting out to save himself by killing the witch and reversing the dreaded corpse sickness.

Chee moved the beam of his light up so that it reflected again from the glazed, angry eyes of Roosevelt Bistie. How did Bistie know the witch was Endocheeney, the man who all at Badwater agreed was a mild and harmless fellow? The shaman would not have known that. And if the two men even knew each other, Chee had seen no sign of it.

Behind him, the state policeman was shouting to Largo, telling him they'd found a body. The wind kicked up again, blowing a flurry of sand against Chee's face. He closed his eyes against it, and when he reopened them, a fragment of dead tumbleweed had lodged itself against Bistie's ear.

Why was Bistie so certain the witch who was killing him was Endocheeney? He had been certain enough to try to kill the man. How had their paths crossed in this fatal way? And where? And when? Now that Bistie was also dead, who could answer those questions? Any of them?

Largo had joined the circle now, and Kennedy. Chee sensed them standing just behind him, staring down at the body.

"There's what killed him," the state policeman said. "Two gunshots through the chest."

Just on the edge of the circle of illumination, Chee could see the healing cut on Bistie's breast. Those two bullets had completed the death of Roosevelt Bistie. But the little wound high on his breast above them had been where Roosevelt Bistie's death had started.

15

THE INDIAN HEALTH service hospital at Gallup is one of the prides of this huge federal bureaucracy—modern, attractive, well located and equipped. It had been built in a period of flush budgeting—with just about everything any hospital needs. Now, in a lean budget cycle, it was enduring harder times. But the shortage of nurses, the overspent supplies budget, and the assortment of other fiscal headaches that beset the hospital's bead counters this particular morning did not affect Joe Leaphorn's lunch, which was everything a sensible patient should expect from a hospital kitchen, nor the view from his window, which was superb. The Health Service had located the hospital high on the slope overlooking Gallup from the south. Over the little hump in the sheet produced by his toes, Leaphorn could see the endless stream of semitrailers moving along Interstate 40. Beyond the highway, intercontinental train traffic rolled east and west on the Santa Fe main trunk. Above and beyond the railroad, beyond the clutter of east Gallup, the red cliffs of Mesa de los Lobos rose—their redness diminished a little by the blue haze of distance, and above them was the gray-green shape of the high country of the Navajo borderlands, where the Big Reservation faded into Checkerboard Reservation. For Joe Leaphorn, raised not fifty miles north of this bed in the grass country near Two Gray Hills, it was the landscape of his childhood. But now he looked at the scene without thinking about it.

He had been awake only a minute or two, having been jarred by the arrival of his lunch tray from a hazy, morphine-induced doze into a panicky concern for the welfare of Emma. He remembered very quickly that Agnes was there, had been there for days, living in the spare bedroom and playing the role of concerned younger sister. Agnes made Leaphorn nervous, but she had good sense. She'd take care of Emma, make the right decisions. He needn't worry. No more than he normally did.

Now he had finished the wit-collection process that follows such awakenings. He had established where he was, remembered why, quickly assessed the unfamiliar surroundings, checked the heavy, still cool and damp cast on his right arm, moved his thumb experimentally, then his fingers, then his hand, to measure the pain caused by each motion, and then he thought about Emma again. Her appointment was tomorrow. He would be well enough to take her, no question of that. And another step would be taken toward knowing what he already knew. What he dreaded to admit. The rest of his life would be spent watching her slip away from him, not knowing who he was, then not knowing who she was. In the material the Alzheimer's Association had sent him, someone had described it as "looking into your mind and seeing nothing there but darkness." He remembered that, as he remembered the case report of the husband of a victim. "Every day I would tell her we'd been married thirty years, that we had four children. . . . Every night when I got into bed she would say, 'Who are you?' " He had already seen the first of that. Last week, he had walked into the kitchen and Emma had looked up from the carrots she was scraping. Her expression had been first startled, then fearful, then confused. And she had clutched Agnes's arm and asked who he was. That was something he'd have to learn to live with—like learning to live with a dagger through the heart.

He groped clumsily with his good left hand for the button to summon an attendant, found it, pressed it, glanced at his watch. Outside the glass, the light was blinding. Far to the east, a cloud was building over Tsoodzil, the Turquoise Mountain. Rain? Too early to tell, and too far east to fall on the reservation if it did develop into a thunderstorm. He swung his legs over the edge of the bed and sat, slumped, waiting for the dizziness to subside, feeling an odd, buzzing sense of detachment induced by whatever they'd given him to make him sleep.

"Well," a voice behind him said. "I didn't expect to find you out of bed."

It was Dilly Streib. He was wearing his FBI summer uniform, a dark blue two-piece suit, white shirt, and necktie. On Streib, all of this managed to look slept in.

"I'm not out of bed yet," Leaphorn said. He gestured toward the closet door. "Look around in there and see if you can find my clothes. Then I'll be out of bed."

Streib was holding a manila folder in his left hand. He dropped it at the foot of Leaphorn's bed and disappeared into the closet. "Thought you'd like to take a look at that," he said. "Anybody tell you what happened?"

It occurred to Leaphorn that he had a headache. He took a deep breath. His lunch seemed to consist of a bowl of soup, which was steaming, a small green salad, and something including chicken which normally would have looked appetizing. But now Leaphorn's stomach felt as if it had been tilted on its side. "I know what happened," Leaphorn said. "Somebody shot me in the arm."

"I meant after that," Streib said. He dumped Leaphorn's uniform at the foot of his bed and his boots on the floor.

"After that I'm blank," Leaphorn said.

"Well, to get to the bottom line, the guy got away and he left behind Bistie's body."

"Bistie's body?" Leaphorn reached for the folder, digesting this.

"Shot," Streib said. "Twice. With a pistol, probably. Probably a thirty-eight or so."

Leaphorn extracted the report from the folder. Two sheets. He read. He glanced at the signature. Kennedy. He handed the report back to Streib.

"What do you think?" Streib asked.

Leaphorn shook his head.

"I think it's getting interesting," Streib said. That meant, Leaphorn understood from half a lifetime spent working with the federals, that people with clout and high civil service numbers were beginning to think they had more bodies than could be politely buried. He took off his hospital gown, picked up his undershirt, and considered the problem of how to get it on without moving his right arm around more than was necessary.

"I think we should have kept that Indian locked up a while," Streib said.

He chuckled. "I guess that's belaboring the obvious." The chuckle turned into a laugh. "I'm sure his doctor would have recommended it."

"You think we could have got him to change his mind? Tell us what he had against Endocheeney?" Leaphorn asked. He thought a moment. If they had taken Bistie back into custody, Leaphorn had planned to try an old, old trick. The traditional culture allows a lie, if it does no harm, but the lie can be repeated only three times. The fourth time told, it locks the teller into the deceit. He couldn't have worked it on Bistie directly, because Bistie would have simply continued to refuse to say anything about Endocheeney, or bone beads, or witchcraft. But maybe he could have worked around the edges. Maybe. Maybe not.

"I'm not so sure," Leaphorn said. He was even less sure he could have talked Streib into signing his name on the sort of complaint they would have needed. This was a notably untidy piece of work, this business of a man who seemed to think he'd shot a man who'd actually been stabbed. And the FBI hadn't fooled the taxpayers all these years by getting itself involved with the messy ones. Streib was a good man, but he hadn't survived twenty years in the Agency jungle without learning the lessons it taught.

"Maybe not," Streib said. "I defer to you redskins on that. But anyhow . . ." He shrugged, letting it trail off. "This is going to put the heat on. Now we don't just have a bunch of singles. Now we got ourselves a double. And maybe more than a double. You know how that works."

"Yeah," Leaphorn said. Doubling homicides didn't double the interest—it was more like squaring it. And if you had yourself genuine serial killings, nicely mysterious, the interest and the pressure and the potential for publicity went right through the roof. Publicity had never been an issue with Navajo Tribal Police—they simply never got any—but for federals, good press brought the billions pouring in and kept the J. Edgar Hoover Building swarming with fat-cat bureaucrats. But it had damned sure better be good press.

Streib had seated himself. He looked at the report and then at Leaphorn, who was pulling on his pants with left-handed awkwardness. Streib's round, ageless, unlined face made it difficult for him to look worried. Now he managed. "Trouble is, among the many troubles, I can't see how the hell to get a handle on this. Doesn't seem to have a handle."

Leaphorn was learning how difficult it can be to fasten the top button of his uniform trousers with his left-hand fingers after a lifetime of doing it with right-hand fingers. And he was remembering the question Jim Chee had raised. ("I heard gossip at Badwater Trading Post," Chee had said. "They say a bone was found in Endocheeney's corpse.") Had the pathologist found the bone?

"The autopsy on Old Man Endocheeney up at Farmington," Leaphorn said. "I think somebody should talk to the pathologist about that. Find out every little thing they found in that stab wound."

Streib put the report back in the folder, the folder on his lap, pulled out his pipe, and looked at the No Smoking sign beside the door. Beside the sign, Little Orphan Annie stared from a poster that read: "Little Orphan Annie's Parents Smoked." Beside that poster was another, a photograph of rows and rows of tombstones, with a legend reading "Marlboro Country." Streib sniffed at the pipe, put it back in his jacket pocket.

"Why?" he asked.

"One of our people heard rumors that a little fragment of bone was found in the wound," Leaphorn said. He kept his eyes on Streib. Would that be enough explanation? Streib's expression said it wasn't.

"Jim Chee found a little bone bead in his house trailer along with the lead pellets after somebody shot the shotgun through his wall," Leaphorn said. "And Roosevelt Bistie was carrying a little bone bead in his wallet."

Understanding dawned slowly, and unhappily, causing Streib's round face to convert itself from its unaccustomed expression of worry to an equally unaccustomed look of sorrow and dismay.

"Bone," he said. "As in skinwalking. As in witchcraft. As in corpse sickness."

"Bone," Leaphorn said.

"Lordy, lordy, lordy," Streib said. "What the hell next? I hate it."

"But maybe it's a handle."

"Handle, shit," Streib said, with a passion that was rare for him. "You remember way back when that cop got ambushed over on the Laguna-Acoma. You remember that one. The agent on that one said something about witchcraft when he was working it, put it in his report. I think they called him all the way back to Washington so the very top dogs could chew him out in person. That was after doing it by letters and telegrams."

"But it was witchcraft," Leaphorn said. "Or it wasn't, of course, but the Lagunas they tried for it said they killed the cop because he had been witching them, and the judge ruled insanity, and they—"

"They went into a mental hospital, and the agent got transferred from Albuquerque to East Poison Spider, Wyoming," Streib said, voice rich with passion. " 'The judge ruled' don't cut it in Washington. In Washington they don't believe in agents who believe in witches."

"I'd do it myself. Look into it, I mean. But I think you'd have more luck talking to the doctor," Leaphorn said. "Getting taken seriously. I go in there, a Navajo, and start talking to the doc about witch bones and corpse sickness and—"

"I know. I know," Streib said. He looked at Leaphorn quizzically. "A bone bead, you said? Human?"

"Cow."

"Cow? Anything special about cow bones?"

"Damn it," Leaphorn said. "Cow or giraffe, or dinosaur or whatever. What difference does it make? Just so whoever we're dealing with thinks it works."

"Okay," Streib said. "I'll ask. You got any other ideas? I got a sort of a feeling that the one at Window Rock—the Onesalt woman—could be some sort of sex-and-jealousy thing. Or maybe the Onesalt gal nosed into some sort of rip-off in the tribal paperwork that caused undue resentment. We know she was a sort of full-time world-saver. Usually you just put her type down as a pain in the ass, but maybe she was irritating the wrong fellow. But I sort of see her as one case and those others as another bag. And maybe now we toss that Chee business in with 'em. You have any fresh thinking about it?"

Leaphorn shook his head. "Just the bone angle," he said. "And probably that leads no place." But he was doing some fresh thinking. Nothing he wanted to talk to Streib about. Not yet. He wanted to find out if Onesalt's agency knew anything about the letter that office had mailed to Dugai Endocheeney. If Onesalt had written it, Dilly might be dead wrong about

Onesalt not being linked to the other homicides. And now he was thinking that Roosevelt Bistie fell into a new category of victim. Bistie had been part of it, part of whatever it was that was killing people on the Big Reservation. Thus the killing of Bistie was something new. Whatever it was, this lethal being, now it seemed to be feeding on itself.

16

THE CAT WAS there when Chee awakened. It was sitting just inside the door, looking out through the screen. When he stirred, rising onto his side in the awkward process of getting up from the pallet he'd made on the floor, the cat had been instantly alert, watching him tensely. He sat, completed a huge yawn, rubbed the sleep from his eyes, and then stood, stretching. To his mild surprise, the cat was still there when he finished that. Its green eyes were fixed on him nervously, but it hadn't fled. Chee rolled up the sleeping bag he'd been using as a pad, tied it, dumped it on his unused bunk. He inspected the irregular row of holes the shotgun blasts had punched through the trailer wall. One day, when he knew who had done it, when he knew it wouldn't be happening again, he would find himself a tin-smith—or whomever one found to patch shotgun holes in aluminum alloy walls—and get them patched more permanently. He peeled off the duct tape he'd used to cover them and held out his hand, feeling the breeze sucking in. Until the rains came, or winter, he might as well benefit from the improved ventilation.

For breakfast he finished a can of peaches he'd left in the refrigerator and the remains of a loaf of bread. It wasn't exactly breakfast, anyway. He'd got to bed just at dawn—thinking he was too tired, and too wired, to sleep. Even though night was almost gone, he avoided the bunk and used the floor. He had lain there remembering the two black holes in the skin of

Roosevelt Bistie's chest, remembering the healing cut higher on Bistie's breast. Those vivid images faded away into a question.

Who had called Janet Pete?

Unless she was lying, it had not been Roosevelt Bistie's daughter. The daughter had driven up just behind the ambulance. She had been following it, in fact—coming home from Shiprock with four boxes of groceries. She had emerged from Bistie's old truck into the pale yellow light of police lanterns, with her face frozen in that expression every cop learns to dread—the face of a woman who is expecting the very worst and has steeled herself to accept it with dignity.

She had looked down at the body as they carried it past her and slid the stretcher into the ambulance. Then she had looked up at Captain Largo. "I knew it would be him," she'd said, in a voice that sounded remarkably matter-of-fact. Chee had watched her, examining her grief for some sign of pretense and thinking that her prescience was hardly remarkable. For whom else could the ambulance have been making this back-road trip? Virtually no one else lived on this particular slope of this particular mountain—and no one else at all on this particular spur of track. The emotion of Bistie's Daughter seemed totally genuine—more shock than sorrow. No tears. If they came, they would come later, when her yard was cleared of all these strangers, and dignity no longer mattered, and the loneliness closed in around her. Now she talked calmly with Captain Largo and with Kennedy—responding to their questions in a voice too low for Chee to overhear, as expressionless as if her face had been carved from wood.

But she had recognized Chee immediately when all that was done. The ambulance had driven away, taking with it the flesh and bones that had held the living wind of Roosevelt Bistie and leaving behind, somewhere in the night air around them, his *chindi*.

"Did Captain Largo tell you where he died?" Chee had asked her. He spoke in Navajo, using the long, ugly guttural sound which signifies that moment when the wind of life no longer moves inside a human personality, and all the disharmonies that have bedeviled it escape from the nostrils to haunt the night.

"Where?" she asked, at first puzzled by the question. Then she understood it, and looked at the house. "Was it inside?"

"Outside," Chee said. "Out in the yard. Behind the house."

It might be true. It takes a while for a man to die—even shot twice through the chest. No reason for Bistie's Daughter to believe her house had been contaminated with her father's ghost. Chee had evolved his own theology about ghost sickness and the *chindi* that caused it. It was, like all the evils that threatened the happiness of humankind, a matter of the mind. The psychology courses he'd taken at the University of New Mexico had always seemed to Chee a logical extension of what the Holy People had taught those original four Navajo clans. And now he noticed some slight relaxation in the face of Bistie's Daughter—some relief. It was better not to have to deal with ghosts.

She was looking at Chee, thoughtfully.

"You noticed when you and the *belagana* came to get him that he was angry," she said. "Did you notice that?"

"But I don't know why," Chee said. "Why was he so angry?"

"Because he knew he had to die. He went to the hospital. They told him about his liver." She placed a hand against her stomach.

"What was it? Was it cancer?"

Bistie's Daughter shrugged. "They call it cancer," she said. "We call it corpse sickness. Whatever word you put on it, it was killing him."

"It couldn't be cured? Did they tell him that?"

Bistie's Daughter glanced around her, looked nervously past Chee into the night. The state policeman's car—on its way back to paved highways—crunched through the weeds at the edge of the yard. Its headlights flashed across her face. She raised her hand against the glare. "You can turn it around," she said. "I always heard you could do that."

"You mean kill the witch and put the bone back in him?" Chee said. "Is that what he was going to do?"

Bistie's Daughter looked at him silently.

"I talked to them already," she said finally. "To the other policemen. To the young *belagana* and the fat Navajo."

Largo would hate hearing that "fat Navajo" description, Chee thought. "Did you tell them that's what your father was doing? When he went to the Endocheeney place?"

"I told them I didn't know what he was doing. I didn't know that man who got killed. All I know is that my father was getting sicker and sicker all the time. He went to see a hand trembler over there between Roof Butte and Lukachukai to find out what kind of cure he would need to have. But the hand trembler had gone off someplace and he wasn't home. He went over on the Checkerboard Reservation, someplace over there by the Nageezi Chapter House, and talked to a listener over there. He told him he had been cooking food over a fire made out of wood struck by lightning and he needed to have a Hail Chant." Bistie's Daughter looked up at Chee with a strained grin. "We burn butane to cook on," she said. "But he charged my father fifty dollars. Then he went to the Badwater Clinic to see if they would give him some medicine. He didn't come back until the next day because they kept him in the hospital. Made X-rays, I think. Things like that. When he came back he was angry. Said they told him he was going to die." Bistie's Daughter stopped talking then, and looked away from Chee. Tears came abruptly but without sound.

"Why angry?" Chee asked, his voice so low she might have thought he meant the question only for himself.

"Because they told him he could not be cured," Bistie's Daughter said in a shaky voice. She cleared her throat, wiped the back of her hand across her eyes. "That man was strong," she continued. "His spirit was strong. He didn't give up on things. He didn't want to die."

"Did he say why he was angry at Endocheeney? Why he blamed Endocheeney? Did he say he thought Endocheeney had witched him?"

"He didn't say hardly anything at all. I asked him. I said, 'My Father, why—' " She stopped.

Never speak the name of the dead, Chee thought. Never summon the *chindi* to you, even if the name of the ghost is Father.

"I asked that man why he was angry. What was wrong. What had they told him at the Badwater Clinic? And finally he told me they said his liver was rotten and they didn't know how to fix it with medicine and he was going to die pretty quick. I told the other policemen all this."

"Did he say anything about being witched?"

Bistie's Daughter shook her head.

"I noticed that he had a cut place on his breast." Chee tapped his uniform shirt, indicating where. "It was healing but still a little sore. Do you know about that?"

"No," she said.

The answer didn't surprise Chee. His people had adopted many ways of the *belagana*, but most of them had retained the Dinee tradition of personal modesty. Roosevelt Bistie would have kept his shirt on in the presence of his daughter.

"Did he ever say anything about Endocheeney?"

"No."

"Was Endocheeney a friend?"

"I don't think so. I never heard of him before."

Chee clicked his tongue. Another door closed.

"I guess the policemen asked you if you know who came here to see your fath—to see him tonight?"

"I didn't know he was home. I was away since yesterday. In Gallup to visit my sister. To buy things. I didn't know he was back from being in jail."

"After we arrested him, did you go and get the lawyer to get him out?"

Bistie's Daughter looked puzzled. "I don't know anything about that," she said.

"You didn't call a lawyer? Did you ask anyone else to call one?"

"I don't know anything about lawyers. I just heard that lawyers will get all your money."

"Do you know a woman named Janet Pete?"

Bistie's Daughter shook her head.

"Do you have any idea who it might have been who came here and shot him? Any idea at all?"

Bistie's Daughter was no longer crying, but she wiped her hand across her eyes again, looked down, and released a long, shuddering sigh.

"I think he was trying to kill a skinwalker," she said. "The skinwalker came and killed him."

And now, as Jim Chee finished the last slice of peach and mopped the residue of juice from the can with the bread crust, he remembered exactly how Bistie's Daughter had looked as she'd said that. He thought she was probably exactly correct. The Mystery of Roosevelt Bistie neatly solved in a sentence. All that remained was another question. Who was the skinwalker who came and shot Bistie? Behind that, how did the witch know Bistie would be home instead of safely jailed in Farmington?

In other words, who called Janet Pete?

He would find out. Right now. The very next step. As soon as he finished breakfast.

He unplugged his coffeepot, filled his coffee cup with water, swirled it gently, and drank it down.

("I never saw anybody do that before," Mary Landon had said.

"What?"

"That with the water you rinsed your cup with." Empty-handed, she had mimicked the swirling and the drinking.

It still had taken him a moment to understand. "Oh," he had said. "If you grow up hauling water, you don't ever learn to pour it out. You don't waste it, even if it tastes a little bit like coffee."

"Odd," Mary Landon said. "What the old prof in Sociology 101 would call a cultural anomaly."

It had seemed odd to Chee that not wasting water had seemed odd to Mary Landon. It still seemed odd.)

He put the pot under the sink. "Look out, Cat," he said. And the cat, instead of diving for the exit flap as it normally did when he came anywhere near this close, moved down the trailer. It sat under his bunk, looking at him nervously.

It took a millisecond for Jim Chee to register the meaning of this.

Something out there.

He sucked in his breath, reached for his belt, extracted his pistol. He could see nothing out the door except his pickup and the empty slope. He checked out of each of the windows. Nothing moved. He went through the door in a crouched run, holding the pistol in front of him. He stopped in the cover of the pickup.

Absolutely nothing moved. Chee felt the tension seep away. But something had driven in the cat. He walked to its den, eyes on the ground. In the softer earth around the juniper there were paw prints. A dog? Chee squatted, studying them. Coyote tracks.

Back in the trailer, the cat was sitting on his bedroll. They looked at each other. Chee noticed something new. The cat was pregnant.

"Coyote's after you, I guess," Chee said. "That right?"

The cat looked at him.

"Dry weather," Chee said. "No rain. Water holes dry up. Prairie dogs, kangaroo rats, all that, they die off. Coyotes come to town and eat cats."

The cat got up from the bedroll, edged toward the doorway. Chee got a better look at it. Not very pregnant yet. That would come later. It looked gaunt and had a new scar beside its mouth.

"Maybe I can fix something up for you," Chee said. But what? Fixing something that would be proof against a hungry coyote would take some thought. Meanwhile he looked through the refrigerator. Orange juice, two cans of Dr. Pepper, limp celery, two jars of jelly, a half-consumed box of Velveeta: nothing palatable for a cat. On the shelf above the stove, he found a can of pork and beans, opened it, and left it on a copy of the Farmington *Times* beside the screen door. When he got back from finding out who called Janet Pete, he'd think of something to do about the coyote. He backed his pickup away from the trailer. In the rearview mirror he noticed that the cat was gulping down the beans. Maybe Janet Pete would have an idea about the cat. Sometimes women were smarter about such things.

But Janet Pete was not at the Shiprock DNA office, a circumstance that seemed to give some satisfaction to the young man in the white shirt and the necktie who answered Jim Chee's inquiry.

"When do you expect her?" Chee asked.

"Who knows?" the young man said.

"This afternoon? Or has she left town or something?"

"Maybe," the man said. He shrugged.

"I'll leave her a message," Chee said. He took out his notebook and his pen and wrote:

"Ms. Pete—I need to know who called you to come and get Roosevelt Bistie out of jail. Important. If I'm not in, please leave message." He signed it and left the tribal police telephone number.

But on the way out, he saw Janet Pete pulling into the parking area. She was driving a white Chevy, newly washed, with the Navajo Nation's seal newly painted on its door. She watched him walk up, her face neutral.

"*Ya-tah-hey*," Chee said.

Janet Pete nodded.

"If you have just a minute or two, I need to talk to you," Chee said.

"Why?"

"Because Roosevelt Bistie's daughter told me she didn't call a lawyer for her father. I need to know who called you."

And I need to know absolutely everything else you know about Roosevelt Bistie, Chee thought, but first things first.

Janet Pete's expression had shifted from approximately neutral to slightly hostile.

"It doesn't matter who called," she said. "We don't have to have a request for representation from the next of kin. It can be anybody." She opened the car door and swung her legs out. "Or it can be nobody, for that matter. If someone needs to have his legal rights protected, we don't have to be asked."

Janet Pete was wearing a pale blue blouse and a tweed skirt. The legs she swung out of the car were very nice legs. And Miss Pete noticed that Chee had noticed.

"I need to know who it was," Chee said. He was surprised. He hadn't expected any trouble with this. "There's no confidentiality involved. Why be—"

"You have another homicide to work on now," she said. "Why not just leave Mr. Bistie alone. He didn't kill anyone. And he's sick. You should be able to see that. I think he has cancer of the liver. Another homicide. And no arrest made. Why don't you work on that?"

Janet Pete was leaning on the car door while she said this, and smiling slightly. But it wasn't a friendly smile.

"Where did you hear about the homicide?"

She tapped the car. "Radio," she said. "Noon news, KGAK, Gallup, New Mexico."

"They didn't say who was shot?"

" 'Police did not reveal the identity of the victim,' " she said, but the smile faded as she said it. "Who was it?"

"It was Roosevelt Bistie," Chee said.

"Oh, no," she said. She sat down on the front seat again, wrinkled her face, closed her eyes, shook her head against this mortality. "That poor man." She put her hands across her face. "That poor man."

"Somebody came to his house last night. His daughter was gone. They shot him."

Janet Pete lowered her hands to listen to this, staring at Chee. "Why?

Do you know why? He was dying, anyway. He said the doctor told him the cancer would kill him."

"We don't know why," Chee said. "I want to talk to you about it. We're trying to find out why."

They left Janet Pete's clean Chevy and got into Chee's unwashed patrol car. At the Turquoise Cafe, Janet Pete ordered iced tea and Chee had coffee.

"You want to know who called me. That's funny, because the man who called lied. I found out later. He said his name was Curtis Atcitty. Spelled with the *A*. Not *E*. I had him spell it for me."

"Did he say who he was?"

"He said he was a friend of Roosevelt Bistie's, and he said Bistie was being held without bond and without any charges being filed against him, and that he was sick and didn't have any lawyer and he needed help." She paused, thinking about it. "And he said that Bistie had asked him to call DNA about a lawyer." She looked at Chee. "That's where he lied. When I told Bistie about it, he said he hadn't asked anybody to call. He said he didn't know anybody named Curtis Atcitty."

Chee clicked his tongue against his teeth, the sound of disappointment. So much for that.

"When you left the jail, I saw you driving back into Farmington. Where did you go? When was the last time you saw him?"

"Down to the bus station. He thought one of his relatives might be there, and they'd give him a ride home. But nobody he knew was there, so I took him back to Shiprock. He saw a truck he recognized at the Economy Washomat and I left him out there."

"Did he ever tell you why he tried to kill Old Man Endocheeney?"

Janet Pete simply looked at him.

"He's dead," Chee said. "No lawyer-client confidentiality left. Now let's try to find out who killed him."

Janet Pete studied her hands, which were small and narrow, with long, slender fingers, and if her fingernails were polished it was with the transparent, colorless stuff. Nice feminine hands, Chee thought. He remembered Mary Landon's hands, strong, smooth fingers intertwined with his own. Mary Landon's fingertips. Mary Landon's small white fist engulfed in his own. Janet Pete's right hand now gripped her left.

"I'm not stalling," she said. "I'm thinking. I'm trying to remember."

Chee wanted to tell her it was important. Very important. But he decided it wasn't necessary to say that to this lawyer. He watched her hands, thinking of Mary Landon, and then her face, thinking of Janet Pete.

"He said very little altogether," she said. "He didn't talk much. He wanted to know if he could go home. We talked about that. I asked him if he knew exactly what he was accused of doing. What law he was supposed to have broken." She glanced at Chee, then turned her eyes away, gazing out the street window through the dusty glass on which THE TURQUOISE CAFE was lettered in reverse. Beyond the glass, the dry wind was chasing a tumbleweed down the street. "He said he had shot a fellow over in the San Juan Canyon. And then he sort of chuckled and said maybe he just scared him. But anyway the man was dead and that was what you had him in jail for." She frowned, concentrating, right hand gripping the left. "I asked him why he had shot at the man and he said something vague." She shook her head.

"Vague?"

"I don't remember. Something like 'I had a reason,' or 'good reason,' or something like that—without saying why."

"Did you press him at all?"

"I said something like 'You must have had a good reason to shoot at a man,' and he laughed, I remember that, but not like he thought it was funny, and I asked him directly what his reason was and he just shut up and wouldn't answer."

"He wouldn't tell us anything, either," Chee said.

Janet Pete had taken a sip from her glass. Now she held it a few inches from her lips. "I told him I was his lawyer—there to help him. What he told me would be kept secret from anyone else. I told him shooting at somebody, even if you missed them, could get him in serious trouble with the white man and if he had a good reason for doing it, he would be smart to let me know about it. To see if we could use it in some way to help keep him out of jail."

She put down the glass and looked directly at Chee. "That's when he told me about being sick. It was easy enough to see anyway, with the way he looked. But anyway, he said the white man couldn't give him any more trouble than he already had, because he had cancer in his liver." She used the Navajo phrase for it—"the sore that never heals."

"That's what his daughter told me," Chee said. "Cancer of the liver."

Janet Pete was studying Chee's face. It was a habit that Chee had learned slowly, and come to tolerate slowly, and that still sometimes made him uneasy. Another of those cultural differences that Mary found odd and exotic.

("That first month or two in class I was always saying: 'Look at me when I talk to you,' and the kids simply wouldn't do it. They would always look at their hands, or the blackboard, or anywhere except looking me in the face. And finally one of the other teachers told me it was a cultural thing. They should warn us about things like that. Odd things. It makes the children seem evasive, deceptive."

And Chee had said something about it not seeming odd or evasive to him. It seemed merely polite. Only the rude peered into one's face during a conversation. And Mary Landon had asked him how this worked for a policeman. Surely, she'd said, they must be trained to look for all those signals facial expressions reveal while the speaker is lying, or evading, or telling less than the truth. And he had said . . .)

"You needed to know who called me," Janet Pete was saying, "because you suspect that whoever called is the one who killed Roosevelt Bistie. Isn't that it?"

Like police academy, Chee thought, law schools teach interrogators a different conversational technique than Navajo mothers. The white way. The way of looking for what the handbook on interrogation called "nonverbal signals." Chee found himself trying to keep his face blank, to send no such signals. "That's possible," he said. "It may have happened that way."

"In fact," Janet Pete said, slowly and thoughtfully, "you think this man used me. Used me to get Mr. Bistie out of jail and home . . ." Her voice trailed off.

Chee had been looking out past the window's painted lettering. The wind had changed direction just a little—enough to pull loose the leaves and twigs and bits of paper it had pinned against the sheep fence across the highway. Now the gusts were pulling these away, sending them skittering along the pavement. Changing winds meant changing weather. Maybe, finally, it would rain. But the new tone in Janet Pete's voice drew his attention back to her.

"Used me to get him out where he could be killed."

She looked at Chee for confirmation.

"He would have gotten out, anyway," Chee said. "The FBI had him, and the FBI didn't charge him with anything. We couldn't have—"

"But I think that man wanted Mr. Bistie out before he would talk to anyone. Doesn't that make sense?"

It was exactly the thought that had brought him looking for Janet Pete.

"Doubtful," Chee said. "Probably no connection at all."

Janet Pete was reading his nonverbal signals. Rude, Chee thought. No wonder Navajos rated it as bad manners. It invaded the individual's privacy.

"It's not doubtful at all," she said. "You are lying to me now." But she smiled. "That's kind of you. But I can't help but feel responsible." She looked very glum. "I am responsible. Somebody wants to kill my client, so they call me and have me get him out where they can shoot him." She picked up her glass, noticed it was empty, put it down again. "He didn't even particularly want to be my client. The guy who wanted to shut him up just put me on the job."

"It probably wasn't that way," Chee said. "Different people, probably. Some friend called you, not knowing that this madman was coming along."

"I'm getting to be a jinx," Janet Pete said. "Typhoid Mary. A sort of curse."

Chee waited for the explanation. Janet Pete offered none. She sat, her square shoulders slumped a little, and looked sadly at her hands.

"Why jinx?" Chee said.

"This is the second time this happened," Janet Pete said, without looking at Chee. "Last time it was Irma. Irma Onesalt."

"The woman who got killed over by . . . You knew her?"

"Not very well," Janet said. She produced a humorless laugh. "A client."

"I want to hear about it," Chee said. Leaphorn seemed to think there might be some connection between the Onesalt killing and the Sam and Endocheeney cases. The lieutenant had been very interested when Chee had told him about the letter Endocheeney received from Onesalt's office. It didn't seem likely, but maybe there was some sort of link.

"That's how I heard about Officer Jim Chee," Janet Pete said, studying him. "Irma Onesalt said you did her a favor, but she didn't like you."

"I don't understand," Chee said. And he didn't. He felt foolish. The only time he'd met Onesalt, the only time he could remember, had been that business about picking up the patient at the clinic—the wrong Begay business.

"She told me you were supposed to deliver a witness to a chapter meeting and you showed up with the wrong man and screwed everything all up. But she said she owed you something. That you'd done her a favor."

"What?"

"She didn't say. I think it must have been some sort of accident. I remember she said you helped her out and you didn't even know it."

"I sure didn't," Chee said. "And don't." He waved at the man behind the counter, signaling a need for refills. "How was she your client?"

"That's pretty vague too," Janet Pete said. "She called one day and made an appointment. And when she came by, she mostly just asked a lot of questions." She paused while her glass was refilled and then stirred sugar into her tea—two teaspoons.

How did she keep so slim? Chee wondered. Nervous, he guessed. Runs it off. Mary was like that. Always moving.

"I don't think she trusted me. Asked a lot of questions about our relationship at DNA with the tribal bureaucracy and the BIA and all that. When we got that out of the way, she had a lot of questions about what I could find out for her. Financial records, things like that. What was public. What wasn't. How to get documents. I asked her what she was working on, and she said she would tell me later. That maybe it wasn't much of anything and then she wouldn't bother me. Otherwise, she would call me back."

"Did she?"

"Somebody shot her," Janet Pete said. "About ten days later."

"Did you report talking to her?"

"Probably no connection, but finally I did. I checked to find out who was handling the case and then called him and told him—Streib I think it was." She shrugged. "The fed at Gallup."

"Dilly Streib," Chee said. "What did he say?"

She made a wry face. "You know the FBI," she said. "Nothing."

"How about you? Any idea what she was after?"

"Not really." She sipped the tea, slim fingers around the tall glass.

A Navajo complexion, Chee thought. Perfect skin. Smooth, glossy.

Janet Pete would never have a freckle. Janet Pete wouldn't have a wrinkle until she was old.

"But she said something that I remembered. It made me curious. Let's see if I can remember just how she put it." She raised a slim hand to her cheek, thinking. "I asked what she would want to look for and she said maybe some answers to some questions, and I said what questions and she said . . . she said how people can look so healthy after they're dead. And then I asked her what that meant. Didn't really ask her exactly, you know. Just looked puzzled, raised my eyebrows or something like that. And she just laughed."

"How people can look healthy after they're dead?"

"That's it," she said. "Maybe not the exact words, but that was the sense of it. Mean anything to you?"

"Absolutely nothing," Chee said, thinking about it so hard that he forgot the refill, and gulped scalding coffee, and spilled it on his uniform shirt—which was not at all what Jim Chee wanted to do in front of Janet Pete.

17

THE FIRST THING Joe Leaphorn noticed when he rolled Emma's old Chevy sedan to a halt in the yard of the Short Mountain Trading Post was that McGinnis had repainted his Sale sign. The sign had been there the first time Leaphorn had seen the place, coming on some long-forgotten assignment when he was a green new patrolman working in the Tuba City subagency. He sat assessing the pain in his forearm. And remembering. Even then the sign had been weather-beaten. Then, as now, it proclaimed in large block letters:

THIS ESTABLISHMENT
FOR SALE
INQUIRE WITHIN

Around Short Mountain, they said that the store on the rim of Short Mountain Wash had been established sometime before the First World War by a Mormon who, it was said, noticed the lack of competition without noticing the lack of customers. It was also said that he had been convinced that the oil prosperity he saw far to the north around Aneth and Montezuma Creek would spread inexorably and inevitably south and west—that the Just Creator must have blessed this area somehow with something. And since the surface itself offered nothing but scanty grass, scarce wood, and a wilderness of erosion, there surely must be a bountiful treasure of oil below those sterile rocks. But his optimism had finally faltered with the Aneth field, and when his church ruled against multiple wives, he'd opted to join the polygamist faction in its trek to tolerant Mexico. Everyone around Short Mountain Wash seemed to remember the legend. No one remembered the man himself, but those who knew McGinnis marveled at the Mormon's salesmanship.

McGinnis now appeared in his doorway, talking to a departing customer, a tall Navajo woman with a sack of cornmeal draped over her shoulder. While he talked he stared at Emma's Chevy. A strange car out here usually meant a stranger was driving it. Among the scattered people who occupied the emptiness of Short Mountain country, strangers provoked intense curiosity. In Old Man McGinnis, almost anything provoked intense curiosity. Which was one reason Leaphorn wanted to talk to Old Man McGinnis, and had been talking to him for more than twenty years, and had become in some odd way his friend. The other reason was more complicated. It had something to do with the fact that McGinnis, alone, without wife, friend, or family, endured. Leaphorn appreciated those who endured.

But Leaphorn was in no hurry. First he would give his arm a chance to quit throbbing. "Don't move it," the doctor had told him. "If you move it, it's going to hurt." Which made sense, and was why Leaphorn had decided to drive Emma's sedan—which had automatic transmission. Emma had been delighted to see him when he'd come home from the hospital. She had fussed over him and scolded and seemed the genuine Emma. But then her face had frozen into that baffled look Leaphorn had come to dread. She said something meaningless, something that had nothing at all to do with the conversation, and turned her head in that odd way she'd developed—looking down and to her right. When she'd looked back, Leaphorn was sure she no longer recognized him. The next few moments formed another of those all too familiar, agonizing episodes of confusion. He and Agnes had taken her into the bedroom, Emma talking in a muddled attempt to communicate something, and then lying on the coverlet, looking lost and helpless. "I can't remember," she'd said suddenly and clearly, and then she'd fallen instantly asleep. Tomorrow they would keep their appointment with the specialist at the Gallup hospital. Then they would know. "Alzheimer's," the doctor would say, and then the doctor would explain

Alzheimer's, all that information Leaphorn had already read and reread in "The Facts About Alzheimer's Disease" sent him by the Alzheimer's Association. Cure unknown. Cause unknown. Possibly a virus. Possibly an imbalance in blood metals. Whatever the cause, the effect was disruption of the cells on the outer surface of the brain, destroying the reasoning process, eroding the memory until only the moment of existence remains, until—in merciful finality—there is no longer a signal to keep the lungs breathing, no longer the impulse to keep the heart beating. Cure unknown. For Emma, he had watched this process of unlearning begin. Where had she left her keys? Walking home from the grocery with the car left parked in the grocery lot. Being brought home by a neighbor after she'd forgotten how to find the house they'd lived in for years. Forgetting how to finish a sentence. Who you are. Who your husband is. The literature had warned him what would be coming next. Fairly early, all speech would go. How to talk. How to dress. Who is this man who says he is my husband? Alzheimer's, the doctor would say. And then Leaphorn would put aside pretense and prepare Emma, and himself, for whatever would be left of life.

Leaphorn shook his head. Now he would think of something else. Of business. Of whatever it was that was killing the people he was paid to protect.

He had the cast propped against the steering wheel, letting the pain drain away, sorting what he hoped to learn from this visit to Old Man McGinnis. Witchcraft, he guessed. Much as he hated to admit it, he was probably involved again in the sick and unreal business of the skinwalker superstition. The bits of bone seemed to link Jim Chee, and Roosevelt Bistie, and Dugai Endocheeney. Dilly Streib's call had confirmed that.

"Jim Chee's gossip had it right," Streib had said. "They found a little bead down in one of the knife wounds. Thread, little dirt, and a bead. I've got it. I'll have it checked to see if it matches the first one." And then Streib had asked Leaphorn what it meant, beyond the obvious connection it made between the Endocheeney and Bistie killings and the attempt on Chee. Leaphorn had said he really didn't know.

And he didn't. He knew what it might mean. It might mean that the killer thought Endocheeney was a witch. He might have thought that Endocheeney, the skinwalker, had given him corpse sickness by shooting the prescribed bit of bone into him. Then, instead of relying on an Enemy

Way ritual to reverse the witchcraft, he had reversed it himself by putting the lethal bone back into the witch. Or it might mean that the killer in some crazy way thought himself to be a witch and was witching Endocheeney, putting the bone into him at the very moment he killed him with the knife. That seemed farfetched, but then everything about Navajo witchcraft seemed farfetched to Leaphorn. Or it might mean that the killer inserted the notion of witchcraft into this peculiar crime simply to cause confusion. If that had been the goal, the project had succeeded. Leaphorn was thoroughly confused. If only Chee had wormed it out of Bistie. If only Bistie had told them why he was carrying the bone bead in his wallet, what he planned to do with it, why he wanted to kill Endocheeney.

The pain in his arm had subsided. He climbed out of the Chevy, and walked across the hardpacked earth toward the sign that proclaimed the willingness of McGinnis to leave Short Mountain Wash for a better world, and stepped through McGinnis's doorway—out of the glare and heat and into the cool darkness.

"Well, now," the voice of McGinnis said from somewhere. "I wondered who it was parked out there. Who sold you that car?"

McGinnis was sitting on a wooden kitchen chair, its back tilted against the counter beside his old black-and-chrome cash register. He was wearing the only uniform Leaphorn had ever seen him wear, a pair of blue-and-white-striped overalls faded by years of washings, and under them a blue work shirt like those that convicts wear.

"It's Emma's car," Leaphorn said.

" 'Cause it's got automatic shift and you got your arm hurt," McGinnis said, looking at Leaphorn's cast. "Old John Manymules was in here with his boys a little while ago and said a cop had got shot over in the Chuskas, but I didn't know it was you."

"Unfortunately it was," Leaphorn said.

"The way Manymules was telling it, old fella got killed up there at his hogan and when the police came to see about it, one of the policemen got shot right in the middle."

"Just the arm." Leaphorn was no longer surprised by the dazzling speed with which McGinnis accumulated information, but he was still impressed.

"What brings you out here to the wrong side of the reservation?" McGinnis said. "Broke arm and all."

"Just visiting," Leaphorn said.

McGinnis eyed him through his wire-rimmed bifocals, expression skeptical. He rubbed his hand across the gray stubble on his chin. Leaphorn remembered him as a smallish man, short but with a barrel-chested strength. Now he seemed smaller, shrunken into his overalls, the sturdiness missing. The face, too, had lost the remembered roundness, and in the dimness of the trading post, his blue eyes seemed faded.

"Well, now," McGinnis said. "That's nice. I guess I ought to offer you a drink. Be hospitable. That is, if my customers can spare me."

There were no customers. The tall woman was gone and the only vehicle in the yard was Emma's Chevy. McGinnis walked to the door, limping a little and more stooped than Leaphorn remembered. He closed it, slipped the bolt lock. "Got to lock her up, then," he said, half to Leaphorn. "Goddam Navajos they'll steal the panes outta the windows if they need it." He limped toward the doorway into his living quarters, motioning Leaphorn to follow. "But only if they need it. White man, now, he'll steal just for the hell of it. I've known 'em to steal something and then just throw it away. You Navajos, now, if you steal a sack of my meal I know somebody's hungry. Screwdriver's missing, I know somebody lost his screwdriver and has a screw that needs driving. I think it was your granddaddy that first explained that to me, when I was new out here."

"Yeah," Leaphorn said. "I think you told me that."

"Get so I repeat myself," McGinnis said, with no sound of repentance in his voice. "Hosteen Klee, they called him before he died. Your mother's father. I knew him when they was still calling him Horse Kicker." McGinnis had opened the door of a huge old refrigerator. "I ain't offering you a drink because you don't drink whiskey, or at least you never did, and whiskey's all I got," he said into the refrigerator. "Unless you want a drink of water."

"No, thanks," Leaphorn said.

McGinnis emerged, holding a bourbon bottle and a Coca Cola glass. He carried these to a rocking chair, sat, poured bourbon into the glass, examined it, then, with the glass close to his eyes, dripped in more until the level reached the bottom of the trademark. That done, he set the bottle on the floor and motioned Leaphorn to sit. The only place open was a sofa upholstered with some sort of green plastic. Leaphorn sat. The stiff plastic crackled under his weight and a puff of dust arose around him.

"You're here on business," McGinnis declared.

Leaphorn nodded.

McGinnis sipped. "You're here because you think old McGinnis knows something about Wilson Sam. He'll tell you, and you'll put it with what you already know and figure out who killed him."

Leaphorn nodded.

"Outta luck," McGinnis said. "I've known that young fella since he was a buck Indian and I don't know anything about him that's going to help."

"You've been thinking about it," Leaphorn said.

"Sure," McGinnis said. "Fella you've known gets killed, you think about it." He sipped again. "Lost a customer," he said.

"Anything in that?" Leaphorn said. "Unusual, I mean. Like him coming in with money to pay off his pawn. Or buying anything unusual. People coming to ask where to find him."

"Nothing," McGinnis said.

"He make any trips? Go anyplace? Been sick? Any ceremonials for him?"

"Nothing like that," McGinnis said. "He used to come in now and then to do his buying. Sell me his wool. Things like that. Get his mail. I remember he cut his hand bad way back last winter and he went into that clinic that Sioux Indian opened there at Badwater Wash and they sewed it up for him and gave him a tetanus shot. But no sickness. No sings for him. No trips anyplace, except he told me couple of months ago he went into Farmington with his daughter to get himself some clothes." McGinnis took another sip of bourbon. "Too damn fashionable to buy his clothes from me anymore. Everybody's wearing designer jeans."

"How about his mail? Do you write his letters for him? He get anything unusual?"

"He could read and write," McGinnis said. "But he ain't bought no stamps this year. Not from me, anyway. Or mailed any letters. Or got any unusual mail. Only thing unusual, couple of months ago he got a letter in the middle of the month." He didn't explain that, or need to. On the far reaches of the reservation, mail consists primarily of subsistence checks, from the tribal offices in Window Rock or some federal agency. They arrive on the second day of the month, in brown stacks.

"In June was it?" That was when Chee had said Endocheeney received his letter from Irma Onesalt's office. "About the second week?"

"That's what I said," McGinnis said. "Two months ago."

Leaphorn had managed to find a way to be fairly comfortable on the sofa. He had been watching McGinnis, who in turn had kept his watery eyes focused on the bourbon while he talked. And while he talked, he rocked, slowly and steadily, coordinating a motion in his forearm with the motion of his chair. The net result of this was that while the bourbon glass seemed to move, the liquid in it remained level and motionless. Leaphorn had noticed this lesson in hydraulic motion before, but it still intrigued him. But what McGinnis had said about the letter regained his full attention. He leaned forward.

"Don't get excited," McGinnis said. "You gonna expect me to tell you that inside that envelope there was a letter from somebody telling Wilson Sam to hold still because he was coming to kill him. Something like that." McGinnis chuckled. "You got your hopes up too high. It wasn't from anybody. It was from Window Rock."

Leaphorn wasn't surprised McGinnis had noticed this, or that he remembered it. A midmonth letter would have been an oddity.

"What was it about?"

McGinnis's placid expression soured. "I don't read folks' mail."

"All right then, who was it from?"

"One of them bureaus there in Window Rock," McGinnis said. "Like I said."

"You remember which one?"

"Why would I remember something like that?" McGinnis said. "None of my business."

Because everything out here is your business, Leaphorn thought. Because the letter would have lain around somewhere for days while you waited for Wilson Sam to come in, or for some relative to come in who could take it to him, and every day you would look at it and wonder what was in it. And because you remember everything.

"I just thought you might," Leaphorn said, overcoming a temptation to tell McGinnis the letter was from Social Services.

"Social Services," McGinnis said.

Social Services. Exactly. He wished he had found time to check. If the letter wasn't in the file, if no one there remembered writing to Endocheeney, or to Wilson Sam, it would be fair circumstantial evidence that

Onesalt had done the writing, and that the letters were in some way unofficial. Why would Social Services be writing to either man?

"Did it have a name on it? I mean on the return address. Or just the office?"

"Come to think of it, yeah." McGinnis sipped again and inspected the bourbon level with watery eyes. "That might be of some interest to you," he said, without taking his eyes off the glass. "Because that woman who had her name on the return address, she was the one that got shot a little later over there in your part of the reservation. Same name, anyway."

"Irma Onesalt," Leaphorn said.

"Yessir," McGinnis said. "Irma Onesalt."

The circle was thus complete. The bone beads linked Wilson Sam and Endocheeney and Jim Chee and Roosevelt Bistie. The letters linked Onesalt into the pattern. Now he had what he needed to solve this puzzle. He had no idea how. But he knew himself. He knew he would solve it.

18

IT WAS A day off for Chee, and in a little while it would be time to leave for the long drive to the place of Hildegarde Goldtooth, to meet with Alice Yazzie. Ninety miles or so, some of it on bad roads, and he intended to leave early. He planned to detour past the Badwater Clinic to see if he could learn anything there. And he didn't want to keep Alice Yazzie waiting. He wanted to do her Blessing Way. Now Chee was passing the time in what Captain Largo called his "laboratory." Largo had laughed about it. "Laboratory, or maybe it's your studio," Largo had said when he found Chee working there. In fact, it was nothing but a flat, hard-packed earthen surface up the slope from Chee's trailer. Chee had chosen it because a gnarled old cottonwood shaded the place. He had prepared it carefully, digging it up, leveling it, raking out bits of gravel and weed roots, making it an approximation of the size and shape of a hogan floor. He used it to practice dry painting the images used in the ceremonials he was learning.

At the moment, Chee was squatting at the edge of this floor. He was finishing the picture of Sun's Creation, an episode from the origin story used in the second night of the Blessing Way. Chee was humming, mouthing the words of the poetry that recounted this episode, letting a controlled trickle of blue sand sift between his fingers to form the tip of the feather that was hung from Sun's left horn.

Sun will be created—they say it is planned to happen.
Sun will be created—they say he has planned it all.
Its face will be blue—they say he has planned it all.
Its eyes will be yellow—they say he planned it all.
Its forehead will be white—they say he planned it all.

Feather finished, Chee rocked back on his heels, poured the surplus blue sand from his palm into the coffee can that held it, wiped his hand on the leg of his jeans, and surveyed his work. It was good. He had left off one of the three plumes that should have extended eastward from the headdress of Pollen Boy, standing against Sun's face—thus not completing the power of the holy image at this inappropriate time and place. Otherwise, the dry painting looked perfect. The lines of sand—black, blue, yellow, red, and white—were neatly defined. The symbols were correct. The red sand was a bit too coarse, but he would fix that by running a can of it through the coffee grinder again. He was ready. He knew this version of the Blessing Way precisely and exactly—every word of every song, every symbol of the dry paintings. It would cure for him. He squatted, memorizing again the complicated formula of symbols he had created on the earth before him, feeling its beauty. Soon he would be performing this old and holy act as it had been intended, to return one of his people to beauty and harmony. Chee felt the joy of that rising in him, and turned away the thought. All things in moderation.

The cat was watching him from the hillside above its juniper. It had been in sight much of the morning, vanishing down the bank of the San Juan for a while but returning after less than an hour to lie in the juniper's shade. Chee had put the shipping case under the tree the previous evening—fitting it beneath the limbs as near to the cat's sleeping place as he could force it. In it he'd put an old denim jacket, which the cat sometimes sat on when it came into the trailer. He had added, as lure, a hamburger patty from his refrigerator. He'd been saving the patty for some future lunch, but the edges had curled and turned dark. This morning he noticed the meat was missing and he presumed the cat had gone into the case to retrieve it. But he could see no sign that the cat had slept there. No problem. Chee was patient.

The case was really a cage with a carrying handle and had cost Chee almost forty dollars with taxes. It had been Janet Pete's idea. He had brought up the problem of cat and coyote as they left the Turquoise Cafe, trying to extend the conversation—to think of something to say that would prevent Miss Pete from getting into her clean white official Chevy sedan and leaving him standing there on the sidewalk.

"I don't guess you'd know anything about cats?" Chee had said, and she'd said, "Not much, but what's the problem?" And he'd told her about the cat and the coyote. Then he'd waited a moment while she thought about it. While he waited (Janet Pete leaning, gracefully, against her Chevy, frowning, lower lip caught between her teeth, taking the problem seriously), he thought about what Mary Landon would have said. Mary would have asked who owned the cat. Mary would have said, Well, silly, just bring the cat in, and keep it in your trailer until the coyote goes away and hunts something else. Perfectly good solutions for a *belagana* cat in a *belagana* world, but they overlooked the nature of Jim Chee, a Navajo, and the role of animals in Dine' Bike'yah, where Corn Beetle and Bluebird and Badger received equal billing when the Holy People emerged into this Earth Surface World.

"I don't guess you'd want a cat," Janet Pete said, looking at Chee.

Chee grinned.

"Can you fix up something out there? So the coyote can't get to it?"

"You know coyotes," Chee said.

Janet Pete smiled, looked wry, brightened. "I know," she said. "Get one of those airline shipping cages." She described one, cat-sized, with her hands. "They're tough. A coyote couldn't get her in that."

"I don't know," Chee said, doubting the cat would get into such a thing. Doubting it would foil a coyote. "I don't think I've ever seen one. Where can you get 'em? Airport?"

"Pet store," Janet Pete said. And she'd driven him to the one in Farmington. The shipping cage Chee eventually bought had been designed for a small dog. It was made of stiff steel wire that looked coyote-proof. And it was large enough, in Chee's opinion, to seem hospitable to the cat. Janet Pete had remembered an appointment and hurried him back to his car at the courthouse.

Even as he was driving to Shiprock with the cage on the seat beside him it was seeming less and less of a good idea. He'd have to narrow the doorway to make it just big enough for the cat and too small for the coyote's head. That looked simple enough. In fact, it had been merely a matter of using some hay baling wire. But there was still the question of whether the cat would accept it as a bedroom, and whether she would be smart enough to recognize the safety it offered when the coyote was stalking her.

Chee thought about that as he swept up the sand, using the feathered wand from his *jish* bundle for the task. After she had created the first of the Navajo clans, Changing Woman had taught them how to perform their curing ceremonials. She'd made the first dry paintings out of the clouds, blowing each away with her breath as its purpose was completed. And she'd taught the first of the Navajos to scatter their painting sand to the winds, just as Chee did now—collecting it on a dustpan and then throwing it into the air to drift away. He brushed the last traces of the picture away and collected the coffee cans in which he kept his supply of unused sands. No use thinking about the cat now. Time would tell. Perhaps the cat would use the cage. If it didn't, there would be the time to seek another solution. And there were other, tougher problems. How would she fare when she grew big with pregnancy? How would the litter survive? Worse, she was hunting less now—or seemed to be. Relying more on the food he provided her. That was exactly what he couldn't allow to happen. If the cat was to make the transition—from someone's property to self-sufficient predator—it couldn't rely on him, or on any person. To do so was to fail. Chee had been surprised when he first realized that he cared how this struggle ended. Now he accepted it. He wanted the cat to tear itself free. He wanted *belagana* cat to become natural cat. He wanted the cat to endure.

Chee stacked the cans of sand back into the outside storage compartment in the wall of his trailer, where he kept all his ceremonial regalia. He would take with him, he decided, his *jish* just in case the circumstances at his meeting with Alice Yazzie required some sort of blessing. Besides, the *jish* case itself and the ceremonial items in it were impressive. In this, Chee was a perfectionist. His prayer sticks were painted exactly right, waxed, polished, with exactly the right feathers attached as they should be attached. The bag that held his pollen was soft doeskin; labeled plastic prescription bottles held the fragments of mica, abalone shell, and the other "hard jewels" his profession required. And his Four Mountain bundle—four tiny bags contained in a doeskin sack—included exactly the proper herbs and minerals, which Chee had collected from the four sacred mountains exactly as the *yei* had instructed. Chee would take his *jish*. He would hope that the opportunity would arise to get it out and open it.

Inside the trailer, he exchanged his dusty jeans for a pair he'd just bought in Farmington. He put on the red-and-white shirt he saved for special occasions, his polished "go-to-town" boots, and his black felt hat. Then he checked himself in the mirror over his washbasin. All right, he thought. Better if he looked a lot older. The Dinee liked their *yataalii* to be old and wise—men like Frank Sam Nakai, his mother's brother. "Don't worry about it," Frank Sam Nakai had told him. "All the famous singers started when they were young. Hosteen Klah started when he was young. Frank Mitchell started when he was young. I started when I was young. Just pay attention and try to learn."

Now, finally, he would be beginning to use what Frank Sam Nakai had been teaching him for so many years. As he drove up the slope away from the river, he noticed that the cloud formation that built every afternoon over the slopes behind Shiprock was bigger today, dark at the bottom, forming its anvil top of ice crystals earlier than usual in this dry summer. Howard Morgan, the weatherman on Channel 7, had said there was a 30 percent chance of rain in the Four Corners today. That was the best odds of the summer so far. Morgan said the summer monsoon might finally be coming. Rain. That would be the perfect omen. And Morgan was often right.

When he turned west on 504, it looked as if Morgan was right again. Thunderheads had merged over the Carrizo range, forming a blue-black wall that extended westward far into Arizona. The afternoon sun lit their tops, already towering high enough to be blowing ice crystals into the jet stream winds. By the time he turned south beyond Dennehotso across Greasewood Flats, he was driving in cloud shadow. Proximity winds were kicking up occasional dust devils. But Chee had been raised with the desert dweller's conditioning to avoid disappointment. He allowed himself to think a while about rain, sweeping its cool, wet blessing across the desert, but not to expect it. And now he needed to think of something else. The Badwater Clinic was over the next ridge.

The quirky wind generated by the thunderstorms' great updrafts bounced a tumbleweed across the unpaved clinic parking lot just as he pulled his truck to a stop. He turned off the engine and waited for the gust to subside. The place had been built only five or so years ago—a long one-story, flat-roofed rectangle set in a cluster of attendant buildings. A cube of concrete housing the clinic's water well was just behind the building, surmounted by a once-white storage tank. Beyond that stood a cluster of those ugly frame-and-brown-plaster housing units that the Bureau of Indian Affairs had scattered by the thousands across Indian reservations from Point Barrow to the Pagago Reservation. New as the clinic compound was, the reservation had already touched it, as it seemed to touch all such unnatural shapes imposed upon it, with an instant look of disrepair. The white paint of the clinic building was no longer white, and blowing sand had stripped patches of it from the concrete-block walls. None of this registered on the consciousness of Chee, who, Navajo fashion, had looked at the setting and not the structures. It was a good place. Beautiful. A long view down the valley toward the cliffs that rose above Chilchinbito Canyon and Long Flat Wash, toward the massive shape of Black Mesa—its dark green turned a cool blue by cloud shadow and distance. The view lifted Chee's spirits. He felt exultant—a mood he hadn't enjoyed since reading Mary Landon's letter. He walked toward the clinic entrance, feeling a gust of sand blown against his ankles and guessing that today it would finally rain and he would be lucky.

He was. The person sitting behind the counterdesk in the entrance foyer was the Woman from the Yoo'l Dinee, the Bead People. Chee's excellent Navajo-trained memory also produced her name—Eleanor Billie. She had been the receptionist on duty that cold late-spring day when he had come with the Onesalt woman to collect the wrong Begay. Her memory seemed to be as good as Chee's.

"Mister Policeman," she said, smiling very slightly. "Who can we get for you today? Do you need another Begay?"

"I just need you to help me understand something," Chee said. "About the time we got the wrong one."

Mrs. Billie had nothing to say to that. That smile, Chee realized, had not been a warm one. Maybe he wasn't so lucky.

"What I need to know is whether the woman who was with me—that woman from Window Rock—if she ever contacted anybody about that.

Wrote a letter. Telephoned. Anything like that. Did she have any questions? Who would I ask about that?"

Mrs. Billie looked surprised. She produced an ironic chuckle. "She raised hell," she said. "She came in here the next day and acted real nasty. Wanted to see Dr. Yellowhorse. I don't know how she acted with him. She acted nasty with me."

"She came back?" Chee laughed. "I guess I shouldn't act surprised. She was mad enough to kill somebody." He laughed again. Mrs. Billie smiled, and now, he noticed, it seemed genuine. In fact, it was spreading into a broad grin.

"I always wondered what happened. To get that bitch in such a rage," Mrs. Billie said.

"Well, we took Begay to the chapter house over at Lukachukai. They were having a meeting—trying to settle whether a family from the Weaver Clan or an outfit from the Many Hogans Dinee had a right to live on some land over there. Anyway, Irma Onesalt had found out that this old Begay man had lived over there for about a thousand years and he was supposed to tell the council that the Many Hogans family had lived there first, and had the grazing and the water and all that. I didn't see all of it, but what I heard was that when they called on that Begay you gave us to talk about it, he gave them this long speech about how he never had lived there at all. He was born to the Coyote Pass People, and born for the Monster People, and him and his outfit lived way over east on the Checkerboard Reservation."

Chee was grinning as he finished, remembering Irma Onesalt's incoherent rage as she stomped out of the chapter house and back to his patrol car. "You should have heard what she said to me," he said. What Irma Onesalt had said would translate precisely from Navajo to English. It was the equivalent of: "You stupid son-of-a-bitch, you got the wrong Begay."

Mrs. Billie's grin showed an array of very white teeth in a very round face.

"I'd like to have seen that," Mrs. Billie said, with Chee now firmly established as a fellow victim. "You should have heard what she said to me. I just reminded her she'd called and said she was picking up Frank Begay to take him to the hearing, and we gave her the only Begay we had. Franklin Begay. Pretty damn close."

"Pretty close," Chee agreed.

"And the only Begay we had," Mrs. Billie said. "Still is, for that matter."

"Wonder what caused her to get the wrong name—or whatever happened."

"Oh, Frank Begay used to be here. He was diabetic, with all sorts of complications. But he died way back in the winter. Earlier than that. It was in October. He was the one from Lukachukai."

"I wonder if that's what caused the confusion," Chee said. "She didn't seem like a woman who'd get confused much."

Mrs. Billie nodded, agreeing. She looked thoughtful. "What she said was that we had our records all screwed up. Said we had him on our list as a patient. I looked, and told her we didn't. And she said, Damn it, yes we did. Maybe not today, she said, but a couple of weeks ago." Mrs. Billie was showing her white teeth in another joyful grin, remembering. "That's why I know just when Frank Begay died. October three. I went back into the files and found it."

Chee allowed himself to imagine for a moment how much pleasure Mrs. Billie had attained by giving that news to Irma Onesalt. He remembered his own discomfort at the chapter house, with the woman leaning on the door of his patrol car, staring at him contemptuously, bombarding him with questions about why he had delivered Franklin Begay when she had told him to deliver Frank Begay. An unusually arrogant woman, Irma Onesalt. He wondered, half seriously, if Dilly Streib, or whoever was working her homicide for the FBI, had considered that as a motive for her murder. Someone might simply have got tired of suffering Irma Onesalt's bad conduct.

"What else did Onesalt say?" Chee asked.

"Wanted to see the doctor to argue about it."

"Dr. Yellowhorse?"

"Yeah. So I sent her on in."

Yellowhorse and Onesalt, Chee thought. Two tough coyotes. For different reasons, he didn't like either of them—but Yellowhorse he respected. His differences with the doctor were purely philosophical—the believer and the agnostic exploiting the belief. Onesalt was, or had been, simply an obnoxious jerk. "I wish I could have seen those two," Chee said. "What happened?"

Mrs. Billie shrugged. "She went in. Maybe five minutes she came out."

The telephone at Mrs. Billie's plump elbow buzzed. "Badwater Clinic," she said. "What? Okay. I'll tell him." She hung up. "Came out steaming," she continued, grinning again. "Pure rage now. The doctor, he can be rough, you get him stirred up."

Chee was remembering what Janet Pete had told him—of Irma Onesalt's remark about the wrong Begay business tipping her off to something. This conversation hadn't opened any doors to what that might be. Or had it?

"She say anything else? Any remarks or anything?"

"No," Mrs. Billie said. "Well, not much. She got almost to the door and then she turned around and came back and asked me what that date was when Frank Begay died."

"You told her October third?"

"No. I hadn't looked it up yet. I told her last fall, I guess. And then she asked me if she could see a list of the patients we had in here." Mrs. Billie's face expressed disapproval of this remembered outrage. "Imagine that kind of brass!" she said. "And I said she'd have to ask the doctor about that and she said to hell with it then, she'd get it another way." Mrs. Billie looked even more disapproving. "Actually she said a little worse than that. Rough-talking woman."

A middle-aged black woman in a nurse's uniform came down the hall with a young Navajo who was pushing a wheelchair. The wheelchair contained a woman with her leg in a cast. "Now tell her again that it will itch, but she's not supposed to scratch it. Just let it itch. Think about something else." The Navajo said, "Don't scratch," in Navajo, and Woman in Cast said, in English, "Don't scratch. You told me that before."

"She speaks English," Mrs. Billie told the nurse. "Better than I do."

"That was it? Nothing else?" Chee asked, getting Mrs. Billie's attention again.

"Just walked out after that," Mrs. Billie said.

"She said she could get the list of patients another way?"

"Yeah," Mrs. Billie said. "I guess she could, too. They'd all be on some sort of medical-cost reimbursement list. Medicare, or Medicaid, or some insurance claim if they had insurance. Most of them wouldn't."

"Just have to go through the red tape?"

"Probably no big deal. She worked in Window Rock with all the other bureaucrats. Probably just get somebody in the right accounting office to get her a Xerox, or let her take a peek."

Chee had been remembering Leaphorn in his trailer, putting the list on his countertop. Leaphorn watching his face as he looked at the list. Leaphorn asking if he knew any of them. Looking disappointed when he didn't. Asking if the names suggested anything to him. They had suggested nothing. But now they did. Now they seemed terribly important.

"I haven't got any friends among the bureaucrats at Window Rock. Any way I could find out who was here that day?"

"You could ask Dr. Yellowhorse."

"Good," Chee said. "Can I get in to see him?"

"He's not here," Mrs. Billie said.

Chee looked as disappointed as possible. He shrugged, made a wry face.

"You're a policeman. I guess you could say it was police business."

"It's police business," Chee said.

"It will take a while," Mrs. Billie said, getting up. "Call me if the telephone rings."

It took about ten minutes and the telephone didn't ring. "I just copied them off for that date," Mrs. Billie said. "I hope you can read my writing."

Mrs. Billie's writing was a beautiful, clear, symmetrical script—a script that would win penmanship competitions, if there were still penmanship competitions. Chee noticed that before he looked at the names.

Ethelmary Largewhiskers
Addison Etcitty
Wilson Sam

This was the list Leaphorn had told him about. The names for which Irma Onesalt was seeking death certificate dates. Wilson Sam's name was third. And second from the bottom Chee saw Dugai Endocheeney.

"Thanks," he said. He folded the paper absently and put it into his billfold, thinking: Sam and Endocheeney were alive when Onesalt was hunting their death certificates. Endocheeney had been into the clinic for that broken leg Iron Woman had told him about, and Sam for God knows what. But they were still alive. What was Onesalt . . . ?

His mind answered the question even before he completed it. He knew why Irma Onesalt had died, and almost all the rest of it. All that remained of the puzzle was why someone had tried to kill him. He glanced at his watch. He'd spent more time here than he'd intended.

"Need to use your telephone," he told Mrs. Billie.

He would call Leaphorn and tell him what he'd learned. Then he had to hurry. He'd been hearing thunder and it seemed to be getting closer. He'd have to leave a little time in case it got muddy. After he made a deal with Alice Yazzie to conduct a Blessing Way, he'd see if he could figure out why Jim Chee's ghost was supposed to join the *chindis* of Onesalt, Sam, and Endocheeney. Now was not the time to be thinking such unpleasant thoughts.

19

THE TELEPHONE WAS buzzing when Leaphorn came through his office door. "You just missed a call," the operator told him. "I took the message for you."

"Okay," Leaphorn said. He was tired. He wanted to clean off his desk in a hurry, go home, take a shower, try to relax for a few minutes, and then drive back to Gallup. Emma had to stay overnight for the tests they were making, for the things they do when something is wrong inside the head. Why? Leaphorn didn't understand that. Uncharacteristically for him, he hadn't insisted on an explanation. Everything about Emma's illness left him feeling helplessly out of control. Things were happening to them that would change their lives—devastate his life—and there was nothing he could do that would affect it. He felt surrounded by inevitability—something new for Joe Leaphorn. It made him feel as he'd heard people felt when caught in earthquakes, with the solid earth no longer solid.

He worked quickly through the "Immediate Action" memos, and found none that required immediate action. The most urgent two concerned the rodeo. First, a bootlegger, a woman in a blue Ford 250 pickup, seemed to be selling more or less openly, according to the complaints, but hadn't been arrested. Second, a problem with traffic management had developed at points where the rodeo grounds access routes tangled with mainstream flow on Navajo Route 3. Leaphorn wrote the necessary order to deal with the traffic first. The bootlegger required thought. Who would the woman be? He sorted through a career-long accumulation of bootlegger knowledge, studied his map briefly. Usually five or six bootleggers would work an event as popular as the rodeo, two or three of them female. One of these women was sick, Leaphorn knew, maybe even in the hospital. Of the other two, the one who lived down at Wide Ruins drove a big pickup. Leaphorn conjured up her family connections. She was born to the Towering House Clan, born for the Rock Gap People? He compared this mentally with the clans of the policemen he had working the rodeo—following the simple and true theory that no one is going to arrest his own clan sister if he can avoid it. He found what he expected to find. The sergeant in charge of internal order was a Towering House man.

Leaphorn tore up the order he'd written to deal with the access problem and wrote another, switching the Towering House sergeant to traffic control and replacing him with the corporal who had been handling traffic. Then he looked at his telephone messages.

The call he had just missed was from Jim Chee.

Lieutenant Leaphorn: Irma Onesalt came back to Badwater Clinic the day after I picked up Franklin Begay there. She was angry. She found out that Frank Begay had died last October. She asked for a list of patients in the clinic, went to see Dr. Yellowhorse about it, got a turndown, said she could get the names elsewhere. I got a list of the names on list on the date Onesalt was there. The list included both Endocheeney and Wilson Sam. I remember hearing that Endocheeney had been in the clinic about then with a broken leg.

The remainder of the message was a listing of all those who had been patients in the Badwater Clinic that April day. They included the names Dr. Jenks had remembered, the quaint names.

Leaphorn read the note again. Then he let it drop from his fingers and picked up the telephone.

"Call Shiprock and get me Chee," he said.

"Doubt if we can," the dispatcher said. "He was calling from the Badwater Clinic. Said he was just leaving. Going over toward Dinebito Wash and he'd be out of touch for a while."

"Dinebito Wash?" Leaphorn said. What the hell would he be doing there? Even on the reservation, where isolation was the norm, Dinebito country was an empty corner. There the desert rose toward the northern limits of the Black Mesa highlands. Leaphorn told the switchboard to get Captain Largo at Shiprock.

He waited, standing by the window. The entire sky, south and west, was black with storm now. Like all people who live a lot out of doors and whose culture depends upon the weather, Leaphorn was a student of the sky. This one was easy enough to read. This storm wouldn't fade away, as storms had been doing all this summer. This one had water in it, and force. It would be raining hard by now across the Hopi mesas, at Ganado and on the grazing country of his cousins around Klagetoh and Cross Canyons and Burntwater. By tomorrow they'd be hearing of the flash floods down Wide Ruins Wash, and the Lone Tule, and Scattered Willow Draw, and those dusty desert-country drains that converted themselves into roaring torrents when the male rains came. Tomorrow would be a busy day for the 120 men and women of the Navajo Tribal Police.

Leaphorn watched the lightning, and the first cold drops splattering themselves across the glass, and did not think of Emma sleeping in her hospital room. Instead he let the links offered in Chee's message click into place. Onesalt's motivation? Malice, of course. Leaphorn thought about it. It was unproductive thought, but it was better than thinking of Emma. Better than thinking about what he would learn tomorrow when the tests were finished.

The telephone rang.

"I've got Captain Largo," the operator said, with Largo's voice behind him saying something about quitting time.

"This is Leaphorn," Leaphorn said. "Do you know where Jim Chee was going today?"

"Chee?" Largo laughed. "I do. Son-of-a-bitch finally got himself a sing. He was going out to see about it. All excited."

"I need to talk to him," Leaphorn said. "Is he working tomorrow? Could you call in and check for me?"

"I am in," Largo said. "I don't have any better luck getting away from the office than you do. Just a minute."

Leaphorn waited, hearing Largo's breathing and the sounds of papers shuffling. "It raining down there yet?" Largo asked. "Looks like we might finally get some up here."

"Just starting," Leaphorn said. He drummed his fingertips against the desktop. Through the rain-streaked window he saw a triple-flash lightning.

"Tomorrow," Largo said. "No, Chee's off."

"Well, hell," Leaphorn said.

"But let's see now. He was supposed to keep in touch. Because of somebody trying to shoot him. I told him, and sometimes Chee does what he's told. Let's see if there's a note on that."

More rustling of papers. Leaphorn waited.

"Be damned. He did it for once." Largo's tone changed from man talking to man reading.

" 'Will go today to the place of Hildegarde Goldtooth out near Dinebito Wash to meet with her and Alice Yazzie about doing a sing for a patient.' " Largo's voice switched back to normal. "He got invited to do that sing last week. Real proud of it. Going around showing everybody the letter."

"Nothing about when he'll be back?"

"With Chee, that'd be asking too much," Largo said.

"I haven't been out there since I worked out of Tuba City," Leaphorn said. "Wouldn't he have to go past Piñon?"

"Unless he's walking," Largo said. "That's the only road."

"Well, thanks," Leaphorn said. "I'll call our man there and get him to catch him going in or out."

The policeman assigned to work out of the Piñon Chapter House was a Sleep Rock Dinee named Leonard Skeet. Leaphorn had worked with him in his younger days at Tuba City and remembered him as reliable if you weren't in a hurry. The voice that said "Hello" was feminine—Mrs. Skeet. Leaphorn identified himself.

"He's gone over to Rough Rock," the woman said.

"When you expect him?"

"I don't know." She laughed, but the storm, or the distance, or the way the telephone line was tied to miles of fence posts to reach this outpost, made it difficult to tell whether the sound was amused or ironic. "He's a policeman, you know."

"I'd like to leave a message for him," Leaphorn said. "Would you tell him Officer Jim Chee will be driving through there. I need your husband to stop Chee and tell him to call me." He supplied his home telephone number. It would be better to wait there until it was time to go back to Gallup.

"About when you think he'll come by? Lenny's going to ask me that."

"It's just a guess," Leaphorn said. "He's gone out somewhere around Dinebito Wash. Out to see Hildegarde Goldtooth. I don't know how far that is."

There was something as close to silence as the crackling of the poorly insulated line allowed.

"You there?" Leaphorn asked.

"That was my father's sister," Mrs. Skeet said. "She's dead. Died last month."

And now it was Leaphorn's turn to produce the long silence. "Who lives out there now?"

"Nobody," Mrs. Skeet said. "The water was bad, anyway. Alkaline. And when she died, there was nobody left but her daughter and her son-in-law. They just moved away."

"The place is empty, then."

"That's right. If anybody moved in, I'd know it."

"Can you tell me exactly how to get there from Piñon?"

Mrs. Skeet could. As Leaphorn sketched out her instructions on his notepad, his mind was checking off other Navajo Police subagency offices that might be able to get someone to Piñon quicker than he could get there himself from Window Rock. Many Farms would be closer. Kayenta would be closer. But who would be working at this hour? And he could think of nothing he could tell them—nothing specific—that would instill in them the terrible sense of urgency that he felt himself.

He could be there in two hours, he thought. Perhaps a little less. And find Chee, and be back here in time to get to Gallup by midnight or so. Emma would be asleep, anyway. He had no choice.

"You taking off for home?" the desk officer asked him when he came down the stairs.

"Going to Piñon," Leaphorn said.

20

IN ALBUQUERQUE, IN the studio of KOAT-TV, Howard Morgan was explaining it. The newscast was picked up and relayed by drone repeater stations to blanket the Checkerboard Reservation and reach into the Four Corners country and into the eastern fringes of the Navajo Big Reservation. Had Jim Chee been at home in his trailer with his battery-powered TV turned on, he would have been seeing Morgan standing in front of a projection of a satellite photograph, explaining how the jet stream had finally shifted south, pulling cool, wet air with it, and this mass was meeting more moisture. The moisture coming up from the south was serious stuff, being pushed across Baja California and the deserts of northwest Mexico by Hurricane Evelyn. "Rains at last," said Morgan. "Good news if you're growing rhubarb. Bad news if you're planning picnics. And remember, the flash flood warnings are out for all of the southern and western parts of the Colorado plateau tonight, and for tomorrow all across northern New Mexico."

But Chee was not at home watching the weathercast. He was more or less racing the storm front—driving through the cloud-induced early twilight with his lights on. Just past Piñon he had run into a quick and heavy flurry of rain—drops the size of peach stones kicking up spurts of dust as they struck the dirt road ahead of him. Then came a bombardment of popcorn snow which moved like a curtain across the road, reflecting his headlights like a rhinestone curtain. That lasted no more than a hundred yards.

Then he was in dry air again. But rain loomed over him. It hung over the northeast slopes of Black Mesa like a wall—illuminated to light gray now and then by sheet lightning. The smell of it came through the pickup vents, mixed with the smell of dust. In Chee's desert-trained nostrils it was heady perfume—the smell of good grazing, easy water, heavy crops of piñon nuts. The smell of good times, the smell of Sky Father blessing Mother Earth.

Chee drove with the map Alice Yazzie had drawn on the back of her letter spread on his lap. The volcanic outcrop rising like four giant clenched fingers just ahead must be the place she'd marked to watch for a left turn. It was. Just beyond it, two ruts branched from the dirt road he'd been following.

Chee was early. He stopped and got out to stretch his muscles and kill a little time, partly to check if the track was still in use and partly for the sheer joy of standing under this huge, violent sky. Once, the track had been used fairly heavily, but not recently. Now the scanty weeds and grass of a dry summer had grown on the hump between the ruts. But someone had driven here today. In fact, very recently. The tires were worn, but what little tread marks they left were fresh. Jagged lightning streaked through the cloud and repeated itself—producing a thunderclap loud as a cannon blast. A damp breeze moved past, pressing the denim of his trousers against his legs and carrying the smell of ozone and wet sage and piñon needles. Then he heard the muted roar of the falling water. It moved toward him like a gray wall. Chee climbed back into the cab, as an icy drop splashed against the back of his wrist.

He drove the final 2.3 miles that Alice Yazzie had indicated on her map with his windshield wipers lashing and the rain pounding on the roof. The track wandered up a wide valley, rising toward the Black Mesa highlands, becoming increasingly rocky. Chee had been worried a little, despite the mud chains he always carried. The rockiness eliminated that worry. He wouldn't get stuck on this. Abruptly, the sky lightened. The rain eased—one of those brief respites common to high-altitude storms. The tracks climbed a ridge lined with eroded granite boulders, followed it briefly, and then turned sharply downward. Below him Chee saw the Goldtooth place. A round stone hogan with a domed dirt roof, a peak-roofed frame house, a pole corral, a storage shed, and a lean-to of poles, planks, and tar-paper, built against the wall of a low cliff. Smoke was coming from the hogan, hanging in the wet air and creating a blue smudge across the narrow cul-de-sac where the Goldtooth outfit had built its place. An old truck was parked beside the plank house. From behind the house, the back end of an ancient Ford sedan was visible. Chee could see a dim light, probably a kerosene lamp, illuminating one of the side windows of the house. Except for that, and the smoke, the place had an abandoned look.

He parked a polite distance from the house and sat for a moment with his headlights on it, waiting. The front door opened and the light outlined a shape, wearing the voluminous long skirt and long-sleeved blouse of the traditional Navajo woman. She stared out into Chee's headlights, then made the traditional welcoming motion and disappeared into the house.

Chee switched off the lights, opened the door, and stepped out into the resuming rain. He walked toward the house, past the parked truck. He could see now that the Ford had no rear wheels. The damp air carried the thousand smells aroused by rain. But something was missing. The acrid smell that fills the air when rain wets the still-fresh manure of corrals and sheep pens. Where was that? Chee's intelligence had its various strengths and its weaknesses—a superb memory, a tendency to exclude new input while it focused too narrowly on a single thought, a tendency to be distracted by beauty, and so forth. One of the strengths was an ability to process new information and collate it with old unusually fast. In a millisecond, Chee identified the missing odor, extracted its meaning, and homogenized it with what he had already noticed about the place of the Goldtooth outfit. No animals. The place was little used. Why use it now? Chee's brain identified an assortment of possible explanations. But all this changed him, midstride, from a man happily walking through the rain toward a long-anticipated meeting, to a slightly uneasy man with a memory of being shot at.

It was just then that Chee noticed the oil.

What he saw was a reflection in the twilight, a slick blue-green sheen where rainwater had washed under the truck and picked up an oil emulsion. It stopped him. He looked at the oily spot, then back at the house. The door was open a few inches. He felt all those odd, intense sensations caused when intense fear triggers the adrenaline glands. Maybe nothing, one corner of his brain said. A coincidence. Leaky oil pans are usual enough among the old trucks so common on the reservation. But he had been foolish. Careless. And he turned back toward his pickup, walking at first, then breaking into a trot. His pistol was locked in the glove compartment.

He was not conscious of any separation between the boom of the shotgun and the impact that staggered him. He stumbled against the hogan, catching the edge of the door lintel for support. Then the second shot hit him, higher this time, the feel of claws tearing against his upper back and neck muscles and the back of his head. It knocked him off balance and he found himself on his knees, his hands in the cold mud. Three shots, he remembered. An automatic shotgun legally choked holds three shells. Three holes torn through the aluminum skin of his trailer. Another shot would be coming. He slammed against the hogan door, pushed his way through it, just as he heard the shotgun again.

He pushed the door shut, sat against it, trying to control the shock and the panic. The hogan was empty, stripped bare and lit by flickering coals of a fire built on the earthen floor under the smoke hole. His ears were ringing with the sound of the shots, but through that he could hear the splashing sound of someone running through the rain. His right side felt numb. With his left hand he reached behind him and slid the wooden latch.

Something pushed, tentatively, against the door.

He pressed his shoulder against it. "If you open the door, I'll shoot you," Chee said.

Silence.

"I am a police officer," Chee said. "Why did you shoot me?"

Silence. The ringing in his ears diminished. He could distinguish a pinging noise—the sound of the rain hitting the metal shield placed over the smoke hole to keep the hogan dry. The sound of feet moving on muddy ground. Metallic sounds. Chee strained to hear them. The shotgun was being reloaded. He thought about that. Whoever had shot him hadn't bothered to reload before running after him. He had seen Chee had been hit, knocked down. Apparently it was presumed the shots had killed him. That Chee was no danger.

The pain was fierce now—especially the back of his head. He touched it gingerly with his fingers and found the scalp slick with blood. He could also feel blood running down his right side, warm against the skin over his ribs. Chee looked at his palm, tilted it so that the weak glow from the coals would reach it. In that light the fresh blood looked almost black. He was going to die. Not right away, probably, but soon. He wanted to know why. This time he shouted.

"Why did you shoot me?"

Silence. Chee tried to think of another way to get an answer. Any response. He tried his right arm, found he could move it. The worst pain was the back of his head. A teeth-gritting ache in what seemed to be twenty places where shotgun pellets had struck the skull bone. Overlying that was the feeling that his scalp was being scalded. The pain made it hard to think. But he had to think. Or die.

Then the voice: "Skinwalker! Why are you killing my baby?"

It was a woman's voice.

"I am not," Chee said, slowly and very plainly.

No reply. Chee tried to concentrate. In not very long, he would bleed to death. Or, before that happened, he would faint, and then this crazy woman would push open the hogan door and kill him with her shotgun.

"You think I'm a witch," he said. "Why do you think that?"

"Because you are an *adan'ti*," she said. "You shot a bone into me before my baby was born, or you shot a bead into my baby, and now it is dying."

That told him just a little. In the Navajo world, where witchcraft is important, where daily behavior is patterned to avoid it, prevent it, and cure it, there are as many words for its various forms as there are words for various kinds of snow among the Eskimos. If the woman thought he was *adan'ti*, she thought he had the power of sorcery—to convert himself into animal form, to fly, perhaps to become invisible. Very specific ideas. Where had she gotten them?

"You think that if I confess that I witched your baby, then the baby will get well and pretty soon I will die," Chee said. "Is that right? Or if you kill me, then the witching will go away."

"You should confess," the woman said. "You should say you did it. Otherwise, I will kill you."

He had to keep her here. Had to keep her talking until he could make his mind work. Until he could learn from her what he had to learn to save his life. Maybe that was impossible. Maybe he was already dying. Maybe his life wind was already blowing out of him—out into the rain. Maybe there was nothing he could learn that would help him. But Chee's conditioning was to endure. He thought, frowning with concentration, willing away the pain and the dreadful consciousness of the blood running down his flanks and puddling under his buttocks. Meanwhile he had to keep her talking.

"It won't help your baby if I confess, because I am not the witch. Can you tell me who told you I was the witch?"

Silence.

"If I were a witch . . . if I had the power of sorcery, did someone teach you what I could do?"

"Yes, I was taught." The voice was hesitant.

"Then you know that if I was a witch, I could turn myself into something else. Into a burrowing owl. I could fly out the smoke hole and go away into the night."

Silence.

"But I am not a witch. I am just a man. I am a singer. A *yataalii*. I have learned the ways to cure. Some of them. I know the songs to protect you against a witching. But I am not a witch."

"They say you are," the woman said.

"Who are they? They who say this?" But he already knew the answer.

Silence.

The back of Chee's head was on fire, and beneath the fire the shattering pain in the skull was beginning to localize itself into a dozen spots of pain—the places where shotgun pellets had lodged in the bone. But he had to think. This woman had been given him as her witch just as Roosevelt Bistie must have been given Endocheeney as his scapegoat. Bistie had been dying of a liver disease. And this woman was watching her infant die. A conclusion took its shape in Chee's mind.

"Where was your baby born?" Chee asked. "And when it got sick, did you take it to the Badwater Clinic?"

He had decided she wouldn't answer before the answer came. "Yes."

"And Dr. Yellowhorse told you he was a crystal gazer, and that he could tell you what caused your baby to be sick, is that right? And Dr. Yellowhorse told you I had witched your child."

It was no longer a question. Chee knew it was true. And he thought he might know how to stay alive. How he might talk this woman into putting down her shotgun, and coming in to help stop his bleeding and to take him to Piñon or someplace where there would be help. He would use what little life he had left telling this woman who the witch really was. Chee believed in witchcraft in an abstract way. Perhaps they did have the power, as the legends claimed and the rumors insisted, to become were-animals, to fly, to run faster than any car. On that score, Chee was a skeptic willing to accept any proof. But he knew witchcraft in its basic form stalked the Dinee. He saw it in people who had turned deliberately and with malice from the beauty of the Navajo Way and embraced the evil that was its opposite. He saw it every day he worked as a policeman—in those who sold whiskey to children, in those who bought videocassette recorders while their relatives were hungry, in the knife fights in a Gallup alley, in beaten wives and abandoned children.

"I am going to tell you who the witch is," Chee said. "First I am going to throw out the keys to my truck. You take 'em and unlock the glove box in the truck, and you will find my pistol there. I said I had it in here with me because I was afraid. Now I am not afraid any more. Go and check, and see that I don't have my pistol with me. Then I want you to come in here where it is warm, and out of the rain, and where you can look at my face while I tell you. That way you can tell whether I speak the truth. And then I will tell you again that I am not a witch who harmed your child. And I will tell you who the witch is that put this curse on you."

Silence. The sound of gusting rain. And then a metallic clack. The woman doing something with the shotgun.

Chee's right arm was numb again. With his left hand he extracted his truck keys, slid back the latch, and eased the door toward him. As he tossed the keys through the opening, he waited for the shotgun. The shotgun didn't fire. He heard the sound of the woman walking in the mud.

Chee exhaled a gust of breath. Now he had to hold off the pain and the faintness long enough to organize his thoughts. He had to know exactly what to say.

21

THE PATROL CAR of Officer Leonard Skeet, born to the Ears Sticking Up Clan, the man in charge of law and order in the rugged vacant places surrounding Piñon, was parked in the rain outside the subagency police station. The station, a double-width mobile home, stood on the bank of Wepo Wash. It also served as home for Leonard Skeet and Aileen Beno, his wife. Leaphorn pulled off the asphalt of Navajo Route 4 and into the mud of Skeet's yard, tapped on Skeet's door, and collected him.

Skeet had seen no sign of Chee's pickup. His house was located with a view of both Navajo 4 and the road that wandered northwestward toward the Forest Lake Chapter House and, eventually, to the Goldtooth place. "He was probably already past here long before I got home," Skeet said. "But he hasn't come back through. I would have seen his truck."

At Emma's car, Skeet hesitated. "This isn't good for mud, and maybe I oughta drive," he said, looking at Leaphorn's cast. "You probably oughta give that arm some rest."

Under the cast, the arm arched from wrist to elbow. Leaphorn stood in the rain, common sense wrestling with his conditioned instinct to be in control. Common sense won. Skeet knew the road. They switched to Skeet's patrol car, left the tiny scattering of buildings that was Piñon behind, left asphalt for gravel, and soon, gravel for graded dirt. It was slick now and Skeet drove with the polished skill of an athletic man who drives the bad back roads every working day. Leaphorn found himself thinking of Emma and turned away from that. Skeet had asked no questions and Leaphorn's policy for years had been to tell people no more than they needed to know. Skeet needed to know a little.

"We may be wasting our time," Leaphorn said. He didn't have to tell Skeet anything about the attempt on Chee's life—everyone in NTP knew everything about that and everyone, Leaphorn guessed, had a theory about it. He told Skeet about Chee being invited to the Goldtooth place to talk about doing a sing.

"Uh huh," Skeet said. "Interesting. Maybe there's some explanation for it." He concentrated on correcting a rear-end skid on the muddy surface. "He didn't know nobody lives there," Skeet said. "No way he could have, I guess. Still, if somebody was shooting at me . . ." He let the statement trail off.

Leaphorn was riding in the back, where he could lean against the driver-side door and keep the cast propped along the top of the backrest. Despite the cushioning, the jolts and jarring of the bumpy road communicated themselves to the bone. He didn't feel like talking, or like defending Chee. "No IQ test required for the job," he said. "But maybe I'm just overnervous. Maybe there's an explanation for having the meeting there."

"Maybe so," Skeet said. His tone was skeptical.

Skeet slowed at an oddly shaped outcrop of volcanic basalt. "If I remember right, the turn-off's here," he said.

Leaphorn retrieved his arm from the backrest. "Let's take a look," he said.

On a clear evening, this lonely landscape would still have been lit by a red afterglow. In steady rain, the dark was almost complete. They used their flashlights.

"Some traffic," Skeet said. "One out pretty recently."

The rain had blurred the track of the tires without erasing them. And the depth of the rut in the softer earth at the juncture showed the vehicle had passed after the moisture had soaked in. And these fresher tracks had partly overlapped earlier, shallower tracks which the rain had almost smoothed away.

"So maybe he's come and gone," Skeet said. But as he said it he doubted it. At least two vehicles had gone in. One had come out since the rain became heavy.

Their headlights reflected first from the rainslick roof of a truck, then they picked up the windows of the Goldtooth house. No lights visible anywhere. Skeet parked fifty yards away. "Leave 'em on?" he said. "What do you think?"

"Turn 'em off for now," Leaphorn said. "Until we make sure that's Chee's truck. And find out who's here."

They found a wealth of half-erased, rain-washed tracks but no sign of anyone outside. "Check the truck," Leaphorn said. "I'll take the house."

Leaphorn pointed his light at the building, holding it gingerly in his left hand, as far from his body as was practical. "Kicked once, double careful," his mother would have told him. And in this case, they might be dealing with a shotgun. Leaphorn thought, wryly, that he should have a telescoping arm, like Inspector Gadget in the television cartoon.

The house door was open. The beam of Leaphorn's light shined through it into emptiness. In front of the door, on the wet, packed earth, it lit a small red cylinder. Leaphorn picked it up, an empty shotgun shell. He switched off the light, sniffed the open end of the cartridge, inhaled the acrid smell of freshly burned powder. "Shit," Leaphorn said. He felt bleak, defeated, conscious of the cold rainwater against his ribs.

Skeet splashed up behind him.

"Truck unlocked," Skeet said. "Glove box open. This was on the seat." He showed Leaphorn a .38 caliber revolver. "That his?"

"Probably," Leaphorn said. He checked the cylinder, sniffed the barrel. It hadn't been fired. He shook his head, showed Skeet the empty shotgun shell. They would find Jim Chee's body and they would call it a homicide. Maybe they should call it suicide. Or death by stupidity.

The house was empty. Absolutely empty. Of people, of furniture, of anything except a scattered residue of trash. They found small footprints around the door, damp but not muddy. Whoever had been here had come before the rain turned heavy. Had left. Hadn't returned.

From the front door, Leaphorn shined his flash on the hogan. Its door was half open.

"I'll check it," Skeet said.

"We will," Leaphorn said.

They found Jim Chee just inside the door, slumped against the wall just south of the entrance—the correct place for a proper Navajo to be if he had entered the hogan properly "sunwise"—which was from east to south to west to north. In the light of the two flashes, the back of his head and his side seemed clotted with grease. In the reflected light, Skeet's long face was pinched and stricken.

Grief? Or was he conscious that he was standing in a ghost hogan, being infected with the virulent ghost of Officer Jim Chee? Leaphorn, who had long since come to terms with ghosts, stared at Skeet's face, trying to separate out the sorrow and find the fear.

"I think he may be alive," Skeet said.

22

AS IT USUALLY does on the Colorado Plateau, night defeated the storm. It drifted northeastward, robbed of the solar power that had fed it, and exhausted its energy in the thin, cold air over the Utah canyons and the mountains of northern New Mexico. By midnight there was no more thunder; the cloud formation had sagged into itself, flattening to a vast general rain—the sort Navajos call female rain—which gently drenched an area from the Painted Desert northward to Sleeping Ute Mountain.

From the fifth-floor windows of the Indian Health Service hospital in Gallup, Joe Leaphorn saw the deep blue of the newly washed morning sky—cloudless except for scraps of fog over the Zuni Mountains to the southeast, and the red cliffs stretching eastward toward Borego Pass. By afternoon, if moisture was still moving in from the Pacific, the towering thunderheads would be building again, bombarding earth with lightning, wind, and rain. But now the world outside the glass where Leaphorn stood was brilliant with sun—clean and calm.

He was hardly aware of it. His mind was full of what the neurologist had told him. Emma did not have Alzheimer's disease. Emma's illness was caused by a tumor pressing against the right front lobe of her brain. The doctor, a young woman named Vigil, had told Leaphorn a great deal more, but what was important was simple enough. If the tumor was cancerous,

Emma would probably die, and die rather soon. If the tumor was benign, Emma would be cured by its removal through surgery. "What are the odds?" Dr. Vigil didn't want to guess. This afternoon she would call a doctor she knew in Baltimore. A doctor she had studied with. Cases like this were his field. He would know.

"I want to discuss it with him before I do any guessing." Dr. Vigil was in her early thirties, Leaphorn guessed. One of those who went to medical school with a government grant and worked it off in the Indian Health Service. She stood, hands on desk, waiting for Leaphorn to leave. "Leave word where I can get in touch with you," she said.

"Call now," Leaphorn said. "I want to know."

"He does his surgery in the mornings," she said. "He won't be in."

"Try it," Leaphorn said. "Just try."

Dr. Vigil said, "Well, now, I don't think . . ." Then her eyes met Leaphorn's. "No harm trying," she said.

He'd waited in the hall, just outside the doctor's door, staring out at the morning, digesting this new data. The news was good. But it left him off balance, trying to live again with hope. It was a luxury he had given up weeks before. The exact moment, he thought, was when he sat at his desk reading the literature the Alzheimer's organization had sent him and seeing Emma's awful confusion described in print. It had been a terrible morning—the worst pain he'd ever endured. Now all his instincts cried out against enduring it again—against reentering that door which hope held open for him. But there was the ultimate fact: Emma might be well again. He wanted to celebrate. He wanted to shout for joy. But he was afraid.

So he waited. To avoid the trap of hope, he thought of Jim Chee. Specifically he thought of what Jim Chee had told them when the ambulance unloaded him at the Badwater Clinic. Just a few words, but a lot of information in them if only Leaphorn knew how to read it.

"Woman," Chee had said, in a voice so weak that Leaphorn had heard it only because he was leaning with his face just inches from Chee's lips.

"Who shot you?" Leaphorn had asked while attendants shifted the stretcher onto the hospital cart. Chee had moved his head. "Do you know?" Chee had moved his head again, a negative motion. And then he had said: "Woman."

"Young?" Leaphorn had asked, and got no response.

"We'll find her," Leaphorn had said, and that had provoked the rest of the information Chee had provided.

"Baby dying," Chee said. He said it clearly, in English. And then he repeated it in mumbled Navajo, his voice fading away.

So it would seem that the person who had shot Chee at the Goldtooth place was a woman with a fatally ill infant. Probably the same person had fired the three shotgun blasts through Chee's trailer wall. When Chee came out of surgery it would be easy enough to find her. He would be able to identify the vehicle she was driving, probably even give them the license number if he had been halfway alert before the shooting. And if he knew she had a sick child, he had to have talked to her face to face. They would also have a physical description. But even if Chee didn't survive to describe her, they could find her. A young woman with a critically ill child who knew about the Goldtooth place, about it being abandoned. That would give them all the narrowing they needed.

They would find the woman. She would tell them why she wanted Jim Chee dead. Then all this insane killing would make sense.

Below Leaphorn, a flock of crows moved toward the center of Gallup, their cawing muted by the glass. Far beyond, an endless line of tank cars moved eastward down the Santa Fe mainline.

Or, Leaphorn thought, they wouldn't find the woman. Or they would find her dead. Or she, like Bistie, would tell them absolutely nothing. And he would be exactly where he was now. And where was that?

The crows disappeared out of his line of vision. The freight crawled inexorably eastward. Leaphorn considered why he was nagged with the feeling that these homicides made perfect sense, that Chee had somehow, in those three words, put the key in the lock and turned it.

"Woman," Chee had said. A woman Chee didn't know. How did that help? Of the victims, only Irma Onesalt was female. She had been killed with a rifle shot, not a shotgun. No apparent connection there. "Baby dying," Chee had said. Presumably the baby of the woman who had shot him. Presumably she had told Chee about it. Why?

"Mr. Leaphorn?" a woman's voice said at Leaphorn's elbow. "She asked me to get you. Dr. Vigil."

Dr. Vigil had come to the door to meet him. "I can give you the statistics now," she said, smiling slightly. "Recovery from the actual surgery, close to ninety-nine percent. Nature of tumor: malignant twenty-three-plus percent, benign seventy-six-plus percent."

And so Joe Leaphorn allowed himself again the heavy risk of hope. He went to Emma's room to tell her, found her sleeping, and left her a note. It told her what Dr. Vigil had told him, and that he loved her, and that he would be back as soon as he could be.

Then he left on the long drive to the Badwater Clinic. He wanted to be there when Chee recovered from the anesthesia. And he wanted to talk to Yellowhorse about Irma Onesalt's list, and learn what Onesalt had said to Yellowhorse about it; specifically if she had told him why she wanted the dates of death of people who had not yet died. The Cambodian doctor who had been in charge when they'd brought Chee in had said Yellowhorse was in Flagstaff—that he would be driving back today, that he should be back by early afternoon.

Leaphorn stopped for gas at Ganado and called the clinic while his tank was being filled. Yes, Chee had survived the surgery. He was still in the recovery room. No, Yellowhorse was not back from Flagstaff yet. But he'd called and they expected him sometime after lunch.

Leaphorn was finding it difficult to think about homicides. He was preoccupied, indeed fascinated, by his own emotions. He had never felt quite like this before—this immeasurable joy. This relief. Emma, who had been lost forever, was found again. She would live. She would be herself again. He thought of Dr. Vigil, watching him receive her hopeful news. Doctors must see a lot of such violent emotional reaction—even more than policemen do. Understanding the intensity love can produce would be a by-product of that profession. Dr. Vigil would understand how a dying infant could motivate a murder. If not yet, she would when she was older. Leaphorn was thinking this as he passed the turnoff to Blue Gap. He moved from that into analyzing his own emotions. Watching what was happening to Emma had caused everything else to recede into triviality. Other values ceased to exist for him. Had there been anything he could do to help her, anything, he would have done it. Beyond the turnoff to Whippoorwill School, his thoughts moved back to a question that had intrigued him earlier. Why had the woman told Chee her baby was dying? He seemed to know the answer. She had told Chee to explain why she was killing him. She was killing him to reverse the witchcraft that was killing her baby. Logical. Why did something keep tugging him back to this?

Just then, Leaphorn saw how it all had worked. All the pins on his map came together into a single cluster at the Badwater Clinic. Four and a half homicides became a single crime with a single motive. His car fishtailed on the muddy road as he jammed down the accelerator. If he didn't reach the clinic before Dr. Yellowhorse, the four and a half homicides would become five.

23

IT WAS ALL very vague to Chee. The nurse who moved him down the hall from the recovery room had shown him a paper cup containing a spoonful of shot. "What Dr. Wu dug out of your back and your neck and your head," she explained. "Dr. Wu thought you'd want to keep it."

Chee, woozy, could think of nothing to say to that. He raised his eyebrows.

"Sort of a souvenir," she explained. "To help you remember." And then she had added something about Dr. Wu being Chinese, but actually a Cambodian Chinese, as if this would clarify why he thought Chee would want a souvenir.

"Um," Chee said, and the nurse had looked at him quizzically and said, "Only if you want to."

The nurse had talked a lot more, but Chee remembered little of it. He recalled wanting to ask her where he was, and what had happened, but he didn't have the energy. Now the back of his head was helping him remember. Whatever painkiller they had used to numb it was wearing off and Chee could isolate and identify about seven places where the surgeon had dug a piece of shot out of the thick bone at the back of his skull. It reminded Chee of a long time ago when a yearling horse they were branding had kicked him squarely on the shinbone. Bruised bone seemed to issue a peculiarly painful protest to the nervous system.

But he kept the pain at bay by celebrating being alive. It surprised him. He could only dimly remember the woman coming hesitantly into the hogan, the shotgun pointing at him. He remembered the seconds when he had thought she would simply shoot him again and that would be the end of it. Perhaps that was what she'd intended to do. But she had let him talk, and he had forced himself into a kind of coherence. Now it was all hazy, much of it simply blank. The medics called it temporary posttrauma amnesia, and Chee had seen it in enough victims of knife fights and traffic accidents to recognize it in himself. He didn't try to force his memory. What was important, obviously, was that the woman had believed him. She seemed to have brought him here, although Chee couldn't remember that happening, or imagine how she had gotten him from the hogan to her truck. The last he remembered was describing for her what must have happened, relying on his recollection of the time he himself had been taken to a crystal gazer as a child, remembering the old man's eye, immensely magnified and distorted, looking into his own eye, remembering his own fear.

"I think I know what happened," Chee had told her. "Yellowhorse pretends to be a crystal gazer. I think you took your sick baby to the Badwater Clinic and Yellowhorse looked at it, and then Yellowhorse got out his crystal, and pretended to be a shaman, and he told you that the baby had been witched. And then he did the sucking ceremony, and he pretended to suck a bone out of your baby's breast." Chee remembered that at this point he began to run out of strength. His eyes were no longer focusing and it was difficult to generate the breath to form the guttural Navajo words. But he had gone on. "Then he told you that I was the skinwalker who had witched your baby and that the only way to cure it was to kill me. And he gave you the bone and told you to shoot it into me."

The woman, hazy and distant, had simply sat there, holding the shotgun. He couldn't see well enough to know if she was listening.

"I think he wants to kill me because I have told people that he is not really a shaman. I told people he had no real powers. But maybe there is some other reason. That doesn't matter. What matters is that I am not the skinwalker. Yellowhorse is the skinwalker. Yellowhorse witched you. Yellowhorse turned you into someone who kills." He had said a lot more, or he thought he had, but maybe that was part of the dream that he had drifted into as he fell asleep. He couldn't separate it.

The nurse was back in the room. She put a tray on the table beside his bed—a white towel, a syringe, other paraphernalia. "You need some of this by now," she said, glancing at her watch.

"First I need to do some things, know some things," Chee said. "Are there any policemen here?"

"I don't think so," the nurse said. "Quiet morning."

"Then I need to make a call," Chee said.

She didn't bother to look at him. "Fat chance," she said.

"Then I need somebody to make a call for me. Call the tribal police headquarters at Window Rock and get a message to a Lieutenant Leaphorn."

"He's one of them who brought you in. With the ambulance," she said. "If you want to tell him who shot you, I'll bet that can wait until you're feeling a little better."

"Is Yellowhorse here? Dr. Yellowhorse?"

"He's in Flag," the nurse said. "Some sort of meeting at the Flagstaff hospital."

Chee felt dizzy, and a little nauseated, and vastly relieved. He didn't understand why Yellowhorse wanted to kill him—not exactly, anyway. But he knew he didn't want to be sleeping in his hospital when Yellowhorse was here.

"Look," he said. Trying to sound like a policeman when your head and your arm and shoulder and side were encased in bandages and you were flat on your back wasn't easy. "This is important. I have to tell Leaphorn some things or a murderer might get away. Might kill somebody again."

"You're serious?" the nurse asked, still doubting it.

"Dead serious."

"What's the number?"

Chee gave her the number at Window Rock. "And if he's not in, call the substation at Piñon. Tell 'em I said we need a policeman out here right away." Chee tried to think of who was stationed at Piñon now, and drew a blank. He was conscious only that his eyes were buzzing and that his head hurt in at least seven places.

"You know that number?"

Chee shook his head.

The nurse went out the door, leaving the tray. "Here he comes now," she said.

Leaphorn, Chee thought. Great!

Dr. Yellowhorse came through the door, moving fast.

Chee opened his mouth, began a yell, and found Yellowhorse's hand clamped across his jaws, cutting off all sound.

"Keep quiet," Yellowhorse said. With his other hand he was pressing something hard against Chee's throat. It was another source of pain—but no competition for the back of his head.

"Struggle and I cut your throat," Yellowhorse said.

Chee tried to relax. Impossible.

Yellowhorse's hand came off his mouth. Chee heard it fumbling in the tray.

"I don't want to kill you," Yellowhorse said. "I'm going to give you this shot so you'll get some sleep. And remember, you can't yell with your windpipe cut."

Chee tried to think. Whatever was pressing against his throat was pressing too hard to make yelling practical. Almost instantly he added the feel of the needle going into his shoulder to the battery of other pains. And then Yellowhorse's hand was over his mouth again.

"I hate to do this," Yellowhorse said, and his expression said he meant it. "It was that damned Onesalt woman. But in the long run, it more than balances out."

Chee's expression, as much as Yellowhorse could see of it around his smothering hand, must have seemed skeptical.

"It balances way out in favor of saving the clinic," Yellowhorse said, voice insistent. "Four lives. Three of them were men past their prime and one of them was dying fast anyway. And on the balance against that, I know for sure we've saved dozens of lives already, and we'll save dozens more. And better than that, we're stopping birth defects, and catching diabetes cases early." Yellowhorse paused, looking into Chee's eyes.

"And glaucoma," he said. "I know we've caught a dozen cases of that early enough to save good vision. That Onesalt bitch was going to put an end to all that."

Chee, who was in no position to talk, didn't.

"You feeling sleepy?" Yellowhorse said. "You should be by now."

Chee was feeling—despite an intense effort of will—very sleepy. There was no question at all that Yellowhorse was going to kill him. If there were any other possibility, Yellowhorse would not be telling him all this, making this apology. Chee tried to gather his strength, tense his muscles for a lunge against the knife. All he had to muster was a terrible weakness. Yellowhorse felt even that and tightened his grip.

"Don't try it," he said. "It won't work."

It wouldn't. Chee admitted it to himself. Time was his only hope, if he had a hope. Stay awake. He made a questioning sound against Yellowhorse's palm. He would ask him why Onesalt and the rest had to be killed. It was to cover up something at the clinic, clearly, but what?

Yellowhorse eased the grip on Chee's mouth.

"What?" he said. "Keep it low."

"What did Onesalt know?" he asked.

The hand gripped again. Yellowhorse looked surprised. "I thought you had guessed," he said. "That day when you came and got the wrong Begay. Onesalt guessed. I figured you would. Or she would tell you."

Chee mumbled against the palm. "You gave us the wrong Begay. I wondered what had happened to the right one. But I didn't guess you were keeping him on your records."

"Well, I thought you were guessing," Yellowhorse said. "I always knew you would guess sooner or later. And once you did, it would take time but it would be inevitable. You would find out."

"Overcharging?" Chee asked. "For patients who weren't here?"

"Getting the government to pay its share," Yellowhorse said. "Have you ever read the treaty? The one we signed at Fort Sumner. Promises. One schoolteacher for every thirty children, everything else. The government never kept any promises."

"Charging for people after they were dead?" Chee mumbled. He simply could not keep his eyes open any longer. When they closed, Yellowhorse would kill him. Not immediately, but soon enough. When his eyes closed they would never open again. Yellowhorse would keep him asleep until he could find a way to make it look normal and natural. Chee knew that. He must keep his eyes open.

"Getting sleepy?" Yellowhorse asked, his voice benign.

Chee's eyes closed. He went to sleep, a troubled sleep, dreaming that something was hurting the back of his head.

24

LEAPHORN PARKED RIGHT at the door, violating the blue handicapped-only zone, and trotted into the clinic. He'd made his habitual instant eyeball inventory of the vehicles present. A dozen were there, including an Oldsmobile sedan with the medical symbol on its license plate, which might be Yellowhorse's car, and three well-worn pickup trucks, which might include the one driven by the woman determined to kill Chee. Leaphorn hurried through the front door. The receptionist was standing behind her half-round desk screaming something. A tall woman in a nurse's uniform was standing across the desk, hands in her hair, apparently terrified. Both were looking down the hallway that led to Leaphorn's right, down a corridor of patients' rooms.

Leaphorn's trot turned into a run.

"She has a gun," the receptionist shouted. "A gun."

The woman stood in the doorway four rooms down, and she did, indeed, have a gun. Leaphorn could see only her back, a traditional dark blue blouse of velvet, the flowing light blue skirt which came to the top of her squaw boots, her dark hair tied in a careful bun at the back of her head, and the butt of the shotgun protruding from under her arm.

"Hold it," Leaphorn shouted, digging with his left hand for his pistol.

Aimed as the shotgun was into the room and away from him, the sound it made was muted. A boom, a yell, the sound of someone falling, glass breaking. With the sound, the woman disappeared into the room. Leaphorn was at the door two seconds later, his pistol drawn.

"The skinwalker is dead," the woman said. She stood over Yellowhorse, the shotgun dangling from her right hand. "This time I killed him."

"Put down the gun," Leaphorn said. The woman ignored him. She was looking down at the doctor, who sprawled face-up beside Jim Chee's bed. Chee seemed to be sleeping. Leaphorn shifted his pistol to the fingers that protruded from his cast and lifted the shotgun from the woman's hand. She made no effort to keep it. Yellowhorse was still breathing, unevenly and raggedly. A man in a pale blue hospital smock appeared at the door—the same Chinese-looking doctor who had been on duty when they delivered Chee. He muttered something that sounded like an expletive in some language strange to Leaphorn.

"Why did you shoot him?" he asked Leaphorn.

"I didn't," Leaphorn said. "See if you can save him."

The doctor knelt beside Yellowhorse, feeling for a pulse, examining the place where the shotgun blast had struck Yellowhorse's neck at point-blank range. He shook his head.

"Dead?" the woman asked. "Is the skinwalker dead? Then I want to bring in my baby. I have him in my truck. Maybe now he is alive again."

But he wasn't, of course.

It took Jim Chee almost four hours to awaken and he did so reluctantly—his subconscious dreading what he would awaken to. But when he came awake he found himself alone in the room. Sunset lit the foot of his bed. His head still hurt and his shoulder and side ached, but he felt warm again. He removed his left hand from under the covers, flexed the fingers. A good strong hand. He moved his toes, his feet, bent his knees. Everything worked. The right arm was another matter. It was heavily bandaged elbow to shoulder and immobilized with tape.

Where was Yellowhorse? Chee considered that. Obviously he had guessed wrong about the doctor. The man hadn't killed him, as common sense said he should have. Apparently Yellowhorse had run for it, or turned himself in, or went to talk to a lawyer, or something. It seemed totally unlikely that Yellowhorse would come back now to finish off Chee. But just in case, he decided he would get up, put on his clothes, and go somewhere else. Call Leaphorn first. Tell him about all this.

Just about then it also occurred to Chee how he would solve the problem of the cat. He would put the cat in the forty-dollar case, and take it to the Farmington airport and send it off to Mary Landon. But first he would write her and explain it all—explain how this *belagana* cat simply wasn't going to make it as a Navajo cat. It would starve, or be eaten by the coyote, or something like that. Mary was a very smart person. Mary would understand that perfectly. Probably better than Chee.

Carefully, slowly, he turned himself onto his good side, swung his feet off the bed, pushed himself upright. Almost upright. Before he completed the move, weakness and faintness overcame him. He was on his side again, the back of his head throbbing, and a metal tray he'd tumbled from the bedside stand still clattering on the floor.

"I see you're awake," a female voice said. "Tell the lieutenant that Officer Chee is awake."

Lieutenant Leaphorn's expression, when he came through the door behind the nurse, could best be described as blank. He sat on the chair beside Chee's bed, resting his cast gingerly on the cover.

"Do you know her name? The woman who shot you?"

"No idea," Chee said. "Where is she? Where's Yellowhorse? Do you know—"

"She shot Yellowhorse," Leaphorn said. "Right here. Did a better job on him than she did on you. We have her in custody, but she won't tell us her name. Anything else, for that matter. Just wants to talk about her baby."

"What's wrong with it?"

"It's dead," Leaphorn said. "The doctors say it's been dead for a couple of days." Leaphorn shifted his cast, which was generally grimy and had a streak of dried blue-black mud on its bottom side.

"She thought it was witched," Chee said. "That's why she wanted to kill me. She thought I was the witch and she could turn the witching around."

Leaphorn looked disapproving. "It had something they call Werdnig-Hoffmann disease," Leaphorn said. "Born with it. The brain never develops properly. Muscles never develop. They live a little while and then they die."

"Well," Chee said. "She didn't understand that."

"No cure for it," Leaphorn said. "Not even by killing skinwalkers like you."

"Do you know why Yellowhorse was doing all this?" Chee asked. "He told me he was trying to get the government to pay its share, or something like that, and Onesalt found out about it, or was finding out, and he figured sooner or later I would understand it too, because of what I knew." Chee paused, slightly abashed by the admission he would be making. "I guess he figured I'm smarter than I am. I guess I was supposed to figure out that he was turning in hospitalization claims on patients after they were dead. I guess that's why Onesalt was looking for those death dates."

"About right," Leaphorn said. "After they died, or long after they'd checked out and gone home. Dilly Streib is in the business office now. They're going through the billing records."

"I began to see how he was doing it," Chee said. "I couldn't see why. Wasn't he using a lot of his own money to run this place?"

"Yeah," Leaphorn said. "Mostly his own money. Through his foundation. And he had other private foundation money. And some tribe support. Medicare. Medicaid. Guess it wasn't enough. Not even with hiring immigrant doctors."

"I understand how he killed Endocheeney and Wilson Sam. How about why?"

"Streib thinks he's going to find they were out of here for months before Yellowhorse stopped billing for them," Leaphorn said. "I guess there were a lot of them like that. But they were the only two on Onesalt's list. After he shot Onesalt, it took the pressure off. No rush anymore. But I guess he figured that since you were with Onesalt, you'd know about the list and sooner or later you'd just naturally find out about it. Or if you didn't, somebody else would. So he decided to get rid of Sam and Endocheeney, and you too."

"He told me it balanced out," Chee said. "Onesalt was going to put an end to the clinic and it was saving more lives than those he had to kill."

Leaphorn had nothing to say to that. He raised his cast off the bed, grimaced, put it down again. "*Anti'll*," he said sourly, using the Navajo word for witchcraft.

Jim Chee just nodded.

"Pretty smart, really," Leaphorn added. "No hurry, so he could pick his people carefully. From desperate people. Like Bistie, who was dying. Or the woman he sent after you. People won't talk about witches, so there wasn't much risk of tracking anything back here."

"I guess he sent two after Endocheeney. Maybe Bistie was too slow and he thought he wasn't going to do it."

"Apparently," Leaphorn said. "And then he found out we'd arrested Bistie, so he had to kill him—just in case we did trick him into talking."

"I guess we could find them now," Chee said. "The one who killed Endocheeney. The one who killed Wilson Sam. Just work down through the records of the caseload here, looking at them the way Yellowhorse would have looked."

"I guess we could," Leaphorn said.

Chee considered that answer awhile. It was, after all, a federal problem.

"You think Streib will think of it?"

"I doubt it," Leaphorn said. He laughed a humorless laugh. "People say I hate witchcraft. Dilly, he hates to even think about witches."

"Doesn't matter, anyway," Chee said. "It's finished."

A Thief of Time

With special thanks to Dan Murphy of the U.S. Park Service for pointing me to the ruins down the San Juan River, to Charley and Susan DeLorme and the other river lovers of Wild River Expeditions, to Kenneth Tsosie of White Horse Lake, to Ernie Bulow, and to the Tom and Jan Vaughn family of Chaco Culture National Historical Park. All characters in this book are imaginary. True, Drayton and Noi Vaughn actually do make the sixty-mile bus ride to school each morning but they are even classier in real life than the fictitious counterparts found herein.

This story is dedicated to Steven Lovato,
firstborn son of Larry and Mary Lovato.
May he always go with beauty
all around him.

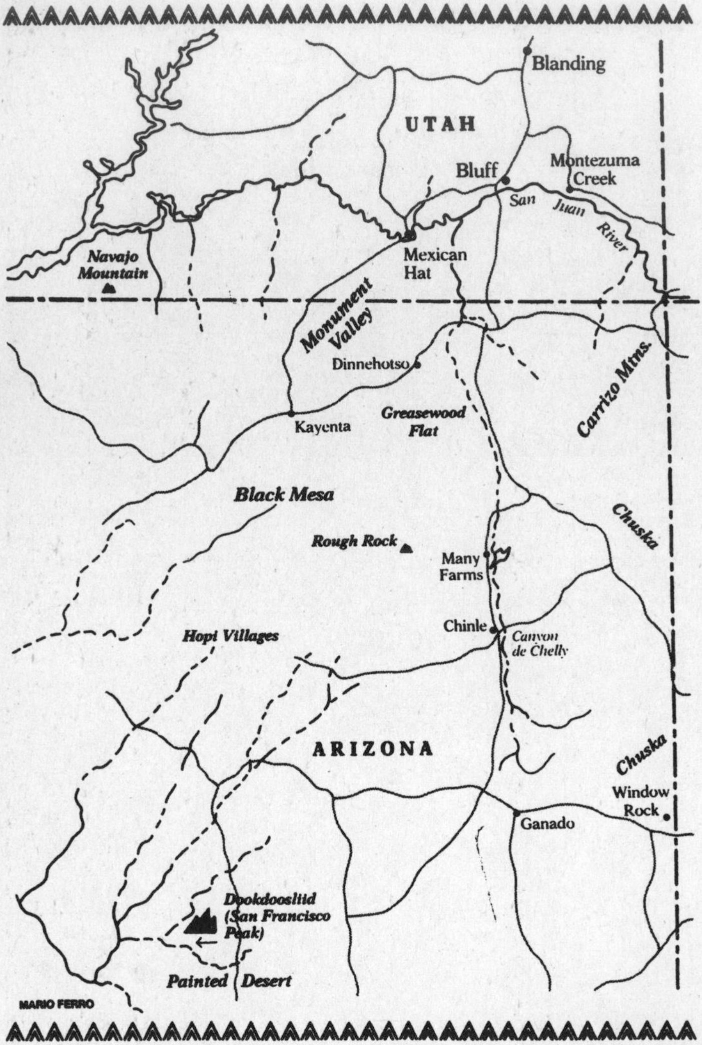
Blanding
UTAH
Montezuma
Creek
Bluff
San Juan River
Navajo
Mountain
Mexican
Hat
Monument
Valley
Dinnehotso
Carrizo Mtns.
Greasewood
Flat
Kayenta
Black Mesa
Chuska
Rough Rock
Many
Farms
Chinle
Canyon
de Chelly
Hopi Villages
ARIZONA
Chuska
Window
Rock
Ganado
Dookdooslííd
(San Francisco
Peak)
Painted Desert
MARIO FERRO

Anasazi Country
Sacred Navajo Mountains
COLORADO
FOUR CORNERS
Dibe
(Mt.
Sis Naajini (Blanca Peak)
Shiprock
Shiprock
Kirtland
Farmington
Dzil Náoodilii
San Juan River
Blanco
Bloomfield
The Hogback
Gobernador Canyon
CARSON NATIONAL FOREST
Blanco Canyon
Chaco River
Bisti
Nageezi
Range
Range
Chaco Mesa
Chaco Wash
Fajardo Wash
CHACO CULTURE NAT'L. HISTORICAL PARK
Chuska Valley
Coyote Canyon
Crown Point
Yah-Ta-Hey
Gallup
NEW MEXICO
Tsoodzil (Mt. Taylor, Turquoise Mtn.)

Author's Note

WHILE MOST OF the places in this volume are real, Many Ruins Canyon has had its name changed and its location tinkered with to protect its unvandalized cliff ruins.

1

THE MOON HAD risen just above the cliff behind her. Out on the packed sand of the wash bottom the shadow of the walker made a strange elongated shape. Sometimes it suggested a heron, sometimes one of those stick-figure forms of an Anasazi pictograph. An animated pictograph, its arms moving rhythmically as the moon shadow drifted across the sand. Sometimes, when the goat trail bent and put the walker's profile against the moon, the shadow became Kokopelli himself. The backpack formed the spirit's grotesque hump, the walking stick Kokopelli's crooked flute. Seen from above, the shadow would have made a Navajo believe that the great *yei* northern clans called Watersprinkler had taken visible form. If an Anasazi had risen from his thousand-year grave in the trash heap under the cliff ruins here, he would have seen the Humpbacked Flute Player, the rowdy god of fertility of his lost people. But the shadow was only the shape of Dr. Eleanor Friedman-Bernal blocking out the light of an October moon.

Dr. Friedman-Bernal rested now, sitting on a convenient rock, removing her backpack, rubbing her shoulders, letting the cold, high desert air evaporate the sweat that had soaked her shirt, reconsidering a long day.

No one could have seen her. Of course, they had seen her driving away from Chaco. The children were up in the gray dawn to catch their school bus. And the children would chat about it to their parents. In that tiny, isolated Park Service society of a dozen adults and two children, everyone knew everything about everybody. There was absolutely no possibility of privacy. But she had done everything right. She had made the rounds of the permanent housing and checked with everyone on the digging team. She was driving into Farmington, she'd said. She'd collected the outgoing mail to be dropped off at the Blanco Trading Post. She had jotted down the list of supplies people needed. She'd told Maxie she had the Chaco fever—needed to get away, see a movie, have a restaurant dinner, smell exhaust fumes, hear a different set of voices, make phone calls back to civilization on a telephone that would actually work. She would spend a night where she could hear the sounds of civilization, something besides the endless Chaco silence. Maxie was sympathetic. If Maxie suspected anything, she suspected Dr. Eleanor Friedman-Bernal was meeting Lehman. That would have been fine with Eleanor Friedman-Bernal.

The handle of the folding shovel she had strapped to her pack was pressing against her back. She stopped, shifted the weight, and adjusted the pack straps. Somewhere in the darkness up the canyon she could hear the odd screeching call of a saw-whet owl, hunting nocturnal rodents. She glanced at her watch: 10:11, changing to 10:12 as she watched. Time enough.

No one had seen her in Bluff. She was sure of that. She had called from Shiprock, just to make doubly sure that no one was using Bo Arnold's old house out on the highway. No one had answered. The house was dark when she'd arrived, and she'd left it that way, finding the key under the flower box where Bo always left it. She'd done her borrowing carefully, disturbing nothing. When she put it back, Bo would never guess it had been missing. Not that it would matter. Bo was a biologist, scraping out a living as a part-timer with the Bureau of Land Management while he finished his dissertation on desert lichens, or whatever it was he was studying. He hadn't given a damn about anything else when she'd known him at Madison, and he didn't now.

She yawned, stretched, reached for her backpack, decided to rest a moment longer. She'd been up about nineteen hours. She had maybe two more to go before she reached the site. Then she'd roll out the sleeping bag and not get out of it until she was rested. No hurry now. She thought about Lehman. Big. Ugly. Smart. Gray. Sexy. Lehman was coming. She'd wine him and dine him and show him what she had. And he would have to be impressed. He'd have to agree she'd proved her case. That wasn't necessary for publication—his approval. But for some reason, it was necessary to her. And that irrationality made her think of Maxie. Maxie and Elliot.

She smiled, and rubbed her face. It was quiet here, just a few insects making their nocturnal sounds. Windless. The cold air settling into the canyon. She shivered, picked up the backpack, and struggled into it. A coyote was barking somewhere over on Comb Wash far behind her. She could hear another across the wash, very distant, yipping in celebration of the moonlight. She walked rapidly up the packed sand, lifting her legs high to stretch them, not thinking of what she would do tonight. She had thought long enough of that. Perhaps too long. Instead she thought of Maxie and Elliot. Brains, both. But nuts. The Blueblood and the Poorjane. The Man Who Could Do Anything obsessed by the woman who said nothing he did counted. Poor Elliot! He could never win.

A flash of lightning on the eastern horizon—much too distant to hear the thunder and the wrong direction to threaten any rain. A last gasp of summer, she thought. The moon was higher now, its light muting the colors of the canyon into shades of gray. Her thermal underwear and the walking kept her body warm but her hands were like ice. She studied them. No hands for a lady. Nails blunt and broken. The skin tough, scarred, callused. Anthropology skin, they'd called it when she was an undergraduate. The skin of people who are always out under the sun, working in the dirt. It had always bothered her mother, as everything about her bothered her mother. Becoming an anthropologist instead of a doctor, and then not marrying a doctor. Marrying a Puerto Rican archaeologist who was not even Jewish. And then losing him to another woman. "Wear gloves," her mother had said. "For heaven's sake, Ellie, you have hands like a dirt farmer."

And a face like a dirt farmer too, she'd thought.

The canyon was just as she remembered from the summer she had helped map and catalog its sites. A great place for pictographs. Just ahead, just beyond the cottonwoods on the sheer sandstone wall where the canyon bottom bent, was a gallery of them. The baseball gallery, they called it, because of the great shaman figure that someone had thought resembled a cartoon version of an umpire.

The moon lit only part of the wall, and the slanting light made it difficult to see, but she stopped to inspect it. In this light, the tapered, huge-shouldered shape of the mystic Anasazi shaman lost its color and became merely a dark form. Above it a clutter of shapes danced, stick figures, abstractions: the inevitable Kokopelli, his humped shape bent, his flute pointed almost at the ground; a heron flying; a heron standing; the zigzag band of pigment representing a snake. Then she noticed the horse.

It stood well to the left of the great baseball shaman, mostly in moon shadow. A Navajo addition, obviously, since the Anasazi had vanished three hundred years before the Spanish came on their steeds. It was a stylized horse, with a barrel body and straight legs, but without the typical Navajo tendency to build beauty into everything they attempted. The rider seemed to be a Kokopelli—Watersprinkler, the Navajos called him. At least the rider seemed to be blowing a flute. Had this addition been there before? She couldn't remember. Such Navajo additions weren't uncommon. But this one puzzled her.

Then she noticed, at each of three feet of the animal, a tiny prone figure. Three. Each with the little circle representing the head separated from the body. Each with one leg cut away.

Sick. And they hadn't been here four years ago. These she would have remembered.

For the first time Eleanor Friedman-Bernal became aware of the darkness, the silence, her total isolation. She had dropped her backpack while she rested. Now she picked it up, put an arm through the carry strap, changed her mind. She unzipped a side pocket and extracted the pistol. It was a .25 caliber automatic. The salesman had shown her how to load it, how the safety worked, how to hold it. He had told her it was accurate, easy to use, and made in Belgium. He had not told her that it took an unusual ammunition that one always had to hunt for. She had never tried it out in Madison. There never seemed to be a place to shoot it safely. But when she came to New Mexico, the first day when there was enough wind to blow away the sound, she'd driven out into the emptiness on the road toward Crownpoint and practiced with it. She had fired it at rocks, and deadwood, and shadows on the sand, until it felt natural and comfortable and she was hitting things, or getting close enough. When she used up most of the box of cartridges, she found the sporting goods store in Farmington didn't have them. And neither did the big place in Albuquerque, and finally she had ordered them out of a catalog. Now she had seventeen bullets left in the new box. She had brought six of them with her. A full magazine. The pistol felt cold in her hand, cold and hard and reassuring.

She dropped it into the pocket of her jacket. As she regained the sandy bottom of the wash and walked up it, she was conscious of the heaviness against her hip. The coyotes were closer, two of them somewhere above her, on the mesa beyond the clifftops. Sometimes the night breeze gusted enough to make its sounds in the brush along the bottom, rattling the leaves on the Russian olives and whispering through the fronds of the tamarisks. Usually it was still. Runoff from the summer monsoons had filled pools along the rocky bottom. Most of these were nearly dry now, but she could hear frogs, and crickets, and insects she couldn't identify. Something made a clicking sound in the darkness where dead tumbleweed had collected against the cliff, and from somewhere ahead she heard what sounded like a whistle. A night bird?

The canyon wound under the cliff and out of the moonlight. She turned on her flash. No risk of anyone seeing it. And that turned her thoughts to how far the nearest human would be. Not far as the bird flies—perhaps fifteen or twenty miles as the crow flew. But no easy way in. No roads across the landscape of almost solid stone, and no reason to build roads. No reason for the Anasazi to come here, for that matter, except to escape something that was hunting them. None that the anthropologists could think of—not even the cultural anthropologists with their notorious talents for forming theories without evidence. But come they had. And with them came her artist. Leaving Chaco Canyon behind her. Coming here to create more of her pots and to die.

From where Dr. Friedman-Bernal was walking she could see one of their ruins low on the cliff wall to her right. Had it been daylight, she remembered, she could have seen two more in the huge amphitheater alcove on the cliff to her left. But now the alcove was black with shadow—looking a little like a great gaping mouth.

She heard squeaking. Bats. She'd noticed a few just after sundown. Here they swarmed, fluttering over places where runoff had filled potholes and potholes had bred insects. They flashed past her face, just over her hair. Watching them, Ellie Friedman-Bernal didn't watch where she was walking. A rock turned under her foot, and she lost her balance.

The backpack cost her enough of her usual grace to make the fall hard and clumsy. She broke it with her right hand, hip, and elbow and found herself sprawled on the stream bottom, hurt, shocked, and shaken.

The elbow was most painful. It had scraped over the sandstone, tearing her shirt and leaving an abrasion that, when she touched it, stained her finger with blood. Then her bruised hip got her attention, but it was numb now and would punish her later. It was only when she scrambled back to her feet that she noticed the cut across the palm of her hand. She examined it in the light of her flash, made a sympathetic clicking sound, and then sat down to deal with it.

She picked out a bit of the gravel imbedded in the heel of her hand, rinsed the cut from her canteen, and bandaged it with a handkerchief, using left hand and teeth to tighten the knot. And then she continued up the wash, more careful now, leaving the bats behind, following a turn back into the full moonlight and then another into the shadows. Here she climbed onto a low alluvial ledge beside the dry streambed and dumped her pack. It was a familiar place. She and Eduardo Bernal had pitched a tent here five summers ago when they were graduate students, lovers, and part of the site-mapping team. Eddie Bernal. Tough little Ed. Fun while it lasted. But not much fun for long. Soon, surely before Christmas, she would drop the hyphen. Ed would hardly notice. A sigh of relief, perhaps. End of that brief phase when he'd thought one woman would be enough.

She removed a rock, some sticks, smoothed the ground with the edge of her boot sole, dug out and softened an area where her hips would be, and then rolled out the sleeping bag. She chose the place where she had lain with Eddie. Why? Partly defiance, partly sentiment, partly because it was simply the most comfortable spot. Tomorrow would be hard work and the cuts on her palm would make digging difficult and probably painful. But she wasn't ready for sleep yet. Too much tension. Too much uneasiness.

Standing here beside the sleeping bag, out of the moonlight, more stars were visible. She checked the autumn constellations, found the polestar, got her directions exactly right. Then she stared across the wash into the darkness that hid what she and Eddie had called Chicken Condo. In the narrow stone alcove, Anasazi families had built a two-story dwelling probably big enough for thirty people. Above it, in another alcove so hidden that they wouldn't have noticed it had Eddie not wondered where an evening bat flight was coming from, the Anasazi had built a little stone fort reachable only by a precarious set of hand- and footholds. It was around the lower dwelling that Eleanor Friedman-Bernal first had found the peculiar potsherds. If her memory didn't fool her. It was there, when it was light enough tomorrow, that she would dig. In violation of Navajo law, of federal law, and of professional ethics. If her memory only had not fooled her. And now she had more evidence than just her memory.

She couldn't wait until daylight. Not now. Not this near. Her flashlight would be enough to check.

Her memory had been excellent. It took her unerringly and without a misstep on an easy climb up the talus slope and along the natural pathway to the rim. There she paused and turned her light onto the cliff. The petroglyphs were exactly as she had stored them in her mind. The spiral that might represent the *sipapu* from which humans had emerged from the womb of Mother Earth, the line of dots that might represent the clan's migrations, the wide-shouldered forms that the ethnographers believed represented kachina spirits. There, too, cut through the dark desert varnish into the face of the cliff, was the shape Eddie had called Big Chief looking out from behind a red-stained shield, and a figure that seemed to have a man's body but the feet and head of a heron. It was one of her two favorites, because it seemed so totally unexplainable even by the cultural anthropologists—who could explain anything. The other was another version of Kokopelli.

Wherever you found him—and you found him everywhere these vanished people carved, and painted, their spirits into the cliffs of the Southwest—Kokopelli looked about the same. His humpbacked figure was supported by stick legs. Stick arms held a straight line to his tiny round head, making him seem to be playing a clarinet. The flute might be pointed down, or ahead. Otherwise there was little variation in how he was depicted. Except here. Here Kokopelli was lying on his back, flute pointed skyward. "At last," Eddie had said. "You have found Kokopelli's home. This is where he sleeps."

But Eleanor Friedman-Bernal hardly glanced at Kokopelli now. The Chicken Condo was just around the corner. That was what had drawn her.

The first things her eyes picked up when the beam of her flash lit the total darkness of the alcove were flecks of white where nothing white should be. She let the flash roam over the broken walls, reflect from the black surface of the seep-fed pool below them. Then she moved the beam back to that incongruous reflection. It was exactly what she had feared.

Bones. Bones scattered everywhere.

"Oh, shit!" said Eleanor Friedman-Bernal, who almost never used expletives. "Shit! Shit! Shit!"

Someone had been digging. Someone had been looting. A pot hunter. A Thief of Time. Someone had gotten here first.

She focused on the nearest white. A human shoulder bone. A child's. It lay atop a pile of loose earth just outside a place where the wall had fallen. The excavation was in the hump of earth that had been this community's trash heap. The common place for burials, and the first place experienced pot hunters dug. But the hole here was small. She felt better. Perhaps not much damage had been done. The digging looked fresh. Perhaps what she was hunting would still be here. She explored with the flash, looking for other signs of digging. She found none.

Nor was there any sign of looting elsewhere. She shined the light into the single hole dug in the midden pile. It reflected off stones, a scattering of potsherds mixed with earth and what seemed to be more human bones—part of a foot, she thought, and a vertebra. Beside the pit, on a slab of sandstone, four lower jaws had been placed in a neat row—three adult, one not much beyond infancy. She frowned at the arrangement, raised her eyebrows. Considered. Looked around her again. It hadn't rained—at least no rain had blown into this sheltered place—since this digging had been done. But then when had it rained? Not for weeks at Chaco. But Chaco was almost two hundred miles east and south.

The night was still. Behind her, she heard the odd piping of the little frogs that seemed to thrive in this canyon wherever water collected. Leopard frogs, Eddie had called them. And she heard the whistle again. The night bird. Closer now. A half-dozen notes. She frowned. A bird? What else could it be? She had seen at least three kinds of lizards on her way from the river—a whiptail, and a big collared lizard, and another she couldn't identify. They were nocturnal. Did they make some sort of mating whistle?

At the pool, her flashlight reflected scores of tiny points of light—the eyes of frogs. She stood watching them as they hopped, panicked by her huge presence, toward the safety of the black water. Then she frowned. Something was strange.

Not six feet from where she stood, one of them had fallen back in midhop. Then she noticed another one, a half-dozen others. She squatted on her heels beside the frog, inspecting it. And then another, and another, and another.

They were tethered. A whitish thread—perhaps a yucca fiber—had been tied around a back leg of each of these tiny black-green frogs and then to a twig stuck into the damp earth.

Eleanor Friedman-Bernal leaped to her feet, flashed the light frantically around the pool. Now she could see the scores of panicked frogs making those odd leaps that ended when a tether jerked them back to earth. For seconds her mind struggled to process this crazy, unnatural, irrational information. Who would . . . ? It would have to be a human act. It could have no sane purpose. When? How long could these frogs live just out of reach of the saving water? It was insane.

Just then she heard the whistle again. Just behind her. Not a night bird. No sort of reptile. It was a melody the Beatles had made popular. "Hey, Jude," the words began. But Eleanor didn't recognize it. She was too terrified by the humped shape that was coming out of the moonlight into this pool of darkness.

2

ELEANOR FRIEDMAN HYPHEN Bernal." Thatcher spaced the words, pronouncing them evenly. "I'm uneasy about women who hyphenate their names."

Lieutenant Joe Leaphorn didn't respond. Had he ever met a hyphenated woman? Not that he could remember. But the custom seemed sensible to him. Not as odd as Thatcher's discomfort with it. Leaphorn's mother, Leaphorn's aunts, all of the women he could think of among his maternal Red Forehead clan, would have resisted the idea of submerging their name or family identity in that of a husband. Leaphorn considered mentioning that, and didn't feel up to it. He'd been tired when Thatcher had picked him up at Navajo Tribal Police headquarters. Now he had added approximately 120 miles of driving to that fatigue. From Window Rock through Yah-Ta-Hey, to Crownpoint, to those final twenty jarring dirt miles to the Chaco Culture National Historical Park. Leaphorn's inclination had been to turn down the invitation to come along. But Thatcher had asked him as a favor.

"First job as a cop since they trained me," Thatcher had said. "May need some advice." It wasn't that, of course. Thatcher was a confident man and Leaphorn understood why Thatcher had called him. It was the kindness of an old friend who wanted to help. And the alternative to going would be to sit on the bed in the silent room and finish sorting through what was left of Emma's things—deciding what to do with them.

"Sure," Leaphorn had said. "Be a nice ride."

Now they were in the Chaco visitors' center, sitting on the hard chairs, waiting for the right person to talk to. From the bulletin board, a face stared out at them through dark sunglasses. A THIEF OF TIME, the legend above it said. POT HUNTERS DESTROY AMERICA'S PAST.

"Appropriate," Thatcher said, nodding toward the poster, "but the picture should be a crowd scene. Cowboys, and county commissioners, and schoolteachers and pipeline workers, and everybody big enough to handle a shovel." He glanced at Leaphorn, looking for a response, and sighed.

"That road," he said. "I've been driving it thirty years now and it never gets any better." He glanced at Leaphorn again.

"Yeah," Leaphorn said. Thatcher had called them ceramic chugholes. "Never gets wet enough to soften 'em up," he'd said. "Rains, the bumps just get greasy." Not quite true. Leaphorn remembered a night a lifetime ago when he was young, a patrolman working out of the Crownpoint subagency. Melting snow had made the Chaco chugholes wet enough to soften the ceramic. His patrol car had sunk into the sucking, bottomless caliche mud. He'd radioed Crownpoint but the dispatcher had no help to send him. So he'd walked two hours to the R.D. Ranch headquarters. He'd been a newlywed then, worried that Emma would be worried about him. A hand at the ranch had put chains on a four-wheel-drive pickup and pulled him out. Nothing had changed since then. Except the roads were a lifetime older. Except Emma was dead.

Thatcher had said something else. He had been looking at him, expecting some response, when he should have been watching the ruts.

Leaphorn had nodded.

"You weren't listening. I asked you why you decided to quit."

Leaphorn had said nothing for a while. "Just tired."

Thatcher had shaken his head. "You're going to miss it."

"No, you get older. Or wiser. You realize it doesn't really make any difference."

"Emma was a wonderful woman," Thatcher had told him. "This won't bring her back."

"No, it won't."

"She were alive, she'd say: 'Joe, don't quit.' She'd say, 'You can't quit living.' I've heard her say things just like that."

"Probably," Leaphorn had said. "But I just don't want to do it anymore."

"Okay," Thatcher drove awhile. "Change the subject. I think women who have hyphenated names like that are going to be rich. Old-money rich. Hard to work with. Stereotyping, but it's the way my mind works."

Then Leaphorn had been saved from thinking of something to say to that by an unusually jarring chughole. Now he was saved from thinking about it again. A medium-sized man wearing a neatly pressed U.S. Park Service uniform emerged from the doorway marked PERSONNEL ONLY. He walked into the field of slanting autumn sunlight streaming through the windows of the visitors' center. He looked at them curiously.

"I'm Bob Luna," he said. "This is about Ellie?"

Thatcher extracted a leather folder from his jacket and showed Luna a Bureau of Land Management law enforcement badge. "L. D. Thatcher," he said. "And this is Lieutenant Leaphorn. Navajo Tribal Police. Need to talk to Ms. Friedman-Bernal." He pulled an envelope from his jacket pocket. "Have a search warrant here to take a look at her place."

Luna's expression was puzzled. At first glance he had looked surprisingly young to Leaphorn to be superintendent of such an important park—his round, good-humored face would be perpetually boyish. Now, in the sunlight, the networks of lines around his eyes and at the corners of his mouth were visible. The sun and aridity of the Colorado Plateau acts quickly on the skin of whites, but it takes time to deepen the furrows. Luna was older than he looked.

"Talk to her?" Luna said. "You mean she's here? She's come back?"

Now it was Thatcher's turn to be surprised. "Doesn't she work here?"

"But she's missing," Luna said. "Isn't that what you're here about? We reported it a week ago. More like two weeks."

"Missing?" Thatcher said. "Whadaya mean missing?"

Luna's face had become slightly flushed. He opened his mouth. Closed it. Inhaled. Young as he looked, Luna was superintendent of this park, which meant he had a lot of experience being patient with people.

"Week ago last Wednesday. . . . That would be twelve days ago, we called in and reported Ellie missing. She was supposed to be back the previous Monday. She hadn't showed up. Hadn't called. She'd gone into Farmington for the weekend. She had an appointment Monday evening, back out here, and hadn't showed up for that. Had another appointment Wednesday. Hadn't been here for that, either. Totally out of character. Something must have happened to her and that's what we reported."

"She's not here?" Thatcher said. He tapped the envelope with the search warrant in it against the palm of his hand.

"Who'd you call?" Leaphorn asked, surprised at himself even as he heard himself asking the question. This was none of his business. It was nothing he cared about. He was here only because Thatcher had wanted him to come. Had wheedled until it was easier, if you didn't care anyway, to come than not to come. He hadn't intended to butt in. But this floundering around was irritating.

"The sheriff," Luna said.

"Which one?" Leaphorn asked. Part of the park was in McKinley County, part in San Juan.

"San Juan County," Luna said. "At Farmington. Anyway, nobody came out. So we called again last Friday. When you showed up, I thought you'd come out to start looking into it."

"I guess we are now," Leaphorn said. "More or less."

"We have a complaint about her," Thatcher said. "Or rather an allegation. But very detailed, very specific. About violations of the Antiquities Preservation Protection Act."

"Dr. Friedman?" Luna said. "Dr. Friedman a pot hunter?" He grinned. The grin almost became a chuckle, but Luna suppressed it. "I think we better go see Maxie Davis," he said.

Luna did the talking as he drove them up the road along Chaco Wash. Thatcher sat beside him, apparently listening. Leaphorn looked out the window, at the late afternoon light on the broken sandstone surface of the Chaco cliffs, at the gray-silver tufts of grama grass on the talus slope, at the long shadow of Fajada Butte stretching across the valley. What will I do tonight, when I am back in Window Rock? What will I do tomorrow? What will I do when this winter has come? And when it has gone? What will I ever do again?

Maxie is Eleanor Friedman's neighbor, Luna was saying. Next apartment in the housing units for temporary personnel. And both were part of the contract archaeology team. Helping decide which of the more than a thousand Anasazi sites in Luna's jurisdiction were significant, dating them roughly, completing an inventory, deciding which should be preserved for exploration in the distant future when scientists had new methods to see through time.

"And they're friends," Luna said. "They go way back. Went to school together. Work together now. All that. It was Maxie who called the sheriff." Today Maxie Davis was working at BC129, which was the cataloging number assigned to an unexcavated Anasazi site. Unfortunately, Luna said, BC129 was on the wrong side of Chaco Mesa—over by Escavada Wash at the end of a very rocky road.

"BC129?" Thatcher asked.

"BC129," Luna repeated. "Just a tag to keep track of it. Too many places out here to dream up names for them."

BC129 was near the rim of the mesa, a low mound that overlooked the Chaco Valley. A woman, her short dark hair tucked under a cap, stood waist-deep in a trench watching. Luna parked his van beside an old green pickup. Even at this distance Leaphorn could see the woman was beautiful. It was not just the beauty of youth and health, it was something unique and remarkable. Leaphorn had seen such beauty in Emma, nineteen then, and walking across the campus at Arizona State University. It was rare and valuable. A young Navajo man, his face shaded by the broad brim of a black felt hat, was sitting on the remains of a wall behind the trench, a shovel across his lap. Thatcher and Luna climbed out of the front seat.

"I'll wait," Leaphorn said.

This was his new trouble. Lack of interest. It had been his trouble since his mind had reluctantly processed the information from Emma's doctor.

"There's no good way to tell this, Mr. Leaphorn," the voice had said. "We lost her. Just now. It was a blood clot. Too much infection. Too much strain. But if it's any consolation, it must have been almost instantaneous."

He could see the man's face—pink-white skin, bushy blond eyebrows, blue eyes reflecting the cold light of the surgical waiting room through the lenses of horn-rimmed glasses, the small, prim mouth speaking to him. He could still hear the words, loud over the hum of the hospital air conditioner. It was like a remembered nightmare. Vivid. But he could not remember getting into his car in the parking lot, or driving through Gallup to

Shiprock, or any of the rest of that day. He could remember only reviving his thoughts of the days before the operation. Emma's tumor would be removed. His joy that she was not being destroyed, as he had dreaded for so long, by the terrible, incurable, inevitable Alzheimer's disease. It was just a tumor. Probably not malignant. Easily curable. Emma would soon be herself again, memory restored. Happy. Healthy. Beautiful.

"The chances?" the surgeon had said. "Very good. Better than ninety percent complete recovery. Unless something goes wrong, an excellent prognosis."

But something had gone wrong. The tumor and its placement were worse than expected. The operation had taken much longer than expected. Then infection, and the fatal clot.

Since then, nothing had interested him. Someday, he would come alive again. Or perhaps he would. So far he hadn't. He sat sideways, legs stretched, back against the door, watching. Thatcher and Luna talked to the white woman in the trench. Unusual name for a woman. Maxie. Probably short for something Leaphorn couldn't think of. The Navajo was putting on a denim jacket, looking interested in whatever was being said, the expression on his long-jawed face sardonic. Maxie was gesturing, her face animated. She climbed out of the trench, walked toward the pickup truck with the Navajo following, his shovel over his shoulder in a sort of military parody. In the deep shadow of the hat brim Leaphorn saw white teeth. The man was grinning. Beyond him, the slanting light of the autumn afternoon outlined the contours of the Chaco Plateau with lines of darkness. The shadow of Fajada Butte stretched all the way across Chaco Wash now. Outside the shadow, the yellow of the cottonwood along the dry streambed glittered in the sun. They were the only trees in a tan-gray-silver universe of grass. (Where had they found their firewood, Leaphorn wondered, the vanished thousands of Old Ones who built these huge stone apartments? The anthropologists thought they'd carried the roof beams fifty miles on their shoulders from forests on Mount Taylor and the Chuskas—an incredible feat. But how did they boil their corn, roast venison, cure their pottery, and warm themselves in winter? Leaphorn remembered the hard labor each fall—his father and he taking their wagon into the foothills, cutting dead piñon and juniper, making the long haul back to their hogan. But the Anasazi had no horses, no wheels.)

Thatcher and Luna were back at the van now. Thatcher slammed the door on his coat, said something under his breath, reopened it and closed it again. When Luna started the engine the seat belt warning buzzed. "Seat belt," Thatcher said.

Luna fastened the seat belt. "Hate these things," he said.

The green pickup pulled ahead of them, raising dust.

"We're going down to look at what's-her-name's stuff," Thatcher said, raising his voice for Leaphorn. "This Ms. Davis doesn't think hyphenated could be a pot hunter. Said she collected pots, but it was for her work. Scientific. Legitimate. Said Ms. . . . Ms. Bernal hated pot hunters."

"Um," Leaphorn said. He could see the big reservation hat of the young man through the back window of the pickup ahead. Odd to see a Navajo digging in the ruins. Stirring up Anasazi ghosts. Probably someone on the Jesus Road, or into the Peyote Church. Certainly a traditional man wouldn't be risking ghost sickness—or even worse, the reputation of being a witch—by digging among the bones. If you believed in the skinwalker traditions, bones of the dead made the tiny missiles that the witches shot into their victims. Leaphorn was not a believer. Those who were were the bane of his police work.

"She thinks something happened to Ms. Bernal," Thatcher said, glancing in the rearview mirror at Leaphorn. "You ought to have that seat belt on."

"Yeah," Leaphorn said. He fumbled it around him, thinking that probably nothing had happened to the woman. He thought of the anonymous call that had provoked this trip. There would be a connection, somewhere. One thing somehow would link Dr. What's-Her-Name's departure from Chaco with the motive for the call. The departure had led to the call, or something had happened that provoked both.

"What do you think?" he would have asked Emma. "Woman takes off for Farmington and drops off the world. Two days later somebody nasty turns her in for stealing pots. It could be she'd done something to make him sore, and knew he'd find out about it and turn her in. So she took off. Or she went to Farmington, made him sore there, and took off. So what you think?"

And Emma would have asked him three or four questions, and found out how little he knew about the woman, or about anything else to do with this, and then she would have smiled at him and used one of those dusty aphorisms from her Bitter Water Clan.

"Only yearling coyotes think there's just one way to catch a rabbit," she'd say. And then she'd say, "About next Tuesday the woman will call and tell her friends she ran away and got married, and it won't have anything to do with stealing pots." Maybe Emma would be right and maybe she'd be wrong, and that didn't really matter. It was a game they had played for years. Emma's astute mind working against his own intelligence, honing his thinking, testing his logic against her common sense. It helped him. She enjoyed it. It was fun.

Had been fun.

Leaphorn noticed it immediately—the cold, stagnant air of abandoned places. He was standing beside Thatcher when Thatcher unlocked the door to the apartment of Dr. Friedman-Bernal and pushed it open. The trapped air flowed outward into Leaphorn's sensitive nostrils. He sensed dust in it, and all that mixture of smells which humans leave behind them when they go away.

The Park Service calls such apartments TPH, temporary personnel housing. At Chaco, six of them were built into an L-shaped frame structure on a concrete slab—part of a complex that included maintenance and storage buildings, the motor pool, and the permanent personnel housing: a line of eight frame bungalows backed against the low cliff of Chaco Mesa.

"Well," Thatcher said. He walked into the apartment with Maxie Davis a step behind him. Leaphorn leaned against the door. Thatcher stopped. "Ms. Davis," he said, "I'm going to ask you to wait outside for a while. Under this search warrant here . . . well, it makes everything different. I may have to take an oath on what was in here when I opened the door." He smiled at her. "Things like that."

"I'll wait," Maxie Davis said. She walked past Leaphorn, smiling at him nervously, and sat on the porch railing in the slanting sunlight. Her face was somber. Again, Leaphorn noticed her striking beauty. She was a small young woman. Cap off now, her dark hair needed combing. Her oval face had been burned almost as dark as Leaphorn's. She stared toward the maintenance yard, where a man in coveralls was doing something to the front end of a flatbed truck. Her fingers tapped at the railing—small, battered fingers on a small, scarred hand. Her blue work shirt draped against her back. Under it, every line of her body was tense. Beyond her, the weedy yard, the maintenance shed, the tumbled boulders along the cliff, seemed almost luminous in the brilliant late-afternoon sunlight. It made the gloom inside Dr. Friedman-Bernal's apartment behind Leaphorn seem even more shadowy than it was.

Thatcher walked through the living room, pulled open the drapes and exposed sliding-glass doors. They framed Fajada Butte and the expanse of the Chaco Valley. Except for a stack of books on the coffee table in front of the bleak brown institutional sofa, the room looked unused. Thatcher picked up the top book, examined it, put it down, and walked into the bedroom. He stood just inside the doorway, shaking his head.

"It would help some," he said, "if you knew what the hell you're looking for."

The room held a desk, two chairs, and two double beds. One seemed to be for sleeping—the covers carelessly pulled back in place after its last use. The other was work space—covered now with three cardboard boxes and a litter of notebooks, computer printouts, and other papers. Beyond this bed other boxes lined the floor along the wall. They seemed to hold mostly broken bits of pottery. "No way on God's green earth of telling where she got any of this stuff," Thatcher said. "Not that I know of. It might be perfectly legal."

"Unless her field notes tell us something," Leaphorn said. "They might. In fact, if she collected that stuff as part of some project or other, they should tell exactly where she picked up every bit of that stuff. And it's going to be legal unless she's been selling the artifacts."

"And of course if she's doing it for a project, it's legal," Thatcher said. "Unless she doesn't have the right permit. And if she's selling the stuff, she sure as hell ain't going to write down anything incriminating."

"Nope," Leaphorn said.

A man appeared at the apartment door. "Finding anything?" he asked. He walked past Leaphorn without a glance and into the bedroom. "Glad to see you people getting interested in this," he said. "Ellie's been missing almost three weeks now."

Thatcher put a fragment of pot carefully back into its box. "Who are you?" he asked.

"My name's Elliot," he said. "I work with Ellie on the Keet Katl dig. Or did work with her. What's this Luna's been telling me? You think she's stealing artifacts?"

Leaphorn found himself interested—wondering how Thatcher would deal with this. It wasn't the sort of thing anticipated and covered in the law enforcement training Thatcher would have received. No chapter covering intrusion of civilian into scene of investigation.

"Mr. Elliot," Thatcher said, "I want you to wait outside on the porch until we get finished in here. Then I want to talk to you."

Elliot laughed. "For God's sake," he said, in a tone that canceled any misunderstanding the laugh might have caused. "A woman vanishes for almost a month and nobody can get you guys off your butts. But somebody calls in with an anonymous . . ."

"Talk to you in a minute," Thatcher said. "Soon as I'm done in here."

"Done what?" Elliot said. "Done stirring through her potsherds? If you get 'em out of order, get 'em mixed up, it will screw up everything for her."

"Out," Thatcher said, voice still mild.

Elliot stared at him.

Maybe middle thirties or a little older, Leaphorn thought. A couple of inches over six feet, slender, athletic. The sun had bleached his hair even lighter than its usual very light brown. His jeans were worn and so were his jean jacket and his boots. But they fit. They had been expensive. And the face fit the pattern—a little weather-beaten but what Emma would have called "an upper-class face." A little narrow, large blue eyes, nothing crooked, nothing bent, nothing scarred. Not the face you'd see looking out of a truckload of migrant workers, or in a roofing crew, or the cab of a road grader.

"Of course this place is full of pots." Elliot's voice was angry. "Studying pots is Ellie's job. . . ."

Thatcher gripped Elliot at the elbow. "Talk to you later," he said mildly, and moved him past Leaphorn and out the door. He closed the door behind him.

"Trouble is," Thatcher said, "everything he says is true. Her business is pots. So she'll have a bunch of 'em here. So what the hell are we looking for?"

Leaphorn shrugged. "I think we just look," he said. "We find what we find. Then we think about it."

They found more boxes of potsherds in the closet, each shard bearing a label that seemed to identify it with the place it had been found. They found an album of photographs, many of them snapshots of people who seemed to be anthropologists working at digs. There were three notebooks—two filled and one almost half filled—in which little pencil drawings of abstract patterns and pots were interposed with carbon rubbings of what they agreed must be the surface patterns of potsherds. The notes that surrounded these were in the special shorthand scientists develop to save themselves time.

"You studied this stuff at Arizona State," Thatcher said. "Can't you make it out?"

"I studied anthropology," Leaphorn admitted. "But mostly I studied cultural anthropology. This is a specialty and I didn't get into it. We went on a few digs in a Southwestern Anthro class, but the Anasazi culture wasn't my thing. Neither were ceramics."

Among the papers on the bed were two Nelson's catalogs, both auctions of American Indian art, African art, and Oceanic art. Both facedown, both open to pages that featured illustrations of Mimbres, Hohokam, and Anasazi pots. Leaphorn studied them. The appraised prices ranged from $2,950 to $41,500 for a Mimbres urn. Two of the Anasazi ceramics had been circled in red in one catalog, and one in the other. The prices were $4,200, $3,700, and $14,500.

"Heard of Nelson's all my life," Thatcher said. "Thought they were just a London outfit. Just auctioned art, masterpieces, the *Mona Lisa*, things like that."

"This is art," Leaphorn said.

"A painting is art," Thatcher said. "What kind of nut pays fourteen grand for a pot?" He tossed the catalog back on the bed.

Leaphorn picked it up.

The cover picture was a stylized re-creation of a pictograph—stick-figure Indians with lances riding horses with pipestem legs across a deerskin surface.

Across the top the legend read:

NELSON'S

FOUNDED 1744

Fine American Indian Art

New York

Auction May 25 and 26

It opened easily to the pottery pages. Ten photographs of pots, each numbered and described in a numbered caption. Number 242 was circled in red. Leaphorn read the caption:

> 242. Anasazi St. John's Polychrome bowl, circa A.D. 1000–1250, of deep rounded form, painted on the interior in rose with wavy pale "ghost lines." Has a geometric pattern enclosing two interlocked spirals. Two hatched, serrated rectangles below the rim. Interior surface serrated. Diameter 7¼ inches (19 cm). $4,000/$4,200.
>
> Resale offer by an anonymous collector.
>
> Documentation.

Inside the scrawled red circle, the same pen had put a question mark over "anonymous collector" and scribbled notations in the margin. What looked like a telephone number. Words that seemed to be names. "Call Q!" "See Houk." Houk. The name made a faint echo in Leaphorn's mind. He'd known someone named Houk. The only notation that meant anything to him was: "Nakai, Slick." Leaphorn knew about Slick Nakai. Had met him a time or two. Nakai was a preacher. A fundamentalist Christian evangelist. He pulled a revival tent around the reservation in a trailer behind an old Cadillac sedan, putting it up here and there exhorting those who came to hear him to quit drinking, leave off fornication, confess their sins, abandon their pagan ways, and come to Jesus. Leaphorn scanned the other names, looking for anything familiar, read the description of a Tonto Polychrome olla valued at $1,400/$1,800. On the next page, a Mimbres black-on-white burial pot, with a "kill hole" in its bottom and its exterior featuring lizards chasing lizards, was advertised for $38,600. Leaphorn grimaced and put down the catalog.

"I'm going to make a sort of rough inventory," Thatcher said, sorting through one of the boxes. "Just jot down some idea of what we have here, which we both know is absolutely nothing that is going to be of any use to us."

Leaphorn sat in the swivel chair and looked at the 365-day calendar on the desk. It was turned to October 11. "What day was it they said Dr. Hyphenated left here? Wasn't it the thirteenth?"

"Yeah," Thatcher said.

Leaphorn flipped over a page to October 13. "Do it!" was written under the date. He turned the next page. Across this was written: "Away." The next page held two notes: "Be ready for Lehman. See H. Houk."

H. Houk. Would it be Harrison Houk? Maybe. An unusual name, and the man fit the circumstances. Houk would be into everything and the Houk ranch—outside of Bluff and just over the San Juan River from the north side of the reservation—was in the heart of Anasazi ruins country.

The next page was October 16. It was blank. So was the next page. That took him to Wednesday. Across this was written: "Lehman!!! about 4 P.M. dinner. sauerbraten, etc."

Leaphorn thumbed through the pages up to the present. So far Dr. Friedman-Bernal had missed two other appointments. She would miss another one next week. Unless she came home.

He put down the calendar, walked into the kitchen, and opened the refrigerator, remembering how Emma liked to make sauerbraten. "It's way too much work," he would say, which was better than telling her that he really didn't like it very well. And Emma would say: "No more work than Navajo tacos, and less cholesterol."

The smell of soured milk and stale food filled his nostrils. The worse smell came from a transparent ovenware container on the top shelf. It held a Ziploc bag containing what seemed to be a large piece of meat soaking in a reddish brown liquid. Sauerbraten. Leaphorn grimaced, shut the door, and walked back into the room where Thatcher was completing his inventory.

The sun was on the horizon now, blazing through the window and casting Thatcher's shadow black against the wallpaper. Leaphorn imagined Eleanor Friedman-Bernal hurrying through the sauerbraten process, getting all those things now shriveled and spoiled lined up on the refrigerator shelves so that fixing dinner for Lehman could be quickly done. But she hadn't come back to fix that dinner. Why not? Had she gone to see Harrison Houk about a pot? Leaphorn found himself remembering the first, and only, time he'd encountered the man. Years ago. He'd been what? Officer Leaphorn working out of the Kayenta substation, obliquely involved in helping the FBI with the manhunt across San Juan.

The Houk killings, they had called them. Leaphorn, who forgot little, remembered the names. Della Houk, the mother. Elmore Houk, the brother. Dessie Houk, the sister. Brigham Houk, the killer. Harrison Houk, the father. Harrison Houk had been the survivor. The mourner. Leaphorn remembered him standing on the porch of a stone house, listening intently while the sheriff talked, remembered him climbing up from the river, staggering with fatigue, when it was no longer light enough to search along the bank for Brigham Houk. Or, almost certainly even then, Brigham Houk's drowned body.

Would it be this same H. Houk now whom Eleanor Friedman-Bernal had noted on her calendar? Was Harrison Houk some part of the reason for the uneaten banquet spoiling in the refrigerator? To his surprise Joe Leaphorn found his curiosity had returned. What had prevented Eleanor Friedman-Bernal from coming home for her party with a guest whose name deserved three exclamation points? What caused her to miss a dinner she'd worked so hard to prepare?

Leaphorn walked back into the closet and recovered the album. He flipped through it. Which one was Eleanor Friedman-Bernal? He found a page of what must have been wedding pictures—bride and groom with another young couple. He slipped one of them out of the corners that held it. The bride was radiant, the groom a good-looking Mexican, his expression slightly stunned. The bride's face long, prominent bones, intelligent, Jewish. A good woman, Leaphorn thought. Emma would have liked her. He had two weeks left on his terminal leave. He'd see if he could find her.

3

IT HAD BEEN a bad day for Officer Jim Chee of the Navajo Tribal Police. In fact, it had been the very worst day of an abysmal week.

It had started going bad sometime Monday. Over the weekend it had dawned upon some dimwit out at the Navajo Tribal Motor Pool that a flatbed trailer was missing. Apparently it had been missing for a considerable time. Sunday night it was reported stolen.

"How long?" Captain Largo asked at Monday afternoon's briefing. "Tommy Zah don't know how long. Nobody knows how long. Nobody seems to remember seeing it since about a month ago. It came in for maintenance. Motor pool garage fixed a bad wheel bearing. Presumably it was then parked out in the lot. But it's not in the lot now. Therefore it has to be stolen. That's because it makes Zah look less stupid to declare it stolen. Better'n admitting he just don't know what the hell they did with it. So we're supposed to find it for 'em. After whoever took it had time to haul it about as far as Florida."

Looking back on it, looking for the reason all of what followed came down on him instead of some other officer on the evening shift, Chee could see it was because he had not been looking alert. The captain had spotted it. In fact, Chee had been guilty of gazing out of the assembly room window. The globe willows that shaded the parking lot of the Shiprock subagency of the Navajo Tribal Police were full of birds that afternoon. Chee had been watching them, deciding they were finches, thinking what he would say to Janet Pete when he saw her again. Suddenly he became aware that Largo had been talking to him.

"You see it out there in the parking lot?"

"Sir?"

"The goddam trailer," Largo said. "It out there?"

"No sir."

"You been paying enough attention to know what trailer we're talking about?"

"Motor pool trailer," Chee said, hoping Largo hadn't changed the subject.

"Wonderful," Largo said, glowering at Chee. "Now from what Superintendent Zah said on the telephone, we're going to get a memo on this today and the memo is going to say that they called our dispatcher way back sometime and reported pilfering out there at night and asked us to keep an eye on things. Long before they mislaid their trailer, you understand. That's to cover the superintendent's ass and make it our fault."

Largo exhaled a huge breath and looked at his audience—making sure his night shift understood what their commanding officer was dealing with here.

"Now, just about now," Largo continued, "they're starting to count all their stuff out there. Tools. Vehicles. Coke machines. God knows what. And sure as hell they're going to find other stuff missing. And not know when they lost it, and claim it got stolen five minutes ago. Or tomorrow if that's handier for 'em. Anyway, it will be at some time after—I repeat, after—we've been officially informed and asked to watch out for 'em. And then I'm going to be spending my weekends writing reports to send down to Window Rock." Largo paused. He looked at Chee.

"So, Chee . . ."

"Yes, sir." Chee was paying attention now. Too late.

"I want you to keep an eye on that place. Hang around there on your shift. Get past there every chance you get. And make chances. Call the dispatcher to keep it on record that you're watching. When they finish their inventory and find out they've lost other stuff, I don't want 'em in a position to blame us. Understand?"

Chee understood. Not that it helped.

That was Monday afternoon. Monday evening it got worse. Even worse than it might have been, because he didn't learn about it until Tuesday.

As instructed, Chee had been hanging close to the motor pool. He would coast out Highway 550 maybe as far as the Hogback formation, which marked the eastern edge of the Big Reservation. Then he would drift back past the motor pool fence and into Shiprock. Stopping now and then to check the gate. Noticing that the summer's accumulation of tumbleweeds piled along the chain-link fence was undisturbed. Drifting down 550 again. Drifting back. Keeping Farmington-Shiprock traffic holding nervously in the vicinity of the speed limit. Boring himself into sleepiness. Calling in now and then to have the dispatcher record that he was diligently watching the motor pool and that all there remained serene.

"Unit Eleven checking at the motor pool," Chee called. "All quiet. No sign of entry."

"Since you're there on five-fifty," the dispatcher said, "see what's going on at the Seven-Eleven. Just had a disturbance call."

Chee had done a quick U-turn, boredom replaced by the uneasiness that always preceded the probability of dealing with a drunk. Or two drunks. Or however many drunks it was taking to disturb the peace at the Shiprock 7-Eleven.

But the parking space in front of the convenience store had been quiet—empty except for an old Dodge sedan and a pickup truck. No drunks. Inside, no drunks either. The woman behind the cash register was reading one of those tabloids convenience stores sell. A green-ink headline proclaimed THE TRUTH ABOUT LIZ TAYLOR'S WEIGHT LOSS. Another declared SIAMESE TWINS BOTH PREGNANT. BLAME MINISTER. A teenaged boy was inspecting the canned soda pop in the cooler.

"What's the trouble?" Chee asked.

The teenager put down the Pepsi he'd selected, looking guilty. The cashier lowered her paper. She was a middle-aged Navajo woman. Towering House Clan, Chee remembered, named Gorman, or Relman, or something like that. Anglo-type name with six letters. Bunker. Walker. Thomas.

"What?" she asked.

"Somebody called in a disturbance here. What's the trouble?"

"Oh," the Towering House woman said. "We had a drunk in here. Where you been?"

"What'd he do? Any damages?"

"She," the woman said. "Old Lady George. She went away when she heard me calling the police."

The cashier's name was Gorman, Chee now remembered. But he was thinking of Old Lady George.

"Which way did she go?"

"Just went," Mrs. Gorman said. She gestured vaguely. "Didn't look. I was picking up the cans she knocked over."

So Chee had gone looking for Old Lady George. He knew her fairly well. She'd been a witness in an automobile theft case he'd worked on—a very helpful witness. Later, when he was looking for one of her grandsons on an assault warrant, she'd helped him again. Sent the boy down to the station to turn himself in. Besides, she was Streams Come Together Clan, which was linked to Chee's father's clan, which made her a relative. Chee had been raised knowing that you watch out for your relatives.

He had watched out for her, first up and down 550 and then up and down side streets. He found her sitting on a culvert, and talked her into the patrol car, and took her home and turned her over to a worried young woman who he guessed must be a granddaughter. Then he had gone back and established that the motor pool remained intact. At least it seemed to be intact as seen from the highway. But seen from the highway, it hadn't been possible to detect that someone had tinkered with the padlock securing the gate. He heard about that the next day when he reported for work.

Captain Largo's usually big voice was unusually quiet—an ominous sign.

"A backhoe," Largo said. "That's what they stole this time. About three tons. Bright yellow. Great big thing. I told Mr. Zah that I had one of my best men watching his place last night. Officer Jim Chee. I told Zah that it must be just another case of forgetting to put it down on the record when somebody borrowed it. You know what he said to me?"

"No, sir," Chee said. "But nobody stole that on my shift. I was driving back and forth past there the whole time."

"Really," Largo said. "How nice." He picked up a sheet from the shift squeal report from his desk. He didn't look at it. "I'm pleased to hear that.

Because you know what Zah said to me? He said"—Largo shifted his voice up the scale—" 'Oh, it was stolen last night all right. The guy that runs the service station across the street there told us about it.' " Largo's voice returned to normal. "This service station man stood there and watched 'em drive out with it."

"Oh," Chee said, thinking it must have been while he was at the 7-Eleven.

"This Zah is quite a comedian. He told me you'd think sneaking a big yellow backhoe out with one of my policemen watching would be like trying to sneak moonrise past a coyote."

Chee flushed. He had nothing to say to that. He had heard the simile before somewhere in another form. Hard as sneaking sunrise past a rooster, it had been. A moonrise without a coyote baying was equally impossible, and relating a coyote to Largo's police added a nicely oblique insult. You don't call a Navajo a coyote. The only thing worse is to accuse him of letting his kinfolks starve.

Largo handed Chee the squeal sheet. It confirmed what Zah had told Largo.

> Subject Delbert Tsosie informed Officer Shorty that while serving a customer at the Texaco station at approximately 10 P.M. he noticed a man removing the chain from the gate of the motor pool maintenance yard across Highway 550. He observed a truck towing a flatbed trailer drive through the gate into the yard. Subject Tsosie said that approximately fifteen minutes later he noticed the truck driving out the gate towing a machine which he described as probably a backhoe or some sort of trenching machine loaded on the trailer. He said he did not report this to police because he presumed tribal employees had come to get the equipment to deal with some sort of emergency.

"That must have been while I was looking for Old Lady George," Chee said. He explained, hurrying through the last stages because of Largo's expression.

"Get to work," Largo said, "and leave this alone. Sergeant Benally will be chasing the backhoe. Don't mess with it."

That was Tuesday morning and should have been the very bottom of the week. The pits. It would have been, perhaps, had not Chee driven past the Texaco station on 550 and seen Delbert Tsosie stacking tires. Benally was handling it, but Chee sometimes bought gasoline from Tsosie. No harm in stopping to talk.

"No," Tsosie said. "Didn't see either one of them well enough to recognize 'em. But you could see one was Dineh—tall, skinny Navajo. Had on a cowboy hat. I know a lot of 'em that works at the motor pool. They come over here and use the Coke machine and buy candy. Wasn't none I knew and I was thinking it was a funny time to be coming to work. But I thought they must have forgotten something and was coming for it. And when I saw the backhoe I figured some pipe broke somewhere. Emergency, you know." Tsosie shrugged.

"You didn't recognize anybody?"

"Bad light."

"Guy in the truck. You see him at all?"

"Not in the truck," Tsosie said. "The skinny Navajo was driving the truck. This guy was following in a sedan. Plymouth two-door. About a '70,'71 maybe. Dark blue but they was doing some bodywork on it. Had an off-color right front fender. Looked white or gray. Maybe primer coat. And lots of patches here and there, like they was getting ready to paint it."

"Driver not a Navajo?"

"Navajo driving the truck. *Belagana* driving the Plymouth. And the white guy, I just barely got a look at him. They all sort of look alike anyway. All I notice is freckles and sunburn."

"Big or little?"

Tsosie thought. "About average. Maybe sort of short and stocky."

"What color hair?"

"Had a cap on. Baseball cap. With a bill."

None of which would have mattered since Benally was handling it, and Tsosie had already told Benally all of this, and probably more. But Saturday morning Chee saw the Plymouth two-door.

It was dark blue, about a '70 model. When it passed him going in the other direction—Shiprock-bound on 550—he saw the mismatched front fender and the patches of primer paint on its doors and the baseball cap on the head of the white man driving it. Without a thought, Chee did a U-turn across the bumpy divider.

He was driving Janet Pete's car. Not exactly Janet Pete's car. Janet had put down earnest money on a Buick Riviera at Quality Pre-owned Cars in Farmington and had asked Chee to test-drive it for her. She had to go to Phoenix Friday and when she got back Monday she wanted to close the deal.

"I guess I've already decided," Janet had told him. "It has everything I need and only fourteen thousand miles on it and the price seems reasonable and he's giving me a thousand dollars on my old Datsun and that seems fair."

To Chee the thousand for the Datsun seemed enough more than fair to arouse suspicion. Janet's Datsun was a junker. But it was clear that Janet was not going to be receptive to discouraging words. She described the Buick as "absolutely beautiful." As she described it, the lawyer in Janet Pete fell away. The girl emerged through the delight and enthusiasm, and Janet Pete became absolutely beautiful herself.

"It has the prettiest blue plush upholstery. Lovely color. Dark blue outside with a real delicate pinstripe down the side, and the chrome is just right." She looked slightly guilty at this. "I don't usually like chrome," she said. "But this . . ." She performed a gesture with shoulder and face that depreciated this lapse from taste. ". . . But this . . . well, I just love it."

She paused, examining Chee and transforming herself from girl to lawyer. "I thought maybe you would check it out for me. You drive all the time and you know all about mechanical things. If you don't mind doing it, and there's something seriously wrong with the engine, or something like that, then I could . . ."

She had left the awful statement unfinished. And Chee had accepted the keys and said sure, he'd be glad to do it. Which wasn't exactly the case. If there was something seriously wrong with the engine, telling her about it wasn't going to make him popular with Janet Pete. And Chee wanted to be popular. He wondered about her. He wondered about a woman lawyer. To be more precise, he wondered if Janet Pete, or any woman, could fill the gap Mary Landon seemed to be leaving in his life.

That was Friday evening. Saturday morning he drove the Buick down to Bernie Tso's garage and put it on the rack. Bernie was not impressed.

"Fourteen thousand miles, my ass," Bernie said. "Look at the tread on those tires. And here." Bernie rattled the universal joint. "Arizona don't have a law about running back the odometer, but New Mexico does," he said. "And she got this junker over in New Mexico. I'd say they fudged the first number a little. Turned her back from forty-four thousand, or maybe seventy-four."

He finished his inspection of the running gear and lowered the hoist. "Steering's slack, too," he said. "Want me to pull the head and take a look there?"

"Maybe later," Chee said. "I'll take it out and see what I can find and then I'll let her decide if she wants to spend any money on it."

And so he had driven Janet Pete's blue Buick out Highway 550 toward Farmington, glumly noting its deficiencies. Slow response to the gas pedal. Probably easy to fix with an adjustment. Tendency to choke on acceleration. Also fixable. Tendency to steer to the right on braking. Suspension far too soft for Chee, who was conditioned to the cast-iron springing of police cars and pickup trucks. Maybe she liked soft suspension, but this one was also uneven—suggesting a bad shock absorber. And, as Bernie had mentioned, slack steering.

He was measuring this slack, swaying down the Farmington-bound lanes of 550, when he saw the Backhoe Bandit. And it was the slack steering, eventually, that did him in.

He noticed the off-color fender first. He noticed that the car approaching him, Shiprock-bound, was a blue Plymouth sedan of about 1970 vintage. As it passed, he registered the patches of gray-white primer paint on its door. He got only a glimpse of the profile of the driver—youngish, long blond hair emerging from under a dark billed cap.

Chee didn't give it a thought. He did a U-turn across the bumpy divider and followed the Plymouth.

He was wearing his off-duty work clothes—greasy jeans and a Coors T-shirt with a torn armpit. His pistol was locked securely in the table beside the cot in his trailer at Shiprock. No radio in the Buick, of course. And it was no chase car. He would simply tag along, determine where the Backhoe Bandit was going, take whatever opportunity presented itself. The Plymouth was in no particular hurry. It did a left turn off 550 on the access road to the village of Kirtland. It crossed the San Juan bridge, did another turn onto a dirt road, and made the long climb up the mesa toward the Navajo Mine and the Four Corners Power Plant. Chee had fallen a quarter-mile back, partly to avoid eating the Plymouth's dust and partly to avoid arousing suspicion. But by the time he reached the escarpment the Backhoe Bandit seemed to have sensed he was being followed. He did another turn onto a poorly graded dirt road across the sagebrush, driving much faster now and producing a rooster tail of dust. Chee followed, pushing the Buick, sending it bouncing and lurching over the humps, fighting the steering where the road was rutted. Through the dust he became belatedly aware the Plymouth had made another turn—a hard right. Chee braked, skidded, corrected the skid, collected the slack in the steering, and made the turn. He was a little late.

Oops! Right wheel onto the rocky track. Left wheel in the sagebrush. Chee bounced painfully against the Buick's blue plush roof, bounced again, saw through the dust the rocks he should have been avoiding, frantically spun the slack steering wheel, felt the impact, felt something go in the front end, and then simply slid along—his hat jammed low onto his forehead by its kiss with the ceiling.

Janet Pete's beautiful blue Buick slid sideways, plowing a sedan-sized gash through the sage. It stopped in a cloud of dirt. Chee climbed out.

It looked bad, but not as bad as it might have been. The left front wheel was horizontal, the tie-rod that held it broken. Not as bad as a broken axle. The rest of the damage was, to Chee's thinking, superficial. Just scrapes, dents, and scratches. Chee found the chrome strip that Janet Pete had so admired about fifteen yards back in the brush, peeled off by a limb. He laid it carefully on the backseat. The plume of dust produced by the Plymouth was receding over the rim of the mesa. Chee watched it, thinking about his immediate problem—getting a tow truck out here to haul in the Buick. Thinking about the five or six miles he would have to walk to get to a telephone, thinking about the seven or eight hundred dollars it was going to cost to patch up the damaged Buick. Thinking about such things was far more pleasant than considering his secondary problem, which was how to break the news to Janet Pete.

"Absolutely beautiful," Janet Pete had said. "I fell in love with it," she'd said. "Just what I'd always wanted." But he would think about that later. He was staring into the diminishing haze of dust, but his vision was turned inward—imprinting the Backhoe Bandit in his memory. The profile, the suggestion of pockmarks on the jaw, the hair, the cap. This had become a matter of pride. He would find the man again, sooner or later.

By midafternoon, with the Buick back at Bernie Tso's garage, it seemed it would be sooner. Tso knew the Plymouth. Had, in fact, once towed it in. And he knew a little about the Backhoe Bandit.

"Everything that goes around comes around," Chee said, happily. "Everything balances out."

"I wouldn't say that," Tso said. "What's it going to cost you to balance out this Buick?"

"I mean catching the son of a bitch," Chee said. "At least I'm going to be able to do that. Lay that on the captain's desk."

"Maybe your girlfriend can take it back to the dealer," Tso said. "Tell 'em she doesn't like the way that front wheel looks."

"She's not my girlfriend," Chee said. "She's a lawyer with DNA. Tribal legal services. I ran into her last summer." Chee described how he had picked up a man who came to be Janet Pete's client, and had tried to have him kept in the Farmington jail until he had a chance to talk to him, and how sore Pete had been about it.

"Tough as nails," Chee said. "Not my type. Not unless I kill somebody and need a lawyer."

"I don't see how you're going to catch him with what little I know about him," Tso said. "Not even his name. All I remember is he works out in the Blanco gas field the other side of Farmington. Or said he did."

"And that you pulled him in when he had transmission troubles. And he paid you with two hundred-dollar bills. And he told you when you got it fixed to leave it at Slick Nakai's revival tent."

"Well, yeah," Tso said.

"And he said you could leave the change with Slick 'cause he saw Slick pretty often."

And now it was Saturday night. Slick Nakai's True Gospel had long since left the place near the Hogback where Tso had gone to tow in the Plymouth. But it was easy enough to locate by asking around. Nakai had loaded his tent, and his portable electric organ, and his sound system into his four-wheel trailer and headed southeast. He had left behind fliers tacked to telephone poles and Scotch-taped to store windows announcing that all hungering for the Word of the Lord could find him between Nageezi and the Dzilith-Na-O-Dith-Hie School.

4

FULL DARKNESS CAME late on this dry autumn Saturday. The sun was far below the western horizon but a layer of high, thin cirrus clouds still received the slanting light and reflected it, red now, down upon the ocean of sagebrush north of Nageezi Trading Post. It tinted the patched canvas of Slick Nakai's revival tent from faded tan to a doubtful rose and the complexion of Lieutenant Joe Leaphorn from dark brown to dark red.

From a lifetime of habit, Leaphorn had parked his pickup a little away from the cluster of vehicles at the tent and with its nose pointing outward, ready for whatever circumstances and duty might require of it. But Leaphorn was not on duty. He would never be on duty again. He was in the last two weeks of a thirty-day "terminal leave." When it ended, his application to retire from the Navajo Tribal Police would be automatically accepted. In fact he was already retired. He felt retired. He felt as if it were all far, far behind him. Faded in the distance. Another life in another world, nothing to do with the man now standing under this red October sunset, waiting for the sounds coming from the True Gospel revival tent to signal a break in the preaching.

He had come to Slick Nakai's revival to begin his hunt. Where had that hyphenated woman gone? Why had she abandoned a meal so carefully prepared, an evening so obviously anticipated? It didn't matter, and yet it did. In a way he couldn't really understand, it would say good-by to Emma. She would have prepared such a meal in anticipation of a treasured guest. Often had done so. Leaphorn couldn't explain it, but his mind made a sort of nebulous connection between Emma's character and that of a woman who probably was quite different. And so he would use the final days of his final leave to find that woman. That had brought him here. That, and boredom, and his old problem of curiosity, and the need for a reason to get away from their house in Window Rock and all its memories.

Whatever had moved him, he was here, on the very eastern fringe of the Navajo Reservation—more than a hundred miles from home. When circumstances allowed, he would talk to a man whose very existence annoyed him. He would ask questions the man might not answer and which might mean nothing if he did. The alternative was sitting in their living room, the television on for background noise, trying to read. But Emma's absence always intruded. When he raised his eyes, he saw the R. C. Gorman print she'd hung over the fireplace. They'd argued about it. She liked it, he didn't. The words would sound in his ears again. And Emma's laughter. It was the same everywhere he looked. He should sell that house, or burn it. It was in the tradition of the Dineh. Abandon the house contaminated by the dead, lest the ghost sickness infect you, and you died. Wise were the elders of his people, and the Holy People who taught them the Navajo Way. But instead, he would play this pointless game. He would find a woman. If alive, she wouldn't want to be found. If dead, it wouldn't matter.

Abruptly, it became slightly more interesting. He had been leaning on the door of his pickup, studying the tent, listening to the sounds coming from it, examining the grounds (another matter of habit). He recognized a pickup, parked like his own behind the cluster of vehicles. It was the truck of another tribal policeman. Jim Chee's truck. Chee's private truck, which meant Chee was also here unofficially. Becoming a born-again Christian? That hardly seemed likely. As Leaphorn remembered it, Chee was the antithesis of Slick Nakai. Chee was a *hatathali*. A singer. Or would be one as soon as people started hiring him to conduct their curing ceremonials. Leaphorn looked at the pickup, curious. Was someone sitting in it? Hard to tell in the failing light. What would Chee be doing here?

The sound of music came from the tent. A surprising amount of music, as if a band were playing. Over that an amplified male voice leading a hymn. Time to go in.

The band proved to be two men. Slick Nakai, standing behind what seemed to be a black plastic keyboard, and a thin guitarist in a blue checked shirt and a gray felt hat. Nakai was singing, his mouth a quarter-inch from a stand-mounted microphone, his hands maintaining a heavy rhythm on the keyboard. The audience sang with him, with much swaying and clapping of hands.

"Jesus loves us," Nakai sang. "That we know. Jesus loves us. Everywhere."

Nakai's eyes were on him, examining him, sorting him out. The guitarist was looking at him, too. The hat looked familiar. So did the man. Leaphorn had a good memory for faces, and for just about everything else.

"We didn't earn it," Nakai sang. "But He don't care. His love is with us. Everywhere."

Nakai emphasized this with a flourish at the keyboard, shifting his attention now from Leaphorn to an elderly woman wearing wire-rimmed glasses who was sway-dancing, eyes closed, too caught up with emotion to be aware she had danced into the tangle of electrical cables linking Nakai's sound system to a generator outside the tent. A tall man with a thin mustache standing by the speaker's podium noticed Nakai's concern. He moved quickly, steering the woman clear of the cables. Third member of the team, Leaphorn guessed.

When the music stopped, Nakai introduced him as "Reverend Tafoya."

"He's Apache. I tell you that right out," Nakai said. "Jicarilla. But that's all right. God made the Apaches, and the *belagana*, and the blacks, and the Hopis, and us Dineh and everybody else just the same. And he inspired this Apache here to learn about Jesus. And he's going to tell you about that."

Nakai surrendered the microphone to Tafoya. Then he poured water from a thermos into a Styrofoam cup and carried it back toward where Leaphorn was standing. He was a short man, sturdily built, neat and tidy, with small, round hands, small feet in neat cowboy boots, a round, intelligent face. He walked with the easy grace of a man who walks a lot.

"I haven't seen you here before," Nakai said. "If you came to hear about Jesus you're welcome. If you didn't come for that you're welcome anyway." He laughed, showing teeth that conflicted with the symphony of neatness.

Two were missing, one was broken, one was black and twisted. Poor people's teeth, Leaphorn thought. Navajo teeth.

"Because that's about all you hear around me anyway . . . Jesus talk," Nakai said.

"I came to see if you can help me with something," Leaphorn said. They exchanged the soft, barely touching handshake of the Navajo—the compromise of the Dineh between modern convention and the need to be careful with strangers who might, after all, be witches. "But it can wait until you're through with your revival. I'd like to talk to you then."

At the podium, Reverend Tafoya was talking about the Mountain Spirits of the Apaches. "Something like your *yei*, like your Holy People. But some different, too. That's who my daddy worshiped, and my mother, and my grandparents. And I did too, until I got this cancer. I don't have to tell you people here about cancer. . . ."

"The Reverend will take care of it for a while," Nakai said. "What do you need to know? What can I tell you?"

"We have a woman missing," Leaphorn said. He showed Nakai his identification and told him about Dr. Eleanor Friedman-Bernal. "You know her?"

"Sure," Nakai said. "For maybe three years, or four." He laughed again. "But not very well. Never made a Christian out of her. It was just business." The laugh went away. "You mean seriously missing? Like foul play?"

"She went to Farmington for the weekend a couple of weeks ago and nobody's heard from her since," Leaphorn said. "What was the business you had with her?"

"She studied pots. That was her business. So once in a while she would buy one from me." Nakai's small, round face was registering concern. "You think something went wrong with her?"

"You never know about that with missing people," Leaphorn said. "Usually they come back after a while and sometimes they don't. So we try to look into it. You a pot dealer?"

Leaphorn noticed how the question sounded, but before he could change it to "dealer in pots," Nakai said, "Just a preacher. But I found out you can sell pots. Pretty big money sometimes. Had a man I baptized over near Chinle give me one. Didn't have any money and he told me I could sell it in Gallup for thirty dollars. Told me where." Nakai laughed again, enjoying the memory. "Sure enough. Went to a place there on Railroad Avenue and the man gave me forty-six dollars for it." He made a bowl of his hands, grinning at Leaphorn. "The Lord provides," he said. "Not too well sometimes, but he provides."

"So now you go out and dig 'em up?"

"That's against the law," Nakai said, grinning. "You're a policeman. I bet you knew that. With me, it's once in a long while people bring 'em in. Several times at revivals I mentioned that fella who gave me the pot, and how it bought gasoline for a week, and the word got around among the born-again people that pots would give me some gasoline money. So now and then when they got no money and want to offer something, they bring me one."

"And the Friedman-Bernal woman buys them?"

"Mostly no. Just a time or two. She told me she wanted to see anything I got when I was preaching over around Chinle, or Many Farms—any of that country over around Chinle Wash. And out around here in the Checkerboard, and if I get up into Utah—Bluff, Montezuma Creek, Mexican Hat. Up in there."

"So you save them for her?"

"She pays me a little fee to take a look at them, but mostly she doesn't buy any. Just looks. Studies them for a couple of hours. Magnifying glass and all. Makes notes. The deal is, I have to know exactly where they came from."

"How do you manage that?"

"I tell the people, 'You going to bring in a pot to offer to the Lord, then you be sure you tell me where you found it.' " Nakai grinned his small, neat grin at Leaphorn. "That way, too, I know it's a legal pot. Not dug up off of government land."

Leaphorn didn't comment on that.

"When's the last time you saw her?" The answer should be late September, or something like that. Leaphorn knew the date he'd seen on Friedman's calendar, but it wasn't something Nakai would be likely to remember.

Nakai extracted a well-worn pocket notebook from his shirt and fingered his way through its pages. "Be last September twenty-third."

"More than a month ago," Leaphorn said. "What did she want?"

Nakai's round face filled with thought. Behind him, the Reverend Tafoya's voice rose into the high tenor of excitement. It described an old preacher at a revival tent in Dulce calling Tafoya to the front, laying on his hands, "right there on the place where that skin cancer was eating into my face. And I could feel the healing power flowing. . . ."

"Well," Nakai said, speaking very slowly. "She brought back a pot she'd gotten from me back in the spring. A piece of a pot, really. Wasn't all there. And she wanted to know everything I knew about it. Some of it stuff I had already told her. And she'd written it down in her notebook. But she asked it all again. Who I'd got it from. Everything he'd said about where he'd found it. That sort of stuff."

"Where was it? I mean where you met. And what did this notebook look like?"

"At Ganado," Nakai said. "I got a place there. I got home from a revival over by Cameron and I had a note from her asking me to call, saying it was important. I called her there at Chaco Canyon. She wasn't home so I left a message when I'd be back at Ganado again. And when I got back, there she was, waiting for me."

He paused. "And the notebook. Let's see now. Little leather-covered thing. Small enough to go in your shirt pocket. In fact that's where she carried it."

"And she just wanted to talk to you about the pot?"

"Mostly where it came from."

"Where was that?"

"Fella's ranch between Bluff and Mexican Hat."

"Private land," Leaphorn said, his voice neutral.

"Legal," Nakai agreed.

"Very short visit then," Leaphorn said. "Just repeating what you had already told her."

"Not really. She had a lot of questions. Did I know where she could find the person who had brought it? Could he have gotten it from the south side of the San Juan instead of the north side? And she had me look at the design on it. Wanted to know if I'd seen any like it."

Leaphorn had discovered that he was liking Nakai a little, which surprised him. "And you told her he couldn't have found it south of the San

Juan because that would be on the Navajo Reservation, and digging up a pot there would be illegal?" He was smiling when he said it and Nakai was smiling when he answered.

"Didn't have to tell Friedman something like that," Nakai said. "That sort of thing, she knew."

"What was special about this pot?"

"It was the kind she was working on, I guess. Anasazi pot, I understand. They look pretty much alike to me, but I remember this one had a pattern. You know, sort of abstract shapes painted onto its surface. That seemed to be what she was interested in. And it had a sort of mixed color. That's what she always had me watching out for. That pattern. It was sort of an impression of Kokopelli, tiny, repeated and repeated and repeated."

Nakai looked at Leaphorn quizzically. Leaphorn nodded. Yes, he knew about Kokopelli, the Humpbacked Flute Player, the Watersprinkler, the fertility symbol. Whatever you called him, he was a frequent figure in strange pictographs the Anasazi had painted on cliffs across the Colorado Plateau.

"Anytime anyone brought one in like that—even a little piece of the pot with that pattern on it—then I was to save it for her and she'd pay a minimum of fifty dollars."

"Who found that pot?"

Nakai hesitated, studied Leaphorn.

"I'm not out hunting pot hunters," Leaphorn said. "I'm trying to find this woman."

"It was a Paiute Clan man they call Amos Whistler," Nakai said. "Lives out there near south of Bluff. North of Mexican Water."

Suddenly Reverend Tafoya was shouting "Hallelujah," his voice loud and hoarse, and the crowd was joining him, and the thin man with the hat was doing something with the guitar.

"Anything else? I can talk to you later," Nakai said. "I need to help out now."

"Was that the last time you saw her? The last contact?"

"Yeah," Nakai said. He started toward the speaker's platform, then turned back. "One other contact," he said. "More or less. A man who works with her came by when I was preaching over at the Hogback there by Shiprock. Fella named . . ." Nakai couldn't come up with the name.

"Anyway he was a *belagana*. An Anglo. He said he wanted to pick up a pot I had for her. I didn't have any. He said he understood I had one, or maybe it was some, from over on the San Juan, around Bluff. I said no." Nakai turned again.

"Was it a tall man? Blond. Youngish. Named Elliot?"

"That's him," Nakai said.

Leaphorn watched the rest of it. He unfolded a chair at the back of the tent and sat, studied Nakai's techniques, and sorted out what he had learned, which wasn't much.

Nakai's congregation here on the fringe of the Checkerboard Reservation included perhaps sixty people—all Navajos apparently, but Leaphorn wouldn't swear that a few of them weren't from the Jicarilla Reservation, which bordered on Navajo territory here. They were about sixty percent women, and most middle-aged or older. That surprised Leaphorn a little. Without really thinking about it, because this aspect of his culture interested Leaphorn relatively little, he had presumed that those attracted to fundamentalist Christianity would be the young who'd been surrounded by the white man's religion off the reservation. That wasn't true here.

At the microphone, Nakai was gesturing toward the north. "Right up the highway here—you could see it from right here if it wasn't dark—right up here you have Huerfano Mesa. We been taught, us Navajos, that that's where First Woman lived, and First Man, and some of the other Holy People, they lived there. An' so when I was a boy, I would go with my uncle and we'd carry a bundle of *aghaal* up there, and we'd stick those prayer sticks up in a shrine we made up there and we'd chant this prayer. And then sometimes we'd go over to Gobernador Knob. . . ." Nakai gestured toward the east. "Over there across Blanco Canyon where First Woman and First Man found the Asdza'a' Nadleehe', and we would leave some of those *aghaal* over there. And my uncle would explain to me how this was a holy place. But I want you to remember something about Huerfano Mesa. Just close your eyes now and remember how that holy place looked the last time you saw it. Truck road runs up there. It's got radio towers built all over the top of it. Oil companies built 'em. Whole forest of those antennae all along the top of our holy place."

Nakai was shouting now, emphasizing each word with a downward sweep of his fist. "I can't pray to the mountain no more," he shouted. "Not after the white man built all over the top of it. Remember what the stories tell us. Changing Woman left us. She's gone away. . . ."

Leaphorn watched the thin man with the guitar, trying to find a place for him in his memory. He studied the audience, looking for familiar faces, finding a few. Even though he'd rarely worked this eastern Checkerboard side of the Big Reservation, this didn't surprise him. The reservation occupied more space than all of New England but it had a population of no more than 150,000. In a lifetime of policing it, Leaphorn had met, in one way or another, a lot of its inhabitants. And these fifty or sixty assembled under Nakai's old canvas to try the Jesus Road seemed approximately typical. Fewer children than would have been brought to a ceremonial of the traditional Navajo religion, none of the teenagers who would have been hanging around the fringes of a Night Chant playing the mating game, none of the drunks, and certainly no one who looked even moderately affluent. Leaphorn found himself wondering how Nakai paid his expenses. He'd collect whatever donations these people would make, but that wouldn't be much. Perhaps the church he represented paid him out of some missionary fund. Leaphorn considered the pots. What he'd seen in the Nelson's catalog made it clear that some of them brought far, far more than fifty-five dollars. But most of them would have little value and Leaphorn couldn't imagine Nakai getting many of them. Even if they were totally converted, still these were born Navajo. The pots came from burials, and Navajos were conditioned almost from infancy to avoid the dead and to have a special dread of death.

It was exactly what Nakai was talking about. Or, more accurately, shouting. He gripped the microphone stand with both of his small, neat hands, and thundered into it.

"The way I was taught, the way you were taught, when my mother died my uncles came there to the place where we lived out there near Rough Rock and they took the body away and put it somewhere where the coyotes and the ravens couldn't get to it." Nakai paused, gripped the microphone stand, looked down. "You remember that?" he asked, in a voice that was suddenly smaller. "Everybody here remembers somebody dying." Nakai looked up, recovering both composure and voice. "And then there's the four days when you don't do nothing but remember. And nobody speaks the name of the dead. . . . Because there's nothing left of them but the *chindi*, that ghost that is everything that was bad about them and nothing that was good. And I don't say my mother's name anymore—not ever again—because that *chindi* may hear me calling it and come back and make me sick. And what about what was good about my mother? What about what was good about your dead people? What about that? Our Holy People didn't tell us much about that. Not that I know about, they didn't. Some of the Dineh, they have a story about a young man who followed Death, and looked down into the underworld, and saw the dead people sitting around down there. But my clan, we didn't have that story. And I think it got borrowed from the Hopi People. It is one of their beliefs."

Early in this discourse, Leaphorn had been interested in Nakai's strategy. Methods of persuasion intrigued him. But there seemed to be nothing particularly unique in it, and he'd let his attention wander. He had reviewed what little he'd learned from Nakai, and what he might do next, if anything, and then simply watched the audience reaction. Now Leaphorn found himself attentive again. His own Red Forehead Clan had no such story either at least he hadn't been told it in his own boyhood introduction into the Navajo Way. He had heard it often in his days as an anthropology student at Arizona State. And he'd heard it since from Navajos around Window Rock. But Nakai was probably right. Probably it was another of the many stories the Dineh borrowed from the cultures that surrounded them—borrowed and then refined into abstract philosophical points. The Navajo Way was devoted to the harmony of life. It left death simply terrifying black oblivion.

"We learn this story about how Monster Slayer corners Death in his pit house. But he lets Death live. Because without death there wouldn't be enough room for the babies, for young people. But I can tell you something truer than that." Nakai's voice had risen again to a shout.

"Jesus didn't let Death live. Hallelujah! Praise the Lord!" Nakai danced across the platform, shouting, drawing from the audience answering shouts. "When we walk through the Valley of Death, he is with us, that's what Jesus teaches. We don't just drift away into the dark night, a ghost of sickness. We go beyond death. We go into a happy world. We go where there ain't no hunger. There ain't no sorrow. Ain't no drunks. No fighting. No seeing relatives run over out here on the highway. We go into a world where last are first, and the poor are the rich, and the sick are well, and the blind, they see again. . . ."

Leaphorn didn't hear the last of it. He was hurrying out through the tent flap into the darkness. He stood for a while, allowing his eyes to adjust, breathing the cool, clean high-altitude air. Smelling dust, and sagebrush, shaken, remembering the day they brought Emma's body home from the hospital.

It had still been unreal to him, what had happened at Gallup, what the doctor had told him. It had left him stunned. Emma's brothers had come to talk to him about it. He'd simply told them that he knew Emma would want a traditional burial, and they'd left.

They'd taken the body to her mother's place over near Blue Gap Chapter House, on the edge of Black Mesa. Under the brush arbor her old aunt had washed her, and combed out her hair, and dressed her in her best blue velvet skirt, and her old squash-blossom necklace, put on her rings, and wrapped her in a blanket. He had sat in the hogan, watching. Her brothers had picked her up then, and put the body in the back of their truck, and driven down the track toward the cliffs. In about an hour they came back without her and took their cleansing sweat bath. He didn't know—would never know—where they'd left her. In a crevice somewhere, probably. High. Protected by deadwood from the predators. Hidden away. He had stayed for two days of the silent days of mourning. Tradition demanded four days, to give the dead time to complete their journey into the oblivion of death. Two days was all he could stand. He'd left them.

And her. But no more of this.

Chee's pickup was still there. Leaphorn walked to it.

"*Ya te'eh,*" Chee said, acknowledging him.

"*Ya te,*" Leaphorn said. He leaned on the truck door. "What brings you out to the Reverend Slick Nakai's revival?"

Chee explained about the backhoe loader, and the abortive chase, and what Tso had told him about where the Backhoe Bandit might be found.

"But I don't think he is going to show up tonight," Chee said. "Getting too late."

"You going to go in and ask Nakai who this fellow is?" Leaphorn asked.

"I'm going to do that," Chee said. "When he's through preaching and when I get a look at the people coming out of the tent."

"You think Nakai would tell you he didn't know this guy, and then tip him off you're looking for him?"

Long silence. "He might," Chee said. "But I think I'll risk it."

Leaphorn didn't comment. It was the decision he would have made. Handle it on Navajo time. No reason to rush in there.

There was no hurry for him either, but he went back into the tent. He'd hear the rest of Nakai's sermon, and see how much money he took in at his collection. And how many, if any, pots. Leaphorn was thinking that maybe he'd learned a little more than he'd first realized. Something had jogged his memory. The thin Navajo with the guitar was the same man he'd seen helping Maxie Davis at the excavation at Chaco Canyon. That answered one small question. A Christian Navajo wouldn't be worrying about stirring up the *chindi* of long-dead Anasazi. But it also made an interesting connection—a man who dug up scientific pots at Chaco worked for a man who sold theoretically legal pots. And a man who sold theoretically legal pots linked to a man who stole a backhoe. Backhoes were machines notoriously useful in uprooting Anasazi ruins and despoiling their graves.

It was just about then, as he walked out of the darkness into the tent, that he became aware of something in his attitude about all this.

He felt an urgency now. The disappearance of Dr. Eleanor Friedman-Bernal had been merely something curious—an oddity. Now he sensed something dangerous. He had never been sure he could find the woman. Now he wondered if she'd be alive if he did.

5

REMEMBER, BOY," UNCLE Frank Sam Nakai would sometimes tell Chee, "when you're tired of walking up a long hill you think about how easy it's going to be walking down." Which was Nakai's Navajo way of saying things tend to even up. For Chee this proved, as his uncle's aphorisms often did, to be true. Chee's bad luck was followed by good luck.

Early Monday a San Juan County sheriff's deputy, who happened to have read the paperwork about the stolen flatbed trailer and backhoe, also happened to get more or less lost while trying to deliver a warrant. He turned off on an access road to a Southern Union pump site and found the trailer abandoned. The backhoe apparently had been unloaded, driven about twenty yards on its own power, and then rolled up a makeshift ramp—presumably into the back of a truck. The truck had almost new tires on its dual rear wheels. The tread pattern was used by Dayton Tire and Rubber, with a single dealer in Farmington and none in Shiprock. The dealer had no trouble remembering. The only truck tires he sold for a month had been to Farmington U-Haul. The company had three trucks out at the moment with dual rear wheels. Two had been recently reshod with Daytons. One was rented to a Farmington furniture company. The other, equipped with a power winch, was rented to Joe B. Nails, P.O. Box 770, Aztec, using a MasterCard.

Farmington police had a record on Nails. One driving while intoxicated. It was enough to provide an employer's name. Wellserve, Inc., a contractor maintaining the Gasco collection system. But Wellserve was a former employer. Nails had quit in August.

Chee learned all of this good news secondhand. He'd spent the morning hanging around Red Rock, worrying about what he'd tell Janet Pete when she got back from Phoenix, and waiting for a witness he was supposed to deliver to the FBI office in Farmington. With that done two hours behind schedule, he had stopped at the Shiprock headquarters and gotten the first half of the news about the trailer. He'd spent the afternoon hunting around Teec Nos Pos for a fellow who'd broken his brother-in-law's leg. No luck on that. When he pulled back into Shiprock to knock off for the day, he ran into Benally going off shift.

"I guess we got your Backhoe Bandit," Benally said. And he filled Chee in on the rest of it. "U-Haul calls us when he checks the truck in."

That struck Chee as stupid. "You think he'll have the backhoe in it when he returns it?" Chee said. "Otherwise, no proof of anything. What you charge him with?"

Benally had thought of that and so had Captain Largo.

"We bring him in. We tell him we have witnesses who saw him taking the thing out, and we can connect it to the truck he rented, and if he'll cooperate and tell us where it is so we can recover it, and snitch on his buddy, then we go light on him." Benally shrugged, not thinking it would work either. "Better than nothing," he added. "Anyway, the call's out on the U-Haul truck. Maybe we catch him with the backhoe in it."

"I doubt it," Chee said.

Benally agreed. He grinned. "The best plan would have been for you to have grabbed him when he was driving out of the yard with it."

Chee called Pete's office from the station phone. He'd break it by degrees. Tell her first that a lot of things were wrong with the Buick, sort of slip into the part about tearing it up. But Miss Pete wasn't in, wasn't back from Phoenix, had called in and said she'd be held over for a day.

Wonderful. Chee felt immense relief. He put the Buick out of his mind. He thought about the Backhoe Bandit, who was going to get away with it. He thought about what the preacher had told him Saturday night.

The preacher said he didn't know the name of the man who owned the patched-up car. He thought he'd heard him called Jody, or maybe Joey. He thought the man worked in the Blanco field—maybe for Southern Union Gas, but maybe not. The man sometimes brought him a pot which the preacher said he sometimes bought. The last time he saw him, the man had asked if the preacher would buy a whole bunch of pots if the man could get them. "And I told him maybe I could and maybe I couldn't. It would depend on whether I had any money."

"So maybe he'll come back again and maybe he won't."

"I think he'll be back," the preacher had said. "I told him if I couldn't handle it, I knew somebody who could." And he told Chee about the woman anthropologist, and that led him to Lieutenant Leaphorn. The preacher was a talkative man.

Chee sat now in his pickup truck beside the willows shading the police parking lot. He felt relief on one hand, pressure on the other. The dreaded meeting with Janet Pete was off, at least until tomorrow. But when it came, he wanted to conclude his story by telling Pete how he had nailed the man to blame for all this. It didn't seem likely that was going to happen. Largo's solution was sensible if you were patient, even though it probably wouldn't produce an indictment. Aside from what it had done to Chee, the crime was relatively minor. Theft of equipment worth perhaps $10,000 in its badly used condition. Hardly an event to provoke all-out deployment of police to run down evidence. So the Backhoe Bandit would get away with it. Unless the rent-a-truck could be found with the backhoe on it. Where would it be?

Chee shifted sideways in the seat, leaned a knee against the dashboard, thought. Nails was a pot hunter. Probably he wanted the backhoe for digging up burials to find a lot of them. With the teeth removed from the shovel to minimize breakage, they were a favorite tool of the professionals. And from what the preacher said, Nails must be going professional. He must have found a likely ruins. What Nails had told the preacher suggested he'd found a wholesale source. Therefore it was a safe presumption that he'd stolen the backhoe to dig them.

So far it was easy. The hard question was where?

The willow branches dangling around Chee's pickup had turned yellow with the season. Chee studied them a moment to rest the brain. Surely he must know something helpful. How about the trailer? Stolen. Then brought back to haul out the backhoe. Then abandoned in favor of the truck? The night the trailer was stolen the backhoe was still being repaired. Had the head off the engine, in fact. So they took the trailer, and brought it back when the backhoe was ready to roll. Pretty stupid, on the face of it. But Chee had checked and learned the trailer was scheduled to haul equipment to a job at Burnt Water the next day. The Backhoe Bandit knew a hell of a lot about what went on in that maintenance yard. Interesting, but it didn't help now.

The next answers did. The question was why steal the trailer at all? Why not simply rent the U-Haul truck earlier, and haul the backhoe out on that? And why not rent the backhoe, instead of stealing it? As Chee thought it through, the answers connected. Rental trucks were easy to trace, so the Backhoe Bandit avoided the risk of having the truck seen at the burglary. A rented backhoe would also be easy to trace. But there would be no reason to trace it if it was checked back in after it was used. So why . . . ? Chee's orderly mind sorted through it. The truck was needed instead of the trailer because the trailer couldn't be pulled where the backhoe was needed. Could it be the dig site was somewhere from which the backhoe couldn't be extricated? Of course. It would be at the bottom of someplace, and that would explain why Nails had rented a truck with a power winch. Running a backhoe down the steep slope of a canyon could well be possible where pulling it out wouldn't be.

Chee climbed out of the cab, trotted into the office, and called the Farmington office of Wellserve, Inc. Yes, they could provide the police with a copy of their well-service route map. Yes, the service superintendent could mark the route Nails had served.

When Chee left Wellserve with the map folded on the seat beside him he had three hours left before sundown. Then there would be a half-moon. A good night for a pot hunter to work, and a good night to hunt pot hunters. He stopped at the sheriff's office and found out who was patrolling where tonight. If Nails was off reservation land, he'd need a deputy along to make an arrest. Then he drove up the San Juan River valley through the little oil town of Bloomfield, and out of the valley into the infinity of sagebrush that covers the Blanco Plateau. He was remembering he'd read somewhere of somebody estimating more than a hundred thousand Anasazi sites on the Colorado Plateau—only a few of them excavated, only a few thousand even mapped. But it wouldn't be impossible. He would guess Nails had found sites along the service roads he traveled and would be looting them. Chee knew some of those sites himself. And he knew what attracted the Anasazi. A cliff faced to catch the winter sun and shaded in the summer, enough floodplain to grow something, and a source of water. That, particularly the water, narrowed it a lot.

He scouted Canyon Largo first, and Blanco Canyon, and Jasis Canyon. He found two sites that had been dug into fairly recently. But nothing new and no sign of the tire tread pattern he was looking for. He moved north then and checked Gobernador Canyon and La Jara and the Vaqueros Wash eastward in the Carson National Forest. He found nothing. He skipped westward, driving far faster than the speed limit down New Mexico Highway 44. The light was dying now—a cloudless autumn evening with the western sky a dull copper glow. He checked out a couple of canyons near Ojo Encino, restricting himself always to the access roads gouged out to reach the gas wells and pump stations Nails had been serving.

By midnight he finished checking the roads leading from the Star Lake Pump Station, driving slowly, using his flashlight to check for tracks at every possible turnoff. He circled back past the sleeping trading post the maps called White Horse Lake. He crossed the Continental Divide, and dropped into the network of arroyos that drain Chaco Mesa. Again he found nothing. He circled back across Chaco Wash and picked up the gravel road that leads northwestward toward Nageezi Trading Post.

Beyond Betonnie Tsosie Wash he stopped the pickup in the middle of the road. He climbed out wearily, stretched, and turned on the flash to check the turnoff of an access trail. He stood in the light of the half-moon, yawning, his flash reflecting from the chalky dust. It showed, clear and fresh, the dual tracks of an almost new Dayton tire tread.

Chee's watch showed 2:04 A.M. At 2:56 he found the place where, maybe a thousand years ago, a little band of Anasazi families had lived, and built their cluster of small stone shelters and living spaces, and died. Chee had been walking for more than a mile. He had left his pickup by a pump site and followed the twin tracks on foot. The pump marked the dead end of this branch of the service road—if two ruts wandering through the sage and juniper could be called that. From here, the dual tires had made their own road. Away from the hard-packed ruts, they were easy to follow now—crushed tumbleweeds, broken brush, the sharp smell of bruised sage.

They led up a long slope, and Chee guessed they wouldn't lead far. He walked carefully and quietly, moon over his shoulder, flash off. The slow huffing of the pump motor diminished behind him. He stopped, listening for the sound the backhoe motor would be making. He heard a coyote, and then its partner. One behind him, one on the ridge to his left. It was work time for predators, with all the little nocturnal rodents out braving death to find a meal.

He didn't see the truck until he was within fifty feet of it. Nails had nosed it into a cluster of juniper just over the crest of the hill. The doors of its van box stood open, a square black shape with the ramp used to unload the backhoe still in place. Chee stared, listening, feeling a mixture of excitement, exultation, and uneasiness. He put his hand on the pistol in his jacket pocket. Chee did not like pistols in general, and the one he had carried since being sworn into the force was no exception. But now the heavy hard metal was reassuring. He walked to the truck, placing each step carefully, stopping to listen. The cab was empty, the doors unlocked. The wire cable from the winch spool extended down the steep slope, slack. If the backhoe was down there, as it must be, the engine wasn't running. The silence was almost total. From far behind him, he could hear the faint sound of the walking beam pump. No coyote sounds now. The air was moving up the slope past his face, a faint coolness.

Chee held the cable in his left hand and started down the slope, following the path broken by the backhoe, trying to keep his weight on his feet, trying to avoid the noise sliding would make.

The slope was too steep. He slid a few feet, regained control. Slid again as the earth gave way under his feet. Then he lay on his back, motionless, breathing dust, cursing under his breath at the noise he had made. He listened, hand gripping the cable. Down here under the ridge, he could no longer hear the distant pump motor. The coyote yipped somewhere off to his left and provoked an answering yip from its partner. He saw the backhoe, partially visible through the brush, its motor silent. The half-moon lit the roof of its cab, the shovel, and part of the jointed arm that controlled it. Nails apparently had been frightened away. It didn't matter. He had the backhoe. He had the truck that had hauled it here, and the record would show Nails had rented the truck.

Chee gripped the cable and shifted his free hand to push himself erect.

He felt cloth under his fingers. And a button. And the hard bone and cold skin of a wrist. He scrambled away from it.

The form lay facedown, head upslope, in the deep darkness cast by a juniper—its left hand stretching out toward the cable. A man, Chee saw. He squatted, controlling the shock. And when it was controlled, he leaned forward and felt the wrist.

Dead. Dead long enough to be stiff. He bent low over the corpse and turned on his flash. It wasn't Nails. It was a Navajo. A young man, hair cut short, wearing a blue checked shirt with two stains on its back. Chee touched one of them with a tentative finger. Stiff. Dried blood. The man had apparently been shot twice. In the middle of the back and just above the hip.

Chee snapped off the light. He thought of the Navajo's ghost, hovering nearby. He turned his mind away from that. The *chindi* was out there, representing all that was evil in the dead man's being. But one did not think of *chindis* out in the darkness. Where was Nails? Most likely, hours away from here. But why did he leave the truck? This Navajo must be the one seen with Nails when they'd stolen the backhoe. Maybe the Navajo had driven the truck, Nails had come in his own car. Odd, but possible.

Chee moved cautiously the few remaining yards to the bottom of the hill. It was full dark here, the moonlight blocked by the high ground. Just enough reflected light to guide his feet. A falling out of thieves, Chee thought. A fight. Nails pulls a gun. The Navajo runs. Nails shoots him. He didn't believe Nails would still be here, or anywhere near here. But he walked carefully.

Even so he almost tripped over the bag before he saw it. It was black plastic, the sort sold in little boxes of a dozen to line wastebaskets. Chee untwisted the wire securing its top and felt inside. Fragments of pottery, just as he'd expected. Between him and the backhoe, more such bags were clustered. Chee walked past them to look at the machine.

It had been turned off with the shovel locked high over the trench it had been digging into a low, brush-covered mound. Scattered along the excavation was a clutter of flat stones. Once they must have formed the wall of an Anasazi settlement. He didn't notice the bones until he turned on his flash.

They were everywhere. A shoulder blade, a thigh bone, part of a skull, ribs, four or five connected vertebrae, part of a foot, a lower jaw.

Jim Chee was modern man built upon traditional Navajo. This was simply too much death. Too many ghosts disturbed. He backed away from the excavation, flashlight still on, careful no longer. He wanted only to be away from here. Into the sunlight. Into the cleansing heat of a sweat bath. To be surrounded by the healing, curing sounds of a Ghostway ceremonial. He started up the slope, pulling himself up by the cable.

The panic receded. First he would check the backhoe cab. He trotted to it, guided by the flash. He checked the metal serial-number plate and the Navajo Nation Road Department number painted on its side. Then he flashed the light into the cab.

A man was sitting there, slumped sideways against the opposite door, his open eyes reflecting white in Chee's flash. The left side of his face was black with what must be blood. But Chee could see his mustache and enough of his face to know that he had found Joe Nails.

6

LEAPHORN CAME HOME to Window Rock long after midnight. He hadn't bothered to turn on the lights. He drank from his cupped palms in the bathroom and folded his clothing over the bedside chair (where Emma had so often sat to read or knit, to do the thousand small things that Emma did). He had turned the bed ninety degrees so that his eyes would open in the morning to the shock of a different view. That broke his lifelong habit, the automatic waking thought of "Where's Emma?" and what then followed. He had moved from his side of the bed to Emma's—which had eliminated that once-happy habit of reaching out to touch her when he drifted into sleep.

Now he lay flat on his back, feeling tired muscles relax, thinking about the food in Eleanor Friedman-Bernal's refrigerator, drifting from that to her arrangement with Nakai to inspect contributed pots and from that to the notebook Nakai had described. He hadn't noticed a pocket-sized leather notebook in her apartment—but then it might be almost anywhere in the room. Thatcher had made no real search. On the long drive homeward across the Checkerboard from Huerfano Mesa, he had thought of why Elliot hadn't mentioned being sent by Friedman to see Nakai and collect a pot. It must have seemed odd to Elliot, this abortive mission. Why not mention it? Before Leaphorn could come to any conclusion, he drifted off to sleep, and it was morning.

He showered, inspected his face, decided he could go another few days without a shave, made himself a breakfast of sausage and fried eggs—violating his diet with the same guilty feelings he always had when Emma was away visiting her family. He read the mail that Saturday had brought him, and the Gallup *Independent*. He snapped on the television, snapped it off again, stood at the window looking out on the autumn morning. Windless. Cloudless. Silent except for a truck rolling down Navajo Route 3. The little town of Window Rock was taking Sunday off. Leaphorn noticed the glass was dusty—a condition Emma had never tolerated. He got a handkerchief from his drawer and polished the pane. He polished other windows. Abruptly he walked to the telephone and called Chaco Canyon.

Until recently telephone calls between the world outside and Chaco had traveled via a Navajo Communications Company telephone line. From Crownpoint northeast, the wire wandered across the rolling grassland, attached mostly to fence posts and relying on its own poles only when no fence was available going in the right direction. This system made telephone service subject to the same hazards as the ranch fence on which it piggybacked. Drifts of tumbleweeds, winter blizzards, dry rot, errant cattle, broke down both fences and communications. When it was operating, voices sometimes tended to fade in and out with the wind velocity. But recently this system had been modernized. Calls were now routed two hundred miles east to Santa Fe, then beamed to a satellite and rebroadcast to a receiving dish at Chaco. The space age system, like the National Aeronautics and Space Administration which made it possible, was frequently out of operation. When it operated at all, voices tended to fade in and out with the wind velocity. Today was no exception.

A woman's voice answered, strong at first, then drifting away into space. No, Bob Luna wasn't in. No use ringing his number because she'd seen him driving away and she hadn't seen him return.

How about Maxie Davis?

Just a minute. She might not be up yet. It was, after all, early Sunday morning.

Maxie Davis was up. "Who?" she asked. "I'm sorry. I can hardly hear you."

Leaphorn could hear Maxie Davis perfectly—as if she were standing beside him. "Leaphorn," he repeated. "The Navajo cop who was out there a couple of days ago."

"Oh. Have you found her?"

"No luck," Leaphorn said. "Do you remember a little leather-covered notebook she used? Probably carried in her shirt pocket?"

"Notebook? Yeah. I remember it. She always used it when she was working."

"Know where she keeps it? When it's not with her?"

"No idea. Probably in a drawer somewhere."

"You've known her long?"

"Off and on, yes. Since we were graduate students."

"How about Dr. Elliot?"

Maxie Davis laughed. "We're sort of a team, I guess you'd say." And then, perhaps thinking Leaphorn would misunderstand, added: "Professionally. We're the two who are going to write the bible on the Anasazi." She laughed again, the sound fading in and out. "After Randall Elliot and me, no more need for Anasazi research."

"Not Friedman-Bernal? She's not part of it?"

"Different field," Davis said. "She's ceramics. We're people. She's pots."

They had decided, he and Emma, to install the telephone in the kitchen. To hang it on the wall beside the refrigerator. Standing there, listening to Maxie Davis, Leaphorn inspected the room. It was neat. No dishes, dirty or otherwise, were in sight. Windows clean, sink clean, floor clean. Leaphorn leaned forward to the full reach of the telephone receiver cord and plucked a napkin from the back of the chair. He'd used it while he'd eaten his eggs. He held the receiver against his ear with his shoulder while he folded it.

"I'm going to come back out there," he said. "I'd like to talk to you. And to Elliot if he's there."

"I doubt it," Maxie Davis said. "He's usually out in the field on Sunday."

But Elliot was there, leaning against the porch support watching Leaphorn as he parked his pickup in the apartment's courtyard.

"Ya tay," Elliot said, getting the pronunciation of the Navajo greeting almost right. "Didn't know policemen worked on Sunday."

"They don't tell you that when they recruit you," Leaphorn said, "but it happens now and then."

Maxie Davis appeared at the door. She was wearing a loose blue T-shirt decorated with a figure copied from a petroglyph. Short dark hair fell around her face. She looked feminine, intelligent, and beautiful.

"I'll bet I know where she keeps that notebook," Davis said. "Do you still have the key?"

Leaphorn shook his head. "I'll get one from headquarters." Or, he thought, failing that, it would be simple enough to get into the apartment. He'd noticed that when Thatcher had unlocked the door.

"Luna's away," Elliot said. "We can get in through the patio door."

Elliot managed it with the long blade of his pocketknife, simply sliding the blade in and lifting the latch.

"Something you learn in graduate school," he said.

Or in juvenile detention centers, Leaphorn thought. He wondered if Elliot had ever been in one of those. It didn't seem likely. Jail is not socially acceptable for prep school boys.

Everything seemed exactly as it had been when he'd been here with Thatcher—the same stale air, the same dustiness, the boxes of pots, the disarray. Thatcher had searched it, in his tentative way, looking for evidence that Dr. Eleanor Friedman-Bernal was a violator of the Federal Antiquities Act. Now Leaphorn intended to search it in his own way, looking for the woman herself.

"Ellie kept her purse in the dresser," Maxie Davis said. She opened a bottom drawer. "In here. And I remember seeing her drop that notebook in it when she came in from work."

Davis extracted a purse and handed it to Leaphorn. It was beige leather. It looked new and it looked expensive. Leaphorn unsnapped it, checked through lipstick, small bottles, package of sugarless gum, Tums, small scissors, odds and ends. No small leather notebook. Emma had three purses—a very small one, a very good one, and a worn one used in the workaday world of shopping.

"She had another purse?" Leaphorn said, making it half a question.

Davis nodded. "This was her good one." She checked into the drawer. "Not here."

Leaphorn's mild disappointment at not finding the notebook was offset by mild surprise. The wrong purse was missing. Friedman-Bernal had not taken her social purse with her for the weekend. She had taken her working purse.

"I want to take a sort of rough inventory," Leaphorn said. "I'm going to rely on your memory. See if we can determine what she took with her."

There were the disclaimers he expected, from both Maxie Davis and Elliot, that they really didn't know much about Ellie's wardrobe or Ellie's possessions. But within an hour, they had a rough list on the back of an envelope. Ellie had taken no suitcase. She had taken a small canvas gym bag. She'd probably taken no makeup or cosmetics. No skirt was missing. No dress. She had taken only jeans and a long-sleeved cotton shirt.

Maxie Davis sat on the bed, examining her jottings, looking thoughtful. "No way of knowing about socks or underwear or things like that. But I don't think she took any pajamas." She motioned toward the chest of drawers. "There's an old blue pair in there I've seen her wear, and a sort of worn-out checked set, and a fancy new pair. Silk." Davis looked at him, checking the level of Leaphorn's understanding of such things. "For company," she explained. "I doubt if she would have a fourth set, or bring it out here anyway."

"Okay," Leaphorn said. "Did she have a sleeping bag?"

"Yeah," Davis said. "Of course." She sorted through the things on the closet shelf. "That's gone too," she said.

"So she was camping out," Leaphorn said. "Sleeping out. Probably nothing social. Probably working. Who did she work with?"

"Nobody, really," Elliot said. "It was a one-woman project. She worked by herself."

"Let's settle down somewhere and talk about that," Leaphorn said.

They settled in the living room. Leaphorn perched on the edge of a sofa that looked and felt as if it would fold outward into a bed, Davis and Elliot on the Park Service Purchasing Office low-bid overstuffed couch. Much of what Leaphorn heard he already knew from his own studies a lifetime ago at Arizona State. He had considered telling the two about his master's degree and decided against it. The time that might have saved had no value to Leaphorn now. And sometimes something might be gained by seeming to know less than you did. And so Leaphorn listened patiently to basic stuff, mostly from Davis, about how the Anasazi culture had risen on the Colorado Plateau, almost certainly a progression from the small, scattered families of hunters and seed collectors who lived in pit houses, and somehow learned to make baskets, and then the rudiments of agriculture, and then how to irrigate their crops by controlling runoff from rain, and—probably in the process of caulking baskets with fire-dried mud to make them waterproof—how to make pottery.

"Important cultural breakthrough," Elliot inserted. "Improved storage possibilities. Opened a door to art." He laughed. "Also gave anthropology something a lot more durable than baskets to hunt, and measure, and study, and all that. But you already know a lot about this, don't you?"

"Why do you say that?" Leaphorn never allowed a subject to shift him from the role of interrogator unless Leaphorn wanted to be shifted.

"Because you don't ask any questions," Elliot said. "Maxie isn't always perfectly clear. Either you're not interested in this background, or you already know it."

"I know something about it," Leaphorn said. "You've said Friedman's interest was in pottery. Apparently she was interested mostly in one kind of pot. Pots which have a kind of corrugated finish. Probably some other revealing details. Right?"

"Ellie thought she had identified one specific potter," Elliot said. "A distinctive individual touch."

Leaphorn said nothing. That sounded mildly interesting. But—even given the intense interest of anthropologists in the Anasazi culture and its mysterious fate—it didn't seem very important. His expression told Elliot what he was thinking.

"One potter. Dead probably seven hundred and fifty years." Elliot put his boots on the battered coffee table. "So what's the big deal? The big deal is, Ellie knows where he lived. Out there at BC57, across the wash from Pueblo Bonito, because she found a lot of his pots there broken in the process of being made. Must have been where he worked. . . ."

"She," Maxie Davis said. "Where she worked."

"Okay, she." Elliot shook his head, regaining his chain of thought, showing no sign of irritation. It was part of a game they played, Leaphorn thought. Elliot's boots were dusty, scarred, flat-heeled, practical. A soft brown leather, perfectly fitted, extremely expensive.

Davis was leaning forward, wanting Leaphorn to understand this. "Nobody before had ever found a way to link the pot with the person who made it—not before Ellie began noticing this peculiar technique repeated in a lot of those BC57 pots. She had already noticed it in a couple of others from other places—and now she had found the source. Where they came from. And she was lucky in another way. Not only was this potter prolific, she was good. Her pots traded around. Ellie tracked one back to the Salmon Ruins over on the San Juan, and she thinks one came out of a burial near the White House Ruin in Canyon de Chelly, and . . ."

If Elliot had any objection to Maxie Davis's commandeering his story, his face hadn't showed it. But now he said: "Get to the important point."

Maxie looked at him. "Well, she's not sure about that," she said.

"Maybe not, but this BC57 site was one of the last ones built—just before everybody disappeared. They dated a roof beam to 1292, and some of the charcoal in what might have been a kiln fire to 1298. So she was working just about the time they turned out the lights here and walked away. And Ellie is beginning to think she might be able to pin down where she went."

"That's the really big deal out here." Davis waved her arms. "Where'd the Anasazi go? The big huge mystery that all the magazine writers write about."

"Among a couple of other big questions," Elliot said. "Like why they built roads when they didn't have wheels, or pack animals, and why they left, and why they lived in this place in the first place with so damn little wood, or water, or good land, and . . ." Elliot shrugged. "The more we learn, the more we wonder."

"This man who was coming out to see her the week after she disappeared, do you know who he was?"

"Lehman," Davis said. "He came." She smiled ruefully. "Plenty sore about it. He came on a Wednesday and it had rained Tuesday night and you know how that road gets."

"And he's . . ." Leaphorn began to ask.

"He's the hotshot in Ellie's field," Elliot said. "I think he was chairman of her dissertation committee when she got her doctorate at Madison. Now he's a professor at University of New Mexico. Two or three books on Mimbres, and Hohokam, and Anasazi pottery evolution. Top guru in the ceramics field."

"Ellie's equivalent of our Devanti," Davis said. "She pretty well had to persuade Lehman she knew what she was talking about. Like in migrations, Elliot and I have to deal with our top honcho."

"Doctor Delbert Devanti," Elliot said. "Arkansas's answer to Einstein." The tone was sardonic.

"He's proved some things," Maxie Davis said, her voice flat. "Even if he didn't go to Phillips Exeter Academy, or Princeton."

There was silence. Elliot's long, handsome face had become stiff and blank. Maxie glanced at him. In the glance Leaphorn read . . . what? Was it anger? Malice? She turned to Leaphorn. "Please note the blue blood's lofty contempt for the plebeians. Devanti is definitely a plebe. He sounds like corn pone."

"And is often wrong," Elliot said.

Davis laughed. "There is that," she said.

"But you give people the right to be wrong if they came out of the cotton patch," Elliot said. His voice sounded normal, or almost normal, but Leaphorn could see the tension in the line of his jaw.

"More of an excuse for it," Maxie said, mildly. "Maybe he overlooked something while he was working nights to feed his family. No tutors to do his digging in the library."

To that, Randall Elliot said nothing. Leaphorn watched. Where would this tension lead? Nowhere, apparently. Maxie had nothing more to say.

"You two work as a team," Leaphorn said. "That right?"

"More or less," Davis said. "We have common interests in the Anasazi."

"Like how?" Leaphorn asked.

"It's complicated. Actually it involves food economics, nutrition tolerances, population sizes, things like that, and you spend a lot more time working on programming statistical projections in the computer than you do digging in the field. Really dull stuff, unless you're weird enough to be into it." She smiled at Leaphorn. A smile of such dazzling charm that once it would have destroyed him.

"And Randall here," she added, "is doing something much more dramatic." She poked him with her elbow—a gesture that almost made what she was saying mere teasing. "He is revolutionizing physical anthropology. He is finding a way to solve the mystery, once and for all, of what happened to these people."

"Population studies," Elliot said in a low voice. "Involves migrations and genetics."

"Rewrites all the books if it works," Maxie Davis said, smiling at Leaphorn. "Elliots do not spend their time on small things. In the navy they are admirals. In universities they are presidents. In politics they are senators. When you start at the top you have to aim high. Or everybody is disappointed."

Leaphorn was uncomfortable. "It would be a problem," he said.

"But not one I had," Maxie Davis said. "I'm white trash."

"Maxie never tires of reminding me of the silver spoon in my crib," Elliot said, managing a grin. "It doesn't have much to do with finding Ellie, though."

"But you have a point," Leaphorn said. "Dr. Friedman wouldn't have missed that appointment with Lehman without a good reason."

"Hell, no," Maxie said. "That's what I told that idiot at the sheriff's office."

"Do you know why he was coming? Specifically."

"She was going to bring him up-to-date," Elliot said.

"She was going to hit him with a bombshell," Maxie said. "That's what I think. I think she finally had it put together."

There was something in Elliot's expression. Maybe skepticism. Or disapproval. But Davis was enthusiastic.

"What did she tell you?"

"Nothing much, really. But I could just sense it. That things were working out. But she wouldn't say much."

"It's not traditional," Elliot said. "Not among us scientists."

Leaphorn found himself as interested in what was going on with Elliot as in the thrust of the conversation. Elliot's tone now was faintly mocking. Davis had caught it, too. She looked at Elliot and then back at Leaphorn, speaking directly to him.

"That's true," she said. "Before one boasts, one must have done something to boast about."

She said it in the mildest of voices, without looking at Elliot, but Elliot's face flushed.

"You think she had found something important," Leaphorn said. "She didn't tell you anything, but something caused you to think that. Something specific. Can you think what it was?"

Davis leaned back on the couch. She caught her lower lip between her teeth. She laid her hand, in a gesture that looked casual, on Elliot's thigh. She thought.

"Ellie was excited," she said. "Happy, too. For a week, maybe a little longer, before she left." She got up from the couch and walked past Leaphorn into the bedroom. Infinite grace, Leaphorn thought.

"She'd been over in Utah. I remember that. To Bluff, and Mexican Hat and—" Her voice from the bedroom was indistinct.

"Montezuma Creek?" Leaphorn asked.

"Yes, all that area along the southern edge of Utah. And when she came back"—Davis emerged from the bedroom carrying a Folgers Coffee carton—"she had all these potsherds." She put the box on the coffee table. "Same ones, I think. At least, I remember it was this box."

The box held what seemed to Leaphorn to be as many as fifty fragments of pots, some large, some no more than an inch across.

Leaphorn sorted through them, looking for nothing in particular but noticing that all were reddish brown, and all bore a corrugated pattern.

"Done by her potter, I guess," Leaphorn said. "Did she say where she got them?"

"From a Thief of Time," Elliot said. "From a pot hunter."

"She didn't say that," Davis said.

"She went to Bluff to look for pot hunters. To see what they were finding. She told you that."

"Did she say which one?" Leaphorn asked. Here might be an explanation of how she had vanished. If she had been dealing directly with a pot hunter, he might have had second thoughts. Might have thought he had sold her evidence that would put him in prison. Might have killed her when she came back for more.

"She didn't mention any names," Davis said.

"Hardly necessary," Elliot said. "Looking for pot hunters around Bluff, you'd go see Old Man Houk. Or one of his friends. Or hired hands."

Bluff, Leaphorn thought. Maybe he would go there and talk to Houk. It must be the same Houk. The surviving father of the drowned murderer. The memories flooded back. Such tragedy burns deep into the brain.

"Something else you might need to know," Davis said. "Ellie had a pistol."

Leaphorn waited.

"She kept it in the same drawer with that purse."

"It wasn't there," Leaphorn said.

"No. It wasn't," Davis said. "I guess she took it with her."

Yes, Leaphorn thought. He would go to Bluff and talk to Houk. As Leaphorn remembered him, he was a most unusual man.

7

JIM CHEE SAT on the edge of his bunk, rubbed his eyes with his knuckles, cleared his throat, and considered the uneasiness that had troubled his sleep. Too much death. The disturbed earth littered with too many bones. He put that thought aside. Was there enough water left in the tank of his little aluminum trailer to afford a shower? The answer was perhaps. But it wasn't a new problem. Chee long ago had developed a method for minimizing its effects. He filled his coffeepot ready for perking. He filled a drinking glass as a tooth-brushing reserve and a mustard jar for the sweat bath he was determined to take.

Chee climbed down the riverbank carrying the jar, a paper cup, and a tarpaulin. At his sweat bath in the willows beside the San Juan, he collected enough driftwood to heat his rocks, filled the cup with clean, dry sand, started his fire, and sat, legs crossed, waiting and thinking. No profit in thinking of Janet Pete—that encounter represented a humiliation that could be neither avoided nor minimized. Any way he figured it, the cost would be $900, plus Janet Pete's disdain. He thought instead of last night, of the two bodies being photographed, being loaded into the police van by the San Juan County deputies. He thought of the pots, carefully wrapped in newspapers inside the garbage bags.

When the rocks were hot enough and the fire had burned itself down to coals, he covered the sweat bath frame with the tarp, slid under it. He squatted, singing the sweat bath songs that the Holy People had taught the first clans, the songs to force contamination and sickness from the body. He savored the dry heat, conscious of muscles relaxing, perspiration seeping from his skin, trickling behind his ears, down his back, wet against his flanks. He poured a palmful of water from the jar into his hand and sprinkled it onto the rocks, engulfing himself in an explosion of steam. He inhaled this hot fog deeply, felt his body slick with moisture. He was dizzy now, free. Concern for bones and Buicks vanished in the hot darkness. Chee was conscious instead of his lungs at work, of open pores, supple muscles, of his own vigorous health. Here was his *bozro*—his harmony with what surrounded him.

When he threw back the tarp and emerged, rosy with body heat and streaming sweat, he felt light of head, light of foot, generally wonderful. He rubbed himself down with the sand he'd collected, climbed back to the trailer, and took his shower. Chee added to the desert dweller's habitual frugality with water the special caution that those who live in trailers relearn each time they cover themselves with suds and find there's nothing left in the reservoir. He soaped a small area, rinsed it, then soaped another, hurried by the smell of his coffee perking. His Navajo genes spared him the need to shave again for probably a week, but he shaved anyway. It was a way to delay the inevitable.

That was delayed a bit more by the lack of a telephone in Chee's trailer. He used the pay phone beside the convenience store on the highway. Janet Pete wasn't at her office. Maybe, the receptionist said, she had gone down to the Justice building, to the police station. She had been worried about her new car. Chee dialed the station. Three call-back messages for him, two from Janet Pete of DNA, the tribal legal service, one from Lieutenant Leaphorn. Leaphorn had just called and talked to Captain Largo. The captain then had left the message for Chee to call Leaphorn at his home number in Window Rock after 6:00 P.M. Had Pete left any messages? Yes, with the last call she had said to tell him she wanted to pick up her car.

Chee called Pete's home number. He tapped his fingers nervously as the telephone rang. There was a click.

"Sorry I can't come to the phone now," Pete's voice said. "If you will leave a message after the tone sounds, I will call you."

Chee listened to the tone, and the silence following it. He could think of nothing sensible to say, and hung up. Then he drove over to Tso's garage. Surely the damage hadn't been as bad as he remembered.

The damage was exactly as he'd remembered. The car squatted on Tso's towing dolly, discolored with dust, the front wheel grotesquely misaligned, paint scraped from the fender, the little clips that once held Janet Pete's favorite chrome strip holding nothing. A small dent in the door. A large dent marring the robin's-egg blue of the rear fender. Looking crippled and dirty.

"Not so terrible," Tso said. "Nine fifty to eleven hundred dollars and it's good as it was. But she really ought to fix all those problems it had when you first drove it in." Tso was wiping the grease from his hands in a gesture that reminded Chee of greedy anticipation. "Grabby brakes, slack steering, all that."

"I'm going to need some credit," Chee said.

Tso thought about that, his face full of remembered debts, of friendships violated. Chee's thoughts of Tso, always warm, began turning cool. While they did, Janet Pete's motor pool sedan pulled up beside the building. The front door opened. Janet Pete emerged. She looked at the Buick, at two other cars awaiting Tso's ministrations, and gave Chee a dazzling smile.

"Where's my Buick?" she asked. "How did it run? Did you . . ."

The question trailed off. Janet Pete looked again at the Buick.

"My God," she said. "Was anybody killed?"

"Well," Chee said. He cleared his throat. "You see, I was driving down . . ."

"Bad shocks," Tso said. "Slack steering. But Chee here took it out anyway. Sort of a safety check." Tso shrugged, made a wry face. "Could have been killed," he said.

Which, if you thought about it right, was perhaps true, Chee thought. His displeasure with Tso was swept away by a wave of gratitude.

He made a depreciating gesture. "I should have been more careful," he said. "Tso warned me."

Janet was staring at the Buick, reconciling what she saw with what she had left. "They told me everything was fine," she said.

"Odometer set back," Tso said. "Brake lining unevenly worn. U-joint loose. Steering loose. Needed lots of work."

Janet Pete bit her lip. Thought. "Can I use your telephone?"

Chee overheard only part of it. Getting past the salesman to the sales manager to the general manager. It seemed to Chee that the general manager mostly listened.

"Officer Chee doesn't seem to be too badly hurt, but I haven't heard from his lawyer . . . mechanic's list of defects shows . . . that's a third-degree misdemeanor in New Mexico, odometer tampering is. Yes, well, a jury can decide that for us. I think the fine is five thousand dollars. You can pick it up at Tso's garage in Shiprock. He tells me he won't release it until you pay his costs. Towing, inspection, I guess. My lawyer told me to make sure that none of your mechanics worked on it until he decides . . ."

On the way to get a cup of coffee in Janet Pete's motor pool sedan, Chee said, "He'll have his mechanics fix everything."

"Probably," Janet said. "Wouldn't be much of a lawsuit anyway. Not worth it."

"Just letting him sweat a little?"

"You know, they wouldn't try that on you. You're a man. They pull that crap on women. They figure they can sell a woman on the baby blue paint and the chrome stripe. Sell us a lemon."

"Um," Chee said, which provoked a period of silence.

"What really happened?" Janet asked.

"Steering failed," Chee said, feeling uneasy.

"Come on," Janet said.

"Tried to make a turn," Chee said. "Missed it."

"How fast? Come on. What was going on?"

So Jim Chee explained it, all about the missing trailer, and the missing backhoe, and Captain Largo, and that led to what he had found last night.

Janet had heard about it on the radio. Over coffee she was full of questions, not all of them about the crime.

"I heard you were a *hatathali*," she said. "That you sing the Blessing Way."

"I'm still learning," Chee said. "The only one I performed was in the family. A relative. But I know it now. If anybody wants one done."

"How do you get time off? Isn't that a problem? Eight days, isn't it? Or do you sing the shorter version?"

"No problem yet. No customers."

"Another thing I hear about you—you have a *belagana* girlfriend. A teacher over at Crownpoint."

"She's gone away," Chee said, and felt that odd sensation of hearing, from some external point, his voice saying the words. "Gone away to be a graduate student in Wisconsin."

"Oh," Janet said.

"We write," Chee said. "I sent her a pregnant cat once."

Janet looked surprised. "Testing her patience?"

Chee tried to think how to explain it. A stupid thing to send to Mary Landon, stupid to mention it now.

"At the time I thought it had some symbolism," he said.

Janet let the silence live, Navajo fashion. If he had more he wanted to say about Mary Landon and the cat, he would say it. He liked her for that. But he had nothing more to say.

"It was that cat you told me about? Last summer when you'd arrested that old man I was representing. The cat the coyote was after?"

Chee was stirring his coffee, head down but conscious that Janet Pete was studying him. He nodded, remembering. Janet Pete had suggested he provide his stray cat with a coyote-proof home and they had gone to a Farmington pet store and bought one of those plastic and wire cages used to ship pets on airliners. He had used it, eventually, to ship the abandoned white man's cat back to the white man's world.

"Symbolism," Janet Pete said. Now she was stirring her coffee, looking down at the swirl the spoon made.

To the top of her head, Chee said: "*Belagana* cat can't adapt to the Navajo ways. Starves. Eaten by coyote. My stray cat experiment fails. I accept the failure. Cat goes back to the world of the *belaganas*, where there's more to eat and the coyote doesn't get you." It was more than Chee had intended to say. He was torn. He wanted to talk about Mary Landon, about the going away of Mary Landon. But he wasn't comfortable talking about it to Janet Pete.

"She didn't want to stay on the reservation. You didn't want to leave," Janet Pete said. "You are saying you understand her problem."

"Our problem," Chee said. "My problem."

Janet Pete sipped her coffee. "Mine was a law professor. Assistant professor, to be technical." She put the cup down and considered. "You know," she said, "maybe it was the same symbolic cat problem. Let me see if I can make it fit."

Chee waited. Like Mary Landon, Janet Pete had large, expressive eyes. Dark brown instead of blue. Now they were surrounded by frown lines as Janet Pete thought.

"Doesn't fit so well," she said. "He wanted a helpmate." She laughed. "Adam's rib. Something to hold back the loneliness of the young man pursuing his brilliant career at law. The Indian maiden." The words sounded bitter, but she smiled at Chee. "You remember. Few years ago, Indian maidens were in with the Yuppies. Like squash-blossom necklaces and declaring yourself to be part Cherokee or Sioux if you wanted to write romantic poetry."

"Not so much now," Chee said. "I gather you agreed to disagree."

"Not really," she said. "The offer remains open. Or so he tells me."

"Fits in a way," Chee said. "I wanted her to be my Navajo."

"She was a schoolteacher? At Crownpoint?"

"For three years," Chee said.

"But didn't want to make a career out of it. I can see her point."

"That wasn't exactly the problem. It was raising kids out here. More than that, too. I could leave. Had an offer from the FBI. Better money. Sort of a choice involved, as she saw it. Did I want her enough to quit being a Navajo?"

Outside the dusty front window of the Navajo Nation Café the dazzling late-day sunlight turned dark with cloud shadow. A Ford 250 pickup rolled past slowly, its front seat crowded with four Navajos, its rear bumper crowded by the van of an impatient tourist. Chee caught the eye of the waitress and got their coffees refilled. What would he say if Janet Pete pressed the question? If she said: "Well, do you?" what would he say?

Instead, she stirred her coffee.

"How has the professor's brilliant career developed?" Chee asked.

"Brilliantly. He's now chief legal counsel of Davidson-Bart, which I understand is what is called a multinational conglomerate. But mostly involved with the commercial credit end of export-import business. Makes money. Lives in Arlington."

Through the dusty window came the faint sound of thunder, a rumble that faded away.

"Wish it would rain," Janet Pete said.

Chee had been thinking exactly the same thing. Sharing a Navajo thought with another Navajo. "Too late to rain," he said. "It's October thirty-first."

Janet Pete dropped him at the garage. He stopped at the station to call Lieutenant Leaphorn on his way back to the trailer.

"Largo told me you found the bodies of those pot hunters," Leaphorn said. "He was a little vague about what you were doing out there."

He left the question implied and Chee thought a moment before answering. He knew Leaphorn's wife had died. He'd heard the man was having trouble coping with that. He'd heard—everybody in the Navajo Tribal Police had heard—that Leaphorn had quit the force. Retired. So what was he doing in this affair? How official was this? Chee exhaled, taking another second for thought. He thought, quit or not, this is still Joe Leaphorn. Our legendary Leaphorn.

"I was looking for that fellow who stole that backhoe here at Shiprock," Chee said. "I found out he was a pot hunter now and then, and I was trying to catch him out digging. With the stolen property."

"And you knew where to look?" Leaphorn, Chee remembered, never believed in coincidence.

"Some guessing," Chee said. "But I knew what gas company he worked for, and where his job would have taken him, and where there might be some sites in the places he would have been."

The word that spread among the four hundred employees of the Navajo Tribal Police was that Joe Leaphorn had lost it. Joe Leaphorn had a nervous breakdown. Joe Leaphorn was out of it. To Jim Chee, Leaphorn's voice sounded no different. Neither did the tone of his questions. A kind of skepticism. As if he knew he wasn't being told all he needed to know. What would Leaphorn ask him now? How he knew the man would be digging last night?

"You have anything else to go on?"

"Oh," Chee said. "Sure. We knew he rented a truck with new tires on double back wheels."

"Okay," Leaphorn said. "Good. So there were tracks to look for." Now his voice sounded more relaxed. "Makes a lot of difference. Otherwise you spend the rest of your life out there running down the roads."

"And I figured he might be out digging last night because of something he said to Slick Nakai. The preacher bought pots from him, now and then. And he sort of told the preacher he'd have some for him quick," Chee said.

Silence.

"Did you know I'm on leave? Terminal leave?"

"I heard it," Chee said.

"Ten more days and I'm a civilian. Right now, matter of fact, I guess I'm unofficial."

"Yes, sir," Chee said.

"If you can make it tomorrow, would you drive out there to the site with me? Look it over with me in daylight. Tell me how it was before the sheriff's people and the ambulance and the FBI screwed everything up."

"If it's okay with the captain," Chee said, "I'd be happy to go."

8

LEAPHORN HAD BEEN aware of the wind most of the night, listening to it blow steadily from the southeast as he waited for sleep, awakening again and again to notice it shifting, and gusting, making *chindi* sounds around the empty house. It was still blowing when Thatcher arrived to pick him up, buffeting Thatcher's motor pool sedan.

"Cold front coming through," Thatcher said. "It'll die down."

And as they drove northward from Window Rock it moderated. At Many Farms they stopped for breakfast, Thatcher reminiscing about Harrison Houk, cattleman, pillar of the Church of Jesus Christ of Latter-day Saints, potent Republican, subject of assorted gossip, county commissioner, holder of Bureau of Land Management grazing permits sprawling across the southern Utah canyon country, legendary shrewd operator. Leaphorn mostly listened, remembering Houk from long ago, remembering a man stricken. When they paid their check, the western sky over Black Mesa was bleak with suspended dust but the wind was down. Fifty miles later as they crossed the Utah border north of Mexican Water, it was no more than a breeze, still from the southeast but almost too faint to stir the sparse gray sage and the silver cheat grass of the Nokaito Bench. The sedan rolled across the San Juan River bridge below Sand Island in a dead calm. Only the smell of dust recalled the wind.

"Land of Little Rain," Thatcher said. "Who called it that?"

It wasn't the sort of friendship that needed answers. Leaphorn looked upstream, watching a small flotilla of rubber kayaks, rafts, and wooden dories pushing into the stream from the Sand Island launching site. A float expedition down into the deep canyons. He and Emma had talked of doing that. She would have loved it, getting him away from any possibility of telephone calls. Getting him off the end of the earth. And he would have loved it, too. Always intended to do it but there was never enough time. And now, of course, the time was all used up.

"One of your jobs?" Leaphorn asked, nodding toward the flotilla below.

"We license them as tour boatmen. Sell 'em trip permits, make sure they meet the safety rules. So forth." He nodded toward the stream. "That must be the last one of the season. They close the river down just about now."

"Big headache?"

"Not this bunch," Thatcher said. "This is Wild Rivers Expeditions out of Bluff. Pros. More into selling education. Take you down with a geologist to study the formations and the fossils, or with an anthropologist to look at the Anasazi ruins up the canyons, or maybe with a biologist to get you into the lizards and lichens and the bats. That sort of stuff. Older people go. More money. Not a bunch of overaged adolescents hoping to get scared shitless going down the rapids."

Leaphorn nodded.

"Take great pride in cleaning up after themselves. The drill now is urinate right beside the river, so it dilutes it fast. Everything else they carry out. Portable toilets. Build their camp fires in fireboxes so you don't get all that carbon in the sand. Even carry out the ashes."

They turned upriver toward Bluff. Off the reservation now. Out of Leaphorn's jurisdiction and into Thatcher's. Much of the land above the bluffs lining the river would be federal land—public domain grazing leases. The land along the river had been homesteaded by the Mormon families who'd settled this narrow valley on orders from Brigham Young to form an outpost against the hostile Gentile world. This stony landscape south of the river had been Leaphorn's country once, when he was young and worked out of Kayenta, but it was too waterless and barren to support the people who would require police attention.

History said 250 Mormons had settled the place in the 1860s, and the last census figures Leaphorn had seen showed its current population was 240—three service stations strung along the highway, three roadside cafés, two groceries, two motels, the office and boathouse of Wild Rivers Expeditions, a school, a ward meetinghouse, and a scattering of houses, some of them empty. The years hadn't changed much at Bluff.

Houk's ranch house was the exception. Leaphorn remembered it as a big, solid block of a building, formed of cut pink sandstone, square as a die and totally neat. It had been connected to the gravel road from Bluff by a graded dirt driveway, which led through an iron gate, curved over a sagebrush-covered rise, and ended under the cottonwoods that shaded the house. Leaphorn noticed the difference at the gate, painted then, rusted now. He unlatched it, refastened it after Thatcher drove through. Then he pulled the chain, which slammed the clapper against the big iron church bell suspended on the pole that took the electric line to the house. That told Houk he had visitors.

The driveway now was rutted, with a growth of tumbleweeds, wild asters, and cheat grass along the tracks. The rabbit fence, which Leaphorn remembered surrounding a neat and lush front yard garden, was sagging now and the garden a tangle of dry country weeds. The pillars that supported the front porch needed paint. So did the pickup truck parked beside the porch. Only the solid square shape of the house, built to defy time, hadn't been changed by the years. But now, surrounded by decay, it stood like a stranger. Even the huge barn on the slope behind it, despite its stone walls, seemed to sag.

Thatcher let the sedan roll to a stop in the shade of the cottonwood. The screen door opened and Houk appeared. He was leaning on a cane. He squinted from the shadows into blinding sunlight, trying to identify who had rung the yard bell. At first look, Leaphorn thought that Houk, like the pink sandstone of his house, had been proof against time. Despite the cane, his figure in the shadow of the porch had the blocky sturdiness Leaphorn remembered. There was still the round bulldog face, the walrus mustache, the small eyes peering through wire-rimmed glasses. But now Leaphorn saw the paunch, the slight slump, the deepened lines, the grayness, the raggedness of the mustache which hid his mouth. And as Houk shifted his weight against the cane, Leaphorn saw the grimace of pain cross his face.

"Well, now, Mr. Thatcher," Houk said, recognizing him. "What brings the Bureau of Land Management all the way out here so soon? Wasn't it only last spring you was out here to see me?" And then he saw Leaphorn. "And who . . ." he began, and stopped. His expression shifted from neutral, to surprise, to delight.

"By God," he said. "I don't remember your name, but you're the Navajo policeman who found my boy's hat." Houk stopped. "Yes I do. It was Leaphorn."

It was Leaphorn's turn for surprise. Almost twenty years since he'd been involved in the hunt for Houk's boy. He had talked to Houk only two or three times, and only briefly. Giving him the wet blue felt hat, soggy with muddy San Juan River water. Standing beside him under the alcove in the cliff that tense moment when the state police captain decided they had Brigham Houk cornered. And finally, on this very porch when it was all over and no hope remained, listening to the man examine his conscience, finding in his own flaws the blame for his boy's murderous rage. Three meetings, and a long, long time ago.

Houk ushered them into what he called the parlor, a neat room that smelled of furniture polish. "Don't use this room much," Houk said loudly, and he pulled back the curtains, raised the blinds, and pushed up the sash windows to admit the autumn. But the room was still dim—its walls a gallery of framed photographs of people, of bookshelves lined mostly with pots. "Don't get much company," Houk concluded. He sat himself in the overstuffed armchair that matched the sofa, creating another faint puff of dust. "In just a minute the girl will be in here with something cold to drink." He waited then, his fingers tapping at the chair arm. It was their turn to speak.

"We're looking for a woman," Thatcher began. "Anthropologist named Eleanor Friedman-Bernal."

Houk nodded. "I know her." He looked surprised. "What she do?"

"She's been missing," Thatcher said. "For a couple of weeks." He thought about what he wanted to say next. "Apparently she came out here just a little while before she disappeared. To Bluff. Did you see her?"

"Let's see now. I'd say it was three, four weeks when she was out here last," Houk said. "Something like that. Maybe I could figure it out exactly."

"What did she want?"

It seemed to Leaphorn that Houk's face turned slightly pinker than its usual hue. He stared at Thatcher, his lip moving under the mustache, his fingers still drumming.

"You fellas didn't take long to get out here," he said. "I'll say that for you." He pushed himself up in the chair, then sat back down again. "But how the hell you connect it with me?"

"You mean her being missing?" Thatcher said, puzzled. "She had your name down in her notes."

"I meant the killings," Houk said.

"Killings?" Leaphorn asked.

"Over in New Mexico," Houk said. "The pot hunters. It was on the radio this morning."

"You think we're connecting those with you?" Leaphorn asked. "Why do you think that?"

"Because it seems to me that every time the feds start thinking about pot stealing, they come nosing around here," Houk said. "Those folks get shot stealing pots, stands to reason it's going to get the BLM cops, and the FBI, and all off their butts and working. Since they don't know what the hell they're doing, they bother me." Houk surveyed them, his small blue eyes magnified by the lenses of his glasses.

"You fellas telling me this visit hasn't nothing to do with that?"

"That's what we're telling you," Leaphorn said. "We're trying to find an anthropologist. A woman named Eleanor Friedman-Bernal. She disappeared the thirteenth of October. Some references in her notes about coming out here to Bluff to see Mr. Harrison Houk. We thought if we knew what she came out here to see you about, it might tell us something about where to look next."

Houk thought about it, assessing them. "She came to see me about a pot," he said.

Leaphorn sat, waiting for his silence to encourage Houk to add to that. But Thatcher was not a Navajo.

"A pot?"

"To do with her research," Houk said. "She'd seen a picture of it in a Nelson auction catalog. You know about that outfit? And it was the kind she's interested in. So she called 'em, and talked to somebody or other, and they told her they'd got it from me." Houk paused, waiting for Thatcher's question.

"What did she want to know?"

"Exactly where I found it. I didn't find it. I bought it off a Navajo. I gave her his name."

A middle-aged Navajo woman came into the room, carrying a tray with three water glasses, a pitcher of what appeared to be ice water, and three cans of Hires root beer.

"Drinking water or root beer," Houk said. "I guess you knew I'm Latter-day Saints."

Everybody took water.

"Irene," Houk said. "You want to meet these fellas. This is Mr. Thatcher here. The one from the BLM who comes out here now and then worrying us about our grazing rights. And this fella here is the one I've told you about. The one that found Brigham's hat. The one that kept those goddam state policemen from shooting up into that alcove. This is Irene Musket."

Irene put down the tray and held her hand out to Thatcher. "How do you do," she said. She spoke in Navajo to Leaphorn, using the traditional words, naming her mother's clan, the Towering House People, and her father's, the Paiute Dineh. She didn't hold out her hand. He wouldn't expect it. This touching of strangers was a white man's custom that some traditional Navajos found difficult to adopt.

"You remember what day it was that anthropology woman was out here?" Houk asked her. "Almost a month ago, I think."

Irene considered. "On a Friday," she said. "Four weeks ago last Friday." She picked up the tray and left.

"Great friend of my wife, Irene was. After Alice passed on, Irene stayed on and looked after things," Houk said.

They sipped the cold water. Behind Houk's gray head, the wall was lined with photographs. Houk and his wife and their children clustered on the front porch. Brigham, the youngest, standing in front. The brother and sister he was destined to kill standing behind him, smiling over his shoulders. Brigham's mouth looked slightly twisted, as if he had been ordered to smile. Houk's face was happy, boyish. His wife looked tired, strain showing in the lines around her mouth. A wedding picture, the bride with the veil raised above her face, Houk with the mustache much smaller, older couples flanking them. A picture of Brigham on a horse, his smile strained and lopsided. A picture of the sister in a cheerleader's uniform. Of the brother in a Montezuma Creek High School football jacket. Of Brigham holding up a dead bobcat by its back legs, his eyes intense. Of Houk in an army uniform. Of the Houks and another couple. But mostly the pictures were of the three children. Dozens of them, at all ages. In most of them, Brigham stood alone, rarely smiling. In three of them, he stood over a deer. In one, over a bear. Leaphorn remembered Houk talking endlessly on the porch the day Brigham had drowned.

"Always outdoors," Houk had said. "From the very littlest. Shy as a Navajo. Wasn't happy around people. We shouldn't have made him go to school there. We should have gotten him some help."

Now Houk put down his glass. Thatcher asked, "When she left here, was she going to see the Navajo? The one who found the pot?"

"I reckon," Houk said. "That was her intention. She wanted to know where he got it. All I knew is what he told me. That he didn't break any law getting it." Houk was talking directly to Thatcher. "Didn't get it off public domain land, or off the reservation. Got to be off private land or I won't have nothing to do with it."

"What was his name?" Thatcher asked.

"Fella named Jimmy Etcitty," Houk said.

"Live around here?"

"South, I think," Houk said. "Across the border in Arizona. Between Tes Nez Iah and Dinnehotso, I think he said." Houk stopped. It seemed to Leaphorn that it was to decide whether he had told them enough. And this time Thatcher didn't interrupt the silence. Houk thought. They waited. Leaphorn studied the room. Everything was dusty except the piano. It glowed with wax. Like most of the bookshelves, a shelf above the piano was lined with pots.

"I think I told her she should stop at the Dinnehotso Chapter House and ask how to get to the Mildred Roanhorse outfit," Houk added. "Etcitty's her son-in-law."

"I noticed in the Nelson catalog that they give the customer some sort of documentation on their artifacts," Leaphorn said. He left the question implied, and Houk let it hang a moment while he thought about how to answer it.

"They do," Houk said. "If I happen to find something myself—or sometimes when I have personal knowledge where it came from—then I fill out this sort of statement, time and place and all that, and I sign it and send it along. Case like this, I just give the documentation form to the finder—whoever I'm buying it from. I have them fill it in and sign it."

"You show that paper to the lady?" Leaphorn asked.

"Didn't have it," Houk said. "Usually I just have the finder send the letter directly to whoever is buying from me. This case, I gave Etcitty the Nelson form and told him to take care of it."

They sat and considered this.

"Cuts out the middleman on that," Houk said.

And, Leaphorn thought, insulates Harrison Houk from any charge of fraud.

"Might as well get it from the horse's mouth," Houk added, somberly. But he winked at Leaphorn.

There was still plenty of the day left to drive south to the Dinnehotso Chapter House and get directions to the Mildred Roanhorse outfit and find Jimmy Etcitty. On the porch Houk touched Leaphorn's sleeve.

"Always wanted to say something to you about what you did," he said. "That evening I wasn't in any condition to think about it. But it was a kindly thing. And brave too."

"It was just my job," Leaphorn said. "That highway patrolman was a traffic man. Green about that kind of work. And scared too, I guess. Somebody needed to keep it cool."

"Turned out it didn't matter," Houk said. "Brigham wasn't hiding up there anyway. I guess he was already drowned by then. But I thank you."

Thatcher was standing at the foot of the steps, waiting and hearing all this. Embarrassing. But he didn't bring it up until they were out of Bluff driving toward Mexican Water into the blinding noontime sun.

"Didn't know you were involved in that Houk case," he said. He shook his head. "Hell of a thing. The boy was crazy, wasn't he?"

"That's what they said. Schizophrenia. Heard voices. Unhappy around anyone but his dad. A loner. But Houk told me he was great at music. That piano in there, that was the boy's. Houk said he was good at it and played the guitar and the clarinet."

"But dangerous," Thatcher said. "Ought to been put in a hospital. Locked up until he was safe."

"I remember that's what Houk said they should've done. He said his wife wanted to, but he wouldn't do it. Said he thought it would kill the boy. Locking him up. Said he wasn't happy except when he was outdoors."

"What'd you do to make such an impression on Houk?"

"Found the boy's hat," Leaphorn said. "Washed up on the reservation side of the river. It was already pretty clear he'd tried to swim across."

Thatcher drove for a while. Turned on the radio. "Catch the noon news," he said. "See what they got to say about those pot hunters getting shot."

"Good," Leaphorn said.

"There was more to it than that," Thatcher said. "More than finding his goddamned hat."

Might as well get it over with. The memories had been flooding back anyway—another of those many things a policeman accumulates in the mind and cannot erase. "You remember the case," Leaphorn said. "Houk and one of his hired hands came home that night, and found the bodies, and the youngest boy, Brigham, missing, with some of his stuff. And the shotgun he'd done it with was missing too. Big excitement. Houk was even more important then than he is now—legislator and all that. Bunches of men out everywhere looking. This Utah highway patrol officer—a captain or lieutenant or something—he and a bunch he was handling thought they had the boy cornered in a sort of alcove-cave up in a box canyon. Saw something or heard something, and I guess the kid had used the place before as a sort of hangout. Anyway, they'd called for him to come out, and no answer, so this dumb captain is going to have everybody shoot into there, and I said first I'd get a little closer and see what I could see, and turned out nobody was in there."

Thatcher looked at him.

"No big deal," Leaphorn said. "Nobody was there."

"So you didn't get shot with a shotgun."

"I happened to have a pretty clear idea of how far a shotgun will shoot. Not very far."

"Yeah," Thatcher said.

The tone irritated Leaphorn. "Hell, man," he said. "The boy was only fourteen."

Thatcher had no comment on that. The woman reading the noon news had gotten to the pot hunter shooting. The San Juan County Sheriff's Office said they had no suspects in the case as yet but they did have promising leads. Casts had been made of the tire tracks of a vehicle believed used by the killer. Both victims had now been identified. They were Joe B. Nails, thirty-one, a former employee of Wellserve in Farmington, and Jimmy Etcitty, thirty-seven, whose address was given as Dinnehotso Chapter House on the Navajo Reservation.

"Well now," Thatcher said. "I guess we can skip stopping at Dinnehotso."

9

THIS IS JUST about where they'd left the U-Haul truck parked," Chee said. He turned off the ignition, set the parking brake. "Pulled up to the edge of the slope with the winch cable run out. Apparently they eased the backhoe down on the cable."

The front of Chee's pickup was pointed down the steep slope. Fifty feet below, the grassy, brushy hump where a little Anasazi pueblo had stood a thousand years ago was a chaos of trenches, jumbled stones, and what looked like broken sticks. Bones reflecting white in the sunlight.

"Where was the backhoe?"

Chee pointed. "See the little juniper? At the end of that shallow trench there."

"The sheriff hauled everything off, I guess," Leaphorn said. "After they got their photographs."

"That was the plan when I left."

Leaphorn didn't comment. He sat silently, considering the destruction below. This ridge was much higher than it had seemed to Chee in the darkness. Shiprock stuck up like a blue thumb on the western horizon seventy miles away. Behind it, the dim outline of the Carrizo Mountains formed the last margin of the planet. The sagebrush flats between were dappled with the shadow of clouds, drifting eastward under the noon sun.

"The bodies," Leaphorn said. "The *belagana* in the backhoe? Right?

Named Nails. And the Navajo partway up this slope under us? Jimmy Etcitty. Which one was shot first?"

Chee opened his mouth, closed it. His impulse had been to say the coroner would have to decide. Or about the same time. But he realized what Leaphorn wanted.

"I'd guess the Navajo was running for his life," he said. "I'd say he'd seen the white man shot in the machine. He was running for the truck."

"Do much checking before you called it in to the sheriff?"

"Hardly any," Chee said.

"But some," Leaphorn said.

"Very little."

"The killer parked up here?"

"Down by the oil well pump."

"Tire tracks mean anything?"

"Car or pickup. Some wear." Chee shrugged. "Dusty dry and in the dark. Couldn't tell much."

"How about his tracks? Or hers?"

"He parked on the sandstone. No tracks right at the vehicle. After that, mostly scuff marks."

"Man?"

"Probably. I don't know." Chee was remembering how shaken he had been. Too much death. He hadn't been using his head. Now he felt guilty. Had he concentrated, he surely could have found at least something to indicate shoe size.

"Not much use going over it again," Leaphorn said. "Too many deputy sheriffs and paramedics and photographers been trampling around."

And so they scrambled down the hill—Leaphorn losing his footing and sliding twenty feet in a shower of dislodged earth and gravel. Standing there, amid the dislodged stones, amid the scattered bones, Chee felt the familiar uneasiness. Too many *chindi* had taken to the air here, finding freedom from the bodies that had housed them. Leaphorn was standing at a narrow trench the backhoe had dug beside a crumbled wall, looking thoughtful. But then Leaphorn didn't believe in *chindi*, or in anything else.

"You studied anthropology, didn't you? At New Mexico?"

"Right," Chee said. So had Leaphorn, if the word around the Navajo Tribal Police was true. At Arizona State. A BA and an MS.

"Get into the Anasazi much? The archaeological end of it?"

"A little," Chee said.

"The point is, whoever did this work knew something about what he was doing," Leaphorn said. "Anasazi usually buried their dead in the trash midden with the garbage, or right against the walls, sometimes inside the rooms. This guy worked the midden. . . ." Leaphorn gestured to the torn earth beyond them. "And he worked along the walls. So I'd guess he knew they buried pottery with their corpses, and he knew where to find the graves."

Chee nodded.

"And maybe he knew this was a late site, and that rule of thumb—the later the site, the better the pot. Glazed, multicolored, decorated, so forth." He bent, picked up a shard of broken pottery the size of his hand and inspected it.

"Most of the stuff I've seen here is like this," he said, handing the shard to Chee. "Recognize it?"

The interior surface was a rough gray. Under its coating of dust the exterior glowed a glossy rose, with ghostly lines of white wavering through it. Chee touched the glazed surface to his tongue—the automatic reaction of a former anthropology student to a potsherd—and inspected the clean spot. A nice color, but his memory produced nothing more than a confused jumble of titles: Classical. Pueblo III. Incised. Corrugated, etc. He handed the shard to Leaphorn, shook his head.

"It's a type called St. John's Polychrome," Leaphorn said. "Late stuff. There's a theory it originated in one of the Chaco outlier villages. I think they're pretty sure it was used for trading."

Chee was impressed and his face showed it.

Leaphorn chuckled. "I can't remember stuff like that either," he said. "I've been doing some reading."

"Oh?"

"We seem to have a sort of overlap here," he said. "You were looking for a couple of men who stole our backhoe. I'm looking for an anthropologist. A woman who works at Chaco and took off one day three weeks ago to go to Farmington and never came back."

"Hadn't heard about that," Chee said.

"She prepared this big, elaborate dinner. Had a guest coming to visit. A man very important to her. She put it in the fridge and she didn't come back." Leaphorn had been looking out across the grassland toward the distant thunderheads. It must have occurred to him that this would sound strange to Chee. He glanced at him. "It's a San Juan County missing person's case," he said. "But I'm on leave, and it sounded interesting."

"You mentioned you were quitting," Chee said. "I mean resigning."

"I'm on terminal leave," Leaphorn said. "A few more days and I'm a civilian."

Chee could think of nothing to say. He didn't particularly like Leaphorn, but he respected him.

"But I'm not a civilian yet," he added, "and what we have here is peculiar. This overlap, I mean. We have Dr. Friedman-Bernal being a ferocious collector of this kind of pottery." Leaphorn tapped the potsherd with his forefinger. "We have Jimmy Etcitty killed here digging up this sort of pot. This same Jimmy Etcitty worked over at Chaco where Friedman-Bernal worked. This same Jimmy Etcitty found a pot somewhere near Bluff which he sold to a collector who sold it to an auction house. This pot got Friedman-Bernal excited enough a month ago to send her driving to Bluff looking for Etcitty. And on top of that we have Friedman-Bernal buying from Slick Nakai, the evangelist, and Nails selling to Slick, and Etcitty playing guitar for Nakai."

Chee waited, but Leaphorn seemed to have nothing to add.

"I didn't know any of that," Chee said. "Just knew Nails and a friend stole the backhoe when I was supposed to be watching the maintenance yard."

"Nice little tangle of strings, and right here is the knot," Leaphorn said.

And none of it any of Leaphorn's business, Chee thought. Not if he had resigned. So why was he out here, sitting on that stone wall with his legs in the sun, with almost two hundred miles of driving already behind him today? He must enjoy it or he wouldn't be here. So why has he resigned?

"Why did you resign?" Chee asked. "None of my business, I guess, but . . ."

Leaphorn seemed to be thinking about it. Almost as if for the first time. He glanced at Chee, shrugged. "I guess I'm tired," he said.

"But you're using leave time out here, chasing after whatever it is we have here."

"I've been wondering about that myself," Leaphorn said. "Maybe it's the fire horse syndrome. Lifelong habit at work. I think it's because I'd like to find this Friedman-Bernal woman. I'd like to find her and sit her down and say: 'Dr. Bernal, why did you prepare that big dinner and then go away and let it rot in your refrigerator?' "

To Chee, the answer to why Dr. Bernal let her dinner spoil was all too easy. Especially now. Dr. Bernal was dead.

"You think she's still alive?"

Leaphorn considered. "After what we have here, it doesn't seem likely, does it?"

"No," Chee said.

"Unless she did it," Leaphorn said. "She had a pistol. She took it with her when she left Chaco."

"What caliber?" Chee asked. "I heard this one was small."

"All I know is small," Leaphorn said. "Small handgun. She carried it in her purse."

"Sounds like twenty-two caliber," Chee said. "Or maybe a twenty-five or a small thirty-two."

Leaphorn rose, stiffly, to his feet. Stretched his back, flexed his shoulders. "Let's see what we can find," he said.

They found relatively little. The investigators from the county had taken the bodies and whatever else had interested them, which probably hadn't been much. The victims seemed to be clearly identified, and that would be checked with people who knew them for confirmation. The FBI would be asked to do a run on their fingerprints, just in case. The backhoe had been hauled away and would be gone over carefully for prints in the event the killer had been careless with his hands when he shot Nails. The rental truck would receive the same treatment. So would the two plastic sacks in which Chee had seen the pots carefully packed. And just in case, a cord had been run around the dig site, with the little tags dangling to warn citizens away from a homicide site. If some afterthought brought an investigator back to check on something, nothing would be disturbed.

What interested Chee was outside the cord—a new cardboard carton bearing the red legend SUPERTUFF and the sublegend WASTEBASKET LINERS, and several other messages: "Why Pay More For Something You'll Throw Away? Six free in this carton. Thirty for the price of twenty-four!"

The cardboard was smudged with white. Chee squatted beside it and recognized fingerprint powder. Someone had checked it and found the cardboard too rough to show prints. Chee picked it up, extracted the carefully folded plastic sacks. Counted them. Twenty-seven. Twenty-seven plus two filled with pots made twenty-nine. He slipped the sacks back into the box and replaced it. One sack unaccounted for. Filled with what? Had the killer taken one set of pots and left the other two? Had Nails's girlfriend, if he had a girlfriend, borrowed one? It was one of those imponderables.

He watched Leaphorn prowling along the trenches, inspecting digging procedures, or perhaps the human bones. Chee had been avoiding the bones without realizing it. Now almost at his foot he noticed the weathered flat surface of a scapula, broken off below the shoulder joint. Just beyond was a very small skull, complete except for the lower jaw. A child, Chee guessed, unless the Anasazi had been even smaller than he remembered. Beyond the skull, partly buried by the excavation dirt, were ribs, and part of a spinal column, the small bones of a foot, three lower jaws placed in a row.

Chee stared. Why had that happened? He strolled over and looked down at them. One was broken, a small jaw with part of its left side missing. The other two were complete. Adult, Chee guessed. An expert would be able to tell the sex of their owners, the approximate ages at death, something about their diet. But why had someone lined them up like this? One of the pot hunters, Chee guessed. It didn't seem the sort of thing one of the deputies would have done. Then Chee noticed another jawbone, and three more, and finally a total of seventeen within a few yards of the juniper where he was standing. He could see only three craniums. Someone—again surely the pot hunters—had sorted out the jaws. Why? Chee walked over to where Leaphorn was standing, studying something in the trench.

"Find anything?" Leaphorn asked, without looking up.

"Nothing much," Chee said. "One of those plastic bags seems to be missing."

Leaphorn looked up at him.

"The box said contents thirty. There were still twenty-seven folded in it. I saw two with pots in them."

"Interesting," Leaphorn said. "We'll ask about that at the sheriff's office. Maybe they took one."

"Maybe," Chee said.

"You notice anything about the skeletons?" Leaphorn was squatting now in the shallow trench, examining bones.

"Somebody seemed to be interested in the jawbones," Chee said.

"Yes," Leaphorn said. "Now why would that be?" He stood up, holding in both hands a small skull. It was gray with the clay of the grave, and the jaw was missing. "Why in the world would that be?"

Chee had not the slightest idea, and said so.

Leaphorn bent into the grave again, poking at something with a stick. "I think this is what they call a Chaco outlier site," he said. "Same people who lived in the great houses over in the canyon, or probably the same. I think there is some evidence, or at least a theory, that these outliers traded back and forth with the great-house people, maybe came into Chaco for their religious ceremonials. Nobody really knows. This was probably one of the sites being reserved for digging sometime in the future." He sounded, Chee thought, like an anthropology lecturer.

"You have anything pressing to do in Shiprock tonight?" Chee denied it with a negative motion of his head.

"How about stopping off at the Chaco Center on the way home then?" Leaphorn said. "Let's see what we can find out about this."

10

FROM THE DESPOILED outlier site to the eastern boundary of the Chaco Culture National Historic Park would be less than twenty-five miles if a road existed across the dry hills and Chaco Mesa. None did. By the oil company roads that carried Leaphorn and Chee back to Highway 44, thence northwest to Nageezi, and then southwest over the bumpy dirt access route, it was at least sixty miles. They arrived at the visitors' center just after sundown, found it closed for the day, and drove up to the foot of the bluff where employee housing was located.

The Luna family was starting supper—the superintendent, his wife, a son of perhaps eleven, and a daughter a year or two younger. Supper centered on an entrée involving macaroni, cheese, tomatoes, and things that Leaphorn could not readily identify. That he and Chee would eat was a foregone conclusion. Good manners demanded the disclaimer of hunger from the wayfarer, but the geography of the Colorado Plateau made it an obvious lie. Out here there was literally no place to stop to eat. And so they dined, Leaphorn noticing that Chee's appetite was huge and that his own had returned. Perhaps it was the smell of the home cooking—something he hadn't enjoyed since Emma's sickness reached the point where it was no longer prudent for her to be in the kitchen.

Bob Luna's wife, a handsome woman with a friendly, intelligent face, was full of questions about Eleanor Friedman-Bernal. After polite feelers established that questions were not out of order, she asked them. The Luna son, Allen, a blond, profusely freckled boy who looked like a small copy of his blond and freckled mother, put down his fork and listened. His sister listened without interrupting her supper.

"We haven't learned much," Leaphorn said. "Maybe the county has done better. It is their jurisdiction. But I doubt it. No sheriff ever has enough officers. In San Juan County it's worse than normal. You're worried to death with everything from vandalism of summer cabins up on Navajo Lake to people tapping distillate out of the gas pipelines, or stealing oil field equipment, things like that. Too much territory. Too few people. So missing persons don't get worked on." He stopped, surprised at hearing himself deliver this defense of the San Juan County Sheriff's Office. Usually he was complaining about it. "Anyway," he added, lamely, "we haven't learned anything very useful."

"Where could she have gone?" Mrs. Luna said. Obviously it was something she had often thought about. "So early in the morning. She told us she was going to Farmington, and got the mail we had going out, and our shopping lists, and then just vanished." She glanced from Chee to Leaphorn and back. "I'm afraid it isn't going to have a happy ending. I'm afraid Ellie got in over her head with a man we don't know about." She attempted a smile. "I guess that sounds odd—to say that about a woman her age—but at this place, it's so small—so few of us live here, I mean—that everybody tells everybody everything. It's the only thing we have to be interested in. One another."

Luna laughed. "It's pretty hard to have secrets here," he said. "You have experienced our telephone. You don't get any secret calls. And you don't get any secret mail—unless it happens to show up at Blanco the day you happen to pick it up." He laughed again. "And it would be pretty hard to have any secret visitors."

But not impossible, Leaphorn thought. No more impossible than driving out to make your calls away from here, or setting up a post office box in Farmington.

"You just get to know everything by accident even if people don't mention it," Mrs. Luna said. "For example, going places. I hadn't thought to tell anybody when I was going to Phoenix over the Fourth to visit my mother. But everybody knew because I got a postcard that mentioned it, and Maxie or somebody picked up the mail that day." If Mrs. Luna resented Maxie or somebody reading her postcard, it didn't show. Her expression was totally pleasant—someone explaining a peculiar, but perfectly natural, situation. "And when Ellie made that trip to New York, and when Elliot went to Washington. Even if they don't mention it, you just get to know." Mrs. Luna paused to sip her coffee. "But usually they tell you," she added. "Something new to talk about." At that she looked slightly abashed. She laughed. "That's about all we have to do, you know. Speculate about one another. TV reception is so bad out here we have to be our own soap operas."

"When was the trip to New York?" Leaphorn asked.

"Last month," Mrs. Luna said. "Ellie's travel agent in Farmington called and said the flight schedule had been changed. Somebody takes the message, so everybody knows about it."

"Does anyone know why she went?" Leaphorn asked.

Mrs. Luna made a wry face. "You win," she said. "I guess there are some secrets."

"How about why Elliot went to Washington?" Leaphorn added. "When was that?"

"No secret there," Luna said. "It was last month. A couple of days before Ellie left. He got a call from Washington, from his project director I think it was. Left a message. There was a meeting of people working on archaic migration patterns. He was supposed to attend."

"Do you know if Ellie's going to New York had anything to do with her pots? Is that logical?"

"Just about everything she did had something to do with her pots," Luna said. "She was sort of obsessive about it."

Mrs. Luna's expression turned defensive. "Well now," she said, "Ellie was about ready to make a really important report. As least she thought so. And so do I. She pretty well had the proof that would connect a lot of those St. John Polychromes from the Chetro Ketl site with Wijiji and Kin Nahasbas. And more important than all that, she was finding that this woman must have moved away from Chaco and was making pots somewhere else."

"This woman?" Luna said, eyebrows raised. "She tell you her potter was a woman?"

"Who else would do all that work?" Mrs. Luna got up, got the coffeepot, and offered all hands, including the children, a refill.

"She was excited, then?" Leaphorn asked. "About something she'd found recently? Did she talk to you about it?"

"She was excited," Mrs. Luna said. She looked at Luna with an expression Leaphorn read as reproach. "I really do believe that she'd found something important. To everybody else those people are just a name. Anasazi. Not even their real name, of course. Just a Navajo word that means . . ." She glanced at Chee. "Old Ones. Ancestors of our enemies. Something like that?"

"Close enough," Chee said.

"But Ellie has identified a single human being in what has always just been statistics. An artist. Did you know that she'd arranged her pots chronologically . . . showing how her technique developed?"

The question was aimed at Luna. He shook his head.

"And it's very logical. You can see it. Even if you don't know much about pots, or glazing, or inscribing, or any of those decorative techniques."

Luna seemed to have decided about then that his self-interest dictated a change in posture on this issue.

"She's done some really original work, Ellie has," he said. "Pretty well pinned down where this potter worked, up Chaco Wash at a little ruins we call Kin Nahasbas. She did that by establishing that a lot of pots made with this potter's technique had been broken there before they were fully baked in the kiln fire. Then she tied a bunch of pots dug up at Chetro Ketl and Wijiji to the identical personal techniques. Trade pots, you know. One kind swapped to people at Chetro Ketl and another sort to Wijiji. Both with this man's—this potter's peculiar decorating strokes. Hasn't been published yet, but I think she has it pinned."

It gave Leaphorn a sense of déjà vu, as if he remembered a graduate student over some supper in a dormitory at Tempe saying exactly these same words. The human animal's urge to know. To leave no mysteries. Here, to look through the dirt of a thousand years into the buried privacy of an Anasazi woman. "To understand the human species," his thesis chairman liked to say. "To understand how we came to behave the way we do." But finally it had seemed to Leaphorn he could understand this better among the living. It was the spring he'd met Emma. When the semester ended in May he'd left Arizona State and his graduate fellowship and his intentions of becoming Dr. Leaphorn, and joined the recruit class of the Navajo Tribal Police. And he and Emma . . .

Leaphorn noticed Chee watching him. He cleared his throat. Sipped coffee.

"Did you have any clear idea of what she was excited about?" Leaphorn asked. "I mean just before she disappeared. We know she drove over to Bluff and talked to a man over there named Houk. Man who sometimes deals in pots. She asked him about a pot she'd seen advertised in an auction catalog. Wanted to know where it came from. Houk told us she was very intense about it. He told her how to get the documentation letter. Did she say why she was going to New York?"

"Not to me, she didn't," Mrs. Luna said.

"Or why she was excited?"

"I know some more of those polychrome pots had turned up. Several, I think. Same potter. Some identical and some with a more mature style. Later work. And it turned out they came from somewhere else—away from the Chaco. She thought she could prove her potter had migrated."

"Did you know Ellie had a pistol?"

Luna and his wife spoke simultaneously. "I didn't," she said. Luna said: "It doesn't surprise me. I'd guess Maxie has one, too. For snakes," he added, and laughed. "Actually it's for safety."

"Do you know if she ever hired Jimmy Etcitty to find pots for her?"

"Boy, that was a shock," Luna said. "He hadn't worked here long. Less than a year. But he was a good hand. And a good man."

"And he didn't mind digging around graves."

"He was a Christian," Luna said. "A fundamentalist born-again Christian. No more *chindi*. But no, I doubt if he worked for Ellie. Hadn't heard of it."

"Had you ever heard he might be a Navajo Wolf?" Leaphorn asked. "Into any kind of witchcraft. Being a skinwalker?"

Luna looked surprised. And so, Leaphorn noticed, did Jim Chee. Not at the question, Leaphorn guessed. That fooling around with the bones they'd found at the ruins would suggest witchcraft to anyone who knew the Navajo tradition of skinwalkers robbing graves for bones to grind into corpse powder. But Chee would be surprised at Leaphorn's thinking. Leaphorn was aware that his contempt for the Navajo witchcraft business was widely known throughout the department. Chee, certainly, was aware of it. They had worked together in the past.

"Well," Luna said. "Not exactly. But the other men who worked here didn't have much to do with him. Maybe that was because he was willing to dig around the burials. Had given up the traditional ways. But they gossiped about him. Not to me but among themselves. And I sort of sensed they were wary of him."

"Davis told me Lehman came. The man she had the appointment with."

"Her project supervisor? Yeah."

"Did he say what the meeting was about?"

"She'd told him she had one more piece of evidence to get and then she'd be ready to publish. And she wanted to show it all to him and talk it over. He stuck around the next day and then drove back to Albuquerque."

"I'll get his address from you," Leaphorn said. "Did he have any idea what that one piece of evidence was?"

"He thought she'd probably found some more pots. Ones that fit. He said she was supposed to have them when they met."

Leaphorn thought about that. He noticed Chee had marked it, too. It seemed to mean that when Ellie left Chaco it was to pick up those final pots.

"Would Maxie Davis or Elliot be likely to know any more about all this?"

Mrs. Luna answered that one. "Maxie, maybe. She and Ellie were friends." She considered that statement, found it too strong. "Sort of friends. At least they'd known each other for years. I don't think they'd ever worked together—as Maxie and Elliot sometimes do. Teamed."

"Teamed," Leaphorn said.

Mrs. Luna looked embarrassed. "Sue," she said. "Allen. Don't you two have any homework? Tomorrow is a school day."

"Not me," Allen said. "I did mine on the bus."

"Me either," Sue said. "This is interesting."

"They're friends," Mrs. Luna said, looking at Sue, but meaning Maxie and Elliot.

"When Mr. Thatcher and I talked to them it seemed pretty obvious that Elliot wanted it that way," Leaphorn said. "I wasn't so sure about Miss Davis."

"Elliot wants to get married," Mrs. Luna said. "Maxie doesn't."

She glanced at her children again, and at Luna.

"Kids," Luna said. "Sue, you better see about your horse. And Allen, find something to do."

They pushed back their chairs. "Nice to have met you," Allen said, nodding to Leaphorn and to Chee.

"Great children," Leaphorn said, as they disappeared down the hallway. "They ride the bus? To where?"

"Crownpoint," Mrs. Luna said.

"Wow!" Chee said. "I used to ride a school bus about twenty-five miles and that seemed forever."

"About sixty miles or so, each way," Luna said. "Makes an awful long day for 'em. But that's the nearest school."

"We could teach them out here," Mrs. Luna said. "I have a teacher's certificate. But they need to see other children. Nothing but grown-ups at Chaco."

"Two young women and one young man," Leaphorn said. "Was there any friction between the women over that? Any sort of jealousy?"

Luna chuckled.

Mrs. Luna smiled. "Eleanor wouldn't be much competition in that race," she said. "Unless the man wants an intellectual, and then it's about even. Besides, I think in Randall Elliot you have one of those one-woman men. He left a job in Washington and worked his way into a project out here. Just following her. I think he's sort of obsessive about it."

"Delete the 'sort of,'" Luna said. "Make it downright obsessive. And sad, too." He shook his head. "Elliot's a sort of macho guy most ways. Played football at Princeton. Flew a navy helicopter in Vietnam. Won a Navy Cross and some other decorations. And he's made himself a good name in physical anthropology for a man his age. Got stuff published about genetics in archaic populations. That sort of stuff. And Maxie refuses to take anything he does seriously. It's the game she plays."

From down the hall came the high, sweet sound of a harmonica—and then the urgent nasal whine of Bob Dylan. Almost instantly the volume was muted.

"Not a game," Mrs. Luna said, thoughtfully. "It's the way Maxie is."

"Reverse snob, you mean?" Luna asked.

"More to it than that. Kind of a sense of justice. Or injustice, maybe."

Luna looked at Leaphorn and Chee. "To explain what we're talking about, and maybe why we're doing this gossiping, there's no way Maxie would be jealous of Dr. Friedman. Or anybody else, I think. Maxie is the ultimate self-made woman from what I've heard about her. Off of some worn-out farm in Nebraska. Her father was a widower, so she had to help raise the little kids. Went to a dinky rural high school. Scholarship to University of Nebraska, working her way through as a housekeeper in a sorority. Graduate scholarship to Madison, working her way through again. Trying to send money home to help Papa and the kids. Never any help for her. So she meets this man from old money, Exeter Academy, where the tuition would have fed her family for two years. Where you have tutors helping you if you need it. And then Princeton, and graduate school at Harvard, all that." Luna sipped his coffee. "Opposite ends of the economic scale. Anyway, nothing Elliot can do impresses Maxie. It was all given to him."

"Even the navy career?"

"Especially the navy," Mrs. Luna said. "I asked her about that. She said, 'Of course, Randall has an uncle who's an admiral, and an aunt who's married to an undersecretary of the navy, and somebody else who's on the Senate Armed Services Committee. So he starts out with a commission.' And I said something like, 'You can hardly blame him for that,' and she said she didn't blame him. She said it was just that Randall has never had a chance to do anything himself." Mrs. Luna shook her head. "And then she said, 'He might be a pretty good man. Who knows? How can you tell?' Isn't that odd?"

"It sounds odd to me," Leaphorn said. "In Vietnam, he was evacuating the wounded?"

"I think so," Luna said.

"That was it," Mrs. Luna said. "I asked Maxie about that. She said, 'You know, he probably could have done something on his own if he had the chance. But officers give each other decorations. Especially if it pleases Uncle Admiral.' 'Uncle Admiral,' that's what she said. And then she told me her younger brother was in Vietnam, too. She said he was an enlisted man. She said a helicopter flew his body out. But no uncles gave him any decorations."

Mrs. Luna looked sad. "Bitter," she said. "Bitter. I remember the night we'd been talking about this. I'd said something about Randall flying a helicopter and she said, 'What chance do you think you or I would have had to be handed a helicopter to fly?' "

Leaphorn thought of nothing to say about that. Mrs. Luna rose, asked about coffee refills, and began clearing away the dishes. Luna asked if they'd like to spend the night in one of the temporary personnel apartments.

"We better be getting back home," Leaphorn said.

The night was dead still, lit by a half-moon. From the visitor camping area up the canyon there was the sound of laughter. Allen was walking up the dirt road toward his house. As he watched him, it occurred to Leaphorn how everyone knew Eleanor Friedman-Bernal had left so early on her one-way trip.

"Allen," Leaphorn called. "What time do you catch the bus in the morning?"

"It's supposed to get here about five minutes before six," Allen said. "Usually about then."

"Down by the road?"

Allen pointed. "At the intersection down there."

"Did you see Ellie drive away?"

"I saw her loading up her car," Allen said.

"You talk to her?"

"Not much," Allen said. "Susy said hello. And she said something about you kids have a good day at school and we said for her to have a good weekend. Something like that. Then we went down and caught the bus."

"Did you know she was going away for the weekend?"

"Well," Allen said, "she was putting her stuff in her car."

"Sleeping bag, too?" Maxie said she owned one, but he hadn't found it in her apartment.

"Yeah," Allen said. "Whole bunch of stuff. Even a saddle."

"Saddle?"

"Mr. Arnold's," Allen said. "He used to work here. He's a biologist. Collects rocks with lichens on them, and he used to live in one of the temporary apartments. Dr. Friedman had his saddle. She was putting it in her car."

"She'd borrowed it from him?"

"I guess so," Allen said. "She used to have a horse. Last year it was."

"Do you know where this Mr. Arnold lives now?"

"Up in Utah," Allen said. "Bluff."

"How'd she sound? Okay? Same as usual? Nervous?"

"Happy," Allen said. "I'd say she sounded happy."

11

FOR MOST OF his life—since his early teens at least—knowing that he was smarter than most people had been a major source of satisfaction for Harrison Houk. Now, standing with his back pressed against the wall of the horse stall in the barn, he knew that for once he had not been smart enough. It was an unusual feeling, and chilling. He thought of that aphorism of southern Utah's hard country—if you want to be meaner than everybody else without dying young, you have to be smarter than everybody else. More than once Harrison Houk had heard that rule applied to him. He enjoyed the reputation it implied. He deserved it. He had gotten rich in a country where almost everybody had gotten poor. It had made him enemies, the way he had done it. He controlled grazing leases in ways that might not have stood grand jury scrutiny. He bought livestock, and sold livestock, under sometimes peculiar circumstances. He obtained Anasazi pots from people who had no idea what they were worth and sometimes sold them to people who only thought they knew what they were getting. He had arranged deals so lopsided that, when daylight hit them, they brought the high councilor of his Latter-day Saints stake down from Blanding to remind him of what was said about such behavior in the Book of Mormon. Even his stake president had written once exhorting him to make things right. But Houk had been smart enough not to die young.

He was old now, and he intended to become very, very old. That was absolutely necessary. Things remained for him to do.

Now more than ever. Responsibilities. Matters of clearing his conscience. He hadn't stopped at much, but he'd never had a human life on his hands before. Not this directly. Never before.

He stood against the wall, trying to think of a plan. He should have recognized the car more quickly, and understood what it must mean. Should have instantly made the link between the killing of Etcitty and the rest of it. He would have when he was younger. Then his mind worked like lightning. Now the killings had made him nervous. They could have been motivated by almost anything, of course. Greed among thieves. Malice over a woman. God knows what. Almost anything. But the instinct that had served him so well for so long suggested something more sinister. An erasing of tracks. A gathering in of strings. That certainly would involve him, and he should have seen. Nor should he have thought so slowly when he saw the car turning through his gate. Maybe he would have had enough time then to hobble back to the house, to the pistol in his dresser drawer or the rifle in the closet. He could only wait now, and hope, and try to think of some solution. There could be no running for it, not with the arthritis in his hip. He had to think.

Quickly. Quickly. He'd left a note for Irene. He thought Irene would be coming back for her squash and she'd wonder where he'd gone. Pinned it on the screen door, telling her he'd be out in the barn working. It was right there in plain view. The worst kind of bad luck.

He looked around him for a hiding place. Houk was not a man subject to panic. He could climb into the loft but there was no cover there. Behind him bales of alfalfa were stacked head-high. He could restack some of them, leave himself a cave. Would there be time? Not without luck. He began a new stack against the wall, leaving a space just wide enough to hold him, groaning as he felt the weight of the heavy bales grinding his hip socket. As he worked, he realized the futility. That would only delay things a few minutes. There was really no place to hide.

He noticed the pitchfork then, leaning beside the door where he'd left it. He limped over, got it, limped back to the horse stall. Maybe there would be some chance to use it. Anyway, it was better than hiding and just waiting.

He gripped the fork handle, listening. His hearing wasn't what it once had been but he could detect nothing except, now and then, the breeze blowing through the slats. The smell of the barn was in his nostrils. Dust. Dry alfalfa. The faint acid of dried horse urine. The smell of a dry autumn.

"Mr. Houk," the voice called. "You in the barn?"

Add it all together, average it out, it had been a good enough life. The first fifty years, close to wonderful, except for Brigham being sick. Even that you could live with, given the good wife he'd been blessed with. Except for the downswings of the schizophrenia, Brigham had been happy enough, most of the time. The rages came and went, but when he was out in the wild country, hunting, living alone, he seemed full of joy. Thinking back, Houk was impressed again with the memory. He'd been pretty good himself outdoors as a kid. But not like The Boy. By the time he was ten, Brigham could go up a cliff that Houk wouldn't have tried with ropes. And he knew what to eat. And how to hide. That brought back a rush of memories, and of the old, old sorrow. The Boy, the summer he was seven, missing long after suppertime. All of them hunting him. Finding him in the old coyote den under the saltbush. He'd been as terrified at being found as if he had been a rabbit dug out by a dog.

That had been the day they no longer lied to themselves about it. But nothing the doctors tried had worked. The piano had helped for a while. He had a talent for it. And he could lose himself for hours just sitting there making his music. But the rages came back. And putting him away had been unspeakable and unthinkable.

"Houk?" the voice said. Now it was just beyond the barn wall. "I need to talk to you."

And now he could hear footsteps, the door with the draggy hinge being pulled open.

One thing he had to do. He couldn't leave it undone. He should have handled it yesterday, as soon as he found out about it. Yesterday—personally. It had to be taken care of. It wasn't something you went away and left—not a human life.

He took out his billfold, found a business card from a well-drilling outfit in it, and began writing on its back, holding the card awkwardly against the billfold.

"Houk," the voice said. It was inside the barn now. "I see you there, through the slats. Come out."

No time now. He couldn't let the note be found, except by the police. He pushed it down inside his shorts. Just as he did, he heard the stall door opening.

12

IT WAS RAINING in New York. L. G. Marcy, the director of public affairs to whom Joe Leaphorn was referred, proved to be a slender, stylish woman with gray hair, and eyes as blue as blade steel. On drier days, the expanse of glass behind her desk looked out upon the rooftops of midtown Manhattan. She examined Leaphorn's card, turned it over to see if the back offered more information, and then glanced up at him.

"You want to see the documentation on an artifact," she said. "Is that correct?" She glanced down at the open catalog Leaphorn had handed her.

"That's all. Just this Anasazi pot," Leaphorn said. "We need to know the site it came from."

"I can assure you it was legal," Ms. Marcy said. "We do not deal in pots collected in violation of the Antiquities Preservation Act."

"I'm sure that's true," said Leaphorn, who was equally sure no sane pot hunter would ever certify that he had taken a pot illegally. "We presume the pot came from private land. We simply need to know which private land. Whose ranch."

"Unfortunately, that pot sold. All pots went in that auction. So we don't have the documentation. The documentation went to the buyer. Along with the pot," L. G. Marcy said. She smiled, closed the catalog, handed it to Leaphorn. "Sorry," she said.

"Who was the buyer?"

"We have a problem there," she said. "It is Nelson's policy to cooperate with the police. It is also Nelson's policy to respect the confidence of our customers. We never tell anyone the identity of buyers unless we have their advance clearance to do so." She leaned across the desk to return Leaphorn's card. "That rarely happens," she said. "Usually, none of the parties concerned wants publicity. They value privacy. On rare occasions, the object involved is so important that publicity is inevitable. But rarely. And in this case, the object is not the sort that attracts the news media."

Leaphorn put the card in the pocket of his uniform shirt. The shirt was damp from the rain Leaphorn had walked through from his hotel toward this office building before ducking for shelter into a drugstore. To his surprise, the store sold umbrellas. Leaphorn had bought one, the first he'd ever owned, and continued his journey under it—tremendously self-conscious—thinking he would own the only umbrella in Window Rock, and perhaps the only umbrella on the reservation, if not in all of Arizona. He was conscious of it now, lying wetly across his lap, while he waited silently for L. G. Marcy to add to her statement. Leaphorn had learned early in his career that this Navajo politeness often clashed with white abhorrence for conversational silences. Sometimes the resulting uneasiness caused *belagana* witnesses to blurt out more than they intended to say. While he waited, he noticed the prints on the wall. All, if Leaphorn could judge, done by female artists. The same for the small abstract sculpture on the Marcy desk. The silence stretched. It wasn't going to work with this *belagana*.

It didn't.

The pause caused L. G. Marcy's smile to become slightly bent. Nothing more. She outwaited him. About his own age, Leaphorn thought, but she looked like a woman in her mid-thirties.

Leaphorn stirred. Moved the umbrella off his lap. "I believe the FBI notified your company that we are investigating two homicides," he said. "This particular pot seems to figure into it. Your client won't be embarrassed. Not in any way. We simply . . ."

"I'm not sure the FBI exactly notified us of anything," Ms. Marcy said. "An FBI agent called from . . ." She examined a notebook. ". . . Albuquerque, New Mexico, and told us that a representative of the Navajo Tribal Police would call today about an artifact we had handled. He said our cooperation would be appreciated. The call was referred to me, and when I questioned him about what the federal government interest might be, this agent, this Mr. Sharkey, he, well . . ." Ms. Marcy hunted politely for a word politer than "weaseled." "He made it appear that his call was not official at all. It was intended as a sort of a personal introduction."

Leaphorn simply nodded. Sharkey hadn't wanted to make the call, had foreseen embarrassment, had been talked into it. Having been caught at it, Sharkey would be angry and hard to deal with. But then in a few more days, nothing like that would matter. Leaphorn would be a civilian. He nodded again.

"There's a system for dealing with problems like this, of course," Ms. Marcy said. "One petitions the appropriate court for an injunction. You then serve this order on us, and we provide you with the information. The requirement that we make available evidence needed in a judicial proceeding supersedes our own need to maintain a confidential relationship with our customers." Her expression was bland.

After a moment, Leaphorn said, "Of course that's a possibility. We'd like to avoid it if we could." He shrugged. "The paperwork. We'd like to avoid all the delay." And, he thought, the problem of persuading the court that an item circled in a Nelson's catalog has anything at all to do with anything.

"That's understandable," Ms. Marcy said. "I think you can also understand our position. Our clients rely on us to keep transactions confidential. For many good reasons." She made an inclusive gesture with small white hands. "Burglars," she said, "for one example. Former wives. Business reasons. So you must understand . . ."

Ms. Marcy began pushing back her chair. When she rises, Leaphorn thought, she will tell me that without a court order she cannot give me any information. He did something he almost never did. He interrupted.

"Our problem is time," he said. "A woman's life may be at stake."

Ms. Marcy lowered herself back into the chair. That little motion brought to Leaphorn's nostrils an awareness of perfume, and powder, and fine feminine things. It reminded him, with overpowering force, of Emma. He closed his eyes, and opened them.

"A woman who was very interested in this particular pot—the woman who drew the circle around it in your catalog—she's been missing for weeks," Leaphorn said. He took out his wallet, extracted his photograph of Dr. Eleanor Friedman-Bernal, the bride. He handed it to Ms. Marcy. "Did she come in to see you? This autumn? Or call?"

"Yes," Ms. Marcy said. "She was in." She studied the photograph, frowning. Leaphorn waited until she looked up.

"Dr. Eleanor Friedman-Bernal," he said. "An anthropologist. Published a lot of papers in the field of ceramics—and of primitive ceramic art. We gather that Dr. Friedman-Bernal believes she has discovered an Anasazi potter whose work she can specifically identify. Did she tell you all that?"

As he related this, Leaphorn was aware of how mundane and unimportant it must sound to a layman. In fact, it sounded trivial to him. He watched Ms. Marcy's face.

"Some of it," Ms. Marcy said. "It would be fascinating if she can prove it."

"From what we can find out, Dr. Friedman-Bernal identified a decorative technique in the finishing of a kind of pottery called St. John Polychrome—a kind made in the last stages of the Anasazi civilization. She found that technique was peculiar to one single specific Anasazi potter."

"Yes. That's what she said."

Leaphorn leaned forward. If his persuasion didn't work, he'd wasted two days on airplanes and a night in a New York hotel.

"I gather that this woman, this Anasazi potter, had some special talent which the doctor spotted. Dr. Friedman-Bernal was able to trace her work backward and forward in time through scores of pots, arranging them chronologically as this talent developed. The potter worked at Chaco Canyon, and her work turned up at several of the villages there. But recently—probably earlier this year—Friedman-Bernal began finding pots that seemed to come from somewhere else. And they were later pots—with the woman's style matured. Your spring auction catalog carried a photograph of one of these pots. We found the catalog in Dr. Friedman-Bernal's room, with the photograph circled."

Ms. Marcy was leaning forward now. "But those pots, they were so stylized," she said. "So much alike. How . . . ?" She didn't complete the question.

"I'm not sure," Leaphorn said. "I think she does it the way graphologists identify handwriting. Something like that."

"It makes sense," Ms. Marcy said.

"From what we know, from what Friedman-Bernal told other anthropologists, she seems to have believed that she could find the place to which this potter moved when the Chaco civilization collapsed," Leaphorn said.

"About right," Ms. Marcy said. "She said she thought this pot was the key. She said she had come across several shards, and one complete pot, which she was sure came from a late phase in this potter's work—an extension and refinement and maturing of her techniques. The pot she'd seen in our catalog seemed to be exactly identical to this work. So she wanted to study it. She wanted to know where she could go to see it, and she wanted to see our documentation."

"Did you tell her?"

"I told her our policy."

"So you didn't tell her who had bought it? Or how to contact the buyer?"

Ms. Marcy sighed, allowed her expression to show a flash of impatience.

"I told her the same thing I am telling you. One of the reasons people have been dealing with Nelson's for more than two hundred years is because of our reputation. They know they can depend, absolutely and without a qualm of doubt, on Nelson's keeping transactions in confidence."

Leaphorn leaned forward.

"Dr. Friedman-Bernal flew back to Albuquerque after she talked to you. Then she drove back to Chaco Canyon, where she lives and works. The following Friday she got up very early, put her sleeping bag into her car, and drove away. She'd told her friends she'd be gone for a day or two. We suspect that somehow she found out where this pot had come from and went to see if she could find something to prove it. Probably to see if there were other such pots, or potsherds, at the place."

He leaned back, folded his hands across his chest, wondering if this would work. If it didn't, he was near a dead end. There was Chee, of course. He'd asked Chee to find the Reverend Slick Nakai—to learn from Nakai everything the man knew about where those damned pots were coming from. Chee seemed interested. Chee would do his best. But how smart was Chee? He should have waited, done it himself, not risked having it all screwed up.

"She vanished," Leaphorn said. "No trace of the woman, or car, or anything. Not a word to anyone. As if Eleanor Friedman-Bernal had never existed."

Ms. Marcy picked up the photograph and studied it. "Maybe she just went away," she said, looking up at Leaphorn. "You know. Too much work. Too much stress. Suddenly you just want to say to hell with it. Maybe that was it." She said it as a woman who knows the feeling.

"Possibly," Leaphorn said. "However, the evening before she left she spent a lot of time fixing a dinner. Marinated the meat entrée, all that. The professor she had worked with was coming in from Albuquerque. She fixed this fancy dinner and put it in the refrigerator. And at dawn the next morning she put her sleeping bag and things like that in her car and drove away."

Ms. Marcy considered. She took the picture of Eleanor Friedman as a bride from the desk and looked at it again.

"Let me see what I can do," she said. She picked up the telephone. "Will you wait outside just a moment?"

The reception room had no view of the rain. Just walls displaying abstract prints, and a receptionist in whom Leaphorn's damp Navajo Tribal Police uniform had aroused curiosity. He sat against the wall, glancing through an *Architectural Digest*, aware of the woman staring at him, wishing he had worn civilian clothes. But maybe it wasn't the uniform. Maybe it was the damp Navajo inside it.

Ms. Marcy came out in a little less than ten minutes. She handed Leaphorn a card. It bore a name, Richard DuMont, and an address on East Seventy-eighth Street.

"He said he would see you tomorrow morning," she said. "At eleven."

Leaphorn stood. "I appreciate this," he said.

"Sure," she said. "I hope you'll let me know. If you find her I mean."

Leaphorn spent the rest of the afternoon prowling through the Museum of Modern Art. He sat, finally, where he could see the patio of sculpture, the rain-stained wall behind it, and the rainy sky above. Like all dry-country people, Leaphorn enjoyed rain—that rare, longed-for, refreshing blessing that made the desert bloom and life possible. He sat with his head full of thoughts and watched the water run down the bricks, drip from the leaves, form its cold pools on the flagstones, and give a slick shine to Picasso's goat.

The goat was Leaphorn's favorite. When they were young and he was attending the FBI Academy, he had brought Emma to see New York. They had discovered Picasso's goat together. He had already been staring at it when Emma had laughed, and plucked at his sleeve, and said: "Look. The mascot of the Navajo Nation."

He had an odd sensation as he remembered this, as if he could see them both as they had been then. Very young, standing by this glass wall looking out into the autumn rain. Emma, who was even more beautiful when she laughed, was laughing.

"Perfect for us Dineh," she'd said. "It's starved, gaunt, bony, ugly. But look! It's tough. It endures." And she had hugged his arm in the delight of her discovery, her face full of the joy, and the beauty, that Leaphorn had found nowhere else. And of course, it was true. That gaunt goat would have been the perfect symbol. Something to put on a pedestal and display. Miserable and starved, true enough. But it was also pregnant and defiant—exactly right to challenge the world at the entrance of the ugly octagonal Tribal Council meeting hall at Window Rock. Leaphorn remembered their having coffee at the museum café and then walking out and patting the goat. The sensation came back to him now—wet, cold metal slick under his palm—utterly real. He got up and hurried out of the museum into the rain, leaving the umbrella hanging forgotten on the chair.

Leaphorn took a cab to the Seventy-eighth Street address, got there a quarter of an hour early, and spent the time prowling the neighborhood—a territory of uniformed doormen and expensive dogs walked by persons who seemed to have been hired for the job. He rang the door chimes at eleven exactly. He waited on the steps, looking at the sky down the street. It would rain again, and soon—probably before noon. An old man, stooped and gray in a wrinkled gray suit, opened the door and stood silently, looking at him patiently.

"My name is Leaphorn," he said. "I have an appointment with Richard DuMont."

"In the study," the man said, motioning Leaphorn in.

The study was a long, high-ceilinged room down a long, high-ceilinged hall. A man in a dark blue dressing gown was sitting at the end of a long library table. Light from a floor lamp beside his chair reflected off the white of a breakfast cloth, and china, and silver.

"Ah, Mr. Leaphorn," the man said, smiling. "You are most punctual. I hope you will excuse me for not getting up to greet you." He tapped the arms of the wheelchair in which he was sitting. "And I hope you will join me for some breakfast."

"No thank you," Leaphorn said. "I've eaten."

"Some coffee, then?"

"I have never refused coffee. Never will."

"Nor I," DuMont said. "Another of my vices. But seat yourself." He gestured toward a blue plush chair. "The woman at Nelson's told me you are hunting a missing woman. An anthropologist. And that murder is involved." DuMont's small gray eyes peered at Leaphorn, avid with interest. Unusual eyes set in a pinched, narrow face under eyebrows almost identical in color to his pale skin. "Murder," he repeated, "and a missing woman." His voice was clear, precise, easy to understand. But like his face it was a small voice. Any background noise would bury it.

"Two pot hunters were killed," Leaphorn said. Something about DuMont was unpleasant. Too much interest? But interest in such a man seemed natural enough. After all, he was a collector. "Including the man who found my pot," DuMont said, with what seemed to Leaphorn to be a sort of pleasure. "Or so that woman at Nelson's told me."

"We think so," Leaphorn said. "Ms. Marcy told me you would be willing to let me see the documentation he sent in. We want to know where he found the pot."

"The document," DuMont said. "Yes. But tell me how the man was killed. How the woman is missing." He raised his arms wide apart, his small mouth grinning. "Tell me all of that."

Behind DuMont, on both sides of a great formal fireplace, shelves formed the wall. The shelves were lined with artifacts. Pots, carved stone images, baskets, fetishes, masks, primitive weapons. Just behind the man, a pedestal held a massive stone head—Olmec, Leaphorn guessed. Smuggled out of Mexico in defiance of that country's antiquities act.

"Mr. Etcitty and a companion were digging up an Anasazi ruin, apparently collecting pots. Someone shot them," Leaphorn said. "An anthropologist named Friedman-Bernal was specializing in this sort of ceramics. In fact, she was interested in this pot you bought. She disappeared. Left Chaco Canyon—she worked there—for a weekend and hasn't come back."

Leaphorn stopped. He and DuMont looked at each other. The stooped, gray man who had admitted Leaphorn appeared at his elbow, placed a small table beside his chair, spread a cloth upon it, put a silver tray on the cloth. The tray held a cup of paper-thin china sitting on a translucent saucer, a silver pot from which steam issued, two smaller silver containers, and a silver spoon. The gray man poured coffee into Leaphorn's cup and disappeared.

"One doesn't buy merely the object," DuMont said. "One wants what goes with it. The history. This head, for example, came out of the jungles in northern Guatemala. It had decorated the doorway to a chamber in a temple. The room where captives were held until they were sacrificed. I'm told the Olmec priests strangled them with a cord."

DuMont covered the lower part of his small face with his napkin and produced a small cough, his avid eyes on Leaphorn.

"And this Anasazi pot of yours. Why is it worth five thousand dollars?" He laughed, a small, tinkling sound. "It's not much of a pot, really. But the Anasazi! Such mysterious people. You hold this pot, and think of the day it was made. A civilization that had grown a thousand years was dying." He stared into Leaphorn's eyes. "As ours is surely dying. Its great houses were standing empty. No more great ceremonials in the kivas. This is about when my pot was made—so my appraisers tell me. Right at the end. The twilight. In the dying days."

DuMont did something at the arm of his wheelchair and said: "Edgar."

"Yes, sir." Edgar's voice seemed to come from under the table.

"Bring me that pot we bought last month. And the documents."

"Yes, sir."

"So stories are important to me," DuMont said to Leaphorn. "What you could tell me has its value here. I show my new pot to my friends. I tell them not just of the Anasazi civilization, but of murder and a missing woman." He grinned a small, prim grin, showing small, perfect teeth.

Leaphorn sipped his coffee. Hot, fresh, excellent. The china was translucent. To the right of DuMont a row of high windows lined the wall.

The light coming through them was dim, tinted green by the vines that covered them. Rain streamed down the glass.

"Did I make my point?" DuMont said.

"I think so," Leaphorn said.

"Tit for tat. You want information from me. In exchange it seems to me only fair that you give me my story. The story to go with my pot."

"I did," Leaphorn said.

DuMont raised two white hands, fluttered them. "Details, details, details," he said. "All the bloody details. The details to pass along."

Leaphorn told him the details. How the bodies were found. How the men had been killed. Who they were. He described the scene. He described the bones. DuMont listened, rapt.

". . . and there we are," Leaphorn concluded. "No leads, really. Our missing woman might be a lead to the killer. More likely she's another victim. But it's all vague. We know just that she was interested in the same pots. Just that she's missing."

Edgar had returned early in this account and stood beside DuMont, holding a pot and a manila folder. The pot was small, about the size of a man's head. A little larger than DuMont's skull.

"Hand the pot to Mr. Leaphorn," DuMont said. "And the documents, please."

Edgar did so. And stood there, stooped and gray, his presence making Leaphorn edgy. Why didn't the man sit down? Leaphorn placed the pot carefully on the table, noticing the smooth feel of the glazing, aware that it had nothing to tell him. He opened the folder.

It contained what appeared to be two bills of sale, one from Harrison Houk to Nelson's and one from Nelson's to DuMont, and a form with its blanks filled in by an awkward hand. It was signed by Jimmy Etcitty.

Leaphorn checked the date. The previous June. He checked the space marked "Place of recovery." The entry read:

> About eight or ten miles down San Juan from Sand Island. From mouth of canyon on north side of river go up the canyon about five and a half miles to the place where there are three ruins on the left side of the canyon at a low level. Right there by the lower ruin are a

bunch of pictures of Anasazi *yei* figures and one looks like a big baseball umpire holding up a pink chest protector. On the north side of the canyon one of the ruins is built against the cliff on the shelf above the canyon bottom. Above it on the higher shelf there is a cave under the cliff with a ruin built in it, and above that in a smaller cave there is another ruin. All these ruins are on private land under lease to my friend Harrison Houk of Bluff, Utah. This pot came from a trench beside the south wall of the ruin against the cliff. It was faceup, with three other pots, all broken, and a skeleton, or part of a skeleton. When found, the pot had nothing but dirt in it.

Leaphorn was surprised at the intensity of his disappointment. It was exactly what he should have expected. He checked the other blanks and found nothing interesting. DuMont was watching him, grinning.

"A problem?"

"A little case of lying," Leaphorn said.

"Just what Dr. Friedman said." DuMont chuckled. "False, false, false."

"You talked to Dr. Friedman?"

"Just like this," DuMont said, delighted with Leaphorn's amazement. "Your missing lady was right here. In that same chair. Edgar, was she drinking from the same cup?"

"I have no idea, sir," Edgar said.

"Same questions, anyway." DuMont gestured. "Fascinating."

"How did she find you?"

"As you did, I presume. Through Nelson's. She called, and identified herself, and made an appointment."

Leaphorn didn't comment. He was remembering her note. "Call Q!" Ellie seemed to have had a pipeline into the auction house that got her past Ms. Marcy.

"She said the certification was false? The location?"

"She said that canyon isn't where Mr. . . . Mr. . . ."

"Etcitty," Edgar said.

"Where Mr. Etcitty said it was." DuMont laughed. "Running the wrong way, she said. Too far down the river. Things like that."

"She was right," Leaphorn said. If that false location had an effect on

DuMont's five-thousand-dollar pot, it had no effect on his humor. He was grinning his small white grin.

"She was quite upset," he said. "Disappointed. Are you?"

"Yes," Leaphorn said. "But I shouldn't be. It's exactly what I should have expected."

"Edgar has made you a copy of that," DuMont said. "To take with you."

"Thank you," Leaphorn said. He pushed himself out of the chair. He wanted to get out of this room. Away. Out into the clean rain.

"And Edgar will give you my card," DuMont said from behind him. "Call me with all the details. When you find her body."

13

FINDING THE REVEREND Slick Nakai had not been easy. At the Nageezi site Chee found only the trampled place where the revival tent had stood, and the trash left behind. He asked around, learned that Nakai was known at the Brethren Navajo Mission. He drove to Escrito. The *belagana* at the mission there knew of Nakai but not his whereabouts. If he had scheduled a revival around there, they hadn't heard of it. Must be a mistake. Chee left, sensing that he wasn't alone in his disapproval of Slick Nakai. At Counselors Trading Post, where people tend to know what's happening on the north side of the Checkerboard Reservation, he hung around until he found someone who knew of a family not only fervently following the Jesus Road, but doing so as prescribed by the tenets of Nakai's sect. It was the family of Old Lady Daisy Manygoats. The Manygoats outfit, unfortunately, lived way over by Coyote Canyon. Chee drove to Coyote Canyon, stopped at the chapter house, got directions down a road that was bad even by reservation standards, and found nobody at home at the Manygoats place except a boy named Darcy Ozzie. Yes, Darcy Ozzie knew about the Reverend Slick Nakai, had in fact gone to his recent revival over at Nageezi.

"They say he was going to preach over between White Rock and Tsaya, over there by the mountains," the boy said, indicating west in the Navajo fashion by a twist of his lips. "And then when he was finished there, he was going way over into Arizona to have a revival over there by Lower Greasewood. Over there south of the Hopi Reservation."

So Chee drove up the Chuska Valley toward Tsaya, with the Chuska Range rising blue to his left and autumn asters forming two lines of color along the opposite sides of the cracked old asphalt of U.S. 666, and snakeweed and chamisa coloring the slopes mottled tan-yellow-gold and the November sky dark blue overhead.

He had quit thinking of Slick Nakai about halfway between Nageezi and Coyote Canyon, having exhausted every possible scenario their meeting might produce. Then he considered Mary Landon. She loved him, he concluded. In her way. But there was love, and then there was love. She would not change her mind about living her life on the reservation. And she was right. Lacking some very basic change in Mary, she would not be happy raising their children here. He wanted Mary to neither change nor be unhappy. Which led him back to himself. She would marry him if he left the reservation. And he could do that. He'd had offers. He could go into federal law enforcement. Work somewhere where their children could go to school with white kids and be surrounded by white culture. Mary would be happy. Or would she? He could still be a Navajo in the sense of blood, but not in the sense of belief. He would be away from family and the Slow Talking Dineh, the brothers and sisters of his maternal clan. He would be outside of Dineh Bike'yah—that territory fenced in by the four sacred mountains within which the magic of the curing ceremonials had its compulsory effect. He would be an alien living in exile. Mary Landon would not enjoy life with that Jim Chee. He could not live with an unhappy Mary Landon. It was the conclusion he always eventually reached. It left him with a sense of anger and loss. That, in turn, moved his thoughts to something else.

He thought of Janet Pete, trying to work what little he knew of her character into the solution she would find to her own problem. Would she allow her lawyer to convert her into an Indian maiden? Not enough data to be sure, but he doubted if Janet Pete would ever buy that.

Who killed Nails and Etcitty? Find the motive. There lies the answer. But there could be a dozen motives and he had no basis for guessing. Leaphorn, obviously, believed Slick Nakai somehow fit into that puzzle.

But then Leaphorn knew a lot more about this business than Chee. All Chee knew was that Nakai bought pots from Etcitty—or perhaps was given them. That Etcitty was one of Nakai's born-again Christians. That Leaphorn believed Nakai sold pots to the woman missing from Chaco Canyon. That was the focus of Chee's assignment. Leaphorn's voice on the telephone had sounded tired. "You want to stick with me a little longer on this Friedman-Bernal business?" he asked. "If you do, I can arrange it with Captain Largo."

Chee had hesitated, out of surprise. Leaphorn had identified the pause as indecision.

"I should remind you again that I'm quitting the department," Leaphorn had interjected. "I'm on terminal leave right now. I already told you that. I tell you now so if you're doing me a favor, remember there's no way I can return it."

Which, Chee had thought, was a nice way of saying the reverse—I can't punish you for refusing.

"I'd like to stay on it," Chee had said. "I'd like to find out who killed those guys."

"That's not what we're working on," Leaphorn had said. "They're connected, I guess. They must be connected. But what I'm after is what happened to the woman missing from Chaco. The anthropologist."

"Okay," Chee had said. It seemed an odd focus. Two murders, apparently premeditated assassinations. And Leaphorn was devoting his leave time, and Chee's efforts, to a missing person case. Same case, probably, the way it looked now. But going at it totally backward. Well, Lieutenant Leaphorn was supposed to be smarter than Officer Chee. He had a reputation for doing things in weird ways. But he also had a reputation for guessing right.

At Tsaya, Chee found he'd missed Slick Nakai, but not by much. Nakai had canceled his planned revival there and headed north.

"Just canceled it?" Chee asked.

He was asking a plump girl of about eighteen who seemed to be in charge of the Tsaya Chapter—since she was the only one present in the chapter house.

"He sort of hurried in, and said who he was, and said he had to cancel a tent meeting that was supposed to be for tonight," she said. "It's over there on the bulletin board." She nodded toward the notices posted by the entrance.

"*NOTICE!*" Nakai had scrawled at the top of a sheet of notepaper:

Due to an unexpected emergency
Reverend Nakai
is forced to cancel his revival for here.
It will be rescheduled later if God wills it.

—Reverend Slick Nakai

"Well, shit!" said Jim Chee, aloud and in English, since Navajo lends itself poorly to such emotional expletives. He glanced at his watch. Almost four-thirty. Where the devil could Nakai have gone? He walked back to the desk where the girl was sitting. She had been watching him curiously.

"I need to find Nakai." Chee smiled at her, happy that he hadn't worn his uniform. A good many people her age looked upon Navajo Tribal Police as the adversary. "Did he say anything else? Like where he was going?"

"To me? Nothing. Just borrowed a piece of paper for his note. You one of his Christians?"

"No," Chee said. "Matter of fact, I'm a *hatathali*. I do the Blessing Way."

"Really?" the girl said.

Chee was embarrassed. "Just beginning," he said. "Just did it once." He didn't explain that the one time had been for a member of his own family. He fished out his billfold, extracted a business card, and handed it to her.

JIM CHEE
HATATHALI
Singer of The Blessing Way
Available for other ceremonials

For consultation call ______________
(P.O. Box 112, Shiprock, N.M.)

Since he had no telephone at his trailer, he'd left the number blank. His plan had been to list the Shiprock police station number, gambling that by the time Largo got wind of it and blew the whistle, he'd have a reputation and a following established. But the dispatcher had balked. "Besides, Jim," she'd argued, "what will the people think? They call for a singer to do a ceremonial and when the phone rings somebody says, 'Navajo Tribal Police.' "

"Give me some more," the girl said. "I'll stick one up on the board, too. Okay?"

"Sure," Chee said. "And give them to people. Especially if you hear of anybody sick."

She took the cards. "But what's a *batathali* doing looking for a Christian preacher?"

"A minute ago, when I asked you if Nakai said anything about where he was headed, you said not to you. Did he tell somebody else?"

"He made a phone call," she said. "Asked if he could borrow the phone here"—she tapped the telephone on her desk—"and called somebody." She stopped, eyeing Chee doubtfully.

"And you overheard some of it?"

"I don't eavesdrop," she said.

" 'Course not," Chee said. "But the man's talking right there at your desk. How can you help it? Did he say where he was going?"

"No," she said. "He didn't say that."

Chee was smart enough to realize he was being teased. He smiled at her. "After a while you are going to tell me what he said," Chee said. "But not yet."

"I just might not tell you at all," she said, grinning a delighted grin.

"What if I tell you a scary story? That I'm not really a medicine man. I'm a cop and I'm looking for a missing woman, and Nakai is not really a preacher. He's a gangster, and he's already killed a couple of people, and I'm on his trail, and you are my only chance of catching him before he shoots everybody else."

She laughed. "That would fit right in with what he said on the phone. Very mysterious."

Chee managed to keep grinning. Just barely.

"Like what?"

She made herself comfortable. "Oh," she said. "He said, did you hear what happened to so-and-so? Then he listened. Then he said something like, it made him nervous. And to be careful. And then he said somebody-else-or-other was who he worried about and the only way to warn him was to go out to his hogan and find him. He said he was going to cancel his revival here and go up there. And then he listened a long time, and then he said he didn't know how far. It was over into Utah." She shrugged. "That's about it."

"About it isn't good enough."

"Well, that's all I remember."

Apparently it was. She was blank on both so-and-so and somebody-else-or-other. Chee left, thinking "over into Utah" was over into the country Leaphorn wanted Nakai cross-examined about—the source of Friedman-Bernal's pot obsession. He was also thinking that heading into the Four Corners would take him past Shiprock. Maybe he would take the night off, if he was tired when he got there. Maybe he would run Slick Nakai to earth tomorrow. But why had Nakai changed his plans and headed for the Utah border? Who knows? "So-and-so" was probably Etcitty. "Somebody-else-or-other" probably another of Nakai's converts who stole pots on the side. To Chee, Nakai was seeming increasingly odd.

He was driving through the Bisti Badlands, headed north toward Farmington, when the five o'clock news began. A woman reporting from the Durango, Colorado, station on the letting of a contract for range improvement on the Ute Mountain Reservation, and a controversy over the environmental impact of an additional ski run at Purgatory, and a recall petition being circulated to unseat a councilman at Aztec, New Mexico. Chee reached up to change the channel. He'd get more New Mexico news from a Farmington station. "In other news of the Four Corners country," the woman said, "a prominent and sometimes controversial Southeast Utah rancher and political figure has been shot to death at his ranch near Bluff."

Chee stopped, hand on the dial.

"A spokesman for the Garfield County Sheriff's Office at Blanding said the victim has been identified as Harrison Houk, a former Utah state senator and one of southern Utah's biggest ranch operators. The body of Houk was found in his barn last night. The sheriff's office said he had been shot twice.

"Some twenty years ago, Houk's family was the victim of one of the Four Corners' worst tragedies. Houk's wife and a son and daughter were shot to death, apparently by a mentally disturbed younger son who then drowned himself in the San Juan.

"Across the line in Arizona, a suit has been filed in federal district court at . . ."

Chee clicked off the radio. He wanted to think. Houk was the man to whom Nakai had sold pots. Houk lived at Bluff, on the San Juan. Maybe Etcitty was Nakai's "so-and-so." More likely it would be Houk. Could Nakai have heard of Houk's murder en route to Tsaya? Probably, on an earlier newscast. That would explain the abrupt change in plans. Or maybe Houk was "somebody-else-or-other"—the man Nakai wanted to warn. Too late for that now. Either way, it seemed clear that Nakai would be headed to somewhere very close to Bluff, to where Houk, his customer for pots, had been killed.

Chee decided he would work overtime. If he could find the elusive Nakai tonight, he would.

It proved to be surprisingly easy. On the road north toward Bluff, far enough north of Mexican Water so he was sure he'd crossed the Arizona border into Utah, Chee saw Nakai's tent trailer. It was parked maybe a quarter-mile up an old oil field road that wanders off U.S. 191 into the rocky barrens south of Caso del Eco Mesa.

Chee made an abrupt left turn, parked by the trailer, and inspected it. The tie-down ropes were in place, all four tires were aired, everything in perfect order. It had simply been unhooked and abandoned.

Chee jolted down the old road, past a silent oil pump, down into the bare stoniness of Gothic Creek, and out of that into a flatland of scattered sage and dwarf juniper. The road divided into two trails—access routes, Chee guessed, to the only two Navajo families who survived in these barrens. It was almost dark now, the western horizon a glowing, luminous copper. Which route to take? Far down the one that led straight ahead he saw Nakai's car.

He drove the five hundred yards toward it cautiously, feeling uneasy. He'd been joking with the girl at Tsaya when he cast Nakai in the role of gangster. But how did he know? He knew almost nothing. That Nakai had been preaching on the reservation for years. That he encouraged his converts to collect pots for him to sell to help finance his operation. Did he have a pistol? A criminal record? Leaphorn probably knew such things, but he hadn't confided in Chee. He slowed even more, nervous.

Nakai was sitting on the trunk of the massive old Cadillac, legs straight out, leaning against the rear window, watching him, looking utterly harmless. Chee parked behind the car, climbed out, stretched.

"*Ya te'eh,*" Nakai said. And then he recognized Chee, and looked surprised. "We meet again—but a long way from Nageezi."

"*Ya te,*" Chee said. "You are hard to find. I heard you were supposed to be"—he gestured southward—"first at Tsaya and then way down beyond the Hopi Country. Down at Lower Greasewood."

"Ran outta gas," Nakai said, ignoring the implied question. "This thing burns gas like a tank." He jumped down from the trunk, with the small man's natural agility. "Were you looking for me?"

"More or less," Chee said. "What brings you up here into Utah? So far from Lower Greasewood?"

"The Lord's business takes me many places," Nakai said.

"You planning a revival out here?"

"Sure," Nakai said. "When I can arrange it."

"But you left your tent," Chee said. And you're lying, he thought. Not enough people out here.

"I was on empty," Nakai said. "Thought I could save enough gas to get where I was going. Then come back and get it." He laughed. "Waited too long to unhook. Burned too much gasoline."

"You forget to look at your gauge?"

"It was already broke when I bought this thing." Nakai laughed again. "Blessed are the poor," he said. "Didn't do no good to look at it. Before I got outta gas, I was outta money."

Chee didn't comment on that. He thought about how he could learn what Nakai was doing out here. Who he came to warn.

"Have a brother lives down there," Nakai explained. "Christian, so he's my brother in the Lord. And he's Paiute. My 'born to' clan. So he's a brother that way, too. I was going to walk. And then I saw you coming."

"So you just got here?"

"Five minutes, maybe. Look, could you give me a ride? Maybe eight miles or so. I could walk it, but I'm in a hurry."

Nakai was looking down the trail, westward. Chee studied his face. The copper light gave it the look of sculpture. Metal. But Nakai wasn't metal. He was worried. Chee could think of no clever way to get him to talk about what he was doing here.

"You found out Harrison Houk was killed," Chee said. "And you headed out here. Why?"

Nakai turned, his face shadowed now. "Who's Houk?"

"The man you sold pots to," Chee said. "Remember? You told Lieutenant Leaphorn about it."

"Okay," Nakai said. "I know about him."

"Etcitty dealt with you, and with Houk, and with these pots, and he's dead. And now Houk. Both shot. And Nails, too, for that matter. Did you know him?"

"Just met him," Nakai said. "Twice, I think."

"Look," Chee said. "Leaphorn sent me to find you because of something else. He wants to locate this Eleanor Friedman-Bernal woman—find out what happened to her. He talked to you about her already. But now he wants more information. He wants to know what she said to you about looking for pots right out here in this part of the country. Along the San Juan. Up around Bluff. Around Mexican Hat."

"Just what I told him. She wanted those smooth polychrome pots. Those pinkish ones with the patterns and the wavy lines and the serration, or whatever you call it. Pots or the broken pieces. Didn't matter. And she told me she was particularly interested in anything that turned up around this part of the reservation." Nakai shrugged. "That was it."

Chee put his hands on hips and bent backward, eliminating a kink in his back. He'd spent ten hours in that pickup today. Maybe more. Too many. "If Joe Leaphorn were here," he said, "he'd say no, that wasn't quite it. She said more than that. You are trying to save time. Summarizing. Tell me everything she said. Let me do the summarizing."

Nakai looked thoughtful. An ugly little man, Chee decided, but smart.

"You're thinking that I am a cop, and that these pots came off the Navajo Reservation where they are *mucho, mucho* illegal. Felony stuff. You're thinking you are going to be careful about what you say." Chee slouched against the pickup door. "Forget it. We are doing one thing at a time and the one thing is finding this woman. Not figuring out who shot

Etcitty. Not catching somebody for looting ruins on Navajo land. Just one single, simple thing. Just find Eleanor Friedman. Leaphorn seems to think she went looking for these pots. At least that's what I think he thinks. He thinks she told you where to find them. Therefore, I'd appreciate it, you'd win my gratitude and a ride to wherever you want to go, if you'll just tell me all of it. Whether or not you think it matters."

Nakai waited awhile, making sure Chee's outburst was finished.

"What matters isn't much," he said. "Let me remember a minute or two."

Behind Nakai the sunset had darkened from glowing pale copper to dark copper. Against that gaudy backdrop, two streaks of clouds were painted, blue-black and ragged. To the left, a three-quarter moon hung in the sky like a carved white rock.

"You want her words," Nakai said. "What she said, what he said, what she said. I don't remember that well. But I remember some impressions. One. She was thinking about very specific ruins. She'd been there. She knew what it looked like. Two. It was illegal. Better than that, it was on the Navajo Reservation. She good as said that. I remember I said something about it being illegal, and she said maybe it shouldn't be. I was a Navajo and it was Navajo land."

Nakai stopped. "How about the ride?"

"What else?"

"That's all I know, really. Did I say it was in a canyon? I'm sure it was. She said she'd been told about it. Didn't say who told her. Somebody she'd bought a pot from, I guess. Anyway, the way she described the place it had to be a canyon. Three ruins, she said. One down by the streambed in the talus, one on the shelf above it, and a third one out of sight in the cliff above the shelf. So that would have to be in a canyon. And that's all I know."

"Not the name of the canyon."

"She didn't know it. Said she didn't think it had one. Canyon *sin nombre*." Nakai laughed. "She didn't tell me much, really. Just that she was very, very interested in pots, or potsherds, even little fragments, but only if they had this pinkish glaze with the wavy light lines and the serration. Said she'd triple her price for them. That she wanted to know exactly where they came from. I wondered why she didn't go try to find the place herself. I guess she didn't want to risk getting caught at it."

"Leaphorn thinks she went. Or, I think he does."

"Now," Nakai said, "I earned my ride."

Chee took him to a hogan built on the slope of a wash that drained into Gothic Creek—using three-quarters of an hour to cover less than eight jarring miles. It was almost full dark when they pulled onto the slick rock surface that formed the hogan yard, but the moon was bright enough to show why the site had been picked. A growth of cottonwoods, tamarisks, and rabbitbrush at the lip of the wash showed where a spring flowed. It was probably the only live water within thirty miles, Chee guessed, and it wasn't lively enough to support a family in the dry season. A row of rusty water barrels on a wooden rack told him that. Chee parked, raced the pickup engine to make sure the hogan's occupants had noticed their arrival, and turned off the engine. A dim light, probably from a kerosene lamp, showed through the side window. The smell of sheep, a smell that always provoked nostalgia in Chee, drifted down from a brush compound behind the house.

"You have another little problem now," Chee said.

"What?"

"This brother of yours who lives here. He steals pots for you. You want to tell him about Etcitty, and Nails, and Houk. You want to tell him to be careful—that somebody's shooting pot hunters. But I'm a cop so you don't want me to hear it."

Nakai said nothing.

"No car. No truck. At least I don't see one. Or see any place to put one on this flat rock where I couldn't see it. So somebody who lives here has gone off with the truck."

Nakai said nothing. He drew in a breath and exhaled it.

"So if I just leave you here, as you'd intended, then you're stuck. No gas and no ride to where you can get some."

"One of his sons probably has the truck," Nakai said. "He probably keeps some gasoline here somewhere. At least a five-gallon can."

"In which case you walk that eight miles back to the Caddy with it," Chee said. "Or maybe he doesn't have any gas."

A blanket hanging over the hogan doorway swung aside. The shape of a man appeared, looking out at them.

"What do you have in mind?" Nakai said.

"You quit playing the game. I'm not going to arrest anyone for stealing pots. But I gotta find out where they came from. That's all I care about. If you don't know where that is, this Paiute Clan man here does. Let him tell me. No more games."

The Paiute Clan man was called Amos Whistler. A skinny man with four of his lower front teeth missing. He knew where the pots had come from. "Way over there, toward the west. Toward Navajo Mountain," he said, indicating the direction. "Maybe thirty miles across the Nokaito Bench." But there were no roads, just broken country, sandstone cut by one wash after another. Whistler said he had heard about the ruins years ago from an uncle, who told him to stay out of the place because the ghosts were bad in there. But he had learned about Jesus, and he didn't believe in ghosts, so he packed in with a couple of horses, but it was tough going. An ordeal. He'd lost a horse. A good one.

Chee owned an excellent U.S. Geological Survey map of the Big Reservation, a book in which each page showed everything in a thirty-two-mile square. "What's the name of the canyon?"

"I don't know if it has a name," Amos Whistler said. "Around here they say its name is Canyon Where Watersprinkler Plays His Flute." It was a long name in Navajo, and Whistler looked embarrassed when he said it.

"Would you take me in there? Rent the horses and lead me in?"

"No," Amos Whistler said. "I don't go there no more."

"I'd hire you," Chee said. "Pay you for using your horses. Good money."

"No," Whistler said. "I'm a Christian now. I know about Jesus. I don't worry about Anasazi ghosts like I did when I was a pagan. Before I walked on the Jesus Road. But I won't go into that place."

"Good money," Chee said. "No problems with the law."

"I heard him in there," Whistler said. He took two steps away from Chee, toward the hogan door. "I heard the Watersprinkler playing his flute."

14

LEAPHORN MANAGED A forward seat by the window when he changed planes in Chicago. There was nothing to see—just the topside of solid cloud cover over the great flat, fertile American heartland. Leaphorn looked down at this gray mass and thought of the river of wet air flowing up from the Gulf of Mexico, and of cold rain, and bleak, featureless landscapes closed in by a sky no more than six feet above one's forehead. At least Emma had saved them from that by holding him on the reservation.

He was depressed. He had done what he had gone to do and achieved nothing useful. All he knew that he hadn't known before was that Etcitty had been too smart to sign a pot documentation admitting a violation of federal law. Leaphorn was fairly sure that the physical description of the site must be accurate. He could think of no reason for Etcitty to have made up such a complicated description. It seemed to flow from memory. An unsophisticated man following the form's instructions, describing reality with the single lie to avoid incrimination. That helped very little. The Utah–Arizona–New Mexico border country was a maze of washes, gulches, draws, and canyons. Thousands of them, and in their sheltered, sun-facing alcoves, literally scores of thousands of Anasazi sites. He'd seen an estimate of more than a hundred thousand such sites on the Colorado Plateau, built over a period of almost a thousand years. What Etcitty had given him was like a description of a house in a big city with no idea of its street address. He could narrow it down some. Probably in southern Utah or extreme northern Arizona. Probably north of Monument Valley. Probably east of Nokaito Mesa. Probably west of Montezuma Creek. That narrowed it to an area bigger than Connecticut, occupied by maybe five thousand humans. And all he had was a site description that might be as false as its location obviously was.

Perhaps Chee had done better. An odd young man, Chee. Smart, apparently. Alert. But slightly . . . slightly what? Bent? Not exactly. It wasn't just the business of trying to be a medicine man—a following utterly incongruous with police work. He was a romantic, Leaphorn decided. That was it. A man who followed dreams. The sort who would have joined that Paiute shaman who invented the ghost dance and the vision of white men withering away and the buffalo coming back to the plains. Maybe that wasn't fair. It was more that Chee seemed to think an island of 180,000 Navajos could live the old way in a white ocean. Perhaps 20,000 of them could, if they were happy on mutton, cactus, and piñon nuts. Not practical. Navajos had to compete in the real world. The Navajo Way didn't teach competition. Far from it.

But Chee, odd as he was, would find Slick Nakai. Another dreamer, Nakai. Leaphorn shifted in the narrow seat, trying vainly for comfort. Chee would find Nakai and Chee would get from Nakai about as much information as Leaphorn would have been able to extract.

Leaphorn found himself thinking of what he would say to Emma about Chee. He shook his head, picked up a *New Yorker*, and read. Dinner came. His seatmate examined it scornfully. To Leaphorn, who had been eating his own cooking, it tasted great. They were crossing the Texas panhandle now. Below, the clouds were thinning, breaking into patches. Ahead, the earth rose like a rocky island out of the ocean of humid air that blanketed the midlands. Leaphorn could see the broken mesas of eastern New Mexico. Beyond, on the western horizon, great cloud-castle thunderheads, unusual in autumn, rose into the stratosphere. Leaphorn felt something he hadn't felt since Emma's death. He felt a kind of joy.

Something like that mood was with him when he awoke the next morning in his bed at Window Rock—a feeling of being alive, and healthy, and interested. He was still weary. The flight from Albuquerque to Gallup in the little Aspen Airways Cessna, and the drive from Gallup, had finished what reserves he had left. But the depression was gone. He cooked bacon for breakfast and ate it with toast and jelly. While he was eating the telephone rang.

Jim Chee, he thought. Who else would be calling him?

It was Corporal Ellison Billy, who handled things that needed handling for Major Nez, who was more or less Leaphorn's boss.

"There's a Utah cop here looking for you," Billy said. "You available?"

Leaphorn was surprised. "What's he want? And what kind of cop?"

"Utah State Police. Criminal Investigation Division," Billy said. "He just said he wants to talk to you. About a homicide investigation. That's all I know. Probably told the major more. You coming in?"

Homicide, he thought. The depression sagged down around him again. Someone had found Eleanor Friedman-Bernal's body. "Tell him ten minutes," he said, which was the time it took for him to drive from his house among the piñons on the high side of Window Rock to police headquarters beside the Fort Defiance Highway.

The desk had two messages for him. One from Jim Chee was short: "Found Nakai near Mexican Hat with a friend who says ruins is located in what the locals call Watersprinkler Canyon west of his place. I will stay reachable through the Shiprock dispatcher."

The other, from the Utah State Police, was shorter. It said: "Call Detective McGee re: Houk. Urgent."

"Houk?" Leaphorn said. "Any more details?"

"That's it," the dispatcher said. "Just call McGee about Houk. Urgent."

He put the message in his pocket.

The door to the major's office was open. Ronald Nez was standing behind his desk. A man wearing a blue windbreaker and a billed cap with the legend LIMBER ROPE on the crown sat against the wall. He got up when Leaphorn walked in, a tall man, middle-aged, with a thin, bony face. Acne or some other scarring disease had left cheeks and forehead pocked with a hundred small craters. Nez introduced them. Carl McGee was the name. He had not waited for a call back.

"I'll get right to it," McGee said. "We got a homicide case, and he left you a note."

Leaphorn kept his face from showing his surprise. It wasn't Friedman-Bernal.

McGee waited for a response.

Leaphorn nodded.

"Harrison Houk," McGee said. "I imagine you know him?"

Leaphorn nodded again, his mind processing this. Who would kill Houk? Why? He could see an answer to the second question. And in general terms to the first one. The same person who had killed Etcitty, and Nails, and for the same reason. But what was that?

"What was the message?"

McGee looked at Major Nez, who looked back, expression neutral. Then at Leaphorn. This conversation was not going as McGee had intended. He extracted a leather folder from his hip pocket, took a business card from it, and handed it to Leaphorn.

BLANDING PUMPS
Well Drilling, Casing, Pulling
General Water System Maintenance
(We also fix your Septic Tanks)

The card was bent, dirty. Leaphorn guessed it had been damp. He turned it over.

The message there was scrawled in ballpoint ink.

It said:

Tell Leaphorn shes still alive up

Leaphorn handed it to Nez, without comment.

"I saw it," Nez said, and handed it back to McGee, who put it back in the folder, and the folder back in his pocket.

"What do you think?" he said. "You got any idea who the 'she' is?"

"A good idea," Leaphorn said. "But tell me about Houk. I saw him just the other day."

"Wednesday," McGee said. "To be exact." He looked at Leaphorn, expression quizzical. "That's what the woman who works for him told us. Navajo named Irene Musket."

"Wednesday sounds right," Leaphorn said. "Who killed Houk?"

McGee made a wry face. "This woman he wrote you about, maybe.

Anyway, it looks like Houk quit trying to find a place to hide to tell you about her. Sounds like you two thought she was dead. Suddenly he sees her alive. He tries to tell you. She kills him."

Leaphorn was thinking that his terminal leave had five more days to run. Actually, only about four and two-thirds. He hadn't been in a mood to screw around like this for at least three months. Not since Emma got bad. He was in no mood for it today. In fact, he had never been tolerant of it. Nor for being polite to this *belagana*, who wanted to act as if Leaphorn was some sort of suspect. But he'd make one more effort to be polite.

"I've been away," he said. "Back east. Just got in last night. You're going to have to skip way back and tell me about it."

McGee told him. Irene Musket had come to work Friday morning and found a note on the screen door telling her that Houk was in the barn. She said she found his body in the barn and called the Garfield County Sheriff's Office, who notified Utah State Police. Both agencies investigated. Houk had been shot twice with a small-caliber weapon, in the center of the chest and in the lower back of the skull. There were signs that Houk had been rearranging bales of hay, apparently into a hiding place. Two empty .25 caliber cartridge casings were found in the hay near the body. The medical examiner said either of the bullets might have caused death. No witnesses. No physical evidence found in the barn except the shell casings. The housekeeper said she found the back screen door lock had been broken and Houk's office was in disarray. As far as she could tell, nothing had been stolen.

"But then, who knows?" McGee added. "Stuff could be gone from his office and she wouldn't know about it." He stopped, looking at Leaphorn.

"Where was the note?"

"In Houk's shorts," McGee said. "We didn't turn it up. The medical examiner found it when they undressed him."

Leaphorn found he was feeling a little better about McGee. It wasn't McGee's attitude. It was his own.

"I went Wednesday to see him about a woman named Eleanor Friedman-Bernal," Leaphorn said. He explained the situation. Who the woman was, her connection with Houk, what Houk had told him. "So I presume he was telling me she was still alive."

"You thought she was dead?" McGee asked.

"Missing two, three weeks. Leaves her clothes. Leaves a big dinner waiting to be cooked in her fridge. Misses important appointments. I don't know whether she's dead or not."

"Pretty fair bet she is," Nez said. "Or it was."

"You and Houk friends?" McGee asked.

"No," Leaphorn said. "I met him twice. Last Wednesday and about twenty years ago. One of his boys wiped out most of the family. I worked a little on that."

"I remember it. Hard one to forget." McGee was staring at him.

"I'm just as surprised as you are," Leaphorn said. "That he left me the note." He paused, thinking. "Do you know why he left the note in the screen door? About being in the barn?"

"Musket said she'd gone off and left some stuff—some squash—she was going to take home. He'd put it in the refrigerator and left the note. It said, 'squash in the icebox, I'm in the barn.' She figured he thought she'd come back for it."

Leaphorn was remembering the setting—the long, weedy drive, the porch, the barn well up the slope behind the house, a loading pen on one side of it, horse stalls on the other. From the barn, Houk would have heard a car coming. He might have seen it, watched its driver open the gate. He must have recognized death coming for him. McGee said he'd started preparing a hiding place—stacking bales with a gap behind them, to form a hidey-hole probably. And then he'd stopped to write the unfinished note. And put it in his shorts. Leaphorn imagined that. Houk, desperate, out of time, sticking the calling card under his belt line. The only possible reason would be to keep his killer from finding it. And that meant the killer would not have left it. And what did that mean? That the killer was Eleanor Friedman-Bernal, who would not want people to know she was alive? Or, certainly, that Houk knew she was alive.

"You have any theories yet?" he asked McGee.

"One or two," he said.

"Involving pot hunting?"

"Well, we know about Etcitty and Nails. They were hunting pots. Houk's been dealing with 'em for years and not particular where what he buys comes from," McGee said. "So, maybe somebody he cheated got tough about it. Houk screwed one person too many. He had a reputation for that. Or maybe it was this woman he was selling to." McGee got up stiffly, adjusted his hat. "Why else the note? He saw her coming. Back from the dead, so to speak. Knew she was after him. Figured she'd already bagged Nails and Etcitty. Started leaving you the note. Put it where she wouldn't find it and get off with it. I'd like you to tell me what you know about that woman."

"All right," Leaphorn said. "Couple of things I have to do and then I'll get with you."

He'd stayed away from his office since Emma's death and now it smelled of the dust that seeps gradually into everything in a desert climate. He sat in his chair, picked up the phone, and called Shiprock. Chee was in.

"This Watersprinkler Canyon," he asked. "Which side of the river?"

"South," Chee said. "Reservation side."

"No question of that?"

"None," Chee said. "Not if this Amos Whistler knew what he was talking about. Or where he was pointing."

"There isn't any Watersprinkler Canyon on my map. What do you think it is?"

"Probably Many Ruins," Chee said.

It was exactly what Leaphorn would have guessed. And getting into the north end of it was damn near impossible. It ran for its last forty miles through a roadless, jumbled stony wilderness.

"You knew Harrison Houk was shot?"

"Yes, sir."

"You want to keep working on this?"

Hesitation. "Yes, sir."

"Get on the telephone then. Call the police at Madison, Wisconsin. Find out if handguns are licensed there. They probably are. If they are, find out who does it and then find out exactly what kind of pistol was licensed to Eleanor Friedman-Bernal. It would have been . . ." He squeezed his eyes shut, recalling what Maxie Davis had told him about the woman's career. "Probably 1985 or '86."

"Okay."

"If she didn't license her gun in Madison, you're going to have to keep checking." He gave Chee other places he knew of where the woman had studied or taught, relying on his memory of his talk with Davis and guessing at the dates. "You may be spending all day on the phone," Leaphorn warned. "Tell 'em three homicides are involved. And then stay close to the phone where I can get you."

"Right."

That done, he sat a moment, thinking. He would go to Bluff and take a look at the barn where Harrison Houk had done the remarkable—written him a note while waiting for his killer. He wanted to see that place. The action jarred on him. Why would Houk care that much about a woman who was merely a customer? "Shes still alive up," the note had said. Up? Up to today? Up what? Up where? Up Watersprinkler Canyon? She had taken her sleeping bag. The boy had seen her loading a saddle. But back to Houk. Starting the note. At that point, almost certainly, Houk had been interrupted by the killer. Had run out of time. Had presumed the killer would destroy the note. Would not want the police to know that "she" was alive. So was "she" Eleanor hyphenated? Who else would care about the note? And yet Leaphorn had trouble putting into the picture the woman who marinated the beef and prepared the dinner so lovingly. He could not see her in that barn, firing her little pistol into the skull of an old man lying facedown in the hay. He shook his head. But that was sentiment, not logic.

Major Nez stood in his door, watching him. "Interesting case," Nez said.

"Yeah. Hard one to figure." Leaphorn motioned him in.

Nez simply leaned against the wall, holding a folded paper in his hand. He was getting fat, Leaphorn noticed. Nez had always been built like a barrel, but now his stomach sagged over his broad uniform belt.

"Doesn't sound like something you can get sorted out in less than a week," Nez said. He tapped the paper against the back of his hand, and it occurred to Leaphorn that it was his letter of resignation.

"Probably not," Leaphorn said.

Nez held out the letter. "You want this back? For now? You can always send it in again."

"I'm tired, Ron. Have been a long time, I guess. Just didn't know it."

"Tired of living," Nez said, nodding. "I get that way now and then. But it's hard to quit."

"Anyway, thanks," Leaphorn said. "You know where McGee went?"

Leaphorn found Detective McGee eating a late breakfast at the Navajo

Nation Inn and told him everything he knew about Eleanor Friedman-Bernal that seemed remotely pertinent. Then he drove back to his house, dug his pistol belt out of the bottom drawer of his dresser, took out the weapon, and dropped it into his jacket pocket. That done, he drove out of Window Rock, heading north.

15

THE YOUNG WOMAN to whom Chee's call was referred at the Madison Police Department had a little trouble believing in the Navajo Tribal Police. But after that was settled, things became most efficient. Yes, handguns were licensed. No, it would be easy to check the record. Just a moment. It was not much more than that.

The next voice was male. Eleanor Friedman-Bernal? Yes, she had been issued a license for a handgun. She had registered a .25 caliber automatic pistol.

Chee noted the details. The pistol was a brand he'd never heard of. Neither had the clerk in Madison. "Portuguese, I think," he said. "Or maybe it's Turkish, or Brazilian."

Step two went almost as quickly. He called the San Juan County Sheriff's Office and asked for Undersheriff Robert Bates, who usually handled homicides. Bates was married to a Navajo, who happened to be "born to" the Kin yaa aanii—the Towering House People—which was linked in some way Chee had never understood to his grandfather's To' aheedlinii'—the Waters Flow Together Clan. That made Chee and Bates vaguely relatives. Just as important, they had worked together a time or two and liked each other. Bates was in.

"If you have the lab report back, I need to know about the bullets that killed Etcitty and Nails," Chee said.

"Why?" Bates asked. "I thought the FBI decided that killing wasn't on reservation land."

"Out on the Checkerboard, the FBI always decides that," Chee said. "We're just interested."

"Why?"

"Ah, hell, Robert," Chee said. "I don't know why. Joe Leaphorn is interested, and Largo has me working with him."

"What's going on with Leaphorn? We heard he had a nervous breakdown. Heard he quit."

"He did," Chee said. "But not yet."

"Well, it was a twenty-five-caliber pistol, automatic judging from the ejection marks on the empties. All the same weapon."

"You have a missing person's report on a woman who owns a twenty-five-caliber automatic pistol," Chee said. "Her name's Dr. Eleanor Friedman-Bernal. She worked out of Chaco Canyon. Anthropologist. Where Etcitty worked." He told Bates more of what he knew about the woman.

"I got her file right here on my desk," Bates said. "I just a minute ago got a call from a Utah State Policeman. They want us to do some checking up on her out at Chaco. Seems they had a fellow shot up at Bluff and he left a note to Leaphorn telling him this woman is still alive. You know about that?"

"Heard about the killing. Not about any note." He was thinking that a few years ago this weird roundabout communication would have surprised him. Now he expected it. He was remembering Leaphorn chewing him out for not passing along all the details. Well, there was no reason for Leaphorn not to have told him about this. Except that Leaphorn considered him merely an errand boy. Chee was offended.

"Tell me about it," he told Bates. "And don't leave anything out."

Bates told him what he'd been told. It didn't take long.

"So Utah State Police think Dr. Friedman showed up and offed Houk," Chee concluded. "Any theories about motive?"

"Big pot hunting conspiracy is what they seem to think. They've had a federal crackdown up there on pot thieves last year. Bunch of arrests. Grand jury sitting in Salt Lake handing down indictments. So they're thinking pots," Bates said. "And why not? Big money in it the way prices are now. Hell, when we was kids and used to go out and dig 'em up around here, you were lucky to get five bucks. Listen," he added, "how you coming on being a medicine man?"

"No clients." It was not a subject Chee wanted to discuss. It was November, already into the "Season When Thunder Sleeps," the season for curing ceremonials, and he hadn't had a single contact. "You going to Chaco now?"

"Soon as I get off the telephone."

Chee gave him a quick rundown on the people he should talk to: Maxie Davis, the Lunas, Randall Elliot.

"They're worried about the woman. Friends of hers. Be sure and tell them about the note."

"Why, sure," Bates said. He sounded slightly offended that Chee had even mentioned it.

There was nothing to do then but stick close to the telephone and wait for Leaphorn's call from Bluff. He dug into his paperwork. A little before noon, the phone rang. Leaphorn, Chee thought.

It was Janet Pete. Her voice sounded odd. Was Chee doing anything for lunch?

"Nothing," Chee said. "You calling from Shiprock?"

"I drove up. Really just went for a drive. Ended up here." She sounded thoroughly down.

"Lunch then," he said. "Can you meet me at the Thunderbird Café?"

She could. And did.

They took a booth by the window. And talked about the weather. A gusty wind was rattling the pane and chasing dust and leaves and now a section of the *Navajo Times* down the highway outside.

"End of autumn, I guess," Chee said. "You watch Channel Seven. Howard Morgan says we're going to get the first blast of winter."

"I hate winter," Janet Pete said. She hugged herself and shivered. "Dismal winter."

"The counselor has the blues," Chee said. "Anything I can do to cheer you up? I'll call Morgan and see if he can postpone it."

"Or call it off altogether."

"Right."

"Or there's Italy."

"Which is warm, I hear," Chee said, and then he saw she was serious.

"You hear from your Successful Attorney?"

"He flew all the way to Chicago, to Albuquerque, to Gallup. I met him at Gallup."

Not knowing what to say, Chee said: "Not exactly meeting him halfway." It sounded flippant. Chee didn't feel flippant. He cleared his throat. "Has he changed? Time does that with people. So I'm told."

"Yes," Janet Pete said. But she shook her head. "But no. Not really. My mother told me a long time ago: 'Don't ever expect a man to change. What you see is what you live with.' "

"I guess so," Chee said. She looked tired, and full of sadness. He reached out and took her hand in his. It was cold. "Trouble is, I guess you love him anyway."

"I don't know," Janet Pete said. "I just . . ." But the sympathy was too much for her. Her voice choked. She looked down, fumbling in her purse.

Chee handed her his napkin. She held it to her face.

"Rough life," Chee said. "Love is supposed to make us happy, and sometimes it makes us miserable."

Through the napkin he heard Janet sniff.

He patted her hand. "This sounds like a cliché, or whatever it is, but I know how you feel. I really do."

"I know," Janet said.

"But you know, I've decided. I'm giving up. You can't go on forever." As he heard himself saying that, he was amazed. When did he decide that? He hadn't realized it. He felt a surge of relief. And of loss. Why can't men cry? he wondered. Why is that not allowed?

"He wants me to go to Italy with him. He's going to Rome. Taking over their legal affairs for Europe. And Africa. And the Middle East."

"He speak Italian?" As he said it, it seemed an incredibly stupid question. Totally beside the point here.

"French," she said. "And some Italian. And he's perfecting it. A tutor."

"How about you?" he said. Why couldn't he think of something less inane? He would be asking her next about her passport. And packing. And airfares. That wasn't what she wanted to talk about. She wanted to talk about love.

"No," she said.

"What did he say? Does he understand now that you want to be a lawyer? That you want to practice it?"

The napkin was in her lap now. Her eyes dry. But they showed she'd been crying. And her face was strained.

"He said I could practice in Italy. Not with his company. It has a nepotism rule. But he could line something up for me after I got the required Italian license."

"He could line something up. For you."

She sighed. "Yeah. That's the way he put it. And I guess he could. At a certain level in law, the big firms feed on one another. There would be Italian firms doing feed out work. The word would go into the good-old-boy network. Tit for tat. I guess once I learned Italian I would be offered a job."

Chee nodded. "I'd think so," he said.

Lunch came. Mutton stew and fry bread for Chee. Janet was having a bowl of soup.

They sat looking at the food.

"You should eat something," said Chee, who had totally lost his appetite. He took a spoonful of the stew, a bite of fry bread. "Eat," he ordered.

Janet Pete took a spoonful of soup.

"Made a decision yet?"

She shook her head. "I don't know."

"You know yourself better than anyone," he said. "What's going to make you happy?"

She shook her head again. "I think I'm happy when I'm with him. Like dinner last night. But I don't know."

Chee was thinking about the dinner and how it had ended, and what happened then. Had she gone to his room with him? Had she spent the night there? Probably. The thought hurt. It hurt a lot. That surprised him.

"I shouldn't let things like this drag on," she said. "I should decide."

"We let ours drag on. Mary and I. And I guess she decided."

He had released her hand when lunch arrived. Now she reached over and put hers on his. "I have your napkin," she said. "Slightly damp but still"—she looked at it, a rumpled square of pale blue paper—"usable in case of emergency."

He realized instantly that this was her bid to change the subject. He took the napkin, dropped it in his lap.

"Have you realized how lucky you are to have been brought to the only café in Shiprock with napkins?"

"Noted and appreciated," she said. Her smile seemed almost natural. "And how are things going with you?"

"I told you about the Backhoe Bandit. And Etcitty?"

She nodded. "That must have been gruesome. How about finding the woman?"

"How much did I tell you about that?"

She reminded him.

He told her about Houk, about the note left for Leaphorn, about Eleanor Friedman-Bernal's pistol and how it was the same caliber used in the killings, about Leaphorn's obsessive interest in finding the Utah site to which Friedman's long-lost potter seemed to have moved.

"You know you have to file for a permit to dig sites like that on the reservation. We have an office in Window Rock that deals with it," Janet Pete said. "Did you check that?"

"Leaphorn might have," Chee said. "But apparently she was trying to find out where the stuff was coming from. You'd have to know that before you could file."

"I guess so. But I think they're all numbered. Maybe she would just guess at it."

Chee grinned and shook his head. "Back when I was an anthropology student, I remember Professor Campbell, or somebody, telling us there were forty thousand sites listed with New Mexico Laboratory of Anthropology numbers. That's in New Mexico alone. And another hundred thousand or so on other registries."

"I didn't mean just pick a number at random," she said, slightly irked. "She could describe the general location."

Chee was suddenly interested. "Maybe Leaphorn already looked into it," he said. He was remembering that probably he would be hearing from Leaphorn soon. He'd left word with the switchboard to relay the call here. "But would it take long to check?"

"I could call," she said, looking thoughtful. "I know the man who runs it. Helped him with the regulations. I think, to dig on the reservation, I think you have to apply to the Park Service and the Navajo Cultural Preservation Office both. I think you have to name a repository for whatever you recover, and get the archive system approved. And maybe . . ."

Chee was thinking how great it would be if, when Leaphorn called, he could tell him the map coordinates of the site he was looking for. His face must have showed his impatience. Janet stopped midsentence. "What?" she said.

"Let's go back to the station and call," he said.

The call from Leaphorn was waiting when they walked in. Chee gave him what he'd learned from the Madison police and from Bates at the San Juan County Sheriff's Office. "They're expecting a report from the Utah State Police," Chee added. "Bates said he would call when he gets it."

"I've got it," Leaphorn said. "It was twenty-five-caliber, too."

"Do you know if Friedman applied for a permit to dig that site you're looking for?"

Long silence. "I should have thought of that," Leaphorn said finally. "I doubt if she did. The red tape takes years and it's a double filing. Park Service clearance plus tribal clearance, and all sorts of checking and screwing around gets involved. But I should have checked it."

"I'll take care of it," Chee said.

The man to call, Janet Pete said, was T.J. Pedwell. Chee reached him just back from lunch. Had he had any applications from Dr. Eleanor Friedman-Bernal to dig on a reserved Anasazi site on the reservation?

"Sure," Pedwell said. "Two or three. On Checkerboard land around Chaco Canyon. She's that ceramics specialist working over there."

"How about over on the north side of the reservation? Up in Utah."

"I don't think so," Pedwell said. "I could check on it. Wouldn't know the site number, would you?"

"'Fraid not," Chee said. "But it might be somewhere near the north end of Many Ruins Canyon."

"I know that place," Pedwell said. "Helped with the Antiquities survey all up through that part of the country."

"You know the canyon the local people call Watersprinkler?"

"It's really Many Ruins," Pedwell said. "It's full of pictographs and petroglyphs of Kokopelli. That's the one the Navajos call the Watersprinkler *yei*."

"I have a description of the site, and it sounds unusual," Chee said. He told Pedwell what Amos Whistler had told him.

"Yeah," Pedwell said. "Sounds familiar. Let me check my files. I have photos of most of them."

Chee heard the telephone click against something. He waited and waited. Sighed. Leaned a hip against the desk.

"Trouble?" Janet Pete asked.

Pedwell's voice was in his ear before he could respond.

"Found it," Pedwell said. "It's N.R. 723. Anasazi. Circa 1280–1310. And there's two other sites right there with it. Probably connected."

"Great!" Chee said. "How do you get there?"

"Well, it ain't going to be easy. I remember that. We packed into some of them on horseback. Others we floated down the San Juan and walked up the canyon. This one I think we floated. Let's see. Notes say it's five point seven miles up from the mouth of the canyon."

"Dr. Friedman. She apply to dig that one?"

"Not her," Pedwell said. "Another of those people out at Chaco did. Dr. Randall Elliot. They working together?"

"I don't think so," Chee said. "Does the application say he was collecting St. John's Polychrome pots?"

"Lemme look." Papers rustled. "Doesn't sound like pots. Says he is studying Anasazi migrations." Mumbling sounds of Pedwell reading to himself. "Says his interest is tracing genetic patterns." More mumbling. "Studying bones. Skull thickness. Six-fingeredness. Aberrant jaw formation." More mumbling. "I don't think it has anything to do with ceramics," Pedwell said, finally. "He's looking at the skeletons. Or will be if your famous Navajo bureaucracy, of which I am a part, ever gets this processed. Six-fingeredness. Lot of that among the Anasazi, but hard to study, because hands don't survive intact after a thousand years. But it sounds like he's found some family patterns. Too many fingers. An extra tooth in the right side of the lower jaw. A second hole where those nerves and blood vessels go through the back of the jaw, and something or other about the fibula. Physical anthropology isn't my area."

"But he hasn't gotten his permit yet?"

"Wait a minute. I guess we weren't so slow on this one. Here's a carbon of a letter to Elliot from the Park Service." Paper rustled. "Turndown,"

Pedwell said. "More documentation needed of previous work in this field. That do it?"

"Thanks a lot," Chee said.

Janet Pete was watching him.

"Sounds like you scored," she said.

"I'll fill you in," he said.

"On the way back to my car." She looked embarrassed. "I'm normally the usual stolid, dull lawyer," she said. "This morning I just ran off in hysterics and left everything undone. People coming in to see me. People waiting for me to finish things. I feel awful."

He walked to the car with her, opened the door.

"I'm glad you called on me," he said. "You honored me."

"Oh, Jim!" she said, and hugged him around the chest with such strength that he caught his breath. She stood, holding him like that, pressed against him. He sensed she was about to cry again. He didn't want that to happen.

He put his hand on her hair and stroked it.

"I don't know what you'll decide about your Successful Attorney," he said. "But if you decide against him, maybe you and I could see if we could fall in love. You know, both Navajos and all that."

It was the wrong thing to say. She was crying as she drove away.

Chee stood there, watching her motor pool sedan speed toward the U.S. 666 junction and the route to Window Rock. He didn't want to think about this. It was confusing. And it hurt. Instead he thought of a question he should have asked Pedwell. Had Randall Elliot also filed an application to dig in that now-despoiled site where Etcitty and Nails had died?

He walked back into the station, remembering those jawbones so carefully set aside amid the chaos.

16

TO LEAPHORN, THE saddle had seemed a promising possibility. She had borrowed it from a biologist named Arnold, who lived in Bluff. Other trails led to Bluff. The site of the polychrome pots seemed to be somewhere west of the town, in roadless country where a horse would be necessary. She would go to Arnold's place. If he could loan her a saddle, he could probably loan her a horse. From Arnold he would learn where Eleanor Friedman-Bernal had headed. The first step was finding Arnold, which shouldn't be difficult.

It wasn't. The Recapture Lodge had been Bluff's center of hospitality for as long as Leaphorn could remember. The man at the reception desk loaned Leaphorn his telephone to call Chee. Chee confirmed what Leaphorn had feared. Whether or not Dr. Friedman was killing pot hunters, her pistol was. The man at the desk also knew Arnold.

"Bo Arnold," he said. "Scientists around here are mostly anthropologists or geologists, but Dr. Arnold is a lichen man. Botanist. Go up to where the highway bends left, and take the right toward Montezuma Creek. It's the little redbrick house with lilac bushes on both sides of the gate. Except I think Bo let the lilacs die. He drives a Jeep. If he's home, you'll see it there."

The lilacs were indeed almost dead, and a dusty early-model Jeep was parked in the weeds beside the little house. Leaphorn parked beside it and stepped out of his pickup into a gust of chilly, dusty wind. The front door opened just as he walked up the porch steps. A lanky man in jeans and faded red shirt emerged. "Yessir," he said. "Good morning." He was grinning broadly, an array of white teeth in a face of weathered brown leather.

"Good morning," Leaphorn said. "I'm looking for Dr. Arnold."

"Yessir," the man said. "That's me." He stuck out a hand, which Leaphorn shook. He showed Arnold his identification.

"I'm looking for Dr. Eleanor Friedman-Bernal," Leaphorn said.

"Me too," Arnold said enthusiastically. "That biddy got off with my kayak and didn't bring it back."

"Oh," Leaphorn said. "When?"

"When I was gone," Arnold said, still grinning. "Caught me away from home, and off she goes with it."

"I want to hear all about that," Leaphorn said.

Arnold held the door wide, welcomed Leaphorn in with a sweep of his hand. Inside the front door was a room crowded with tables, each table crowded with rocks of all sizes and shapes—their only common denominator being lichens. They were covered with these odd plants in every shade from white through black. Arnold led Leaphorn past them, down a narrow hall.

"No place to sit in there," he said. "That's where I work. Here's where I live."

Where Arnold lived was a small bedroom. Every flat surface, including the narrow single bed, was covered with boards on which flat glass dishes were lined. The dishes had something in them that Leaphorn assumed must be lichens. "Let me make you a place," Arnold said, and cleared off chairs for each of them.

"Why you looking for Ellie?" he asked. "She been looting ruins?" And he laughed.

"Does she do that?"

"She's an anthropologist," Arnold said, his chuckle reduced again to a grin. "You translate the word from academic into English and that's what it means: ruins looter, one who robs graves, preferably old ones. Well-educated person who steals artifact in dignified manner." Arnold, overcome by the wit of this, laughed. "Somebody else does it, they call 'em vandals. That's the word for the competition. Somebody gets there first, gets off with the stuff before the archaeologists can grab it, they call 'em

Thieves of Time." His vision of such hypocrisy left him in high good humor, as did the thought of his missing kayak.

"Tell me about that," Leaphorn said. "How do you know she took it?"

"She left a full, signed confession," Arnold said, fumbling in a box from which assorted scraps of papers overflowed. He extracted a small sheet of lined yellow notepaper and handed it to Leaphorn.

> Here's your saddle, a year older but no worse for wear. (I sold that damned horse.) To keep you caring about me, I am now borrowing your kayak. If you don't get back before I do, ignore the last part of this note because I will put the kayak right back in the garage where I got it and you'll never know it was gone.
>
> Don't let any lichens grow on you!
>
> Love,
> Ellie

Leaphorn handed it back to him. "When did she leave it?"

"I just know when I found it. I'd been up there on Lime Ridge collecting specimens for a week or so and when I got back, the saddle was on the floor in the workroom up front with this note pinned on it. Looked in the garage, and the kayak was gone."

"When?" Leaphorn repeated.

"Oh," Arnold said. "Let's see. Almost a month ago."

Leaphorn told him the date Eleanor Friedman-Bernal had made her early-morning departure from Chaco Canyon. "That sound right?"

"I think I got back on a Monday or Tuesday. Three or four days after that."

"So the saddle might have been sitting there three or four days?"

"Could have been." Arnold laughed again. "Don't have a cleaning lady coming in. Guess you noticed that."

"How did she get in?"

"Key's over there under the flower box," Arnold said. "She knew where. Been here before. Go all the way back to the University of Wisconsin." Abruptly Arnold's amusement evaporated. His bony, sun-beaten face became somber. "She's really missing? People worried about her? She didn't just walk off for a few days of humanity?"

"I think it's serious," Leaphorn said. "Almost a month. And she left too much behind. Where would she go in your kayak?"

Arnold shook his head. "Just one place to go. Downstream. I use it to play around with. Like a toy. But she'd have been going down the river. Plenty of sites along the river until you get into the deep canyon where there's nothing to live on. And then there's hundreds of ruins up the side canyons." There was no humor at all left in Arnold's face. He looked at least his age, which Leaphorn guessed at forty. He looked worn and worried.

"Ceramics. That's what Ellie would be looking for. Potsherds." He paused, stared at Leaphorn. "I guess you know we had a man killed here just the other day. Man named Houk. The son of a bitch was a notorious pot dealer. Somebody shot him. Any connection?"

"Who knows?" Leaphorn said. "Maybe so. You have any more specific idea where she took your kayak?"

"Nothing more than I said. She borrowed it before and went down into the canyons. Just poking around in the ruins looking at the potsherds. I'd guess she did it again."

"Any idea how far down?"

"She'd ask me to pick her up the next evening at the landing upstream from the bridge at Mexican Hat. Only place to get off the river for miles. So it would have to be between Sand Island and Hat."

Her car too could be found between Sand Island and Mexican Hat, Leaphorn was sure. She would have to have hauled the kayak within dragging distance of the river. But there was no reason now to look for the car.

"That narrows it down quite a bit," Leaphorn said, thinking Ellie's trips were into the area Etcitty had described in his falsified documentation, the area Amos Whistler had pointed to in his talk with Chee. He would find a boat and go looking for Arnold's kayak. Maybe, when he found it, he would find Eleanor Friedman, and what Harrison Houk meant in that unfinished note. ". . . shes still alive up." But first he wanted a look at that barn.

Irene Musket came to the door at Harrison Houk's old house. She recognized him instantly and let him in. She was a handsome woman, as Leaphorn remembered, but today she looked years older, and tired. She told him about finding the note, about finding the body. She confirmed that she had found absolutely nothing missing from the house. She told him nothing he didn't already know. Then she walked with him up the long slope toward the barn.

"It happened right in here," she said. "Right in that horse stall there. The third one."

Leaphorn looked back. From the barn you could see the driveway, and the old gate with its warning bell. Only the front porch was obscured. Houk might well have seen his killer coming for him.

Irene Musket stood at the barn door. Kept out, perhaps, by her fear of the *chindi* Harrison Houk had left behind him and the ghost sickness it would cause her. Or perhaps by the sorrow that looking at the spot where Houk had died would bring to her.

Leaphorn's career had made him immune to the *chindi* of the dead, immune through indifference to all but one of them. He walked out of the wind and into the dimness.

The floor of the third horse stall had been swept clean of the old alfalfa and prairie-hay straw that littered the rest of the place. That debris now formed a pile in one corner, where the Utah crime lab crew had dumped it after sorting through it. Leaphorn stood on the dirt packed by a hundred years of hooves and wondered what he had expected to find. He walked across the barn floor, inspected the piles of alfalfa bales. It did, indeed, seem that Houk might have been rearranging them to form a hiding place. That touched him oddly, but taught him nothing. Nothing except that Houk, the hard man, the scoundrel, had set aside a chance to hide to make time to leave him a message. "Tell Leaphorn shes still alive up"—up the canyon? That seemed likely. Up which canyon? But why would Houk have put his own life at greater risk to help a woman who must have been nothing more than one of his many customers? It seemed out of character. Not the Houk he knew about. That Houk's only weakness seemed to have been a schizophrenic son, now long dead.

Outside the barn the wind shifted direction slightly and howled through the cracks, raising a small flurry of straw and dust on the packed floor and bringing autumn smells to compete with the ancient urine. He was wasting his time. He walked back toward where Irene Musket was standing, checking the stalls as he passed. In the last one, a black nylon kayak was leaning against the wall.

Bo Arnold's kayak. Leaphorn stared at it. How could it have gotten here? And why?

It was inflated, standing on one pointed end in the stall corner. He walked in for a closer look. Of course it wasn't Arnold's kayak. He had described his as dark brown, with what he called "white racing stripes."

Leaphorn knelt beside it, inspecting it. It seemed remarkably clean for this dusty barn. He felt inside, between the rubber-coated nylon of its bottom and the inflated tubes that formed its walls, hoping to find something telltale left behind. His fingers encountered paper. He pulled it out. The crumpled, water-stained wrapper from a Mr. Goodbar. He ran his fingers down toward the bow.

Water.

Leaphorn pulled out his hand and examined his wet fingers. Whatever water had been left in the kayak had drained down into this crevice. How long could it have been there? How long would evaporation take in this no-humidity climate?

He walked to the door.

"The inflated kayak in there. You know when it was used?"

"I think four days ago," Irene Musket said.

"By Mr. Houk?"

She nodded.

"His arthritis didn't bother him?"

"His arthritis hurt all the time," she said. "It didn't keep him from that boat." She sounded as if this represented an argument lost, an old hurt.

"Where did he go? Do you know?"

She made a vague gesture. "Just down the river."

"Do you know how far?"

"Not very far. He would have me pick him up down there near Mexican Hat."

"He did this a lot?"

"Every full moon."

"He went down at night? Late?"

"Sometimes he would watch the ten o'clock news and then we would go down to Sand Island. We'd make sure nobody was there. Then we'd put it in." The wind whipped dust around Mrs. Musket's ankles and blew up her long skirt. She held it down, pressed back against the barn door. "We would put it in, and then the next morning, I would drive the pickup down to that landing place upstream from Mexican Hat and I'd wait for him there. And then . . ." She paused, swallowed. Stood a moment, silently. Leaphorn noticed her eyes were wet, and looked away. Hard as he was, Harrison Houk had left someone to grieve for him.

"Then we would drive back to the house together," she concluded.

Leaphorn waited awhile. When he had given her enough time, he asked: "Did he tell you what he did when he went down the river?"

The silence lasted so long that Leaphorn wondered if his question had been lost in the wind. He glanced at her.

"He didn't tell me," she said.

Leaphorn thought about the answer.

"But you know," he said.

"I think so," she said. "One time he told me not to guess. And he said, 'If you guess anyway, then don't ever tell anybody!' "

"Do you know who killed him?"

"I don't," she said. "I wish they would have killed me, instead."

"I think we will find the one who did it," Leaphorn said. "I really do."

"He was a good man. People talked about how mean he was. He was good to good people and just mean to the mean ones. I guess they killed him for that."

Leaphorn touched her arm. "Would you help me put the kayak in? And then tomorrow, drive my truck down to Mexican Hat and pick me up?"

"All right," Irene Musket said.

"First I have to make a telephone call. Can I use your telephone?"

He called Jim Chee from Houk's house. It was after six. Chee had gone home for the day. No telephone, of course. Typical of Chee. He left Houk's number for a call back.

They slid the kayak into the back of his truck, with its double-bladed paddle and Houk's worn orange jacket, tied it down, and drove south to Sand Island launch site. Bureau of Land Management signs there warned that the river was closed for the season, that a license was required, that the San Juan catfish was on the extinction list and taking it was prohibited.

With the kayak in the water, Leaphorn stood beside it, feet in the cold water, doing a last-minute inventory of possibilities. He wrote Jim Chee's name and the Shiprock police station number on one of his cards and gave it to her.

"If I don't meet you by noon tomorrow down at Mexican Hat, I hope you will call this man for me. Tell him what you told me about Mr. Houk and this kayak. And that I took it down the river."

She took it.

He climbed into the kayak.

"You know how to run that thing?"

"Years ago I did. I think I'll remember."

"Well, put on the life jacket and buckle it. It's easy to turn over."

"Right," Leaphorn said. He did it.

"And here," she said. She handed him a heavy canteen with a carrying strap and a plastic bread sack. "I got something for you to eat out of the kitchen," she said.

"Well, thanks," Leaphorn said, touched.

"Be careful."

"I can swim."

"I didn't mean the river," Mrs. Musket said.

17

TRAILERS ARE POOR places to sleep on those nights when seasons are changing on the Colorado Plateau. All night Jim Chee's narrow bed quivered as the gusts shook the thin walls of his home. He slept poorly, wrestling with the problem of Elliot's application while he was awake, dreaming of jawbones when he dozed. He rose early, made coffee, and found four Twinkies abandoned in his otherwise empty bread box to round out his breakfast. It was his day off, and time to buy groceries, do the laundry, check three overdue books back into the Farmington library. He'd refilled his water reservoir, but his butane supply was low. And he needed to pick up a tire he'd had repaired. And, come to think of it, drop by the bank and see about the $18.50 difference between his checkbook balance and their records.

Instead he looked in his notebook and found the number Dr. Pedwell had given him for the Laboratory of Anthropology in Santa Fe. "That would have an MLA number," Pedwell had told him when he'd asked if Elliot had also applied to excavate the site where Etcitty and Nails had been killed. "It's in New Mexico, and apparently on public land. If it's on a Navajo section, we record it. If it's not, Laboratory of Anthropology handles it."

"Sounds confusing," Chee had said.

"Oh, it is," Pedwell had agreed. "It's even more confusing than that."

And he'd started explaining other facets of the numbering system, the Chaco numbers, the Mesa Verde, until Chee had changed the subject. Now he realized he should have asked for a name at Santa Fe.

He made the call from the station, drawing a surprised look from the desk clerk, who knew he was off. And it took three transfers before he connected with the woman who had access to the information he needed. She had a sweet, distinct middle-aged voice.

"It's easier if you know the MLA number," she said. "Otherwise I have to check through the applicant files."

And so he waited.

"Dr. Elliot has eleven applications on file. You want all of them?"

"I guess so," Chee said, not knowing exactly what to expect.

"MLA 14,751. MLA 19,311. MLA—"

"Just a moment," Chee said. "Do they have site locations? What county they're in. Like that?"

"On our map, yes."

"The one I'm interested in would be in San Juan County, New Mexico."

"Just a minute," she said. The minute passed. "Two of them. MLA 19,311 and MLA 19,327."

"Could you pin the location down any more?"

"I can give you the legal description. Range, township, and section." She read them off.

"Was he issued the permits?"

"Turned down," she said. "They're saving those sites to be dug sometime in the future when they have better technology. It's hard to get permission to dig them now."

"Thanks a lot," Chee said. "It's exactly what I need."

And it was. When he checked the legal description on the U.S. Geological Survey map in Captain Largo's office, MLA 19,327 proved to share range, township, and section with the oil well pump beyond which he'd found the U-Haul truck.

He had less luck trying to call Chaco Canyon. The phone was suffering some sort of satellite relay problem that produced both fade-out and echo. Randall Elliot was out of reach at one of the down-canyon ruins. Maxie Davis was somewhere. Luna was doing something, unintelligible to Chee, at Pueblo Bonito.

Chee glanced at his watch. He calculated the distance to Chaco. About a hundred miles. He remembered the condition of that last twenty-five miles of dirt. He groaned. Why was he doing this on his day off? But he knew why. Much as Leaphorn irritated him, he wanted the man to pat him on the head. To say, "Good job, kid." Might as well admit it. Also he might as well admit another fact. He was excited now. That grotesque line of lower jaws suddenly seemed to mean something. Perhaps something important.

The strange weather slowed him a little, rocking his truck when he stretched the limit on the fast pavement of N.M. 44 across the sagebrush flats of Blanco Plateau. End of autumn, he thought. Winter coming out of the west. Behind him over Colorado's La Plata range, the sky was dark, and when he left the pavement at Blanco Trading Post, he had a direct side wind to deal with—and the tiring business of steering against it as he fought chugholes and ruts. And tumbleweeds and blowing sand chased him across the parking lot at the Chaco visitors' center.

The woman he'd talked to was at the desk, looking trim in her park ranger uniform and glad to have Chee break the boredom of a day, and a season, that brought few visitors. She showed him on the Chaco map how to get to Kin Kletso, the site where Randall Elliot would be working today, "if he can work in this wind." Where Maxie Davis was seemed a mystery, "but maybe she'll be working with Randall." Luna had driven into Gallup and wouldn't be back until tonight.

Chee went back to his truck, leaning into the wind, squinching his eyes against the dust. At Kin Kletso, he found a Park Service truck parked and an employee sitting in the shelter of one of the walls.

"Looking for Dr. Randall Elliot," Chee said. "Did I miss him?"

"A mile," the man said. "He didn't show up today."

"You know where . . ."

The man waved a dismissive wave. "No idea," he said. "He's independent as a hog on ice."

Maybe he was home. Chee drove to the temporary housing. Nothing in the parking area. He knocked at the door marked Elliot. Knocked again. Walked around the building to the back. Randall Elliot hadn't pulled the drapes across his sliding-glass patio door. Chee peered into what must be the living room. Elliot seemed to have converted it into a work area. Sawhorses supported planks on which cardboard cartons were lined. Those that Chee could see into seemed to contain bones. Skulls, ribs, jawbones. Chee pressed his forehead against the cool glass, shading his eyes with both hands, straining to see. Against the wall, boxes were lined. Books on shelves against the kitchen partition. No sign of Elliot.

Chee glanced down at the lock that held the door. Simple enough. He looked around him. No one visible. He dug out his penknife, opened the proper blade, slipped the catch.

Once inside he closed the drapes and turned on the light. He hurried through a quick search of the bedroom, kitchen, and bath, touching hardly anything and using his handkerchief to avoid leaving prints. This made him nervous. Worse, it made him feel dirty and ashamed.

But back in the living room he lingered over the boxes of bones. They seemed to be arranged in groups, tagged by site. Chee checked the tags, looking for either N.R. 723 or MLA 19,327. On the makeshift table by the kitchen door he found the N.R. number.

The tag was tied through the eye socket of a skull, number on one side, notes on the other. They seemed to be in some sort of personal shorthand, with numbers in millimeters. Bone thickness, Chee guessed, but the rest of it meant nothing to him.

The N.R. 723 box contained four lower jaws, one apparently from a child, one broken. He examined them. Each contained an extra molar, or a trace of one, on the right side. Each had two of the small holes low in the bones through which Elliot's petition had stated nerves and blood vessels grow.

Chee put the jaws back in the box exactly as he had found them, wiped his fingers on his pants legs, and sat down to sort out the significance of this. It seemed clear enough. Elliot's genetic tracking had led him to the same site as had Eleanor Friedman-Bernal's pottery chase. No. That didn't state it accurately. In their mutual fishing expeditions, both had struck pay dirt in the same ruins. Perhaps, Chee thought, one of the jawbones belonged to the potter.

He thought about site MLA 19,327, the lined jawbones, the missing plastic sack from the box of thirty. Thinking about that, he made another search of the apartment.

He found a black plastic sack in the bottom of a wastebasket in the kitchen. He carefully set aside the table scraps and wadded papers that had buried it and put it on the counter beside the sink. The top was tied in a knot. Chee untied it and examined the plastic. SUPERTUFF was printed around the top. The missing sack.

Inside it were seven human mandibles, two of them child-sized, two broken. Chee counted teeth. Each had seventeen—one more than standard—and in each the superfluous molar was second from the back and out of line.

He put the sack back in the wastebasket, recovered it with waste, and picked up the telephone.

No, the woman at the visitors' center said, Elliot hadn't reported in. Nor had Luna or Maxie Davis.

"Can you get me Mrs. Luna?"

"Now that's easy," she said.

Mrs. Luna answered on the third ring and remembered Chee instantly. How was he? How was Mr. Leaphorn? "But this isn't what you called about."

"No," Chee said. "I came out to talk to Randall Elliot but he's away somewhere. I remembered you said he went to Washington last month. You said his travel agent called and you took the message. Do you remember the name of the agency?"

"Bolack's," Mrs. Luna said. "I think just about everybody out here uses Bolack's."

Chee called Bolack Travel in Farmington.

"Navajo Tribal Police," he told the man who answered. "We need to confirm the dates of an airline ticket. Don't know the airline, but the tickets were issued by your agency to Randall Elliot, address at Chaco Canyon."

"You know about when? This year? This month? Yesterday?"

"Probably late last month," Chee said.

"Randall Elliot," the man said. "Randall Elliot. Let's see." Chee heard the clacking sound of a computer keyboard. Silence. More clacking. More silence.

"That's funny," the man said. "We issued them, but he didn't pick them up. It was an October eleven departure, with an October sixteen return. Mesa from Farmington to Albuquerque, American from Albuquerque to Washington. You just need the dates?"

"The tickets weren't picked up? You're certain?"

"I sure am. Makes a lot of work for nothing."

Chee called Mrs. Luna again. Listening to the ring, he felt a sense of urgency. Randall Elliot wasn't in Washington that morning Eleanor Friedman-Bernal drove away to oblivion. He didn't go. But he pretended to go. He arranged it so that everyone in this gossipy place would think he was in Washington. Why? So they wouldn't be curious about where he'd actually gone. And where was that? Chee thought he knew. He hoped he was wrong.

"Hello," Mrs. Luna said.

"Chee again," he said. "Another question. Did a deputy sheriff come out here yesterday to talk to people?"

"He did. About a month late, I'd say."

"Did he tell you about the note left for Lieutenant Leaphorn? The one that sounded like Dr. Friedman might still be alive."

"Is alive," Mrs. Luna said. "He said the note said, 'Tell Leaphorn she is still alive.' "

"Does everybody here know about that? Does Elliot?"

"Of course. Because everybody was beginning to have their doubts. You know, that's a long time to just disappear unless something bad has happened."

"You sure about Elliot?"

"He was right here when he told Bob and me."

"Well, thanks a lot," Chee said.

The wind had fallen now into something near a calm. Which was lucky for Chee. He drove back to Blanco Trading Post much faster than the rutted dirt roadbed made wise, and then much faster than the law allowed on N.M. 44 to Farmington. He was worried. He had told Undersheriff Bates to tell the people at Chaco about Houk's note. He should not have done that. But maybe these suspicions were groundless. He thought of a way he could check—a call he should have made before he left Chaco.

He pulled into the grocery store at Bloomfield and ran to the pay phone, then ran back to his truck for the supply of quarters he kept in the glove box. He called the Farmington airport, identified himself, asked the woman who answered who there rented helicopters. He jotted down the two names she gave him, and their numbers. The line was busy at Aero Services. He dialed Flight Contractors. A man who identified himself as Sanchez answered. Yes, they had rented a copter that morning to Randall Elliot.

"Pretty sorry weather for flying, even in a copter," Sanchez said. "But he's got the credentials and the experience. Flew for the navy in Nam."

"Did he say where he was going?"

"He's an anthropologist," Sanchez said. "We been renting to him for two, three years now. Said he was going down over the White Horse Lake country hunting one of them Indian ruins. If you're going to fly in this kind of weather, that's a good place to fly. Just grass and snakeweed down that way."

It was also just about exactly the opposite direction from where Elliot was really flying, Chee thought. Southeast instead of northwest.

"When did he leave?"

"I'd say maybe three hours ago. Maybe a little longer."

"Do you have another one to rent? With a pilot."

"Have the chopper," Sanchez said. "Have to see about the pilot. When's it for?"

Chee made some instant calculations. "Thirty minutes," he said.

"I doubt it by then," Sanchez said. "I'll try."

It took Chee a little less than that, at considerable risk of a speeding ticket. Sanchez had found a pilot, but the pilot hadn't arrived.

"He's the substitute pilot for the air ambulance service," Sanchez said. "Man named Ed King. He didn't care much for this weather, but then the wind's been dying."

In fact the wind had moderated to a steady breeze. It seemed to be dying away as the weather front that brought it moved southeast. But now the sky to the north and west was a solid dark overcast.

While they waited for King, he'd see if he could get hold of Leaphorn. If he couldn't, he'd leave word for him. Tell him about finding the missing wastebasket liner hidden in Elliot's kitchen with the bones in it, and about Elliot's rejected applications to dig those sites. He'd tell Leaphorn that Elliot hadn't taken the flight to Washington the weekend that Friedman-Bernal disappeared. That provoked another thought.

"Mr. Sanchez. Could you check and see if Dr. Elliot took out a helicopter on, let's see, the thirteenth of October?"

Sanchez looked as doubtful as he had when Chee had said he should bill the copter rental to the Navajo Tribal Police. The look had hardened, and Chee had finally presented his MasterCard and waited while Sanchez checked his credit balance. It seemed to have reached the minimum guarantee. ("Now," said Sanchez, cheerful again, "if it's okay with the tribal auditors you can get your money back.")

"I don't know that I'm supposed to be telling all this stuff," Sanchez said. "Randall's a regular customer of ours. It might get back to him."

"It's police business," Chee said. "Part of a criminal investigation."

"About what?" Sanchez looked stubborn.

"Those two men shot out in the Checkerboard. Nails and Etcitty."

"Oh," Sanchez said. "I'll check."

"While you do, I'll call my office."

Benally was in charge of the shift. No, Benally knew no way to get in touch with Leaphorn.

"Matter of fact, you have a message from him. Woman named Irene Musket called from Mexican Hat. She said Leaphorn headed down the San-Juan—" Benally paused, chuckling. "You know," he said, "this sounds just like the screwy stuff you get mixed up in, Jim. Anyway, she said Leaphorn took off down the San Juan yesterday evening in a boat, looking for a boat this anthropologist you're looking for took. She was supposed to pick him up this morning at Mexican Hat, and call you if he didn't show up. Well, he didn't show up."

And just then the door opened behind Chee, letting in the cold breeze.

"Somebody here want a chopper ride?"

A burly, bald-headed man with a great yellow mustache was standing holding it open, looking at Chee. "You the daredevil who wants to fly out into this weather? I'm the daredevil here to take you."

18

FINDING THE KAYAK Eleanor Friedman-Bernal had borrowed seemed simple enough to Leaphorn. She could have gone only downriver. The cliffs that walled in the San Juan between Bluff and Mexican Hat limited takeout places to a few sandy benches and the mouths of perhaps a score of washes and canyons. Since Leaphorn's reason and instincts told him her target ruin was on the reservation side of the river, his hunting grounds were further limited. And the description he had been given of the woman suggested she wouldn't be strong enough to pull the heavy rubber kayak very far out of the water. Therefore, finding it, even in the gathering darkness with only a flashlight, would be easy. Finding the woman would be the tough part.

Leaphorn had calculated without the wind. It treated Houk's little craft like a sail, pushing against its sides and forcing Leaphorn into a constant struggle to keep it in the current. About four miles below the Bluff bridge, he let the kayak drift into a sandbar on the north side of the river, as much to stretch cramping muscles and give himself a rest as in any hope of finding something. On the cliffs here he found an array of petroglyphs cut through the black desert varnish into the sandstone. He studied a row of square-shouldered figures with chevron-like stripes above their heads and little arcs suggesting sound waves issuing from their mouths. If they hadn't predated the time his own people had invaded this stone wilderness, he would have thought they represented the Navajo *yei* called Talking God. Just above them was the figure of a bird—an unambiguous representation of the snowy egret. Above that, Kokopelli played his flute, bent so far forward that it pointed at the earth. The ground here was littered with shards of pottery but Leaphorn found no sign of the kayak. He hadn't expected to.

Relaunched, he paddled the kayak back into the current. Twilight now, and he found himself relaxing. Someone had said that "the rush of the river soothes the mind." It did seem to, in contrast to the sound of wind, which always made him tense. But the wind was moderating now. He heard the call of a bird behind him, and a coyote somewhere on the Utah side, and the distant voice of rapids from the darkness ahead.

He checked two possible landing points on the reservation side, and spent more time than he'd planned looking at the mouths of Butler Wash and Comb Creek on the Utah side. When he pushed off again, it was into the light of the rising moon—a little past full. Leaphorn heard an abrupt flurry of sound. A snowy egret had been startled from its roosting place. It flew away from him into the moonlight, a graceful white shape moving against the black cliff, solitary, disappearing into the darkness where the river bent.

Egrets, he thought, were like snow geese and wolves and those other creatures—like Leaphorn himself—that mated only once and for life. That would explain its presence here. It was living out its loneliness in this empty place. Leaphorn's kayak slid out of the darkness under the cliff and into a moonlit eddy. His shadow streaked out from that of the kayak, making a strange elongated shape. It reminded him of the bird, and he waved the paddle to magnify the effect. As he rested with his arms relaxed, he became the stick figure of the *yei* Black God as Navajo shamans represented him in the dry painting of the Night Chant. Bent over the paddle, pulling his weight against the water, he was Kokopelli, with his hunched back full of sorrows. He was thinking that, as the current swept him around the cliff into the dark. Here, with all black except the stars directly overhead, the shout of the river drowned out everything.

As the San Juan drops toward its rendezvous with the mighty Colorado, its rapids are relatively mild. It is the goal of those who run rivers for joy to nose their tough little kayaks into the throats of these cataracts for the thrill of being buried under the white water. It was Leaphorn's goal to skirt the bedlam and keep dry. Even so, he emerged soaked from the waist down and well splashed elsewhere. The river here had cut through the Comb Ridge anticline—what millions of years of erosion had left of the Monument Upwarp. Here, eons ago, the earth's crust had bulged outward in a massive bubble of bending stone layers. Leaphorn drifted past slanting layers of stone which, even in this dim light, gave the eerie impression of sliding toward the center of the earth.

Beyond the anticline, he used his flashlight to check another sandy bench and the mouth of two washes. Then, around another bend and through another rapids, he guided the kayak into the eddy where Many Ruins Wash drained a huge expanse of the Navajo Reservation into the San Juan. If he had a specific destination when he left Sand Island, this was it.

Leaphorn had long since stopped trying to keep dry. He waded knee-deep through the eddy, pulled the kayak well ashore, and sat on the sand beside it, catching his breath. He was weary. He was wet. He was cold. Abruptly, he was very, very cold. He found himself shaking and unable to control the motion. His hands shook. So did his legs. His teeth chattered. Hypothermia. Leaphorn had suffered it before. It frightened him then and it frightened him now.

He pushed himself to his feet, staggered down the sand, the flashlight beam jittering erratically ahead of him. He found a place where a flash flood had left a tangle of twigs. He fumbled the lip balm tube in which he kept kitchen matches out of his jacket, managed to get his shaking fingers to open it, managed to stuff desiccated grass under a pile of twigs, managed on the third match to get the fire going. He added driftwood, fanned the fire into a blaze with his hat, and stood beside it, panting and shaking.

In his panic he had made the fire in the wrong place. Now, with his jeans steaming and some warmth returning to his blood, he looked around for a better place. He built this new fire where two walls of stone formed a sand-floored pocket, collecting enough heavy driftwood to keep it going until morning. Then he dried his clothing thoroughly.

This was where he'd expected to find the kayak. Up this canyon somewhere he expected to find the site that had drawn Eleanor Friedman-Bernal. When the river delayed him, he'd decided to wait for daylight to hunt the kayak. But now he couldn't wait. Tired as he was, he picked up the flashlight and walked back to the water.

She had hidden it carefully, dragging it with more strength than he credited her with far up under the tangled branches of a cluster of tamarisks. He searched, expecting to find nothing, and finding only a little nylon packet jammed under the center tube. It held a red nylon poncho. Leaphorn kept it. Back at the fire, he kicked himself a loosened place in the sand, spread the poncho as a ground cloth and lay down to sleep, leaving his boots close enough to the flames to complete the drying process.

The flames attracted flying insects. The insects attracted the bats. Leaphorn watched them fluttering at the margin of the darkness, darting to make their kill, flashing away. Emma had disliked bats. Emma had admired lizards, had battled roaches endlessly, had given names to the various spiders that lived around their house and—all too often—in it. Emma would have enjoyed this trip. He had always planned to take her, but there was never time, until now, when time no longer mattered. Emma would have been intensely interested in the affair of Eleanor Friedman-Bernal, would have felt a rapport with her. Would have asked him, if he'd forgotten to report, what progress was being made. Would have had advice for him. Well, tomorrow he would find that woman. A sort of gift, it would be.

He shifted himself into the sand. A chunk of driftwood fell, sending a shower of sparks up toward the stars. Leaphorn slept.

The cold awakened him. The fire had burned to dim embers, the moon was down, and the sky over him was an incredible dazzle of stars humans can see only when high altitude, clear, dry air, and an absence of ground light combine. Below these black thousand-foot cliffs, it was like looking into space from the bottom of a well. Leaphorn rebuilt the fire and dozed off again, listening to the night sounds. Two coyotes were on their nocturnal hunt now somewhere up the canyon and he could hear another pair very distant across the river. He heard a saw-whet owl high in the cliffs, a cry as shrill as metal rubbing metal. Just as he fell into sleep he heard the sound of a flute. Or perhaps it was just part of his dream.

When he awoke again, he was shivering with cold. It was late dawn, with the coldest air of night settled into this canyon slot. He got up, flinching against the stiffness, restarted the fire, drank from his canteen, and looked for the first time into the sack of food Irene Musket had sent with him—a great chunk of fry bread and a coil of boiled Polish sausage. He was hungry, but he would wait. He might need it much more later.

Despite their age, he found a fair set of Eleanor Friedman-Bernal's tracks pressed into the hard sand under the tamarisks—where the hanging vegetation had protected them from the moving air. Then he methodically searched the rest of this junction of canyons. He wanted to confirm that this was the place Houk had come, and he did. In fact, Houk seemed to have come here often. Probably it was his monthly destination. Someone, presumably Houk, had repeatedly slid a kayak up the sloping sand at the extreme upper end of the bench and left it under a broken-off cottonwood. From there a narrow trail took an unlikely course about five hundred yards through the brush, through the little dunes of blown sand, and down into the bottom of Many Ruins. It stopped at a little cul-de-sac of boulders.

Leaphorn spent a half-hour in that much-used spot, partly because he could find no sign that Houk had gone beyond it. This sheltered place seemed to be where Houk's moonlit journeys ended. Again, he was looking for confirmation of what he was now sure must be true. This damp and protected place held footprints well, and Houk's were everywhere. Many were fresh, evidence of the final visit before his murder. On these Leaphorn focused his attention, narrowing it finally to two prints. Both had been pressed upon by something heavy and partly erased. A soft, edgeless pressure. But not a moccasin. Something odd about it. Finally, looking at both prints from every possible angle, Leaphorn realized what caused the strange lines. Fur. But they weren't animal tracks. When patched together in Leaphorn's mind, the pressed places had the shape of a man's foot.

With nothing else to learn, Leaphorn started up-canyon. While he walked he considered what he was now almost certain were the facts. Brigham Houk probably had not drowned. Somehow he had managed to get across the river. Brigham Houk, the boy who had slaughtered his mother, his brother, and his sister, was somewhere in this canyon. Had been here almost twenty years, living away from people as he had longed to live. Houk had found the boy after the hue and cry of murder died away, had sustained him secretly all these years with whatever this born hunter had needed to stay alive. Nothing else seemed to explain Houk's note. Nothing else Leaphorn could think of would have motivated the man to stop an admittedly futile effort to build a hiding place to write a note. Houk didn't want this mad son of his abandoned here. He wanted him found by the same policeman who had once shown some awareness of the boy's humanity. He wanted him cared for, and he'd given up whatever minuscule chance he'd had of living to write his note. The writing had been tiny, Leaphorn remembered, and started at one end of the card. What would Houk have said had time allowed? Would he have explained about Brigham? He'd never know.

About two miles up the twisting canyon Leaphorn found the only sign of modern human occupancy. The bare poles of an old sweat bath stood on the broad shelf above the canyon floor. The ashes under it suggested it hadn't been used for years. If the canyon had ever been grazed, it hadn't been recently. He found no tracks of horses, sheep, or goats. The only hoofprints he found were mule deer, and there seemed to be plenty of rabbits, porcupines, and small rodents. He noticed three game trails leading to a deep spring-fed pothole at the canyon bottom. Four miles up, he stopped in a shady place and ate a small piece of the bread and a couple of inches of the sausage. There was heavy cloud cover over the northwest sky now. It was colder and yesterday's wind was back again now with a vengeance. It blew cross-canyon, forming powerful eddies of air that swirled this way here, and that way there. It made the odd sounds wind makes when it pours through stony crevices. It sent whirlwinds of fallen leaves sweeping around Leaphorn's legs. It blotted out all other sound.

The wind made walking difficult, and the crooked, erratic nature of the canyon bottom made estimating distance—even for one as experienced as Leaphorn—little more than guesswork. Double guesswork, he thought. He had to guess how much of this climbing over tumbled boulders and detouring around brush would have added to the five and a half miles Etcitty had estimated. It would be less than that, he was sure, and he'd been looking for the landmarks Etcitty had mentioned since about mile three. Just ahead, where the canyon bottom made a sharp bend, he saw a crevice in the cliff walled in with stones—an Anasazi storeroom. On the cliff below it, half obscured by tall brush, he saw pictographs. He climbed the soft earth to the floor of the bench and pushed his way through the heavy growth of nettles for a closer look.

The dominant shape was one of those broad-shouldered, pin-headed figures that anthropologists believe represented Anasazi shamans. It looked, as Etcitty had described it, "like a big baseball umpire holding up a pink chest protector." Leaphorn recrossed the canyon bottom and climbed the shelf on the other side. He saw what he had come to find.

Near its beginnings in the Chuska Mountains, Many Ruins Canyon is cut deep and narrow through the Chinle sandstone formation of that plateau. There its cliffs rise sheer and vertical almost a thousand feet above a narrow, sandy bottom. It is much shallower by the time it emerges into Chinle Valley and becomes a mere drainage wash as it meanders northward toward Utah through the Greasewood Flats. But the cut deepens again in its passage through the Nokaito Bench to the San Juan. Here the crazy mishmash geology of the earth's crust had given Many Ruins a different shape. One climbed out of it on a series of steps. First the low, sometimes earthen cliffs that crowded its narrow streambed, then a broken sandstone shelf hundreds of yards wide, then more cliffs, rising to another shelf, and still more cliffs rising to the flat top of Nokaito Mesa.

In the spring when the snowpack melts a hundred miles away in the Chuska Mountains, Many Ruins carries a steady stream. In the late-summer thunderstorm season it rises and falls between a trickle and booming flash floods, which send boulders tumbling like marbles down its bottom. In late autumn it dries. The life that occupied it finds water then only in spring-fed potholes. From where he stood on the sandstone shelf above such a pothole, Leaphorn could see the second of the ruins Etcitty had described. Two ruins, in fact.

Part of the wall of one was visible in an alcove in the second level of cliffs above him. Another, reduced to little more than a brushy hump, had been built along the base of the cliff not two hundred yards from the alcove.

All this day he had fought down his sense of excitement and urgency. He had a long ways to go and he went at a careful walk. Now he trotted across the sandstone bench.

He stopped when the alcove came in full view. Like those invariably picked as building sites by the Anasazi, it faced the low winter sun, with enough overhang to shade it in the summer. A cluster of brushy vegetation grew under it, telling him it was also the site of seep. He walked toward it, more slowly now. He didn't consider Brigham Houk particularly dangerous. Houk had called him schizophrenic—unpredictable but not likely to be a threat to a stranger. Still, he had killed once in an insane rage. Leaphorn unsnapped the flap that held his pistol in its holster.

Eons of water running down the inner face of the alcove had worn a depression several feet into the sandstone below it. Water stains indicated this held a pool about four feet deep in wetter seasons. Now only a foot or two was left—still fed by a tiny trickle from a mossy crevice in the cliff, and now green with algae. It was also the home of scores of tiny leopard frogs, which hopped away from Leaphorn's feet.

Only some of them hopped.

Leaphorn squatted, grunted with surprise. He studied the small scattered frog bodies, some already shriveled, some newly dead, each with a leg secured by a yucca thread to a tiny peg cut from a twig. He stood, trying to make sense of this. The pegs followed a series of faint concentric circles drawn around the pothole, the outside one perhaps four feet from the water. Some sort of game, Leaphorn guessed. He tried to understand the mind that would be amused by it. He failed. Brigham Houk was insane, probably dangerous.

He considered. Brigham Houk almost certainly would already know he was here.

Leaphorn made a megaphone of his hands. "Eleanor," he shouted. "Ellie. Ellie." Then he listened.

Nothing. Outside the alcove, the wind made whimpering sounds.

He tried again. Again, nothing.

The Anasazi had built their structure on a stone shelf above the pool. About a dozen small rooms once, Leaphorn estimated, with part of it at two levels. He skirted around the pool, climbed over the tumbled walls, peered into the still-intact rooms. Nothing. He walked back to the pool, puzzled. Where to look next?

At the edge of the alcove, a worn set of footholds had been cut into the sandstone—a climbway leading to the shelf above the alcove. Perhaps that led to another site. He walked out of the alcove around the cliff to the brushy hump. Immediately he saw it had been plundered. A ditch had been dug along the outside wall. Bones were scattered everywhere. The digging had been recent—hardly any rain since the earth was disturbed. Leaphorn inspected it. Was this why Eleanor Friedman-Bernal had slipped away from Chaco, slipped down the San Juan? To search this site for her polychrome pots? So it would seem. And what had happened then? What had interrupted her? He checked in the disturbed earth for shards and collected a handful. They might be the sort that interested her. He couldn't be sure. He looked down in the trench. Jutting from the earth was part of a pot. And another. In the bottom were a half-dozen shards, two of them large. Why had she left them there? Then he noticed an oddity. Among the bones littering the trench he saw no skulls. On the earth outside more than a dozen were scattered. None had jawbones. Natural, probably. The mandible would be attached only by muscle and gristle, which wouldn't survive an eight-hundred-year burial. Then where were the missing mandibles? He saw five of them together beside the trench, as if discarded there. It reminded him of the jawbones lined so neatly at the dig site where Etcitty and Nails had died.

But where was the woman who had dug the trench? He went back to the pool and inspected the footholds. Then he started climbing, thinking as he did that he was far too old for this. Fifty feet up the cliff, he was aware of two facts. These Anasazi footholds were in regular current use, and he was a damn fool to have attempted the climb. He clung to the stone, reaching blindly for the next handhold, wondering how many remained. Finally the slope eased. He looked up. He had done it. His head was almost even with the top. He pulled himself up, his upper body over the edge.

Standing there, watching him, was a man. He wore a beard cut straight across, a nylon jacket so new it still had the creases of its folds, a pair of tattered jeans, and moccasins that seemed to have been sewn together from deer hide.

"Mr. Leaphorn," the man said. "Papa said you coming."

19

As Harrison Houk's message to him had promised, Dr. Eleanor Friedman-Bernal was still alive. She lay dozing under a gray wool blanket and a covering of sewn-together rabbit skins. She looked very, very ill.

"Can she talk?" he asked Brigham.

"A little," he said. "Sometimes."

It occurred to Leaphorn that Brigham Houk might have been describing himself. He talked very little and sometimes not at all. What you'd expect, Leaphorn thought, after twenty years of no one to talk to except once every full moon.

"How bad is it? Her injuries I mean?"

"Knee's hurt," he said. "Arm broken. Place in her side. Place in her hip."

And probably all infected, Leaphorn thought. Thin as her face was, it was flushed.

"You found her and brought her here?"

Brigham nodded. Like his father, he was a small man, tightly built, with short arms and legs and a thick, strong torso.

"Do you know what happened to her?"

"The devil came and hurt her," Brigham said in an odd, flat voice. "He hit her. She ran away. He chased. She fell down. He pushed her off. She fell into the canyon. Broke everything."

Brigham had made a bed for her by digging a coffin-shaped pit in the sand that had drifted into a room of the sheltered ruin. He'd filled it with a two- or three-foot layer of leaves. Open as it was to the air, it had the sick-room smell of urine and decay.

"Tell me about this," Leaphorn said.

Brigham was standing at what had been the entry door to the little room—now a narrow gap into a roofless space. Behind him the sky was dark. The wind, which had fallen during the afternoon, was blowing again now. It blew steadily out of the northwest. Winter, Leaphorn thought. He kept his eyes locked with Brigham's. The young man's eyes were the same odd blue-gray as his father's. Had the same intensity about them. Leaphorn looked into them, searching for insanity. Looking for it, he found it.

"This devil came," Brigham said, speaking very slowly. "He dug up the bones, and sat on the ground there looking at them. One after another he would look at them. He would measure them with a tool he had. He was looking for the souls of people who never had been prayed for. He would suck the souls out of the skulls and then he would throw them away. Or some of them he would take away in his sack. And then one day the last time the moon was full—" He paused and his somber bearded face converted into an expression of delight. "When the moon is full, that's when Papa comes and talks to me, and brings me what I need." The smile drifted away. "A little after that, this woman came." He nodded at Friedman-Bernal. "I didn't see her come and I think maybe the angel Moroni brought her because I didn't see her come and I see everything in this place. Moroni left her to fight with that devil. She had come to the old cliff house down below here where I keep my frogs. I didn't know she was there. I was playing my flute and I frightened her and she ran away. But the next day, she came to where the devil was digging up the bones. I saw them talking."

Brigham's mobile face became fierce. His eyes seemed to glitter with the anger. "He knocked her down, and he was on top of her, fighting with her. He got up and was searching through her pack, and she jumped up and ran over to the edge where the cliff drops down to the streambed and then she fell down. That devil, he went over and pushed her over with his foot." Brigham stopped, his face wet with tears.

"He just left her there, where she fell?"

Brigham nodded.

"You kept her alive," Leaphorn said. "But now I think she is starting to die. We have to get her out of here. To a hospital where doctors can give her medicine."

Brigham stared at him. "Papa said I could trust you." The statement was reproachful.

"If we don't get her out, she dies," Leaphorn said.

"Papa will bring medicine. The next time the moon is full he will come with it."

"Too long," Leaphorn said. "Look at her."

Brigham looked. "She's asleep," he said, softly.

"She has fever. Feel her face. How hot. She has infections. She has to have help."

Brigham touched Eleanor Friedman-Bernal's cheek with the tips of his fingers. He jerked them away, looking frightened. Leaphorn thought of the shriveled bodies of the frogs and tried to square that image with this tenderness. How do you square insanity?

"We need to make something to carry her on," Leaphorn said. "If you can find two poles long enough, we can tie the blanket between them and carry her on that."

"No," Brigham Houk said. "When I try to move her, to clean her after she does number one or number two, she screams. It hurts too bad."

"No choice," Leaphorn said. "We have to do it."

"It's terrible," Brigham said. "She screams. I can't stand that, so I had to leave her dirty." He looked at Leaphorn for understanding. Houk had apparently given him a haircut and trimmed his beard on the last visit. The old man was no barber. He had simply left the hair about an inch long everywhere, and whacked the beard off a half-inch under Brigham's chin.

"It was better to leave her dirty," Leaphorn said. "You did right. Now, can you find me two poles?"

Brigham nodded. "Just a minute. I have poles. It's close." He disappeared, making no sound at all.

Here is how it must have been when man lived as predator, Leaphorn thought. He developed the animal skills, and starved with his children when the skill failed him. How had Brigham hunted? Traps, probably, and a bow to kill larger game. Perhaps his father had brought him a gun—but someone might have heard gunshots. He listened to the sound of Eleanor Friedman's shallow breathing, and over that, the wind sounds. Suddenly he heard a thumping. Steady at first, then louder. He leaped to his feet. A helicopter. But before he could get into the open there was only the wind. He stared into the grayness, frustrated. He had found her. He must get her out of here alive. The risk lay in carrying such a fragile load over such rough terrain. It would be difficult. It might be impossible. A helicopter would save her. Why hadn't Houk done more to get her out? No time, Leaphorn guessed. His son had told him of this injured woman, but perhaps not how near she was to death. Houk would have wanted a way to save the woman without giving up this mad son to life (or perhaps death) in a prison for the criminally insane. Even Houk needed time to solve such a puzzle. He was too crippled to bring her out himself. If he did, she would talk of the man who had nursed her, and Brigham would be found—an insane triple murderer in the eyes of the law. The only solution Leaphorn saw would be to find Brigham another hideaway. That would take time, and the killer had allowed Houk no time.

The woman stirred, moaned. He and Brigham would have to carry her to the canyon bottom, then five miles down to the river. They could tie the kayaks together, put her litter on one of them, and float her to Mexican Hat. Five or six hours at least, and then an ambulance would come for her. Or the copter would come from Farmington if the weather allowed. It hadn't been too bad for whatever had just flown over.

He walked out under the dark sky. He smelled ozone. Snow was near. Then he saw Randall Elliot walking toward him.

Elliot raised his hand. "I saw you from up there," he said, pointing past Leaphorn to the rim of the mesa. "Came down to see if you needed help."

"Sure," Leaphorn said. "Lots of help."

Elliot stopped a few feet away. "You find her?"

Leaphorn nodded toward the ruin, remembering Elliot was a copter pilot.

"How is she?"

"Not good," Leaphorn said.

"But alive at least?"

"In a coma," Leaphorn said. "She can't talk." He wanted Elliot to know that immediately. "I doubt if she'll live."

"My God," Elliot said. "What happened to her?"

"I think she fell," Leaphorn said. "A long ways. That's what it looks like."

Elliot was frowning. "She's in there?" he said. "How did she get here?"

"A man lives out here. A hermit. He found her and he's been trying to keep her alive."

"I'll be damned," Elliot said. He moved past Leaphorn. "In here?"

Leaphorn followed. They stood, Elliot staring at Friedman-Bernal, Leaphorn watching Elliot. He wanted to handle this just exactly right. Only Elliot could fly the helicopter.

"A hermit found her?" he said softly, posing the question to himself. He shook his head. "Where is he?"

"He went to get a couple of poles. We're going to make a litter. Carry her down to the San Juan. Her kayak's there, and mine. Float her down to Mexican Hat and get help."

Elliot was looking at her again, studying her. "I have a helicopter up on the mesa. We can carry her up there. Much quicker."

"Great," Leaphorn said. "Lucky you found us."

"Really, it was stupid," Elliot said. "I should have remembered about this place. She'd told me once she'd found the polychrome pattern she was chasing on potsherds in here. Back when she was helping inventory these sites. I knew she'd planned to come back." He turned away from the woman. His eyes locked with Leaphorn's.

"As a matter of fact, she said some things that made me think she had come here earlier. She didn't exactly say it, but I think she did some illegal digging in here. I think she found what she was looking for, and she came back to get some more."

"I think you're right," Leaphorn said. "She dug up that ruins on the shelf down below here. Dug up a bunch of graves."

"And got careless," Elliot added, looking at her.

Leaphorn nodded. Where was Brigham? He'd said just a minute. Leaphorn walked out of the ruin, looking along the talus slope under the cliff. Two poles leaned against the wall not ten feet away. Brigham had returned and seen his devil, and gone away. The poles were fir, apparently, and weathered. Driftwood, Leaphorn guessed, carried down Many Ruins all the way from the mountains by one of its flash floods. On the ground beside them was a loop of rawhide rope. He hurried back into the room with them.

"A very skittish man," Leaphorn said. "He left the poles and disappeared again."

"Oh," Elliot said. He looked skeptical.

They doubled the blanket, made lacing holes, and tied it securely to the poles.

"Be very careful," Leaphorn said. "Knee probably broken. Broken arm, all sorts of internal injuries."

"I used to collect the wounded," Elliot said, without looking up. "I'm good at this."

And Elliot seemed to be careful. Even so, Eleanor Friedman-Bernal uttered a strangled moan. Then she was unconscious again.

"I think she fainted," Elliot said. "Do you really think she's dying?"

"I do," Leaphorn said. "I'm giving you the heavy end because you're younger and stronger and not so exhausted."

"Fair," Elliot said. He picked up the end of the poles at the woman's head. "You know the way back to your copter, so you lead the way."

They carried Eleanor Friedman-Bernal carefully down the talus, then toward a long rock slide which sloped down from the rim. Beyond the slide—probably the cause of it—was a deep erosion cut which carried runoff water down from the top. Elliot turned toward the cut.

"Rest a minute," Leaphorn said. "Put her down on this slab."

He was fairly sure now what Elliot planned. Somewhere between here and the helicopter, wherever that was, something fatal had to happen to Eleanor Friedman-Bernal. Elliot simply could not risk having her arrive at a hospital alive. Ideally, something fatal would also happen to Leaphorn. If Elliot was smart, he would wait until they had climbed a hundred feet or so up the cut. Then he would push the litter backward, tumbling Friedman-Bernal and Leaphorn down the jumble of boulders. Then he would climb back down and do whatever was needed, if anything, to finish them off. A bang of the head on a rock would do it and leave nothing to arouse the suspicion of a medical examiner. Figuring that out had been easy enough. Knowing what to do about it was another matter. He could think of nothing. Shooting Elliot was shooting the copter pilot. Pointing a gun at him to force him to fly them out wasn't practical. Elliot would know Leaphorn wouldn't shoot him once they were airborne. He'd be able to make the helicopter do tricks that Leaphorn couldn't handle. And he probably had the little pistol. And yet, once they started that steep climb, Elliot had simply to drop his end of the litter and Leaphorn would be helpless.

"Is this the only way up?" Leaphorn asked.

"Only one I could see," Elliot said. "It's not as bad as it looks. We can take it slow."

"I'll wait here with the lady," Leaphorn said. "You fly the copter down here, land it somewhere where we don't have to make the climb." You could land a copter on this shelf if you had to, Leaphorn guessed. You'd have to be good, but someone who'd flown evacuations in Vietnam would be very good.

Elliot seemed to consider. "That's a thought," he said.

He reached into his jacket, extracted a small blue automatic pistol, and pointed it at Leaphorn's throat. "Unbuckle your belt," he said.

Leaphorn unbuckled it.

"Pull it out."

Leaphorn pulled it out. His holster fell to the ground.

"Now kick the gun over here to me."

Leaphorn did.

"You make it tough," Elliot said.

"Not tough enough."

Elliot laughed.

"You'd rather not have a bullet hole in me," Leaphorn said. "Or her either."

"That's right," Elliot said. "But I don't have any choice now. You seem to have figured it out."

"I figured you were going to get us far enough up the rocks to make it count and then tumble us down."

Elliot nodded.

"I'm not sure of your motive for all this. Killing so many people."

"Maxie told you that day," Elliot said. The good humor was suddenly gone, replaced by bitter anger. "What the hell can a rich kid do to impress anyone?"

"Impress Maxie," Leaphorn said. "A truly beautiful young woman." And he was thinking, maybe I'm like you. I don't want this to go wrong now because of Emma. Emma put little value on finding people to punish them. But this would really have impressed her. You love a woman, you want to impress her. The male instinct. Hero finds lost woman. The life saved. He didn't want it to go wrong now. But it had. In a very little while, wherever and whenever it was most convenient, Randall Elliot would kill Eleanor Friedman-Bernal and Joe Leaphorn. He could think of nothing to prevent it. Except maybe Brigham Houk.

Brigham must be somewhere near. It had taken him only minutes to get the poles and return. He had seen his devil, recognized him, and slipped away. Brigham Houk was a hunter. Brigham Houk was also insane, and afraid of this devil. What would he do? Leaphorn thought he knew.

"We'll leave her here for now and we'll walk over there," Elliot said, pointing with the pistol toward the edge of the shelf. It was exactly the direction Leaphorn wanted to go. It was the only way that led to convenient shelter. It must be the way Brigham had gone.

"It's going to look funny if too many people fall off things," Leaphorn said. "Two is too many."

"I know," Elliot said. "Do you have a better idea?"

"Maybe," Leaphorn said. "Tell me your motive for all this."

"I think you guessed," Elliot said.

"I guess Maxie," Leaphorn said. "You want her. But she's a self-made, class-conscious woman with a lot of bad memories of being put down by the upper class. On top of that, she's a tough one, a little mean. She resents you, and everybody like you, because it's all handed to you. So I think you're going to do something that has nothing to do with being born to the upper, upper, upper class. Something that neither Maxie nor anybody else can ignore. From what you told me at Chaco it's something to do with tracing what happened to these Anasazi by tracking genetic flaws."

"How about that," Elliot said. "You're not as dumb as you try to act."

"You found the flaw you were hunting in the bones here, and over at the site on the Checkerboard, too, I guess. You were digging here illegally, and our friend here came in and caught you at it."

Elliot held up his empty hand. "So I tried to kill her and screwed it up."

"Curious about something," Leaphorn said. "Were you the one who called in the complaint about Eleanor being a pot hunter?"

"Sure," Elliot said. "You figured why?"

"Not really," Leaphorn said. Where the devil was Brigham Houk?

Maybe he'd run. Leaphorn doubted it. His father wouldn't have run. But then his father wasn't schizophrenic.

"You can't get a permit to dig," Elliot said. "Not in your lifetime. These asshole bureaucrats are always saving it for the future. Well, if a site is being vandalized, that puts it in a different category. Not so tough then, after it's already been messed up. I was going to follow up later with some hints about where to find digs Eleanor was stealing from. They'd find her body, so they'd have their Thief of Time. They wouldn't have to be looking for one and maybe suspecting me. And then I'd get my dig permit." He laughed. "Roundabout way, but I've seen it work."

"You were getting your bones anyway," Leaphorn said. "Buying some, digging some up yourself."

"Wrong category, friend," Elliot said. "Those are unofficial bones. Not 'in site.' I was finding 'em unofficially, so I'd know where to find 'em officially when I got my permit. You understand that?" Elliot peered at him, grinning. He was enjoying this. "When I get my permit to excavate, I come back and the bones I find then are registered in place. Photographed. Documented." He grinned again. "Same bones, maybe, but now they're official."

"How about Etcitty," Leaphorn asked, "and Nails?" Over Elliot's shoulder, Leaphorn had seen Brigham Houk. He saw Houk because the man wanted Leaphorn to see him. He was behind a fallen sandstone slab, screened by brush. He held something that might have been a curved staff and he motioned Leaphorn toward him.

"That was a mistake," Elliot said.

"Killing them?"

Elliot laughed. "That was correcting the mistake. Nails was too careless. And too greedy. Once the silly bastards stole that backhoe they were sure to get caught." He glanced at Leaphorn. "And Nails was sure to tell you guys everything he knew."

"Which would have been bad for your reputation," Leaphorn said.

"Disastrous," Elliot said. He waved the pistol. "But hurry it up. I want to get out of here."

"If you're working on what I think," Leaphorn said, "there's something I want to show you. Something Friedman-Bernal found. You're interested in jaw deformities. Something like that?"

"Well, a little like that," Elliot said. "You understand how the human chromosome works? Fetus inherits twenty-three from its mother, twenty-three from its father. Genetic characteristics handed down in the genes. Once in a while polyploidy occurs in the genetic crossover points. Someone gets multiple chromosomes, and you get a characteristic change. Inheritable. But you need more than one to do a trace which has any real meaning. At Chaco, in some of the early Chaco burials, I found three that were passed along. A surplus molar in the left mandible. And that went along with a thickening of the frontal bone over the left eye socket, plus—" Elliot stopped. "You understanding this?"

"Genetics wasn't my favorite course. Too much math," Leaphorn said. What the devil was Brigham Houk doing? Was he still behind that slab up ahead?

"Exactly," Elliot said, pleased by this. "It's one percent digging and ninety-nine percent working out statistical models for your computer. Anyway, the third thing, which sort of mathematically proves the pass-along genes, is that hole in the mandible through which the blood and nerve tissue passes. At Chaco, from about 650 A.D. until they turned out the lights, this family had two holes in the left mandible and the usual one in the right. Plus those other characteristics. And out here, I'm still finding it among these exiles. Can you see why it's important?"

"And fascinating," Leaphorn said. "Dr. Friedman must have known what you were looking for. She saved a lot of jawbones." He was almost to the great sandstone slab. "I'll show you."

"I doubt if she found anything I overlooked," Elliot said. He followed Leaphorn, keeping the pistol level. "But this is the way we were going anyway."

They were passing the sandstone now. Leaphorn tensed. If nothing happened here, he would have to try something else. It wouldn't work, but he wouldn't simply stand still to be shot.

"Right over here," Leaphorn said.

"I think you're just—"

The sentence ended with a grunt, a great exhalation of breath. Leaphorn turned. Elliot was leaning slightly forward, the pistol hanging at his side. About six inches of arrow shaft and the feathered tip protruded from his jacket.

Leaphorn reached for him, heard the whistle and thump of the second arrow. It went through Elliot's neck. The pistol clattered on the stone. Elliot collapsed.

Leaphorn retrieved the pistol. He squatted beside the man, turned him on his back. His eyes were open but he seemed to be in shock. Blood trickled from the corner of his mouth.

There was snow in the wind now, little dry flakes that skittered along the surface like white dust. Leaphorn tested the arrow. It was the sort bow hunters buy in sporting goods stores and it was lodged solidly through Elliot's neck. Pulling it out would just make things worse. If they could be worse. Elliot was dying. Leaphorn stood, looking for Brigham Houk. Houk was standing beside the slab now, holding a great ugly bow of metal, wood, and plastic, looking upward. From somewhere Leaphorn heard the clatter of a helicopter. Brigham Houk had heard it earlier. He stood very close to cover, ready to vanish.

The helicopter emerged over the rim of the mesa almost directly overhead. Leaphorn waved, saw an answering wave. The copter circled and disappeared over the mesa again.

Leaphorn checked Elliot's pulse. He didn't seem to have one. He looked for Brigham Houk, who seemed never to have existed. He walked over to the litter where Dr. Eleanor Friedman-Bernal lay. She opened her eyes, looked at him without recognition, closed them again. He tucked the rabbit fur cloak around her, careful to apply no pressure. Now it was snowing harder, still blowing like dust. He walked back to Elliot. No pulse now. He opened his jacket and shirt and felt for a heartbeat. Nothing. The man was no longer breathing. Randall Elliot, graduate of Exeter, of Princeton, of Harvard, winner of the Navy Cross, was dead by arrow shot. Leaphorn gripped him under the arms and pulled him into the cover of the slab where Brigham Houk had hidden. Elliot was heavy, and Leaphorn was exhausted. By pulling hard and doing some twisting, he extracted the arrows. He wiped the blood off as well as he could on Elliot's jacket. Then he picked up a rock, hammered them into pieces, and put the pieces in his hip pocket. That done, he found dead brush, broke it off, and made an inefficient effort to cover the body. But it didn't matter. The coyotes would find Randall Elliot anyway.

Then he heard the clatter of someone scrambling down the cut. It proved to be Officer Chee, looking harassed and disheveled.

It took some effort for Leaphorn not to show he was impressed. He pointed to the litter. "We need to get Dr. Friedman to the hospital in a hurry," he said. "Can you get that thing down here to load her?"

"Sure," Chee said. He started back toward the cut at a run.

"Just a second," Leaphorn said.

Chee stopped.

"What did you see?"

Chee raised his eyebrows. "I saw you standing beside a man slumped down on the ground. I guess it was Elliot. And I saw the litter over there. And maybe I saw another man. Something jumping out of sight back there just as we came over the top."

"Why did you think it was Elliot?"

Chee looked surprised. "The helicopter he rented is parked up there. I figured when he heard she was still alive he'd have to come out here and kill her before you got here."

Leaphorn again was impressed. This time he made a little less effort to conceal it. "Do you know how Elliot knew she was alive?"

Chee made a wry face. "I more or less told him."

"And then made the connection?"

"Then I found out he had filed for permission to dig this site, and the site where he killed Etcitty. Turned down on both of them. I went out there to talk to him and found—you remember the box of plastic waste-basket liners at the Checkerboard site. One missing from it. Well, it was hidden in Elliot's kitchen. Had jawbones in it."

Leaphorn didn't ask how Chee had gotten into Elliot's kitchen.

"Go ahead, then, and get the copter down here. And don't say anything."

Chee looked at him.

"I mean don't say anything at all. I'll fill you in when we get a chance."

Chee trotted toward the cut.

"Thank you," Leaphorn said. He wasn't sure if Chee heard that.

It was snowing hard by the time they had the litter loaded and the copter lifted off the shelf. Leaphorn was jammed against the side. He looked down on a stone landscape cut into vertical blocks by time and now blurred by snow. He looked quickly away. He could ride the big jets, barely. Something in his inner ear made anything less stable certain nausea. He closed his eyes, swallowed. This was the first snow. They would come when the weather cleared to recover the copter and look for Elliot. But they wouldn't look hard because it was so obviously hopeless. Snow would have covered everything. After the thaw, they would come again. Then they would find the bones, scattered like the Anasazi skeletons he looted. There would be no sign of the arrow wounds then. Cause of death unknown, the coroner would write. Victim eaten by predators.

He glanced back. Chee was jammed in the compartment beside the litter, his hand on Dr. Eleanor Friedman-Bernal's arm. She seemed to be awake. I will ask him what curing ceremony he would recommend, Leaphorn thought, and knew at once that his fatigue was making him silly. Instead he said nothing. He thought of the circumstances, of how proud Emma would be of him tonight if she could be home to hear about this woman brought safely to the hospital. He thought about Brigham Houk. In just about twenty-four more days, the moon would be full again. Brigham would be waiting at the mouth of Many Ruins Canyon, but Papa wouldn't come.

I will go, Leaphorn thought. Someone has to tell him. And that meant that he would have to postpone his plan to leave the reservation, probably a long postponement. Solving the problem of what to do about Brigham Houk would take more than one trip down the river. And if he had to stick around, he might as well withdraw that letter. As Captain Nez had said, he could always write it again.

Jim Chee noticed Leaphorn was watching him.

"You all right?" Chee asked.

"I've felt better," Leaphorn said. And then he had another thought. He considered it. Why not? "I hear you're a medicine man. I heard you are a singer of the Blessing Way. Is that right?"

Chee looked slightly stubborn. "Yes, sir," he said.

"I would like to ask you to sing one for me," Leaphorn said.

Coyote Waits

For my great friend and brother-in-law, Charles Unzner,

and

For our world-class next-door neighbors—

Jim and Mary Reese, and Gene and Geraldine Bustamante

1

OFFICER JIM CHEE was thinking that either his right front tire was a little low or there was something wrong with the shock on that side. On the other hand, maybe the road grader operator hadn't been watching the adjustment on his blade and he'd tilted the road. Whatever the cause, Chee's patrol car was pulling just a little to the right. He made the required correction, frowning. He was dog-tired.

The radio speaker made an uncertain noise, then produced the voice of Officer Delbert Nez. ". . . running on fumes. I'm going to have to buy some of that high-cost Red Rock gasoline or walk home."

"If you do, I advise paying for it out of your pocket," Chee said. "Better than explaining to the captain why you forgot to fill it up."

"I think . . ." Nez said and then the voice faded out.

"Your signal's breaking up," Chee said. "I don't read you." Nez was using Unit 44, a notorious gas hog. Something wrong with the fuel pump, maybe. It was always in the shop and nobody ever quite fixed it.

Silence. Static. Silence. The steering seemed to be better now. Probably not a low tire. Probably . . . And then the radio intruded again.

". . . catch the son-of-a-bitch with the smoking paint gun in his hand," Nez was saying. "I'll bet then . . ." The Nez voice vanished, replaced by silence.

"I'm not reading you," Chee said into his mike. "You're breaking up."

Which wasn't unusual. There were a dozen places on the twenty-five thousand square miles the Navajos called the Big Rez where radio transmission was blocked for a variety of reasons. Here between the monolithic volcanic towers of Ship Rock, the Carrizo Range, and the Chuska Mountains was just one of them. Chee presumed these radio blind spots were caused by the mountains but there were other theories. Deputy Sheriff Cowboy Dashee insisted that it had something to do with magnetism in the old volcanic necks that stuck up here and there, like great black cathedrals. Old Thomasina Bigthumb had told him once that she thought witches caused the problem. True, this part of the Reservation was notorious for witches, but it was also true that Old Lady Bigthumb blamed witches for just about everything.

Then Chee heard Delbert Nez again. The voice was very faint at first. ". . . his car," Delbert was saying. (Or was it ". . . his truck"? Or ". . . his pickup"? Exactly, precisely, what had Delbert Nez said?) Suddenly the transmission became clearer, the sound of Delbert's delighted laughter. "I'm gonna get him this time," Delbert Nez said.

Chee picked up the mike. "Who are you getting?" he said. "Do you need assistance?"

"My phantom painter," Nez seemed to say. At least it sounded like that. The reception was going sour again, fading, breaking up into static.

"Can't read you," Chee said. "You need assistance?"

Through the fade-out, through the static, Nez seemed to say "No." Again, laughter.

"I'll see you at Red Rock then," Chee said. "It's your turn to buy."

There was no response to that at all, except static, and none was needed. Nez worked up U.S. 666 out of the Navajo Tribal Police headquarters at Window Rock, covering from Yah-Ta-Hey northward. Chee patrolled down 666 from the Ship Rock subagency police station, and when they met they had coffee and talked. Having it this evening at the service station–post office–grocery store at Red Rock had been decided earlier, and it was upon Red Rock that they were converging. Chee was driving down the dirt road that wandered back and forth across the Arizona–New Mexico border southward from Biklabito. Nez was driving westward from 666 on the asphalt of Navajo Route 33. Nez, having pavement, would have been maybe fifteen minutes early. But now he seemed to have an arrest to make. That would even things up.

There was lightning in the cloud over the Chuskas now, and Chee's patrol car had stopped pulling to the right and was pulling to the left. Probably not a tire, he thought. Probably the road grader operator had noticed his maladjusted blade and overcorrected. At least it wasn't the usual washboard effect that pounded your kidneys.

It was twilight—twilight induced early by the impending thunderstorm—when Chee pulled his patrol car off the dirt and onto the pavement of Route 33. No sign of Nez. In fact, no sign of any headlights, just the remains of what had been a blazing red sunset. Chee pulled past the gasoline pumps at the Red Rock station and parked behind the trading post. No Unit 44 police car where Nez usually parked it. He inspected his front tires, which seemed fine. Then he looked around. Three pickups and a blue Chevy sedan. The sedan belonged to the new evening clerk at the trading post. Good-looking girl, but he couldn't come up with her name. Where was Nez? Maybe he actually had caught his paint-spraying vandal. Maybe the fuel pump on old 44 had died.

No Nez inside either. Chee nodded to the girl reading behind the cash register. She rewarded him with a shy smile. What was her name? Sheila? Suzy? Something like that. She was a Towering House Dineh, and therefore in no way linked to Chee's own Slow Talking Clan. Chee remembered that. It was the automatic checkoff any single young Navajo conducts—male or female—making sure the one who attracted you wasn't a sister, or cousin, or niece in the tribe's complex clan system, and thereby rendered taboo by incest rules.

The glass coffee-maker pot was two-thirds full, usually a good sign, and it smelled fresh. He picked up a fifty-cent-size Styrofoam cup, poured it full, and sipped. Good, he thought. He picked out a package containing two chocolate-frosted Twinkies. They go well with the coffee.

Back at the cash register, he handed the Towering House girl a five-dollar bill.

"Has Delbert Nez been in? You remember him? Sort of stocky, little mustache. Really ugly policeman."

"I thought he was cute," the Towering House girl said, smiling at Chee.

"Maybe you just like policemen?" Chee said. What the devil was her name?

"Not all of them," she said. "It depends."

"On whether they've arrested your boyfriend," Chee said. She wasn't married. He remembered Delbert had told him that. ("Why don't you find out these things for yourself," Delbert had said. "Before I got married, I would have known essential information like that. Wouldn't have had to ask. My wife finds out I'm making clan checks on the chicks, I'm in deep trouble.")

"I don't have a boyfriend," the Towering House girl said. "Not right now. And, no Delbert hasn't been in this evening." She handed Chee his change, and giggled. "Has Delbert ever caught his rock painter?"

Chee was thinking maybe he was a little past dealing with girls who giggled. But she had large brown eyes, and long lashes, and perfect skin. Certainly, she knew how to flirt. "Maybe he's catching him right now," he said. "He said something on the radio about it." He noticed she had miscounted his change by a dime, which sort of went with the giggling. "Too much money," Chee said, handing her the dime. "You have any idea who'd be doing that painting?" And then he remembered her name. It was Shirley. Shirley Thompson.

Shirley shuddered, very prettily. "Somebody crazy," she said.

That was Chee's theory too. But he said: "Why crazy?"

"Well, just because," Shirley said, looking serious for the first time. "You know. Who else would do all that work painting that mountain white?"

It wasn't really a mountain. Technically it was probably a volcanic throat—another of those ragged upthrusts of black basalt that jutted out of the prairie here and there east of the Chuskas.

"Maybe he's trying to paint something pretty," Chee said. "Have you ever gone in there and taken a close look at it?"

Shirley shivered. "I wouldn't go there," she said.

"Why not?" Chee asked, knowing why. It probably had some local legend attached to it. Something scary. Probably somebody had been killed there and left his *chindi* behind to haunt the place. And it was tainted by witchcraft gossip. Delbert had been raised back in the Chuska high country west of here and he'd said something about that outcrop—or maybe one nearby—being one of the places where members of the skinwalker clan were supposed to meet. It was a place to be avoided—and that was part of what had fascinated Officer Delbert Nez with its vandalism.

"It's not just that it's such a totally zany thing to do," Delbert had said. "Putting paint on the side of a rocky ridge, like that. There's a weirdness to it, too. It's a scary place. I don't care what you think about witches, nobody goes there. You do, somebody sees you, and they think you're a skinwalker yourself. I think whoever's doing it must have a purpose. Something specific. I'd like to know who the hell it is. And why."

That had been good enough for Chee, who enjoyed his own little obsessions. He glanced at his watch. Where was Delbert now?

The door opened and admitted a middle-aged woman with her hair tied in a blue cloth. She paid for gasoline, complained about the price, and engaged Shirley in conversation about a sing-dance somebody was planning at the Newcomb school. Chee had another cup of coffee. Two teenaged boys came in, followed by an old man wearing a T-shirt with DON'T WORRY, BE HAPPY printed across the chest. Another woman came, about Shirley's age, and the sound of thunder came through the door with her. The girls chatted and giggled. Chee looked at his watch again. Delbert was taking too damned long.

Chee walked out into the night.

The breeze smelled of rain. Chee hurried around the corner into the total darkness behind the trading post. In the car, he switched on the radio and tried to raise Nez. Nothing. He started the engine, and spun the rear wheels in an impatient start that was totally out of character for him. So was this sudden sense of anxiety. He switched on his siren and the emergency flashers.

Chee was only minutes away from the trading post when he saw the headlights approaching on Route 33. He slowed, feeling relief. But before they reached him, he saw the car's right turn indicator blinking. The vehicle turned northward, up ahead of him, not Nez's Navajo Tribal Police patrol car but a battered white Jeepster. Chee recognized it. It was the car of the Vietnamese (or Cambodian, or whatever he was) who taught at the high school in Ship Rock. Chee's headlights briefly lit the driver's face.

The rain started then, a flurry of big, widely spaced drops splashing the windshield, then a downpour. Route 33 was wide and smooth, with a freshly painted centerline to follow. But the rain was more than Chee's wipers could handle. He slowed, listening to the water pound against the roof. Normally rain provoked jubilation in Chee—a feeling natural and primal, bred into dry-country people. Now this joy was blocked by worry and a little guilt. Something had delayed Nez. He should have gone looking for him when the radio blacked out. But it was probably nothing much. Car trouble. An ankle sprained chasing his painter in the dark. Nothing serious.

Lightning illuminated the highway ahead of him, showing it glistening with water and absolutely empty. The flash lit the ragged basalt shape of the formation across the prairie to the south—the outcrop on which Nez's vandal had been splashing his paint. Then the boom of thunder came. The rain slackened, flurried again, slackened again as the squall line of the storm passed. Off to the right Chee saw a glow of light. He stared. It came from down a dirt road that wandered from 33 southward over a ridge, leading eventually to the "outfit" of Old Lady Gorman. Chee let the breath whistle through his teeth. Relief. That would probably be Nez. Guilt fell away from him.

At the intersection, he slowed and stared down the dirt road. Headlights should be yellow. This light was red. It flickered. Fire.

"Oh, God!" Chee said aloud. A prayer. He geared the patrol car down into second and went slipping and sliding down the muddy track.

2

UNIT 44 WAS parked in the center of the track, its nose pointed toward Route 33, red flames gushing from the back of it, its tires burning furiously. Chee braked his car to a stop, skidding it out of the muddy ruts and onto the bunch grass and stunted sage. He had his door open and the fire extinguisher in his hand while the car was still sliding.

It was raining hard again, the cold drops splashing against his face. Then he was engulfed in the sickening black smoke of burning rubber, burning oil, burning upholstery. The driver's-side window had been shattered. Chee fired the extinguisher through it, seeing the white foam stream through the smoke, and seeing through the smoke the dark shape of Nez slumped over the steering wheel.

"Del!"

Chee snatched at the door handle, barely conscious of the searing pain. He jerked the door open and found himself engulfed in a gust of flames. He jumped back, whacking at the fire burning his uniform shirt. "Del," he shouted again. He sprayed the extinguisher foam into the car again, dropped the extinguisher, reached through the open door, clutched the arm of Officer Delbert Nez and pulled.

Nez was wearing his seat belt.

Chee fumbled for the catch, released it, pulled with all his strength, aware as he did that his palm was hurting in a way he had never experienced before. He tumbled backward into the driving rain, he and Delbert Nez. He lay for a moment, gasping, lungs full of smoke, conscious that something was wrong with the hand, and of the weight of Delbert Nez partly across him. Then he was aware of heat. His shirt sleeve burning. He put it out, struggled out from under the weight of Nez.

Nez lay on his back, arms and legs sprawled. Chee looked at him and looked away. He picked up the extinguisher, sprayed the burning places on the officer's trousers. He used what was left in the tank to put out the fire. "Running on fumes," Nez had said. That was lucky. Chee had seen enough car fires to know what a full tank would do. Lucky? Fumes had provided enough fire to kill Delbert Nez.

He was on the radio, calling this in to Ship Rock, asking for help, before he was fully aware of the pain of his own burns.

"There was blood, too," Chee was saying. "He might have been shot. I think blood on the back of his shirt, and blood on the front, too."

Captain Largo happened to be in, doing his perpetual paperwork. While Chee was saying that, Largo took over the radio in the Ship Rock dispatcher's office.

"We'll send all we have from here," Largo was saying. "And from Window Rock, and we'll see if anybody from Crownpoint is patrolling out your direction. Blood still fresh?"

Chee looked at his hand and grimaced. "It's still sticky," he said. "Somewhere between slick and sticky." A chunk of skin had flapped off the palm of his hand. The door handle, he thought. That had done it. It felt like it had burned all the way to the bone.

"You saw no other car lights?"

"One car. Just as I was leaving Red Rock a white Jeepster was turning off 33 onto the road toward Biklabito. One man in it. I think it was that Vietnamese math teacher at Ship Rock High School. I think that's his car, anyway." Chee's throat hurt. So did his lungs. So did his eyes. And his face. He felt with numb fingers. No eyebrows.

"We'll handle that part then," Largo said. "Save any looking for tracks for daylight. Do not mess anything up around the car. You got that?" Largo paused. "Do not," he repeated.

"Okay," Chee said. He wanted to end this. He wanted to go find whoever had killed Delbert Nez. He should have been with Nez. He should have gone to help him.

"You came down 33 from the west? From Red Rock? Get back on 33 and head east. All the way to 666. See if you can pick up anything that way. If the guy had a vehicle that's the only way he could have gone." Largo paused. "Unless he was your Vietnamese schoolteacher."

Chee didn't get all the way to U.S. Highway 666. Three miles east of the intersection, the high beams of his headlights reflected from the back of a man walking down the asphalt. Chee braked and stared. The man was walking erratically down the center of the westbound lane. He was bareheaded, his gray hair tied in a bun, his rain-soaked shirt plastered to his back. He seemed totally oblivious of Chee's headlights, now just a few yards behind him. Without a backward glance, with no effort to move to the side of the road, he walked steadily onward, swinging something in his right hand, zigzagging a little, but with the steady, unhurried pace of a man who has walked great distances, who will walk great distances more.

Chee pulled up beside him, rolled down his window. The object the man was swinging was a squat bottle, held by the neck. "*Yaa' eh t'eeh!*" Chee shouted, the standard Navajo greeting. The man ignored him, plodding steadily down the asphalt. As he moved past the police car and back into the glare of the headlights Chee saw he had something bulky stuck under his belt in the back of his trousers. It looked like the butt of a pistol.

Chee unsnapped his own pistol, took it out of its holster, and laid it on the seat beside him. He touched the siren button, producing a sudden howling. The gray-haired man seemed not to hear it.

Chee picked up the mike, raised Ship Rock, gave his location. "I have a male, about five feet eight inches tall, elderly, gray-haired, walking down the westbound lane away from the Nez site. He has what appears to be a pistol stuck under his belt and what appears to be a whiskey bottle in his right hand and is acting in a peculiar manner."

"Peculiar manner," the dispatcher said.

"I think he's drunk," Chee said. "He acts like he doesn't hear me or see me."

"Subject is drunk," the dispatcher said.

"Maybe," Chee said. "I will apprehend him now."

Which might be easier said than done, he thought. He pulled the patrol car past the walker and spun it around so its lights shone directly into the man's face. He got out with his pistol in his hand. He felt dizzy. Everything was vague.

"Hold it right there," Chee said.

The walker stopped. He looked intently at Chee, as if trying to bring him into focus. Then he sighed and sat on the pavement. He screwed the cap off the bottle, and took a long, gurgling drink. He looked at Chee again and said:

"*Baa yanisin, shiyaazh.*"

"You are ashamed?" Chee repeated. His voice choked. "Ashamed!" With his good hand he reached over the walker's shoulder, jerked the pistol out of the man's belt. He sniffed the muzzle of the barrel and smelled burned powder. He checked the cylinders. All six contained cartridges, but three of the cartridges were empty. They had been fired. He jammed the pistol under his belt, snatched the bottle out of the walker's hand, and hurled it into the sagebrush beside the road.

"Dirty coyote," Chee said in Navajo. "Get up." His voice was fierce.

The man stared up at him, expression puzzled. The glare of the headlights reflected off the streaks of rainwater running down his face, dripping from his hair, from his eyebrows.

"Get up!" Chee screamed.

He jerked the man to his feet, hurried him to the patrol car, searched him quickly for another weapon, took a pocketknife and some coins from a front pocket and a worn wallet from his hip pocket. He handcuffed him, conscious of the man's thin, bony wrists, conscious of the numbness in his own right hand, and the pain in his left palm. He helped the man into the backseat, closed the door behind him, and stood for a moment looking through the glass at him.

"*Shiyaazh,*" the man said again. "*Baa yanisin.*" *My son, I am ashamed.*

Chee stood with his head bowed, the rain beating against his shoulders. He wiped the back of his hand across his wet face and licked his lips. The taste was salty.

Then he walked into the sagebrush, looking for the bottle. It would be needed as evidence.

3

THERE WAS NOTHING Lieutenant Joe Leaphorn dreaded more than this—this unpleasant business of pretending to help people he could not possibly help. But those involved today were a family in Emma's clan, his in-laws, people from Bitter Water clan. By the Navajos' extended definition of kinship, they were Emma's brothers and sisters. He'd rarely heard Emma speak of them but that was beside the point. It was beside the point, too, that Emma would never have asked him to interfere. Certainly not in this case, with one of their own policemen murdered. She would have tried to help them herself, though. Tried very quietly—and she would have been no less impotent than Leaphorn. But Emma was dead now and that left only him.

"We know he didn't kill that policeman," Mary Keeyani had said. "Not Ashie Pinto."

By the white man's way of reckoning kinship, the Keeyani woman was Ashie Pinto's niece. In fact, she was the daughter of Ashie's sister, which gave her among the Turning Mountain People the same status as a daughter. She was a small, bony woman dressed in her old-fashioned, traditional, going-to-town best. But the long-sleeved velvet blouse hung on her loosely, as if borrowed from fatter times, and she wore only a single bracelet of narrow silver and a squash blossom necklace which used very little turquoise.

She sat stiffly upright in the blue plastic chair across from Leaphorn's desk, looking embarrassed and uncomfortable.

While Mary Keeyani explained her relationship to Ashie Pinto, and therefore to Hosteen Pinto's problem, in the proper fashion of a traditional Navajo, Louisa Bourebonette had not explained herself at all. She sat next to Mary Keeyani, looking determined.

"There is absolutely no doubt that this is all some sort of mistake," Louisa Bourebonette said in a slow, precise, slightly southern voice. "But we haven't had any success talking with the FBI. We tried to talk to someone at the Farmington office and then we went to Albuquerque. They simply won't discuss it. And we don't know who to get to look for evidence to prove he's innocent. We thought we could hire a private detective. We thought maybe you could recommend someone who would be reliable."

Louisa Bourebonette had given Leaphorn her card. He picked it up now and glanced at it again.

LOUISA BOUREBONETTE, PH.D.
ASSOCIATE PROFESSOR,
AMERICAN STUDIES
NORTHERN ARIZONA UNIVERSITY
FLAGSTAFF, ARIZONA

This wasn't the information he wanted. He wanted to know how this trim, gray-haired, sharp-eyed woman was connected to the sorrowful business of Delbert Nez, a young man murdered and an old man destroyed. It was partly the wisdom Leaphorn had accumulated in a long life of police work that people have reasons for whatever they do—and the more effort required, the stronger the reason must be. Among Navajos, family is an overpowering reason. Bourebonette was not Navajo. What she was doing required a lot of effort. He put the card in his desk drawer.

"Have you talked to Hosteen Pinto's attorney?"

"She didn't seem to know much," Bourebonette said. She made a small, self-deprecatory face and shook her head. "Of course, they turned Mr. Pinto over to someone brand new in the job. She'd just moved in from

Washington. Had just been hired. She told us the Federal Public Defender's office had two investigators who might be helpful. But . . ."

Professor Bourebonette let the sentence trail off, intending to let the skepticism in her tone finish it. Leaphorn sat silently behind his desk. He glanced at her. And away. Waiting.

Bourebonette shrugged. "But I got the impression that she didn't think they would be very helpful. I don't think she knew them well yet. In fact, she didn't give us much reason to believe that Mr. Pinto will be well represented."

Leaphorn knew one of the federal defender cops. A good, solid, hard-working Hispano named Felix Sanchez. He used to be with the El Paso police department and he knew how to collect information. But there wasn't much of anything Sanchez could do to help these women. And nothing Leaphorn could do, either. He could give them the names of private detectives in Farmington, or Flagstaff, or Albuquerque. White men. What could they do? What could anyone do? An old man had been turned mean by whiskey and had killed a policeman. Why waste what little money his family might have? Or this abrasive white woman's money. How did she fit into this?

"If you hire a private detective it's going to be expensive," Leaphorn said. "He would want some money in advance as a retainer. I'd guess at least five hundred dollars. And you'd be paying his expenses. Mileage, meals, motels, things like that. And so much an hour for his fee."

"How much?" Professor Bourebonette asked.

"I'm not sure. Maybe twenty-five, thirty dollars an hour."

Mrs. Keeyani sucked in her breath. She looked stricken. Dr. Bourebonette put a comforting hand on Mrs. Keeyani's arm.

"That's about what I'd expected," Professor Bourebonette said, in a stiff, unnatural-sounding voice. "We can pay it. Who would you recommend?"

"It would depend," Leaphorn said. "What do you—"

Professor Bourebonette interrupted him.

"One would expect, or should expect if she didn't know better, that you people would take care of this yourselves. That the family wouldn't have to hire someone to find out the facts in a murder case."

The anger left Leaphorn with nothing to say. So he said the obvious.

"In a case like this, a felony committed on a reservation, the jurisdiction . . ."

She held up her hand. "The Federal Bureau of Investigation has the jurisdiction. We know that. We've already been told, and we knew it already, being reasonably intelligent. But after all, one of your own men was killed." A trace of sarcasm crept into Bourebonette's tone. "Aren't you a little bit curious about who actually killed him?"

Leaphorn felt himself flushing. Surely this arrogant white woman didn't expect him to answer that. Not in the presence of the murderer's niece.

But the professor was waiting for an answer. Let her wait. Leaphorn waited himself. Finally he said: "Go on."

"Since you don't seem to be investigating, and since the Federal Bureau of Investigation is content to simply bring Ashie Pinto to trial without any effort to find the actual criminal, we hope you can at least give us some advice about who to hire. Somebody honest."

Leaphorn cleared his throat. He was trying to imagine this haughty woman in the beautifully finished office of the agent-in-charge at Albuquerque. Nothing but politeness and good manners there, he was sure.

"Yes," he said. "That's what we were discussing. And to give you that advice I must know some things. What do you have to tell this private detective? What can you give him to work on? Would it be leads he'd be following on the Reservation—around where Hosteen Pinto lived? Or around Ship Rock and Red Rock where the—where it happened? In other words, what do you know that can help? What do you know that would help him find a witness, something to prove, for example, that Hosteen Pinto was somewhere else when this crime happened? What can you give him to give him a place to start looking?"

Leaphorn paused, thinking he shouldn't pull himself into this. It was not his case, not his business. Interfering was certain to cause offense in a department that wanted the death of a brother officer balanced with a conviction of his killer. He shouldn't open the door he was about to open. He should simply tell these women he couldn't help them. Which just happened to be the sad truth. Still, Mary Keeyani was Emma's kin. And, still, there were some unanswered questions in that Nez business—as much as he knew about it.

"As a matter of fact," he said, "if you have any useful information—any witnesses, anything that would lead to concrete evidence that the FBI wouldn't listen to—you can tell me. I'll see to it that the Bureau pays the proper attention. Anything you know."

"We know he didn't do it," Bourebonette said. But the anger was used up now. She attempted a small, wan smile. "All we can tell you is *why* we know he couldn't have killed the policeman, and that's nothing more concrete than telling you about the kind of man Ashie Pinto is. Always has been."

But he did kill a man, Leaphorn was thinking, *a long time ago. If I remember what I read in that report, he was convicted, years ago, went to prison for killing a man.*

"Are you a relative?" he asked Bourebonette.

"I am a friend," Bourebonette said.

Leaphorn looked at her over his glasses, waiting for more than that.

"For twenty-five years," she added. "At least."

"Ah," Leaphorn said.

Professor Bourebonette looked impatient, as if it probably wasn't worth her time to explain. But she decided to.

"My interest is in comparative mythology. The evolution of myth inside cultures. The evolution of myth as cultures meet and intermix. The relationship of a society's mythology with its economic base. Its environment. Mr. Pinto has been one of my informants. For years." She paused.

Leaphorn glanced at her. Was she finished? No. She was remembering.

"He wouldn't kill anyone," she added. "He has a great sense of humor. A great memory for the funny things. A great memory for everything." She looked into Leaphorn's eyes and said it slowly, as if he was the judge. As if he was the jury. Could whiskey not make a killer out of a funny man, just as it did of sad men and angry men?

"He has a great sense of humor," Bourebonette repeated.

It didn't prove anything, Leaphorn thought. But it was interesting. It was also interesting that she was telling him this. A long way to come, a lot of time used, a lot of money to be spent if she was serious about hiring an investigator. And a very flimsy explanation of why she was doing it.

And so Leaphorn had asked the Turning Mountain woman and the professor to wait. He called downstairs and asked for the file marked HOMICIDE; DELBERT NEZ.

He had been away when it happened, waiting in a motel room in Phoenix to be called as a witness in a case being tried on appeal in the federal court there. Even so, he remembered a lot of it. He had read about it every day in the Phoenix *Gazette* and the *Arizona Republic*, of course. He had called the Ship Rock subagency station and talked to Captain Largo about it. The Navajo Tribal Police included only about 110 sworn officers, making the murder of any one of them not only memorable but close and personal. He had barely known Delbert Nez and remembered him as a small, quiet, neat young officer. But, like Leaphorn, Nez had worked out of the Window Rock office and Leaphorn had seen him often. Nez had been trying to grow a mustache. That was not an easy task for Navajos, with their lack of facial hair, and his sparse growth had provoked teasing and ribald jokes.

Leaphorn had known the arresting officer much better. Jim Chee. He had run across Chee several times on other investigations. An unusually bright young man. Clever. Some good qualities. But he had what might be a fatal flaw for a policeman. He was an individualist, following the rules if and when they agreed with him. On top of that, he was a romantic. He even wanted to be a medicine man. Leaphorn smiled at the idea. A Tribal Policeman-Shaman. The two professions were utterly incongruous.

Leaphorn found himself wondering if he had been Chee's first client. After a tough case, in the awful malaise that had followed Emma's death, he'd hired Chee to do a Blessing Way for him. An impulsive decision—unusual for him. He'd done it partly to give the young man a chance to try his hand as a shaman and partly as a gesture toward Emma's people. The Yazzies were Bitter Water clansmen and traditionalists. The ceremony would be sort of an unspoken apology for the hurt he must have caused them. He'd left Emma's mother's place on the second morning after they'd carried the body out into the canyon—unable to endure the full four days of silent withdrawal among her relatives that tradition required. It had been rude, and he'd regretted it. And so he had called Agnes and told her he'd hired a singer. He asked her to arrange the ceremony. She had gladly done it, not needing a reminder that his own clan, the Slow Talking Dinee, was now scattered and almost extinct, or that there was little left of his own family. He'd been uneasy around Agnes. Agnes had never married and, as

Emma's sister, he would have been expected to marry her under the old tradition.

He glanced up at the two women waiting patiently across the desk and then looked back at the report. But he was thinking of Officer Chee, his hair tied in a knot at the back of his head arranging his equipment on the swept earthen floor of the Yazzie hogan. Chee had been nervous, showing Leaphorn where to sit with his back against the west wall of the hogan, spreading a small rug in front of him. Then Chee had extracted from his deerskin *jish* the little leather sack that was his Four Mountain bundle, two pairs of "talking prayersticks," a snuff can containing flint arrow points, and a half dozen pouches of pollen. He had solemnly formed the shape of footprints on the earth and marked on them with the pollen the symbols of the sunrays on which Leaphorn would walk. Beyond Chee, through the hogan doorway to the east he could see the rugged ramparts of the Carrizo Mountains reflecting the rosy twilight. He had smelled the piñon smoke from the cooking fires of Emma's kinfolks and of his own friends who had come to join him in this venture into the spirit world of his people.

At that moment he had wished desperately for a way to call it all off. He was a hypocrite. He did not believe that the ritual poetry that Officer Jim Chee would chant, or the dry paintings he would form on the hogan floor, would control the powers and force them to restore Joe Leaphorn to a life with "beauty all around him." The beauty had gone somewhere up in the canyon rocks with Emma's body. Gone forever. He wanted only to follow her.

But there had been no way out of it. And on the second dawn, after the long night of chanting, he had sucked in the four great ceremonial breaths of cold morning air feeling different than he had felt for weeks. It had not cured him, but it had started the healing. He could thank Shaman Jim Chee for that, he guessed. Or for part of it. But Officer Jim Chee was another matter. If Officer Chee had done his duty, Delbert Nez might still be alive.

"Shot high in the left chest," the report said. "Apparently at very close range."

Leaphorn glanced up at Mary Keeyani and the professor. "Sorry I'm taking so long," he said.

"There is time enough," Mary Keeyani said.

Captain Largo had told him that Chee wanted to resign after the homicide. Getting Nez out of the car, Chee had been burned on both hands, one arm, one leg, and the chest. Largo had gone to the hospital at Farmington to see him. Largo was an old friend. He'd told Leaphorn about it.

"He didn't just offer to resign," Largo had told Leaphorn. "He insisted on it. He gave me his badge. Said he'd screwed up. That he should have gone to assist Nez when he knew Nez was in pursuit. And of course he should have gone."

"Why the devil didn't he go?" Leaphorn had asked. "The silly son-of-a-bitch. What was his excuse?"

"He didn't offer any excuses," Largo had said, his voice resenting Leaphorn's judgmental tone. "But I reminded him that his report showed Nez had been laughing. From what little he heard on the radio Nez wasn't taking it seriously. Like it was a joke. And I told him he couldn't resign anyway. He can't resign until we get Pinto tried."

Thinking of that conversation now as he turned the page in the report, Leaphorn remembered that Largo had some sort of vague clan kinship link with Officer Chee. At least he'd heard that. Navajo Tribal Police regulations prohibited nepotism in the chain of command. But the rules were just picked up from *biligaana* personnel regulations. The white rules didn't recognize clan connections.

The next sheet was the report of Sergeant Eldon George. When George arrived he had found Chee sprawled in the front seat of his vehicle, half-unconscious from shock. Pinto was asleep on the back seat, handcuffed. George had attempted to treat Chee's burns with his first aid kit. Another Navajo Police unit had arrived, and a San Juan County Sheriff's car, and a New Mexico State Police patrolman and then the ambulance that Chee had called to pick up Nez. Instead, it had taken Officer Chee. Pinto had been transported to the county jail at Aztec and booked on an assault charge—the toughest rap possible for a crime committed on federal trust land until the federals got involved and filed their felony homicide complaint.

Leaphorn glanced up at Mrs. Keeyani. She sat with her hands clenched in her lap, lower lip caught between her teeth, watching him.

"I must refresh my memory before I can tell you anything," he said.

Mrs. Keeyani nodded.

The next page reminded Leaphorn that Ashie Pinto had not made a statement. When apprehended, he had said, according to the report:

"Officer, I have done something shameful."

Sounded stilted. Leaphorn considered it. Pinto would have spoken to Chee in Navajo, probably. Chee, probably no better than half-conscious, would have passed along a translation to George. George had jotted it into his notebook, retyped it into his report. What had Pinto actually said?

According to the report, nothing else. He had admitted nothing, denied nothing, remained absolutely silent, refusing to answer any question except to confirm his identity with a nod, declining to call a lawyer, to name anyone who he might wish to be informed of his arrest. When asked to submit to the taking of a blood sample, "Subject Pinto was seen to nod in the affirmative."

The test showed a blood alcohol level of 0.211. The percentage of alcohol in the blood that made one formally and legally drunk in New Mexico was 0.10.

There followed the Federal Bureau of Investigation report dated eleven days following the arrest. Leaphorn scanned it. Ballistics confirmed that the bullet fired into the chest of Nez had come from the pistol confiscated from Pinto, a .38 caliber revolver. It confirmed that holes in Pinto's trousers were caused by burns. There was more, including the autopsy. Leaphorn knew what it said. Nez had been alive when the fire suffocated him. Probably unconscious, but alive. Leaphorn sighed, turned to the next page. It summarized a statement taken from Chee at the hospital. He scanned it quickly. Familiar stuff. But wait. He lingered on a paragraph. Reread it.

"Officer Chee said that for several weeks Nez had been interested in apprehending an unidentified subject who had been vandalizing and defacing a basaltic outcrop east of Red Rock and south of Ship Rock. Chee said he believed from what he heard on the radio that Nez had seen this person and expected to apprehend the subject. He said the radio signal was breaking up but that he heard Nez laughing and Nez did not appear to want a backup."

Leaphorn snorted, an angry sound and unintentionally loud. He glanced up to see if the women had noticed. They had.

He covered his embarrassment with a question. "Did anyone tell you about the circumstances?"

"They said he was arrested out there where it happened," Mrs. Keeyani said. "They said he had the gun that killed that policeman."

"Did they tell you that he hasn't denied it?" Leaphorn asked. But he was thinking of Jim Chee. Irritated. Nez did not appear to want a backup. Whether he wanted one or not, the rules said Chee should be there. But that was Chee's reputation. He made his own rules. Smart. Unusually smart. But not a team player. So he was sitting in the trading post at Red Rock drinking coffee while Nez, alone, was dealing with a homicidal drunk armed with a pistol.

"I don't know what my uncle told them," Mary Keeyani said. She shook her head. "But I know he didn't do it. Not Hosteen Pinto. He wouldn't kill anybody."

Leaphorn waited, watching her face, giving her a chance to say more. She simply sat, looking down at her hands.

Finally she said: "A long, long time ago, before I was born. . . . He got in a fight then, when he was young, and a man was killed. But he was a wild boy then, and drunk. Now he is an old man. He doesn't drink now. Not for years."

It was not something to argue about. Instead Leaphorn said, "He won't tell them anything at all. That's what I'm told. Not a word. Not even to his lawyer."

Mrs. Keeyani looked at her hands. "That wasn't his gun," she said. "My uncle had an old .22 rifle. A single-shot rifle. He still has that. It's in his hogan."

Leaphorn said nothing. This interested him. That pistol Pinto had was a Ruger, an expensive model and not what you would expect a man like Pinto to own. On the other hand, there could be a thousand explanations of why he did own it.

"Perhaps you didn't know about this pistol," Leaphorn said.

Now it was Mrs. Keeyani's turn to be surprised. "He is my mother's brother," she said. "He never got married. His place was there at our grandmother's place behind Yon Dot Mountain."

Leaphorn needed no more explanation. If Ashie Pinto had owned an expensive Ruger revolver, his relatives would have known it. He glanced back at the FBI report, looking for the name of the investigating officer. Agent Theodore Rostik. He'd never heard of Rostik, which meant he was a newcomer to the Gallup office—either fresh and green from the FBI Academy, or an older agent exiled as a lost cause. Up-and-comers in the agency were not sent to places like Farmington, or Fargo, or Gallup, or other towns considered Siberian by the Bureau hierarchy. These were the billets for new men without political connections in the agency, or those who had fallen from grace—perhaps having caused bad publicity (the agency's mortal sin) or shown signs of original thinking. For Leaphorn the point was that Rostik might be unusually stupid, or unusually smart—either of which might cause his exile. But most likely he was simply green.

"I'll tell you what I think you should do," he said to Mrs. Keeyani without looking up from the report. "Hosteen Pinto has a lawyer who may be green but will be smart. The Federal Public Defender just hires the smart ones. Work with her. Tell her the strange things that trouble you. She will send out one of the investigators to learn the facts. I know one of them personally, a very good man. You should work with them."

Leaphorn read on, not looking up, waiting for a response. He heard Mrs. Keeyani shift in her chair. But the voice he heard was Dr. Bourebonette's. "Are they Navajos?" she asked. "Would they understand that Hosteen Pinto's family would certainly know if Hosteen Pinto owned that pistol?"

"Maybe not," Leaphorn said. He didn't look up because he didn't want to show his resentment. Mrs. Keeyani he could tolerate. He respected her reason for being here—even though it wasted her time and his. Professor Bourebonette was another matter. But it was an astute question.

"Probably they wouldn't understand that," he agreed.

He was looking for something in the report that would tell him how Ashie Pinto had gotten from his place behind Yon Dot Mountain to Navajo Route 33 south of Ship Rock, New Mexico. Two hundred miles, more or less. Nothing in the report mentioned an abandoned car or pickup.

Dr. Bourebonette cleared her throat politely. "Does that report tell how Hosteen Pinto got over into New Mexico?"

"I was looking for that," Leaphorn said, glancing up at her. "Do you know?"

"Someone came and got him," she said.

"Who?"

Dr. Bourebonette glanced at Mary Keeyani.

"I don't know," Mary Keeyani said. "But I know somebody came and got him. I had gone over to the store at the Gap to get some kerosene for the light. And my husband, he was out with the sheep. Everybody was gone somewhere except my youngest daughter. She had come home on the school bus and she'd gone out to catch her horse and go help with the sheep and she saw dust from the car."

"It wasn't Pinto's car?"

Mrs. Keeyani laughed. "Hosteen Pinto's car broke a long time ago," she said. "The chickens sleep in it." Her amusement left as quickly as it had come. "She was up on the side of the hill with the horse and all she saw was the dust and maybe just a glimpse. It had come from Hosteen Pinto's shack. The road, it runs right by my mother's hogan and past our house and then out toward Twenty-nine Mile Canyon and connects up with the road to Cedar Ridge Trading Post. She said it might be a light-colored car, or maybe a pickup, or maybe it was just dusty."

"When was this?"

"It was the evening before Hosteen Pinto got arrested over in New Mexico."

Leaphorn flipped back through the report. He found nothing about any of this.

"Did a policeman come to talk to you?"

"A young white man," she said. "With those little spots on his face. And a Navajo to translate for him."

Freckles, Leaphorn thought. A culture unafflicted with freckles has no noun for them. "What did they want to know?"

"They asked about the pistol. They asked about what Hosteen Pinto was doing over there. Where did Pinto get the pistol? Where did he get the two fifty-dollar bills he had in his pocket? Did Hosteen Pinto know Delbert Nez—the man they say he shot? They asked questions like they thought Hosteen Pinto was bootlegging wine. Like how did Hosteen Pinto act when he was drunk? Did he get into fights? How did he make a living? Was he a bootlegger?" Mrs. Keeyani had been looking down at her hands. Now she looked up. "They seemed to think for sure he was a bootlegger." She shook her head.

"How did you answer?"

"I said maybe the fifty-dollar bills were his fee. From the one who came and got him."

"Fee?"

"He had his crystals with him," Mrs. Keeyani said. "When he was younger he used to work finding things for people. When I was a little girl they would come from as far away as Tuba City, and even Kayenta and Leupp. He was pretty famous then."

"He was a crystal gazer," Leaphorn said. He leaned forward. If this man was working as a shaman, maybe there was more to this than just another senseless, sordid whiskey killing. "He still worked at it?"

"Not much." She thought about it. "Last year he found a horse for a man who works over at Copper Mine, and then he did a little work for a white man. And he would work with Dr. Bourebonette." She nodded at the professor. "That was about all I know about."

"What had the white man lost?"

"I think he was hunting old-time stories."

Leaphorn wasn't sure what she meant. He waited for an explanation. None came.

"Was Hosteen Pinto someone the anthropologists came to see to learn the old stories? Like Professor Bourebonette?"

"Yes. Many times in the old days. Not so much now. He learned most of them from Narbona Begay I think. The brother of his mother."

"You think it was this white man looking for stories who came for him the day before the shooting?"

Mrs. Keeyani shook her head. "I don't know who it was. Maybe."

Or maybe not, Leaphorn thought. And how does it help anyway? His mind kept returning to Dr. Bourebonette's reason for being here. She knew the man, obviously. She said she liked him, had worked with him. But being here involved a lot of time and effort if you worked in Flagstaff. And she also seemed ready to pay for the expense of a private investigator.

"Are you still working with Hosteen Pinto?" he asked her. "I mean something current? Going on right now?"

She nodded. "We have been collaborating on a book," she said.

"About mythology?"

"About the evolution of witchcraft beliefs," she said. "Ashie Pinto had noticed it himself. How the stories had changed since his boyhood. He went to Albuquerque with me and we listened to the tapes. . . ." She paused. Decided this needed explanation. "The oral history tapes in the University of New Mexico collection. Interviews with elderly Navajos. And not just Navajos. With the other Native American cultures and the Spanish-American old people. Tapes that were made back in the thirties and forties that were recording memories that go way back into the 1880s. And if you allow secondhand, second-person memories—what we call grandfather stories—some of the memories went back before the Long Walk. We'd listen to these and look at the transcripts and that would refresh Hosteen Pinto's memories of the tales he had been told."

Dr. Bourebonette had an austere face. The only expressions Leaphorn had identified in it were skepticism, anger, and determination—the face of a woman used to getting her way who doubted she would get it from him. Now Bourebonette's face had changed. As she talked of this book there was animation and enthusiasm.

Leaphorn decided he might know what motivated Dr. Bourebonette.

". . . It's remarkable," she was saying. "What Hosteen Pinto can remember. How well he commands the little nuances of those old stories. The differences in attitudes of the teller toward the witch, for example. The shift in importance if the variation came from outside the Navajo culture. For example, from the Zuni sorcery tradition. Or the Hopi 'two-heart' legends, or—" Dr. Bourebonette stopped, midphrase. She looked embarrassed.

"You were still working with Hosteen Pinto? You hadn't finished?"

"More or less. I was to pick him up later that week. The week it happened. In fact that's how I found out he was arrested. I had read about the crime, but they hadn't released Hosteen Pinto's name. So I went out to his place and Mrs. Keeyani told me he was in jail."

In jail, Leaphorn thought. Unavailable to answer professorial questions. A book put on hold. Perhaps never to be finished. Professor Bourebonette's motivations seemed much less mysterious.

"Can the book be finished without him?" Leaphorn asked. His voice was as neutral as he could make it. But Professor Bourebonette read him exactly. Her sharp blue eyes stared into his. "Of course," she said. But she nodded, conceding his point and accepting the accusation. "But it might not be as solid a work."

Leaphorn looked away from her, back at the report, impressed with her astuteness and feeling slightly guilty. If he told Emma of this exchange, as he would have, she would have clucked her tongue, disapproving of his conduct. He turned the page, looking for the answer to the obvious question these women had posed. How had the old man gotten from the west side of the Reservation to Ship Rock country? At least he could try to find that out for them.

"It was mostly his book," Professor Bourebonette said, as if to herself.

Leaphorn glanced up, directly into her eyes. And saw what? Anger? Disappointment?

He flipped through the remaining pages. The question that seemed so obvious to him and his visitors had not seemed so intriguing to Agent Rostik. It simply wasn't dealt with. Well, perhaps there was some simple, irrelevant answer.

He had intended to ignore the manila envelope of photographs in the back of the folder. They weren't the sort of images he'd want to share with these women. But now he was curious. He slid the stack out on his desk.

Nez's body beside the burned car. More burned car, with Chee's fire extinguisher lying beside it. The pistol, shiny and new looking. A half-dozen shots of the locale taken in daylight, with the tortured, ugly shape of a basaltic outcrop rising in the background over the grassy ridge, a liquor bottle, a pocketknife, odds and ends that the police photographer, or the officer running the investigation, thought might be relevant.

Relevant. Leaphorn picked up the photograph of the bottle. A typical Scotch bottle—nothing to distinguish it from most any other, except the cost. He put on his glasses and examined the label.

DEWARS WHITE LABEL

He turned over the photograph. The label on the back confirmed that this was the bottle Ashie Pinto was carrying when apprehended by Officer Chee. "One quart capacity," the notation added, "approx. five sixth empty."

Scotch. Expensive Scotch.

"Mrs. Keeyani," Leaphorn said. "Do you know what Hosteen Pinto likes to drink? Wine? Whiskey?"

Mrs. Keeyani's face said she resented the question. "He doesn't drink," she said.

"He had been drinking that night," Leaphorn said. "Alcohol was in his blood."

"He used to drink," Mrs. Keeyani said. "Just now and then. He'd say if he took one little spoonful he just couldn't stop. For a long time, he wouldn't drink, and then somebody would have to go into Flagstaff or Winslow or some place and bring him home from jail. And then he wouldn't drink any more for a long time. For months. But finally four-five years ago, he did it again, and he got sick in the jail at Flag. Had to go to the hospital and the doctor said it would kill him. And after that—" She paused, shook her head. "No more drinking after that."

"But when he drank, what did he drink?"

Mrs. Keeyani shrugged. "Wine," she said. "Anything. Whatever was cheap."

"How about Scotch?"

Mrs. Keeyani looked puzzled. "Is it sweet?"

"No. It's very strong and expensive, but not sweet. Why?" Leaphorn asked.

Mrs. Keeyani smiled, remembering. "My uncle had a sweet tooth," she said. "We used to call him Sugarman. Anything sweet, he loved it. If she saw Hosteen Pinto's pickup coming, my mother would say, hurry up children, hide that cake I baked. Hide the candy. Hide the sugar sack. Here comes my brother the Sugarman." She chuckled at the memory. Then, not wanting her mother misjudged, added, "She'd give him a piece of cake."

"But you don't know if he drank Scotch?"

"If it was sweet, he drank it. If it was cheap."

Leaphorn glanced at the photograph of the bottle. The Scotch that came in that was definitely not cheap.

Leaphorn sighed. After a lifetime in police work, he understood himself well enough to know he wouldn't tolerate this apparent violation of the natural order. He had been curious about how Pinto came to be two hundred miles away from home with no way of getting there, or getting back. But that could be explained by hitchhiking. He could think of no such easy explanation for this bottle of Dewars Scotch. Or two fifty-dollar bills. Or how he got that pistol.

Leaphorn stood.

"Ladies," he said, "I will see what I can find out."

4

JIM CHEE CAME slouching out of the Burn Doctor's examining room at the University of New Mexico Hospital Burn and Trauma Center feeling distinctly down. Predictions concerning his hand had been ambiguous. Then he noticed the woman sitting against the wall in the waiting room. Something about her reminded him of Janet Pete. She was immersed in a *Newsweek*, her sleek, dark hair visible above the cover and her very nice legs neatly crossed. He stared. She turned the page of the magazine, giving him a look at more than her forehead.

Depression vanished, replaced by delight. It *was* Janet Pete.

"Hey," Chee said. "Janet. What are you doing here?"

"I was waiting for you," Janet Pete said, grinning at him. "I wanted to see how you look toasted."

"Not much improvement," Chee said, displaying the bandage on his hand. He used his good arm to hug her.

Janet hugged back, hard against Chee's damaged chest.

"Aaagh!"

Janet recoiled. "Oh. I'm sorry."

"Just a play for sympathy," Chee said, breathing hard.

"I didn't notice the bandages under your shirt," Janet said, repentant.

"One on my leg, too," Chee said, tapping his thigh and grinning at her.

"The doctor said that altogether if you average it out, I was somewhere between medium rare and medium."

"I just heard about it," she said. "It happened just when I was moving. Back in Washington, they have so much local homegrown homicide that one way out here doesn't make the paper. Not even if it's a policeman."

"I'd heard you'd come back home," Chee said. "Or almost home. I was going to hunt you up when I got all these bandages off." He was looking down at her, conscious that he was smiling like an ape, conscious that the receptionist was watching all this, conscious that Janet Pete had come to see him. "But how did you find me here?"

"I called your office in Ship Rock. They told me you were on sick leave. And the dispatcher asked around for me and found out you'd come to the burn center here for a checkup." She touched the bandage with a tentative finger. "Is it better? Are you going to be all right?"

"Mostly just scars. Except for this hand. They think it will be all right, too. Probably. Or close enough so I can use it. But let's get out of here. You have time for coffee?"

Janet Pete had time.

Walking from the university hospital, across the campus to the Frontier Restaurant, Janet touched gently on the death of Nez and deduced that Chee wasn't ready to talk about it. Chee touched on Janet's coming home from her law-firm job in Washington, and sensed this was a subject better returned to later. And so as they walked through the mild Albuquerque morning, they skipped further back in time and reminisced.

"Remember that day we met?" Janet said. "At the San Juan County jail. You were trying to keep my client locked up without charging him with anything. And I was being righteously indignant about it. Remember that?" She was laughing.

"I remember how I outsmarted you," Chee said.

"Like hell you did," Janet said. She stopped laughing. She stopped walking. "How? What do you mean?"

Chee looked back at her, grinning.

"What do you mean?" Janet demanded.

"Remember, you were getting your man out of lockup, and you had gotten his sack of stuff from the booking desk, and you got sore at me, thinking I was trying to worm some incriminating information out of him in the interrogation room. So when you went to call the FBI to complain about my conduct and get me called off, you took your client to the telephone with you."

Janet was frowning. "I remember that," she said. "The agent-in-charge said you didn't have FBI authorization to talk to the man. What was his name?"

"Bisti," Chee said. "Roosevelt Bisti."

"Yes," Janet said. "I remember he was sick. And I remember the fed said he wanted to talk to you and he told you to butt out. Didn't he? So how did you outsmart me, wise guy?"

"When you went to the phone you took along Bisti, but you left his sack behind."

Janet digested this. She walked toward him, shaking her head.

"You searched through his stuff," she said, accusingly. "Is that what you're telling me? That's not outslicking me. That's cheating."

They were walking again, Chee still grinning. His hand hurt a little, and so did the burn on his chest, but he was enjoying this. He was happy.

"Whose rules?" he asked. "You're a lawyer so you have to play by the *biligaana* rules. But you didn't ask me what rules I was using."

Janet laughed. "Okay, Jim," she said. "Anyway, I got Old Man Bisti out of jail and out of your unfair clutches."

"You enjoyed that job, didn't you? I mean your work out on the Big Rez? Why don't you go back to it? They're short-handed. I'll bet you could get your job back in a minute."

"I am going back to it."

"With the DNA?" Chee's delight was in his voice. The Dinebeiina Nahiilna be Agaditahe was the Navajo Tribe's version of a legal aid society—providing legal counsel for those who couldn't afford to pay. He'd be seeing Janet Pete a lot.

"Same sort of work but not the DNA," she said. "I'll be working for the Department of Justice. With the Federal Public Defender here in Albuquerque. I'll be one of the court-appointed defense attorneys in federal criminal cases."

"Oh," Chee said. His quick mind formed two conclusions. Janet Pete, being Navajo and being the most junior lawyer on the staff, would have been given Ashie Pinto to represent. From that conclusion, the second was instantaneous and took the joy from the morning. Janet Pete had come to see Officer Jim Chee, not Friend Jim Chee.

"I went to school here, you know," Chee said, simply to have something to say, to cover his disappointment.

They were walking under the sycamores that shaded the great brick expanse of the central mall. A squadron of teenaged skateboarders thundered past. Janet Pete glanced at him, curious about the change of subject and the sudden silence which had preceded it.

"After four years," she said, "a campus starts to feel like home."

"Seven for me," Chee said. "You go a couple of semesters and then run out of money, and come back again when you've stacked some up again. That's the average here, I think. About seven years to get a bachelor's degree. But it never started to feel like home."

"It was different at Stanford," Janet said. "People either had money or they had the big scholarships. You lived around the campus, so you got acquainted, made friends. It's more a community, I guess." She glanced at him again. "What's wrong?"

"Nothing. Everything's fine."

"Your mood changed. A cloud over the sun."

"I shifted from the social mode into strictly business," Chee said.

"Oh?" Puzzlement in her voice.

"You're representing Ashie Pinto. Right?" The tone was a little bleaker than he'd intended.

They walked past the Student Union without an answer to that, toward the fountain formed of a great slab of natural stone. Chee remembered the local legend that the university architect, lacking funds for an intended sculpture, had scrounged the monolithic sheets of rough marble from a quarry and arranged them in something that might suggest Stonehenge, or raw nature, or whatever your imagination allowed.

It worked beautifully and usually it lifted Chee's spirits.

"I came to see you because I like you," Janet Pete said. "If you weren't my friend, which you happen to be, I would have come looking for you because you're the arresting officer and it's my job."

Chee thought about that.

"So I had two reasons," she said. "Is that one too many reasons for you?"

"What did I say?" Chee asked. "I didn't say anything."

"Hell you didn't. Then why am I feeling like I'm on the defensive?" Janet said. "And not exactly knowing why." She hurried a little faster. "Boy," she said. "Boy, I can see why that white girl of yours went back to Wisconsin."

Chee caught up with her.

"What was her name? Mary?"

"Mary Landon," Chee said. "Look, I'm sorry. I know how it is. Somebody has to represent Pinto and naturally it would be you. So what do you want to know?"

Janet Pete, still walking fast, was out of the trees now, angling across the parking lot past Popejoy Hall. Chee followed her out under a morning sky that was dark blue and sunny—with just enough of those puffy forenoon clouds to suggest autumn was not too far along to produce afternoon thunderheads.

"FBI's not cooperating, huh?" Chee said. "What do you want to know?"

"Nothing," Janet said.

"Come on, Janet. I said I was sorry."

"Well," she said. And then she laughed up at him, squeezed his arm.

"I can be as touchy as you are," she said. "I can be a real bitch." She laughed again. "But notice how neatly I put you in the wrong. Did you appreciate that?"

"Not much," Chee said. "Is that something you learn in law school?"

"It's something you learn from your mother."

Jim Chee's taste for coffee had been brutalized by years of drinking the version he used to make for himself in his trailer under the cottonwood trees at Ship Rock—recently he'd taken to using little filter things that fit over his cups. The Frontier coffee tasted fresh but weak. Over a second refill they decided that he would cash in his return ticket on the Mesa Airlines flight and ride back to Ship Rock with Janet Pete. Tomorrow he'd show her the scene of the crime. By tomorrow, he thought, he would feel like talking about it.

"Did you know Hosteen Pinto still won't say anything about what happened?" Janet asked. "He'll talk to me about other things but not about the crime. He just shuts up."

"What's there to say?"

"Well, everything. Whether he did it, for one thing. Why he did it, if he did. What he was doing out there. Did you know he's a shaman, a crystal gazer? He finds things for people. That seems to be his only income. That and getting fees as an informant. From scholars, I mean. He's sort of an authority on old stories, legends, what happened when. So the history professors, and the mythologists, and the sociologists, and that sort of people are always having him remember things on tape for them. He has a car, but it doesn't run, so how did he get there? I mean where he was when you arrested him. What was he doing about two hundred miles from home? That's what I want him to tell me. And if he did it, why. Everything."

"He did it because he was drunk," Chee said. "Nez picked him up to get him out of the rain, tried to put him in the backseat of the patrol car, and Pinto got sore about it."

"That seems to be the official 'theory of the crime.' I know that's what the U.S. attorney is going to trial with," Janet said.

"And that seems to be pretty much what went on," Chee said.

"But why didn't Nez take that pistol away from him? You guys have a sort of standard procedure for things like that, don't you? For handling drunks?"

Chee had wondered about that himself. "He wasn't arresting him," he said. "We take drunks in for their own protection. So they don't freeze. Or drown." As Janet Pete knew very well.

She sipped her coffee. Her dark eyes looked skeptical over the rim.

"He didn't take the pistol because he didn't see the pistol," Chee added. "The old man had it stuck in his belt, behind him."

Janet sipped. "Come on," she said. "Gimme a break. Isn't that sort of a usual place to stick a pistol?"

Chee shrugged.

"So how did Pinto get there?" she asked.

"I don't know. Maybe the guy in the white car brought him," Chee said. "You've seen the FBI report, haven't you? What did they say?"

Janet had put her cup down. "White car? What white car?"

"When I was driving down from Red Rock, I met a white—anyway a light-colored vehicle. It was raining and getting dark. But I think I recognized it. It's an old banged-up Jeepster that one of the teachers at Ship Rock drives. What'd they say about that in the report?"

"They didn't mention it," Janet said. "All news to me."

"They didn't run that down?" Chee said. He shook his head. "I can't believe it."

"I can," Janet said. "You gave them all they needed. Their suspect, arrested at the scene of the crime, holding the murder weapon. All that's missing is the motive. Being drunk takes care of that. He doesn't even deny he did it. So why waste time and complicate things by digging out all the facts?" The question sounded bitter.

"How about that fancy bottle he was carrying? Does the report show where that came from?"

"Nothing. I didn't know it was fancy."

"Like something you'd give a fancy drinker for Christmas. If you wanted to impress him. It wasn't what a drunk would be buying."

Janet finished her coffee, put down the cup, looked at him for a while.

"You know, Jim, you don't have to do any of this. I know how you must feel. And I'm having trouble separating friend from lawyer when . . ."

He held up his right palm, interrupting her.

"When I think I'm hearing a lawyer, I'll shut up," he said. The thing about Janet Pete was that he could talk to her about things that were hard to talk about. She wasn't Mary Landon. No soft, pale hair, no bottomless blue eyes, no talent for making him feel like the ultimate male. But by tomorrow, he thought, he could talk to her about listening to Delbert Nez laughing on the radio. He could talk to her about how the dreadful feeling grew as he sat over his coffee at the Red Rock Trading Post, and waited, and waited, and waited. He could tell her how long it had taken him to sense that he had made an unforgivable, irredeemable mistake. She would understand why, when Ashie Pinto was convicted, he would resign from the tribal police and find some job that he was fitted for. She would understand why he had to see the old drunk convicted. He hadn't done his job. He hadn't kept Delbert Nez alive. But at least he had arrested his killer. Done one thing right.

She'd have to defend the old man, get him a light sentence—or perhaps some sort of an insanity plea bargain that would put him in a hospital for a while. He had no problem with that. It didn't matter to him if the old man was punished. That would do no possible good.

But he needed Janet Pete to understand that a verdict finding Pinto innocent would make Jim Chee doubly guilty.

5

JOE LEAPHORN STOOD at the door of Ashie Pinto's house reexamining his understanding of what the law allowed in a criminal investigation. He was sure that only the most genial judge would tolerate what was going on here. It would be labeled as a search without a warrant, perhaps as downright breaking and entering. However, Mary Keeyani and Louisa Bourebonette had not been impressed with such niceties, nor with Leaphorn's uneasiness.

"I thought we were just going to check around out here," Leaphorn had said. "Ask some questions. See if anyone had seen anything. We don't have any legal right to break into the suspect's house."

"He's my uncle," Mary Keeyani had said. She was using the tire tool from Professor Bourebonette's car, prying at the padlock hasp that secured Ashie Pinto's door.

"It's not as if we were actually breaking in," Bourebonette said. "We're here for his own benefit."

Joe Leaphorn wasn't exactly sure why he was here. Partly curiosity, partly some irrational sense of responsibility to Emma's clan sister—sort of a family gesture to soothe his conscience. Certainly he had no reason to be here that would sound either plausible or professional if this meddling into a federal homicide case caused any complications. True, that seemed extremely unlikely. But he stood aside as Mary Keeyani opened the violated door. The women filed in past him.

"He keeps his papers in a tin box," Mary Keeyani said. "It's in here somewhere if I can find it."

Leaphorn left the women to their questionable task. He walked across the hardpacked earth behind Pinto's house and inspected Pinto's truck. It was a 1970-vintage Ford short-bed pickup with the left front tire flat, the left rear critically low, the glass missing from the driver's-side window, and chicken manure on the seat. He released the hood catch and raised it. The battery was missing—the first thing taken on the back side of the Reservation when a truck gets too worn out to fix. Obviously, Ashie Pinto hadn't driven this truck for a long, long time.

He closed the hood and walked down the slope through the snakeweed to Pinto's outhouse. The raw planks used to build it a lifetime ago had shrunk and warped. Through the gaping cracks Leaphorn admired Pinto's view while he urinated—a grand expanse of tan-silver grass and black-silver sage sloping down Blue Moon Bench toward the cliffs of the Colorado River Canyon. On the way back to the house he made another stop at the hogan that adjoined it. It was round and windowless, built of stone, its tarpaper roof insulated with a layer of earth. Leaphorn pulled open the board door and peered into the darkness. He saw an iron cot, boxes, an old icebox apparently used for storage, nothing that looked interesting.

Nor was there anything interesting under Ashie Pinto's brush arbor—just an old bridle hanging from a crossbar, the bit rusted, the leather stiff and cracked. Leaphorn took it down, looked at it, hung it back where he'd found it, yawned. A wasted day, he thought. The only useful thing Leaphorn could think of that might be found here was something that would tell them how Pinto got from here on the western fringe of the Big Reservation over to Ship Rock territory. Probably at least two hundred miles. Someone with a vehicle must have taken him. Logically they would have sent word they were coming. Probably mailed to Pinto at the Short Mountain Trading Post. Possibly, as Mary Keeyani believed, this letter would have been saved in Pinto's repository of documents.

"When you just get maybe one letter a year—or maybe just eight or ten your whole life—then probably you save them," Mary Keeyani had explained. True enough. He walked back to the house.

In Leaphorn's experience, men who lived alone tended to be either totally sloppy or totally neat—one extreme or the other. Ashie Pinto was neat. From his vantage point leaning against the doorjamb, Leaphorn could see everything in the living room–bedroom of Pinto's two-room house. The bedstead stood on the cracked and worn linoleum, a blue-and-white J. C. Penney blanket folded across it; beside the single window, a three-drawer chest, beside the chest an armchair, the upholstery of its back and seat water-stained; a metal-and-Formica table, two wooden chairs; a tall cabinet with double doors which, since the room had no closet, must hold Pinto's spare clothing. There was nothing on the table, nothing on the chairs, nothing on the bed, but the top of the chest held a cigar box; a framed photograph which seemed, from Leaphorn's viewpoint, to be of Pinto himself; a large wash basin of white ceramic; and something flat, black, and metallic.

Mary Keeyani was looking through the drawers of the chest and Professor Bourebonette was making clattering noises in the kitchen.

"A tin box?" she said. "Square or round?"

"Round," Mary Keeyani said. "I think a fruitcake came in it. Maybe cookies."

Leaphorn struggled with his sense of official decorum on one hand and his curiosity on the other. What was that atop the chest? He reached a compromise.

"Mrs. Keeyani. What's that black thing on top of the chest there? Beside the cigar box."

"It's a tape recorder," Mrs. Keeyani said. She retrieved it, came to the door, and handed it to him with a plastic sack containing five cassettes. "My uncle did a lot of that. Taping stuff for those *biligaana* he worked for."

Professor Bourebonette appeared in the kitchen door. She displayed a round tin can with a cluster of red roses decorating the lid.

"That's it," Mary Keeyani said.

The tape recorder was of the bulky, heavy sort sold about twenty years ago. It contained a cassette. Leaphorn pushed the play button. He heard the faint sound of friction recorders make when running over blank tape. He pushed Stop, and Rewind, waited for the reversing process to stop and pushed Play again.

The speaker produced an old man's voice, speaking in Navajo.

"They say Coyote is funny, some of those people say that. But the old people

who told me the stories, they didn't think Coyote was funny. Coyote was always causing trouble. He was mean. He caused hardship. He hurt people. He caused people to die. That's the way the stories go that I was told by my uncles when I was a boy. These uncles, they say . . ."

Professor Bourebonette was standing beside him. Leaphorn pushed the stop button, looked up at her.

"He was doing that for me," she said. "I asked him for that story. I wonder how far he got."

"Ashie Pinto? For your book?"

"Not really. He told me he knew the original correct version of one of the Coyote myths. The one about the red-winged blackbirds and the game they play with their eyeballs. Throwing them up in the air and catching them, and Coyote forcing them to teach him the game." She glanced at Leaphorn, quizzical. "You know the story?"

"I've heard it," Leaphorn said. He looked at the tin she was holding. "Are you going to open Mr. Pinto's box?"

Bourebonette read into Leaphorn's tone some hint of disapproval. She looked at the box and at Leaphorn and said, "I'll just give it to Mary. She's his niece."

Mary Keeyani had no qualms. She worked off the lid. Inside Leaphorn could see a jumble of papers: envelopes, receipts, what seemed to be a car title, odds and ends. She put it on the table where she and Bourebonette sorted through it.

"Here's a letter from me," Bourebonette said, extracting an envelope. "And another one." She glanced at Leaphorn. "That's all of them. We didn't do much business by mail."

Mary Keeyani stopped sorting. "Here's all he has in here for this year," she said. She displayed two envelopes. "No use going back any further than that." She extracted a single sheet of notepaper from one envelope, read it, slipped it back into the envelope, and dropped it back into the box. She repeated the process, put the lid on the box, and stood, looking disappointed.

"Nothing helpful?" Bourebonette said.

Nothing helpful, Mrs. Keeyani had agreed. Nothing that would tell them who had driven out here over this awful rocky track and hauled an old man across the Reservation to commit a murder. Leaphorn drove carefully over that rocky track now, sorting out his reaction to this. It was what he had expected, or should have, and yet he felt disappointed. Why? He hadn't thought a search through Pinto's documents, if he had any, would be revealing. But if you give luck a chance, sometimes it rewards you.

His real hope was in finding a witness. The FBI seemed to have decided its case was made and hadn't looked for one. And strange vehicles came so rarely down these tracks—which were really little more than miles and miles of shared driveways—that people remembered them. A visit from a stranger to anyone on your side of the mountain was exciting. But, unfortunately, Ashie Pinto's place, even though it was four miles from the road, was the first place on this track. Mary Keeyani's outfit, where he was about to park now, occupied a little cluster of shacks with a shared hogan, out of sight more than a mile down the slope. It was only by chance that one of the children out with the sheep had noticed the dust raised by the vehicle that took Pinto away. There had been no one else to see it.

Leaphorn stifled a yawn. It was almost sundown. A long day. He was tired. He had driven more than two hundred and fifty miles, and two hundred and fifty miles with two strange women is more exhausting than that distance in the relaxing solitude to which he was accustomed. And before he was done with this day, he had to drive another four hours back to Window Rock. A day wasted. Nothing accomplished. Well, almost nothing. He stopped the car beside Mrs. Keeyani's house, a weathered mobile home set on concrete blocks. At least, he would get rid of this sense of family responsibility—and get rid of these two women—when he wrapped this up.

So wrap it up.

"Mrs. Keeyani," he said, "who all had Hosteen Pinto worked with? I mean in recent years. Besides Dr. Bourebonette."

Mrs. Keeyani was sitting beside him, getting her stuff together.

"He used to work with a man from Tucson. Somebody named Dr. Drabner. But not this year, I think. And then there was an old professor from the University of Utah. I don't remember his name but he spoke pretty good Navajo."

"I think that was a Dr. Justin Milovich," Bourebonette said. "He was into linguistics."

"Milovich," Mrs. Keeyani said. She climbed out of the car, where three dogs greeted her with much tail wagging, jumping, and rowdy enthusiasm. "That was him."

"Anyone else? That's it?"

"Nobody else I knew of."

"How about that history professor from the University of New Mexico?" Bourebonette said. "Tagert. How about Tagert? Hosteen Pinto used to work with him a lot."

"Not no more he don't," Mary Keeyani said.

Her tone and her face raised a question and Professor Bourebonette asked it. "Something happened?"

"He would give my uncle whiskey."

"Oh," Bourebonette said. "The son-of-a-bitch." She turned to Leaphorn. "When he drinks he just about kills himself."

Or someone else, Leaphorn thought.

"I told that man not to ever give my uncle any whiskey but he did it anyway," Mary Keeyani said. "So when the last time he wrote my uncle a letter about working for him, when my uncle brought it to me, I wouldn't even read it for him. I just tore it up. And I made my uncle promise not to work for him any more."

"When was that?" Leaphorn asked.

"Last year. Way last spring a year ago."

"When was the last time he heard from Milovich or Drabner? Can you remember?"

"Long time for Milovich," she said. "Drabner, I think it was last winter. Maybe even last fall. It was that letter in the box."

They were back on U.S. 89, Bourebonette and he, rolling southward toward the Tuba City junction, when the turnoff to Short Mountain reminded Leaphorn of Old Man McGinnis and his Short Mountain Trading Post.

He slowed, looked at Bourebonette. "I'm thinking of that bottle of whiskey Ashie Pinto had. The bottle he had when Chee arrested him. Remember what Mary Keeyani said about that New Mexico historian giving him booze?"

"I thought about that, too," she said. "Maybe Pinto picked up his mail himself, and there was a letter from Dr. Tagert and Ashie didn't let Mary see it. Maybe he got somebody else to read it for him and help him answer it."

"Exactly," Leaphorn said, pleased with her. "Maybe not, too. But didn't the Pintos do their trading at Short Mountain?"

"That was his mailing address."

"Let's go check."

The road from Highway 89 to Short Mountain Trading Post was a little better than Leaphorn remembered it from his days as a patrolman working out of Tuba City. It had been improved by gravel and grading from terrible to fairly bad. Leaphorn maneuvered the patrol car back and forth across its washboard surface, avoiding the worst of the bumps such roads develop. It was twilight when they dropped down into Short Mountain Wash and parked on the hard-packed earth that formed the trading post yard.

It was empty. Leaphorn parked near the porch, turned off the ignition and sat. He had brought Emma here once, long ago, to see this place and to meet Old John McGinnis. He'd described McGinnis as he'd known him, honorable in his way but notoriously grouchy, pessimistic, perverse, quick with insults and overflowing with windy stories and gossip. Over the front door nailed to the porch beam a faded sign proclaimed:

THIS ESTABLISHMENT FOR SALE
INQUIRE WITHIN

The sign had been there at least fifty years. According to local legend, McGinnis had hung it there within weeks after he'd bought the store from the Mormon who'd established it. The legend had it that young McGinnis had been outsmarted in the deal. Those who knew him found that incredible.

"He's rude," he'd told Emma. "No manners at all and he may snap at you. But look him over. I'd like to know what you think of him."

So, of course, McGinnis had been courtly, charming, full of smiles and compliments, showing Emma the best of his pawn goods and his collection of lance points, pots, and assorted artifacts—perverse as always. Emma had been charmed.

"I don't see why you say those bad things about him," she'd said. "He's a good man."

As always when it came to judging people, Emma was correct. In his prickly, eccentric way, John McGinnis was a good man.

Leaphorn was aware that Professor Bourebonette had glanced at him and glanced away. He supposed she was wondering why he was just sitting here. But she said nothing, and made no move to open her door. Willing to wait, sensing the value of this moment to him. He found himself favorably impressed with the woman. But then this sort of sensitivity would be something one in her profession would polish—part of their technique for establishing rapport with those they need to use. How long would her formula cause her to wait?

Cold evening air settling into Short Mountain Wash pushed a breeze across the yard, moving a tumbleweed languidly toward the porch. A water barrel stopped it. The buildings here had looked tired and decrepit the first time he'd seen the place. In the red light of the sunset they looked worse. A plaster-and-stone building behind the main post had been partially burned and left unrepaired, the shed where hay was stored leaned to the left. Even the porch seemed to have sagged under the weight of age and loneliness.

Now a naked light bulb hanging over the trading post door went on, a feeble yellow glow in the twilight.

"Well," Leaphorn said. "He's ready to receive a customer. Let's go talk to him."

"I only met him once," Bourebonette said. "He helped me find some people. I remember he seemed fairly old."

"He knew my grandfather," Leaphorn said. "Or so he claims."

Bourebonette looked at him. "You sound skeptical."

Leaphorn laughed, shook his head. "Oh, I guess he really did know him. But with McGinnis—" He laughed again.

The front door opened and McGinnis stood in it, looking out at them.

"After closing time," he said. "What you want?"

He was smaller than Leaphorn remembered—a white-haired, bent old man in faded blue overalls. But he identified Leaphorn as soon as he climbed out of the car.

"Be damned," McGinnis said. "Here comes the Sherlock Holmes of the Navajo Tribal Police. And I betcha I can guess what brought him out here to the poor side of the Reservation."

"*Yaa' eh t'eeh,*" Leaphorn said, "I think you know Dr. Bourebonette here."

"Why, yes indeed I do," McGinnis said. To Leaphorn's amazement, he made something like a bow. "And it's good to see you back again, Ma'am.

Can you come on in and have something to drink? Or maybe join me at my supper. It's only some stew but there's plenty of it."

Professor Bourebonette was smiling broadly. "Mr. McGinnis," she said, "I hope you got my letter, thanking you for your help." She held out her hand.

McGinnis took it, awkwardly, his face expressing an emotion Leaphorn had never seen there before. Shyness? Embarrassment? "I got it," McGinnis said. "Wasn't necessary. But much appreciated."

He ushered them through the gloomy dimness of his store toward his living quarters in the back. Not much stock, Leaphorn noticed. Some shelves were bare. The case where McGinnis had always kept his pawn goods locked behind glass held only a scattering of concha belts, rugs, and the turquoise and silver jewelry by which the Navajos traditionally measured and preserved their meager surplus. There was a sense of winding down in the store. Leaphorn felt the same sensation when he stepped through the doorway into the big stone-walled room where McGinnis lived.

"You want to talk about Hosteen Pinto," McGinnis said. "What I know about him." McGinnis had removed a pile of *National Geographics* from a faded red plush chair for Bourebonette, motioned Leaphorn toward his plastic-covered sofa, and lowered himself into his rocking chair. "Well, I don't know why he killed that policeman of yours. Funny thing for him to do." McGinnis shook his head at the thought of it. "They say he was drunk, and I've seen him drunk a time or two. He was a mean drunk. Cranky. But no meaner than most. And he told me he'd quit that drinking. Wonder what he had to burn up that officer for. What did he say about that?"

Leaphorn noticed that Professor Bourebonette looked surprised and impressed. He was neither. McGinnis was shrewd. And why else would Leaphorn be coming here to talk to him? Now McGinnis was pouring water from a five-gallon can into his coffee-pot. He struck a match to light his butane stove and put the pot on it.

"I understand he won't talk about it," Leaphorn said.

McGinnis stopped adjusting the flame. He straightened and looked at Leaphorn. He looked surprised. "Won't say why he did it?"

"Or whether he did it. Or didn't do it. He just won't talk about it at all."

"Well, now," McGinnis said. "That makes it interesting." He sorted through the odds and ends stacked on a shelf above the stove, extracted two cups and dusted them. "Won't talk," McGinnis said. "And old Ashie was always a forthcoming man."

"That's what the FBI report says. He won't admit it, won't deny it, won't discuss it," Leaphorn said. Professor Bourebonette stirred in her chair.

"What was he doing way over there anyhow?" asked McGinnis. "Didn't his folks know? Mary Keeyani keeps a close eye on him. He don't get away with much that she don't know about."

"Mary doesn't know," Bourebonette said. "Somebody came and got him. Must have been that."

"But Mary don't know who?" McGinnis chuckled. "I know who then. Or, I'll bet I do."

"Who?" Leaphorn said. He tried to make it sound casual, resisted the impulse to lean forward. He remembered how McGinnis loved to drag things out and the more you wanted it, the longer he made you wait.

"If it was somebody he was working for, that is," McGinnis said. "He'd been working for Professor Bourebonette here—" he nodded toward her "—and for somebody from the University of New Mexico. I think his name was Tagert. And for a couple of others off and on. People who wanted his folk tales like the professor, or wanted to put down some of his memories."

McGinnis stopped, tested the side of the coffeepot for temperature with the back of his finger and looked at Leaphorn. Waiting.

"Which one was it?"

McGinnis ignored Leaphorn's question. "You sure Mary didn't know?" he asked Bourebonette.

"Absolutely sure."

"Had to be Tagert then." He waited again.

"Why Tagert?" Leaphorn asked.

"Tagert used to give him whiskey. Mary found out about it. She wouldn't let him work for Tagert any more."

Leaphorn considered this. It fit with what Mrs. Keeyani had said. And it made a certain amount of sense, even though the way McGinnis told it, it seemed nothing more than a guess. But McGinnis knew more than he'd told. Leaphorn was sure of that. He was also tired, with hours of driving ahead of him. He didn't want to sit here while McGinnis amused himself.

"Did you write a letter for him? For Hosteen Pinto?"

McGinnis tested the coffeepot again, found the heat adequate, filled one cup, handed it to Professor Bourebonette.

"If you like sugar in it, I can get you that. I'm all out of milk unless I have some condensed out in the store."

"This is fine," she said. "Thank you."

"You known Lieutenant Leaphorn long? If I might ask such a question."

"You may. We met just this morning."

"Notice how he gets right to the point. That's unusual in a Navajo. Usually they're more polite about it." McGinnis glanced at Leaphorn. "We got plenty of time."

"Pinto got a letter from Tagert here," Leaphorn said. "He happened to pick it up himself, didn't he? You read it to him and then you answered it for him. That about right?"

McGinnis poured Leaphorn's coffee into a mug that bore the legend JUSTIN BOOTS. It reminded Leaphorn that the boots Emma had bought him for his birthday after they were married were Justins. They couldn't afford them then. But he'd worn them almost twenty years. Emma. The sure knowledge that he would never see her again sat suddenly on his shoulders, as it sometimes did. He closed his eyes.

When he opened them, McGinnis was holding the mug out to him, expression quizzical.

Leaphorn took it, nodded.

"You had it about right," McGinnis said. "He was in the store when the mail came, as I remember it. Tagert wanted to interview him about something. He wanted to know if he could come and get him on some date or other. He asked Ashie to let him know if that date was all right or to name another if it wasn't."

"Anything else?" Leaphorn asked. He sipped the coffee. Even by the relaxed standards of the Window Rock Tribal Police headquarters it was bad coffee. Made this morning, Leaphorn guessed, and reheated all day.

"Just a short letter," McGinnis said. "That was it."

"What was the date?"

"I don't remember. Would have been early in August."

"And Pinto agreed?"

"Yeah," McGinnis said. He frowned, remembering—the plump, round face Leaphorn remembered from a decade ago shrunken now into a wilderness of lines and creases. Then he shrugged. "Anyway, the upshot was he asked me to write Tagert back and tell him he'd be ready in the afternoon."

Professor Bourebonette, either politer or more starved for caffeine than Leaphorn, was sipping her coffee with no apparent distaste. She put down the cup.

"So now we know how he got to Ship Rock," she said. "Tagert came and got him."

But Leaphorn was studying McGinnis. "Pinto said something about it, or something like that? He didn't just immediately say write him back?"

"I'm trying to remember," McGinnis said, impatiently. "I'm trying to get it all back in my mind. We was in this room, I remember that much. Ashie's getting too damn old to amount to much but I've known him for years and when he comes in we usually come back here for a talk. Find out what's going on over by the river, you know."

He rocked forward in his chair, got up clumsily. He opened the cabinet above the stove and extracted a bottle. Old Crow.

"The lieutenant here don't drink," McGinnis said to Professor Bourebonette. He glanced at Leaphorn. "Unless he's changed his ways. But I will offer you a sip of bourbon."

"And I will accept it," the professor said. She handed McGinnis her empty coffee cup and he poured the whiskey into it. Then he fumbled at the countertop, came up with a Coca-Cola glass and filled it carefully up to the trademark by the label. That done, he sat again, put the bottle on the floor beside him, and rocked.

"I didn't offer Hosteen Pinto a drink. I remember that. Wouldn't be the thing to do, him being alcoholic. But I poured myself one, and sat here and sipped at it." McGinnis sipped his bourbon, thinking.

"I read the letter to him and he said something strong." McGinnis examined his memory. "Strong. I think he called Tagert a coyote, and that's about as strong as a Navajo will get. And at first he wasn't going to work for him. I remember that. Then he said something like Tagert paid good.

And that's what had brought him in here in the first place. Money. You notice that belt out in the pawn case?"

McGinnis pushed himself out of the rocker and disappeared through the doorway into the store.

Leaphorn looked at Bourebonette. "I'll tell the FBI about Tagert," he said.

"You think they'll do anything?"

"They should," he said. But maybe they wouldn't. Why would they? Their case was already made. And what difference did it make anyway?

McGinnis reappeared carrying a concha belt. The overhead light reflected dimly off the tarnished silver.

"This was always old Pinto's fallback piece. The last thing he pawned when he was running low." McGinnis's gnarled hand stroked the silver disks. "It's a dandy."

He handed it to Professor Bourebonette.

Leaphorn could see it was indeed a dandy. An old, heavy one made of the turn-of-the-century silver Mexican five-peso pieces. Worth maybe two thousand dollars from a collector. Worth maybe four hundred in pawn credit.

"Trouble is he'd already pawned it," McGinnis said. "Not only pawned it. He'd been in twice to bump up the loan. He wanted another fifty dollars in groceries on it and we was jawing about that when the mail truck came up."

McGinnis was rocking while he remembered, holding the Coca-Cola glass in left hand, tilting it back and forth in compensation for the rocking motion. Exactly as he'd seen him do it when Leaphorn was twenty years younger, coming in here to learn where families had moved, to collect gossip, just to talk. Leaphorn felt a dizzying sense of dislocation in time. Everything was the same. As if twenty years hadn't ticked away. The cluttered old room, the musty smell, the yellow light, the old man grown older, as if in the blink of an eye. Suddenly he knew just what McGinnis would do next, and McGinnis did it.

He leaned, picked up the Old Crow bottle by the neck, and carefully recharged his glass, dripping the last of the recharge until it was exactly up to the trademark.

"I've seen Pinto poor before. Many times. But that day he was totally tapped out. Said he was out of coffee and cornmeal and lard and just about everything and Mary wasn't in any shape to help him with her own bunch to feed."

McGinnis fell silent, rocking, tasting the whiskey on his tongue.

"So he took the job," Professor Bourebonette said.

"So he did," McGinnis said. "Had me write Tagert right back." He took another tiny sip, and savored it in a silence that made the creaking of his rocker seem loud.

A question hung in Leaphorn's mind: *Why had Pinto called Tagert a coyote?* It was a hard, hard insult among the Navajos—implying not just bad conduct but the evil of malice. Mary Keeyani said Tagert had given him whiskey. Would that be the reason? Leaphorn noticed his interest in this affair growing.

"But I know he didn't want to," McGinnis added. "I said, What's wrong with this fella? He looks all right to me. He pays you good money, don't he? He's just another one of them professors. And old Ashie said Tagert wants me to do something I don't want to do. And I said what's that, and he said he wants me to find something for him. And I said well hell, you do that all the time, and he was quiet a while. And then he said, you don't have to go looking for Coyote. Coyote's always out there waiting."

Professor Bourebonette had offered to share driving on the way home and Leaphorn had explained to her that Tribal Police rules prohibited it. Now, about fifty miles east of Tuba City, Leaphorn began wishing he hadn't. He was exhausted. Talking had helped keep sleep at bay for the first hour or so. They talked about McGinnis, about what Tagert might have wanted Hosteen Pinto to find, about Pinto's reluctance. They discussed how Navajo mythology related to the origin story of the Old Testament, and to myths of the Plains Indians, and police techniques in criminal investigations, and civil rights, and academic politics. She had told him about the work she had done studying mythology in Cambodia, Thailand, and Vietnam, before the intensifying war made it impossible. And now Leaphorn was talking about his days as a graduate student at Arizona State, and specifically about a professor who was either weirdly absent-minded or over the hill into senility.

"Trouble is, I'm beginning to notice I'm forgetting things myself," he concluded.

The center stripe had become double, waving off in two directions. Leaphorn shook his head, jarring himself awake. He glanced at Bourebonette to see if she'd noticed.

Professor Bourebonette's chin was tilted slightly forward, her head leaned against the door. Her face was relaxed in sleep.

Leaphorn studied her. Emma had slept like that sometimes on late night returns. Relaxed. Trusting him.

6

THE BATTERED WHITE Jeepster proved remarkably easy to locate. It sat in space number seventeen in a weedy parking lot guarded by a sign that declared:

SHIP ROCK HIGH SCHOOL
TEACHER/STAFF PARKING ONLY

Janet Pete parked her little Toyota two-door beside the jeep. She'd changed out of her go-see-a-sick-friend skirt into jeans and a long-sleeved blue shirt.

"There it is. Exactly as you planned," she said. "You want to wait here for the owner?" She motioned to the cars streaming out of the teacher/staff parking lot, a surprising number it seemed to Chee. "It shouldn't be long."

"I want to know who I'm talking to," Chee said, climbing out. "I'll go ask."

The secretary in the principal's office looked at Jim Chee's badge, and through the window to where he was pointing, and said "Which one?" and then said, "Oh."

"That's Mr. Ji's," she said. "Are you going to arrest him?" Her voice sounded hopeful.

"Gee," Chee said. "How does he spell it?"

"It's H-U-A-N J-I," she said, "so I guess if you pronounced it the way we pronounce 'na-va-*ho*' it would be 'Mr. Hee.' "

"I heard he was a Vietnamese. Or Cambodian," Chee said.

"Vietnamese," the secretary said. "I think he was a colonel in their army. He commanded a Ranger battalion."

"Where could I find him?"

"His algebra class is down in room nineteen," she said, gesturing down the hallway. "School's over but he usually keeps part of them overtime." She laughed. "Mr. Ji and the kids have a permanent disagreement over how much math they are going to learn."

Chee paused at the open door of room nineteen. Four boys and a girl were scattered at desks, heads down, working on notebooks. The girl was pretty, her hair cut unusually short for a young Navajo woman. The boys were two Navajos, a burly, sulky-looking white, and a slender Hispano. But Chee's interest was in the teacher.

Mr. Huan Ji stood beside his desk, his back to the class and his profile to Chee, staring out the classroom window. He was a small man, and thin, rigidly erect, with short-cropped black hair and a short-cropped mustache showing gray. He wore gray slacks, a blue jacket, and a white shirt with a tie neatly in place and looked, therefore, totally misplaced in Ship Rock High School. His unblinking eyes studied something about level with the horizon. Seeing what? Chee wondered. He would be looking across the tops of the cottonwoods lining the San Juan and southwestward toward the sagebrush foothills of the Chuskas. He would be seeing the towering black shape of Ship Rock on the horizon, and perhaps Rol-Hai Rock, and Mitten Rock. No. Those landmarks would be beyond the horizon from Mr. Ji's viewpoint at the window. Chee was creating them by looking into his own memory.

Mr. Ji's expression seemed sad. What was Huan Ji seeing in his own memory? Perhaps he was converting the gray-blue desert mountains of Dinetah into the wet green mountains of his homeland.

Chee cleared his throat.

"Mr. Ji," he said.

Five students looked up from their work, staring at Chee. Mr. Ji's gaze out the window didn't waver.

Chee stepped into the classroom. "Mr. Ji," he said.

Mr. Ji jerked around, his expression startled.

"Ah," he said. "I'm sorry. I was thinking of something else."

"I wonder when I might talk to you," Chee said. "Just for a moment."

"We're about finished here," Ji said. He looked at the five students, who looked back at him. He looked at his watch. "You can go now," he said. "If you have finished, give me your papers. If not, bring them in tomorrow—finished and corrected." He turned to Chee. "You are a parent?"

"No sir," Chee said. "I'm Officer Chee. With the Navajo Tribal Police." As he said it, he was conscious of Mr. Ji noticing the thick bandage on his hand, his denims, his short-sleeved sport shirt. "Off duty," he added.

"Ah," Mr. Ji said. "What can I tell you?"

Chee heard hurrying footsteps—Janet Pete coming down the hallway toward them. Hosteen Pinto would be legally represented in this conversation, he thought. Well, why not? But it bothered him. Where does friend end and lawyer start?

"Mr. Ji?" Janet asked, slightly breathless.

"This is Janet Pete," Chee said. "An attorney."

Mr. Ji bowed slightly. If Mr. Ji ever allowed confusion to show, it would have shown now. "Is this about one of my students?" he said.

The last of Mr. Ji's students hurried past them, the urge to be away overcoming curiosity.

"Miss Pete represents Ashie Pinto," Chee said.

It seemed to Jim Chee that Mr. Ji momentarily stopped breathing. He looked at Janet Pete, his face showing no emotion at all.

"Is there a place we could talk?" Chee asked.

Someone was in the teachers' lounge. They walked out to where Janet's Toyota was parked.

"Is this your car?" Chee pointed to the Jeepster.

"Yes," Ji said.

"It was seen out on Navajo 33 the night Officer Delbert Nez was killed."

Ji said nothing. Chee waited.

Ji's face was blank. (The inscrutable Oriental, Chee thought. Where had he heard that? Mary Landon had used it once to describe him. "You are, you know. You guys came over the icecap from the steppes of Mongolia or Tibet or someplace like that. We came out of the dark forests of Norway.")

"What was the date?" Ji asked.

Chee told him. "That was the night of the rain. Good hard rain. It would have been between seven-thirty and eight. But getting dark because the storm was coming."

"Yes," Ji said. "I remember it. I was there."

"Did you see anyone? Anything?" Janet Pete asked.

"Where?" Ji asked.

Chee suppressed a frown. It seemed a stupid question.

"Where you were. Out beyond Ship Rock," he said. "East of Red Rock on Route 33."

"I don't remember seeing anything," Ji said.

"How about after you turned north on Route 63?"

"Route 63?" Ji looked genuinely puzzled. Not too surprising. Not many people, including those who routinely drove that dusty, bumpy route, would know its map number.

"The gravel road close to Red Rock that goes north toward Biklabito and Ship Rock."

"Oh," Ji said, nodding. "No. I saw nothing. Not that I remember."

"You didn't see the fire, Nez's car burning?"

"I think I saw a glow. I thought it was the lights of a car. I really don't remember much about that now."

"Do you remember what you were doing out there?"

Ji smiled and nodded. "I remember that," he said. "It looked like it might rain. Rain clouds back over the mountains. It rains a lot in my country and I miss it out here. I thought I would drive out and enjoy it."

"How did you go?" Chee asked.

Ji thought. "I drove south on U.S. 666 toward Gallup, and then I turned west on that paved road over to Red Rock, and then circled back on the gravel road."

"Did you see a Tribal Police car?"

"Ah, yes," Ji said. "One passed me."

"Where?"

"On the Red Rock road."

That would have been Delbert's Unit 44. "Did you see it again?"

"No."

"You would have passed it," Chee said. "It had pulled off the left side of the road and driven down a dirt track."

"I didn't notice it," Ji said. "I think I would have remembered that."

"Did you meet anyone, I mean on your way home?"

Mr. Ji thought about it. "Probably," he said. "But I don't remember."

And that was exactly all they learned.

From the parking lot, they drove southward down 666, across the San Juan bridge.

"You want to go see where it happened?" he asked Janet.

She looked at him, surprised. "Do you?"

"Not exactly," he said. "But yes, I guess I do."

"You haven't been back?"

"I was in the hospital in Albuquerque for weeks," Chee said. "And then, I don't know, there just wasn't any reason."

"Okay," Janet said. "I think I should see it."

"You have a better reason than I do," Chee said. "I've got nothing to do with it anymore. It's FBI business. I'll just testify as the arresting officer."

Janet nodded. She saw no reason to comment on any of this. Chee knew she already knew it.

"I didn't do any of the investigating," he added, knowing she would have known that, too.

"Do you think the FBI took a statement from Mr. Ji?"

Chee shook his head. "He would have mentioned it."

"Doesn't it surprise you that they didn't?"

He shook his head. "Not now. Remember? You explained it to me. They have all they need for a conviction. Why waste their time?"

She was frowning. "I know I said that. But they'd seen your statement. They knew you'd met that car driving away from the scene. You described it as a white Jeepster, said who owned it. I'd think just simple curiosity . . ." She let it trail off.

"They had their man, and their evidence," Chee said. "Why make things complicated?"

Janet thought about that. "Justice," she said.

Chee let it pass. Justice, he thought, wasn't a concept that fit very well in this affair. Besides, the sun was just dipping behind the Chuskas now. On the vast, rolling prairie that led away from the highway toward the black shape of Ship Rock every clump of sagebrush, every juniper, every snakeweed, every hummock of bunch grass cast its long blue shadow—an infinity of lines of darkness undulating across the glowing landscape. Beautiful. Chee's spirit lifted. No time to think of justice. Or of the duty he had left undone.

Janet's Toyota topped the long climb out of the San Juan Basin and earth sloped away to the south—empty, rolling gray-tan grassland with the black line of the highway receding toward the horizon like the mark of a ruling pen. Miles to the south, the sun reflected from the windshield of a northbound vehicle, a blink of brightness. Ship Rock rose like an oversized, free-form Gothic cathedral just to their right, miles away but looking close. Ten miles ahead Table Mesa sailed through its sea of buffalo grass, reminding Chee of the ultimate aircraft carrier. Across the highway from it, slanting sunlight illuminated the ragged black form of Barber Peak, a volcanic throat to geologists, a meeting place for witches in local lore.

They did the right turn off 666 onto Navajo 33, driving into the setting sun.

"Here's probably about where he was when we first made radio contact," Chee said. "Just about here." His voice sounded stiff in his own ears.

Janet nodded.

He slowed, pointing. "I was way over there, twenty-five, thirty miles behind Ship Rock, driving south on the road from Biklabito. I was back there behind the rock. Something like that screws up radio communication. It keeps fading in and out."

Chee cleared his throat. He pulled down the sunshade. Janet flipped down the one on the driver's side, found she was too short to be helped by it, and fished out her sunglasses. She was thinking that Chee wasn't as ready to talk about this as he'd thought he was.

"Going to be quite a sunset," she said. "Look north."

North, over Sleeping Ute Mountain in Colorado, over Utah's Abajo Mountains, great thunderheads were reaching toward their evening climax. Their tops, reflecting in the direct sun, were snowy white and the long streamers of ice crystals blown from them seemed to glitter. But at lower levels the light that struck them had been filtered through the clouds over the Chuskas and turned into shades of rose, pink, and red. Lower still, the failing light mottled them from pale blue-gray to the deepest blue. Overhead, the streaks of high-level cirrus clouds were being ignited by the sunset. They drove through a fiery twilight.

"There's where it happened," Chee said, nodding to the left. "He pulled off the pavement right up there, and the car was burning over by that cluster of junipers, way off there."

Janet nodded. Chee noticed her forehead, her cheeks rosy in the reflected light. Skin as smooth as silk. Her eyes were intense, staring at something. An intelligent face. A classy face. She frowned.

"What's that over on those rocks?" She gestured. "Those white marks up in that formation over there?"

"That's what was bothering Delbert," Chee said, and made a chuckling sound. "That's the artwork of our phantom vandal. Delbert noticed somebody had been painting those formations maybe six weeks ago. He wanted to catch the guy."

"It bothered him? I don't guess there's a law against it. Nothing specific anyway," she said. "But it bothers me too. Why ugly up something natural?"

"With Nez, I think it was a mixture of being bothered and thinking it was sort of weird. Who would climb up in there and waste all that time and paint turning black basalt into white? Anyway, Delbert was always talking about it. And that night, it sounded like he thought he'd seen the guy. He was laughing about it."

"Maybe he did see him," Janet said. She was staring out at the formation. "What caused all that? I know it must be volcanic but it doesn't look like the normal ones. Frankly, they don't teach you anything about geology in law school."

"In anthropology departments either," Chee said. "But from what I've been told, the volcanic action that formed Ship Rock lasted for tens of thousands of years. The pressure formed a lot of cracking in the earth's surface, and every thousand years or so—or maybe it's millions of years—there would be another bubbling up of melted rock and new ridges would form. Sometimes right beside the old ones."

"Oh," Janet said.

"These run for miles and miles," Chee said. "Sort of parallel the Chuska Mountains."

"Is there a name for them?"

Chee told her.

She made a wry face. "My parents wanted me to speak perfect English. They didn't talk Navajo much around me."

"It means something like 'Long Black Ridges.' Something like that." He glanced at Janet, not knowing where she stood on the issue of Navajo witchcraft. "Lot of traditional Navajos wouldn't want to go around those lava formations—especially at night. According to Navajo mythology, at least on the east side of the Reservation, those lava flows are the dried blood of the monsters killed by the Hero Twins. I think that's one of the things that got Nez so interested. You know. Who was breaking that taboo?"

"Maybe Nez caught whoever it was, and the guy killed him," Janet said.

"And gave the pistol to Hosteen Pinto," Chee said. "You're going to have trouble selling that one."

Janet shrugged. "It's as good as anything else I've thought of," she said. "Let's take a look at it." She glanced at Chee, looking suddenly doubtful. "Or would there be a lot of snakes this time of year?"

"Always some snakes in places like that," Chee said. "But they're no problem if you use your head."

"Just thinking about snakes is a problem," Janet said. But she turned the Toyota off the asphalt.

Getting to part of the formation where the painter worked involved maneuvering the little Toyota across about a mile of trackless stone, cactus, Russian thistle, buffalo grass, sage, and snakeweed. After dropping a wheel with a rattling jolt into a little wash, Janet switched off the ignition.

"It's easier to walk," she said. "Especially easier on my poor car."

It wasn't quite as easy as it looked. As with all large objects seen through the thin, dry, high desert air, the outcrop was bigger and more distant than it seemed. The sun had dipped well below the horizon when they climbed the steep final slope toward its base. Overhead the high clouds had faded from rose to dark red. Far to the west across Arizona, clouds over the Kaibito Plateau were blue-black, outlined by fiery yellow.

Janet stopped to stare.

"Did you miss these sunsets in Washington?" Chee asked.

"I'm looking at that car," she said, pointing.

Pulled behind a clump of junipers was a dark green Ford Bronco II, dirty, dented, and several years old. They detoured to walk behind it. It wore a New Mexico vanity license plate.

"REDDNEK," Janet read. "You think the irony was intended?"

Chee shrugged. He didn't catch the irony. The vehicle was empty. What was it doing here? Where was the driver?

"A redneck who can't spell it," she explained.

"Oh."

On the ridge beyond the vehicle, Janet stopped again. She stood, head tilted back, staring up at the massive, unbroken slab of basalt which confronted them here.

"I don't see any sign of paint," Janet said. The red light changed the color of her shirt, and her faded jeans, and her face. Her hair was disheveled, her expression intent, and, taken all together, she looked absolutely beautiful to Jim Chee. It would be a lot better, he thought, if friends didn't look like that.

"Let's see if we can find where he climbed up," he said.

That wasn't easy. The first upward possibility dead-ended on a shelf that led absolutely nowhere except up a vertical face of stone. The second, a pathway that opened inside a split in a basaltic slab, took them perhaps seventy-five yards upward and in before it finally dwindled away into an impossibly narrow crack. They found the third atop a sloping hump of debris by ducking under a tilted roof of fallen stone.

"I haven't brought up the subject of snakes," Janet said. She was brushing the dirt from her hands on her pant legs. "If I do, I hope you'll try to say something positive."

"Okay," Chee said. He thought for a minute, catching his breath. "If you like snakes, this is a fine example of the places you come to find them."

"I don't like snakes," Janet said. "I know all that BS about Navajos and snakes being friends, but I don't like them. They scare me."

"We're not supposed to be friends," Chee said. "The way it goes in the legend, First Man and Big Snake learned to respect one another. The way you do that is by not putting your hand, or your foot, or any other part of you where you can't see. That way you don't step on your little brother, or sit on him, or poke him in the eye. And in return, he buzzes his rattlers to tell you if you're getting in dangerous territory. Very efficient."

"I still don't like them," Janet said, but she was staring up into the formation. "Look. I think that's paint."

It was. Above them and to their left, Chee could see a face of the basalt cliff reflecting white. Reaching it involved climbing up a deep crack into a long, narrow pocket. But eons of erosion had filled it with enough fallen rocks and blown dust to form a floor. There Chee leaned against the stone, breathing hard, the bottom level of the paint just above his head.

"Look here," Janet said. She was kneeling on the dirt. "Can you believe this? I think somebody carried a ladder in here."

If Janet was breathing hard it didn't show. But Chee was, and was embarrassed by it. It was being out of shape, he thought. Too long in the hospital bed. Too many weeks without exercise. Climbing with one hand in a bandage hadn't been easy. He would have to get back into doing some exercises.

He took a long, deep breath and squatted beside her. Two narrow, rectangular shapes had been pressed into the earth, the proper distance apart to have been made by the feet of a ladder.

"A determined painter," Janet said. "With a plan, obviously. Why else haul a ladder way up in here? He had to know he was going to be reaching up somewhere where he'd need it."

Chee was examining the holes the ladder had left. He was wishing they'd climbed in here when the light was better.

"I think that's interesting," Janet said.

He stood and brushed off his jeans with his good hand, wondering if Nez actually caught the son-of-a-bitch. Did Nez chase him? Did he even know Nez was after him?

"Did this crazy rock painter kill Nez?" Janet asked.

"Ashie Pinto shot Nez in the chest," Chee said. "But did this nutty rock painter have anything to do with it? Did he see it happen?"

"He seems nutty all right," Janet said. She had climbed halfway out of the pocket and was staring up into the broken, slanted wilderness of slabs, crags, boulders, and cliffs of the upthrust. "You can see several painted places back in there. One big squarish place, and a narrow vertical strip and some other small places."

Chee climbed up beside her.

"If he saw it happen, and I can find him, then you could just plead Pinto guilty," Chee said. "No use letting it go to trial. Just make a deal for him."

Janet let it pass, staring up into the formation. "Odd," she said.

"It doesn't seem to form any pattern," Chee agreed. "Or communicate anything or make any sense." With his knife, he scraped at the painted stone where they were standing, collecting a sample from the lower edge of the brush mark. Then he bent close, examining it in the dimming red glow of the twilight.

"He's sending some sort of signal to flying saucers," Janet said. "Or when the Mesa airliner comes over here flying down to Gallup, this says 'YOU'RE LOST' to the pilot. Or the guy who is doing it, they lost his luggage and when you look down from the airplane this is some sort of awful obscene insult."

"Look at this," Chee said.

Janet bent closer. "What?"

"It washed down a little," Chee said, indicating the flow with his finger.

"So?"

"So I think the paint was fresh when it started raining. He was still painting when the rain began."

"Ah," Janet Pete said. "So maybe there was a witness. Maybe . . ." Her voice trailed off, turning squeaky. She shrank away from the slab where she had been leaning, away from a buzzing sound.

"Jim," she whispered. "Don't tell me that's what I think it is."

"Only if you don't think it's a rattlesnake," Chee said. "Move back toward me. It's under the edge of that slab. See it?"

Janet made no effort to see it. "Let's go," she said. And went, and it was still light enough to see that the old green Bronco II was no longer parked behind the junipers.

She rolled the Toyota to a halt under the cottonwood tree that shaded Jim Chee's home—a well-scuffed and dented aluminum trailer parked on the low north bluff of the San Juan River. Chee made no move to get out. He was waiting for her to turn off the ignition. She left the motor running and the headlights on.

"The only other time I was here you had a pregnant cat," she said. "Remember that? It seems like a long time ago."

"I didn't have a cat," Chee said. "It was just hanging out here."

"You were looking out after it." She grinned at him. "Remember? You were afraid a coyote was going to get it. And I thought about getting one of those cases they ship animals in on airplanes to use as a cat house. Coyote-proof. And you bought one in Farmington. What happened?"

"You moved away," Chee said. "You followed your boyfriend to Washington and joined his law firm and got rich and came home again."

"I meant what happened to the cat," Janet said.

"I couldn't deal with the cat," Chee said. "It was a *biligaana* cat. Ran away from some tourists I guess. And I thought maybe it could become a natural Navajo Reservation–type cat and live on its own. But it wasn't working."

"But what happened?"

"I put it in the shipping case and sent it to Mary Landon," Chee said.

"Your white schoolteacher," Janet said.

"White schoolteacher, but not mine," Chee said. "She moved back to Wisconsin. Going to graduate school."

"Not yours anymore?"

"I guess maybe she never was."

They sat in the Toyota considering this, listening to the engine run.

Janet looked at him. "You all right now?"

"More or less," Chee said. "I guess so."

They considered that.

"How about you?" Chee said. "How about your ambitious lawyer? I don't remember his name. How about your own ambitions?"

"He's back in Washington. Getting rich, I guess. And here I am, trying to defend a destitute drunk who won't even tell me he didn't do it."

Chee, who had been listening very, very carefully, heard nothing much in her voice. Just a flat statement.

"You're all right now? Is that the message you're sending me?"

"We don't write," she said, voice still flat. "I guess so. Except it leaves you feeling stupid. And used. And confused."

"I'll make some coffee," Chee said.

No response. Janet Pete merely looked out the windshield, as if she was seeing something in the darkness under the cottonwoods.

"Maybe somebody told you about my coffee," Chee said. "But I don't boil it anymore. Now I've got some of these things where you put a little container on top of the cup, and coffee grounds in the container, and pour boiling water through. It's much better."

Janet Pete laughed and turned off the ignition.

The coffee was, in fact, excellent. Hot and fresh. She was tired and she sipped it gratefully, surveying Jim Chee's narrow quarters. Neat, she noticed. That surprised her. Everything in place. She glanced at his bed—a blanket-covered cot suspended from the wall. Monastic was the word for it. And above it, a shelf overflowing with books. She recognized Joseph Campbell's *The Power of Myth*, Buchanan's *A Shining Season*, Momaday's *The Way to Rainy Mountain*, and Zolbrod's *Dine Bahane*, which had seemed to her to be the best translation of the Navajos' origin story. Odd that Chee would be reading a white man's version of the Navajo Bible.

"You still planning to be a medicine man?" she asked.

"Someday," Chee said. "If I live long enough."

She put down her cup. "It's been a long day," she said. "I don't think I learned much useful. I don't think I answered any questions about Ashie Pinto. Like how he got there. Or why. Or who killed Officer Nez."

"That's the only one I can answer," Chee said. "Your client did it. I don't know why. Neither does he, exactly. But the reason was rooted in whiskey. The Dark Water. That's what the Navajo word for it means in English."

Janet let all that pass. "How about you?" she asked. "You think we solved any mysteries?"

Chee was leaning against the stove, holding his cup clumsily in his left hand. He sipped. "I think we added a new one. Why Mr. Ji lied to us."

"How?"

"He said he didn't meet anyone on the way home. He must have seen me coming toward him, just as he was turning off Route 33 onto the gravel."

"Maybe he forgot," Janet said. "It's been weeks."

"I had my siren going and my cop lights blinking."

Janet considered that. "Oh," she said. "You'd think he'd remember that."

"He would have just driven past a fire. A big one not far off the road. Then here comes a cop car, siren going. This isn't Chicago. Nothing much happens out here. He would have remembered."

She frowned. "So what does it mean—that he was pretending he was there when he actually wasn't? Or pretending he didn't see your patrol car? That wouldn't make sense. Or, maybe somebody else was driving his car and he was covering for them. Or . . . what?" She rubbed the back of her hand across her forehead, picked up the cup again and drained it. "I'm too damn tired to think about it," she said. "And I've got to go. Got to drive down to Window Rock tonight."

"That's too far," Chee said. "Two hard hours. Just stay here." He paused, gestured. "I'll roll my sleeping bag out on the floor."

They looked at each other. Janet sighed.

"Thanks," she said. "But Emily's expecting me."

Emily. Chee vaguely remembered the name. Someone Janet had shared an apartment with when she worked in Window Rock.

He stood in the doorway watching the Toyota on its climb back up to the road, then sat on the bunk and removed his shoes. He was tired, but the coffee would keep him awake. He unbuttoned his shirt and slipped it off over the bandage, yawning.

Three new questions added today, he thought. Not just why Mr. Ji had lied. There was also the methodical insanity of the painter to puzzle over. And most important of all, there was Janet Pete.

7

THE VOICE OF Ashie Pinto had an odd sort of singsong quality through the earphones Jim Chee was wearing. It rose and fell, recounting the time in myth when Changing Woman had her second menstrual period.

"They say that much time had passed but I don't know how much in days as we count them now. The old men would tell about this very carefully. Careful not to make any mistakes, they would tell it, but if they told the number of the days I do not remember that now. They told how First Man had instructed Changing Woman, and First Woman had watched after her, and I think they must have told Changing Woman to tell them when her second period began. And when it did, Talking God came to the place there where the Holy People were staying near Huerfano Mesa. He came to the hogan First Man had built east of the mesa. They say that Calling God came with him but they say Talking God was in charge of it."

Pinto's voice shifted from singsong into a creaky-voiced chant. Chee recognized one of the Talking God songs from the Blessing Way. He had memorized that ceremonial himself, and given it twice when his ambition to be a medicine man had been alive and thriving.

" *'e ne ya!* Now I am the child of Changing Woman. My moccasins are of white shell . . ."

The earpiece of the tape player was hurting Chee's earlobe. He listened to another couple of minutes of the tape, noticing that Pinto's version was just a little different in phrasing from the chant Frank Sam Nakai had taught him. His maternal uncle was Hosteen Nakai, and he was a medicine man of good reputation. Chee tended to consider Nakai's versions correct and to disapprove of variations. He pushed the fast-forward button and looked around him.

The reading room of the Reserve Section of the University of New Mexico Library was almost empty. The row of tables was vacant except for him and a skinny, middle-aged man working his way methodically through boxes that seemed to be filled with old postcards and letters. In the silence, the sound of the tape racing over the reel seemed loud. Chee stopped it sooner than he had intended and listened again.

". . . way out there north of Ladron Butte. That's what my grandfather told me. He said that the Utes used to cross the San Juan River upstream from where Montezuma Creek is now, and they'd come down Tsitah Wash. That's the route they liked to take in those days. They'd ride up the wash and come out there where Red Mesa school is now, and then go east of Tohatin Mesa and try to catch the people who lived around Sweetwater. He said a lot of the Mud Clan People used to grow corn and beans and peaches there in those days, and the Utes would try to kill the men and steal the horses and the women and children. He said in those days when his father was a boy the Mexicans used to pay sometimes a hundred dollars for a Navajo child there in Santa Fe where they sold them. And then when the *biligaana* came in the price got higher and . . ."

Chee took off the headset and pushed the rewind button. He was wasting his time. All he had accomplished by coming here was to confirm what Janet Pete had told him. Ashie Pinto had been discovered long ago by the academic world as a source of what academics treasure. He knew the old tales that contain the history of the Dinee. And he knew the story of how the Holy People had created the humans who were to become the Navajo clans. Wonderful. But what did it have to do with the murder of Delbert Nez?

Chee shifted his weight in the hard chair, stretched his legs and thought about that—reexamining the thinking that had led him here. The question that troubled him most wasn't motive for murder. He knew the motive. Whiskey. *Todilhil*, the Navajos had named it. Water of Darkness if you translated that word into *biligaana* language. But Navajos sometimes mispronounced it. *Todilhaal,* they'd say. Making it mean "sucking in darkness," and enjoying the wry irony of the pun. The savagery of whiskey erased the need for a motive. No Navajo policeman—or any policeman—had to relearn that message. Death slept in the bottle, only waiting to be released, and every policeman knew it. The question that nagged at Chee was a different one. What motivated the old man to come halfway across Arizona into New Mexico to an empty place beside a lonely road? There had to be a reason for that. And how the devil did he get there? Pinto made tapes for the scholars. Maybe he had been working for a scholar that day. Maybe a check of scholars who harvested Ashie Pinto's vast memory would provide a list of names. Leads. Maybe listening to the tapes these harvesters of memory collected would tell him what attracted Pinto to the Ship Rock country. Maybe not. Whatever the truth of that, Chee now had his list of who had made these tapes.

He looked at the notebook.

Professor Christopher Tagert, University of New Mexico, Department of History.

Professor Roger Davenport, University of Utah, Department of Anthropology.

Professor Louisa Bourebonette, Northern Arizona University, Department of American Studies.

Professor Alfonso Villareal, University of New Mexico, Language and Linguistics.

Perhaps there were others. These names simply represented tapes of Pinto's recollections available in this library. If others existed in any library they could be found, copied, and sent here. The very pleasant woman at the Special Collections desk had assured him of that. Chee decided not to bother. The only thing that seemed even vaguely promising was one of the Tagert tapes. In it, Pinto was remembering what his grandfather had told him about two white men being killed somewhere south of the San Juan and east of the Chuska. Tagert's cross-examination focused on where the two had come from, when it had happened, and where they had died. Pinto's answers had seemed vague but Tagert hadn't pursued it.

Perhaps there was a later tape. He'd look Tagert up in the faculty directory, call him, and ask about it.

He checked in the tapes and the tape player at the desk.

"I noticed you didn't sign the register," the woman at the desk told him. "We ask people to do that." She pointed to the ledger open on the table beside the door.

Chee filled in his name and address, left the space for "academic department" blank, and jotted "Ashie Pinto tapes" in the "material required" space, and then noted the date and the hour checked out and in. The name on the line above was John Todman. He noticed the old pictures Todman was examining were listed as "Golightly mining camp photographs."

Who else, he wondered, would be interested in Ashie Pinto's old tapes? Probably no one. He turned the page, scanned it. Turned it again. And again. And again. Six pages back, on a page where the first dates were mid-July, he found the legend "Navajo language tapes—Pinto."

The person who signed for them was William Redd.

Chee pursed his lips. He turned the page again. William Redd had also required the same tapes the previous day, and the day before, and the day before that. He jotted the name and address in his notebook and glanced at his watch.

It was still early. He would drive past that address and see if an old green Bronco II was parked there, with REDDNEK vanity plates.

8

JIM CHEE IN Albuquerque was Jim Chee separated from his vehicle—a duck out of water. He had left his pickup at the Farmington airport yesterday, flown Mesa to Albuquerque, and taken a taxi to his motel. This morning he'd called a cab again to get to the University Medical Center for his appointment at the Burn and Trauma Center. His medical insurance would pay for all that. But taxis were expensive and, like all cities of the trans-Mississippi West, Albuquerque had grown on the presumption that humans over fourteen were driving themselves around in their own cars. There was some bus service if you understood how to use it. Chee didn't, and taxicabs made Chee uneasy.

Now, afoot at the university library, Chee did a typical Western thing. He called a friend to ask for a ride.

"I'm supposed to be working," Janet Pete said.

"This will be working. Pick me up in the parking lot behind Zimmerman Library and we'll go work some more on the Ashie Pinto business."

"Like what?" Janet sounded suspicious.

"Remember you noticed that REDDNEK vanity plate on the Bronco parked out by the lava? Well, I was in the Reserve Room listening to Ashie Pinto tapes and I noticed a guy named Redd had been checking them out. R-E-D-D. Like on the plate. He'd checked them out for four consecutive days just about a week before the murder."

As Chee said it, it sounded monumentally trivial. He expected Janet to say something like "So what?" Instead she said nothing at all.

"Well?" Chee said. "Is that a good enough excuse?"

"I can't right now, Jim. I'm right in the middle of finishing something. With people waiting. Can I pick you up in an hour? Hour and a half?"

"Good enough," Chee said, trying to keep from feeling disgruntled, thinking that Janet was doing something important while he was killing idle time, wondering what she was thinking. "I'll walk over to the Union and drink coffee."

Walking across the brick-paved mall he had another idea. Since he couldn't check on Redd now, he'd go find Professor Tagert, while he was waiting, and see if Tagert could tell him anything.

The Department of History had moved since Chee's days on the campus. He found it in a handsome old building he remembered as a dormitory.

The woman at the desk in the department office looked at him curiously, taking in the bandage on his hand first, and his being a Navajo second. "Dr. Tagert?" she said, and chuckled. She sorted quickly through papers on the desk and extracted what looked like a list. "He has office hours this afternoon. Right now in fact. And his office is room 217." She gestured down the hallway and chuckled again. "I wish you luck."

The door of 217 was open.

Chee looked into a cluttered room, lit by two dusty windows, divided by two long desks placed back to back in its center. Books were everywhere, jamming bookcases that occupied the walls, stacked on chairs, tumbled out of untidy piles on the desks. Behind the nearest desk, her back to Chee, a woman was typing.

Chee tapped at the door.

"He's still not here," the woman said without looking around at him. "We haven't heard from him."

"I'm looking for Professor Tagert," Chee said. "Any idea where I could find him?"

"None," she said, and turned around, looking at Chee over the tops of reading glasses. "Which class are you in?"

"I'm a cop," he said. He fished out his identification and handed it to her. Not a worry in the world if the Bureau bitched about him nosing into an FBI case. He was going to quit anyway.

She looked at the identification, at him, at his damaged hand. She was a plump woman in her late twenties, Chee guessed, with a round, good-natured face and short brown hair.

"On duty?"

Shrewd, Chee thought. "More or less," he said. "I'm working on a case that involves a man Dr. Tagert did some business with. I wanted to see what Dr. Tagert could tell me about this guy."

"Who is it?" She smiled at him, shrugged. "None of my business, maybe. But I'm Tagert's teaching assistant. Maybe I could help."

"Where would Tagert be, this time of day?"

She laughed. "I can't help you with that. He's supposed to be sitting right there—" she pointed across the desk "—having his office hours. And he was supposed to be here all last week, meeting his classes. And the week before that, attending the presemester faculty meetings. Nobody knows where the hell he is." She pointed across the desk at a stack of envelopes overflowing a wire basket on the adjoining desk. "Unopened mail," she said.

Chee looked at the stack. A lot of mail.

"From when? How long has he been gone?"

"I saw him at the end of summer session." She laughed again but there was no humor in it. "Or almost the end. He usually manages to quit a little early. Had me grade his papers for him and turn in his grades. He said he had to get going on some research."

Chee found himself a lot more interested. "My name's Jim Chee," he said.

"Oh," she said. "I'm Jean Jacobs." She held out her hand.

Chee shook it.

"Can I sit down?"

She gestured toward a chair. "Move the books."

He sat. "Doesn't anybody know where he is? How about Mrs. Tagert?"

"They're separated," Jacobs said. "I called her when the department chairman first got excited about finding him. She said she didn't know and she didn't want to know and if I found him to please not tell her about it."

"Strange," Chee said.

"Not really," Jacobs said. "Dr. Tagert wouldn't be a happy man to live with. In fact . . ." She let that trail off, unfinished.

"I meant strange nobody knows where he is," Chee said. "You'd think he'd keep the department informed."

"No you wouldn't," Jacobs said. "Not if you knew him."

Chee was remembering his own days as an undergraduate here. Usually things had been fairly well organized, but not always. And it had seemed to him that the tenure/academic freedom system made faculty members almost totally independent.

"What's the chairman doing about it?"

"He's pissed off. He got me to start Tagert's Trans-Mississippi West class. And I met with his seminars just to tell those poor souls what he'll expect, hand out the reading lists, and all that. And then the dean called and wanted to know when he'd be back, and what he was doing—as if it was my fault." Jean Jacobs's expression soured at the memory. "I hope the Navajos got him," she added.

"Is that where he was going? To the Navajo Reservation?"

"Who knows?" she said. "Or gives a damn. But that's where he'd been working."

"You know what he was working on?"

"Vaguely. It had to be cops and robbers. That's his field. 'Law and Order in the Old West.' He's The Authority in that particular category." She paused. "Or so he tells everybody."

"Do you know if he was working on that with a Navajo named Ashie Pinto?"

"Sure," she said. "Pinto was one of his informants this summer. For old stories and things like that." Her eyes went from Chee's hand to his face. "Chee," she said, recognition dawning. "You're the one who arrested Mr. Pinto. You got yourself burned trying to pull that other policeman out of the car."

Clearly Jean Jacobs was impressed.

"I'm on leave," Chee said, indicating the hand and feeling embarrassed. "But I'm trying to find out what Pinto was doing out there. Where the crime was committed. How he got there. So forth. And Pinto won't talk about it."

Jean Jacobs had another question. "Why did he kill the policeman?"

"He was drunk," Chee said. It irritated him that it didn't sound like a convincing motive. "Very drunk."

Jean Jacobs was looking at Chee. Smiling. Approving.

"I thought maybe Professor Tagert could tell me something helpful. Maybe he was doing something for Tagert. Working with him on something."

"It might show in his calendar," Jean Jacobs said. "Let's look."

Tagert's desk calendar was open to the second week in August. The spaces under Monday through Thursday were mostly filled with jottings—Friday, Saturday, and Sunday were blank except for a diagonal line drawn across them and the legend "Go hunting." Just above the Wednesday space the words "pick up Oldfart" were written in a neat, precise hand.

Chee indicated it with his finger.

"I don't know who that means," Jacobs said. "I'm not his TA because I like him," she explained. "He's chairman of my dissertation committee. I'm trying to get a doctorate in history. Doing it on the impact of the trading post system on the Western tribes. That falls into Doctor Tagert's field so he's chairman of my committee—like it or not."

"He was here when I was a student," Chee said. "I remember now. One of my friends told me to avoid Professor Tagert."

"Good thinking," Jacobs said. "Sound advice."

"Except now. Now it looks like he had himself scheduled to pick up somebody, maybe Mr. Pinto, the day before Mr. Pinto shot a policeman. Now I think Tagert could tell me a lot."

"Well," Jean Jacobs said, "I wish I could help you find him." She sorted aimlessly through the papers on the desktop, as if some clue to Tagert's whereabouts might be among them. Chee flipped forward in the desk calendar. The next week was blank. The following page was cluttered with notations of committee meetings, luncheon engagements, numbers to be called. "Looks like he intended to get back before classes started," Chee said.

"I noticed that."

He flipped the pages backward, reentering August, moving out of the time when Nez was dead, to the day Nez died because Chee hadn't done his job. That page was blank.

Jean Jacobs must have been watching his face.

"What's wrong?"

"Nothing," Chee said. "Just remembering."

He turned the pages back to the date where Tagert had left it, and back another page to a week when Chee had been a happy man. That week, too, was cluttered with the busy Tagert's notations.

Among them, near the bottom, in the space left for Friday, Tagert had written: "Find out what Redd wants." That and a telephone number.

9

REDD ANSWERED THE telephone.

"Jim Chee?" he said. "Chee. Are you the cop who arrested Old Man Pinto?"

"Right," Chee said. He was surprised. But after all, there had been a lot in the paper about it. And Redd seemed to be involved, somehow, in this odd affair. "That's what I'd like to talk to you about. What you know about Pinto."

"Damn little," Redd said. "But go ahead and ask. What do you want to know?"

"How about me coming over? I hate to talk on the telephone."

"Sure," Redd said, and he gave Chee his address.

Janet Pete was waiting in the lot behind Zimmerman Library, with the unhappy, nervous look of people who are parked in loading zones.

"You're late," she said. "You said an hour. The cops already made me move twice."

"It was you who said, and you said an hour and a half or so," Chee said. "By Navajo time it is now just a tiny bit past the so."

Janet snorted. "Get in," she said. "You're sure getting a lot of mileage out of that sore hand."

Redd's address was in Albuquerque's student ghetto—a neighborhood of small frame-stucco bungalows left over from the 1940s with weedy yards and sagging fences. Redd's residence was behind such a bungalow in what had once been a double garage. The rusty Bronco II with the REDDNEK plate was parked beside it, and Redd himself was standing in the door watching them as Janet Pete pulled up.

He was a tall man with athlete's shoulders, but the first thing Chee noticed was red hair, a red mustache, and a long, narrow face sprinkled with freckles.

"Yaa' eh t'eeh," he said, handling the Navajo glottal sounds perfectly. "William Odell Redd," the man said, holding out his hand to Janet Pete, "but people call me Odell. And you'd be?"

"Janet Pete," she said, "and this is Jim Chee."

Odell Redd was grinning broadly at Chee. "That's the hand you got burned," Redd said. "I read about that. But come on in. You want a drink?"

The interior of Redd's apartment was jammed but orderly. Except for books. Most of them concerned linguistics. Dictionaries were everywhere, English and foreign, ranging from French to Quechua. There was a Cherokee dictionary and beside it *Navajo Tonal Syntax*. Books were stacked on all flat surfaces. There was even a dictionary on the battered table in the center of what served as both Redd's living room and bedroom. But that was an incongruous *Dictionary of Stamps*. Other books cluttering the tabletop involved coins. The *Macmillan Encyclopedic Dictionary of Numismatics* was open, surrounded by tidy rows of pennies. More pennies were piled into three cigar boxes.

"Take that there," Redd told Janet, pointing to an overstuffed chair in the corner. The burden of books it had once held now stood in a tidy stack on the linoleum floor beside it—cleared away, Chee guessed, to make room for his coming. "I'll fix a place here for Mr. Chee to sit."

Redd lifted a huge Spanish-English dictionary and two smaller ones from a kitchen chair and pushed aside enough pennies to make room for them on the table. Then he sat down himself, reversed on a kitchen chair, leaning across its wooden back, looking first at Janet Pete and then at Chee.

"Didn't I see you two out there south of Ship Rock the other evening? Out there south of Highway 33?"

"That's right," Chee said.

"Interesting country," Redd said. "You probably know more about it than I do—being Navajos. All those lava flow ridges and outcrops and things. There's supposed to be a place out there somewhere where witches get together. Initiate people as skinwalkers. That sort of thing."

"You have any idea what Pinto was doing out there?" Janet asked.

Redd smiled at her. "I'll bet you're his kinfolks," he said. "Pinto, he's Mud Clan. Are you related?"

"I'm his lawyer," Janet said.

"Won't he tell you, then? I mean what he was doing out there that night. When he shot the policeman."

Janet hesitated. She glanced at Chee, uncertain. Chee said: "Pinto won't talk about it."

"I sort of got that impression from the papers," Redd said. "It said he was drunk. Said double the legal level. Maybe he just doesn't remember."

"Maybe not," Chee said. "Any idea how he could have gotten out there?"

Redd denied it with a shake of his head. "But the old man had to get there some way or other. Two hundred miles, more or less, is too far to walk. Even for a Navajo. You wouldn't think somebody would just drop him off way out there and leave him. And otherwise, you'd think the cops would have seen somebody driving away."

"Nobody saw anything as far as we know," Janet said. "Jim got there just after it happened and he didn't see anybody. And Mr. Ji came by just about before that, and he didn't either."

Redd looked puzzled. "Mr. Gee?"

"Mr. Ji," Janet said. "J-I but it sounds like 'Gee.' It's Vietnamese. He's a teacher at Ship Rock."

"Oh," Redd said. "Anyway, the best I can do about what Pinto was doing out there is guess at it. I think he was working for Professor Tagert."

Chee waited for some expansion of that. None came.

"Like how?" he asked. He held up his hand. "But first answer me another one. What were you doing out there when you saw Janet and me?"

Redd laughed. "I was exercising my curiosity. I kept thinking there'd be more in the papers. You know, after the police finished their investigation, explaining what the hell was going on. There wasn't, and I kept thinking about it and I came up with a theory. So I went out to take a look and it didn't pay off."

"What's the theory?"

"I had the notion that Pinto had found Butch Cassidy for Tagert," Redd said.

He smiled at them, waiting.

Finally, Janet said: "Butch Cassidy?"

Redd nodded. "What do you know about Western history?" he asked. "I mean about the academic politics of Western history."

"Little bit of the history. No politics," Chee said.

"Well, the guru for years in that field was Frederick Jackson Turner. He died back in the thirties, I think. Taught at Harvard and way back at the end of the nineteenth century he came up with this theory that the wide open western frontier had free land, gold, silver, grazing for anybody who could take it—" Redd paused, looking slightly abashed "—take it away from the Indians, I mean. Anyway, he thought this changed European immigrants into a new kind of people. Made democracy work. Turner and his followers dominated academic Western history down through this century. The Anglo white man was the hero and there wasn't much attention paid to the Spanish, or the French, or the Indians. But now there's a new wave. Donald Worster at the University of Kansas, Patricia Limerick at Colorado University, Tagert here, a guy named Henderson at UC Berkeley, and a few others are the leaders. Or, at least Tagert would like to be one."

Redd paused, looking from one to the other. "This takes a little time to explain."

"No rush," Janet said.

"Well, the way I understand this feud started, this Dr. Henderson wrote a textbook, and Tagert did a paper criticizing part of it, and then Henderson took a whack in *Western History Quarterly* at a paper Tagert had done about the Hole-in-the-Wall Gang." Redd paused again. "I should have explained that Tagert and Henderson both specialize in law and order—or the lack of it—on the frontier. To get to the point, they hate each other's guts. And Tagert thinks he's onto something that will put Henderson down. It involves something he learned from Pinto."

"You're one of Tagert's students?" Janet asked.

Chee felt his jaw tighten. This interruption broke the flow of whatever Redd was trying to tell them. And, by Navajo standards, such an interruption was rude. One let a speaker finish, and then waited to make sure he was indeed finished, before one spoke. But then Janet Pete was really

Navajo only by blood and birth. She hadn't been raised on the Reservation in the Navajo Way. Had never had a *kinaalda* to celebrate her puberty, had never been taught . . .

"No way," Redd said. "I studied it down at UTEP. But you can't make a living at it. Now I'm working on a doctorate in linguistics. There's a better chance of a teaching job and if you can't get that, you can be a translator. Lot of people need them. Oil companies. Export-import. Law firms. Lots of jobs."

"But you know a lot about history, and Tagert," Janet said.

"I know a lot about Tagert," Redd replied. "A lady who works for him is a good friend of mine."

"Jean Jacobs?" Janet said. "Jim told me he met her today at Tagert's office. She was very helpful."

"Nice gal," Redd said, with an expression that said he meant it. "We go way back."

Chee found himself feeling impatience—a rare emotion with him. Wishing he had left Janet Pete behind. Wanting to get on with it.

"Do you know enough about Tagert to have any idea where he might be?" He noticed his tone wasn't right. So did Redd. So did Pete.

"No," Redd said. "No idea, really." He got up, turned his chair around, and sat again.

The conversation had become formal. Ah, well, Chee thought, I've screwed up. He sensed Janet Pete's eyes on him. Time to pull the rabbit from the hat. But he had no rabbit. He felt disgusted with himself. "You said you'd seen us out near the place where Pinto killed Delbert Nez. You said you were checking on a theory."

"I was just curious," Redd said. "I know Mr. Pinto some. I wondered what he could be doing out there."

"You started to tell us that Pinto was working for Dr. Tagert. To tell us what he was doing. Something about Western history and a professor named Henderson, and—"

"Oh, yeah. I drifted away from the point I was trying to make. Well, this Henderson is out with a new book, about banditry, organized gangs, so forth, but mostly it's about the Pinkerton organization." Redd paused, glanced at them. "You know about the Pinkertons?"

Chee nodded.

"Well, they're supposed to have hounded Butch Cassidy out of the country. About 1901. Down to Argentina and then to Bolivia. Well, Henderson had gone down there and dug into the records at La Paz, old military records, and established from the official report all the details of how this Bolivian mounted infantry patrol caught the two of 'em in a little village and shot 'em. Nothing much new in it, except the details. Thing is, Tagert doesn't think it happened that way."

Redd paused, awaiting some reaction. In a second or two he got one.

"That's the way it was in the movie," Janet said.

Redd looked surprised. "Movie?"

"*Butch Cassidy and the Sunshine Kid*, I think it was. Robert Redford and somebody-or-other. And the Bolivian army kills them." Janet shuddered. "Blows them all to pieces. Gruesome."

It wasn't the reaction Redd had expected, but he went on. Enjoying the attention, Chee thought sourly, and then was disgusted with himself for his bad temper. Redd could hardly be more cooperative. He seemed to be one of those perpetual graduate students who inhabit the fringes of every university—but a decent sort of fellow.

Redd was telling them that Tagert didn't believe Cassidy had been killed in Bolivia. Tagert believed part of the tale told by Cassidy's kinfolks. The family claimed that Cassidy had slipped back into the United States in 1909, had bought a farm under an assumed name, had lived out his life as a law-abiding citizen, and had finally died as an old, old man about 1932. Tagert believed some of that. But not the law-abiding part.

"He published a paper in *Western Archives* about ten years ago, connecting Cassidy with a 1909 bank robbery in Utah," Redd said. "In stuffy old history faculties that stirred up a controversy, and Henderson blew him out of the water. He found out that Tagert had relied on some old trial testimony that had since been discredited. That infuriated Tagert. And this new book . . ." Redd grinned broadly. "Jean said Tagert was absolutely livid. In a downright rage. Stomping around the office, having a regular tantrum." He laughed, shook his head, savoring the memory.

"I take it that Jean Jacobs doesn't care much for the professor," Janet said.

Redd's delight vanished. "Does the slave love her master?" Redd asked. "That's what we are. Lincoln didn't mention graduate students when he issued the Emancipation Proclamation. We're the Grand Republic's last vestige of indentured labor. We do the master's research for him, or we don't get our dissertation approved. Then you don't get the union card."

Chee swallowed. How did all this Cassidy stuff relate to Ashie Pinto? How could it? But he wasn't going to show impatience again. He would behave like a Navajo. He would endure.

"I remember how it was in law school," Janet said. "If you were working your way through."

"Anyway," Redd said, "old Tagert had dug out an old newspaper account of a train robbery up in Utah. I think it was the newspaper at Blanding. Three men, one of them killed, and the other two getting away and some people on the train claiming one of the robbers was Cassidy. He found a later account reporting that the two bandidos had turned up in Cortez, and got away again, and the posse had chased them south and lost track of 'em south and west of Sleeping Ute Mountain. Again, one of the cops said the blond bandit was Butch Cassidy. He claimed he'd known him way back when Cassidy was connected with the Hole-in-the-Wall Gang."

Redd paused. Shook his head. "Pretty slim evidence, but it was all Tagert had, and he used it in that paper, along with what Cassidy's kinfolks had said, and—like I said—he got blown out of the water by Henderson's Bolivian stuff." Redd shook his head again, expression wry.

Being raised Navajo, Jim Chee understood how human nature affected storytellers and how they worked an audience. Now, at last, Redd would tell them something pertinent.

"He had nothing but that." Redd looked at Chee. The dramatic pause. "Then Ashie Pinto picked up Butch Cassidy's trail on the Big Reservation."

10

JOE LEAPHORN—A practical man—handled it by telephone. He got Professor Tagert's home number in Albuquerque from information. No one answered. He called the university switchboard for Tagert's office number. There a woman answered. She said her name was Jean Jacobs, Tagert's teaching assistant. From Jacobs, Leaphorn learned two interesting facts.

First, Tagert was two weeks overdue for his academic duties and—if Jacobs knew what she was talking about—no one seemed to know his whereabouts.

Second, the arresting officer in the Pinto case, Jim Chee, off duty and on convalescent leave, was performing as Chee performed all too often—a mile outside the rules. He had presented himself at Tagert's office asking questions. How could Chee have come to know about Tagert?

Thinking of this, Leaphorn found himself violating one of his own rules. He was allowing his mind to shift back and forth between two problems—Tagert and Chee—and thus getting nowhere on either. Chee could wait. First he would see if he could fit Tagert's absence from his university classrooms into this puzzle.

Leaphorn swiveled his chair to face the map that dominated his wall behind his desk. It was a magnified version of the "Indian Country" map produced by the Automobile Club of Southern California. Smaller versions were used throughout the Four Corners territory for its details and its accuracy. Leaphorn had hired a photographer to copy it and make him a double-sized print on a matte paper. Emma had pasted this to a sheet of corkboard. For years, he had sprinkled it with coded pins, using it, so he said, to reinforce his memory. Actually Leaphorn's memory was remarkable, needing no reinforcement. He used the map in his endless hunt for patterns, sequences, order—something that would bring a semblance of Navajo *hohzho* to the chaos of crime and violence.

From his desk, Leaphorn extracted a box of pins, the sort mapping companies provide. He selected three with large yellow heads—yellow being Leaphorn's code for problems with no priority beyond their inherent oddity. He stuck one in the map between Bekahatso Wash and Yon Dot Mountain, at about the place where Ashie Pinto's hogan stood. Another he placed between Birdsprings Trading Post and Jadito Wash. There Nez had lived. He put the third south of Navajo Route 33 on a line between Ship Rock and Beautiful Mountain, the place where Pinto had shot Delbert Nez. Then he leaned back and inspected his work.

The triangle formed by the pins was huge. It emphasized two points in Leaphorn's mind. The Nez home was at least 150 miles south of the Pinto place in a part of the Reservation where intercourse with both the Hopis and the busy world of the *biligaana* was easy if not inevitable. Pinto lived in a different world of the pure, traditional Navajo culture. Everything separated them. Distance. Age. Culture. And yet they had come together violently at the point of the triangle—two hundred miles from either one's home. Duty had taken Nez to that rendezvous. But what had taken Pinto there?

That was the second point. The pins made it clear he could hardly have been there by chance. One could not get from pin A at Pinto's hogan to pin C beside Navajo Route 33 without changing roads a half-dozen times. Pinto could not have simply happened past en route to somewhere else. He had gone there for a purpose. And Leaphorn's reasoning said Pinto's purpose must be linked to why the old man had killed Delbert Nez.

But three pins were not enough to tell him anything. So Leaphorn, being Leaphorn, studied the map to see if they would fit into any other pattern.

He noticed only one thing that interested him. While Leaphorn rejected traditional Navajo witchcraft beliefs and detested them, they were part of his job. Belief in witches, and fear of them, lay at the root of many of the troubles, many of the tragedies, that occupied him as a policeman.

Pin C, where Delbert Nez had died, was very close to a rugged volcanic outcropping, nameless on the map, but which local families called Tse A'Digash. Witchery Rock. Around this long irregular ridge were clustered a measles rash of red pins marked with the letter *a*. The *a* stood for *A'Digash*. Witchcraft. Each pin in the quarter-century accumulation marked some sort of disturbance, assault, threat, or misdemeanor in which fear of these so-called skinwalkers had played some part.

Leaphorn's eyes were on the map but he was seeing Tse A'Digash in his memory—an ugly black ridge of old lichen-covered lava that ran for three or four miles south of Navajo 33. Now a yellow pin stuck out in the cluster of red ones. A coincidence? Perhaps. Leaphorn had learned to be skeptical of coincidences. Perhaps that pin, too, should be red with an *a* in its center.

In fact Leaphorn had learned to be skeptical in general. He took another yellow pin from the desk drawer and stuck it in just south of Flagstaff. Professor Bourebonette had said she lived south of town. Her motivation, so she said, was merely friendship. He had absolutely no way to calculate how she actually fit into this.

Then Leaphorn picked up his phone, dialed the records office downstairs, and asked for the file on the Delbert Nez homicide.

While he waited for it, he shuffled through the folders Bolack Travel had sent him on China. One concerned a tour sponsored by the Audubon Society, which would focus on visits to bird sanctuaries. He reread parts of that. Emma had been an amateur bird watcher—keeping three feeders stocked in their backyard. The others on the trip would be interesting people, probably. But he would have nothing to talk to them about. Nothing in common. Another tour simply involved visits to cities. That left him cold. His best alternative seemed to be going alone. He would see if any of his old professors were left on the anthropology faculty at Arizona State. It wasn't likely, but it was possible. If not, maybe someone else there would help him. He'd explain he was an alum, with their master of science in anthropology degree from way back when, and he wanted to go into Asia and see if he could find any roots to his Athabaskan origins. He'd wanted to do that for years, ever since he'd become conscious as an anthropology student that his forebears had probably emerged from Mongolia. It had faded into the subconscious after he'd met Emma and married her. Emma was no traveler. Three days in Albuquerque made her vaguely uneasy, yearning for home. Three days in New York made her miserable. She would have gone with him without a murmur. But taking her would have been cruel.

When the Nez folder arrived, he was examining a picture of a Shanghai street scene, seeing himself there amid the stampede of bicycles. It depressed him.

He spent almost an hour rereading the file and jotting reminders in the slim notebook he always carried in his uniform pocket.

> Chee met car. Was it the schoolteacher's? What did he see?
> Expensive whiskey? How? Where bought?
> Pistol. Where did he get it?
> Two fifty-dollar bills? McGinnis said he was broke.
> Did Pinto have his *jish* with him? Where is it?

Then he called the FBI office at Gallup, got Jay Kennedy, and invited him to lunch.

"What do you want this time?" Kennedy asked.

"Wait a minute," Leaphorn said. "Remember. Last time somebody wanted something it was you. You wanted me to check a homicide scene for tracks."

"Which you didn't find," Kennedy said.

"Because there weren't any," Leaphorn said. "Besides, I'll buy."

"I'll have to cancel something," Kennedy said. "Is it important?"

Leaphorn considered. And reconsidered.

"Well?"

"No," Leaphorn said. He considered again. "Probably not."

He heard Kennedy sigh. "So what are we talking about? Just in case I need to look something up. Or dig into something so confidential that it might cost me my job."

"Delbert Nez," Leaphorn said.

"Oh, shit," Kennedy said. "Naturally."

"Why?"

"It was a sloppy job," Kennedy said. "Even worse than usual."

They met at the International Pancake House on old U.S. 66 and sat a while sipping coffee. The autumn sun warmed Leaphorn's shoulders through his uniform jacket and the traffic streamed by off Interstate 40. He noticed how gray Kennedy had become, how—uncharacteristic of FBI agents and of Kennedy himself—he needed a haircut. Old cops, Leaphorn thought. Two old dogs getting tired of watching the sheep. Old friends. How rare they are. The Bureau would be glad to see the last of Kennedy—exiled here years ago for some violation of the old J. Edgar Hoover prohibition against bad publicity, liberalism, or innovative thinking. The story was that Kennedy's ex-wife had been active in the American Civil Liberties Union. She had left him to marry a real estate broker, but the stigma remained.

For that matter, Leaphorn suspected there were those in his Navajo Tribal Police hierarchy who would be happy to celebrate his own retirement. He wouldn't make them wait much longer.

Kennedy had been talking about one of those endless interagency shoving matches which involve public employees—this one an effort of the Bureau of Land Management, the Forest Service, the Bureau of Indian Affairs, and "The Bureau" to make one or another of them responsible for protecting Anasazi ruins under the Antiquities Act. Leaphorn had heard a lot of it before.

Kennedy quit talking. "I'm not holding your attention," he said.

"You ever been to China?" Leaphorn asked.

Kennedy laughed. "Not yet," he said. "If the Bureau opens an office there—say in North Manchuria—I'll get the assignment."

"Think you'd like to go?"

Kennedy laughed again. "It's on my wish list," he said. "Right after Angola, Antarctica, Bangladesh, Lubbock, Texas, and the Australian outback. Why? Are you planning to go?"

"I guess not," Leaphorn said. "Always sort of wanted to. Wanted to go out in the steppe country. Outer Mongolia. The part of the world where they think the Athabaskans originated."

"I used to want to go back to Ireland," Kennedy said. "Where my great-grandfather came from. I outgrew that notion."

"Yeah," Leaphorn said. "Do you know if anybody checked on that pistol Pinto used?"

"Somebody checked," Kennedy said. "It was a common type, but I don't remember the brand. American made, I think it was, and an expensive model. It had been recently fired. The slug in Nez came from it. Check of Pinto's hand showed he'd recently fired something."

"Where did it come from?"

"No idea," Kennedy said. "The old man isn't saying. Totally silent from what I hear. I guess he bought it at some pawnshop."

"I don't think so," Leaphorn said.

Kennedy peered at him, expression quizzical. "You've been asking around," he said. "Any reason for that?"

Leaphorn made a wry face. "Turns out Ashie Pinto is sort of shirttail, linked-clan kinfolks of mine," he said. "Through Emma's clan."

"You know him?"

"Never heard of him."

"But you got roped in."

"Right," Leaphorn said. "I don't think he bought the pistol because he was broke. Not even eating money. What do you know about those two fifties he had?"

"Nothing."

"Where did Pinto get his hands on them?"

"No idea." Kennedy looked irritated. "How would we know something like that?"

"Did anybody check on the driver of the car Chee met going to the fire?"

Kennedy shook his head. "I told you it was a sloppy job. But damn it, Joe, why would they check on that? Look what you had there. No big mystery. A drunk gets arrested and kills the policeman. Doesn't even deny it. What's to investigate? I know you think we loaf around a lot, but we do have things to do."

"Did Pinto have his *jish* with him? You know where that is?"

"*Jish?*" Kennedy said. "His medicine bundle? I don't know."

"He was a shaman. A crystal gazer. If he was on a job, he'd have his crystals with him, and his *jish*."

"I'll find out," Kennedy said. "Probably he wasn't working. Left it home."

"We didn't find it at his place."

Kennedy looked at him. "You been out to his place, then."

The waitress delivered the waffles, which smelled delicious. Leaphorn applied butter, poured on syrup. He was hungry and he hadn't been hungry much lately. This Ashie Pinto business must be good for him.

Kennedy had hardly looked at his waffle. He was still looking at Leaphorn.

"We?" he said. "You been out searching Pinto's hogan? Who's we?"

"Pinto's niece," Leaphorn said. "And a woman named Bourebonette. A professor at Northern Arizona University. You guys turn up anything about her?"

"Bourebonette? No. Why would we? How would she fit into this?"

"That's what bothers me," Leaphorn said. "She says Pinto was one of her sources for myths, legends, so forth. That's her field. Mythology. She says she's into it because he's a friend. Just that."

Kennedy peered at him. "You sound like you have trouble believing that."

Leaphorn shrugged. "Sophisticated, urbane university professor. Old illiterate Navajo. And she's going to a hell of a lot of trouble."

"You're getting even worse with age," Kennedy said. "Emma used to make you a little more human." He buttered his waffle. "Okay, then. What do you think motivates the woman?"

Leaphorn shrugged again. "Maybe she's working on a book. Needs more out of him to finish it off."

"She could get to him in prison. They're not going to put somebody like that in solitary. Not even for killing a policeman."

"I don't know then. What do you think?"

"Why not just believe she's nuts? Likes the old bastard. She's doing it for humanitarian reasons. You actually went all the way out there and searched the old man's hogan?"

"I didn't search. No warrant."

"You're getting serious about this, aren't you?" Kennedy said. "You think there's something more to it than just Pinto being drunk and killing your man?"

"No," Leaphorn said. "I'm just curious." The waffle was wonderful. He chewed a second bite, swallowed, sipped his coffee. "Have you found that car that Chee saw? The old white Jeepster?"

"Didn't we already cover that? You asked me about the driver."

"And I noticed how you didn't exactly answer. You just sort of nodded, and said it had been sloppy work, and then did your little sermon about why waste time on a made case." Leaphorn was grinning at him. "When the Bureau dumps you I hope you don't get into playing poker for a profession."

Kennedy made a wry face. He chewed for a while.

"It took you longer to get to it than I expected," Kennedy said. "But you never fail to get there. Right to the touchy spot."

"Touchy?"

"How much do you know about the car?"

"Nothing," Leaphorn said. "Just what was in the report. Chee saw an old white Jeepster coming from the direction of the crime, turning on a gravel road toward Ship Rock. Chee thought it belonged to an Oriental who teaches at the high school. There was nothing in the report about checking on that car."

"They found it," Kennedy said. He eyed Leaphorn. "This is one of those 'you don't remember where you heard it' times."

"Sure," Leaphorn said.

"The car belonged to a man named Huan Ji. He teaches math at Ship Rock High School. Just been there four years. No way he'd have anything to do with this crime. He couldn't have known Pinto or Nez."

Leaphorn waited for more. Kennedy sipped the last of his coffee, signaled the pretty Zuni girl who was their waitress.

"Ready for a refill," he said, indicating his cup.

Kennedy had said all he wanted to say about Juan Gee and the car. Why?

"What was this Gee doing way out there in the rain?" Leaphorn asked. "What did he see? What did he tell you?"

Kennedy grimaced and peered across his coffee cup at Leaphorn.

"You remember the Howard case in Santa Fe. The defrocked CIA agent who was working for the State of New Mexico, and the CIA thought he had sold out to the Russians, and we had him staked out watching him until somebody could get around to filing charges. You remember."

"I remember," Leaphorn said, grinning. "The part I remember best was the ingenious way he slipped away from you guys. Had his wife drive the car."

Kennedy grinned, too, even broader than Leaphorn. "Embarrassment squared. Embarrassment to the third power," he said. The grin turned into a chuckle. "Can you imagine what it was like in the Albuquerque office when the powers found out Howard was safely behind the Iron Curtain? Hell was raised. Fits thrown. Carefully written reports were sent out explaining why it hadn't occurred to the Bureau that Howard might have his wife driving the car on the escape run."

"I can imagine the CIA people were rubbing it in."

"I think you can be sure of it," Kennedy said.

"Can I be sure that all of this is going to have some bearing on why nobody talked to this Juan Gee?"

"You can," Kennedy said. "It seems the Bureau was aware that Huan Ji was a friend of the Agency. He was a colonel in the South Vietnamese Army. In intelligence, and he was working for Washington as well as Saigon. We have this vague, scuttlebutt impression that he was one of the very hard people, involved with the sort of stuff we used to hear the horror stories about."

"Like dropping Vietcong out of helicopters so the one you didn't drop would be willing to talk?"

"I don't know," Kennedy said. "It was just gossip. But anyway he was a client, so to speak, of the CIA and so when everything went to hell over there in 1975 and the Saigon government collapsed, they got him out and helped him get started in the States."

"A Vietnamese named Juan?" Leaphorn asked.

"It's H-U-A-N and J-I. Sounds like 'Gee.' "

"So why didn't the FBI talk to him?" Leaphorn asked, thinking he already knew the answer.

Kennedy looked slightly defensive. "Why talk to him? The case was all locked up. The arrest was made. We had the smoking gun. No mystery. Nothing to resolve. We didn't really need another witness." He stopped.

"And bothering this guy would look bad to the CIA. Would maybe irritate the CIA, which is already sneering at you guys for letting Howard walk away."

"More or less, I'd say," Kennedy admitted. "I'm not privy to the upper councils, but I'd say that is a close guess."

Leaphorn ate more waffle.

"And what the hell's wrong with that? Why waste everybody's time? Why piss off the Agency? Why bother Mr. Ji?"

"I just wonder what he was doing out there," Leaphorn said. "That's all."

Kennedy finished his waffle. "I've got to go to Farmington," he said. "A hundred bumpy miles up Route 666. And then a night in a Holiday Inn."

"You sure you don't want to go to China?"

"About as much as I want to go to Farmington," Kennedy said. "And don't forget to leave a generous tip."

Leaphorn watched Kennedy leave. He saw his car pull out of the Pancake House parking lot onto old 66, heading for the long drive north to Farmington. He was still wondering what Colonel Ji was doing out in the rain by the rock where the witches gather.

11

THE HAND MAN'S reputation was as good as they get in modern medicine. He had identified himself as an "Indian Indian," smiling as he said it and giving Chee a name which Chee instantly forgot. His voice carried a slight British accent with a trace of lilt in it, and he asked his questions in a soft, gentle voice without looking at Chee, never taking his eyes off the ugly, puckered cavity burned across Chee's left palm. With the Burn Doctor, a woman named Johns, the Hand Man discussed tendon damage, ligament damage, nerve damage, regeneration of tissue, "prognosis for usage," and "viability of surgical techniques."

"You clutched the handle of a car door? Is that how I understand it? And the car was burning?" He glanced at Chee's right hand.

"But you are right-handed, is it not true? Why did you use your left hand?"

"I guess because it's natural to open the driver's door that way," Chee said. "If I had another reason I don't remember it."

"It's almost as if your subconscious sensed the forthcoming damage and protected the hand most useful to you." The Hand Man said it in a clipped, didactic tone, still staring at the angry red mass of scarring on Chee's palm, never glancing up. "Would you agree?"

"I doubt it," Chee said. "I'd guess it was also because I was going to pull

Delbert out of there with my right hand. But it's all sort of hazy to tell the truth."

"Ah, well," the Hand Man said, no longer interested. And that was that. The Burn Doctor put on a new bandage, using a different wrapping technique. She gave Chee a prescription and instructions, and said she would see him in a week.

"Well, what do you think?" he asked the Burn Doctor.

"Think?"

"About surgery. About how much use I'll regain of my fingers. Things like that?"

"We'll have to decide," the Burn Doctor said. "You'll be informed."

"Appreciate it," Chee said, but the Burn Doctor didn't notice the irony.

He used the pay telephone again. This time Janet Pete was out. She was in Santa Fe, the receptionist at the Federal Public Defender's office told him. She was involved with picking a jury for a forthcoming trial. Would she be home this evening? The receptionist had no idea.

Chee called Professor Tagert's office. Jean Jacobs answered. No, Tagert still hadn't checked in.

"Can I come over? Do you have time to talk?"

"Sure," Jacobs said. "About what?"

"Mr. Redd told us about Tagert's interest in Butch Cassidy. He said Ashie Pinto had helped Tagert find what might be Cassidy's trail. Out on the Reservation."

"Okay," Jacobs said. "I know he's obsessed with Cassidy but I don't know much about it."

Chee walked, feeling disgruntled. Janet Pete knew he would be back in Albuquerque today. He'd written her a note, telling her. So, maybe she couldn't avoid the Santa Fe duty. On the other hand, maybe she could have. Chee had been around long enough to know how priorities worked when there was a conflict between duty and desire.

He crossed the mall with fallen sycamore leaves blowing around his feet. His hand hurt. His fingers wouldn't respond properly. He felt discouraged. Blue. Bored. Undecided. He found the door of Dr. Tagert's office open. Jean Jacobs sat, elbows on desk, chin on hands, staring out the window. She looked blue, bored, and undecided.

"I'm glad to see you," Jean Jacobs said. "I've got a million things to do."

She slapped an angry palm onto a pile of paperwork. "All this goddamn Tagert work, and all my own work and—oh, to hell with it."

"Yeah," Chee said. "Sometimes that's about it."

"So screw it all," she said. "I hope you have just walked in here with something that is not only totally time-wasting but mysterious. We'll figure out how to find the vanished professor of history." She paused. "Even better, we'll figure out where they hid the bastard's body."

"I guess he's not back yet then," Chee said. He decided she wasn't going to ask him to sit down, even though she obviously expected him to stay. So he moved a stack of folders off a chair and sat.

"I think he's dead," Jacobs said. "I'll bet your Mr. Pinto shot him the same time he shot the officer."

"I think that's possible," Chee said. "But then, what happened to his body?"

Jacobs made a "who knows" gesture. "Did Odell tell you anything interesting? Or useful?"

"I'm not sure how useful. He told us all about Tagert's disagreement about Butch Cassidy with that other professor. And he told us that Pinto knew an old story about Cassidy, or some other bandido, coming across the Reservation after a robbery in Utah and getting killed by some of us Navajos. Tagert thought that maybe he could find some proof of that. And he'd given up on trying to prove Cassidy died of old age."

"I heard a little about that yarn," Jacobs said. "Not much. But I think Tagert was excited about it. That was last summer." She paused, looked at Chee, a shy look. "What did you think of him?"

"Of Redd? He seemed like a nice guy. He said you were a friend."

"Ummm," she said. "A friend."

Her expression was so sad, so close to matching Chee's own mood, that he said: "Having troubles?"

And she heard the sympathy in his voice.

"I'm just down today," she said, and laughed a shaky laugh. "You too, I'll bet. You didn't look all that cheerful anyway when you walked in."

"Yeah," Chee said. "It hasn't been one of my better days."

"Hand hurt?"

"A little."

"You look down," Jacobs said. "Troubles?"

"Not really," Chee said. He shrugged. "I was hoping to meet a friend. She had to go to Santa Fe." He considered that. "At least she said she had to go to Santa Fe."

Jacobs was frowning. "She didn't go?"

"Oh, I guess she went. I meant maybe she didn't really *have* to go."

"Oh," Jacobs said. She made a wry face. "I know *exactly* what you mean."

"I'm not sure I do," Chee said.

"I was just guessing. With me, I think it's more important for me to be with Odell than it is for Odell to be with me."

"Okay," Chee said. He laughed. "We're on the same wavelength."

"You've got a bad hand. You fly all the way in from Farmington or wherever, and your girlfriend thinks going to Santa Fe is more important."

"Maybe she couldn't get out of it. And she's not exactly my girlfriend. We're more just friends."

"Uh-huh," Jacobs said. "Like Odell said."

Chee wanted to get off this subject.

"You work for Tagert. Part-time anyway. Did you ever notice anything in the paperwork that would give you any idea what he and Pinto were doing out there?"

"I wasn't that interested, to tell the truth," she said. "You know, it seems pretty mean to me that they still have you working on this when your hand's like that. You should be on sick leave."

"Actually, I am," Chee said. "I'm doing this on my own time."

Jacobs lowered her chin, peering at him over her reading glasses, her smooth, round face furrowed by a frown. "Why? Why are you doing it?"

"I'm curious," Chee said. "I just want to find out how Hosteen Pinto got out there, and what he was doing. Things like that. It doesn't really need to be done. Not for the trial. Pinto doesn't even deny he killed Delbert. I'm just doing it because I don't have anything else to do. And nobody else gives a damn."

"Somebody else is doing it, too," Jacobs said.

"What? Who?"

"I got a call a couple of days ago. From a Navajo tribal policeman in Window Rock. He wanted to talk to Tagert. Wanted to know where he could find him."

"Who was it? You sure it was a Navajo tribal policeman? Not the FBI? Or maybe an investigator from the Federal Public Defender's office."

"It was from Window Rock. He said Navajo Tribal Police."

"What was the name?"

"A funny name. I don't remember. I remember he was a lieutenant."

"Leaphorn!"

"That was it," Jacobs said. "Lieutenant Leaphorn. Do you know him?"

Chee was thinking. He came to the only possible conclusion. "That son-of-a-bitch," he said.

Jacobs looked startled at the bitterness. She looked away, picked up a pen. Put it down.

"Sorry," Chee said.

"It sounds like you know him. Is he your boss?"

"I know him. No, he's not my boss."

"He just asked if Tagert was here. If I knew where to find him." She studied Chee. "Is it bad?"

"No," Chee said. "I don't know. It's just—"

He sighed. "You don't want to hear all this," he said.

"Yes," she said. "I do."

"It's more than curiosity with me," he began, and told her about his radio conversation with Nez, the fading in and out, the nut who painted basalt, the laughter that led him to fail his friend. He told her of arresting Pinto. He told her about Janet Pete back from Washington taking the Federal Public Defender's job and representing Pinto.

"I know she was assigned to do it. It's her job. But Janet lets me know she halfway believes Pinto didn't do it. She sees a lot of unanswered questions. What's his motive, she says. He was drunk, and he'd killed someone before when he was drunk and served time for it. And he was caught redhanded and doesn't even deny it. But for her, that's not enough." Chee shook his head.

"You think it would be kinda nice if it was enough just because you were the one who nabbed him," Jacobs said. "But you've got to consider she's his defense attorney. And she's a woman in a field men have dominated. And so she feels like she's got something to prove. At least I would. Maybe she feels like she has to prove something to you, too." Jacobs made a wry face. "You know, you've been a cop awhile. Into law enforcement. She's brand new at the game." She shrugged. "I don't know. I'm just talking."

"You are missing the implication," Chee said. He stood up. His voice had sounded stiff, but to hell with it. This woman felt like listening. He felt like letting some of this anger out. "You see, I screwed up on this. If I hadn't screwed up, I would have been there when Nez was making this arrest—or whatever he was doing—and he wouldn't have been killed. But I was over in Red Rock drinking coffee, thinking all was good because I heard Delbert laughing."

He was standing with his arms hanging by his side. That made his hand hurt. He folded his arms.

"But I did get there. Too late to help Delbert, but I got there in time to catch the man who killed him. I was a good enough cop for that."

Jacobs was silent for a while, thinking about it, her face full of sympathy. She was a talented listener. He had noticed it before. When you talked to this woman, she attended. She had all her antennae out, focused on the speaker. The world was shut out. Nothing mattered but the words she was hearing. Listening was ingrained in the Navajo culture. One didn't interrupt. One waited until the speaker was finished, gave him a moment or two to consider additions, or footnotes or amendments, before one responded. But even Navajos too often listened impatiently. Not really listening, but framing their reply. Jean Jacobs *really listened*. It was flattery, and Chee knew it, but it had its effect.

"I can see why you'd want to find Tagert. I can see why you'd want to make sure."

"Sure!" Chee said it louder than he intended. "I *am* sure. How sure can I be? The killer at the scene, drunk, with the smoking gun. He doesn't even deny it. How goddamn sure can you be?"

"It sounds sure to me," Jacobs said.

"And the FBI is happy. They took it to the federal grand jury, and got the indictment. They're ready for trial."

"This Lieutenant Leaphorn, is he—"

"A vote of no confidence," Chee said.

"The tribal police think you got the wrong man?"

"Maybe. More likely Leaphorn is freelancing. He does that some. He's sort of our supercop. Old as the hills. Knows everybody. Remembers everything. Forgets nothing. I worked with him a time or two before. Everybody does sooner or later because he handles the tough investigations wherever they are."

"You didn't get along?"

"I don't think he held me in extremely high regard," Chee said. "But we got along all right. To be fair about it. He even hired me to do a Blessing Way for him."

He saw the question in Jacobs's face.

"It's a curing ceremonial," he explained. "I'm a would-be shaman. A singer. A medicine man. *Hataalii* is the Navajo word for it. I was going to be one of the people who conducts the curing ceremonies to restore people to harmony. Or I was trying to be. Nobody seemed to want my services." He produced a humorless chuckle. "And Lieutenant Leaphorn was my only legitimate patient. Only one outside the family."

"You do sand paintings," Jacobs said. "Is that right? That's about all I know about it."

Even while he was speaking, Chee had the sensation of standing outside himself, watching and listening. He saw self-pity, and heard it. Some anger, yes. But mostly he saw a man who felt sorry for himself. He hated that in others, hated it even more in himself. Now he felt ashamed. And beyond his anger, he was suddenly aware of the implications of Leaphorn's involvement. It couldn't be merely casual. How had the lieutenant found out about Tagert? That must have taken some digging. Chee felt his anger seeping away, replaced by a sense of urgency.

"Sorry about unloading my troubles," he said. "I didn't come in here for that. I came in to see if I could look at some of the paperwork. See if maybe it would tell us what Tagert and Pinto were working on. Tell us if Tagert was with him that day."

"We can look," Jean Jacobs said. "But I don't think it's going to help much."

Look they did. But first Jean Jacobs closed the door. And locked it. "I feel sort of sneaky," she said. "Looking through the old bastard's stuff. Even though I work with a lot of it every day."

"Just remember, I'm the arresting officer," Chee said, and felt his mood improving.

The out-basket was empty. They checked the in-basket.

The mail, the memos, were a month old and, as far as Chee could tell, without relevance.

"How does he file things?" Chee asked.

"By subject, usually. Sometimes mail gets filed by name of the correspondent. Mostly by subject."

"Let's see if he has a Pinto file."

No Pinto file.

"How about a Cassidy file?"

Cassidy folders occupied half a drawer in Tagert's filing cabinet. Chee and Jacobs stacked them on his desktop and started sorting.

"What am I looking for?" Jacobs asked.

"Good question," Chee said. "Anything related to Pinto, I'd say, for starters. Anything that relates to this robbery up in Utah and the chase. Stuff like—"

"Here's stuff about the Utah robbery," Jacobs said. "Copies of newspaper stories."

The headline in the *Blanding Defender* was multiple lines, in turn-of-the-century newspaper fashion:

OLD HOLE IN WALL
GANG BELIEVED
INVOLVED IN
TRAIN ROBBERY
WITNESS SAYS HE SAW
BUTCH CASSIDY AMONG
GANG WHICH BOARDED
COLORADO & SOUTHERN
TRAIN AT FRY CREEK

WOUNDED BANDIT SAYS IT IS TRUE

DEAD BANDIT IS IDENTIFIED
AS RUDOLPH "RED" WAGONSTAFF
HIS FRIENDS SAY HE USED TO
RUSTLE CATTLE WITH CASSIDY
AND THE WYOMING WILD BUNCH

The story below repeated all that with more details and with a rehashing of what happened in the robbery. Three men had boarded the train when it stopped to pick up mail at Fry Creek. They had entered the mail car, and engaged in a gunfight with the two mail clerks. One clerk was killed, the other wounded in the upper chest. The bandit now identified as Wagonstaff was shot in the neck and died the next day in the Blanding hospital.

The bandits had stopped the train north of Blanding where an accomplice was waiting with horses. An off-duty Garfield County deputy sheriff had fired from the train window at the departing robbers. His bullet struck one in the back, causing him to fall from his horse.

The newspaper account continued:

> As their bad luck had it, this fellow was carrying the bags which contained most of the loot which had attracted the bandits. He is now in the hospital here in Blanding but the doctor has little hope for him. He told Sheriff Lester Ludlow that his name is Davis and that Butch Cassidy was leading the group.
>
> Sheriff Ludlow said most of the loot taken in the robbery was recovered in the bags Davis had been carrying—which was the payroll money for the Parker Mine. He said the bandits probably got away with no more than three or four hundred dollars—mostly in bank notes, stamps and other supplies being delivered to post offices along the route south from Salt Lake City.

The rest of the story was mostly information about the dead and wounded mail clerks and about the posse formed to pursue the bandits. Chee skipped through it hurriedly and went on to the next item. It was dated a week later. Davis had died. The posse had tracked the two survivors southward. They had been seen by a Mormon rancher near Montezuma Creek—two men with four horses. Sheriff Ludlow expressed optimism. "The Sheriff said in his telegram to this newspaper: 'They will be caught.' "

A week later, Ludlow was not making such optimistic statements. "They have slipped away onto the Navajo Reservation. We have wired authorities throughout Arizona and New Mexico to look for them."

The only mention of the robbery the following week concerned the wounded mail clerk. He was released from the hospital.

"Finding anything?" Jacobs asked. "Reading these old papers is like eating peanuts. You can't stop. Here's a piece about a stagecoach robbery. Imagine!"

"Wonder why he saved that?" Chee was thinking of motivations.

"One of the passengers said it was Butch Cassidy."

Chee was still thinking of motivations, remembering the bandits had gotten away with very little money. That led to a thought of the coin-collector books at Redd's place, the pennies on his table. If coins were involved, they'd be antiques now. And valuable.

"Redd had about a million pennies when we were there," he said. "Do you know what that's all about?"

"It's all about how a graduate student stays alive," Jacobs said. "Pays the rent. When Odell gets his paycheck, he cashes it at the bank and buys all the pennies he can afford. And then he sorts through them looking for keepers. Some of them are worth something to the collectors. Certain dates, certain mints. Maybe, for example, you find a 1947 penny minted in Baltimore might be worth a dime, or a '54 minted in Denver maybe would be worth twenty cents. He keeps those out and sells them to the coin stores, and takes the others back and buys more pennies."

"Hey," Chee said. "That's smart. How much does he make?"

She laughed. "You don't get rich. One week he found an Indian head worth almost four dollars. That week he made about five dollars an hour for his time."

"What if you found coins taken in that train robbery? Would it be like a gold mine?"

"Not really," Jacobs said. "Odell talked about that—how great it would be to find all those old coins. But he looked it up and it was a bad time for coins. They made tons of silver dollars and five-dollar gold pieces during those years. Scarcity is what makes coins expensive."

"Like how much would a nineteen-hundred silver dollar be worth?"

"Maybe twenty dollars to a coin dealer, if it was in perfect condition," she said. "And the newspaper said most of the money was bank notes."

So much for that idea. And while he was thinking that, he found what he'd been looking for without knowing he'd been looking for it.

The manila folder was labeled PINTO/CASSIDY. In it was a thick sheaf of paper, typed double-spaced.

"They say it was the summer my brother was born. That's when they say this thing happened." Penciled in the margin was the notation "1909/10?"

They say the Utes had been bad about coming down that year. They would come down that trail past Thieving Rock and Blue Hill and at night they would steal horses and sheep from the people around Teec Nos Pos in the flats around the San Juan River, and even as far over as Cineza Mesa. They say this happened several times, and one time the Utes shot at a Navajo man over there. He was out there with his sheep and those Utes shot at him and he ran away. They say it was a Piaute Clan man named Left-handed.

Now Left-handed had a son named Delbito Willie and he had married a woman of the Yucca Fruit Clan and he was living with her over on the other side of the Carrizo Mountains. But he had come over there around Teec Nos Pos to see about his brothers and sisters and everybody told him about the Utes shooting at his father.

They say this Delbito Willie talked to two of his wife's brothers, and some young men in his own Piaute Clan, and he told them they should go up north, go up there around Sleeping Ute Mountain, and they should steal some Ute horses and get all their sheep and goats back.

The Piaute Clan headman over there in those days was an old fellow they called Kicks His Horse and they talked about this idea with him, and he said they should wait. They say he said that because it was in *Yaiisjaastsoh* season, which in the *biligaana* language is Season to Plant Late Crops. They call it July. At that time there is lightning and the snakes are out feeding and then you can have the kind of curing ceremonial they would need before they went on that kind of a raid. And when they got back they would need to have an Enemy Way sing to cure them, and that could not be held either because you can't hold those ceremonials until the Season When the Thunder Sleeps. You can't hold them until the ground is frozen and the snakes are in the ground.

> But they say Delbito Willie he was angry about the Utes shooting at his father and he wanted to go anyway. He didn't care what anybody said. They say the Piaute Clan men listened to their headman and wouldn't go, so Delbito Willie went back to his wife's Yucca Fruit people and talked to them about it. He got seven of them to listen to him, mostly young men, they say, but one of them was Old Man Joseph. And so they got their best horses and they went off to the north toward Sleeping Ute Mountain. They say they forded the San Juan there at—

"Find something interesting?" Jean Jacobs was leaning over his shoulder.

"I think this is what Redd was telling us about," Chee said. "Pinto's story that puts Cassidy on the Navajo Reservation. Anyway it's about a raid to steal Ute horses. And the dates would be about right."

Chee flipped through the pages, read about Old Man Joseph being thrown from his horse. Flipped again, read about Delbito Willie deciding that they should take only horses and mules from the pastures west of Sleeping Ute Mountain and not try to drive the goats because the Utes would chase them. Flipped again, read about the two of the men splitting off from the party to head west to Teec Nos Pos, taking eleven of the Ute horses. One of the Piaute Clan men had been shot in the leg somewhere back in one of the pages Chee had skipped. But a fight with the Utes wasn't what he was looking for. He flipped again, scanning rapidly. Then he stopped.

> They say there were Hosteen Joseph and Delbito Willie and the young men from the Yucca Fruit People still on their way home then, and they were camped out for the night somewhere between Rol Hai Rock and Littlewater Wash. They say Delbito Willie had gone out to get some firewood because they were cooking two rabbits they had shot. He saw dust over to the northeast. They put out their fire and watched. These two men were riding toward Beautiful Mountain, leading a mule. It is said that these were white men. They saw where Delbito Willie had left the Ute ponies, on their hobbles down below the cliffs of that place. These two white men, they scouted all around, looking for the people who owned those

ponies, but they never did see Delbito Willie or the Yucca Fruit People with him. So they started to steal the horses. They were cutting the hobbles when Hosteen Joseph shot one of them, and the two men got back on their horses and rode away. Delbito Willie and the Yucca Fruit men were chasing them. They were shooting at them and the two men were shooting and one of them, the white man with the yellow mustaches they say it was, he shot Hosteen Joseph. The bullet hit Old Man Joseph in the chest, right below the nipple they say, and it killed him.

After that they chased the two white men. They almost got away once, but the one Hosteen Joseph had shot fell off his horse and the other one had to stop and help him back on. After that they say Delbito Willie shot the other man, but didn't kill him. And then the two white men rode their horses out into a place where there is lava flow. Where it's dangerous to ride a horse even in the daylight. The Yucca Fruit men followed slowly, keeping way back where they wouldn't get shot because that man with the yellow mustaches, they said he was a good shot even riding on a horse. Finally they found where the white men had left their horses and went up into the rocks.

Chee skipped rapidly through the rest of it. The next morning, one of the white men had tried to come out and one of the Yucca Fruit boys shot him again—they thought in the arm this time—and he went back up into the rocks. The Navajos had waited all that day, and the next. They drank up their own water, and the water canteens the white men had left on their horses, and finally—on the morning of the fourth day—Delbito Willie had climbed up into the rocks. He followed the bloody spots back into the formation until he could see the bodies of the two men. Then the group had taken the horses and returned to their place on the other side of the Carrizo Mountains. An Enemy Way was held for all of them because of their contamination with the Utes and the white men.

Chee lingered over the section in which Ashie Pinto had described the ceremonial curing—an Enemy Way and a section of the Ghostway done, apparently, for Delbito Willie alone. It stirred his memory of an Enemy Way he'd attended as a child. The cure had been conducted by a *hataalii* who had been very tall and had seemed to him then to be incredibly ancient. The patient had been Chee's paternal grandmother, a woman he had loved with the intensity of a lonely child, and the event had formed one of his earliest really vivid memories. The cold wind, the starlight, the perfume of the piñon and juniper burning in the great fires that illuminated the dance ground. Even now, he could see it all and the remembered aroma overpowered the mustiness of this office. Most of all, he remembered the *bataalii* standing gray and thin and tall over his grandmother, holding a tortoiseshell rattle and a prayer plume of eagle feathers, chanting the poetry from the emergence story, making Old Lady Many Mules one with White Shell Girl, restoring her to beauty and harmony.

And restore her it had. Chee remembered staying at the old woman's place, playing with his cousins and their sheepdogs, seeing his grandmother happy again, hearing her laughter. She had died, of course. The disease was lung cancer, or perhaps tuberculosis, and people with such diseases died—as all people do. But it had been that cure that had caused him to think that he would learn the great curing ways, the songs and the sand paintings, and become a *bataalii* for his people. Unfortunately, his people showed no sign of wanting him as one of their shamans. He must have laughed because Jacobs asked, "Something funny? You find something interesting?"

"Just thinking," Chee said.

"About what?" Jacobs said. "You're not supposed to be holding out on me."

"I was reading what Ashie Pinto told Tagert about these Navajo horse thieves," Chee said. "They had a curing ceremonial for them when they got home and I was remembering my own boyish dreams about becoming a medicine man."

Jacobs was looking at him, eyes curious. Or perhaps sympathetic. Perhaps both. Their eyes held. Chee made a wry mouth. Jacobs looked down.

"Anything in there that helps get Tagert home so I can quit doing all his work?" she asked.

Chee shrugged. "No," he said. "Or if there is, I don't understand it."

But he was thinking about the Ghostway. He didn't know it. Frank Sam Nakai, who was a respected *bataalii* and Chee's maternal uncle and mentor in all things metaphysical, didn't know it either. Why would part of it have been done for Delbito Willie and for no one else on the raiding party? And why had Ashie Pinto, with his Navajo storyteller's predilection for telling everything in exhaustive detail, skipped so quickly over this?

Maybe Pinto would tell him that, even if he would tell him nothing else.

12

As was his fashion (except when it violated his sense of order), Leaphorn went through channels. The former Vietnamese colonel named Huan Ji lived in Ship Rock, which was in the jurisdiction of the Ship Rock subagency of the Navajo Tribal Police. Leaphorn dialed the Ship Rock Tribal Police office and asked for Captain Largo.

"I've heard of him," Largo said. "He teaches at the Ship Rock High School. Math, I think it is, or maybe one of the sciences. But we never had any business with him. What's he up to?"

Leaphorn told him about the conversation with Kennedy.

"I remember now," Largo said. "It was his car Jim Chee met when he was going to the Nez killing. The Bureau had us run it down for them. What'd he tell them?"

"They didn't talk to him," Leaphorn said.

"They didn't?" Largo said, surprised. Then, "Oh, yeah." He laughed—which with Largo was a deep, rumbling sound. "From what I hear he's sort of an untouchable. Supposed to have worked for the CIA in Nam."

"I think somebody ought to talk to the man," Leaphorn said. "I think I'll come and do it."

"You want me to save you the drive?"

"No use you pissing off the Bureau," Leaphorn said. "I'll do it."

"That sounds like you're still thinking of retiring," Largo said, and laughed again.

"One of these days. Anyway, I'm at the point where if a yelling match started with the feds, anybody who decided to fire me would have to move fast."

Largo didn't comment on that. He said, "Let me know when you're coming, and if you need any help. Right now, I'll just look that address up for you."

"I'll probably come this afternoon," Leaphorn said. "Just as soon as I get my paperwork done."

But just as he was moving the penultimate report from in-basket to out-basket, the telephone rang.

"A woman down here to see you," the desk clerk said. "A Professor Bourebonette."

"Ah," Leaphorn said. He thought a moment. "Ask her to come on up."

He put down the telephone, pulled the ultimate report out of the basket, opened it on his desk, and then stared out the window at the sun and shadows on Window Rock Ridge. A question of motive again. What brought the professor here? A long drive from Flagstaff. Either she had risen in the predawn darkness or she had spent the night somewhere. At the Window Rock motel perhaps, or at Gallup. A strong motive. Friendship, she said. Friendship might well be part of it. But what else?

As she came through his door, Professor Bourebonette's words were apologetic. But her expression wasn't.

"I realize we're imposing on your time. Hosteen Pinto isn't your responsibility. But I wondered if you could bring me up to date. Have you learned anything?"

Leaphorn was standing. "Please," he said, motioning her to a chair. He sat, too, closed the waiting folder. "I haven't learned anything very useful."

"What did Professor Tagert say? I called his office and they told me he wasn't in. They didn't know when to expect him. That seems awfully odd. Their semester started two or three weeks ago. He'd have to be keeping office hours."

"Dr. Tagert seems to have jumped ship," Leaphorn said. "I got the same information you did."

"He's missing?" Dr. Bourebonette sounded incredulous. "Are the police looking for him?"

This was something that always had to be explained. Leaphorn did it, patiently.

"It doesn't work that way with adults. You have a right to be missing if you want to be. It's nobody's business but your own. The police 'look' only if there's some crime involved. Or some reason to suspect foul play."

Professor Bourebonette was frowning at him. "There's certainly a crime involved here. And isn't he what you call a material witness?"

"He might be," Leaphorn said. "If he is, nobody knows it. The crime is the Nez homicide. There's nothing to connect him to that. Absolutely nothing."

Bourebonette absorbed this statement, her eyes on Leaphorn but her thoughts, obviously, on something else. She nodded, agreeing with some inner notion. Leaphorn considered her. What was she thinking? It would be something intelligent, he was sure of that. He wished the thought, whatever it was, would provoke some remark that would give him a clue to what she was doing here.

"Have you considered that Tagert might be dead?" she asked. "Have you considered that whoever killed your officer also killed Tagert? Have you thought of that?"

Leaphorn nodded. "I have."

Bourebonette was silent again, thinking. Long silences didn't seem to bother her. Unusual in a white. From downstairs Leaphorn could hear a telephone ringing. He smelled coffee brewing. Professor Bourebonette was wearing a cologne of some sort. The aroma was very, very faint. So faint it might be his imagination.

"The trial should be postponed," Bourebonette said suddenly. "Until they can find Professor Tagert." She stared at Leaphorn, her eyes demanding. "How can we arrange that? Surely they can't try Mr. Pinto without knowing what's going on. Nobody knows what actually happened out there."

Leaphorn shrugged. But the shrug wasn't good enough.

"I think we have a right to expect some sort of effort toward simple justice," Bourebonette said. Her voice sounded stiff. "Mr. Pinto has a right to demand that."

"I'll admit I would have liked a little solider investigation," Leaphorn said. "But it's not my responsibility. It's a federal case and the federals have all they need to convince a jury beyond any reasonable doubt. The game is played a little—"

"Game!"

Leaphorn interrupted the interruption with an upraised palm. He, too, could be aggressive. "—a little differently when the defendant does not deny the crime," he continued. "In the first place, that reduces any worry that you have that you might have arrested the wrong person. In the second place, it leaves you without the defendant's story to check. So there's much less the arresting agency can do, even when it has the very best of intentions."

Bourebonette was studying him. "And you think they've done all that's necessary?"

He hesitated. "Well," he said, "I would want to talk to Tagert, and there's another loose end or two."

"Like what? Lack of a motive?"

Leaphorn closed his eyes. Memory has no temporal limits. When he opened them again two seconds later memory had shown him a score of bloody scenes.

"Whiskey is the perfect motive," he said.

"Then what?"

He wanted to turn the question around, to ask this woman to tell him why this drunken shooting was worth so much of her time. It was probably the book. Friendship and the book. She needed Pinto free to finish it. But maybe there was something deeper. If he asked her, she would simply repeat that Pinto was innocent, that Pinto was a friend.

"Well, Officer Chee met a car when he was driving toward the crime scene. This car might have driven past the scene. Perhaps not, but most likely it did. Maybe the driver saw something. Probably not, but I would have found him and asked."

"Of course," Bourebonette said. "You mean nobody did."

"I hear they didn't."

"But why not?"

"Why not? Because they had their case. Smoking gun. Motive. No denial. They have other work to do, stacked on their desks." He made an illustrative gesture at his own desk. Except for the single folder it was uncharacteristically, point-defeatingly clean.

"Too much trouble running him down. Too much trouble finding the car. When an old man is being tried for murder." Her voice was bitter.

"We found the car," Leaphorn said. "It belongs to a schoolteacher at Ship Rock. I'm going to talk to him today."

"I'll go with you," Bourebonette said.

"I'm afraid that—" Then he stopped. Why not? No damage to be done. It wasn't his case anyway. If the Bureau got mad, it would get no madder because this woman was along. And he wanted to know what she was after. This business was interesting him more and more.

They took the road that wanders over Washington Pass via Red Lake, Crystal, and Sheep Springs. Winding down the east slope of the Chuskas, Leaphorn stopped at an overlook. He pointed east and swept his hand northward, encompassing an immensity of rolling tan and gray grasslands. Zuni Mountains to the south, Jemez Mountains to the east, and far to the north the snowy San Juans in Colorado.

"*Dinetah*," he said. She would know the meaning of the word. "Among the People." The heartland of the Navajos. The place of their mythology, the Holy Land of the Dinee. How would she react?

Professor Bourebonette said nothing at all for a moment. Then: "I won a bet with myself," she said. "Or part of a bet. I bet you would stop here and enjoy the view. And I bet you'd say something about naming this pass after Washington."

This wasn't what Leaphorn had expected.

"And what would I have said?"

"I wasn't sure. Maybe something angry. I would be bitter if I was a Navajo to have anything in my territory named after Colonel John Macrae Washington. It's like naming a mountain pass in Israel after Adolf Hitler."

"The colonel was a scoundrel," Leaphorn agreed. "But I don't let the nineteenth century worry me."

Bourebonette laughed. "If you don't mind my saying so, that's typically Navajo. You stay in harmony with reality. Being bitter about the past isn't healthy."

"No," Leaphorn said. "It's not."

He thought: Professor Bourebonette is flattering me. Why? What will she want from this?

"I would be thinking of the insult," Bourebonette said. "Every time I took this route it would rankle. I would think, why does the white man do this? Why does he honor the man who was our worst enemy and rub our noses in it? The colonel who murdered Narbona, that honorable and peaceable man. The colonel who broke treaty after treaty, and protected the people who captured your children and sold them into slavery in New Mexico and argued for a policy of simply exterminating your tribe, and did everything he could to carry it out. Why take such a bastard and name a mountain pass right in the middle of your country after him? Is that just the product of ignorance? Or is it done as a gesture of contempt?"

There was anger in Bourebonette's voice and in her face. This wasn't what Leaphorn had expected, either.

"I would say ignorance," Leaphorn said. "There's no malice in it." He laughed. "One of my nephews was a Boy Scout. In the Kit Carson Council. Carson was worse in a way, because he pretended to be a friend of the Navajos." He paused and looked at her. "Washington didn't pretend," he said. "He was an honest enemy."

Professor Louisa Bourebonette showed absolutely no sign that she sensed the subtle irony Leaphorn intended in that.

The sun was halfway down the sky when they started down the long slope that drops into the San Juan River basin and Ship Rock town. They had discussed Arizona State University, where Leaphorn had been a student long ago, whether the disease of alcoholism had racial/genetic roots, the biography-memoir-autobiography of Hosteen Ashie Pinto the professor had been accumulating for twenty years, drought cycles, and law enforcement. Leaphorn had listened carefully as they talked about the Pinto book, guiding the conversation, confirming his thought that the Pinto effort was the top priority in this woman's life but learning nothing more. He had noticed that she was alert to what he was noticing and that she had no problem with long silences. They were enjoying such a silence now, rolling down the ten-mile grade toward the town. The cottonwoods along the river formed a crooked line of dazzling gold across a vast landscape of grays and tans. And beyond, the dark blue mountains formed the horizon, the

Abajos, Sleeping Ute, and the San Juans, already capped with early snow. It was one of those still, golden days of high desert autumn.

Then Leaphorn broke the mood.

"I told the captain in charge of the Ship Rock subagency I'd let him know when I got here," he said, and picked up the mike.

The dispatcher said Captain Largo wasn't in.

"You expect him soon?"

"I don't know. We had a shooting. He went out on that about an hour ago. I think he'll be back pretty quick."

"A homicide?"

"Maybe. We sent an ambulance. You want me to call the captain?"

"Don't interrupt him," Leaphorn said. "When he comes in, tell him I went directly out to the Huan Ji residence. Tell him I'll fill him in if I learn anything."

"Huan Ji," the dispatcher said. "That's where the shooting was reported. That's where we sent the ambulance."

13

THEY MET THE ambulance returning to the Ship Rock Public Health Service Hospital as they turned off onto Huan Ji's street. The emergency lights were flashing and the siren growling. Leaphorn had been around violence too long to be deceived by that. The driver was in no hurry. He recognized Leaphorn as they passed, and raised a hand in salute. Whoever had been shot at Huan Ji's place was either in no danger or he was already dead.

Ji's house was a rectangular frame-and-stucco bungalow in a block of such structures. They had been designed long ago by a Bureau of Indian Affairs bureaucrat to house Bureau of Indian Affairs employees. As they had weathered and sagged, they had passed from that existence and become tribal property—occupied now by schoolteachers, hospital clerks, road-grader operators, and similar folk. Ji's house was instantly recognizable. It had attracted a cluster of police cars and a scattering of neighbors watching from their yards. Even without the magnet of this temporary tragedy, it would have stood out.

It was surrounded by a neat chain-link fence and flanked by a tidy gravel driveway that led to an empty carport. Inside the fence was a flower bed, precisely bordered by a perfectly aligned row of bricks. Six rose bushes were spaced on each side of the concrete sidewalk. Autumn had turned the Bermuda-grass lawn gray, but it was trimmed and ready for spring.

The house itself was a clone of its neighbors and as alien as a Martian. In a row of houses frayed, faded, and weary, its fresh white paint and fresh blue trim seemed a reproach to the dusty street.

Captain Largo, as neat as the house but somewhat smaller, was standing on the porch. He was talking to a skinny tribal policeman and a neat young man in a felt hat and a dark gray business suit—which meant in Four Corners country that he was either an agent of the Federal Bureau of Investigation or a young man making his mission for the Church of Jesus Christ of Latter-day Saints. Largo's bulk made them both look unnaturally small. He recognized Leaphorn and waved.

Leaphorn glanced at Bourebonette, thinking of how to phrase his request.

She anticipated it.

"I'll wait in the car," she said.

"I won't be long," Leaphorn said.

On the porch, Largo introduced him. The skinny policeman was Eldon Roanhorse, who Leaphorn vaguely remembered from some affair out of the past, and Gray Suit was Theodore Rostik of the Farmington office of the Federal Bureau of Investigation.

"Mr. Rostik just transferred in this summer," Largo said. "Lieutenant Leaphorn is with our criminal investigation division. Out of Window Rock."

If Rostik was impressed by Leaphorn or his title, he concealed it. He nodded to Leaphorn, turned back to Largo.

"Window Rock," he said. "How'd he know about this? How did he get here so quick?"

Once this rudeness would have irritated Leaphorn. That was a long time ago. He said, "I just happened to be up here on another matter. What do you have?"

"Homicide," Largo said. "Somebody shot the owner here. Twice. No witnesses. Mailman heard him moaning. Looked in and saw him on the floor and turned it in."

"Any suspects?"

"We're talking to neighbors but nobody much seems to have been around when it happened," Largo said.

"This will be a federal case," Rostik said. "Felony on a federal reservation."

"Of course," Leaphorn said. "We'll help any way we can. Interpreting, things like that. Where's his wife?"

"Neighbors say he's a widower," Roanhorse said. "He was a teacher down at the high school. He lived here with his boy. Teenaged kid."

"If we need help—" Rostik began, but Leaphorn held up his hand.

"Just a second," he said. "Where's his car?"

"Car?" Rostik said.

"We've got a call out on it," Largo said, looking solemnly at Leaphorn. "I understand it's an old white Jeepster."

"The son wasn't here?"

"Not unless he did it," Rostik said. "When the mailman got here there was just Mr. Ji."

"Mr. Rostik," Leaphorn said, "if you don't have any objection, I'd like to look around inside. Nothing will be touched."

"Well, now," Rostik said. He cleared his throat. "I don't see what—"

Captain Largo, who almost never interrupted, interrupted now. "The lieutenant is usually our liaison with the Bureau in cases like this. He'd better see what you have here," he said, and led the way inside.

The homicide team had drawn a chalk outline of where Colonel Huan Ji's body had fallen against the front room's wall. A great splotch of blood drying on the polished hardwood floor made the chalk redundant. Except for that, and a scrabble of reddish marks on the tan wallpaper, the room was as neat as the yard. Immaculate. And cool as the autumn afternoon outside.

Leaphorn avoided the blood and squatted beside the defaced wallpaper. "He left a message?"

"He left two," Rostik said.

" 'Save Taka,' " Leaphorn read. "Is that what it says?"

"His son's name is Taka," Rostik said. "According to the neighbors."

Leaphorn was far more interested by the other message. Ji apparently had written them in his own blood by moving a shaky finger across the wall. SAVE TAKA above, and below it: LIED TO CHEE.

"Any theories about this bottom one?" Leaphorn asked.

"Not yet," Rostik said.

Leaphorn pushed himself erect, grunting. He was getting old for the squatting position. He looked at Captain Largo. Largo looked back, expressionless.

"Unfortunately, Chee is a common name among Navajos," Largo said. "Like Smith in Chicago, or Martinez in Albuquerque."

Leaphorn drifted into the kitchen, looking at tidiness, touching nothing. Huan Ji's bedroom was fairly large, but suggested a monastery cell—a narrow bed tightly made, a chair, a small desk, a dresser, a chest of drawers with what seemed to be a camera bag on top of it. Everything tidy. Nothing to suggest someone lived here. He stood at the desk, looking down at the blotter, the little cup holding paper clips, the pen in its holder.

Behind him, Rostik cleared his throat. "Don't touch anything. We'll go through all of this later," Rostik said. "Everything in here. Everything in the house. With trained people."

"Of course," Leaphorn said.

Taka's room was tidy by Leaphorn's standards, if not by Huan Ji's. An identical narrow bed, covers tight. Similar furniture. But the boy's desk was cluttered with books and papers and his dresser was a gallery of photographs. Leaphorn, hands in his jacket pockets, examined these pictures. Most of them were of a girl, a moderately pretty Navajo of perhaps sixteen. One of these seemed to be a school yearbook portrait, rephotographed and blown up to eleven-by-fourteen-inch size. The others were candid shots, apparently taken when the subject wasn't looking. Some included two or three other youngsters, but always with the girl. Many of them had been taken, judging from the compressed background, with a telescopic lens.

The back porch was screened, a repository for stored items. A door opened from it into a side room which Leaphorn guessed had been tacked on as a third bedroom. The door bore the stenciled legend: DARKROOM. KNOCK BEFORE OPENING. He glanced at Rostik, nodded at him, turned the knob. It was dark inside, the windows covered with opaque plastic, the air heavy with the smell of acids. Leaphorn switched on the overhead light. It was a small room, sparsely furnished. Along one side, a table bore a small enlarger, a set of developing tanks, and an array of the inevitable chemical containers. Beside that was another table and on it an open-faced cabinet held boxes which Leaphorn presumed held photographic paper. His gaze wandered over all of this and returned to the developing trays and the electric print dryer beside them. Eight-by-ten prints were stacked in the basket below the dryer.

Leaphorn picked up the top one by the edges. It was a black-and-white photograph of what seemed to be a rugged, irregular outcropping of rock. He replaced the print and picked up the one below it. At first he thought it was identical. Then he saw it was apparently another segment of the same outcropping, with some overlapping. He replaced it and reached for a third print.

Rostik touched his elbow.

"I don't want anything touched," he said. "The experts may want to go over this room."

"Then I will leave it for the experts," Leaphorn said.

On the porch again, he suddenly remembered the professor waiting in the car. He wanted to talk to Largo about Officer Jim Chee, but he didn't want to wash any Tribal Police laundry in front of Agent Rostik of the Federal Bureau of Investigation. First he would explain things to Bourebonette. He'd tell her to start the engine and turn on the heater. He'd tell her that he wouldn't be much longer.

As he started across the street, he saw the old white Jeepster turn the corner. It rolled halfway down the block, stopped, began backing away from the cluster of police cars at the Huan Ji house. Then it stopped again, remaining motionless on the street. Guilt, Leaphorn thought. Or perhaps fear struggling with curiosity. Whatever the driver's motivations, the Jeepster rolled forward again. Leaphorn trotted across the street in front of it to his own car. Bourebonette had rolled down the window. She was watching him.

"It was about what we thought," he said. "Someone shot Mr. Ji twice. Fatally. No one saw it or heard anything. No suspects. And this—" he nodded toward the Jeepster now pulling into the gravel driveway at the Ji residence "—will probably be Taka, who is Mr. Ji's son."

Professor Bourebonette was looking past him at the car. "Does he know?"

"Probably not. Not unless he did it."

Bourebonette looked down. "How sad," she said. "How terrible. Is his mother home? Do you think this could—" She stopped.

"Be connected with the Nez homicide?" Leaphorn finished. "Who knows. You don't see anything on the surface, but—" He shrugged.

Across the street, Rostik and Largo were talking to a slender boy in jeans and a black leather jacket. Largo had his large hand on the boy's shoulder. They moved through the front door and disappeared into the house.

"I think I'll go back over there," Leaphorn said.

"Do they need your help?"

Leaphorn chuckled. "The man in charge is the young man in the gray suit," he said. "If he wants my help he has shown absolutely no sign of it. I'll be quick this time."

Roanhorse was waiting on the porch.

"Was that Ji's son?"

"Right," Roanhorse said. "Name's Taka. Something like that."

"He okay?"

"Looked like somebody hit him with a club when Rostik told him," Roanhorse said.

Taka Ji was sitting stiffly on the edge of a recliner chair. Rostik was facing him, perched on the arm of the sofa. Largo leaned against the wall, his round, dark face devoid of expression. Leaphorn stopped just inside the door. Rostik glanced at him, looked irritated, chose to ignore him, continued his questioning.

He was good at it, Leaphorn noticed. Young, obviously. Probably inexperienced. But well trained in the job, and smart. Some of the questions replowed old ground from new angles. Some were new. Huan Ji's son, still looking as if he had been hit by a club, answered them tersely.

He had not seen his father since he'd driven to school with him in the Jeepster. Right?

Taka nodded. "Yes," he said. His voice was so small that Leaphorn could barely hear him.

And how had he gotten the Jeepster?

"My father, he said I could use it after school. He would walk home. He liked to walk. So after my biology class, I got it from the parking lot."

"The key was left in it?"

"I have a key. My father has a key. I have one."

"And where did you go?"

"I drove out toward Ship Rock. I am taking pictures out there. Photographs."

"Pictures of who?"

Taka was looking straight ahead, seeing something in the wallpaper across the room. His face was pale. He closed his eyes. "I take pictures of landscapes," he said.

"Who was with you?"

Leaphorn thought Taka hadn't heard the question. But he had. Finally he said: "No one. I go alone."

A Vietnamese in a Navajo school. A long time ago Leaphorn had been a Navajo in white Arizona State University. He understood what Taka had not quite said. What was it that Colonel Ji had written on the wall in his own blood? "Help Taka." Something like that.

Rostik changed the subject.

"Did your father have enemies?"

Taka shrugged. "He was a man," he said. "A long time ago he was a colonel in the army." He looked up at Rostik. "The Army of the Republic of Vietnam."

"But do you know of any enemies? Had he received any threats?"

Again it seemed Taka wouldn't answer. Then he tilted his head, frowned. "I don't think he would have told me." This knowledge seemed to surprise him.

"No threat you know of then?"

"No."

"Do you know anyone named Chee?"

"Like I told you, there is a boy on the basketball team. There is a girl in my history class."

"Does your father have any friends named Chee? Any enemies?"

"I don't know," Taka said. "There is a teacher. In junior high school. Her name I think is Miss Dolores Chee."

"A friend of your father's?"

"I don't think so," Taka said. "There are lots of Chees."

Leaphorn glanced at Captain Largo and found Captain Largo glancing at him. Largo made a wry face.

And so it went. Leaphorn listened and watched. He assessed Rostik, and reassessed him. A smart young man. He assessed Taka as best he could. This was not the normal Taka. This was a stunned teenager. The death of his father was still unreal, an incredible but abstract fact. Rostik now was covering yesterday. How had Taka's father behaved? What had he said? Leaphorn noticed the boy was shivering.

Leaphorn interrupted.

"Mr. Rostik," he said. "Just a moment, if you don't mind." And he turned to Taka.

"Son. Do you have any relatives here? Anybody to go to?"

"Not here," the boy said. "Not here at Ship Rock."

A stranger alone in a strange land, Leaphorn thought. He asked: "Where?"

"My aunt and uncle. They live in Albuquerque."

"Are they the ones you are closest to?" As he asked it, Leaphorn thought how different this would be for a Navajo boy. He would be smothered by family. But maybe it would have been that way for Taka Ji, too, if his people had not been uprooted by war. Perhaps the Vietnamese had not, like the *biligaana*, lost the value of the family.

Taka was nodding. "They are all there is," he said.

"We'll call them when you are finished here," Leaphorn said, glancing at Rostik.

"I'm finished," Rostik said to Taka. "I'll just need to know where we can reach you if we need to know something else."

"How about a friend here? Somebody you can stay with tonight?"

Taka thought. He gave Leaphorn a name, the son of another of the high school teachers.

Rostik left. They made the calls on the colonel's telephone and Roanhorse took Taka in hand. He'd deliver him to the house of the friend.

"I'll lock the place up," Captain Largo said. "We'll keep an eye on it until the feds go over it."

"One last look at the darkroom," Leaphorn said. "No one will ever know."

With Largo peering over his shoulder, he went through the stack of prints in the dryer basket—eleven photographs of segments of the same outcropping of what seemed to be part of a long basaltic ridge. They were taken—or seemed to be—from the same viewpoint, as if the camera with a telescopic lens had been shifted slightly on a tripod for each exposure.

"Landscapes," Largo said. "If those are his landscapes he's not going to get rich with them."

"No," Leaphorn said, and placed them back in the dryer basket. "You recognize the place?"

"They could have been taken any of a hundred places," Largo said. "It just looked like a big bunch of extruded lava. Fairly old. Could be out there around Ship Rock. Could be down in the malpais south of Grants. Could be over east of Black Mesa. Could be lots of places."

On the porch, Largo paused to lock the front door.

"Can you think of any reason those pictures might have been taken?" Leaphorn asked.

"None," Largo said. "No idea why any teenage kid does anything."

"They might have been taken by the colonel," Leaphorn said. "He was a photographer, too."

Largo nodded. "True," he said. But he wasn't particularly interested.

"Odd though," Leaphorn said. "When he feels better I might ask him."

"Maybe the colonel did take them," Largo said. "But so what. People are always taking pictures of rocks. They think they see a shape like a duck, or Ronald Reagan, or God knows what."

"You think the boy did it?"

"The killing? I don't. How about you?"

Leaphorn shook his head. The sort of a shake that avoids an answer.

"I've got another question," Leaphorn said. "While Chee is a common name among us Dinee, unfortunately, it is not all that damn common. How the hell did your Jim Chee get himself mixed up with this?"

Largo's expression was grim. "I intend to find out."

"So do I," Leaphorn said.

14

JANET PETE HAD not liked the idea. Basically, no matter what she said, Jim Chee understood that she hadn't liked it because she hadn't trusted him. At worst, she thought he might betray her. Chee doubted that she really believed that, although the possibility that she did lingered in his memory. And rankled. At best, she wasn't certain she could depend on his discretion. On his good judgment. That rankled, too. In a way, that was even worse.

Chee had finally let his temper show. That was a weakness new to him, and he realized it. He explained it to himself as a product of raw nerves; of a hand which, with every twinge, reminded him it might never be fully useful again; of traumatic memories which recalled his failure to perform his duty. However he explained it, he didn't like the way it felt.

"Janet," he said. "Spare me all that lawyer talk. I've told you I won't ask the old man for a confession. I won't ask him what he was doing out there that night. Or how he got there. Or what the hell caused him to shoot Nez. I just want to ask him about the story he told to the professor. Just why he thinks the Enemy Way sing was done for all those horse thieves, and the Ghostway Chant added for one of them. I won't ask him anything that would make any sense to the FBI. Or to you either, for that matter."

That had touched a nerve. Janet's voice turned chilly.

"I'll spare you the lawyer talk. You spare me the 'I'm more Indian than you are' crap. Okay?"

Chee hesitated. "Right," he said. "Sorry about that."

"Okay, then," she said. "But you play by the rules. I'm going to be there every minute. Ashie Pinto only answers what I want him to answer. You two speak better Navajo than I do, so if I want you to explain a question, you by God explain it until I understand what you're getting at or it doesn't get answered. Understood?"

Chee had understood perfectly.

Janet Pete set it up for three that afternoon and Chee took a cab down to the County Detention Center where federal prisoners were being held. It was a sunny, windless autumn afternoon with a fringe of high clouds drifting in from the northwest, reminding him that the TV weatherman had reported snow in Flagstaff last night and the front—as always—was drifting eastward. He showed his credentials to the desk clerk and a deputy jailer escorted him to the visitors' room.

Janet Pete was waiting. She sat behind a long wooden table in a straight wooden chair looking small and tired and beautiful.

"*Yaa' eh t'eeh*," Chee began, and swallowed it and said, "Hello, Janet," instead.

She smiled at him. "*Yaa' eh t'eeh*," she said. "I do know a little Navajo."

"As much as I do," Chee said, which was a blatant lie, but a guard ushered in Hosteen Ashie Pinto before she could say so.

Here, in this still, sterile room lit by a battery of fluorescent tubes, Ashie Pinto was not the man Chee remembered. He remembered a stumbling drunk illuminated in the yellow glare of his headlights, wet with rain, blurred by Chee's own shock and Chee's own pain. Now he was smaller, desiccated, frail, dignified, and terribly old. He sat in the chair next to Janet Pete, acknowledged her with a nod. He looked at Chee, and then at the heavy bandages wrapped on Chee's left hand. Then Ashie Pinto repeated the only thing Chee had ever heard him say.

"I am ashamed," he said, and looked down.

Chee looked down, too. And when he looked up, Janet was watching him. He wondered if she had understood the Navajo phrase.

"I think I told you Mr. Pinto speaks hardly any English at all," she said. "I told him you were coming, of course, so he remembers who you are. He still does not want to say anything at all about the crime and I told him not to answer any questions until I tell him to."

"Okay," Chee said. "The question I want to ask him takes some explaining. Stop me if you get lost."

And so Chee began.

"My uncle," he said, "I think you may have heard of Frank Sam Nakai, who is a singer of the Blessing Way and the Mountain Top Chant and many of the other curing songs. This man is the brother of my mother, and he has tried to teach me to follow him and become a *hataalii*. But I am still an ignorant man. I have much yet to learn. I have learned a little of the Ways of the Holy People. And what I have learned has brought me here to ask you a question. It is a question about something you told to a professor named Tagert."

Chee stopped, eyes on Pinto. The man sat as still as death, waiting. His skin was drawn tight over the skull bones, seeming almost transparent in its thinness. The desiccation made his eyes seem protuberant, larger than they were. They were black eyes, but the cornea of one was clouded by a film of cataract.

Sure now that Chee had finished his statement, Pinto nodded. Chee was to continue.

"You were telling the professor about a time, perhaps before you were born, when some young men of the Yucca Fruit People rode over to Sleeping Ute Mountain to get back some horses the Utes had stolen from them. Do you remember that?"

Pinto remembered.

Chee summarized the rest of the adventure, taking time to tell it carefully. He wanted to draw Pinto's consciousness out of this room, out of his role as prisoner and into his past. Finally he had reached the place which had puzzled him.

"The way the *biligaana* professor wrote down what you told him may not be exactly what you told him. But what he wrote down is like this. That you said the *hataalii* the Yucca Fruit People called decided that an Enemy Way sing should be held for all of those young men. Is that true?"

Pinto considered. He smiled slightly, nodded.

"Then the *biligaana* professor wrote down that you told him that this singer decided he should also hold a Ghostway Chant for the man they called Delbito Willie. Is that true?"

There was no hesitation now. Hosteen Pinto nodded.

"That is the first of my questions," Chee said. "Do you know why this Ghostway was needed?"

Pinto studied Chee's face, thinking. He smiled slightly, nodded again.

"My uncle," Chee said, "will you tell me why?"

"Not yet," Janet Pete said. "I didn't understand a lot of that. What are you driving at?"

"Basically, why a certain cure was prescribed for one of those men and not for the others. That suggests he broke a specific taboo. I wonder what it was?"

Janet Pete was obviously lost. "But how . . . ? Oh, go ahead and answer it."

Hosteen Pinto glanced at Janet Pete, then back at Chee, then at something out the window beside Chee's shoulder. Chee waited. Through the glass came the sound of an ambulance siren, the sound of brakes applied. Somewhere in the building a door slammed, the clang of steel on steel. Chee could smell dust, an astringent floor cleaner, the aroma peculiar to old, old men. Pinto released his breath, a sighing exhalation. He looked at Janet Pete again, smiling. *This man,* Chee thought, *this kindly old man is the man who murdered Delbert Nez. The man who burned my friend in his car. The man whose actions caused this terrible burn across my hand. Why did he do it? Whiskey.* Todilhil. *The Water of Darkness. Twice it had turned this old man into a coyote.*

Hosteen Pinto shifted in his chair, seeking some comfort for old bones. "This young woman has become like a granddaughter to me," he said. "She tells me that she knows you. She says that you are an honorable man. She says you follow the Navajo Way."

He paused to give Chee a chance to respond to that. Then drew a deep breath.

"These things I told Hosteen Professor. I think they wrote these things all down on paper. And you read that paper? Is that right?"

"Yes. I read it all."

Pinto looked puzzled.

"And you know the Navajo Way?"

"I have studied it some," Chee said.

Pinto's expression was slightly skeptical, as if he wondered how much Chee had studied.

"They say there were many skinwalkers then," Hosteen Pinto began. "Even more than now. Do you understand skinwalkers?"

"I know something about them," Chee said. He settled himself in his chair. This was going to take a long time. Pinto would begin in the beginning and talk his way through it. And the longer he talked the better the chance that he'd cast some light on this murky business. If, that is, anything connected with anything.

"They teach us that everything has two forms," Hosteen Pinto said, starting even further back than Chee had expected. "There is the mountain we see there beside Grants, the mountain the *biligaana* call Mount Taylor. That is the outer form. And then they say there is the inner form, the sacred Turquoise Mountain that was there with the Holy People in the First World, the Dark World at the very beginning. And First Man brought it up from the Third World and built it on his magic robe, and decorated it with turquoise. And then there is the yucca. We see the outer form all around us, but it is the inner form of yucca that we offer the prayer plume for when we dig its roots to make the soap to clean ourselves."

He paused, studying Chee. "You understand?"

Chee nodded. This was basic Navajo metaphysics. But he wondered if Janet had ever heard it.

"Bluebird has two forms, and the deer and the beetle. Two forms. They have the form of the *yei* and they have the outer form that we see. All living things. You too. And I. Two forms."

Hosteen Ashie Pinto leaned forward, tiny in the yellow coveralls of the county prisoner, intent on Chee's understanding.

"And then there is Coyote," he said. "Do you know about Coyote?"

"I know something about Coyote," Chee said. He glanced at Janet Pete. She was focused on Pinto, concentrating on what he was saying. Wondering, Chee imagined, where all this was leading. "I know about his tricks. I have heard the stories. How he snatched the blanket and scattered the stars into the Milky Way. How he stole the baby of the Water Monster. How he tricked the sister of the bears into marrying him. How—"

The amusement on Pinto's face stopped him.

"The children are told the funny stories about Coyote so they will not be afraid," Pinto said. The amusement went away. Pinto smiled a tight, grim smile and launched into the explanation—as old as the culture of the People—of why Coyote was not funny. Chee listened, wishing, as he had come to wish many times in such sessions with old taletellers, that Navajos did not have to start everything at the very beginning. He glanced at Janet again. She looked bemused, probably wondering what the devil he was hoping to learn from all this—a wonder Chee was beginning to share. But at least she couldn't accuse him of trying to learn anything incriminating. Unless, of course, the old man talked long enough to tell him what Chee had come here to learn.

Now Hosteen Pinto was talking about how the name for Coyote in the Fourth World was not *atse'ma'ii*, or First Coyote, but *atse' hashkke*, or First Angry, and what that implied symbolically in an emerging culture in which peace and harmony were essential to survival. He talked of Coyote as the metaphor for chaos among a hungry people who would die without order. He talked of Coyote as the enemy of all law, and rules, and harmony. He talked of Coyote's mythic power. He reminded Chee how Coyote always sat in the doorway of the hogan when the Holy People met in Council, neither quite part of these representatives of cosmic power, nor totally allied with the wilderness of evil outside. And finally he reminded Chee that other wise people, like the old men in the Hopi kiva societies, knew that there was a time when humans had two hearts. Thus they were able to move back and forth from one form to the other—from natural to supernatural.

"I think your uncle must have taught you about the power of skin," Pinto said. He looked up for confirmation in Chee's face and, seeing it, went on:

"They say that's how Changing Woman created the first Navajos. From the skin rubbed from her breast, she formed the Salt People, and the Mud Clan, and the Bitter Waters and the Bead People. I have heard of your uncle, of Frank Sam Nakai. They say he is a great *hataalii*. He must have taught you how Coyote transformed First Man into a skinwalker by blowing his hide over him. You know about that? About how First Woman wouldn't sleep with him because now he had all the evil ways of Coyote, smelled like coyote urine, licked himself and tried to lick her, and did all those dirty things that coyotes do. And how the Holy People cured First Man by passing him through the magic hoops to strip away his coyote skin. Your uncle taught you that?"

"Some of it," Chee said. He remembered a little of it. It was something reenacted in part of the Ghostway ceremony—a cure for the most virulent form of witch sickness.

"So then you know why this fellow had to have the Ghostway sing," Pinto said. "He had to have it because he had been with the *yenaldlooshi*."

"No," Chee said. "I don't understand that."

Janet Pete raised a hand. "Wait a minute. I don't understand this either. *Yenaldlooshi?* That is the word for animals that trot, isn't it?"

Chee nodded. "Animals that trot on four legs. But it is also used for skinwalkers. Witches."

"Where is this conversation going?" she asked. "Are you leading Mr. Pinto into something? Do you remember what you promised?"

Pinto was watching, puzzled.

Janet Pete switched to Navajo. "I wanted to make sure that Mr. Chee was not trying to get you to say something that would hurt your chance in the trial," she explained. "I want you to be careful about that."

Hosteen Pinto nodded. "We are talking about something that happened a long time ago," he said.

"I don't understand, my uncle," Chee said. "Why did they do the Ghostway sing for the one they called Delbito Willie when they did the Enemy Way for the others?"

"Because he went in there," Hosteen Pinto said. His tone was patient. "He went in there—into Tse A'Digash. He went in there where the witches gather. He went in there among the corpses and the skinwalkers. He went in to the place where the *yenaldlooshi* do their ceremonies, where they do incest, where they kill their relatives."

Silence. Chee thought about this. He frowned, glanced at Janet Pete. She was watching him. Well, he would ask it anyway.

"My uncle, would you tell me just where this Tse A'Digash is located?"

Pinto's expression changed. "I cannot tell you that."

"Could you tell me if Professor Tagert hired you to show him where it was?"

Hosteen Pinto stared at Chee. "When you arrested me that night, I could smell the fire in your clothing. I could smell where your flesh had burned. I said I was ashamed. I am still ashamed of that. But these things you ask me now, I cannot tell you."

"What's going on?" Janet asked.

Hosteen Pinto stood, limped toward the doorway, his old bones stiff from the sitting.

"Could you just tell me who gave you that whiskey?"

Hosteen Pinto tapped on the glass. The jailer was coming.

"Don't say anything," Janet said. Then to Chee, angrily, "So much for your promises."

"I just want some of the truth," Chee said. "Maybe the truth will make him free."

15

JIM CHEE HAD not flown enough to learn to think creatively on an airplane. He spent the time on this Mesa Airlines turboprop flight looking down from his seat by the window at the early snow on the Jemez Mountain ridges below, and the great broken expanse of tan and gray of the Chaco Mesa country and finally, at the ribbon of fading yellow and black that marked the San Juan River Valley. His mind was on Janet Pete, who had been irritated with him—but not nearly as irritated as he had expected her to be. He decided, tentatively, that this was because Hosteen Pinto had told him nothing incriminating.

Still, she should have been furious because he'd tried to take advantage of her. That could be explained if Janet didn't give a damn how he behaved. Chee didn't like that explanation. It was true, perhaps, but he rejected it. More and more, he was giving a damn about Janet.

He retrieved his pickup from the airport parking lot and drove down off the mesa into the heavy after-work traffic on 550. He'd stop at the police station in Ship Rock and see if the captain was in. Largo had been around a lot longer than Chee and knew a lot more people in this part of the Reservation. He might have heard of the Tse A'Digash that Ashie Pinto had mentioned. It would be somewhere south of Ship Rock, Chee guessed. Somewhere in the volcanic outcrop country. Probably not too far from where he'd arrested the man. And if Largo didn't know, he'd be likely to know some old-timer who would.

But Largo wasn't at the station.

Angie was at the desk.

"Hey, man, how's the hand?" she asked, grinning at him. And without waiting for an answer: "The captain's been looking for you. Like he has something heavy on his mind."

"What?" Chee asked, starting the automatic examination of conscience that such statements provoke. "I'm on sick leave."

"I don't know what. He didn't say. But Lieutenant Leaphorn was with him. Up from Window Rock. And he looked pissed off."

"Leaphorn?"

"Captain Largo," Angie said. "Come to think of it, the lieutenant, too, I guess."

"Was that today?"

Angie nodded. "They left here just a little bit ago."

To hell with it, Chee thought. He'd see Largo when he saw him. The Leaphorn news disturbed him more. Leaphorn had been trying to reach Tagert. There could be just one explanation for that. The lieutenant, the supercop, had invited himself into the Pinto investigation. Not at the invitation of the FBI, Chee guessed. That wasn't likely. More likely he'd guessed Officer Jim Chee had screwed it up. Well, to hell with Leaphorn.

"Angie, you've been here awhile. Do you know any places around this part of the Reservation that people call Tse A'Digash?"

Angie just looked at him.

Chee persisted. "A place with a bad reputation for witches? Sort of place people stay away from?"

"Sort of place people don't talk about to strangers, either," Angie said. "I'm from over near Leupp. Over on the southwest side of the Reservation. Three hundred miles from here."

"I know," Chee said. "But you've lived here ten or twelve years."

Angie shook her head. "That's not long enough," she said. "Not to talk about skinwalkers with you."

And it wasn't. Chee knew that.

Chee drove home thinking about who, among his friends, was enough of a Ship Rock territory old-timer to know what he needed to know. He had three names in mind, with Largo the fourth. Largo was sore at him, apparently, at the moment. But that was not unusual. And Largo would tell him what he knew. He wondered what had upset the captain, and Lieutenant Leaphorn. And at the thought of Leaphorn, he was irritated himself.

As he tilted his pickup off gravel and onto the steep track that led downward through the rabbitbrush toward his trailer house, he saw he had a visitor. A car was just pulling away from the trailer, coming toward him. A Navajo Tribal Police patrol car.

It stopped, went into reverse, reparked just where Chee usually parked his pickup. He parked beside it.

Captain Largo was driving, another policeman beside him.

"Glad to see you," Largo said, hoisting himself out. "We've been looking for you."

"That's what Angie said," Chee said. "You want to come in?"

"Why not," Largo said.

The other policeman emerged from the passenger door, putting his uniform hat back on a head of short-cropped gray hair. Lieutenant Leaphorn.

"*Yaa' eh t'eeh,*" Leaphorn said.

The afternoon sun still lit the high side of Ship Rock town but here in the cottonwoods beside the river Chee's trailer had been in shadow for long enough to be cold. Chee turned on the propane heater, filled his coffeepot with water, got out three cups and three of the paper filters he was now using to brew the stuff right in the cups. Why had the captain been looking for him? Why was Leaphorn here, so far from his desk at Window Rock? Chee lit the fire under the coffeepot, conscious that he was more cautious with fire than he used to be. The captain and the lieutenant occupied his two chairs. Chee took a seat on the edge of his bunk.

"We have to wait until the water boils," he said. "Just takes a few minutes."

Largo cleared his throat, producing a rumble.

"We had a man killed here in Ship Rock today," Largo said. "Shot."

This was not anything like what Chee had expected.

"Shot? Who?"

"Fellow named Huan Ji," Largo said. "You know him?"

"Wow," Chee said. He sat stock still, digesting this. Digesting how he was learning it, too. "Yeah," he said. "I don't exactly know him, but I've talked to him. Once. Last week. It was his car I saw out there where Delbert was killed." Then another thought. "Who shot him?"

He noticed Leaphorn sitting, arms folded across his chest, watching him.

"No suspects," Largo said. "Apparently somebody came to his house this afternoon. It must have been very soon after he got home from school. Or maybe they were there waiting for him. Anyway, whoever it was shot him twice. Left him on the floor in the front room."

"Son-of-a-bitch," Chee said. "Any idea why anybody'd shoot him?"

"None," Largo said. He was leaning his chair back against the wall, looking at Chee over his glasses. "How about you? Any ideas?"

"None," Chee said.

"What did you talk to him about?"

"About what he might have seen that night Nez got killed."

"What did he see?"

"He said he didn't see anything."

"He left a note," Largo said. "Wrote it on the wallpaper there where he was lying. He wrote 'Take care of Taka' and under that he wrote 'Tell Chee I lied.' He put his finger in his own blood and wrote it."

"Be damned," Chee said.

"What do you think he meant?"

Chee hesitated. "Well, I knew he lied about one thing. He said he didn't see any other cars. He had to have seen my police car. He was coming toward me, his Jeepster was, and he did a right turn just before we met. My siren was going and the flasher. And my headlights were right on him. No way he wouldn't have seen me."

The three of them considered that.

Leaphorn said: "Odd thing to lie about."

"I thought so, too," Chee said. "I wondered why."

"Did you ask him?"

"No."

"Why not?"

"I didn't think it would lead anywhere."

Leaphorn considered this, and nodded. He said: "Why did you go talk to him? You're on convalescent leave. And it's a federal case."

Chee felt himself flushing. "The FBI hadn't talked to him," Chee said. "I thought he might have seen something."

Leaphorn didn't comment on that. He said: "The water's boiling for your coffee."

Once Joe Leaphorn had been addicted to cigarettes—smoking unfiltered Pall Malls at a rate of two packs a day and, when he shifted to filters in response to Emma's concern, three packs a day. He had broken that habit early in Emma's terminal illness. He had bitten the nicotine deprival bullet as a sort of offering to her, who loved him. And to the gods—that this small, lovely woman would be left with him. As the yearning for cigarettes faded he had found it replaced by a delight in coffee. Now he awoke each morning in his lonely bed anticipating that first sip and savoring it. His working day was measured out in the intervals between the cups. Being Leaphorn, being logical, he'd known that this obsessive affair with coffee represented a flaw in his character, a weakness, as well as a risk to his health. He'd made a logical compromise: no more than four cups before noon and nothing but decaffeinated stuff after lunch. With that he lived fairly happily.

But today he'd had almost no coffee. He had drunk his usual two cups with what was left of last night's mutton stew for breakfast. He had stopped at the store beside the highway at the Newcomb junction for another cup. But none had been available. At lunch in Shiprock the product served had been a reheated stale brew obviously left over from breakfast and undrinkable even by Leaphorn's relaxed standards. And then the homicide of Huan Ji had interfered. Now, as Jim Chee poured boiling water through the coffee grounds, the aroma that reached Leaphorn's nostrils was indescribably delicious.

He'd never seen coffee made that way before. Chee had arrayed three mugs beside the sink, put a little black cone-shaped gadget atop one of them, inserted a paper filter into it, dumped a spoonful of Folger's into that, and poured the water through. Then he replaced the grounds and repeated the process in the other cups. Wasteful, Leaphorn thought, and time-consuming. But when he tasted the results, he was impressed. Downright fine. As good as any he'd ever tasted. He studied Chee over the rim of the cup. Odd young man. Good-looking in a way, with the sort of long, sensitive face women seemed to like. A fairly good cop, excellent in some categories, weak in others. He remembered that Largo had tried him out as an acting sergeant once. It hadn't lasted long for some reason he had forgotten or, more likely, had never known. But he could guess the reason. Chee wasn't an organization man. He was a loner. Liked to freelance. A man who worked inside the system only until the system interfered. One of those who marched to his private drummer. This business of trying to be a *hataalii* and a policeman at the same time, for example. It wasn't just impractical. How the hell could a cop get time off at the drop of a hat for a nine-day sing? It was incongruous. It was like being an investment banker and a Catholic priest at the same time. Or a rabbi and a clown. People wouldn't accept it. They expect a shaman or a priest to be different from ordinary humans, expect him to live in the shadow on the dangerous mystical fringe of the supernatural.

Now Chee was refilling the pot, the heavy bandage on his left hand making it a clumsy project. The fruit of freelancing, Leaphorn thought. But in fairness he should say a dead policeman was the result of the rules-bending, the burned hand the product of Chee's bravery. He wondered if he would have walked into that fire, gripped that red-hot door handle, to save another man's life. He wasn't sure he would have. He might have stood there, calculating the odds of success—trying to do what was rational.

"Is it still painful?" Leaphorn asked. "The hand?"

"Not much." Chee sat on the bunk again. "Not if I'm careful."

"You mentioned one thing Ji lied about when you talked to him. Do you think that's what the message was about?"

Chee was tucking a stray end of the gauze back into the bandage—concentrating on that.

"No," he said. "I doubt it."

Smart, Leaphorn thought. Of course it wasn't that. "What do you think it was?"

Chee hesitated. "This is new to me," he said. "I need a minute to get it together."

Leaphorn sipped, enjoyed it. Wonderful coffee.

"Take your time," he said.

Chee looked up from the bandage. His face was full of anger.

"I have a question for you. What pulled you into this? Into the Delbert Nez homicide?"

Leaphorn considered Chee's expression, the anger in his voice. "Somebody shot Huan Ji," he said. "That pulled me into it."

"No," Chee said, shaking his head. "Last week you were looking for a professor named Tagert. What's up? You think I arrested the wrong man? You think I screwed that up, too?"

Captain Largo shifted in his chair. "Take it easy," he said.

Chee's emotion was interesting. What motivated it? Leaphorn turned his cup in his hands.

"I wondered how Pinto got where you found him," he said. "The FBI didn't check it out. They didn't see any reason to, I guess, since you gave them the man with the smoking gun." Leaphorn was silent a moment, looking into Chee's anger. There was absolutely no reason for him to tell this young man anything. No reason except the bandaged hand and what it represented.

"I wondered about that," Leaphorn continued, "and then Pinto's niece came to see me. She's Turning Mountain Clan. A relative of my late wife. She wanted to hire a private detective to find out who gave the old man the ride. I decided to do it for her."

Chee nodded, unmollified.

"You wondered, too, I noticed," Leaphorn said. "You went to the trouble of finding out about Tagert hiring him, too."

"Did he hire him?" Chee said. "All I knew was that Tagert had used him in the past. As a source for old legends. That sort of thing. Had Tagert hired him this time?"

"Yes," Leaphorn said. He told Chee about the letter Old Man McGinnis had written, about the vehicle seen driving away from Pinto's place. "How did you make the Tagert connection?"

Chee told him about Janet Pete, about climbing into the formation where the crazy painter Nez hoped to catch had been defacing the rocks. He told him what they had seen there, that the painter had carried a ladder into the formation, painting high places, ignoring low ones, painting part of the surface of one formation, skipping the next one. He told him about the car with the REDDNEK plate, about going to the library at UNM to listen to Pinto's tapes, noting who had taped them. He told Leaphorn about what he had learned from Jean Jacobs and Odell Redd.

"You think Tagert is chasing down something about Butch Cassidy then?" Leaphorn asked.

"They think so," Chee said. "That seems to be his connection with Pinto. That old story about the horse thieves and the two whites."

"So what do you think Ji lied to you about?"

The abrupt change of subject didn't seem to bother Chee.

"I don't think Ji was driving the car," Chee said. "I think he lied about that."

"Why?" Leaphorn asked. "Why do you think that?"

"He didn't see my car. He didn't see the fire. He was very cautious about the way he answered questions. He didn't volunteer anything that would catch him out. He just waited for a question and then gave a very careful, limited answer."

"Why would he lie about that? You have any theories?"

"What else did you say he wrote on the wall?" Chee asked.

Captain Largo answered that. " 'Take care of Taka.' "

"No," Leaphorn said. "It was 'Save Taka.' "

"That's his kid?" Chee asked. "Right?"

Leaphorn smiled slightly, approving of the way Chee's mind was working. "So you're thinking that Taka was driving the car? I think that's not a bad guess. He was driving it after school today. He drives it a lot, I think. He told me he even has his own key to it."

"I suspect he didn't want the boy pulled into a police investigation," Chee said. "I don't know why."

"He seems to have been a special friend of the Central Intelligence Agency. Back from his days in Vietnam," Leaphorn said. He explained what Kennedy had told him.

"So maybe Colonel Ji was just the nervous sort. Is that what you're thinking?" Chee asked.

Leaphorn shrugged. "A man makes a career out of playing hard games, it would be difficult to get over that sort of thinking. A policeman gets killed. You don't want your child touched by something like that." He shrugged again. "Good a guess as any. We just don't know enough."

"No," Largo said. "We don't know a damned thing. Except homicide is a felony and we don't have jurisdiction in any of this. Nez nor Colonel Ji."

"We have jurisdiction in a vandalism case," Leaphorn said. "Tell me about that?"

Largo looked puzzled. "What vandalism?"

Chee said, "You mean the painting on the rocks? You know what was in the report. Well, Delbert noticed this maybe two or three weeks earlier. Somebody putting white paint here and there in a rock formation out there between Ship Rock and the Chuska Range. He got interested in it and he started swinging past there whenever his patrol would allow it. He was hoping to catch the guy. But he never did."

"And he thought he saw him that night?"

"That's what he said."

"And it sounded like he was going after him?"

"That's how it sounded."

Leaphorn put down his coffee cup. He glanced at the stove. Steam was jetting from Chee's pot, but this wasn't the time to break this chain of thought.

"What do you think?" Leaphorn asked. "You see any connection? Was Ashie Pinto painting rocks? That seems totally unlikely. Did Pinto being there have something to do with the painting? Anything at all to do with it? Or was it just that Nez, thinking he was chasing his painter, turned out to be chasing Pinto? And he catches himself a homicidal drunk. Or what? What do you think?"

Silence.

Largo got up and turned down the burner under the coffeepot. He picked up the funnel that held the grounds. "How do you make this stuff?" he asked. "And as far as the painter and Ashie Pinto are concerned, I pick number two. Nez thought he was chasing his nut and he catches Pinto."

Chee scratched the back of his neck. "Yeah," he said slowly, "that sounds the most probable."

"No connection otherwise, then?" Leaphorn said. "Neither of you can think of any?"

Chee got up, collected the cups, lined them beside the sink, and picked out a fresh filter.

Another cup of coffee would be fine, Leaphorn thought. And then he would go and pick up Professor Bourebonette and be on his way. She had come up with a graceful way to get out of his way when he'd come out of Ji's house and returned to the car.

"You're going to be busy for a while," she had said. "Just drop me off at the community college. I have a friend in the library there I'd like to see."

Nothing more was going to come out of this conversation. He would drink his coffee, drop by the library to pick up the professor, and then head back to Window Rock. Neither Chee nor Largo seemed to be able to think of any connection between a rock painter and a policeman's murder. But there must be one. Because Leaphorn's logic told him that somehow Colonel Ji had tried to tell them that with his blood-smeared finger. The man must have known he was dying. Protect his son, he'd told them, and then that he had lied to Chee. There must be a connection, and the connection—as Chee thought, too—must be that the boy had been driving his car that night. Driving it out where an old drunk was killing a policeman and a madman was painting random patterns on an outcrop of lava.

Random, Leaphorn thought. Random. When he was a young man, a junior at Arizona State, running around, drinking, chasing the girls, he had gone to a sing-dance once over between Kinlichee and Cross Canyon. It had rained that night, and he and Haskie Jim, his father's older brother, had watched the first drops pattering into the dust. He had been full of the mathematics he was studying, and of his own wisdom, and he had talked to his old uncle of probabilities and of randomness. He had always remembered the scene.

"You think these raindrops are random?" his uncle had asked. And Leaphorn had been surprised. He'd said of course they were random. Didn't his uncle think they were random?

"The stars," Haskie Jim said. "We have a legend about how First Man and First Woman, over by Huerfano Mesa, had the stars in their blanket and were placing them carefully in the sky. And then Coyote grabbed the blanket and whirled it around and flung them into the darkness and that is how the Milky Way was formed. Thus order in the sky became chaos. Random. But even then . . . Even then, what Coyote did was evil, but was there not a pattern, too, in the evil deed?"

That had not been the time in Leaphorn's life when he had patience for the old metaphysics. He remembered telling Haskie Jim about modern astronomy and the cosmic mechanics of gravity and velocity. Leaphorn had said something like "Even so, you couldn't expect to find anything except randomness in the way the rain fell." And Haskie Jim had watched the rain awhile, silently. And then he had said, and Joe Leaphorn still remembered not just the words but the old man's face when he said them: "I think from where we stand the rain seems random. If we could stand somewhere else, we would see the order in it."

After he had thought about the meaning in that, Leaphorn had looked for order in everything. And he usually found it. Except in the events of insanity. Joe Leaphorn didn't think a man—or a woman—who carried a ladder along with a paint gun into the hills would be insane.

There was a pattern there, and a motive, if he could only find them.

16

DEPUTY T. J. BIRDIE was on duty when Jim Chee arrived at the San Juan County jail at Aztec. T. J. said he was just too busy right now.

"We're short-handed. I got the desk and the telephone switchboard, and the radio and everything all to myself. Just George back there in the jail and me. Come in tomorrow during regular hours and somebody will do it for you. It's not as easy as you make it sound. All that sorting around. Putting stuff back where it was."

"Come on, T. J.," Chee said. "Don't act like a horse's ass. All you got to do is pull the file on booking Ashie Pinto and let me take a look at the inventory of what stuff he had."

"Can't leave the phone," T. J. said. "Sheriff'd hang me up by the balls if he calls in here and I'm not on it." Deputy Birdie was a stubby young man with his black hair cut short—half Apache. It was gossiped in political circles that the sheriff had hired him in the interest of attracting votes from the nearby Jicarilla Apache Reservation and still didn't know Birdie was a Mescalero, whose numerous kinfolks and clansmen voted two hundred miles south and east in Otero County. Chee knew that Birdie was actually White Mountain Apache whose folks voted in Arizona and he was pretty sure the sheriff had hired him because he was smart. Unfortunately he was also lazy.

"Come on, damn it," Chee said. He came around behind the counter.

"Just get in there and pull out the Ashie Pinto file. I'll answer the telephone for you."

"Well, hell," T.J. said. "What's the big hurry?"

But he left, muttering. And when he returned five minutes later he handed Chee the folder.

The inventory of Hosteen Ashie Pinto's impounded possessions was short:

wallet containing:
  two fifty-dollar bills
  photo of woman
  photo of two men
  one pocketknife
  one comb
one tin chewing tobacco containing:
  corn meal
one leather pouch (jish) containing:
  two crystals
  feathers
  mineral stones
  bull durham pouch of pollen
  assorted small jish items

Chee handed the folder back to Birdie.

"That it?" Birdie said. "Can I get back to doing my duty for San Juan County now?"

"Thanks, T.J.," Chee said.

"What were you looking for? Did you find it?"

"His *jish*. The old man is a crystal gazer," Chee said. "I wanted to see if he was working. If he had his medicine bundle with him."

"Well, hell," Birdie said. "I was here the night they brought him in. I could have told you that. Saved me all that work if you'd just asked."

It was late but Chee decided to make the four-hour drive to Albuquerque, turning the new information over in his mind. First, there was the fact that Tagert had hired Pinto. Presumably he'd picked up Pinto at his hogan and taken him to the vicinity of whatever he was hunting. Pinto had taken along his crystals—the tools of his profession as a finder of the lost and seer of the unseen. Some white men around the Reservation used crystal gazers but Tagert didn't seem the sort. He guessed the historian was more interested in the old man's memory than in his shamanistic powers. Memory of what? Logically it would be connected to Tagert's interest in two white men who seemed to have died a long lifetime ago in a rock formation on the Navajo Reservation. Presumably Tagert would be hunting their bodies, for evidence that one of them was the notorious Butch Cassidy. Logic suggested that the rock formation would be somewhere fairly close to where he'd arrested Pinto. There were plenty of them around—the product of the same paroxysm of volcanic action that cracked the earth and formed the basaltic spires of Ship Rock. It might be the same formation into which he and Janet Pete had taken their stroll to study the work of Delbert Nez's nutty vandal. If all else failed, he might search that formation again. Given a day or two to cover it better and more daylight he might find something. Or get snakebit. But Pinto's old tale suggested witches were involved. First he would see where that could lead him.

And then there was the business of Colonel Ji. Who? Why? Probably Ji had lied to protect his son, Chee guessed. What had his son done? Or was it just a father's concern that his kid might be involved in something dangerous?

He turned it over, and over, and over. And the thinking kept him awake while he drove the endless miles of N.M. 44 toward Albuquerque. He had relied on a translator's transcript of Hosteen Pinto's tale of horse theft and homicide. He wanted to hear it for himself in the old man's own voice.

17

THE YELLOW TAPE used to isolate the scene of a crime dangled loosely across Colonel Ji's front gate. Leaphorn detached it, ushered Professor Bourebonette through, and reconnected it behind them.

"You're sure this is all right?"

"The people from the Bureau are all finished in here," Leaphorn said. "But keeping your hands in your pockets, not moving anything—that's a good idea."

Actually, it wasn't exactly all right. It would be better if Bourebonette waited in the car. Better still if he had made this recheck of the colonel's darkroom before he picked her up at the library. But he hadn't thought of it until too late for that. And then the idea pressed on him. A feeling of urgency that he couldn't really understand.

He unlocked the door, felt the little sigh of cold air that empty houses release when he opened it. It was a familiar sensation to Leaphorn—one he felt each evening when he unlocked his own house in Window Rock.

Nothing had changed in the front room, except it was silent now and the sills and surfaces bore the faint gray stains of fingerprint powder. He noticed Professor Bourebonette looking at the chalk lines that marked where the colonel's body had been. He noticed the colonel's messages were still on the wall, looking blacker now under the artificial yellow glare of the ceiling bulb. He noticed the professor's expression. Strained? Sad? Mournful? Obviously this is unpleasant for her. Why was she here?

Everything in the darkroom was as he remembered it—a cramped, airless space, musty, nostrils filled with the acid smell of print-developing fluids. The prints were where he had seen them but now they also wore traces of gray powder. Would an FBI lab technician be sorting out Joe Leaphorn's fingerprints? He checked his memory. No, he had handled everything carefully, by the edges.

Now he spread the prints on the cabinet top in two neat rows and examined them methodically. They were all the standard eight by ten inches on black-and-white glossy paper. All seemed to be exposures of parts of the same dark basaltic outcrop. They seemed to have been shot from a considerable distance through a telescopic lens. Or perhaps they had been magnified in the enlarger. The same negative had been used to make several of the prints, each blown up to a different magnification. But the angle in all was almost exactly the same—as if all the negatives had been exposed from the same location, but had been made by using lenses of different focal lengths and by shifting the camera on the tripod. All included the same segment of that outcrop. Some more of it, some less, depending on the lens. But in all, the same features were near the center of the print.

Leaphorn showed them to Bourebonette and explained what he was thinking.

"Why telescopic?" she asked.

"Notice this juniper in the foreground here in this one? Here it is in this other one. Notice how the relationship in size has changed. A telescopic lens compresses the distance like that."

Bourebonette nodded. "Sure," she said. "That's the way the optics would work."

"You know the Reservation pretty well. Does this look familiar?"

She studied the prints. "They're all the same place, obviously. But we don't get enough of it to put it in the landscape."

"Have you seen it?"

She laughed. "Probably. Or something like it. It could be about forty places in the malpais down around Grants. Or maybe out in the Bisti badlands, or in the Zuni Mountains, or on the Black Mesa side of Monument

Valley, or down around the Hopi Buttes, or out here beyond Ship Rock toward Littlewater or Sanostee. Or one of those volcanic throats east of Mount Taylor, or—" She shook her head, and handed the prints to Leaphorn. "Hard to tell. Any place that lava bubbled up through the cracks during a volcanic period. And that happened a lot out here."

"It would be near here someplace, I think," Leaphorn said. "We can presume Ji or his son shot them. Do you have any idea why either one would do that? Or make all these prints?"

"No idea," she said. "But they certainly weren't taken for the beauty of the landscape. Could you call the boy and ask him? Didn't you say he was staying with some friends here?"

"They decided against that. They're taking him to Albuquerque to stay with some relatives instead. He won't be there yet. But let's see if we can locate the negatives. Maybe they'll include enough background to tell us where this is."

They spent almost thirty minutes sorting negative files without finding anything useful.

Leaphorn pulled the wastebasket from under the sink, sorted through it, and extracted a crumpled sheet of photographic paper. It was part of the same scene, blown up larger on an eleven-by-fourteen-inch sheet. The print was much darker. Overexposed in the enlarger, Leaphorn guessed, and thrown away. He spread it on the cabinet, looked at Bourebonette, raised his eyebrows in a question.

"I don't know," she said. "Maybe big enough to work with." She looked at Leaphorn and grinned. "But work on what?"

"I think maybe we're just wasting our time," he said and put the picture back in the wastebasket.

"I'm thinking you're in a strange business," she said.

"Oh, not usually," he said. "All this is an oddity."

"A single-minded photographer," she said. "Rocks and this girl." She touched the portrait of the teenager Leaphorn had noticed earlier. "Several of these. Probably the boy's girlfriend, I'd guess."

"It looks like it's a photocopy," Leaphorn said. "Not very good."

"Out of this, maybe," she said. The Ship Rock High School yearbook was on the shelf behind the enlarger.

They found the girl's portrait among the cheerleaders. She was a junior. Jenifer Dineyahze.

"I think we should go find Jenifer Dineyahze," Leaphorn said. "Maybe she can tell us something useful." But even as he said it, he doubted it.

Jenifer Dineyahze proved to be a rider of the Ship Rock school bus.

"It's a little tough to tell you exactly where the Dineyahzes live," the acting assistant principal told them, and he dug a map out of his desk drawer and showed them which school bus she rode and just about where the bus picked her up. "Back in here," he said, putting the tip of his pencil on the slope of Beautiful Mountain. "Or here, maybe." And he moved it a little toward Sanostee. "You'll see the place where the track takes off to the left."

Before they left Ship Rock, Leaphorn filled the tank of his patrol car—as he always did on junkets that would take him onto the back roads. But at least this errand took them south and west, toward Window Rock and home. And it would take them past the place where Jim Chee had arrested Ashie Pinto. It would give him a look at the rock formation where the painter had done his vandalism.

"What do you think you're going to learn?" Bourebonette asked.

"Frankly, nothing," Leaphorn said. "I think tomorrow I'll get on the telephone and try to get hold of the boy in Albuquerque and I'll ask him about the pictures. But it's sort of on the way home—or back to your car. And you never know."

They turned west off Route 666 toward Red Rock on Navajo 33.

Bourebonette pointed south toward Rol Hai Rock and then toward Barber Peak across the highway. "Those pictures," she said. "It could be a little piece of either one of those."

"Or even of some of those rays that run out from Ship Rock," he said. "Any new ideas by now of why he took them?"

"No. Not even an old idea. How about you?"

"I have an old idea," Leaphorn said. "I'm thinking that when we get to that rock formation Nez's vandal was painting, maybe it will turn out to be the same formation Ji, or Ji's boy, was photographing."

Bourebonette thought about this. "Why?"

Leaphorn chuckled. "I was afraid you'd ask me that," he said. "I think it's because since my wife died I've started watching television. That's the way the plot ought to work out."

Bourebonette didn't comment for a while. And then she said: "Well, there had to be some reason for somebody to shoot Colonel Ji. He was up around where the painter was working the night Mr. Nez was killed. At least his car was. And he took pictures of the rocks. So maybe there's a connection."

Leaphorn glanced at her, caught her looking at him. She shrugged. "Sounds silly, but the same rocks—" she said, "—that would be some connection."

Leaphorn made a left turn off the asphalt onto a dirt road which hadn't been on this year's road grading schedule. They bumped down it, raising dust. "Well," he said. "We'll soon know."

Leaphorn parked at the place the car of Officer Nez had burned. It had been hauled away—an unusual fate for a derelict vehicle on a reservation where they commonly rusted away where they died—but the place was marked by the skeletons of partially burned junipers and scorched cactus.

"There it is," Bourebonette said, pointing. "See the painted places?"

The formation rose to the southeast, one of many old volcanic extrusions scattered along the flanks of the great upthrusts that form the multitude of mountain ridges of the southern Rockies. "Where?" Leaphorn asked and, as he said it, saw a stripe of white, and another, and another, where no white should be.

"Ah," he said, and reached behind the seat of his car for his binoculars. But before he used them, he studied the formation, looking for the same pattern of shapes he memorized from the photographs. He didn't see it.

The formation seemed to have been produced by a series of eruptions. In some places the basalt had been worn smooth by eons of time and softened by growths of lichens—its cracks sprouting buffalo and bunch grass, cactus, and even scraggly junipers. Elsewhere it was newer, still ragged and black. A couple of miles long, Leaphorn guessed, with a smaller formation beyond it extending perhaps another quarter of a mile.

Through the binoculars the formation seemed even rougher and more complex. In places the upthrust seemed to have forced overlying sandstone upward, producing broken walls and leaning slabs in a chaotic labyrinth. There, in the highest part of the ridge, the painting had been done.

Done carefully. Despite what Chee had told him, that surprised Leaphorn. At the point where the binoculars were focused, the black of the basaltic surface and the white of the paint formed a slight curve, not perfect but generally clean-cut. He shifted his vision to the next spot. The shape seemed irregular. Perhaps that was because of his perspective. But here, too, the margin was clean. He could see too little of the other painted surfaces to form a judgment.

He handed the binoculars to Professor Bourebonette. "Notice the edges. Notice how carefully done," he said. While she looked, he thought about what she was seeing. As he did he understood exactly where the photographs had been taken.

His uncle had been right. Things seem random only because we see them from the wrong perspective.

He told Bourebonette about it as they drove down the bumpy road toward the Dineyahze place.

"It still sounds crazy as hell," he said, "but I think either Ji or the boy took all those photographs and blew them up to plan where to put the paint."

Professor Bourebonette looked suitably surprised. She considered. Leaphorn slowed, let the car roll across the borrow ditch and onto a road, which quickly became simply two parallel tracks through the bunch grass and snakeweed.

"Okay," Bourebonette said finally. "If you wanted to paint something regular on a totally irregular surface, I guess that's how you could do it."

"I think so," Leaphorn said. "You'd pick the spot you wanted to see it from, and take the photographs, mark out the places where the paint had to go. Little bit here on this corner of this slab, and then back here, and up there and so forth."

"That leaves the really big question, though," she said. "The big question is why anybody sane would want to paint something out here. And what it would be." She looked at him. "You have that part of it figured out?"

"Afraid not," Leaphorn said.

"I think that would take some real genius."

The patrol car eased up a long slope, jolting over rocky places. The windshield was coated with dust, but the sun was low in the southwest now, out of their faces. Leaphorn shifted down, and up, and down again. And suddenly he found another answer. Or maybe he did.

"I have another thought," he said. "About 'what.' Or more about 'why.' "

Bourebonette looked at him, waiting.

Leaphorn considered whether he would look stupid if he was wrong. It occurred to him that he was showing off. And enjoying it. He considered that. Why would he be showing off? Why enjoying this?

"Are you going to tell me?" Bourebonette asked.

Leaphorn shifted up again as the tracks leveled off. "When we get to the top of this ridge here, we're going to be able to see that formation again. From a different perspective now. I think we're going to see those painted spaces coming together. Forming a unity."

"Oh? Like what?"

"Something to do with this little girl we're going out to visit." And as he said it, realized that it sounded absurd. It would be wrong. The painting would remain, forever, a crazy jumble.

They reached the summit of the ridge. The shoulder was wide here, blocking their view of the formation. But they could see the Dineyahze place. It was built on the slope opposite them. The Dineyahze outfit included a small oblong of house with a tar-paper roof weighed down against windy weather by a scattering of old automobile tires, a hogan built of stone, a mobile home set on concrete blocks, and the usual brush arbors, corrals, and storage sheds.

"If I'm guessing right, the Ji boy took those photographs from the ridge above the house. He wanted the same view that Jenifer would have from her yard." He glanced at Bourebonette, who was looking impressed.

"If I am guessing wrong," he added, feeling sudden embarrassment, "then I have made myself look foolish."

"Right or wrong," Bourebonette said, "I'd say you have made yourself look like an innovative thinker. None of that occurred to me at all."

The rock formation emerged slowly into view as the car moved along the ridge. And then they could see the paint.

Leaphorn stopped the car. He pulled on the parking brake. He stared.

Jubilation!

It wasn't perfect from this perspective. But you could easily make it out. The white-against-black read:

I LOVE JEN

"Can you see it?" he asked. "Can you read it?"

"How about that?" Professor Bourebonette said. "Congratulations to you, Lieutenant Leaphorn."

Her smile engulfed him with warm approval.

"I should have thought of it sooner," he said. "I had all the information I needed. As soon as I knew where the girl lived, I should have guessed."

"Modesty," Bourebonette said. "I think that was right out of Sherlock Holmes."

"To tell you the truth, I'm sort of proud of it myself," he said.

"I wonder what the girl thinks?" Bourebonette said. "I think I'll ask her."

"I don't see much need to bother her now," Leaphorn said. "We were going to ask her if she had any idea what would be going on with Taka. Now we know."

"We sure do," Bourebonette said.

She was silent while he backed the car around. Then she said: "What we don't know is why somebody shot his father."

"No, we don't," Leaphorn said.

But he was beginning to think he might know that, too.

18

CHEE HAD HOPED to catch Janet Pete before the federal court session convened. But there was the problem of finding a parking place in downtown Albuquerque. So he emerged from the elevator just in time to see the U.S. marshals ushering Hosteen Pinto into the courtroom.

"Jury selection today," the receptionist at the Federal Public Defender's office had told him. "She'll be over in Judge Downey's court in the new Federal Building. On Gold."

"How long will that take?" Chee had asked, and the answer had been "Maybe all day. Maybe tomorrow. Probably you can catch her before it starts. If you hurry."

He'd hurried, but not quite enough. Maybe, he thought, there would be a recess and he could talk to her then. He nodded to the bailiff at the door and started in.

"You'll have to sit over by the wall, and about the fourth row," the bailiff told him. "All the front rows are for the jury panel, and they use the back rows until their names get called."

Chee sat against the wall in the fourth row and watched the panel being ushered in. There would be sixty of them if he remembered the procedure—men and women from around New Mexico with nothing much in common except that they lived in this judicial district and had registered to vote. Thus their names had been drawn for this duty.

When the last one was seated a middle-aged woman in a dark blue dress began spinning the bingo cage on a table beside the judge's bench, pulling out names. An elderly Hispano named Martinez was first. He came down the aisle through the gate in the railing, turned right, and took the first chair in the row inside the railing.

"Mrs. Eloise Gibbons," Blue Woman read, and a slender young woman in a gray pantsuit came down the aisle and took the chair next to Martinez.

"Mr. William Degenhardt," Blue Woman said, and a conservative-looking man with a conservative haircut and a conservative gray suit took the chair to her right.

Blue Woman continued the litany, filling the row of chairs inside the railing, and then the two rows behind it. Slightly more women than men, Chee estimated. Altogether, seven Anglos and Hispanics, a Vietnamese or Cambodian, a middle-aged Navajo woman, a man who might be an Apache, and two who were clearly Pueblo Indians, although Chee couldn't identify which of the Pueblos.

Janet Pete and a man who Chee guessed must be the federal prosecutor assigned to this case were standing in front of the high desk where the judge sat. The three were discussing something with her. Would that be an advantage? Woman judge, woman lawyer? Chee doubted it. It would be fairly common these days.

Chee felt tremendously drowsy. It was warm in the courtroom and he'd slept very little last night. He thought of his hand, which was itching under the bandage. How much use of it would he recover? He thought of what he wanted to tell Janet Pete—about Ji's son being the driver of the car he'd seen the night Nez was killed. About Ji's message on the wall. He thought of how Janet Pete looked. She was wearing something dark green with a skirt that came far below her knees. She had pretty knees, not that he'd seen them often, and pretty ankles.

Janet was standing facing the jury panel now and the judge was asking if any panelist knew her, knew her family, had had any dealing with her. A very classy woman, Chee thought. He felt a wave of affection, and of chauvinistic Navajo pride in her. And more than that, he felt a hunger for her. And a sense of failure. Since the day she'd come to the hospital to see him he'd lost ground with her. He was sure of that. She liked him less now than she did that morning.

The prosecutor was standing, undergoing the same scrutiny from the jury panel. One man on the front row put up his hand, and said he knew the man. They were members of the same church. He was excused.

Then Ashie Pinto stood. The business suit issued by the Bernalillo County jail for this appearance was too large for him, making him look even thinner than Chee had remembered.

"Face the jury panel, please, Mr. Pinto," the judge said.

Hosteen Pinto reacted to his name. He looked back at the judge, puzzled.

"Interpreter!"

The interpreter responded to the impatience in Judge Downey's voice. He awoke from whatever had been occupying his thoughts, stood, said something in Navajo too low for Chee to understand.

Hosteen Pinto looked at the man, cupped a hand behind his ear.

"She wants you to look out at those people," the interpreter said, much louder now. "So they can see you."

Pinto looked out at them, his expression sometimes embarrassed, sometimes determined. Pinto's eyes moved across the courtroom, hesitating a moment when they came to the Navajo panelist, hesitating another moment when they met the eyes of Jim Chee.

Chee looked away, down at his itching hand.

No one knew Hosteen Ashie Pinto. The whites didn't know him, nor the Hispanics, nor the Apache, nor the Pueblos, nor the Asian. *Nor Janet Pete, nor me. He is a shaman. He is a stranger to us all.*

The prosecutor looked at his notes then looked up. "Mrs. Greyeyes, I believe you live at Nakaibito. On the Navajo Reservation. Is that correct?"

"Actually, closer to Coyote Canyon," Mrs. Greyeyes said.

"But on the Reservation?"

"Yes."

"Are you a Navajo?"

"Yes."

"Do you have any clan relationships with the defendant?"

"I don't know what he is."

The prosecutor looked at his notes.

"I have two clans written down here. Turning Mountain Dinee and the Bitter Water People." He looked at the interpreter. "Is that right? Two clans?"

"Mother's and father's," the interpreter said. "Two clans."

"I am born to the Sage Brush Hill People," the woman said. "And born for Towering House Clan."

"So there is no connection? Correct?"

"We're not kinfolks," the woman said.

Judge Downey leaned forward and stared at the interpreter. "Miss Pete," she said, "do you think your client should know what is going on here? Shouldn't it be interpreted for Mr. Pinto?"

Janet Pete looked abashed.

"I would like to have it interpreted," she said.

"So ordered," said Judge Downey.

The interpreter was a man of perhaps forty with a disheveled look that was probably genetic. He explained in loud and precise Navajo the exchange between Mrs. Greyeyes and the prosecutor.

Chee began to doze. Snapped awake. The man with the conservative look was being questioned now by Janet Pete.

"Mr. Degenhardt, I want you to tell me if you have ever had or if anyone in your family, or even a close friend, has ever had any unpleasant experience involving a member of the Navajo Tribe. Have you ever been in a fight with a Navajo? Anything like that?"

Mr. Degenhardt thought about it.

The interpreter said: "She asked him if he ever been in a fight with a Navajo."

Mr. Degenhardt shook his head. "No."

"Can you think of any reason why you could not give this gentleman here, Mr. Pinto, a fair trial?"

"She say you be fair?" the interpreter said.

"No, Ma'am," Degenhardt said.

"He say yes, he be fair," the interpreter said.

Chee stopped listening. Who was the interpreter who translated Ashie Pinto's words from the tape to the transcript? Had he been as lazy as this one? Skipping? Summarizing? Or, if he was a traditional Navajo, perhaps leaving out unpleasant parts about witches and skinwalkers? He was remembering he'd decided yesterday to hear Hosteen Pinto's story in Hosteen Pinto's very own words. This business of selecting a jury would take hours. Chee got up and moved quietly out the door.

Finding a parking place near the Federal Building downtown was child's play compared to finding a place to park anywhere near the university library. Finally Chee left his pickup in a POLICE VEHICLES ONLY space behind the campus police station. He identified himself to the duty sergeant, explained his business, and got reluctant approval to leave it there.

By the time he climbed the stairs to the Reserve Room in Zimmerman Library, checked out the tapes and transcripts, and went to work, it was almost noon. He was hungry. He should have stopped for lunch.

He started with the horse thief tape. He'd listened to some of it already, with a lot of skipping around, and he'd read a copy of the transcript in Tagert's office. Now as he listened to Pinto's voice droning the same story into his earphones his sleepiness returned. But he fought it off, checking what he was hearing with the library's copy of the transcript. When he came to a discrepancy, he stopped the tape and replayed it. The revisions tended to be minor corner-cuttings or sometimes eliminations of repetition. By one P.M. he'd found nothing that changed the meaning or left out anything significant.

Sleepiness was almost overpowering. His stomach grumbled with hunger. He put down the transcript, took off the earphones, yawned and stretched. The air around him had the deadness common to rooms without open windows, common to rooms where old things are stored. The silence was absolute, the place empty except for himself and the young woman who sat behind the desk at the entrance, working on files.

He would walk across the mall to the Union and get something to eat. No, he would walk across Central Avenue to the Frontier and have a green chile enchilada. But first he would skip ahead and see if the translator had cheated when the subject became witchcraft. When he'd read the transcript before, it had seemed that Pinto had said remarkably little about why the Ghostway cure had been needed for Delbito Willie. Perhaps he'd actually said more.

He ran the tape fast forward, listening to Pinto's old voice quacking in his ears until he found the proper place.

". . . And then the two white men rode their horses out into a place where there was a lava flow. It is dangerous to ride a horse in there, even in daylight, because, you know, he might get his hoof in one of those cracks—just a little slip, you know, and break his leg and throw you onto the rocks."

Chee stopped the tape and checked the translation. Just as he remembered, the copy he'd read omitted the digression about the horse breaking its leg. He started the tape again.

". . . The Yucca Fruit Clan men followed very slowly. The lava was rough there and they kept way back anyway because of the man with the yellow mustache. They say he was a very good shot even riding on a horse. Finally they found where the white men had tied up their horses and went up into the rocks. Right there, Delbito Willie and the Yucca Fruit Clan men they stopped, too, because they knew Yellow Mustache would be protecting his horses with his rifle and because they saw then where it was the white men had gone. It was up there in the place where the witches gather. It was up there in the cave where the evil ones come to make somebody into a skinwalker. Some of those Yucca Fruit Clan men knew about it. They lived over on the other side of the Carrizo Mountains, but they had heard about this place. And you could tell it was this place because of the way the rocks were formed there. They say it looked like the ears of a mule sticking up. If you looked at it from the west, that's the way it looked. Two sharp spires with a low saddle between them. They say it looked like a saddle, like one of those McClellan saddles, with the steep rise up the back side and the horn sticking up on the other side. Reminded people of a saddle."

Chee stopped the tape. None of this, not a word of it, was in the transcript he'd read at Tagert's office. He turned the pages of the library copy. None of it was here, either. Two pages were missing, cut out with a very sharp knife or a razor blade.

He ran the tape again, hearing how Delbito Willie wanted to go in after the white men, to see if they were dead. If they were he would take the rifle of Yellow Mustache—a very fine rifle. The argument had lasted two days, with all of the Yucca Fruit men against it until finally, when they all agreed the white men must be dead by now, one of the Yucca Fruit Clan agreed to go partway with Willie—but not as far as the witches' cave. And Willie had gone in and had come out with the rifle of Yellow Mustache, and the word that both men were indeed dead.

He checked the tape and transcript in at the desk.

"Is there a way to find out who did the translating? Any record kept of that?"

"Just a minute," the woman said. "I think so."

She disappeared into a door marked STAFF ONLY.

Chee waited, rechecking his reasoning. He thought he knew who the translator would be.

He was right.

The woman reappeared, holding a file card.

"Someone named William Redd," she said.

19

LEAPHORN WAS HAVING one of those frustrating mornings which cause all bureaucrats to wish the telephone had never been invented.

At first, he got nothing but a no answer at the number of Mr. Doan Van Ha, the Albuquerque uncle to whom Taka Ji had been sent for safekeeping. Finally, when someone did pick up the phone it proved to be an elderly woman who identified herself as Khanh Ha. Her command of English was barely rudimentary. After a few minutes of total failure to communicate, Khanh Ha said: "You stay. I get boy."

Leaphorn stayed, telephone receiver held to his ear, listening to the silence in the home of the Ha family. Minutes ticked away. He noticed his windows were dusty. Through them he noticed that one of the crows that used the cottonwoods across the road from the Justice Building had lost some wing feathers and flew out of balance. He noticed that the high clouds he had seen when he came to work had thickened and spread from the northern horizon across most of the sky. Maybe it would snow. They needed it. It was late. He thought of Emma, of how she gloried in these days when time hung stalled between the seasons, urging winter on, then cheering for spring, then happily announcing that tomorrow it would be summer and thunderstorm season. Then pleased to see the summer die, anxious for the peaceful gold of autumn. Emma. Happiness was always on her side of the horizon, safely in Dinetah, safely between the Sacred Mountains. She never felt any need to learn what lay beyond them.

A door slammed faintly in distant Albuquerque. Then came the sound of footsteps on a hard floor, and a boyish voice said: "Hello?"

"This is Lieutenant Leaphorn, Taka," Leaphorn said. "Remember? We talked at your house in Ship Rock."

"You have the wrong number," the boy said. "I think so."

"I am calling for Taka Ji," Leaphorn said.

"This is Jimmy Ha," the boy said. "I think they took Taka to my aunt's house. Down in the South Valley."

"Do you have that number?"

Jimmy Ha had it, but it took another five minutes to find it. Then, when Leaphorn dialed it, he got another no answer.

He fiddled ineffectively with his paperwork, passing enough time to make another try sensible. Again, no answer. He hung up, dialed the Federal Public Defender's office in Albuquerque.

No, Jim Chee wasn't there. He had been in this morning but he'd left.

"To go where?" Leaphorn asked.

To the federal courthouse.

"How about Janet Pete? Is she in?"

Janet Pete was at the courthouse, too. A jury was being selected.

"When she comes in would you tell her that I have to get a message to Jim Chee. Tell her to get word to him that I have to talk to him. Tell her it's important."

When he hung up, he made no pretense of doing paperwork. He simply sat and thought. Why had Colonel Ji been killed? He swiveled in his chair and stared at his map. It told him nothing. Nothing except that everything seemed to focus on a rock formation south of Ship Rock. Nothing made any sense. And that, he knew, was because he was seeing it all from the wrong perspective.

He thought about Professor Bourebonette.

He thought about Jim Chee. Unreliable perhaps. But a good mind.

He noticed his wastebasket. The maintenance man who had been neglecting to wash his windows had also neglected to empty it. Leaphorn leaned over and fished out the brochure describing the wonders of the People's Republic of China. He spread it on the desk and studied the pictures again.

Then he threw it back in the wastebasket.

20

ODELL REDD WAS not at home. Or if he was, he didn't respond to Jim Chee's persistent knocking. Chee gave up. He found a vacant parking place in a loading zone behind the Biology Building and walked over to the History Department.

No, Jean Jacobs hadn't seen him, either.

"Not this morning. He came in yesterday. We went out to lunch." Jean Jacobs's expression made it clear that this was a happy event.

"No idea where he is?"

"He should be working on his dissertation. Maybe in the library."

The idea of hunting through the labyrinthine book stacks at Zimmerman held no appeal to Chee. He sat down.

"How about your boss? Still missing?"

"Nary a word," Jacobs said. "I'm beginning to seriously think he died someplace. Maybe his wife killed him, or one of his graduate students." She laughed. "They'd draw straws. Stand in line for it if they thought they had any chance of getting away with it."

"What kind of car does he drive?"

"I don't know." She opened a drawer and extracted a file. "I've seen him driving a white four-door sedan, and sometimes a sexy sports car. Whorehouse red."

She extracted a card from the file.

"I think that's when his wife gave up on him, after he bought that red one. Let's see, now. Oldsmobile Cutlass. Nineteen ninety. Corvette coupe. That's a 1982 model. But cool, you know. Impresses the cute little coeds looking for a father figure to take them to bed."

Jean Jacobs laughed when she said it, but it didn't sound like the thought amused her.

"That's his application for a parking permit?"

"Right," Jacobs said. "It covers both cars. You just hang it on the one you're driving."

Chee looked down at his hand which was itching furiously. He resisted an impulse to rub it, adjusted the bandage instead. Jacobs was watching him.

"Healing up okay?"

Chee nodded. He was thinking about a low-slung Corvette, or a brand-new Oldsmobile, banging over those tracks south of Ship Rock.

"Which car did he drive mostly? Which one was he driving that last day you saw him, that evening when he came in to pick up his mail? You have any way of knowing what he was driving?"

"No," Jacobs said. She hesitated. "He just came in and got his mail. And stuff."

"Stuff?"

"Well, he took some stuff he'd collected for a paper he was doing. It had been on his desk there. And a couple of letters that were in his out-basket."

"Was he all right? What did he say?"

Jacobs sat looking out of the window. She glanced at him and back out the window again.

"Were you here when he came in?"

"No."

"Just the next day you noticed he'd been in and picked up stuff?"

Jacobs nodded.

They considered each other.

"But he left me a note," she said. She rummaged in her desk drawer, extracted a salmon-colored WHILE YOU WERE OUT slip, handed it to Chee.

Scrawled across it was:

"Jacobs—Call admissions. Get class lists on time for a change. Tell maintenance to clean up this pigpen, get windows washed."

"He doesn't sign his notes?" Chee asked.

Jacobs laughed. "No please. No thank you. That's Tagert's signature."

"But it's his handwriting?"

She glanced at the note. "Who else?"

He used Tagert's telephone to call the Federal Public Defender's office for Janet Pete. The receptionist's voice boomed in his ear, telling him that Miss Pete was still at the courthouse. He held the receiver away from his ear, frowning.

Jean Jacobs was smiling about it. "The professor is hard of hearing," she said. "He kept complaining to the telephone people about their equipment mumbling so they came in finally and put in that high-volume phone."

"Wow," Chee said.

"Just hold it a little way from your ear. It's easy once you know how to handle it."

The receptionist was talking again, less painfully now that he was following Jacobs's advice.

"But there's a message for you," she was saying. "For her actually. She's supposed to tell you to call Window Rock. 'Please tell Mr. Chee to call Lieutenant Joe Leaphorn at his office.' "

Chee called.

"You in Albuquerque?" Leaphorn asked.

Chee said he was.

"We've got sort of a funny situation," the lieutenant said. "It turns out that Taka Ji is the rock painter that Delbert Nez was after."

"Oh," Chee said. He digested the thought. "How'd you find out?"

Leaphorn told him.

"Has anyone talked to him?"

"I can hardly hear you," Leaphorn said. "It sounds like you're standing out in the hall."

Chee pulled the mouthpiece closer to his lips. "I said has anyone talked to him? He was out there the night Nez was killed. Maybe he saw something."

Leaphorn explained that the boy had been taken to Albuquerque to stay with relatives. He gave Chee the name and the number. "Nobody home when I called. But I think somebody should talk to him in person."

"Did you tell the FBI?"

Chee's question provoked an extended silence. Finally Leaphorn chuckled. "The Bureau was not particularly interested in a vandalism case at the moment."

"They don't see the connection?"

"With what? The agent handling the Ji killing is new out here, and pretty new in the business for that matter. I got the impression that he'll talk to the boy one of these days but I don't think he could see how painting his romantic message on rocks had anything to do with somebody shooting the colonel. I think they see some sort of link back to Vietnam. And what he did there."

"How about with somebody shooting Officer Delbert Nez?" Chee asked.

Another pause. Then Leaphorn said: "Yeah. That's what troubles me, too. I think that's the key to it. Have you got it figured out?"

Chee found, to his surprise, that being asked that question by Lieutenant Joe Leaphorn pleased him. The question was clearly serious. The famous Joe Leaphorn, asking him that. Unfortunately he didn't have an answer. Not a good one.

"Not really," he said. "But I think once we understand it, we're going to find there was more to the Nez homicide than we know about."

"Exactly. Has the trial started yet?"

"They're picking the jury. Maybe they'll start it tomorrow. Or the day after."

"You'll be one of the first witnesses, I'd say. That right?"

"I'm under subpoena. The prosecutor wants me to tell about the arrest. What I saw."

"So you'll be in Albuquerque," Leaphorn said. "I know you're on leave but I think you ought to go see the Ji kid. See what he'll tell you. See if he saw anything."

"I was planning to do that," Chee said.

"Unofficially," Leaphorn said. "Not our case, of course." There was a pause. "And get that telephone fixed."

21

THE ADDRESS LEAPHORN had given him for the Ha residence was in the opposite direction from the Tagert address. But Tagert's house wasn't far from the university campus and Chee made the detour. He had a hunch he wanted to check.

It was a single-story, brick-fronted house on the lower end of the middle class—the sort of house history professors can afford if they are frugal with their grocery buying. Chee parked on the street, walked up the empty driveway, and rang the bell. No answer. He rang it four times. Still no answer. Then he walked across the yard and peered through the garage window. It was dirty, but not too dirty for Chee to see a red Corvette parked inside and beyond it a white Oldsmobile sedan.

The Ha residence was neat, standing out for its tidiness in a weed-grown neighborhood which was on the upper end of the lower class. There was no car in the driveway, but as Chee parked his truck at the curb, an elderly blue Chevy sedan pulled up beside the carport. The boy sitting beside the young woman who was driving was Taka Ji.

They started their talking in the driveway, Chee leaning on the sedan door, the boy standing stiffly facing him, and Miss Janice Ha, the driver, standing beside Taka—a silent, disapproving observer.

"I was the officer who made the arrest out there that night," Chee told the boy. "I saw you driving your father's car. I was in the police car you met just before you turned off the pavement toward Ship Rock."

Taka Ji simply looked at him.

"Now we know some more," Chee said. "We know you're the one who painted those rocks. It might help us catch the man who shot your father if you tell me what you saw."

Janice Ha put her hand on the boy's shoulder. "I think we should go inside," she said.

The front room of the house was almost as small as Chee's own cramped lodgings—but there was space in it, between the two front windows, for a shrine. The shrine featured a foot-tall plaster statue of the Blessed Virgin in her traditional blue-and-white robes looking down serenely at two small candles and two small pots of chrysanthemums. A woman who reminded Chee of a smaller, slightly older, and female version of Colonel Ji was sitting on the sofa beside it.

She was Thuy Ha, and she bowed deeply to Chee when Janice Ha introduced him.

"Taka's father was my mother's younger brother," Janice Ha explained. "Her English is not yet good. It was a long time before we could get her released by the Communists. She joined us only last year."

"I hate to intrude at this bad time," Chee said. He looked at Taka Ji. "But I think Mr. Ji here might be able to help us."

Janice spoke to the woman—translating Chee presumed—and Thuy Ha said something in response. "She said he will help you any way he can," Janice Ha said.

The older woman spoke again, a longer statement this time. The girl responded briefly and the older woman responded. Her voice sounded angry.

"Mrs. Ha asked me to tell you that the Communists killed Colonel Ji," Janice Ha said. She looked embarrassed. "She said I should tell you Colonel Ji worked faithfully for the Americans, and made many enemies because of that, and the Communists sent someone all the way over here to America just to kill him."

The woman was watching Chee intently.

"Would you ask her if she knows who might have done it?"

Janice Ha translated. Mrs. Ha spoke a single word.

"Communists," Janice Ha said.

Taka Ji broke the brief silence that followed that.

"I didn't see very much," he said. "It was getting dark, and the storm was coming."

"Just tell me what you saw," Chee said.

First he had heard a car. He had climbed down from the ladder and was sitting on the sand beside it, looking at the blown-up photograph of the rocks, deciding exactly where he should add the next section of paint. He had heard the engine of a vehicle, revving up, driving in very low gear, coming in closer to this formation than vehicles usually come. He had folded up the ladder and put it out of sight. Then he had hidden himself. But after a while he heard voices, and he climbed up to where he could see what was going on.

"There were three people. They had left the truck, or whatever it was, parked back behind some of those junipers on the slope. I could just see the roof. And three of them were walking toward the formation. Not toward me, but more toward the west. At first I thought it was one man and two women because one was larger than the other two. But then I saw when they got a little closer that one of them was a real thin old man."

"Ashie Pinto?"

"Yes," Taka Ji said. "I saw his picture in the Farmington *Times* that Sunday, after he was arrested. It looked like the man who killed the policeman."

"The other two? Did you recognize them?"

The boy shook his head.

"Could you, if you saw them again?"

"One of them, I think. The bigger one. I got a better look at him. The other one, I don't know."

"But the other one was a woman?"

"I don't know. I think I thought that just because of the size. They had on a dark-colored felt hat, and a big jacket, and jeans." Taka stopped, looking doubtful. His aunt said something terse in Vietnamese.

"Okay," Taka said. "After that, they disappeared up into the rocks. I just stayed there awhile, where I was. I was thinking I should go, because I didn't want anybody to know what I was doing." He stopped, glanced at his Mrs. Ha, said something haltingly in Vietnamese.

She nodded, smiled at him, reached over and patted his knee.

"He said he was afraid people would think what he was doing was silly," Janice Ha said. Her expression said she agreed with her cousin. They would think it was silly.

"I thought if I left now, they would maybe see me driving away. I always left the car down in the arroyo where nobody could see it, but they would see me driving away. So I decided I would wait until they left." He stopped again.

"Go on," Janice said. "Tell us what happened." She looked at Chee. "We didn't know anything about this either. He should have told the police."

Taka flushed. "My father told me not to tell anybody. He said it sounded like something I should not be mixed up in. He said to just be quiet about it."

"Well, better late than never," Janice said. "Tell us."

"I wondered what was happening over there, so I decided to get closer so I could see. I know that place real well by now, or the part of it where I was working anyway. It's full of snakes. They come in there when the weather starts getting cold because those black rocks stay warm even in the winter and the field mice move in there too. And, normally, those snakes hunt at night because that's when the kangaroo rats and the little mice come out to eat, but in the winter it's cold at night and the snakes are cold-blooded reptiles so they stay in their holes after . . ."

Taka had noticed Janice's expression—impatient with this digression into natural science.

"Anyway," he said hurriedly, "I know where to walk and how not to get snakebit. So I went over in the direction I had seen the three people go and in a little while I could hear voices. Talking up there in the rocks. So I moved around there—it was just beginning to get dark now and there was lightning up in the mountains. And then I saw the one who killed the policeman. He hadn't gone up in there with the other two. He was sitting out by a piñon tree on the ground. I watched him awhile, and he didn't do anything except once in a while he would drink out of a bottle he had with him.

"I thought about that for a while and I decided that if that one was drunk, then when it got just a little darker, I could get down to the arroyo and get my car and slip away without being seen. I just sat there and waited a little while. I heard the two who went up into the rocks yelling. It sounded like they were really excited. I thought they had stirred up some of the snakes back in there."

Taka Ji stopped, looked at his aunt, and at Janice, and finally at Chee. He cleared his throat.

"Then I heard a shot," he said. "And I got out of there and got the car and went home."

The boy looked around him again. Finished. Waiting for questions.

Janice Ha was looking startled. "A shot! Did you tell your dad? You should have told the police."

Mrs. Ha said something in Vietnamese to Janice, got an explanation, responded to that. Then Janice said to her mother: "Well, I don't care. We're living in America now."

"Where did the sound of the shot come from?" Chee asked.

"It sounded like from back in the rocks. Back in there where they had been yelling. I thought maybe they had shot at a snake."

"Just one shot?"

"One," Taka said.

"Were you still there when Officer Nez came?"

"I heard the car. I heard it coming. There's a track that runs along there west of that rocky ridge where we were. It was coming along that. Toward us."

"Did he have his siren going? His red light on?"

"No, but when I saw it, I saw it was a Navajo Tribal Police car. I decided I better go. Right away. I got away from there and went to the arroyo and got the car and went home."

"Do you remember meeting me?"

"It scared me," Taka said. "I saw your police car, coming fast, toward me." He paused. "I should have stopped. I should have told you I heard the shot."

"It wouldn't have made any difference," Chee said. But he was thinking that it might have saved Colonel Ji's life.

Mrs. Ha was watching them, listening to every word. Chee thought that she must know a little English.

"I want you to give me some directions," Chee said. "I have a big-scale map out in my truck. I want to show you that and have you mark on it exactly where those people were in that rock formation."

Taka Ji nodded.

Mrs. Ha said something in Vietnamese, said it directly to Jim Chee and then glanced at her daughter, awaiting the translation.

"She said: 'We have a saying in Vietnam—' " Janice Ha hesitated. "I'm not sure of the word for that animal in English. Oh, yes. The saying is that fate is as gentle with men as the mongoose is with mice."

Chee shook his head, nodded to the woman. "Would you tell your mother that Navajos say the same thing in different words. We say: 'Coyote is always out there waiting, and Coyote is always hungry.' "

It was obvious when the elevator doors opened that federal district court was recessing for lunch. People were milling in the hallway. Janet Pete was hurrying for the elevator, directly toward him. He let her in, along with twenty or thirty other citizens.

"I found Colonel Ji's boy," Chee told her. "I just came from talking with him." He explained what Leaphorn had learned—that Taka Ji was the elusive painter of stone, that Taka Ji had been out on the basalt ridge the evening Delbert Nez was killed.

"You're going to tell me that you have your witness now. That that boy saw Ashie Pinto shoot Delbert Nez."

She was pressed against him, sideways, in the jam-packed elevator. All Chee could see was the top of her head and part of her cheek. But if he could see her face, the expression would be disappointed. He could tell that from her tone.

"No," Chee said. "As a matter of—" The fat man with the briefcase and the Old Spice cologne leaned against his hand, causing Chee to suck in his breath. He raised the hand gingerly and held it above his head, preferring looking silly to risking the pain.

"As a matter of fact, I wanted to tell you I may have arrested the wrong man. Could you get the trial postponed a little? Maybe a few days?"

"What?" Janet said, so loudly that the buzz of competing conversations surrounding them hushed. "We shouldn't be talking about the case in here," she said. But then she whispered, "What did he see?"

"Before Nez got there, there were three people out there. Pinto and two other people. Maybe two other men, maybe a man and a woman."

Janet had managed to turn herself in the crush of people about forty-five degrees—a maneuver which Chee found most pleasant—and looked up at him. Her face was full of questions. He went on, "He said Pinto sat down by a tree on the grass and was drinking from a bottle. The others climbed up in the rocks. He heard them yelling up in there, and then he heard a shot. He thought they'd killed a rattlesnake. Remember those?"

Janet's face expressed distaste. She remembered them all too well.

"Then he heard Nez's police car. And he left."

Chee had his chin tucked against his chest, looking down at her. He was conscious of her faint perfume, of her hip pressed against him, of hair which smelled of high country air and sunshine. He could see her face now. But he couldn't read her expression. It baffled him.

"You think that helps prove you caught the wrong man? Helps Hosteen Pinto?"

"Helps Hosteen Pinto? Well, sure it does. Somebody else had the pistol, or at least a gun of some kind, before Nez was shot. All Pinto had, as far as the boy could see, was the bottle. Sure it helps. It creates a reasonable doubt. Don't you think so?"

Janet Pete had put her arms around his waist and hugged him fiercely.

"Ah, Jim," she said. "Jim."

And it took Chee, bandaged hand held high over his head, several seconds to realize that everyone on the elevator who faced the right way must be staring at them. And when he realized it he didn't care.

22

TAKA JI PROVED to be as efficient at marking Jim Chee's map as he had been plotting out his romantic signal to Jenifer Dineyahze. Chee drove almost directly to the site and found the place in the adjoining arroyo where Taka had hidden his father's vehicle. He climbed out of his pickup and stood beside it for a moment, stretching cramped muscles and plotting the most efficient way to climb into the outcrop.

Somewhere back in those black rocks was what Professor Tagert was looking for—probably the skeleton of Butch Cassidy. There was also something that had caused Redd to change a translation to foil Tagert, something that eighty years ago had caused a stubborn Navajo to undergo a cure for exposure to witches. Back in there two *biligaana* bandits had probably died a long time ago. And back in there, Taka Ji last month had heard someone shoot a snake, or perhaps another human, or perhaps nothing.

Since leaving Albuquerque in the early afternoon, Chee had been racing against the weather as well as the sun. As far south as the point where Highway 44 entered the Jicarilla Reservation, he'd been conscious of the darkness on the northwestern horizon. "A slow-moving storm, this one, and that means we might get some substantial snow," Howard Morgan had told them on the Channel 7 news. "But of course, if the jet stream moves north, it could miss most of New Mexico." The storm had indeed moved slowly, much more slowly than the reckless seventy to eighty Chee had been pushing his pickup in defiance of law and common sense. Even so, by the time he passed the Huerfano Mesa two-thirds of the sky was black with storm and the smell of snow was in the air.

His nostrils were still full of that aroma of cold wetness as he stood beside the truck. The sun was almost on the horizon, shining through a narrow slot not closed in the west between cloud and earth. The slanting light outlined every crevasse in shadowy relief, making apparent the broken ruggedness of the ridge. It rose, ragged and tumbled shapes in black and gray, out of a long sloping hummock—what a million years or so of erosion had left of the mountain of volcanic ash that had once buried the volcano's core. From where Chee stood there seemed to be dozens of ways up into the ridge. Most of them would dead-end at walls of lava.

He found what traces of Taka Ji's tracks the rain that night had left and followed them—helped by the angle of the light. Then he found other tracks, easy-to-follow high-heeled cowboy boots among them. They led up into the malpais.

They led, as Chee was thinking, into Tse A'Digash. That was the term Hosteen Pinto had used—the rocks where witches gathered. There was that to think of. That, and the variety of rattlesnakes which would have been accumulating here since the first autumn cold snaps, taking advantage of a final few days of warmth from the rocks before hibernating for the winter. Maybe they would already be in hibernation. Chee doubted it. The old shamans watched such things closely. And they would not have yet started scheduling those curing rituals which could only be held when the snakes were safely asleep. Ah, well. Snakes preyed on animals small enough to be swallowed, not on men. But snakes struck men in self-defense. With that thought in mind, with the reputation this place had earned—even a hundred years ago—for witches, Chee moved cautiously.

The first path he chose led into a pocket of rocks with no exits. The second, after he climbed a difficult tilted slab of stone, led him higher and higher into the ridge. The dying sunlight no longer reached this path but the going was relatively easy. Obviously this walkway had been used for many years by animal and man. Here a cactus had been broken by a careless step, and healed with time. There a clump of buffalo grass had been distorted by the pressure of footsteps. Now and then, where the rocky formation fended off the rain, Chee picked up recent boot prints. The high-heeled boot marks were no longer evident. They must have been Ashie Pinto's boots. Ashie Pinto had been too wise to enter here. Pinto had sat beside a piñon on the grass, not taking any chances with destiny. But Coyote had been waiting out there, too.

Chee was high in the rocks before he saw his first snake. It was a smallish prairie rattler which had been moving slowly across the pathway just as he turned a corner between shoulder-high boulders. Chee stopped. Snake stopped. It formed itself into a coil, but the motion was lethargic. Chee stepped back to where his human smell would be less likely to reach the reptile. Waited a moment, looked around the rock. The snake was gone.

Chee paused as he stepped over the snake's track across the sand and took time to erase the zigzag marking with his toe. He couldn't remember the reason for this action, just that it was one of the litany of taboos and their counters his grandmother had taught him—a small courtesy to Big Snake.

Not fifty feet beyond where the snake had been, he found the place he had come to find.

In some forgotten time, a great upsurge of molten magma had produced a cul-de-sac walled in by slabs of weathered, lichen-covered basalt. At the wide end, a bubble of this molten rock had burst—forming a small cave. Eons of migrating sand, dust, and organic material had been trapped here, borne directly in by the wind or washed down from the rocks above. It had formed a flat floor on which bunch and needle grass grew when enough water seeped in from above. At the near edge of this little floor, Chee saw the weathered ruins of what had been a saddle.

Chee stopped and studied the place.

Even from where he stood, yards away, he could see the floor had been disturbed by foot tracks. He heard a scraping sound. Or thought he did. When he had left his truck there had been a breeze, the edge of what weather people call "proximity wind" stirred up on the edges of a storm. Now that had died away, leaving the dead calm that so often comes just as the first flakes fall.

Had he heard something? Chee couldn't be sure. Probably just nerves—the proximity of witches. Witches. That caused him to think of Joe Leaphorn, to whom belief in witches was superstitious anathema. Chee had come to terms with them in another way. He saw what the origin mythology said of them as a metaphor. Some choose to violate the Way of the People, choosing incest, murder, and material riches over the order and harmony of the Navajo Way. Call them what you like, Chee knew they existed. He knew they were dangerous.

Now Chee listened and heard almost nothing. A meadowlark somewhere out of sight ran its soprano meadowlark scales. Down near the arroyo where he'd parked, the crows were quarreling. He heard nothing to explain his nervousness.

The sun was down now just below the horizon, and was coloring the bottom of the storm cloud a dazzling yellow in the far west and dull rose over Chee's head. Reflected light washed the rocky landscape with a dull red tint—making vision deceptive. No time to waste.

He walked past the old saddle into the cul-de-sac. And stopped again.

First he saw the hat. Sand had drifted over most of it, but part of the brim and much of the crown were visible. Apparently a very old hat of once-black felt now faded into mottled gray. Beyond the hat, over a low partition of sloping rock, he saw a pant leg and a boot—also mostly buried under the drifted dust.

Chee drew a deep breath and let it out, steadying himself. Apparently, old Hosteen Pinto's story was true. At least one man had died here a long time ago. In a moment, he would check for the second one. No terrible hurry. Chee, like most Navajos who hold to the traditions of the People, would avoid a corpse as diligently as an orthodox Jew or Moslem would avoid roast pork. They were taboo. They caused sickness.

But there were cures for such sickness if it couldn't be avoided. Chee walked over to inspect the corpse.

The man who wore the pant leg lay mostly far under an overhang of stone—seeking shade probably when he was dying. Now, too late, it protected him from wind and weather. But the desiccating heat had converted him into a shriveled mummy swaddled in faded clothing.

There should be another man, Chee thought. He found him in the little cave.

This had been a bigger man, and he, too, had been partly mummified by the dry heat. His hat had been placed on his face but under its brim Chee could see a long mustache, bleached a gray-white. This body had been moved, pulled out flat on the sand. It still wore a gun belt but the holster was empty. Here seemed to be Professor Tagert's famous Butch Cassidy. Here was Tagert's revenge upon his detractors.

He stood studying the body. Part of the man's vest had been torn away and part of the other clothing had pulled apart when it had been dragged from under the sheltering rocks. Or perhaps, totally rotten, had fallen away by its own weight. Or perhaps Tagert had gone through Mr. Cassidy's pockets in search of identification.

Had Tagert been here? He must have been one of the two people Taka Ji had seen. Chee checked for tracks. They were everywhere. Tracks of two people. Flat-heeled boots with pointed toes, about size ten, and something much smaller made by patterned rubber soles.

Where were their saddlebags? One had been strong enough to carry his saddle up. Surely he would have brought the bags. He looked for a place they might be hidden. The shelf behind him—the most logical place to toss them—was empty. He noticed a deep slot about shoulder high between two layers of rock. He peered into it—cautiously, because it was a perfect place for a snake to rest. Indeed, a snake was coiled back in the crack. It looked like a full-grown diamondback rattler. To the left of the snake, where the slot was a little deeper, Chee could see the tannish-gray color of old canvas. A saddlebag had been pushed back there out of sight. He could reach it, he thought, if he didn't mind risking irritating the snake.

He looked around for an adequate stick and settled for a limb broken from an overhanging juniper.

"*Hohzho,* Hosteen Snake," Chee said. "Peace. Live with beauty all around you." He moved the stick into the slot. "Just take it easy. Don't mean to trouble you."

He could reach the saddlebag without getting his hand in range of the snake. But he couldn't move it.

The snake tested the air with its tongue, didn't like the human aroma it detected, and began readjusting its coil. The tip of its tail emerged. It rattled.

"*Hohzho,*" Chee said. He withdrew hand and stick and looked around, seeking something more suitable for extracting the saddlebags.

Then he noticed drag marks.

They were fresh. Something large and heavy had been pulled across the sandy space to his left and into the rocks.

Chee followed. He turned the corner.

William Odell Redd was standing there. He had an oversized revolver in his hand, pointing more or less at Chee's knees. And there, at Redd's feet, was the body of a small man, face up, as if Redd had dragged him by the shoulders.

"I wish you hadn't come back here," Redd said.

Chee thought, So do I. But he said: "What are you doing here?"

"I came after some things of mine," Redd said. "I guessed you'd be coming. I was going to be gone before you got here."

"I guess Jean Jacobs mentioned it to you," Chee said.

"A great girl," Redd said. "Really."

"I thought so too."

Redd was looking down at Tagert. "He treated her like dirt," Redd said. "He treated everybody like dirt. The son-of-a-bitch."

"Is that why you shot him?"

"No," Redd said, still looking down at the professor. "Probably should have. Long ago."

Chee was looking at the pistol. It looked about a hundred years old. It probably was. Probably it had come from the holster of Butch Cassidy, or whoever the bandit turned out to be. What mattered was whether it would still work. It looked ancient and dusty. But not rusty. It was cocked. The hammer had gone backward so it would probably come forward. Fast enough to detonate the cartridge? Maybe. Would the cartridge still be good after all these years? It seemed doubtful, but this arid climate preserved almost everything. Taka had heard a shot up here. This pistol? Shooting Professor Tagert? Chee found it difficult to think of anything but what Redd planned to do with the weapon. But he didn't want to ask.

It was snowing now. Small dry flakes drifted in, hanging in the air, disappearing. Chee found his mind working in an odd way. It had deduced why Colonel Ji had been killed, which was not at this moment a high-priority question. He and Janet had talked about Ji in Redd's house, about Ji being the owner of the car seen leaving this area after Nez's death. Redd must have seen it that night, too. Must have presumed the murder of Tagert had been observed. Must have gone to Ship Rock and killed Ji as soon as he'd learned from them (or thought he had learned) the identity of the witness. And killed the wrong person. But there was no right person. Taka hadn't seen the killing either.

Now, suddenly, Chee saw how this information might be useful. If he could be subtle enough. He said:

"Did you see the boy in here that night? The boy who was painting the rocks?"

"What boy?" Redd looked surprised.

"The Ship Rock High School boy," Chee said. "He saw your car in here. Saw you with Hosteen Pinto and," Chee glanced at the body, "with the professor. Climbing up here. The two of you, he said. Not Pinto. He said Pinto stayed behind and got drunk."

Redd looked stricken. "It was the math teacher," he said. "Not a boy."

"We were wrong about that. It wasn't the math teacher. It was a high school kid."

"Ah, shit," Redd said. "Ah, shit." He leaned back against the rock. "So they'll be after me, then. No matter what."

"Best thing would be to turn yourself in," Chee said.

Redd wasn't listening. He was shaking his head. "Weird," he said. "Weird. The way this all started."

"How did it?"

"I was just going to squeeze a thousand bucks out of the old bastard. Just what he owed me for the overtime he was always working me and not paying me for."

"By holding out part of the translation?" Chee asked. "You knew he wanted to find this place. These dead cowboys, or whoever."

"Butch Cassidy," Redd said, absently. "Yeah. I left that part of the story out. The part that located this place. Then I told Tagert that since I know Navajo and can talk to people I'd be able to find it. He gave me a five-hundred-dollar advance." Redd looked up at Chee, and laughed. "I found this ridge all right. That was easy enough with the details Pinto had in his story. But I couldn't find this spot. The son-of-a-bitch wanted his money back. Then I got the idea of hiring Pinto. As a crystal gazer, you know. Sometimes that works, I heard, especially if the shaman knows something he's not telling."

"So Pinto found it for you?"

"We brought him here. He looked in his crystals. Put 'em on the ground, used pollen, did some chanting and looked into them and told us where to climb up into here. He was very vague about it at first but Tagert poured the whiskey into him. Loosened him up."

"So why did you kill Tagert? He wouldn't give you the other five hundred bucks?"

Redd was staring at him. "You said the boy saw me shoot Tagert? That's right?"

Chee nodded.

"You bastard," Redd said. "No he didn't." He laughed. Relieved. Delighted.

"What do you mean?"

"I mean I didn't kill the son-of-a-bitch. I didn't shoot Tagert. The boy couldn't have seen that. I'll bet he didn't see a damned thing."

"He saw you," Chee said, but Redd wasn't listening.

"I do believe this is going to work out after all," Redd said, half to himself. He stepped over Tagert's body, looked down at it.

"I'll tell you why I should have shot him, though. Not for any five hundred dollars." He poked Tagert's shoulder with the toe of his boot. "For lots of money."

The pistol was now pointed directly at Chee and Redd was looking at him over it.

"Do you know about the robbery? The one these two bandidos were running from?"

"A train robbery, I think. Up in Utah, wasn't it?" Chee asked. But he was asking himself what Redd meant. That he hadn't shot Tagert. If he hadn't, who had?

"Right," Redd said. "Not much money in it, and they lost most of that because the third man in the bunch was carrying it and he got shot. But the train was making stops at all the little post offices out here, stocking them up with stamps and stuff. There were just twenty or thirty silver dollars and some five-dollar gold pieces in the bag they had. But there were a dozen or so packages of stamps. You know what that means?"

Chee was remembering the stamp collector's book he'd seen in Redd's house.

"I'd guess it means a lot of money," he said.

"A lot of money! Dozens of sheets of uncancelled stamps. All kinds. I'm no stamp man but I looked some of them up. Five-cent William McKinleys worth like four hundred dollars for a block of four. Ten-cent Louisiana Purchase memorials worth eight hundred bucks for a block of four. Some of those one-centers worth over a hundred bucks apiece. I didn't add it all up, but we're talking about three or four hundred thousand dollars."

"Lot of money," Chee said, but he was thinking about whether the old pistol Redd was pointing at him would work, about how the hell to get out of here. And he must not have sounded properly impressed.

"It may not sound like much to you, with a regular job. But if you're starving your way through graduate school, it sounds like a hell of a lot," Redd said. "It sounds like an escape from never having a dime and doing slave labor for bastards like this one."

"What was the problem, then? Did Tagert want to keep it all?"

Redd laughed. "He didn't need money. He had it. He needed fame. And getting even with the other historians who don't agree he's God. No. He was going to leave it all here—just like I found it for him. Then he was going to call in the authorities. Most especially he was going to call in somebody important from the U.S. Post Office. He wanted official certification that this mailbag and all in it came off that Colorado and Southern train."

"Oh," Chee said. "I guess I see. He wanted a solid connection between these bodies here and that identification of Cassidy as the train robber. To make those other historians eat crow."

"I think he'd found some sort of identification on the body. And he measured it. Can you believe that? Laid it out straight as he could and measured it. He said Cassidy was five foot nine inches and so was the mummy with the mustache. He said Cassidy had a scar under one eye. And two deep scars on the back of his head. He claimed he found those, too, but the thing's so dried-up I couldn't tell."

"I say it would be safe to say he's Cassidy without all that. How you going to prove it isn't?"

"You don't know historians," Redd said. "And Tagert's a single-minded bastard. I told him what it would do—if he called in the authorities. The Post Office would claim the mailbags, and the stamps. Face value of those stamps to them, maybe a hundred dollars, and we lose a fortune."

"What did you want to do?"

"Split it," Redd said. "Just split it. Fifty-fifty. That would be fair. After all, he never could have found it without me."

Chee was thinking, How about thirds? How about Ashie Pinto sitting out there under his tree with his bottle? You wouldn't have found anything without Pinto. But he said: "What did Tagert say?"

"He just sneered at me. Said I had made a deal for a thousand and I had five hundred coming out of that."

"So you shot him?"

"I didn't shoot him. I grabbed the mailbag and it turns out he had a pistol in his coat pocket. He pulled it out. Said he would shoot me if I didn't leave things alone." Chee watched Redd's face register surprise at this manufactured memory. "You know, I think he would have done it too."

Play along, Chee thought. Play along. "I wouldn't be surprised. What I've heard about him."

Redd laughed. "No," he said. "Talk about irony. Old Ashie shot him."

Of course. And Nez, too. Lay the blame on old, drunk Ashie Pinto.

But Chee said: "Pinto. What's ironic about that?"

After the first flurry, the snow had stopped. But now it began again, brushing Chee's cheek with flakes and swirling them around the knees of Redd.

Redd had been thinking, not listening. Sorting things out in his mind. He motioned Chee with his pistol.

"Let me have your gun," he said.

Chee shrugged. "No gun," he said. "I'm off duty."

"Don't bull me," Redd said. "You cops always carry guns."

"No we don't. I'm on convalescent leave." He held up his left hand, displaying the wrappings. "Because of this."

"You have a gun," Redd said. "Lean up against that rock there. Use your good hand. I'll see."

"No gun," Chee said. Which, unfortunately, was true. Chee's pistol was where it always seemed to be when he wanted it—in the glove box of his truck.

Redd checked his pockets, his pant legs, the tops of his boots.

"Okay," he said. "I noticed you looking at this old hogleg. If you're thinking it won't work, it will. I tried it."

"What are you planning to do?" Chee asked. "You didn't shoot anybody. So, why not turn yourself in?"

Redd had walked to the cleft in the basalt where he had hidden the saddlebag. He was pointing the pistol at Chee, reaching in, leaning against the stone, trying to give his fingers a grip on the canvas, eyes still on Chee, a sardonic grin on his face.

"Turn myself in for what?" he asked. He grunted as his fingers slipped off the canvas. "Damned thing's jammed back in there," he said. "I didn't want somebody to happen in here and find it. Like whoever was watching."

"Why didn't you take it with you?" Chee asked. Every nerve was tense. When Redd pulled the bag out, that would be the time to make a run for it. He had ruled out jumping the man long ago. Redd outweighed him by forty pounds and had two good hands.

"Because that goddam cop car came rolling up. First it was Nez. And then you." Redd pulled the arm out, empty-handed again. "I didn't have time to decide what to do. I just wanted to get away from here."

"Why burn him?" Chee's voice was strained.

"That crazy bastard," Redd said, and Chee presumed he meant Pinto—not Nez. He stared into the crevice, estimating distance. "I shouldn't have pushed it in there so far," he said, half to himself. "The cop was already dead. The fire—he was shooting . . . I don't know what happened. Dealing with a drunk, I guess you could call it an accident. Everything that's happened has been sort of accidental when you think about it." He laughed. "Kismet," he said. "Fate."

"Fate," Chee said. "Yeah. Blame it on old Coyote."

"Like you and the girl coming out here the day I came back to pick up the mailbag. I figured the cops would find it and stake the place out. And when I finally decided that hadn't happened and came out to get it, it was the same day you and that woman came out. So I thought I'd just leave it until after the trial. Get it when everything got cooled down and forgotten."

While he talked, he was looking around for something to pry the saddlebag with. He looked at Chee's stick and rejected it. "It had been here like almost a century. What's another few months?"

"What did you mean, ironic that Pinto shot the professor?" Chee asked.

"Well, hell," Redd said, and leaned into the cavity as far as he could reach. "I meant Tagert gave the old man the whiskey. Coaxed him. Had him smell it. Told him he'd brought a really sweet kind because he knew Pinto liked it sweet." He laughed. "I think he put Nutrisweet in Scotch." Redd raised his voice, mimicking Tagert. " 'Just taste it. You don't have to get drunk. Just take a taste.' Just to make him drunk so he'd tell us more than he wanted to. When we were driving over to pick Pinto up, Tagert told me he did that. He said: 'The old devil always tries to leave stuff out when you hire him to tell you something, but he can't handle whiskey. So when he starts getting coy, I get him started drinking and once he's drunk he tells me—' " Suddenly Redd grunted. He was leaning into the cleft, straining to reach. "Ah," he said. "Now I got it."

Just then the rattlesnake struck.

Redd jerked away from the rocks, gripping the saddlebag by some sort of reflex action. The great gray snake dangled, writhing, from the side of his neck, its fangs hooked through the neck muscles just below Redd's left ear. Redd screamed, a terrified, gargling sound. He dropped the bag, grabbed the diamondback by its flat, triangular head, pulled it loose, and threw it back among the basalt boulders.

Chee wasted perhaps two seconds watching this—first too startled to move and then thinking Redd would drop the pistol. He didn't. Chee ran.

Moving fast over rough country comes naturally to young men raised in a culture in which skill at running is both respected and useful. Within a minute, Chee was sure enough that Redd couldn't find him, so he stopped, looked back and listened. It was snowing hard now, the flakes no longer tiny or dry. They stuck to the black rocks for long seconds before warmth from the stone converted them to water.

Redd wasn't following him. Chee hadn't really expected him to. Redd didn't seem to know much about snakes but he'd know a rattlesnake when he saw one. And he'd probably know the neck was a hell of a poor place to get bitten. The venom had only a few inches to move to reach the brain. Redd would be running for help.

Chee climbed, looking for a place from which he could see something. He found one, and he saw Redd almost immediately despite the blowing snow. He was out of the ridge formation, running down the grassy slope toward the arroyo, and then up the arroyo. Probably to his Bronco II, Chee thought. He was still carrying the saddlebag.

Chee climbed down, found the path, and found his way through the snow to his pickup truck.

The driver's-side window had been broken out.

Chee climbed in and tried the starter. Nothing happened. He pulled the hood release, climbed out, and found exactly what he had feared he'd find.

Redd had torn loose the wiring.

Chee stood beside the truck, creating a map of this landscape in his mind. Where would be the nearest telephone? Red Rock Trading Post. How far? Maybe fifteen miles, maybe twenty. If he walked all night he could be there about opening time tomorrow morning.

23

CHEE PUSHED THE up button of the elevator in the Albuquerque Federal Building a little after ten thirty. He looked like a man who had spent a sleepless night walking out in the snow, which he had. The minuscule amount of nighttime traffic that Navajo Route 33 normally carries had been cut to zero by the storm. A disappointing storm as it turned out, depositing less than two inches of snow across the arid Four Corners landscape, but enough to keep people at home. Chee had finally reached Red Rock Trading Post and got to a telephone a little after dawn. He'd called the station at Ship Rock and reported everything that had transpired. Then he called Mesa Airlines and reserved a seat on its nine A.M. flight. Finally he'd persuaded an early-rising Navajo rancher who'd stopped for gasoline to give him a ride to his trailer and from there to the airport. From the airport, he'd tried to call both Janet Pete and Hugh Dendahl, who was prosecuting this case for the U.S. attorney. Both of them had already left for the courthouse. He left messages for them both.

A U.S. marshal in a suit that had been big enough last year spotted Chee as he headed for the courtroom door.

"Where the hell you been?" he asked. "Dendahl has been looking for you."

"He get my message?"

The marshal looked blank. "No message. He was making sure all his witnesses were ready."

"He said he wouldn't need me until this afternoon," Chee said. "Maybe not then if they had trouble getting a jury." Maybe not at all when he finds out about Redd, Chee was thinking. They'll have to start over on this one.

"They got themselves a jury," the marshal said. "Opening arguments this morning. He may need you right after lunch."

"Well, I'm here," Chee said.

The marshal was looking him over. No sign of approval.

"You live close?" he asked. "Maybe you could go home and clean up a little. Shave."

"I live at Ship Rock," Chee said. "Let me borrow your pen. And have you got a piece of paper?"

The marshal had a notebook in his coat pocket. Chee wrote hurriedly. Two almost identical notes to Janet Pete and Dendahl. He was thinking that as a witness they wouldn't want him in the courtroom now. But what the hell. This trial wasn't going to be held now anyway.

"Thanks," he said, and handed the marshal his pen. "I have to get this note to Dendahl."

The bailiff stopped him at the door.

Chee folded the notes, handed them to the bailiff. "This one goes to Dendahl," he said. "This one to Janet Pete."

Something was going on in the courtroom. The jury was being brought in. Janet, Dendahl, and another assistant district attorney who Chee didn't know were huddled in front of Judge Downey. The judge looked irritated.

"What's going on?" Chee asked.

"I don't know," the bailiff said. "I think the old man's going to change his plea, or something. But he demanded that the jury be in here to hear it. He wants to make a statement."

"Change his plea?" Chee said, incredulous. "You mean plead guilty?"

"I don't know," the bailiff said, giving Chee a "you dumb bastard" look. "She has him pleaded not guilty, so if he changes it, I guess that's what you'd get."

"Look," Chee said. "Those notes are important, then. They have to get that information right away."

The bailiff looked skeptical. "All right," he said, and waddled down the aisle.

Chee moved inside, found a back-row seat, and watched.

Hosteen Ashie Pinto was sitting, too. Waiting. He noticed Chee, looked at him, nodded. The conference at the bench ended. Janet sat next to Pinto, whispering something to him. Pinto shook his head. Judge Downey tapped tentatively with her gavel, looking out of sorts with it all. The bailiff waited patiently for the proper opportunity to deliver his messages.

"The record will show the defendant wishes to change his plea," Judge Downey said. "Let the record show the defendant, after consultation with counsel, requested that the jury be brought in. The record will show defendant wishes to make a statement to the court."

Janet Pete motioned to Ashie Pinto. He stood, looked around him, wiped his hand across his lips.

"I am an old man, and ashamed," Hosteen Pinto began. His voice was surprisingly strong. "I want everybody to know, all of you to know, how it was that I killed that policeman. And how it was—"

Pinto's interpreter signaled him to stop. He stood, looking surprised and uncomfortable, and converted Pinto's confession into English, and nodded to Pinto when he was finished and said: "Go on now."

Chee sat stunned. Did the old man kill Nez? Not Redd? He'd presumed Redd was lying. He'd presumed—

"And how it was when I was a young man," Pinto continued, "I killed a man in my father's clan at a sing-dance out at Crooked Ridge. Every time it was the same thing. Every time it was whiskey." There are several words in Navajo for whiskey in its various forms. Pinto used the one that translates to "water of darkness." Then he stopped, stood, head slightly bowed, while the interpreter translated.

Chee was watching Janet Pete. She looked sad, but not surprised. Pinto must have finally confided in her. He had wanted to do this and she had arranged it. When?

Pinto was talking again, to a silent, intent audience.

". . . When they came out of the rocks there, Mr. Redd and the man I would kill, that man had a pistol in his hand. He was pointing that pistol at Mr. Redd. Now that man with the pistol was the man who gave me the whiskey. He gave it to me some other times. Before, when I worked for him. He knew how it was for me. This whiskey. He knew that when I drank it I would do wrong things. I would tell him what I didn't want to tell him. He knew it made my tongue loose and he knew that when it was in me it took over my mind. It made the wind that blows inside me blow as dark as night."

The interpreter was tugging at Pinto's sleeve.

"Going too fast," he said, and Pinto stopped.

Pinto had gone too fast. The interpreter missed a little of it, cut some corners.

Pinto told them Redd was a good young man, that Redd had signaled him to get the man's pistol, and when they were all three getting into his car to drive away, he had gotten it.

"So I shot him," Pinto said. "By the car. Then I shot him again."

The interpreter translated.

"Then Mr. Redd he carried the body of that man away. I think he didn't want the police to find it. The man I shot is a very little man and Mr. Redd is big and he carried him back up into the rocks where nobody would find him. And I was waiting there by the car when the policeman came. He was talking to me about painting things. I didn't know what he was talking about but he acted like he wanted to arrest me so I shot him, too."

The interpreter translated but Chee didn't wait to hear it. He still wondered why Pinto had set the car on fire. Maybe the old man would explain that, but he didn't want to hear the answer. Not now. He hurried out the door and down the elevator.

He'd taken a taxi from the airport. This lack of wheels was an oddity he had little experience dealing with. He stopped in the main-floor coffee shop, ordered a cup, and thought about it. He had a headache, which was as unusual as the lack of transportation. Probably the product of lack of sleep last night. Or maybe lack of breakfast. He wasn't really hungry but he ordered a hamburger.

Redd would be arrested by now, probably. Or dead. If he hadn't checked into a hospital fast to have that venom dealt with it had probably killed him. Chee considered that. That and the value of three or four hundred thousand dollar's worth of old stamps. What would Redd have bought with it that he didn't now have? A better car? A better house? Then he faced the fact that he was thinking of this because he didn't want to think of the note he'd sent to Janet. To Dendahl, too, for that matter, but to hell with Dendahl.

"Ask for a recess," he'd told them both. "I don't think Pinto did it. Redd was there. He killed Colonel Ji. I think he killed Tagert and Nez. I think he can prove all of it."

Wrong again. Redd had killed Colonel Ji because he thought Ji had seen too much. Ji would find the bodies, and the stamps.

Wrong about it all. Looking foolish. Feeling foolish.

He ate his hamburger slowly, thinking of Janet hugging him in the elevator. Was that before or after Pinto had told her? Something about his memory of the moment made him think it was after. That she already knew Pinto was guilty. But why, then, the hug? Quite a hug it was, with her pressing against him like that. The hug was about the only bright spot of this whole business.

Then Janet came hurrying up.

"I saw you in here," she said, and sat beside him in the booth. "How much of that did you hear before you left?"

"Up to where he said he shot Delbert," Chee said. "I left then. Did I miss anything?"

"You missed part of Mr. Pinto's speech about whiskey. How it destroys everything it touches. He asked the jury to have all whiskey everywhere poured out on the ground. That's what he was waiting for. Why he wouldn't say anything before. He remembered the time he was tried before, and sent to prison. He thought that this would be the time to warn the world about whiskey."

"Good as any, I guess," Chee said. "Anyway, it's just about what you'd expect from a nutty old Navajo shaman. The spoken word has great power, you know." He sounded bitter.

She was grinning at him. "Don't be sarcastic. It does have power. Did you notice the press was here? He wasn't so nutty."

The grin disappeared. "I got your note. I want to hear all about that. About Odell Redd."

"All right," Chee said. "You want something to eat?"

"Maybe some coffee." She signaled the waitress. "How did you figure Redd out?"

"You mean about him shooting Delbert Nez? How did I get that wrong, too?"

She noticed his tone. She was serious now.

"You didn't get it wrong. You arrested Ashie Pinto. Hurt as you were, you arrested him. It was me. I thought he didn't do it."

"Yeah," Chee said. "Okay."

"I was wrong about something else, too," she said.

"Like what?"

"Like about you," she said. "You made me think for a while that all you cared about was proving you were right."

"What do you mean?" Chee asked.

"Oh, forget it," she said. And to his amazement Janet Pete hugged him again, even harder this time.

24

LEAPHORN HAD SPENT all morning in his office. By a little after ten, he'd leaned back in his chair and spent a long moment just enjoying the scene—his in-basket was empty, his out-basket full but neat, the surface of the desk bare. Wood visible. Nothing cluttering the blotter except a ballpoint pen.

He picked up the pen, dropped it in the top drawer, and looked at the desk again. Even better.

Then he worked through the Nez homicide again. He fished the Gallup *Independent* out of the wastebasket where it had landed in this paroxysm of housecleaning. He reread the story of Ashie Pinto's confession and his indictment of alcohol. Leaphorn agreed with every word of it. Death in a bottle, Pinto had called it. Exactly. Death, sorrow, and misery. The story said Judge Downey had delayed his sentencing pending a medical and psychiatric examination of Pinto. The worst the law allowed under the circumstances would be life in prison. Downey would probably give him something less. But it wouldn't matter, life or ten years. The story said he was "about eighty."

Satisfaction from the clean desk waned. Leaphorn considered Officer Jim Chee. A screwup, but an interesting young man. Intelligent, the way he had made the connections to tie everything in. But he'd never make a good administrator. Never. Nor a team player, and law enforcement often required that. Maybe he would work better in criminal investigations. Like Leaphorn. He smiled at the thought. Where screwing up didn't matter much if you had a creative thought now and then. He would talk to Captain Largo about it. Largo knew Chee better than he did.

He considered everything about the affair of Delbert Nez.

His mother would have said Coyote was waiting for Nez. Bad luck. For that matter for Redd as well. All he seemed to have wanted was some decent pay for his skills as a linguist. And he ended his game killing the wrong person for the wrong reason. Anyway, Coyote ate Redd. They'd found the old Bronco in a ditch and got him to the hospital, another Dead on Arrival.

He turned to his map and pulled out the few pins this business had inspired. They hadn't helped much this time.

Even a pin for Professor Bourebonette. The question of her motive. He smiled to himself, thinking of that. Emma had always accused him of being too cynical. She was right this time, as she often was. He had checked on Bourebonette. He'd called an old friend in the anthropology department at Arizona State. Did he know someone at Northern Arizona who would know Bourebonette, the mythologist in American Studies there? Could this person determine how she was coming on her new book? She could. The manuscript was off to the publishers. It should be out early next year. So much for that. He would get a copy. He'd like to read it.

They'd talked of mythology on their way back from Short Mountain Trading Post that night. She had talked a little, and slept a bit, and when she awoke she was full of conversation. She'd questioned him about his own knowledge of Navajo myth and where he had learned it. And then they had covered the nature of imagination. How the human intelligence works. The difference between mind and brain. It had been a pleasant ride. She had talked, too, of the time she'd spent in Cambodia and Thailand collecting animism myths and working with the shamans who select the exact place where the bones of one's crucial ancestor must be kept to ensure good family fortune.

From his window, Leaphorn could see four cattle semitrailers in a convoy rolling to a stop at the tribal barns across Navajo Route 3. That would be rodeo livestock for the Tribal Fair. He made a face. The fair was an annual problem for every cop on the Reservation. Then, too, it meant winter was coming. This year he dreaded winter.

He would go to lunch. Alone. He picked up his cap, put it on. Took it off again. Picked up the telephone. Dialed information.

She answered the telephone on the second ring.

"Hello."

"This is Joe Leaphorn," he said. "How are you?"

"Very well," she said. "Are you here in Flag?"

"Window Rock," he said. "My office."

"Oh? By the way, I found out you did some checking up on me. About my book."

"I was skeptical about your motives," Leaphorn said. "It's one of my flaws. Cynicism. Emma used to fuss at me about it."

"Well, I guess that's reasonable. For a policeman."

"Professor Bourebonette, I think I'm going to China," Leaphorn said. "Would you like to go along?"